THE WRITINGS OF HERMAN MELVILLE

The Northwestern–Newberry Edition

VOLUME FIVE

EDITORS
HARRISON HAYFORD, *General Editor*
HERSHEL PARKER, *Associate General Editor*
G. THOMAS TANSELLE, *Bibliographical Editor*

BIBLIOGRAPHICAL ASSOCIATE
RICHARD COLLES JOHNSON

CONTRIBUTING SCHOLARS

WALTER E. BEZANSON
MERLIN BOWEN
WATSON G. BRANCH
RICHARD HARTER FOGLE
ELIZABETH S. FOSTER
WILLIAM H. GILMAN
HOWARD HORSFORD
LEON HOWARD
WILLIAM H. HUTCHINSON

LELAND PHELPS
AMY PUETT
GORDON ROPER
ROMA ROSEN
ROBERT C. RYAN
MERTON M. SEALTS, JR.
MORRIS STAR
WILLARD THORP
NATHALIA WRIGHT

ADVISORY BOARD
JOHN HURT FISHER   *For the Modern Language Association of America*
WILLIAM M. GIBSON   *For the Center for Editions of American Authors*
LEON HOWARD   *For the MLA American Literature Section*
WILLARD THORP   *For the MLA American Literature Section*
MOODY E. PRIOR   *For Northwestern University*
ROBERT PLANT ARMSTRONG   *For Northwestern University Press*
LAWRENCE W. TOWNER   *For The Newberry Library*

White-Jacket

This volume edited by
HARRISON HAYFORD
HERSHEL PARKER
G. THOMAS TANSELLE

Historical Note by
WILLARD THORP

White-Jacket

or

The World in a Man-of-War

HERMAN MELVILLE

NORTHWESTERN UNIVERSITY PRESS
and
THE NEWBERRY LIBRARY
Evanston and Chicago
1970

THE RESEARCH *reported herein was prepared pursuant to a contract with the United States Department of Health, Education, and Welfare, Office of Education, under the provisions of the Coöperative Research Program, and is in the public domain.*

Publication of the Northwestern–Newberry Edition of THE WRITINGS OF HERMAN MELVILLE *has been made possible through the financial support of Northwestern University and its Research Committee, and of The Newberry Library. This edition originated with Northwestern University Press, Inc., which reserves all rights against commercial reproduction by offset-lithographic or equivalent copying processes.*

LIBRARY OF CONGRESS CATALOG CARD NUMBER 67-21603

PRINTED IN THE UNITED STATES OF AMERICA

FIRST PRINTING, 1970
SECOND PRINTING, 1981

Cloth Edition, SBN   8101-0257-9
Paper Edition, SBN   8101-0258-7

CENTER FOR EDITIONS OF
AMERICAN AUTHORS

AN APPROVED TEXT

MODERN LANGUAGE
ASSOCIATION OF AMERICA

®

PS
2380
.F68
vol. 5

Melville, Herman.
White-jacket.

35,939

CONCEIVE HIM *now in a man-of-war; with his letters of mart, well armed, victualed, and appointed, and see how he acquits himself.*

FULLER's "Good Sea-Captain."

CAMROSE LUTHERAN COLLEGE
LIBRARY

Note

IN THE YEAR 1843 I shipped as "ordinary seaman" on board of a United States frigate, then lying in a harbor of the Pacific Ocean. After remaining in this frigate for more than a year, I was discharged from the service upon the vessel's arrival home. My man-of-war experiences and observations are incorporated in the present volume.

NEW YORK, *March*, 1850.

Contents

EDITORIAL APPENDIX

White-Jacket

Chapter 1

The Jacket

I T WAS NOT a *very* white jacket, but white enough, in all conscience, as the sequel will show.

The way I came by it was this.

When our frigate lay in Callao, on the coast of Peru—her last harbor in the Pacific—I found myself without a *grego*, or sailor's surtout; and as, toward the end of a three years' cruise, no pea-jackets could be had from the purser's steward; and being bound for Cape Horn, some sort of a substitute was indispensable; I employed myself, for several days, in manufacturing an outlandish garment of my own devising, to shelter me from the boisterous weather we were so soon to encounter.

It was nothing more than a white duck frock, or rather shirt; which, laying on deck, I folded double at the bosom, and by then making a continuation of the slit there, opened it lengthwise—much as you would cut a leaf in the last new novel. The gash being made, a metamorphosis took place, transcending any related by Ovid. For, presto! the shirt was a coat! —a strange-looking coat, to be sure; of a Quakerish amplitude about the skirts; with an infirm, tumble-down collar; and a clumsy fullness about the wristbands; and white, yea, white as a shroud. And my shroud it afterward came very near proving, as he who reads further will find.

3

But, bless me, my friend, what sort of a summer jacket is this, in which to weather Cape Horn? A very tasty, and beautiful white linen garment it may have seemed; but then, people almost universally sport their linen next to their skin.

Very true; and that thought very early occurred to me; for no idea had I of scudding round Cape Horn in my shirt; for *that* would have been almost scudding under bare poles, indeed.

So, with many odds and ends of patches—old socks, old trowser-legs, and the like—I bedarned and bequilted the inside of my jacket, till it became, all over, stiff and padded, as King James's cotton-stuffed and dagger-proof doublet; and no buckram or steel hauberk stood up more stoutly.

So far, very good; but pray, tell me, White-Jacket, how do you propose keeping out the rain and the wet in this quilted *grego* of yours? You don't call this wad of old patches a Mackintosh, do you?—You don't pretend to say that worsted is water-proof?

No, my dear friend; and that was the deuce of it. Water-proof it was not, no more than a sponge. Indeed, with such recklessness had I bequilted my jacket, that in a rain-storm I became a universal absorber; swabbing bone-dry the very bulwarks I leaned against. Of a damp day, my heartless ship-mates even used to stand up against me, so powerful was the capillary attraction between this luckless jacket of mine and all drops of moisture. I dripped like a turkey a' roasting; and long after the rain storms were over, and the sun showed his face, I still stalked a Scotch mist; and when it was fair weather with others, alas! it was foul weather with me.

Me? Ah me! Soaked and heavy, what a burden was that jacket to carry about, especially when I was sent up aloft; dragging myself up, step by step, as if I were weighing the anchor. Small time then, to strip, and wring it out in a rain, when no hanging back or delay was permitted. No, no; up you go: fat or lean: Lambert or Edson: never mind how much avoirdupoise you might weigh. And thus, in my own proper person, did many showers of rain reascend toward the skies, in accordance with the natural laws.

But here be it known, that I had been terribly disappointed in carrying out my original plan concerning this jacket. It had been my intention to make it thoroughly impervious, by giving it a coating of paint. But bitter fate ever overtakes us unfortunates. So much paint had been stolen by the sailors, in daubing their overhaul trowsers and tarpaulins, that by the time I an honest man—had completed my quiltings, the paint-pots were banned, and put under strict lock and key.

Said old Brush, the captain of the *paint-room*—"Look ye, White-Jacket," said he, "ye can't have any paint."

Such, then, was my jacket: a well-patched, padded, and porous one; and in a dark night, gleaming white, as the White Lady of Avenel!

Chapter 2

Homeward-Bound

ALL HANDS UP ANCHOR! Man the capstan!"

"High die! my lads, we're homeward bound!"

Homeward bound!—harmonious sound! Were you ever homeward bound?—No?—Quick! take the wings of the morning, or the sails of a ship, and fly to the uttermost parts of the earth. There, tarry a year or two; and then let the gruffest of Boatswains, his lungs all goose-skin, shout forth those magical words, and you'll swear "the harp of Orpheus were not more enchanting."

All was ready; boats hoisted in, stun' sail gear rove, messenger passed, capstan-bars in their places, accommodation-ladder below; and in glorious spirits, we sat down to dinner. In the ward-room, the lieutenants were passing round their oldest Port, and pledging their friends; in the steerage, the *middies* were busy raising loans to liquidate the demands of their laundress, or else—in the navy phrase—preparing to pay their creditors *with a flying fore-topsail*. On the poop, the captain was looking to windward; and in his grand, inaccessible cabin, the high and mighty commodore sat silent and stately, as the statue of Jupiter in Dodona.

We were all arrayed in our best, and our bravest; like strips of blue sky, lay the pure blue collars of our frocks upon our shoulders, and our pumps were so springy and playful, that we danced up and down as we dined.

It was on the gun-deck that our dinners were spread; all along between the guns; and there, as we cross-legged sat, you would have thought a hundred farm-yards and meadows were nigh. Such a cackling of ducks, chickens, and ganders; such a lowing of oxen, and bleating of lambkins, penned up here and there along the deck, to provide sea repasts for the officers. More rural than naval were the sounds; continually reminding each mother's son of the old paternal homestead in the green old clime; the old arching elms; the hill where we gambolled; and down by the barley banks of the stream where we bathed.

"All hands up anchor!"

When that order was given, how we sprang to the bars, and heaved round that capstan; every man a Goliath, every tendon a hawser!—round and round—round, round it spun like a sphere, keeping time with our feet to the time of the fifer, till the cable was straight up and down, and the ship with her nose in the water.

"Heave and pall! unship your bars, and make sail!"

It was done:—bar-men, nipper-men, tierers, veerers, idlers and all, scrambled up the ladder to the braces and halyards; while like monkeys in Palm-trees, the sail-loosers ran out on those broad boughs, our yards; and down fell the sails like white clouds from the ether—top-sails, top-gallants, and royals; and away we ran with the halyards, till every sheet was distended.

"Once more to the bars!"

"Heave, my hearties, heave hard!"

With a jerk and a yerk, we broke ground; and up to our bows came several thousand pounds of old iron, in the shape of our ponderous anchor.

Where was White-Jacket then?

White-Jacket was where he belonged. It was White-Jacket that loosed that main-royal, so far up aloft there, it looks like a white albatross' wing. It was White-Jacket that was taken for an albatross himself, as he flew out on the giddy yard-arm!

Chapter 3

A Glance at the principal Divisions, into which a Man-of-war's Crew is divided

HAVING JUST DESIGNATED the place where White-Jacket belonged, it must needs be related how White-Jacket came to belong there.

Every one knows that in merchantmen the seamen are divided into watches—starboard and larboard—taking their turn at the ship's duty by night. This plan is followed in all men-of-war. But in all men-of-war, besides this division, there are others, rendered indispensable from the great number of men, and the necessity of precision and discipline. Not only are particular bands assigned to the three *tops*, but in getting under weigh, or any other proceeding requiring all hands, particular men of these bands are assigned to each yard of the tops. Thus, when the order is given to loose the main-royal, White-Jacket flies to obey it; and no one but him.

And not only are particular bands stationed on the three decks of the ship at such times, but particular men of those bands are also assigned to particular duties. Also, in tacking ship, reefing top-sails, or "coming to," every man of a frigate's five-hundred-strong, knows his own special place, and is infallibly found there. He sees nothing else, attends to nothing else, and will stay there till grim death or an epaulette orders him away. Yet there are times when, through the negligence of the officers, some exceptions are found to this rule. A rather serious circumstance growing out of such a case will be related in some future chapter.

Were it not for these regulations a man-of-war's crew would be nothing but a mob, more ungovernable stripping the canvass in a gale than Lord George Gordon's tearing down the lofty house of Lord Mansfield.

But this is not all. Besides White-Jacket's office as looser of the main-royal, when all hands were called to make sail; and besides his special offices, in tacking ship, coming to anchor, &c.; he permanently belonged to the Starboard Watch, one of the two primary, grand divisions of the ship's company. And in this watch he was a main-top-man; that is, was stationed in the main-top, with a number of other seamen, always in readiness to execute any orders pertaining to the main-mast, from above the main-yard. For, including the main-yard, and below it to the deck, the main-mast belongs to another detachment.

Now the fore, main, and mizen-top-men of each watch—Starboard and Larboard—are at sea respectively subdivided into Quarter Watches; which regularly relieve each other in the tops to which they may belong; while, collectively, they relieve the whole Larboard Watch of top-men.

Besides these topmen, who are always made up of active sailors, there are Sheet-Anchor-men—old veterans all—whose place is on the forecastle; the fore-yard, anchors, and all the sails on the bowsprit being under their care.

They are an old weather-beaten set, culled from the most experienced seamen on board. These are the fellows that sing you "*The Bay of Biscay Oh!*" and "*Here a sheer hulk lies poor Tom Bowling!*" "*Cease, rude Boreas, blustering railer!*" who, when ashore, at an eating-house, call for a bowl of tar and a biscuit. These are the fellows, who spin interminable yarns about Decatur, Hull, and Bainbridge; and carry about their persons bits of "Old Ironsides," as Catholics do the wood of the true cross. These are the fellows, that some officers never pretend to damn, however much they may anathematize others. These are the fellows, that it does your soul good to look at;—hearty old members of the Old Guard; grim sea grenadiers, who, in tempest time, have lost many a tarpaulin overboard. These are the fellows, whose society some of the youngster midshipmen much affect; from whom they learn their best seamanship; and to whom they look up as veterans; if so be, that they have any reverence in their souls, which is not the case with all mid-shipmen.

Then, there is the *After-guard*, stationed on the Quarter-deck; who, under the Quarter-Masters and Quarter-Gunners, attend to the main-sail and spanker, and help haul the main-brace, and other ropes in the stern of the vessel.

The duties assigned to the After-Guard's-Men being comparatively light and easy, and but little seamanship being expected from them, they are composed chiefly of landsmen; the least robust, least hardy, and least sailor-like of the crew; and being stationed on the Quarter-deck, they are generally selected with some eye to their personal appearance. Hence, they are mostly slender young fellows, of a genteel figure and gentlemanly address; not weighing much on a rope, but weighing considerably in the estimation of all foreign ladies who may chance to visit the ship. They lounge away the most part of their time, in reading novels and romances; talking over their lover affairs ashore; and comparing notes concerning the melancholy and sentimental career which drove them—poor young gentlemen—into the hard-hearted navy. Indeed, many of them show tokens of having moved in very respectable society. They always maintain a tidy exterior; and express an abhorrence of the tar-bucket, into which they are seldom or never called to dip their digits. And pluming themselves upon the cut of their trowsers, and the glossiness of their tarpaulins, from the rest of the ship's company, they acquire the name of "*sea-dandies*" and "*silk-sock-gentry*."

Then, there are the *Waisters*, always stationed on the gun-deck. These haul aft the fore and main-sheets, besides being subject to ignoble duties; attending to the drainage and sewerage below hatches. These fellows are all Jimmy Duxes—sorry chaps, who never put foot in ratlin, or venture above the bulwarks. Inveterate "*sons of farmers*," with the hay-seed yet in their hair, they are consigned to the congenial superintendence of the chicken-coops, pig-pens, and potato-lockers. These are generally placed amidships, on the gun-deck of a frigate, between the fore and main hatches; and comprise so extensive an area, that it much resembles the market-place of a small town. The melodious sounds thence issuing, continually draw tears from the eyes of the Waisters; reminding them of their old paternal pig-pens and potato-patches. They are the tag-rag and bob-tail of the crew; and he who is good for nothing else is good enough for a *Waister*.

Three decks down—spar-deck, gun-deck, and berth-deck—and we come to a parcel of Troglodytes or "*holders*," who burrow, like rabbits in warrens, among the water-tanks, casks, and cables. Like Cornwall miners, wash off the soot from their skins, and they are all pale as ghosts. Unless upon rare occasions, they seldom come on deck to sun themselves. They may circumnavigate the world fifty times, and they see about as much of it as Jonah did in the whale's belly. They are a lazy, lumpish, torpid set; and when going ashore after a long cruise, come out into the day, like terrapins from their caves, or bears in the spring, from tree-trunks. No one ever knows the names of these fellows; after a three years' voyage, they still remain strangers to you. In time of tempests, when all hands are called to save ship, they issue forth into the gale, like the mysterious old men of Paris, during the massacre of the Three Days of September; every one marvels who they are, and whence they come; they disappear as mysteriously; and are seen no more, until another general commotion.

Such are the principal divisions into which a man-of-war's crew is divided; but the inferior allotments of duties are endless, and would require a German commentator to chronicle.

We say nothing here of Boatswain's mates, Gunner's mates, Carpenter's mates, Sail-maker's mates, Armorer's mates, Master-at-Arms, Ship's corporals, Cockswains, Quarter-masters, Quarter-gunners, Captains of the Forecastle, Captains of the Fore-top, Captains of the Main-top, Captains of the Mizen-top, Captains of the After-Guard, Captains of the Main-Hold, Captains of the Fore-Hold, Captains of the Head, Coopers, Painters, Tinkers, Commodore's Steward, Captain's Steward, Ward-Room Steward, Steerage Steward, Commodore's cook, Captain's cook, Officers' cook, Cooks of the range, Mess-cooks, hammock-boys, messenger boys, cot-boys, loblolly-boys, and numberless others, whose functions are fixed and peculiar.

It is from this endless subdivision of duties in a man-of-war, that, upon first entering one, a sailor has need of a good memory, and the more of an Arithmetician he is, the better.

White-Jacket, for one, was a long time rapt in calculations, concerning the various "numbers" allotted him by the *First Luff*, otherwise known as the First Lieutenant. In the first place, White-Jacket was given the *number of his mess*; then, his *ship's number*, or the number to which he must answer when the watch-roll is called; then, the number of his hammock; then, the number of the gun to which he was assigned; besides a variety of other numbers; all of which would have taken Jedediah Buxton himself some time to arrange in battalions, previous to adding up. All these numbers, moreover, must be well remembered, or woe betide you.

Consider, now, a merchant-sailor altogether unused to the tumult of a man-of-war, for the first time stepping on board, and given all these numbers to recollect. Already, before hearing them, his head is half stunned with the unaccustomed sounds ringing in his ears; which ears seem to him like belfries full of tocsins. On the gun-deck, a thousand scythed chariots seem passing; he hears the tread of armed marines; the clash of cutlasses and curses. The Boatswain's mates whistle round him, like hawks screaming in a gale, and the strange noises under decks, are like volcanic rumblings in a mountain. He dodges sudden sounds, as a raw recruit falling bombs.

Well-nigh useless to him, now, all previous circumnavigations of this terraqueous globe; of no account his arctic, antarctic, or equinoctial experiences; his gales off Beachy Head, or his dismastings off Hatteras. He must begin anew; he knows nothing; Greek and Hebrew could not help him, for the language he must learn has neither grammar nor lexicon.

Mark him, as he advances along the files of old ocean-warriors; mark his debased attitude, his deprecating gestures, his Sawney stare, like a Scotchman in London in King James's time; his—*"cry your mercy, noble seignors!"* He is wholly nonplused, and confounded. And when, to crown all, the First Lieutenant, whose business it is to welcome all new-comers, and assign them their quarters; when this officer—none of the most bland or amiable either—gives him number after number to recollect—246—139—478—351—the poor fellow feels like decamping.

Study, then, your mathematics, and cultivate all your memories, oh ye! who think of cruising in men-of-war.

Chapter 4

Jack Chase

THE FIRST NIGHT out of port was a clear, moonlight one; the frigate gliding through the water, with all her batteries.

It was my Quarter Watch in the top; and there I reclined on the best possible terms with my top-mates. Whatever the other seamen might have been, these were a noble set of tars, and well worthy an introduction to the reader.

First and foremost was Jack Chase, our noble First Captain of the Top. He was a Briton, and a true-blue; tall and well-knit, with a clear open eye, a fine broad brow, and an abounding nut-brown beard. No man ever had a better heart or a bolder. He was loved by the seamen and admired by the officers; and even when the Captain spoke to him, it was with a slight air of respect. Jack was a frank and charming man.

No one could be better company in forecastle or saloon; no man told such stories, sang such songs, or with greater alacrity sprang to his duty. Indeed, there was only one thing wanting about him; and that was, a finger of his left hand, which finger he had lost at the great battle of Navarino.

He had a high conceit of his profession as a seaman; and being deeply versed in all things pertaining to a man-of-war, was universally regarded as an oracle. The main-top, over which he presided, was a sort of oracle of Delphi, to which, many pilgrims ascended, to have their perplexities or differences settled.

There was such an abounding air of good sense and good feeling about the man, that he who could not love him, would thereby pronounce himself a knave. I thanked my sweet stars, that kind fortune had placed me near him, though under him, in the frigate; and from the outset Jack and I were fast friends.

Wherever you may be now rolling over the blue billows, dear Jack! take my best love along with you; and God bless you, wherever you go!

Jack was a gentleman. What though his hand was hard, so was not his heart, too often the case with soft palms. His manners were easy and free; none of the boisterousness, so common to tars; and he had a polite, courteous way of saluting you, if it were only to borrow your knife. Jack had read all the verses of Byron, and all the romances of Scott. He talked of Rob Roy, Don Juan, and Pelham; Macbeth and Ulysses; but, above all things, was an ardent admirer of Camoens. Parts of the Lusiad, he could recite in the original. Where he had obtained his wonderful accomplishments, it is not for me, his humble subordinate, to say. Enough, that those accomplishments were so various; the languages he could converse in, so numerous; that he more than furnished an example of that saying of Charles the Fifth—*he who speaks five languages is as good as five men*. But Jack, he was better than a hundred common mortals; Jack was a whole phalanx, an entire army; Jack was a thousand strong; Jack would have done honor to the Queen of England's drawing-room; Jack must have been a by-blow of some British Admiral of the Blue. A finer specimen of the island race of Englishmen could not have been picked out of Westminster Abbey of a coronation day.

His whole demeanor was in strong contrast to that of one of the Captains of the fore-top. This man, though a good seaman, furnished an example of those insufferable Britons, who, while preferring other countries to their own as places of residence; still, overflow with all the pompousness of national and individual vanity combined. "When I was on board the Audacious"—for a long time, was almost the invariable exordium to the fore-top Captain's most cursory remarks. It is often the custom of men-of-war's-men, when they deem any thing to be going on wrong aboard ship, to refer to *last cruise*, when of course every thing was done *ship-shape and Bristol fashion*. And by referring to the *Audacious*—an expressive name by the way— the fore-top Captain meant a ship in the English navy, in which he had had the honor of serving. So continual were his allusions to this craft with the amiable name, that at last, the *Audacious* was voted a bore by his shipmates. And one hot afternoon, during a calm, when the fore-top Captain, like many others, was standing still and yawning on the spar-deck; Jack Chase, his own countryman, came up to him, and pointing at his open mouth, politely inquired, whether that was the way they caught *flies* in Her Britannic Majesty's ship, the *Audacious?* After that, we heard no more of the craft.

Now, the tops of a frigate are quite spacious and cosy. They are railed in behind so as to form a kind of balcony, very pleasant of a tropical night. From twenty to thirty loungers may agreeably recline there, cushioning themselves on old sails and jackets. We had rare times in that top. We accounted ourselves the best seamen in the ship; and from our airy perch, literally looked down upon the landlopers below, sneaking about the deck, among the guns. In a large degree, we nourished that feeling of *"esprit de corps,"* always pervading, more or less, the various sections of a man-of-war's crew. We main-top-men were brothers, one and all; and we loaned ourselves to each other with all the freedom in the world.

Nevertheless, I had not long been a member of this fraternity of fine fellows, ere I discovered that Jack Chase, our captain, was—like all prime favorites and oracles among men—a little bit of a dictator; not peremptorily, or annoyingly so, but amusingly intent on egotistically mending our manners and improving our taste, so that we might reflect credit upon our tutor.

He made us all wear our hats at a particular angle—instructed us in the tie of our neck handkerchiefs; and protested against our wearing vulgar *dungeree* trowsers; besides giving us lessons in seamanship; and solemnly conjuring us, forever to eschew the company of any sailor we suspected of having served in a whaler. Against all whalers, indeed, he cherished the unmitigated detestation of a true man-of-war's man. Poor Tubbs can testify to that.

Tubbs was in the After-Guard; a long, lank Vineyarder, eternally talking of line-tubs, Nantucket, sperm oil, stove boats, and Japan. Nothing could silence him; and his comparisons were ever invidious.

Now, with all his soul, Jack abominated this Tubbs. He said he was vulgar, an upstart—Devil take him, he's been in a whaler. But like many men, who have been where *you* haven't been; or seen what *you* haven't seen; Tubbs, on account of his whaling experiences, absolutely affected to look down upon Jack, even as Jack did upon him; and this it was that so enraged our noble captain.

One night, with a peculiar meaning in his eye, he sent me down on deck to invite Tubbs up aloft for a chat. Flattered by so marked an honor—for we were somewhat fastidious, and did not extend such invitations to every body—Tubbs quickly mounted the rigging, looking rather abashed at finding himself in the august presence of the assembled Quarter-Watch of main-top-men. Jack's courteous manner, however, very soon relieved his embarrassment; but it is no use to be courteous to *some* men in this world. Tubbs belonged to that category. No sooner did the bumpkin feel himself at ease, than he lanched out, as usual, into tremendous laudations of whale-men; declaring that whalemen alone deserved the name of sailors. Jack stood it some time; but when Tubbs came down upon men-of-war, and particularly upon main-top-men, his sense of propriety was so outraged, that he lanched into Tubbs like a forty-two pounder.

"Why, you limb of Nantucket! you train-oil man! you sea-tallow strainer! you bobber after carrion! do *you* pretend to vilify a man-of-war? Why, you lean rogue, you, a man-of-war is to whalemen, as a metropolis to shire-towns, and sequestered hamlets. *Here's* the place for life and commotion; *here's* the place to be gentlemanly and jolly. And what did you know, you bumpkin! before you came on board this *Andrew Miller?* What knew you of gun-deck, or orlop, mustering round the capstan, beating to quarters, and piping to dinner? Did you ever roll to *grog* on board your greasy bally-hoo of blazes? Did you ever winter at Mahon? Did you ever '*lash and carry?*' Why, what are even a merchant-seaman's sorry yarns of voyages to China after tea-caddies, and voyages to the West Indies after sugar puncheons, and voyages to the Shetlands after seal-skins—what are even these yarns, you Tubbs you! to high life in a man-of-war? Why, you dead-eye! I have sailed with lords and marquises for captains; and the King of the Two Sicilies has passed me, as I here stood up at my gun. Bah! you are full of the fore-peak and the forecastle; you are only familiar with Burtons and Billy-tackles; your ambition never mounted above pig-killing! which, in my poor opinion, is the proper phrase for whaling! Topmates! has not this Tubbs here been but a misuser of good oak planks, and a vile desecrator of the thrice holy sea? turning his ship, my hearties! into a fat-kettle, and the ocean into a whale-pen? Begone! you graceless, godless knave! pitch him over the top there, White-Jacket!"

But there was no necessity for my exertions. Poor Tubbs, astounded at these fulminations, was already rapidly descending by the rigging.

This outburst on the part of my noble friend Jack made me shake all over, spite of my padded surtout; and caused me to offer up devout thanks-givings, that in no evil hour had I divulged the fact of having myself served in a whaler; for having previously marked the prevailing prejudice of men-of-war's-men to that much-maligned class of mariners, I had wisely held my peace concerning stove boats on the coast of Japan.

Chapter 5

Jack Chase on a Spanish Quarter-deck

HERE, I MUST FRANKLY TELL A STORY about Jack, which, as touching his honor and integrity, I am sure, will not work against him, in any charitable man's estimation. On this present cruise of the frigate Neversink, Jack had deserted; and after a certain interval, had been captured.

But with what purpose had he deserted? To avoid naval discipline? to riot in some abandoned sea-port? for love of some worthless signorita? Not at all. He abandoned the frigate from far higher and nobler, nay, glorious motives. Though bowing to naval discipline afloat; yet ashore, he was a stickler for the Rights of Man, and the liberties of the world. He went to draw a partisan blade in the civil commotions of Peru; and befriend, heart and soul, what he deemed the cause of the Right.

At the time, his disappearance excited the utmost astonishment among the officers, who had little suspected him of any such conduct as deserting.

"What? Jack, my great man of the main-top, gone!" cried the Captain: "I'll not believe it."

"Jack Chase cut and run!" cried a sentimental middy. "It must have been all for love, then; the signoritas have turned his head."

"Jack Chase not to be found?" cried a growling old sheet-anchor-man, one of your malicious prophets of past events: "I thought so; I know'd it;

I could have sworn it—just the chap to make sail on the sly. I always s'pected him."

Months passed away, and nothing was heard of Jack; till at last, the frigate came to anchor on the coast, alongside of a Peruvian sloop of war.

Bravely clad in the Peruvian uniform, and with a fine, mixed martial and naval step, a tall, striking figure of a long-bearded officer was descried, promenading the Quarter-deck of the stranger; and superintending the salutes, which are exchanged between national vessels on these occasions.

This fine officer touched his laced hat most courteously to our Captain, who, after returning the compliment, stared at him, rather impolitely, through his spy-glass.

"By Heaven!" he cried at last—"it is he—he can't disguise his walk— that's his beard; I'd know him in Cochin China.—Man the first cutter there! Lieutenant Blink, go on board that sloop of war, and fetch me yon officer."

All hands were aghast—What? when a piping-hot peace was between the United States and Peru, to send an armed body on board a Peruvian sloop of war, and seize one of its officers, in broad daylight?—Monstrous infraction of the Law of Nations! What would Vattel say?

But Captain Claret must be obeyed. So off went the cutter, every man armed to the teeth, the lieutenant commanding having secret instructions, and the midshipmen attending looking ominously wise, though, in truth, they could not tell what was coming.

Gaining the sloop of war, the lieutenant was received with the customary honors; but by this time the tall, bearded officer had disappeared from the Quarter-deck. The Lieutenant now inquired for the Peruvian Captain; and being shown into the cabin, made known to him, that on board his vessel was a person belonging to the United States Ship Neversink; and his orders were, to have that person delivered up instanter.

The foreign captain curled his mustache in astonishment and indignation; he hinted something about beating to quarters, and chastising this piece of Yankee insolence.

But resting one gloved hand upon the table, and playing with his sword-knot, the Lieutenant, with a bland firmness, repeated his demand. At last, the whole case being so plainly made out, and the person in question being so accurately described, even to a mole on his cheek, there remained nothing but immediate compliance.

So the fine-looking, bearded officer, who had so courteously doffed his chapeau to our Captain, but disappeared upon the arrival of the Lieutenant, was summoned into the cabin, before his superior, who addressed him thus:—

"Don John, this gentleman declares, that of right you belong to the frigate Neversink. Is it so?"

"It is even so, Don Sereno," said Jack Chase, proudly folding his gold-laced coat-sleeves across his chest—"and as there is no resisting the frigate, I comply.—Lieutenant Blink, I am ready. Adieu! Don Sereno, and Madre de Dios protect you! You have been a most gentlemanly friend and captain to me. I hope you will yet thrash your beggarly foes."

With that he turned; and entering the cutter, was pulled back to the frigate, and stepped up to Captain Claret, where that gentleman stood on the quarter-deck.

"Your servant, my fine Don," said the Captain, ironically lifting his chapeau, but regarding Jack at the same time with a look of intense displeasure.

"Your most devoted and penitent Captain of the Main-top, sir; and one who, in his very humility of contrition is yet proud to call Captain Claret his commander," said Jack, making a glorious bow, and then tragically flinging overboard his Peruvian sword.

"Reinstate him at once," shouted Captain Claret—"and now, sir, to your duty; and discharge that well to the end of the cruise, and you will hear no more of your having run away."

So Jack went forward among crowds of admiring tars, who swore by his nut-brown beard, which had amazingly lengthened and spread during his absence. They divided his laced hat and coat among them; and on their shoulders, carried him in triumph along the gun-deck.

Chapter 6

The Quarter-deck Officers, Warrant Officers, and Berth-deck Underlings of a Man-of-war; where they Live in the Ship; how they Live; their Social Standing on Ship-board; and what sort of Gentlemen they are

SOME ACCOUNT HAS BEEN GIVEN of the various divisions into which our crew was divided; so it may be well to say something of the officers; who they are, and what are their functions.

Our ship, be it known, was the flag-ship; that is, we sported a *broad pennant*, or *bougee*, at the main, in token that we carried a Commodore—the highest rank of officers recognized in the American navy. The bougee is not to be confounded with the *long pennant* or *coach-whip*, a tapering, serpentine streamer worn by all men-of-war.

Owing to certain vague, republican scruples, about creating great officers of the navy, America has thus far had no admirals; though, as her ships of war increase, they may become indispensable. This will assuredly be the case, should she ever have occasion to employ large fleets; when she must adopt something like the English plan, and introduce three or four grades of flag-officers, above a Commodore—Admirals, Vice-Admirals, and Rear-Admirals of Squadrons; distinguished by the colors of their flags, —red, white, and blue, corresponding to the centre, van, and rear. These rank respectively with Generals, Lieutenant Generals, and Major Generals in the army; just as a Commodore takes rank with a Brigadier General. So that the same prejudice which prevents the American Government from creating Admirals should have precluded the creation of all army officers above a Brigadier.

An American Commodore, like an English Commodore, or the French *Chef d'Escadre*, is but a senior Captain, temporarily commanding a small number of ships, detached for any special purpose. He has no permanent rank, recognized by Government, above his captaincy; though once employed as a Commodore, usage and courtesy unite in continuing the title.

Our Commodore was a gallant old man, who had seen service in his time. When a lieutenant, he served in the Late War with England; and in the gun-boat actions on the Lakes near New Orleans, just previous to the grand land engagements, received a musket-ball in his shoulder; which, with the two balls in his eyes, he carries about with him to this day.

Often, when I looked at the venerable old warrior, doubled up from the effect of his wound, I thought what a curious, as well as painful sensation, it must be, to have one's shoulder a lead-mine; though, sooth to say, so many of us civilized mortals convert our mouths into Golcondas.

On account of this wound in his shoulder, our Commodore had a body-servant's pay allowed him, in addition to his regular salary. I can not say a great deal, personally, of the Commodore; he never sought my company at all; never extended any gentlemanly courtesies.

But though I can not say much of him personally, I can mention something of him in his general character, as a flag-officer. In the first place, then, I have serious doubts, whether, for the most part, he was not dumb; for, in my hearing, he seldom or never uttered a word. And not only did he seem dumb himself, but his presence possessed the strange power of making other people dumb for the time. His appearance on the Quarter-deck seemed to give every officer the lock-jaw.

Another phenomenon about him was the strange manner in which every one shunned him. At the first sign of those epaulets of his on the weather side of the poop, the officers there congregated invariably shrunk over to leeward, and left him alone. Perhaps he had an evil eye; may be he was the Wandering Jew afloat. The real reason probably was, that, like all high functionaries, he deemed it indispensable religiously to sustain his dignity; one of the most troublesome things in the world, and one calling for the greatest self-denial. And the constant watch, and many-sided guardedness, which this sustaining of a Commodore's dignity requires, plainly enough shows that, apart from the common dignity of manhood, Commodores, in general, possess no real dignity at all. True, it is expedient for crowned heads, generalissimos, Lord-high-admirals, and Commodores, to carry themselves straight, and beware of the spinal complaint; but it is not the less veritable, that it is a piece of assumption, exceedingly uncomfortable to themselves, and ridiculous to an enlightened generation.

Now, how many rare good fellows there were among us main-topmen, who, invited into his cabin over a social bottle or two, would have rejoiced our old Commodore's heart, and caused that ancient wound of his to heal up at once.

Come, come, Commodore, don't look so sour, old boy; step up aloft here into the *top*, and we'll spin you a sociable yarn.

Truly, I thought myself much happier in that white jacket of mine, than our old Commodore in his dignified epaulets.

One thing, perhaps, that more than any thing else helped to make our Commodore so melancholy and forlorn, was the fact of his having so little to do. For as the frigate had a captain; of course, so far as *she* was concerned, our Commodore was a supernumerary. What abundance of leisure he must have had, during a three years' cruise! how indefinitely he might have been improving his mind!

But as every one knows that idleness is the hardest work in the world, so our Commodore was specially provided with a gentleman to assist him. This gentleman was called the *Commodore's secretary*. He was a remarkably urbane and polished man; with a very graceful exterior, and looked much like an Embassador Extraordinary from Versailles. He messed with the Lieutenants in the Ward-room, where he had a state-room, elegantly furnished as the private cabinet of Pelham. His cot-boy used to entertain the sailors with all manner of stories about the silver-keyed flutes and flageolets, fine oil paintings, morocco bound volumes, Chinese chess-men, gold shirt-buttons, enameled pencil cases, extraordinary fine French boots with soles no thicker than a sheet of scented note-paper, embroidered vests, incense-burning sealing-wax, alabaster statuettes of Venus and Adonis, tortoise-shell snuff-boxes, inlaid toilet-cases, ivory-handled hair-brushes and mother-of-pearl combs, and a hundred other luxurious appendages scattered about this magnificent secretary's state-room.

I was a long time in finding out what this secretary's duties comprised. But it seemed, he wrote the Commodore's dispatches for Washington, and also was his general amanuensis. Nor was this a very light duty, at times; for some Commodores, though they do not *say* a great deal on board ship, yet they have a vast deal to write. Very often, the regimental orderly, stationed at our Commodore's cabin-door, would touch his hat to the First Lieutenant, and with a mysterious air hand him a note. I always thought these notes must contain most important matters of state; until one day, seeing a slip of wet, torn paper in a scupper-hole, I read the following:

"Sir, you will give the people pickles to-day with their fresh meat.
"To Lieutenant Bridewell.
"By command of the Commodore.
"ADOLPHUS DASHMAN, Priv. Sec."

This was a new revelation; for, from his almost immutable reserve, I had supposed that the Commodore never meddled immediately with the concerns of the ship, but left all that to the captain. But the longer we live, the more we learn of Commodores.

Turn we now to the second officer in rank, almost supreme, however, in the internal affairs of his ship. Captain Claret was a large, portly man, a Harry the Eighth afloat, bluff and hearty; and as kingly in his cabin as Harry on his throne. For a ship is a bit of terra firma cut off from the main; it is a state in itself; and the captain is its king.

It is no limited monarchy, where the sturdy Commons have a right to petition, and snarl if they please; but almost a despotism, like the Grand Turk's. The captain's word is law; he never speaks but in the imperative mood. When he stands on his Quarter-deck at sea, he absolutely commands as far as eye can reach. Only the moon and stars are beyond his jurisdiction. He is lord and master of the sun.

It is not twelve o'clock till he says so. For when the sailing-master, whose duty it is to take the regular observation at noon, touches his hat, and reports twelve o'clock to the officer of the deck; that functionary orders a midshipman to repair to the captain's cabin, and humbly inform him of the respectful suggestion of the sailing-master.

"Twelve o'clock reported, sir," says the middy.

"*Make* it so," replies the captain.

And the bell is struck eight by the messenger-boy, and twelve o'clock it is.

As in the case of the Commodore, when the captain visits the deck, his subordinate officers generally beat a retreat to the other side; and, as a general rule, would no more think of addressing him, except concerning the ship, than a lackey would think of hailing the Czar of Russia on his throne, and inviting him to tea. Perhaps no mortal man has more reason to feel such an intense sense of his own personal consequence, as the captain of a man-of-war at sea.

Next in rank comes the First or Senior Lieutenant, the chief executive officer. I have no reason to love the particular gentleman who filled that post aboard of our frigate, for it was he who refused my petition for as much black paint as would render water-proof that white jacket of mine. All my soakings and drenchings lie at his state-room door. I hardly think I shall ever forgive him; every twinge of the rheumatism, which I still occasionally feel, is directly referable to him. The Immortals have a reputation for clemency; and *they* may pardon him; but he must not dun me to be merciful. But my personal feelings toward the man shall not prevent me from here doing him justice. In most things, he was an excellent seaman; prompt, loud, and to the point; and as such, was well fitted for his station. The First Lieutenancy of a frigate demands a good disciplinarian, and, every way, an energetic man. By the captain he is held responsible for every thing; by that magnate, indeed, he is supposed to be omnipresent; down in the hold, and up aloft, at one and the same time.

He presides at the head of the Ward-room officers' table, who are so called from their messing together in a part of the ship thus designated. In a frigate it comprises the after part of the berth-deck. Sometimes it goes by the name of the Gun-room, but oftener is called the Ward-room. Within, this Ward-room much resembles a long, wide corridor in a large hotel; numerous doors opening on both hands to the private apartments of the officers. The first time I had a look at it, the Chaplain was seated at the table in the centre, playing chess with the Lieutenant of Marines. It was mid-day, but the place was lighted by lamps.

Besides the First Lieutenant, the Ward-room officers include the junior lieutenants, in a frigate six or seven in number, the Sailing-master, Purser, Chaplain, Surgeon, Marine officers, and Midshipmen's Schoolmaster, or "the Professor." They generally form a very agreeable club of good fellows; from their diversity of character, admirably calculated to form an agreeable social whole. The Lieutenants discuss sea-fights, and tell anecdotes of Lord Nelson and Lady Hamilton; the Marine officers talk of storming fortresses, and the siege of Gibraltar; the Purser steadies this wild conversation by occasional allusions to the rule of three; the Professor is always charged with a scholarly reflection, or an apt line from the classics, generally Ovid; the Surgeon's stories of the amputation-table judiciously serve to suggest the mortality of the whole party as men; while the good chaplain stands ready at all times to give them pious counsel and consolation.

Of course these gentlemen all associate on a footing of perfect social equality.

Next in order come the Warrant or Forward officers, consisting of the Boatswain, Gunner, Carpenter, and Sail-maker. Though these worthies sport long coats and wear the anchor-button; yet, in the estimation of the ward-room officers, they are not, technically speaking, rated gentlemen. The First Lieutenant, Chaplain, or Surgeon, for example, would never dream of inviting them to dinner. In sea parlance, "they come in at the hawse holes;" they have hard hands; and the carpenter and sail-maker practically understand the duties which they are called upon to superintend. They mess by themselves. Invariably four in number, they never have need to play whist with a dummy.

In this part of the category now come the "reefers," otherwise "middies" or midshipmen. These boys are sent to sea, for the purpose of making commodores; and in order to become commodores, many of them deem it indispensable forthwith to commence chewing tobacco, drinking brandy and water, and swearing at the sailors. As they are only placed on board a sea-going ship to go to school and learn the duty of a Lieutenant; and until qualified to act as such, have few or no special functions to attend to; they are little more, while midshipmen, than supernumeraries on board. Hence, in a crowded frigate, they are so everlastingly crossing the path of both men and officers, that in the navy it has become a proverb, that a useless fellow is *"as much in the way as a reefer."*

In a gale of wind, when all hands are called and the deck swarms with men, the little "middies" running about distracted and having nothing particular to do, make it up in vociferous swearing; exploding all about under foot like torpedoes. Some of them are terrible little boys, cocking their caps at alarming angles, and looking fierce as young roosters. They are generally great consumers of Macassar oil and the Balm of Columbia; they thirst and rage after whiskers; and sometimes, applying their ointments, lay themselves out in the sun, to promote the fertility of their chins.

As the only way to learn to command, is to learn to obey, the usage of a ship of war is such that the midshipmen are constantly being ordered about by the Lieutenants; though, without having assigned them their particular destinations, they are always going somewhere, and never arriving. In some things, they almost have a harder time of it than the seamen themselves. They are messengers and errand-boys to their superiors.

"Mr. Pert," cries an officer of the deck, hailing a young gentleman forward. Mr. Pert advances, touches his hat, and remains in an attitude of deferential suspense. "Go and tell the boatswain I want him." And with this perilous errand, the middy hurries away, looking proud as a king.

The middies live by themselves in the steerage, where, nowadays, they dine off a table, spread with a cloth. They have a castor at dinner; they have some other little boys (selected from the ship's company) to wait upon them; they sometimes drink coffee out of china. But for all these, their modern refinements, in some instances the affairs of their club go sadly to rack and ruin. The china is broken; the japanned coffee-pot dented like a pewter mug in an ale-house; the pronged forks resemble tooth-picks (for which they are sometimes used); the table-knives are hacked into hand-saws; and the cloth goes to the sail-maker to be patched. Indeed, they are something like collegiate freshmen and sophomores, living in the college buildings, especially so far as the noise they make in their quarters is concerned. The steerage buzzes, hums, and swarms like a hive; or like an infant-school of a hot day, when the schoolmistress falls asleep with a fly on her nose.

In frigates, the ward-room—the retreat of the Lieutenants—immediately adjoining the steerage, is on the same deck with it. Frequently, when the middies, waking early of a morning, as most youngsters do, would be kicking up their heels in their hammocks, or running about with double-reefed night-gowns, playing *tag* among the "clews;" the Senior Lieutenant would burst among them with a—"Young gentlemen, I am astonished. You must stop this sky-larking. Mr. Pert, what are you doing at the table there, without your pantaloons? To your hammock, sir. Let me see no more of this. If you disturb the ward-room again, young gentlemen, you shall hear of it." And so saying, this hoary-headed Senior Lieutenant would retire to his cot in his state-room, like the father of a numerous family after getting up in his dressing-gown and slippers, to quiet a daybreak tumult in his populous nursery.

Having now descended from Commodore to Middy, we come lastly to a set of nondescripts, forming also a "mess" by themselves, apart from the seamen. Into this mess, the usage of a man-of-war thrusts various subordinates—including the master-at-arms, purser's steward, ship's corporals, marine sergeants, and ship's yeomen, forming the first aristocracy above the sailors.

The master-at-arms is a sort of high constable and schoolmaster, wearing citizen's clothes, and known by his official rattan. He it is whom all sailors hate. His is the universal duty of a universal informer and hunter-up of delinquents. On the berth-deck he reigns supreme; spying out all grease spots made by the various cooks of the seamen's messes, and driving the laggards up the hatches, when all hands are called. It is indispensable that he should be a very Vidocq in vigilance. But as it is a heartless, so is it a thankless office. Of dark nights, most masters-at-arms keep themselves in readiness to dodge forty-two pound balls, dropped down the hatchways near them.

The ship's corporals are this worthy's deputies and ushers.

The marine sergeants are generally tall fellows with unyielding spines and stiff upper lips, and very exclusive in their tastes and predilections.

The ship's yeoman is a gentleman who has a sort of counting-room in a tar-cellar down in the fore-hold. More will be said of him anon.

Except the officers above enumerated, there are none who mess apart from the seamen. The "*petty officers*," so called; that is, the Boatswain's, Gunner's, Carpenter's, and Sail-maker's mates, the Captains of the Tops, of the Forecastle, and of the After-Guard, and of the Fore and Main holds, and the Quarter-Masters, all mess in common with the crew, and in the American navy are only distinguished from the common seamen by their slightly additional pay. But in the English navy they wear crowns and anchors worked on the sleeves of their jackets, by way of badges of office. In the French navy they are known by strips of worsted worn in the same place, like those designating the Sergeants and Corporals in the army.

Thus it will be seen, that the dinner-table is the criterion of rank in our man-of-war world. The Commodore dines alone, because he is the only man of his rank in the ship. So too with the Captain; and the Ward-room officers, warrant officers, midshipmen, the master-at-arms' mess, and the common seamen;—all of them, respectively, dine together, because they are, respectively, on a footing of equality.

For the same reason, the Commodore has his own steward and cook, who wait upon nobody but him; also his own stove, where nothing is cooked but for his meals. So, too, with the Captain. The ward-room officers, also, have their own steward and cook; also, the midshipmen. The cooking for these two classes is done at a distinct part of the great galley—the forward end—a place called "the range." This is a wide grate, several feet long.

Chapter 7

Breakfast, Dinner, and Supper

NOT ONLY IS THE DINNER-TABLE a criterion of rank on board a man-of-war, but also the dinner hour. He who dines latest is the greatest man; and he who dines earliest is accounted the least. In a flag-ship, the Commodore generally dines about four or five o'clock; the Captain about three; the Lieutenants about two; while *the people** (by which phrase the common seamen are specially designated in the nomenclature of the quarter-deck) sit down to their salt beef exactly at noon.

Thus it will be seen, that while the two estates of sea-kings and sea-lords dine at rather patrician hours—and thereby, in the long run, impair their digestive functions—the sea-commoners, or *the people*, keep up their constitutions, by keeping up the good old-fashioned, Elizabethan, Franklin-warranted dinner hour of twelve.

Twelve o'clock! It is the natural centre, key-stone, and very heart of the day. At that hour, the sun has arrived at the top of his hill; and as he seems to hang poised there a while, before coming down on the other side, it is but reasonable to suppose that he is then stopping to dine; setting an eminent example to all mankind. The rest of the day is called *afternoon*; the very sound of which fine old Saxon word conveys a feeling of the lee bulwarks

* In the same nomenclature, they are also especially designated as "the men."

and a nap; a summer sea—soft breezes creeping over it; dreamy dolphins gliding in the distance. *Afternoon!* the word implies, that it is an after-piece, coming after the grand drama of the day; something to be taken leisurely and lazily. But how can this be, if you dine at five? For, after all, though Paradise Lost be a noble poem, and we men-of-war's men, no doubt, largely partake in the immortality of the immortals; yet, let us candidly confess it, shipmates, that, upon the whole, our dinners are the most momentous affairs of these lives we lead beneath the moon. What were a day without a dinner? a dinnerless day! such a day had better be a night.

Again: twelve o'clock is the natural hour for us men-of-war's men to dine, because at that hour the very time-pieces we have invented arrive at their terminus; they can get no further than twelve; when straightway they continue their old rounds again. Doubtless, Adam and Eve dined at twelve; and the Patriarch Abraham in the midst of his cattle; and old Job with his noon mowers and reapers, in that grand plantation of Uz; and old Noah himself, in the Ark, must have gone to dinner at precisely *eight bells* (noon), with all his floating families and farm-yards.

But though this antediluvian dinner hour is rejected by modern Commodores and Captains, it still lingers among "*the people*" under their command. Many sensible things banished from high life find an asylum among the mob.

Some Commodores are very particular in seeing to it, that no man on board the ship dare to dine after his (the Commodore's) own dessert is cleared away.—Not even the Captain. It is said, on good authority, that a Captain once ventured to dine at five, when the Commodore's hour was four. Next day, as the story goes, that Captain received a private note; and in consequence of that note, dined for the future at half past three.

Though in respect of the dinner hour on board a man-of-war, *the people* have no reason to complain; yet they have just cause, almost for mutiny, in the outrageous hours assigned for their breakfast and supper.

Eight o'clock for breakfast; twelve for dinner; four for supper; and no meals but these; no lunches and no cold snacks. Owing to this arrangement (and partly to one watch going to their meals before the other, at sea), all the meals of the twenty-four hours are crowded into a space of less than eight! Sixteen mortal hours elapse between supper and breakfast; including, to one watch, eight hours on deck! This is barbarous; any physician will tell you so. Think of it! Before the Commodore has dined, you have supped. And in high latitudes, in summer-time, you have taken your last meal for the day, and five hours, or more, daylight to spare!

Mr. Secretary of the Navy, in the name of *the people*, you should interpose in this matter. Many a time have I, a main-top-man, found myself actually faint of a tempestuous morning watch, when all my energies were demanded—owing to this miserable, unphilosophical mode of allotting the government meals at sea. We beg of you, Mr. Secretary, not to be swayed in this matter by the Honorable Board of Commodores, who will no doubt tell you that eight, twelve, and four are the proper hours for *the people* to take their meals; inasmuch, as at these hours the watches are relieved. For, though this arrangement makes a neater and cleaner thing of it for the officers, and looks very nice and superfine on paper; yet, it is plainly detrimental to health; and in time of war is attended with still more serious consequences to the whole nation at large. If the necessary researches were made, it would perhaps be found that in those instances where men-of-war adopting the above-mentioned hours for meals have encountered an enemy at night, they have pretty generally been beaten; that is, in those cases where the enemies' meal times were reasonable; which is only to be accounted for by the fact that *the people* of the beaten vessels were fighting on an empty stomach instead of a full one.

Chapter 8

Selvagee contrasted with Mad-Jack

H AVING GLANCED AT THE GRAND DIVISIONS of a man-of-war, let us now descend to specialties; and, particularly, to two of the junior lieutenants; lords and noblemen; members of that House of Peers, the gun-room. There were several young lieutenants on board; but from these two—representing the extremes of character to be found in their department—the nature of the other officers of their grade in the Neversink must be derived.

One of these two quarter-deck lords went among the sailors by a name of their own devising—Selvagee. Of course, it was intended to be characteristic; and even so it was.

In frigates, and all large ships of war, when getting under weigh, a large rope, called a *messenger*, is used to carry the strain of the cable to the capstan; so that the anchor may be weighed, without the muddy, ponderous cable itself going round the capstan. As the cable enters the hawse-hole, therefore, something must be constantly used, to keep this traveling chain attached to this traveling *messenger*; something that may be rapidly wound round both, so as to bind them together. The article used is called a *selvagee*. And what could be better adapted to the purpose? It is a slender, tapering, unstranded piece of rope; prepared with much solicitude; peculiarly flexible; and wreathes and serpentines round the cable and messenger like an elegantly-modeled garter-snake round the twisted stalks of a vine. Indeed, *Selvagee* is the exact type and symbol of a tall, genteel, limber, spiralizing exquisite. So much for the derivation of the name which the sailors applied to the Lieutenant.

From what sea-alcove, from what mermaid's milliner's shop, hast thou emerged, Selvagee! with that dainty waist and languid cheek? What heartless step-dame drove thee forth, to waste thy fragrance on the salt sea-air?

Was it *you*, Selvagee! that, outward-bound, off Cape Horn, looked at Hermit Island through an Opera-glass? Was it *you*, who thought of proposing to the Captain, that when the sails were furled in a gale, a few drops of lavender should be dropped in their "bunts," so that when the canvass was set again, your nostrils might not be offended by its musty smell? I do not *say* it was you, Selvagee; I but deferentially inquire.

In plain prose, Selvagee was one of those officers whom the sight of a trim-fitting naval coat had captivated in the days of his youth. He fancied, that if a sea-officer dressed well, and conversed genteelly, he would abundantly uphold the honor of his flag, and immortalize the tailor that made him. On that rock many young gentlemen split. For upon a frigate's quarter-deck, it is not enough to sport a coat fashioned by a Stultz; it is not enough to be well braced with straps and suspenders; it is not enough to have sweet reminiscences of Lauras and Matildas. It is a right down life of hard wear and tear, and the man who is not, in a good degree, fitted to become a common sailor will never make an officer. Take that to heart, all ye naval aspirants. Thrust your arms up to the elbow in pitch, and see how you like it, ere you solicit a warrant. Prepare for white squalls, living gales and Typhoons; read accounts of shipwrecks and horrible disasters; peruse the Narratives of Byron and Bligh; familiarize yourselves with the story of the English frigate Alceste, and the French frigate Medusa. Though you may go ashore, now and then, at Cadiz and Palermo; for every day so spent among oranges and ladies, you will have whole months of rains and gales.

And even thus did Selvagee prove it. But with all the intrepid effeminacy of your true dandy, he still continued his Cologne-water baths, and sported his lace-bordered handkerchiefs in the very teeth of a tempest. Alas, Selvagee! there was no getting the lavender out of you.

But Selvagee was no fool. Theoretically he understood his profession; but the mere theory of seamanship forms but the thousandth part of what makes a seaman. You can not save a ship by working out a problem in the cabin; the deck is the field of action.

Well aware of his deficiency in some things, Selvagee never took the trumpet—which is the badge of the deck officer for the time—without a tremulous movement of the lip, and an earnest, inquiring eye to the windward. He encouraged those old Tritons, the Quarter-masters, to discourse with him concerning the likelihood of a squall; and often followed their advice as to taking in, or making sail. The smallest favors in that way were thankfully received. Sometimes, when all the North looked unusually lowering, by many conversational blandishments, he would endeavor to prolong his predecessor's stay on deck, after that officer's watch had expired. But in fine, steady weather, when the Captain would emerge from his cabin, Selvagee might be seen, pacing the poop with long, bold, indefatigable strides, and casting his eye up aloft with the most ostentatious fidelity.

But vain these pretences; he could not deceive. Selvagee! you know very well, that if it comes on to blow pretty hard, the First Lieutenant will be sure to interfere with his paternal authority. Every man and every boy in the frigate knows, Selvagee, that you are no Neptune.

How unenviable his situation! His brother officers do not insult him, to be sure; but sometimes their looks are as daggers. The sailors do not laugh at him outright; but of dark nights they jeer, when they hearken to that mantua-maker's voice ordering *a strong pull at the main brace*, or *hands by the halyards!* Sometimes, by way of being terrific, and making the men jump, Selvagee raps out an oath; but the soft bomb stuffed with confectioner's kisses seems to burst like a crushed rose-bud diffusing its odors. Selvagee! Selvagee! take a main-top-man's advice; and this cruise over, never more tempt the sea.

With this gentleman of cravats and curling irons, how strongly contrasts the man who was born in a gale! For in some time of tempest—off Cape Horn or Hatteras—*Mad Jack* must have entered the world—such things have been—not with a silver spoon, but with a speaking-trumpet in his mouth; wrapped up in a caul, as in a main-sail—for a charmed life against shipwrecks he bears—and crying, *Luff! luff, you may!—steady!—port! World ho!—here I am!*

Mad Jack is in his saddle on the sea. *That* is his home; he would not care much, if another Flood came and overflowed the dry land; for what would it do but float his good ship higher and higher and carry his proud nation's flag round the globe, over the very capitals of all hostile states! Then would masts surmount spires; and all mankind, like the Chinese boatmen in Canton River, live in flotillas and fleets, and find their food in the sea.

Mad Jack was expressly created and labelled for a tar. Five feet nine is his mark, in his socks; and not weighing over eleven stone before dinner.

Like so many ship's shrouds, his muscles and tendons are all set true, trim, and taut; he is braced up fore and aft, like a ship on the wind. His broad chest is a bulk-head, that dams off the gale; and his nose is an aquiline, that divides it in two, like a keel. His loud, lusty lungs are two belfries, full of all manner of chimes; but you only hear his deepest bray, in the height of some tempest—like the great bell of St. Paul's, which only sounds when the King or the Devil is dead.

Look at him there, where he stands on the poop—one foot on the rail, and one hand on a shroud—his head thrown back, and his trumpet like an elephant's trunk thrown up in the air. Is he going to shoot dead with sound, those fellows on the main-topsail-yard?

Mad Jack was a bit of a tyrant—they *say* all good officers are—but the sailors loved him all round; and would much rather stand fifty watches with him, than one with a rose-water sailor.

But Mad Jack, alas! has one fearful failing. He drinks. And so do we all. But Mad Jack, *he* only drinks brandy. The vice was inveterate; surely, like Ferdinand, Count Fathom, he must have been suckled at a puncheon. Very often, this bad habit got him into very serious scrapes. Twice was he put off duty by the Commodore; and once he came near being broken for his frolics. So far as his efficiency as a sea-officer was concerned, on shore at least, Jack might *bouse away* as much as he pleased; but afloat it will not do at all.

Now, if he only followed the wise example set by those ships of the desert, the camels; and while in port, drank for the thirst past, the thirst present, and the thirst to come—so that he might cross the ocean sober; Mad Jack would get along pretty well. Still better, if he would but eschew brandy altogether; and only drink of the limpid white-wine of the rills and the brooks.

Chapter 9

Of the Pockets that were in the Jacket

I MUST MAKE SOME FURTHER MENTION of that white jacket
of mine.

And here be it known—by way of introduction to what is to follow—
that to a common sailor, the living on board a man-of-war is like living in
a market; where you dress on the door-steps, and sleep in the cellar. No
privacy can you have; hardly one moment's seclusion. It is almost a physical
impossibility, that you can ever be alone. You dine at a vast *table d'hôte;*
sleep in commons, and make your toilet where and when you can. There
is no calling for a mutton chop and a pint of claret by yourself; no selecting
of chambers for the night; no hanging of pantaloons over the back of a
chair; no ringing your bell of a rainy morning, to take your coffee in bed.
It is something like life in a large manufactory. The bell strikes to dinner,
and hungry or not, you must dine.

Your clothes are stowed in a large canvas bag, generally painted black,
which you can get out of the "rack" only once in the twenty-four hours;
and then, during a time of the utmost confusion; among five hundred other
bags, with five hundred other sailors diving into each, in the midst of the
twilight of the berth deck. In some measure to obviate this inconvenience,
many sailors divide their wardrobes between their hammocks and their
bags; stowing a few frocks and trowsers in the former; so that they can shift

35

at night, if they wish, when the hammocks are piped down. But they gain very little by this.

You have no place whatever but your bag or hammock, in which to put any thing in a man-of-war. If you lay any thing down, and turn your back for a moment, ten to one it is gone.

Now, in sketching the preliminary plan, and laying out the foundation of that memorable white jacket of mine, I had had an earnest eye to all these inconveniences, and resolved to avoid them. I proposed, that not only should my jacket keep me warm, but that it should also be so constructed as to contain a shirt or two, a pair of trowsers, and divers knickknacks—sewing utensils, books, biscuits, and the like. With this object, I had accordingly provided it with a great variety of pockets, pantries, clothes-presses, and cupboards.

The principal apartments, two in number, were placed in the skirts, with a wide, hospitable entrance from the inside; two more, of smaller capacity, were planted in each breast, with folding-doors communicating, so that in case of emergency, to accommodate any bulky articles, the two pockets in each breast could be thrown into one. There were, also, several unseen recesses behind the arras; insomuch, that my jacket, like an old castle, was full of winding stairs, and mysterious closets, crypts, and cabinets; and like a confidential writing-desk, abounded in snug little out-of-the-way lairs and hiding-places, for the storage of valuables.

Superadded to these, were four capacious pockets on the outside; one pair to slip books into when suddenly started from my studies to the main-royal-yard; and the other pair, for permanent mittens, to thrust my hands into of a cold night-watch. This last contrivance was regarded as needless by one of my top-mates, who showed me a pattern for sea-mittens, which he said was much better than mine.

It must be known, that sailors, even in the bleakest weather, only cover their hands when unemployed; they never wear mittens aloft; since aloft, they literally carry their lives in their hands, and want nothing between their grasp of the hemp, and the hemp itself.—Therefore, it is desirable, that whatever things they cover their hands with, should be capable of being slipped on and off in a moment. Nay, it is desirable, that they should be of such a nature, that in a dark night, when you are in a great hurry—say, going to the helm—they may be jumped into, indiscriminately; and not be like a pair of right-and-left kids; neither of which will admit any hand, but the particular one meant for it.

My top-mate's contrivance was this—he ought to have got out a patent for it—each of his mittens was provided with two thumbs, one on each side; the convenience of which needs no comment. But though for clumsy seamen, whose fingers are all thumbs, this description of mitten might do very well, White-Jacket did not so much fancy it. For when your hand was once in the bag of the mitten, the empty thumb-hole sometimes dangled at your palm, confounding your ideas of where your real thumb might be; or else, being carefully grasped in the hand, was continually suggesting the insane notion, that you were all the while having hold of some one else's thumb.

No; I told my good top-mate to go away with his four thumbs, I would have nothing to do with them; two thumbs were enough for any man.

For some time after completing my jacket, and getting the furniture and household stores in it; I thought that nothing could exceed it, for convenience. Seldom now did I have occasion to go to my bag, and be jostled by the crowd who were making their wardrobe in a heap. If I wanted any thing in the way of clothing, thread, needles, or literature, the chances were that my invaluable jacket contained it. Yes: I fairly hugged myself, and reveled in my jacket; till alas! a long rain put me out of conceit of it. I, and all my pantries and their contents, were soaked through and through, and my pocket-edition of Shakspeare was reduced to an omelet.

However, availing myself of a fine sunny day that followed, I emptied myself out in the main-top, and spread all my goods and chattels to dry. But spite of the bright sun, that day proved a black one. The scoundrels on deck detected me in the act of discharging my saturated cargo; they now knew that the white jacket was used for a store-house. The consequence was that, my goods being well dried and again stored away in my pockets, the very next night, when it was my quarter watch on deck, and not in the top (where they were all honest men), I noticed a parcel of fellows skulking about after me, wherever I went. To a man, they were pickpockets, and bent upon pillaging me. In vain I kept clapping my pockets like nervous old gentlemen in a crowd; that same night I found myself minus several valuable articles. So, in the end, I masoned up my lockers and pantries; and save the two used for mittens, the white jacket ever after was pocketless.

Chapter 10

From Pockets to Pickpockets

A S THE LATTER PART of the preceding chapter may seem strange to those landsmen, who have been habituated to indulge in high-raised, romantic notions of the man-of-war's man's character; it may not be amiss, to set down here certain facts on this head, which may serve to place the thing in its true light.

From the wild life they lead, and various other causes (needless to mention), sailors, as a class, entertain the most liberal notions concerning morality and the Decalogue; or rather, they take their own views of such matters, caring little for the theological or ethical definitions of others concerning what may be criminal, or wrong.

Their ideas are much swayed by circumstances. They will covertly abstract a thing from one, whom they dislike; and insist upon it, that, in such a case, stealing is no robbing. Or, where the theft involves something funny, as in the case of the white jacket, they only steal for the sake of the joke; but this much is to be observed nevertheless, i. e., that they never spoil the joke by returning the stolen article.

It is a good joke, for instance, and one often perpetrated on board ship, to stand talking to a man in a dark night watch, and all the while be cutting the buttons from his coat. But once off, those buttons never grow on again. There is no spontaneous vegetation in buttons.

Perhaps it is a thing unavoidable, but the truth is that, among the crew of a man-of-war, scores of desperadoes are too often found, who stop not at the largest enormities. A species of highway robbery is not unknown to them. A *gang* will be informed, that such a fellow has three or four gold pieces in the monkey-bag, so called, or purse, which many tars wear round their necks, tucked out of sight. Upon this, they deliberately lay their plans; and in due time, proceed to carry them into execution. The man they have marked is perhaps strolling along the benighted berth-deck to his mess-chest; when, of a sudden, the foot-pads dash out from their hiding-place, throw him down, and while two or three gag him, and hold him fast, another cuts the bag from his neck, and makes away with it, followed by his comrades. This was more than once done in the Neversink.

At other times, hearing that a sailor has something valuable secreted in his hammock, they will rip it open from underneath while he sleeps, and reduce the conjecture to a certainty.

To enumerate all the minor pilferings on board a man-of-war would be endless. With some highly commendable exceptions, they rob from one another, and rob back again, till, in the matter of small things, a community of goods seems almost established; and at last, as a whole, they become relatively honest, by nearly every man becoming the reverse. It is in vain that the officers, by threats of condign punishment, endeavor to instill more virtuous principles into their crew; so thick is the mob, that not one thief in a thousand is detected.

Chapter 11

The Pursuit of Poetry under Difficulties

T HE FEELING OF INSECURITY concerning one's possessions in the Neversink, which the things just narrated begat in the minds of honest men, was curiously exemplified in the case of my poor friend Lemsford, a gentlemanly young member of the After-Guard. I had very early made the acquaintance of Lemsford. It is curious, how unerringly a man pitches upon a spirit, any way akin to his own, even in the most miscellaneous mob.

Lemsford was a poet; so thoroughly inspired with the divine afflatus, that not even all the tar and tumult of a man-of-war could drive it out of him.

As may readily be imagined, the business of writing verse is a very different thing on the gun-deck of a frigate, from what the gentle and sequestered Wordsworth found it at placid Rydal Mount in Westmoreland. In a frigate, you can not sit down and meander off your sonnets, when the full heart prompts; but only, when more important duties permit: such as bracing round the yards, or reefing top-sails fore and aft. Nevertheless, every fragment of time at his command was religiously devoted by Lemsford to the Nine. At the most unseasonable hours, you would behold him, seated apart, in some corner among the guns—a shot-box before him, pen in hand, and eyes "*in a fine frenzy rolling.*"

"What's that 'ere born nat'ral about?"—"He's got a fit, hain't he?"
were exclamations often made by the less learned of his shipmates. Some
deemed him a conjurer; others a lunatic; and the knowing ones said, that
he must be a crazy Methodist. But well knowing by experience the truth
of the saying, that *poetry is its own exceeding great reward*, Lemsford wrote on;
dashing off whole epics, sonnets, ballads, and acrostics, with a facility which,
under the circumstances, amazed me. Often he read over his effusions to me;
and well worth the hearing they were. He had wit, imagination, feeling,
and humor in abundance; and out of the very ridicule with which some
persons regarded him, he made rare metrical sport, which we two together
enjoyed by ourselves; or shared with certain select friends.

Still, the taunts and jeers so often leveled at my fine friend the poet,
would now and then rouse him into rage; and at such times the haughty
scorn he would hurl on his foes, was proof positive of his possession of that
one attribute, irritability, almost universally ascribed to the votaries of
Parnassus and the Nine.

My noble Captain, Jack Chase, rather patronized Lemsford, and he
would stoutly take his part against scores of adversaries. Frequently, inviting him up aloft into his top, he would beg him to recite some of his
verses; to which he would pay the most heedful attention, like Mecænas
listening to Virgil, with a book of the Æneid in his hand. Taking the liberty
of a well-wisher, he would sometimes gently criticise the piece, suggesting
a few immaterial alterations. And upon my word, noble Jack, with his
native-born good sense, taste, and humanity, was not ill qualified to play
the true part of a *Quarterly Review;*—which is, to give quarter at last, however severe the critique.

Now Lemsford's great care, anxiety, and endless source of tribulation
was the preservation of his manuscripts. He had a little box, about the size
of a small dressing-case, and secured with a lock, in which he kept his papers
and stationery. This box, of course, he could not keep in his bag or hammock, for, in either case, he would only be able to get at it once in the
twenty-four hours. It was necessary to have it accessible at all times. So
when not using it, he was obliged to hide it out of sight, where he could.
And of all places in the world, a ship of war, above her *hold*, least abounds
in secret nooks. Almost every inch is occupied; almost every inch is in plain
sight; and almost every inch is continually being visited and explored.
Added to all this, was the deadly hostility of the whole tribe of ship-
underlings—master at-arms, ship's corporals, and boatswain's mates,—
both to the poet and his casket. They hated his box, as if it had been

Pandora's, crammed to the very lid with hurricanes and gales. They hunted out his hiding-places like pointers, and gave him no peace night or day.

Still, the long twenty-four-pounders on the main-deck offered some promise of a hiding-place to the box; and, accordingly, it was often tucked away behind the carriages, among the side tackles; its black color blending with the ebon hue of the guns.

But Quoin, one of the quarter-gunners, had eyes like a ferret. Quoin was a little old man-of-war's man, hardly five feet high, with a complexion like a gun-shot wound after it is healed. He was indefatigable in attending to his duties; which consisted in taking care of one division of the guns, embracing ten of the aforesaid twenty-four-pounders. Ranged up against the ship's side at regular intervals, they resembled not a little a stud of sable chargers in their stalls. Among this iron stud little Quoin was continually running in and out, currying them down, now and then, with an old rag, or keeping the flies off with a brush. To Quoin, the honor and dignity of the United States of America seemed indissolubly linked with the keeping his guns unspotted and glossy. He himself was black as a chimney-sweep with continually tending them, and rubbing them down with black paint. He would sometimes get outside of the port-holes and peer into their muzzles, as a monkey into a bottle. Or, like a dentist, he seemed intent upon examining their teeth. Quite as often, he would be brushing out their touch-holes with a little wisp of oakum, like a Chinese barber in Canton, cleaning a patient's ear.

Such was his solicitude, that it was a thousand pities he was not able to dwarf himself still more, so as to creep in at the touch-hole, and examining the whole interior of the tube, emerge at last from the muzzle. Quoin swore by his guns, and slept by their side. Woe betide the man whom he found leaning against them, or in any way soiling them. He seemed seized with the crazy fancy, that his darling twenty-four-pounders were fragile, and might break, like glass retorts.

Now, from this Quoin's vigilance, how could my poor friend the poet hope to escape with his box? Twenty times a week it was pounced upon, with a "here's that d—d pill-box again!" and a loud threat, to pitch it overboard the next time, without a moment's warning, or benefit of clergy. Like many poets, Lemsford was nervous, and upon these occasions he trembled like a leaf. Once, with an inconsolable countenance, he came to me, saying that his casket was nowhere to be found; he had sought for it in his hiding-place, and it was not there.

I asked him where he had hidden it?

"Among the guns," he replied.

"Then depend upon it, Lemsford, that Quoin has been the death of it."

Straight to Quoin went the poet. But Quoin knew nothing about it. For ten mortal days the poet was not to be comforted; dividing his leisure time between cursing Quoin and lamenting his loss. The world is undone, he must have thought; no such calamity has befallen it since the Deluge; —my verses are perished.

But though Quoin, as it afterward turned out, had indeed found the box, it so happened that he had not destroyed it; which no doubt led Lemsford to infer that a superintending Providence had interposed to preserve to posterity his invaluable casket. It was found at last, lying exposed near the galley.

Lemsford was not the only literary man on board the Neversink. There were three or four persons who kept journals of the cruise. One of these journalists embellished his work—which was written in a large blank account-book—with various colored illustrations of the harbors and bays at which the frigate had touched; and also, with small crayon sketches of comical incidents on board the frigate itself. He would frequently read passages of his book to an admiring circle of the more refined sailors, between the guns. They pronounced the whole performance a miracle of art. As the author declared to them that it was all to be printed and published so soon as the vessel reached home, they vied with each other in procuring interesting items, to be incorporated into additional chapters. But it having been rumored abroad that this journal was to be ominously entitled "*The Cruise of the Neversink, or a Paixhan Shot into Naval Abuses;*" and it having also reached the ears of the Ward-room that the work contained reflections somewhat derogatory to the dignity of the officers, the volume was seized by the master-at-arms, armed with a warrant from the Captain. A few days after, a large nail was driven straight through the two covers, and clinched on the other side, and, thus everlastingly sealed, the book was committed to the deep. The ground taken by the authorities on this occasion was, perhaps, that the book was obnoxious to a certain clause in the Articles of War, forbidding any person in the Navy to bring any other person in the Navy into contempt, which the suppressed volume undoubtedly did.

Chapter 12

The Good or Bad Temper of Men-of-war's men, in a great Degree, attributable to their Particular Stations and Duties aboard Ship

QUOIN, THE QUARTER-GUNNER, was the representative of a class on board the Neversink, altogether too remarkable to be left astern, without further notice, in the rapid wake of these chapters.

As has been seen, Quoin was full of unaccountable whimsies; he was, withal, a very cross, bitter, ill-natured, inflammable little old man. So, too, were all the members of the gunner's gang; including the two gunner's mates, and all the quarter-gunners. Every one of them had the same dark brown complexion; all their faces looked like smoked hams. They were continually grumbling and growling about the batteries; running in and out among the guns; driving the sailors away from them; and cursing and swearing as if all their consciences had been powder-singed, and made callous, by their calling. Indeed they were a most unpleasant set of men; especially Priming, the nasal-voiced gunner's mate, with the hare-lip; and Cylinder, his stuttering coadjutor, with the clubbed foot. But you will always observe, that the gunner's gang of every man-of-war are invariably ill-tempered, ugly featured, and quarrelsome. Once when I visited an English line-of-battle ship, the gunner's gang were at work fore and aft, polishing up the batteries, which, according to the Admiral's fancy, had been painted white as snow. Fidgeting round the great thirty-two-pounders, and

44

making stinging remarks at the sailors and each other, they reminded one of a swarm of black wasps, buzzing about rows of white head-stones in a church-yard.

Now, there can be little doubt, that their being so much among the guns is the very thing that makes a gunner's gang so cross and quarrelsome. Indeed, this was once proved to the satisfaction of our whole company of main-top-men. A fine top-mate of ours, a most merry and companionable fellow, chanced to be promoted to a quarter-gunner's berth. A few days afterward, some of us main-top-men, his old comrades, went to pay him a visit, while he was going his regular rounds through the division of guns allotted to his care. But instead of greeting us with his usual heartiness, and cracking his pleasant jokes, to our amazement, he did little else but scowl; and at last, when we rallied him upon his ill-temper, he seized a long black rammer from overhead, and drove us on deck; threatening to report us, if we ever dared to be familiar with him again.

My top-mates thought that this remarkable metamorphose was the effect produced upon a weak, vain character, suddenly elevated from the level of a mere seaman to the dignified position of a *petty-officer*. But though, in similar cases, I had seen such effects produced upon some of the crew; yet, in the present instance, I knew better than that;—it was solely brought about by his consorting with those villainous, irritable, ill-tempered cannon; more especially from his being subject to the orders of those deformed blunderbusses, Priming and Cylinder.

The truth seems to be, indeed, that all people should be very careful in selecting their callings and vocations; very careful in seeing to it, that they surround themselves by good-humored, pleasant-looking objects; and agreeable, temper-soothing sounds. Many an angelic disposition has had its even edge turned, and hacked like a saw; and many a sweet draught of piety has soured on the heart, from people's choosing ill-natured employments, and omitting to gather round them good-natured landscapes. Gardeners are almost always pleasant, affable people to converse with; but beware of quarter-gunners, keepers of arsenals, and lonely light-house men. And though you will generally observe, that people living in arsenals and light-houses endeavor to cultivate a few flowers in pots, and perhaps a few cabbages in patches, by way of keeping up, if possible, some gayety of spirits; yet, it will not do; their going among great guns and muskets, everlastingly mildews the blossoms of the one; and how can even cabbages thrive in a soil, whereunto the moldering keels of shipwrecked vessels have imparted the loam?

It would be advisable for any man, who from an unlucky choice of a profession, which it is too late to change for another, should find his temper souring, to endeavor to counteract that misfortune, by filling his private chamber with amiable, pleasurable sights and sounds. In summer time, an Æolian harp can be placed in your window at a very trifling expense; a conch-shell might stand on your mantel, to be taken up and held to the ear, that you may be soothed by its continual lulling sound, when you feel the blue fit stealing over you. For sights, a gay-painted punch-bowl, or Dutch tankard—never mind about filling it—might be recommended. It should be placed on a bracket in the pier. Nor is an old-fashioned silver ladle, nor a chased dinner-castor, nor a fine portly demijohn, nor any thing, indeed, that savors of eating and drinking, bad to drive off the spleen. But perhaps the best of all is a shelf of merrily-bound books, containing comedies, farces, songs, and humorous novels. You need never open them; only have the titles in plain sight. For this purpose, Peregrine Pickle is a good book; so is Gil Blas; so is Goldsmith.

But of all chamber furniture in the world, best calculated to cure a bad temper, and breed a pleasant one, is the sight of a lovely wife. If you have children, however, that are teething, the nursery should be a good way up stairs; at sea, it ought to be in the mizzen-top. Indeed, teething children play the very deuce with a husband's temper. I have known three promising young husbands completely spoil on their wives' hands, by reason of a teething child, whose worrisomeness happened to be aggravated at the time by the summer-complaint. With a breaking heart, and my handkerchief to my eyes, I followed those three hapless young husbands, one after the other, to their premature graves.

Gossiping scenes breed gossips. Who so chatty as hotel-clerks, market-women, auctioneers, bar-keepers, apothecaries, newspaper-reporters, monthly-nurses, and all those who live in bustling crowds, or are present at scenes of chatty interest.

Solitude breeds taciturnity; *that* every body knows; who so taciturn as authors, taken as a race?

A forced, interior quietude, in the midst of great outward commotion, breeds moody people. Who so moody as rail-road-brakemen, steam-boat engineers, helmsmen, and tenders of power-looms in cotton factories? For all these must hold their peace while employed, and let the machinery do the chatting; they can not even edge in a single syllable.

Now, this theory about the wondrous influence of habitual sights and sounds upon the human temper, was suggested by my experiences on board our frigate. And although I regard the example furnished by our quarter-gunners—especially him who had once been our top-mate—as by far the strongest argument in favor of the general theory; yet, the entire ship abounded with illustrations of its truth. Who were more liberal-hearted, lofty-minded, gayer, more jocund, elastic, adventurous, given to fun and frolic, than the top-men of the fore, main, and mizzen masts? The reason of their liberal-heartedness was, that they were daily called upon to expatiate themselves all over the rigging. The reason of their lofty-mindedness was, that they were high lifted above the petty tumults, carping cares, and paltrinesses of the decks below.

And I feel persuaded in my inmost soul, that it is to the fact of my having been a main-top-man; and especially my particular post being on the loftiest yard of the frigate, the main-royal-yard; that I am now enabled to give such a free, broad, off-hand, bird's-eye, and, more than all, impartial account of our man-of-war world; withholding nothing; inventing nothing; nor flattering, nor scandalizing any; but meting out to all—commodore and messenger-boy alike—their precise descriptions and deserts.

The reason of the mirthfulness of these top-men was, that they always looked out upon the blue, boundless, dimpled, laughing, sunny sea. Nor do I hold, that it militates against this theory, that of a stormy day, when the face of the ocean was black, and overcast, that some of them would grow moody, and chose to sit apart. On the contrary, it only proves the thing which I maintain. For even on shore, there are many people, naturally gay and light-hearted, who, whenever the autumnal wind begins to bluster round the corners, and roar along the chimney-stacks, straight become cross, petulant, and irritable. What is more mellow than fine old ale? Yet thunder will sour the best nut-brown ever brewed.

The *Holders* of our frigate, the Troglodytes, who lived down in the tarry cellars and caves below the berth-deck, were, nearly all of them, men of gloomy dispositions, taking sour views of things; one of them was a blue-light Calvinist. Whereas, the old sheet-anchor-men, who spent their time in the bracing sea-air and broad-cast sunshine of the forecastle, were free, generous-hearted, charitable, and full of good-will to all hands; though some of them, to tell the truth, proved sad exceptions; but exceptions only prove the rule.

The "steady-cooks" on the berth-deck, the "steady-sweepers," and "steady-spit box-musterers," in all divisions of the frigate, fore and aft, were a narrow-minded set; with contracted souls; imputable, no doubt, to their groveling duties. More especially was this evinced in the case of those odious ditchers and night scavengers, the ignoble "Waisters."

The members of the band, some ten or twelve in number, who had nothing to do but keep their instruments polished, and play a lively air now and then, to stir the stagnant current in our poor old Commodore's torpid veins, were the most gleeful set of fellows you ever saw. They were Portuguese, who had been shipped at the Cape De Verd islands, on the passage out. They messed by themselves; forming a dinner-party, not to be exceeded in mirthfulness, by a club of young bridegrooms, three months after marriage, completely satisfied with their bargains, after testing them.

But what made them, now, so full of fun? What indeed but their merry, martial, mellow calling. Who could be a churl, and play a flageolet? who mean and spiritless, braying forth the souls of thousand heroes from his brazen trump? But still more efficacious, perhaps, in ministering to the light spirits of the band, was the consoling thought, that should the ship ever go into action, they would be exempted from the perils of battle. In ships of war, the members of the "music," as the band is called, are generally noncombatants; and mostly ship, with the express understanding, that as soon as the vessel comes within long gun-shot of an enemy, they shall have the privilege of burrowing down in the cable-tiers, or sea coal-hole. Which shows that they are inglorious, but uncommonly sensible fellows.

Look at the barons of the gun-room—Lieutenants, Purser, Marine officers, Sailing-master—all of them gentlemen with stiff upper lips, and aristocratic cut noses. Why was this? Will any one deny, that from their living so long in high military life, served by a crowd of menial stewards and cot-boys, and always accustomed to command right and left; will any one deny, I say, that by reason of this, their very noses had become thin, peaked, aquiline, and aristocratically cartilaginous? Even old Cuticle, the Surgeon, had a Roman nose.

But I never could account how it came to be, that our gray-headed First Lieutenant was a little lop-sided; that is, one of his shoulders disproportionately drooped. And when I observed, that nearly all the First Lieutenants I saw in other men-of-war, besides many Second and Third Lieutenants, were similarly lop-sided; I knew, that there must be some general law which induced the phenomenon; and I put myself to studying it out, as an interesting problem. At last, I came to the conclusion—to which I still adhere— that their so long wearing only one epaulet (for to only one does their rank entitle them) was the infallible clew to this mystery. And when any one reflects upon so well-known a fact, that many sea Lieutenants grow decrepit from age, without attaining a Captaincy and wearing *two* epaulets, which would strike the balance between their shoulders, the above reason assigned will not appear unwarrantable.

Chapter 13

A Man-of-war Hermit in a Mob

THE ALLUSION to the poet Lemsford in a previous chapter, leads me to speak of our mutual friends, Nord and Williams, who, with Lemsford himself, Jack Chase, and my comrades of the main-top, comprised almost the only persons with whom I unreservedly consorted while on board the frigate. For I had not been long on board ere I found that it would not do to be intimate with every body. An indiscriminate intimacy with all hands leads to sundry annoyances and scrapes, too often ending with a dozen at the gang-way. Though I was above a year in the frigate, there were scores of men who to the last remained perfect strangers to me, whose very names I did not know, and whom I would hardly be able to recognize now should I happen to meet them in the streets.

In the dog-watches at sea, during the early part of the evening, the main-deck is generally filled with crowds of pedestrians, promenading up and down past the guns, like people taking the air in Broadway. At such times, it is curious to see the men nodding to each other's recognitions (they might not have seen each other for a week); exchanging a pleasant word with a friend; making a hurried appointment to meet him somewhere aloft on the morrow, or passing group after group without deigning the slightest salutation. Indeed, I was not at all singular in having but comparatively few acquaintances on board, though certainly carrying my fastidiousness to an unusual extent.

My friend Nord was a somewhat remarkable character; and if mystery includes romance, he certainly was a very romantic one. Before seeking an introduction to him through Lemsford, I had often marked his tall, spare, upright figure stalking like Don Quixote among the pigmies of the After-guard, to which he belonged. At first I found him exceedingly reserved and taciturn; his saturnine brow wore a scowl; he was almost repelling in his demeanor. In a word, he seemed desirous of hinting, that his list of man-of-war friends was already made up, complete, and full; and there was no room for more. But observing that the only man he ever consorted with was Lemsford, I had too much magnanimity, by going off in a pique at his cold-ness, to let him lose forever the chance of making so capital an acquaintance as myself. Besides, I saw it in his eye, that the man had been a reader of good books; I would have staked my life on it, that he seized the right meaning of Montaigne. I saw that he was an earnest thinker; I more than suspected that he had been bolted in the mill of adversity. For all these things, my heart yearned toward him; I determined to know him.

At last I succeeded; it was during a profoundly quiet midnight watch, when I perceived him walking alone in the waist, while most of the men were dozing on the carronade-slides.

That night we scoured all the prairies of reading; dived into the bosoms of authors, and tore out their hearts; and that night White-Jacket learned more than he has ever done in any single night since.

The man was a marvel. He amazed me, as much as Coleridge did the troopers among whom he enlisted. What could have induced such a man to enter a man-of-war, all my sapience can not fathom. And how he man-aged to preserve his dignity, as he did, among such a rabble rout was equally a mystery. For he was no sailor; as ignorant of a ship, indeed, as a man from the sources of the Niger. Yet the officers respected him; and the men were afraid of him. This much was observable, however, that he faithfully dis-charged whatever special duties devolved upon him; and was so fortunate as never to render himself liable to a reprimand. Doubtless, he took the same view of the thing that another of the crew did; and had early resolved, so to conduct himself as never to run the risk of the scourge. And this it must have been—added to whatever incommunicable grief which might have been his—that made this Nord such a wandering recluse, even among our man-of-war mob. Nor could he have long swung his hammock on board, ere he must have found that, to insure his exemption from that thing which alone affrighted him, he must be content for the most part to turn a man-hater, and socially expatriate himself from many things, which might have rendered his situation more tolerable. Still more, several events that took place must have horrified him, at times, with the thought that, however he might isolate and entomb himself, yet for all this, the improbability of his being overtaken by what he most dreaded never advanced to the infallibility of the impossible.

In my intercourse with Nord, he never made allusion to his past career— a subject upon which most high-bred castaways in a man-of-war are very diffuse; relating their adventures at the gaming-table; the recklessness with which they have run through the amplest fortunes in a single season; their alms-givings, and gratuities to porters and poor relations; and above all, their youthful indiscretions, and the broken-hearted ladies they have left behind. No such tales had Nord to tell. Concerning the past, he was barred and locked up like the specie vaults of the Bank of England. For any thing that dropped from him, none of us could be sure that he had ever existed till now. Altogether, he was a remarkable man.

My other friend, Williams, was a thorough-going Yankee from Maine, who had been both a peddler and a pedagogue in his day. He had all manner of stories to tell about nice little country frolics, and would run over an end-less list of his sweet-hearts. He was honest, acute, witty, full of mirth and good humor—a laughing philosopher. He was invaluable as a pill against the spleen; and, with the view of extending the advantages of his society to the saturnine Nord, I introduced them to each other; but Nord cut him dead the very same evening, when we sallied out from between the guns for a walk on the main-deck.

Chapter 14

A Drought in a Man-of-war

W E WERE NOT MANY DAYS out of port, when a rumor was set afloat that dreadfully alarmed many tars. It was this: that, owing to some unprecedented oversight in the Purser, or some equally unprecedented remissness in the Naval-store-keeper at Callao, the frigate's supply of that delectable beverage, called "grog," was well-nigh expended.

In the American Navy, the law allows one gill of spirits per day to every seaman. In two portions, it is served out just previous to breakfast and dinner. At the roll of the drum, the sailors assemble round a large tub, or cask, filled with the liquid; and, as their names are called off by a midshipman, they step up and regale themselves from a little tin measure called a "tot." No high-liver helping himself to Tokay off a well-polished side-board, smacks his lips with more mighty satisfaction than the sailor does over this *tot*. To many of them, indeed, the thought of their daily *tots* forms a perpetual perspective of ravishing landscapes, indefinitely receding in the distance. It is their great "prospect in life." Take away their grog, and life possesses no further charms for them. It is hardly to be doubted, that the controlling inducement which keeps many men in the Navy, is the unbounded confidence they have in the ability of the United States government to supply them, regularly and unfailingly, with their daily allowance of this beverage. I have known several forlorn individuals, shipping as landsmen, who have

53

confessed to me, that having contracted a love for ardent spirits, which they could not renounce, and having by their foolish courses been brought into the most abject poverty—insomuch that they could no longer gratify their thirst ashore—they incontinently entered the Navy; regarding it as the asylum for all drunkards, who might there prolong their lives by regular hours and exercise, and twice every day quench their thirst by moderate and undeviating doses.

When I once remonstrated with an old toper of a top-man about this daily dram-drinking; when I told him it was ruining him, and advised him to *stop his grog* and receive the money for it, in addition to his wages, as provided by law, he turned about on me, with an irresistibly waggish look, and said, "Give up my grog? And why? Because it is ruining me? No, no; I am a good Christian, White-Jacket, and love my enemy too much to drop his acquaintance."

It may be readily imagined, therefore, what consternation and dismay pervaded the gun-deck at the first announcement of the tidings that the grog was expended.

"The grog gone!" roared an old Sheet-anchor-man.

"Oh! Lord! what a pain in my stomach!" cried a Main-top-man.

"It's worse than the Cholera!" cried a man of the After-guard.

"I'd sooner the water-casks would give out!" said a Captain of the Hold.

"Are we ganders and geese, that we can live without grog?" asked a Corporal of Marines.

"Ay, we must now drink with the ducks!" cried a Quarter-master.

"Not a tot left?" groaned a Waister.

"Not a toothful!" sighed a Holder, from the bottom of his boots.

Yes, the fatal intelligence proved true. The drum was no longer heard rolling the men to the tub, and deep gloom and dejection fell like a cloud. The ship was like a great city, when some terrible calamity has overtaken it. The men stood apart, in groups, discussing their woes, and mutually condoling. No longer, of still moon-light nights, was the song heard from the giddy tops; and few and far between were the stories that were told.

It was during this interval, so dismal to many, that, to the amazement of all hands, ten men were reported by the master-at-arms to be intoxicated. They were brought up to the mast, and at their appearance the doubts of the most skeptical were dissipated; but whence they had obtained their liquor no one could tell. It was observed, however, at the time, that the tarry knaves all smelled of lavender, like so many dandies.

After their examination they were ordered into the "brig," a jail-house between two guns on the main-deck, where prisoners are kept. Here they laid for some time, stretched out stark and stiff, with their arms folded over their breasts, like so many effigies of the Black Prince on his monument in Canterbury Cathedral.

Their first slumbers over, the marine sentry who stood guard over them had as much as he could do to keep off the crowd, who were all eagerness to find out how, in such a time of want, the prisoners had managed to drink themselves into oblivion. In due time they were liberated, and the secret simultaneously leaked out.

It seemed that an enterprising man of their number, who had suffered severely from the common deprivation, had all at once been struck by a brilliant idea. It had come to his knowledge that the purser's steward was supplied with a large quantity of *Eau-de-Cologne*, clandestinely brought out in the ship, for the purpose of selling it, on his own account, to the people of the coast; but the supply proving larger than the demand, and having no customers on board the frigate but Lieutenant Selvagee, he was now carrying home more than a third of his original stock. To make a short story of it, this functionary, being called upon in secret, was readily prevailed upon to part with a dozen bottles, with whose contents the intoxicated party had regaled themselves.

The news spread far and wide among the men, being only kept secret from the officers and underlings, and that night the long, crane-necked Cologne bottles jingled in out-of-the-way corners and by-places, and, being emptied, were sent flying out of the ports. With brown sugar, taken from the mess-chests, and hot water begged from the galley-cooks, the men made all manner of punches, toddies, and cocktails, letting fall therein a small drop of tar, like a bit of brown toast, by way of imparting a flavor. Of course, the thing was managed with the utmost secrecy; and as a whole dark night elapsed after their orgies, the revelers were, in a good measure, secure from detection; and those who indulged too freely had twelve long hours to get sober before daylight obtruded.

Next day, fore and aft, the whole frigate smelled like a lady's toilet; the very tar-buckets were fragrant; and from the mouth of many a grim, grizzled old quarter-gunner came the most fragrant of breaths. The amazed Lieutenants went about snuffing up the gale; and, for once, Selvagee had no further need to flourish his perfumed handkerchief. It was as if we were sailing by some odoriferous shore, in the vernal season of violets. Sabæan odors!

"For many a league,
Cheered with the grateful smell, old Ocean smiled."

But, alas! all this perfume could not be wasted for nothing; and the master-at-arms and ship's corporals, putting this and that together, very soon burrowed into the secret. The purser's steward was called to account, and no more lavender punches and Cologne toddies were drank on board the Neversink.

Chapter 15

A Salt-Junk Club in a Man-of-war, with a Notice to Quit

IT WAS ABOUT THE PERIOD of the Cologne-water excitement that my self-conceit was not a little wounded, and my sense of delicacy altogether shocked, by a polite hint received from the cook of the mess to which I happened to belong. To understand the matter, it is needful to enter into preliminaries.

The common seamen in a large frigate are divided into some thirty or forty messes, put down on the purser's books as *Mess No.* 1, *Mess No.* 2, *Mess No.* 3, &c. The members of each mess club their rations of provisions, and breakfast, dine, and sup together in allotted intervals between the guns on the main-deck. In undeviating rotation, the members of each mess (excepting the petty-officers) take their turn in performing the functions of cook and steward. And for the time being, all the affairs of the club are subject to their inspection and control.

It is the cook's business, also, to have an eye to the general interests of his mess; to see that, when the aggregated allowances of beef, bread, &c., are served out by one of the master's mates, the mess over which he presides receives its full share, without stint or subtraction. Upon the berth-deck he has a chest, in which to keep his pots, pans, spoons, and small stores of sugar, molasses, tea, and flour.

But though entitled a cook, strictly speaking, the head of the mess is no cook at all; for the cooking for the crew is all done by a high and mighty functionary, officially called the "*ship's cook*," assisted by several deputies. In our frigate, this personage was a dignified colored gentleman, whom the men dubbed "*Old Coffee;*" and his assistants, negroes also, went by the poetical appellations of "*Sunshine,*" "*Rose-water,*" and "*May-day.*"

Now the *ship's cooking* required very little science, though old Coffee often assured us that he had graduated at the New York Astor House, under the immediate eye of the celebrated Coleman and Stetson. All he had to do was, in the first place, to keep bright and clean the three huge coppers, or caldrons, in which many hundred pounds of beef were daily boiled. To this end, Rose-water, Sunshine, and May-day every morning sprang into their respective apartments, stripped to the waist, and well provided with bits of soap-stone and sand. By exercising these in a very vigorous manner, they threw themselves into a violent perspiration, and put a fine polish upon the interior of the coppers.

Sunshine was the bard of the trio; and while all three would be busily employed clattering their soap-stones against the metal, he would exhilarate them with some remarkable St. Domingo melodies; one of which was the following:

> "Oh! I los' my shoe in an old canoe,
>   Johnio! come Winum so!
> Oh! I los' my boot in a pilot-boat,
>   Johnio! come Winum so!
> Den rub-a-dub de copper, oh!
> Oh! copper rub-a-dub-a-oh!"

When I listened to these jolly Africans, thus making gleeful their toil by their cheering songs, I could not help murmuring against that immemorial rule of men-of-war, which forbids the sailors to sing out, as in merchant-vessels, when pulling ropes, or occupied at any other ship's duty. Your only music, at such times, is the shrill pipe of the boatswain's mate, which is almost worse than no music at all. And if the boatswain's mate is not by, you must pull the ropes, like convicts, in profound silence; or else endeavor to impart unity to the exertions of all hands, by singing out mechanically, *one, two, three,* and then pulling all together.

Now, when Sunshine, Rose-water, and May-day have so polished the ship's coppers, that a white kid glove might be drawn along the inside and show no stain, they leap out of their holes, and the water is poured in for the coffee. And the coffee being boiled, and decanted off in buckets-full, the cooks of the messes march up with their salt beef for dinner, strung upon strings and tallied with labels; all of which are plunged together into the self-same coppers, and there boiled. When, upon the beef being fished out with a huge pitch-fork, the water for the evening's tea is poured in; which, consequently, possesses a flavor not unlike that of shank-soup.

From this it will be seen, that, so far as cooking is concerned, a "*cook of the mess*" has very little to do; merely carrying his provisions to and from the grand democratic cookery. Still, in some things, his office involves many annoyances. Twice a week butter and cheese are served out—so much to each man—and the mess-cook has the sole charge of these delicacies. The great difficulty consists in so catering for the mess, touching these luxuries, as to satisfy all. Some guzzlers are for devouring the butter at a meal, and finishing off with the cheese the same day; others contend for saving it up against *Banyan Day*, when there is nothing but beef and bread; and others, again, are for taking a very small bit of butter and cheese, by way of dessert, to each and every meal through the week. All this gives rise to endless disputes, debates, and altercations.

Sometimes, with his mess-cloth—a square of painted canvas—set out on deck between the guns, garnished with pots, and pans, and *kids*, you see the mess-cook seated on a match-tub at its head, his trowser legs rolled up and arms bared, presiding over the convivial party.

"Now, men, you can't have any butter to-day. I'm saving it up for to-morrow. You don't know the value of butter, men. You, Jim, take your hoof off the cloth! Devil take me, if some of you chaps haven't no more manners than so many swines! Quick, men, quick; bear a hand, and '*scoff*' (eat) away.—I've got my to-morrow's *duff* to make yet, and some of you fellows keep *scoffing* as if I had nothing to do but sit still here on this here tub here, and look on. There, there, men, you've all had enough; so sail away out of this, and let me clear up the wreck."

In this strain would one of the periodical cooks of mess No. 15 talk to us. He was a tall, resolute fellow, who had once been a breakman on a rail-road, and he kept us all pretty straight; from his fiat there was no appeal.

But it was not thus when the turn came to others among us. Then it was, *look out for squalls*. The business of dining became a bore, and digestion was seriously impaired by the unamiable discourse we had over our *salt horse*.

I sometimes thought that the junks of lean pork—which were boiled in their own bristles, and looked gaunt and grim, like pickled chins of half-famished, unwashed Cossacks—had something to do with creating the bristling bitterness at times prevailing in our mess. The men tore off the tough hide from their pork, as if they were Indians scalping Christians.

CAMROSE LUTHERAN COLLEGE
LIBRARY

Some cursed the cook for a rogue, who kept from us our butter and cheese, in order to make away with it himself in an underhand manner; selling it at a premium to other messes, and thus accumulating a princely fortune at our expense. Others anathematized him for his slovenliness, casting hypercritical glances into their pots and pans, and scraping them with their knives. Then he would be railed at for his miserable "duffs," and other short-coming preparations.

Marking all this from the beginning, I, White-Jacket, was sorely troubled with the idea, that, in the course of time, my own turn would come round to undergo the same objurgations. How to escape, I knew not. However, when the dreaded period arrived, I received the keys of office (the keys of the mess-chest) with a resigned temper, and offered up a devout ejaculation for fortitude under the trial. I resolved, please Heaven, to approve myself an unexceptionable caterer, and the most impartial of stewards.

The first day there was "*duff*" to make—a business which devolved upon the mess-cooks, though the boiling of it pertained to Old Coffee and his deputies. I made up my mind to lay myself out on that *duff;* to centre all my energies upon it; to put the very soul of art into it, and achieve an unrivaled *duff*—a *duff* that should put out of conceit all other *duffs*, and forever make my administration memorable.

From the proper functionary the flour was obtained, and the raisins; the beef-fat, or "*slush*," from Old Coffee; and the requisite supply of water from the scuttle-butt. I then went among the various cooks, to compare their receipts for making "duffs;" and having well weighed them all, and gathered from each a choice item to make an original receipt of my own, with due deliberation and solemnity I proceeded to business. Placing the component parts in a tin pan, I kneaded them together for an hour, entirely reckless as to pulmonary considerations, touching the ruinous expenditure of breath; and having decanted the semi-liquid dough into a canvas-bag, secured the muzzle, tied on the talley, and delivered it to Rose-water, who dropped the precious bag into the coppers, along with a score or two of others.

Eight bells had struck. The boatswain and his mates had piped the hands to dinner; my mess-cloth was set out, and my messmates were assembled, knife in hand, all ready to precipitate themselves upon the devoted *duff*. Waiting at the grand cookery till my turn came, I received the bag of pudding, and gallanting it into the mess, proceeded to loosen the string.

It was an anxious, I may say, a fearful moment. My hands trembled;

every eye was upon me; my reputation and credit were at stake. Slowly I undressed the *duff*, dandling it upon my knee, much as a nurse does a baby about bed-time. The excitement increased, as I curled down the bag from the pudding; it became intense, when at last I plumped it into the pan, held up to receive it by an eager hand. Bim! it fell like a man shot down in a riot. Distraction! It was harder than a sinner's heart; yea, tough as the cock that crowed on the morn that Peter told a lie.

"Gentlemen of the mess, for heaven's sake! permit me one word. I have done my duty by that duff—I have—"

But they beat down my excuses with a storm of criminations. One present proposed that the fatal pudding should be tied round my neck, like a mill-stone, and myself pushed overboard. No use, no use; I had failed; ever after, that duff lay heavy at my stomach and my heart.

After this, I grew desperate; despised popularity; returned scorn for scorn; till at length my week expired, and in the duff-bag I transferred the keys of office to the next man on the roll.

Somehow, there had never been a very cordial feeling between this mess and me; all along they had nourished a prejudice against my white jacket. They must have harbored the silly fancy that in it I gave myself airs, and wore it in order to look consequential; perhaps, as a cloak to cover pilferings of tit-bits from the mess. But to out with the plain truth, they themselves were not a very irreproachable set. Considering the sequel I am coming to, this avowal may be deemed sheer malice; but for all that, I can not avoid speaking my mind.

After my week of office, the mess gradually changed their behavior to me; they cut me to the heart; they became cold and reserved; seldom or never addressed me at meal-times, without invidious allusions to my *duff*, and also to my jacket, and its dripping in wet weather upon the mess-cloth. However, I had no idea that any thing serious, on their part, was brewing; but alas! so it turned out.

We were assembled at supper one evening, when I noticed certain winks and silent hints tipped to the cook, who presided. He was a little, oily fellow, who had once kept an oyster-cellar ashore; he bore me a grudge. Looking down on the mess-cloth, he observed that some fellows never knew when their room was better than their company. This being a maxim of indiscriminate application, of course I silently assented to it, as any other reasonable man would have done. But this remark was followed up by another, to the effect that, not only did some fellows never know when their room was better than their company, but they persisted in staying when their company wasn't wanted; and by so doing disturbed the serenity of society at large. But this, also, was a general observation that could not be gainsayed. A long and ominous pause ensued; during which I perceived every eye upon me, and my white jacket; while the cook went on to enlarge upon the disagreeableness of a perpetually damp garment in the mess, especially when that garment was white. This was coming nearer home.

Yes, they were going to black-ball me; but I resolved to sit it out a little longer; never dreaming that my moralist would proceed to extremities, while all hands were present. But bethinking him that by going this round-about way he would never get at his object, he went off on another tack; apprising me, in substance, that he was instructed by the whole mess, then and there assembled, to give me warning to seek out another club, as they did not longer fancy the society either of myself or my jacket.

I was shocked. Such a want of tact and delicacy! Common propriety suggested that a point-blank intimation of that nature should be conveyed in a private interview; or, still better, by note. I immediately rose, tucked my jacket about me, bowed, and departed.

And now, to do myself justice, I must add that, the next day, I was received with open arms by a glorious set of fellows—mess No. 1!— numbering, among the rest, my noble Captain Jack Chase.

This mess was principally composed of the headmost men of the gun-deck; and, out of a pardonable self-conceit, they called themselves the "*Forty-two-pounder Club;*" meaning that they were, one and all, fellows of large intellectual and corporeal calibre. Their mess-cloth was well located. On their starboard hand was *Mess No.* 2, embracing sundry rare jokers and high livers, who waxed gay and epicurean over their salt fare, and were known as the "Society for the *Destruction of Beef and Pork*." On the larboard hand was *Mess No.* 31, made up entirely of fore-top-men, a dashing, blaze-away set of men-of-war's-men, who called themselves the "*Cape Horn Snorters and Neversink Invincibles.*" Opposite, was one of the marine messes, mustering the aristocracy of the marine corps—the two corporals, the drum-mer and fifer, and some six or eight rather gentlemanly privates, native-born Americans, who had served in the Seminole campaigns of Florida; and they now enlivened their salt fare with stories of wild ambushes in the everglades; and one of them related a surprising tale of his hand-to-hand encounter with Osceola, the Indian chief, whom he fought one morning from daybreak till breakfast time. This slashing private also boasted that he could take a chip from between your teeth at twenty paces; he offered to bet any amount on it; and as he could get no one to hold the chip, his boast remained forever good.

Besides many other attractions which the *Forty-two-pounder Club* furnished, it had this one special advantage, that, owing to there being so many *petty officers* in it, all the members of the mess were exempt from doing duty as cooks and stewards. A fellow called a *steady-cook*, attended to that business during the entire cruise. He was a long, lank, pallid varlet, going by the name of Shanks. In very warm weather this Shanks would sit at the foot of the mess-cloth, fanning himself with the front flap of his frock or shirt, which he inelegantly wore over his trowsers. Jack Chase, the President of the Club, frequently remonstrated against this breach of good manners; but the *steady-cook* had somehow contracted the habit, and it proved incurable. For a time, Jack Chase, out of a polite nervousness touching myself, as a newly-elected member of the club, would frequently endeavor to excuse to me the vulgarity of Shanks. One day he wound up his remarks by the philosophic reflection—"But White-Jacket, my dear fellow, what can you expect of him? Our real misfortune is, that our noble club should be obliged to dine with its cook."

There were several of these *steady-cooks* on board; men of no mark or consideration whatever in the ship; lost to all noble promptings; sighing for no worlds to conquer, and perfectly contented with mixing their *duffs*, and spreading their mess-cloths, and mustering their pots and pans together three times every day for a three years' cruise. They were very seldom to be seen on the spar-deck, but kept below out of sight.

Chapter 16

General Training in a Man-of-war

TO A QUIET, CONTEMPLATIVE CHARACTER, averse to uproar, undue exercise of his bodily members, and all kind of useless confusion, nothing can be more distressing than a proceeding in all men-of-war called *"general quarters."* And well may it be so called, since it amounts to a general drawing and quartering of all the parties concerned.

As the specific object for which a man-of-war is built and put into commission is to fight and fire off cannon, it is, of course, deemed indispensable that the crew should be duly instructed in the art and mystery involved. Hence these "general quarters," which is a mustering of all hands to their stations at the guns on the several decks, and a sort of sham-fight with an imaginary foe.

The summons is given by the ship's drummer, who strikes a peculiar beat—short, broken, rolling, shuffling—like the sound made by the march into battle of iron-heeled grenadiers. It is a regular tune, with a fine song composed to it; the words of the chorus, being most artistically arranged, may give some idea of the air:

"Hearts of oak are our ships, jolly tars are our men,
    We always are ready, steady, boys, steady,
    To fight and to conquer, again and again."

In warm weather this pastime at the guns is exceedingly unpleasant, to say the least, and throws a quiet man into a violent passion and perspiration. For one, I ever abominated it.

I have a heart like Julius Cæsar, and upon occasion would fight like Caius Marcius Coriolanus. If my beloved and forever glorious country should be ever in jeopardy from invaders, let Congress put me on a war-horse, in the van-guard, and *then* see how I will acquit myself. But to toil and sweat in a fictitious encounter; to squander the precious breath of my precious body in a ridiculous fight of shams and pretensions; to hurry about the decks, pretending to carry the killed and wounded below; to be told that I must consider the ship blowing up, in order to exercise myself in presence of mind, and prepare for a real explosion; all this I despise, as beneath a true tar and man of valor.

These were my sentiments at the time, and these remain my sentiments still; but as, while on board the frigate, my liberty of thought did not extend to liberty of expression, I was obliged to keep these sentiments to myself; though, indeed, I had some thoughts of addressing a letter, marked *Private and Confidential*, to his Honor the Commodore, on the subject.

My station at the batteries was at one of the thirty-two-pound carro-nades, on the starboard side of the quarter-deck.*

I did not fancy this station at all; for it is well known on shipboard that, in time of action, the quarter-deck is one of the most dangerous posts of a man-of-war. The reason is, that the officers of the highest rank are there stationed; and the enemy have an ungentlemanly way of target-shooting at their buttons. If we should chance to engage a ship, then, who could tell but some bungling small-arm marksman in the enemy's tops might put a

---

* For the benefit of a Quaker reader here and there, a word or two in explanation of a carronade may not be amiss. The carronade is a gun comparatively short and light for its calibre. A carronade throwing a thirty-two-pound shot weighs considerably less than a long-gun only throwing a twenty-four-pound shot. It further differs from a long-gun, in working with a joint and bolt underneath, instead of the short arms or *trunnions* at the sides. Its *carriage*, likewise, is quite different from that of a long-gun, having a sort of sliding apparatus, something like an extension dining-table; the goose on it, however, is a tough one, and villainously stuffed with most indigestible dumplings. Point-blank, the range of a carronade does not exceed one hundred and fifty yards, much less than the range of a long-gun. When of large calibre, however, it throws within that limit, Paixhan shot, all manner of shells and combustibles, with great effect, being a very destructive engine at close quarters. This piece is now very generally found mounted in the batteries of the English and American navies. The quarter-deck armaments of most modern frigates wholly consist of carronades. The name is derived from the village of Carron, in Scotland, at whose celebrated founderies this iron Attila was first cast.

bullet through *me* instead of the Commodore? If they hit *him*, no doubt he would not feel it much, for he was used to that sort of thing, and, indeed, had a bullet in him already. Whereas, *I* was altogether unaccustomed to having blue pills playing round my head in such an indiscriminate way. Besides, ours was a flag-ship; and every one knows what a peculiarly dangerous predicament the quarter-deck of Nelson's flag-ship was in at the battle of Trafalgar; how the lofty tops of the enemy were full of soldiers, peppering away at the English Admiral and his officers. Many a poor sailor, at the guns of that quarter-deck, must have received a bullet intended for some wearer of an epaulet.

By candidly confessing my feelings on this subject, I do by no means invalidate my claims to being held a man of prodigious valor. I merely state my invincible repugnance to being shot for somebody else. If I am shot, be it with the express understanding in the shooter that I am the identical person intended so to be served. That Thracian who, with his compliments, sent an arrow into the King of Macedon, superscribed "*For Philip's right eye*," set a fine example to all warriors. The hurried, hasty, indiscriminate, reckless, abandoned manner in which both sailors and soldiers nowadays fight is really painful to any serious-minded, methodical old gentleman, especially if he chance to have systematized his mind as an accountant. There is little or no skill and bravery about it. Two parties, armed with lead and old iron, envelop themselves in a cloud of smoke, and pitch their lead and old iron about in all directions. If you happen to be in the way, you are hit; possibly, killed; if not, you escape. In sea-actions, if by good or bad luck, as the case may be, a round shot, fired at random through the smoke, happens to send overboard your fore-mast, another to unship your rudder, there you lie crippled, pretty much at the mercy of your foe; who, accordingly, pronounces himself victor, though that honor properly belongs to the Law of Gravitation operating on the enemy's balls in the smoke. Instead of tossing this old lead and iron into the air, therefore, it would be much better amicably to toss up a copper and let heads win.

The carronade at which I was stationed was known as "Gun No. 5," on the First Lieutenant's quarter-bill. Among our gun's crew, however, it was known as *Black Bet*. This name was bestowed by the captain of the gun —a fine negro—in honor of his sweet-heart, a colored lady of Philadelphia. Of Black Bet I was rammer-and-sponger; and ram and sponge I did, like a good fellow. I have no doubt that, had I and my gun been at the battle of the Nile, we would mutually have immortalized ourselves; the ramming-pole would have been hung up in Westminster Abbey; and I, ennobled by the king, besides receiving the illustrious honor of an autograph letter from his majesty through the perfumed right hand of his private secretary.

But it was terrible work to help run in and out of the port-hole that amazing mass of metal, especially as the thing must be done in a trice. Then, at the summons of a horrid, rasping rattle, swayed by the Captain in person, we were made to rush from our guns, seize pikes and pistols, and repel an imaginary army of boarders, who, by a fiction of the officers, were supposed to be assailing all sides of the ship at once. After cutting and slashing at them a while, we jumped back to our guns, and again went to jerking our elbows.

Meantime, a loud cry is heard of "Fire! fire! fire!" in the fore-top; and a regular engine, worked by a set of Bowery-boy tars, is forthwith set to playing streams of water aloft. And now it is "Fire! fire! fire!" on the main-deck; and the entire ship is in as great a commotion as if a whole city ward were in a blaze.

Are our officers of the Navy utterly unacquainted with the laws of good health? Do they not know that this violent exercise, taking place just after a hearty dinner, as it generally does, is eminently calculated to breed the dyspepsia? There was no satisfaction in dining; the flavor of every mouthful was destroyed by the thought that the next moment the cannonading drum might be beating to quarters.

Such a sea-martinet was our Captain, that sometimes we were roused from our hammocks at night; when a scene would ensue that it is not in the power of pen and ink to describe. Five hundred men spring to their feet, dress themselves, take up their bedding, and run to the nettings and stow it; then hie to their stations—each man jostling his neighbor—some alow, some aloft; some this way, some that; and in less than five minutes the frigate is ready for action, and still as the grave; almost every man precisely where he would be were an enemy actually about to be engaged. The Gunner, like a Cornwall miner in a cave, is burrowing down in the magazine under the Ward-room, which is lighted by battle-lanterns, placed behind glazed glass bull's-eyes inserted in the bulkhead. The *powder-monkeys*, or boys, who fetch and carry cartridges, are scampering to and fro among the guns; and the *first and second loaders* stand ready to receive their supplies.

These *Powder-monkeys*, as they are called, enact a curious part in time of action. The entrance to the magazine on the berth-deck, where they procure their food for the guns, is guarded by a wooden screen; and a gunner's mate, standing behind it, thrusts out the cartridges through a small arm-hole in this screen. The enemy's shot (perhaps red hot) are flying in all directions; and to protect their cartridges, the powder-monkeys hurriedly wrap them up in their jackets; and with all haste scramble up the ladders to their respective guns, like eating-house waiters hurrying along with hot cakes for breakfast.

At *general quarters* the shot-boxes are uncovered; showing the grape-shot—aptly so called, for they precisely resemble bunches of the fruit; though, to receive a bunch of iron grapes in the abdomen would be but a sorry dessert; and also showing the canister-shot—old iron of various sorts, packed in a tin case, like a tea-caddy.

Imagine some midnight craft sailing down on her enemy thus; twenty-four pounders leveled, matches lighted, and each captain of his gun at his post!

But if verily going into action, then would the Neversink have made still further preparations; for however alike in some things, there is always a vast difference—if you sound them—between a reality and a sham. Not to speak of the pale sternness of the men at their guns at such a juncture, and the choked thoughts at their hearts, the ship itself would here and there present a far different appearance. Something like that of an extensive mansion preparing for a grand entertainment, when folding-doors are withdrawn, chambers converted into drawing-rooms, and every inch of available space thrown into one continuous whole. For previous to an action, every bulk-head in a man-of-war is knocked down; great guns are run out of the Commodore's parlor windows; nothing separates the ward-room officers' quarters from those of the men, but an ensign used for a curtain. The sailors' mess-chests are tumbled down into the hold; and the hospital cots—of which all men-of-war carry a large supply—are dragged forth from the sail-room, and piled near at hand to receive the wounded; amputation-tables are ranged in the *cock-pit* or in the *tiers*, whereon to carve the bodies of the maimed. The yards are slung in chains; fire-screens distributed here and there; hillocks of cannon-balls piled between the guns; shot-plugs suspended within easy reach from the beams; and solid masses of wads, big as Dutch cheeses, braced to the cheeks of the gun-carriages.

No small difference, also, would be visible in the ward-robe of both officers and men. The officers generally fight as dandies dance, namely, in silk stockings; inasmuch as, in case of being wounded in the leg, the silk-hose can be more easily drawn off by the Surgeon; cotton sticks, and works into the wound. An economical captain, while taking care to case his legs in silk, might yet see fit to save his best suit, and fight in his old clothes. For, besides that an old garment might much better be cut to pieces than a new one, it must be a mighty disagreeable thing to die in a stiff, tight-breasted coat, not yet worked easy under the armpits. At such times, a man should feel free, unencumbered, and perfectly at his ease in point of straps and suspenders. No ill-will concerning his tailor, should intrude upon his thoughts of eternity. Seneca understood this, when he chose to die naked in a bath. And men-of-war's-men understand it, also; for most of them, in battle, strip to the waist-bands; wearing nothing but a pair of duck trowsers, and a handkerchief round their head.

A captain combining a heedful patriotism with economy, would probably "bend" his old topsails before going into battle, instead of exposing his best canvass to be riddled to pieces; for it is generally the case that the enemy's shot flies high. Unless allowance is made for it in pointing the tube, at long-gun distance, the slightest roll of the ship, at the time of firing, would send a shot, meant for the hull, high over the top-gallant yards.

But besides these differences between a sham-fight at *general quarters* and a real cannonading, the aspect of the ship, at the beating of the retreat, would, in the latter case, be very dissimilar to the neatness and uniformity in the former.

Then our bulwarks might look like the walls of the houses in West Broadway in New York, after being broken into and burned out by the Negro Mob. Our stout masts and yards might be lying about decks, like tree boughs after a tornado in a piece of woodland; our dangling ropes, cut and sundered in all directions, would be bleeding tar at every yarn; and strewn with jagged splinters from our wounded planks, the gun-deck might resemble a carpenter's shop. *Then*, when all was over, and all hands would be piped to take down the hammocks from the exposed nettings (where they play the part of the cotton bales at New Orleans), we might find bits of broken shot, iron bolts, and bullets in our blankets. And, while smeared with blood like butchers, the surgeon and his mates would be amputating arms and legs on the berth-deck, an underling of the carpenter's gang would be new-legging and arming the broken chairs and tables in the Commodore's cabin; while the rest of his *squad* would be *splicing* and *fishing* the shattered masts and yards. The scupper-holes having discharged the last rivulet of blood, the decks would be washed down; and the galley-cooks would be going fore and aft, sprinkling them with hot vinegar, to take out the shambles' smell from the planks; which, unless some such means are employed, often create a highly offensive effluvia for weeks after a fight.

Then, upon mustering the men, and calling the quarter-bills by the light of a battle-lantern, many a wounded seaman, with his arm in a sling, would answer for some poor shipmate who could never more make answer for himself:

"Tom Brown?"

"Killed, sir."

"Jack Jewel?"

"Killed, sir."

"Joe Hardy?"

"Killed, sir."

And opposite all these poor fellows' names, down would go on the quarter-bills the bloody marks of red ink—a murderer's fluid, fitly used on these occasions.

Chapter 17

Away! Second, Third, and Fourth Cutters, away!

I T WAS THE MORNING succeeding one of these *general quarters*
that we picked up a life-buoy, descried floating by.

It was a circular mass of cork, about eight inches thick and four feet in
diameter, covered with tarred canvas. All round its circumference there
trailed a number of knotted ropes'-ends, terminating in fanciful Turks'
heads. These were the life-lines, for the drowning to clutch. Inserted into
the middle of the cork was an upright, carved pole, somewhat shorter than
a pike-staff. The whole buoy was embossed with barnacles, and its sides
festooned with sea-weed. Dolphins were sporting and flashing around it,
and one white bird was hovering over the top of the pole. Long ago, this
thing must have been thrown overboard to save some poor wretch, who
must have been drowned; while even the life-buoy itself had drifted away
out of sight.

The forecastle-men fished it up from the bows, and the seamen thronged
round it.

"Bad luck! bad luck!" cried the Captain of the Head; "we'll number
one less before long."

The ship's cooper strolled by: he, to whose department it belongs to see
that the ship's life-buoys are kept in good order.

In men-of-war, night and day, week in and week out, two life-buoys are kept depending from the stern; and two men, with hatchets in their hands, pace up and down, ready at the first cry to cut the cord and drop the buoys overboard. Every two hours they are regularly relieved, like sentinels on guard. No similar precautions are adopted in the merchant or whaling service.

Thus deeply solicitous to preserve human life are the regulations of men-of-war; and seldom has there been a better illustration of this solicitude than at the battle of Trafalgar, when, after "several thousand" French seamen had been destroyed, according to Lord Collingwood, and, by the official returns, sixteen hundred and ninety Englishmen were killed or wounded, the Captains of the surviving ships ordered the life-buoy sentries from their death-dealing guns to their vigilant posts, as officers of the Humane Society.

"There, Bungs!" cried Scrimmage, a sheet-anchor-man,* "there's a good pattern for you; make us a brace of life-buoys like that; something that will save a man, and not fill and sink under him, as those leaky quarter-casks of yours will the first time there's occasion to drop 'em. I came near pitching off the bowsprit the other day; and, when I scrambled inboard again, I went aft to get a squint at 'em. Why, Bungs, they are all open between the staves. Shame on you! Suppose you yourself should fall overboard, and find yourself going down with buoys under you of your own making—what then?"

"I never go aloft, and don't intend to fall overboard," replied Bungs.

"Don't believe it!" cried the sheet-anchor-man; "you lopers that live about the decks here are nearer the bottom of the sea than the light hand that looses the main-royal. Mind your eye, Bungs—mind your eye!"

"I will," retorted Bungs; "and you mind yours!"

Next day, just at dawn, I was startled from my hammock by the cry of "*All hands about ship and shorten sail!*" Springing up the ladders, I found that an unknown man had fallen overboard from the chains; and darting a glance toward the poop, perceived, from their gestures, that the life-sentries there had cut away the buoys.

It was blowing a fresh breeze; the frigate was going fast through the water. But the one thousand arms of five hundred men soon tossed her about on the other tack, and checked her further headway.

---

* In addition to the *Bower-anchors* carried on her bows, a frigate carries large anchors in her fore-chains, called *Sheet-anchors*. Hence, the old seamen stationed in that part of a man-of-war are called *Sheet-anchor-men*.

"Do you see him?" shouted the officer of the watch through his trumpet, hailing the main-mast-head. "Man or *buoy*, do you see either?"

"See nothing, sir," was the reply.

"Clear away the cutters!" was the next order. "Bugler! call away the second, third, and fourth cutters' crews. Hands by the tackles!"

In less than three minutes the three boats were down. More hands were wanted in one of them, and, among others, I jumped in to make up the deficiency.

"Now, men, give way! and each man look out along his oar, and look sharp!" cried the officer of our boat. For a time, in perfect silence, we slid up and down the great seething swells of the sea, but saw nothing.

"There, it's no use," cried the officer; "he's gone, whoever he is. Pull away, men—pull away! they'll be recalling us soon."

"Let him drown!" cried the strokesman; "he's spoiled my watch below for me."

"Who the devil is he?" cried another.

"He's one who'll never have a coffin!" replied a third.

"No, no! they'll never sing out, '*All hands bury the dead!*' for him, my hearties!" cried a fourth.

"Silence," said the officer, "and look along your oars." But the sixteen oarsmen still continued their talk; and, after pulling about for two or three hours, we spied the recall-signal at the frigate's fore-t'-gallant-mast-head, and returned on board, having seen no sign even of the life-buoys.

The boats were hoisted up, the yards braced forward, and away we bowled—one man less.

"Muster all hands!" was now the order; when, upon calling the roll, the cooper was the only man missing.

"I told you so, men," cried the Captain of the Head; "I said we would lose a man before long."

"Bungs, is it?" cried Scrimmage, the sheet-anchor-man; "I told him his buoys wouldn't save a drowning man; and now he has proved it!"

Chapter 18

A Man-of-war Full as a Nut

I T WAS NECESSARY to supply the lost cooper's place; accordingly, word was passed for all who belonged to that calling to muster at the main-mast, in order that one of them might be selected. Thirteen men obeyed the summons—a circumstance illustrative of the fact that many good handicraftsmen are lost to their trades and the world by serving in men-of-war. Indeed, from a frigate's crew might be culled out men of all callings and vocations, from a backslidden parson to a broken-down comedian. The Navy is the asylum for the perverse, the home of the unfortunate. Here the sons of adversity meet the children of calamity, and here the children of calamity meet the offspring of sin. Bankrupt brokers, boot-blacks, blacklegs, and blacksmiths here assemble together; and castaway tinkers, watch-makers, quill-drivers, cobblers, doctors, farmers, and lawyers compare past experiences and talk of old times. Wrecked on a desert shore, a man-of-war's crew could quickly found an Alexandria by themselves, and fill it with all the things which go to make up a capital.

Frequently, at one and the same time, you see every trade in operation on the gun-deck—coopering, carpentering, tailoring, tinkering, blacksmithing, rope-making, preaching, gambling, and fortune-telling.

In truth, a man-of-war is a city afloat, with long avenues set out with guns instead of trees, and numerous shady lanes, courts, and by-ways. The quarter-deck is a grand square, park, or parade ground, with a great Pitts-field elm, in the shape of the main-mast, at one end, and fronted at the other by the palace of the Commodore's cabin.

Or, rather, a man-of-war is a lofty, walled, and garrisoned town, like Quebec, where the thoroughfares are mostly ramparts, and peaceable citizens meet armed sentries at every corner.

Or it is like the lodging-houses in Paris, turned upside down; the first floor, or deck, being rented by a lord; the second, by a select club of gentlemen; the third, by crowds of artisans; and the fourth, by a whole rabble of common people.

For even thus is it in a frigate, where the commander has a whole cabin to himself on the spar-deck, the lieutenants their ward-room underneath, and the mass of sailors swing their hammocks under all.

And with its long rows of port-hole casements, each revealing the muzzle of a cannon, a man-of-war resembles a three-story house in a suspicious part of the town, with a basement of indefinite depth, and ugly-looking fellows gazing out at the windows.

Chapter 19

The Jacket aloft

AGAIN MUST I CALL ATTENTION to my white jacket, which about this time came near being the death of me.

I am of a meditative humor, and at sea used often to mount aloft at night, and, seating myself on one of the upper yards, tuck my jacket about me and give loose to reflection. In some ships in which I have done this, the sailors used to fancy that I must be studying astronomy—which, indeed, to some extent, was the case—and that my object in mounting aloft was to get a nearer view of the stars, supposing me, of course, to be short-sighted. A very silly conceit of theirs, some may say, but not so silly after all; for surely the advantage of getting nearer an object by two hundred feet is not to be underrated. Then, to study the stars upon the wide, boundless sea, is divine as it was to the Chaldean Magi, who observed their revolutions from the plains.

And it is a very fine feeling, and one that fuses us into the universe of things, and makes us a part of the All, to think that, wherever we ocean-wanderers rove, we have still the same glorious old stars to keep us company; that they still shine onward and on, forever beautiful and bright, and luring us, by every ray, to die and be glorified with them.

Ay, ay! we sailors sail not in vain. We expatriate ourselves to nationalize with the universe; and in all our voyages round the world, we are still accompanied by those old circumnavigators, the stars, who are shipmates and fellow-sailors of ours—sailing in heaven's blue, as we on the azure main. Let genteel generations scoff at our hardened hands, and finger-nails tipped with tar—did they ever clasp truer palms than ours? Let them feel of our sturdy hearts, beating like sledge-hammers in those hot smithies, our bosoms; with their amber-headed canes, let them feel of our generous pulses, and swear that they go off like thirty-two-pounders.

Oh, give me again the rover's life—the joy, the thrill, the whirl! Let me feel thee again, old sea! let me leap into thy saddle once more. I am sick of these terra firma toils and cares; sick of the dust and reek of towns. Let me hear the clatter of hailstones on icebergs, and not the dull tramp of these plodders, plodding their dull way from their cradles to their graves. Let me snuff thee up, sea-breeze! and whinny in thy spray. Forbid it, sea-gods! intercede for me with Neptune, O sweet Amphitrite, that no dull clod may fall on my coffin! Be mine the tomb that swallowed up Pharaoh and all his hosts; let me lie down with Drake, where he sleeps in the sea.

But when White-Jacket speaks of the rover's life, he means not life in a man-of-war, which, with its martial formalities and thousand vices, stabs to the heart the soul of all free-and-easy honorable rovers.

I have said that I was wont to mount up aloft and muse; and thus was it with me the night following the loss of the cooper. Ere my watch in the top had expired, high up on the main-royal-yard I reclined, the white jacket folded around me like Sir John Moore in his frosted cloak.

Eight bells had struck, and my watchmates had hied to their hammocks, and the other watch had gone to their stations, and the *top* below me was full of strangers, and still one hundred feet above even *them* I lay entranced; now dozing, now dreaming; now thinking of things past, and anon of the life to come. Well-timed was the latter thought, for the life to come was much nearer overtaking me than I then could imagine. Perhaps I was half conscious at last of a tremulous voice hailing the main-royal-yard from the *top*. But if so, the consciousness glided away from me, and left me in Lethe. But when, like lightning, the yard dropped under me, and instinctively I clung with both hands to the "*tie*," then I came to myself with a rush, and felt something like a choking hand at my throat. For an instant I thought the Gulf Stream in my head was whirling me away to eternity; but the next moment I found myself standing; the yard had descended to the *cap*; and shaking myself in my jacket, I felt that I was unharmed and alive.

Who had done this? who had made this attempt on my life? thought I, as I ran down the rigging.

"Here it comes!—Lord! Lord! here it comes! See, see! it is white as a hammock."

"Who's coming?" I shouted, springing down into the top; "who's white as a hammock?"

"Bless my soul, Bill, it's only White-Jacket—that infernal White-Jacket again!"

It seems they had spied a moving white spot there aloft, and, sailor-like, had taken me for the ghost of the cooper; and after hailing me, and bidding me descend, to test my corporeality, and getting no answer, they had lowered the halyards in affright.

In a rage I tore off the jacket, and threw it on the deck.

"Jacket," cried I, "you must change your complexion! you must hie to the dyers and be dyed, that I may live. I have but one poor life, White Jacket, and that life I can not spare. I can not consent to die for *you*, but be dyed you must for me. You can dye many times without injury; but I can not die without irreparable loss, and running the eternal risk."

So in the morning, jacket in hand, I repaired to the First Lieutenant, and related the narrow escape I had had during the night. I enlarged upon the general perils I ran in being taken for a ghost, and earnestly besought him to relax his commands for once, and give me an order on Brush, the captain of the paint-room, for some black paint, that my jacket might be painted of that color.

"Just look at it, sir," I added, holding it up; "did you ever see any thing whiter? Consider how it shines of a night, like a bit of the Milky Way. A little paint, sir, you can not refuse."

"The ship has no paint to spare," he said; "you must get along without it."

"Sir, every rain gives me a soaking;—Cape Horn is at hand—six brushes-full would make it water-proof; and no longer would I be in peril of my life!"

"Can't help it, sir; depart!"

I fear it will not be well with me in the end; for if my own sins are to be forgiven only as I forgive that hard-hearted and unimpressible First Lieutenant, then pardon there is none for me.

What! when but one dab of paint would make a man of a ghost, and a Mackintosh of a herring-net—to refuse it!

I am full. I can say no more.

Chapter 20

How they Sleep in a Man-of-war

N O MORE OF MY LUCKLESS JACKET for a while; let me
speak of my hammock, and the tribulations I endured therefrom.
Give me plenty of room to swing it in; let me swing it between two date-trees on an Arabian plain; or extend it diagonally from
Moorish pillar to pillar, in the open marble Court of the Lions in Granada's
Alhambra: let me swing it on a high bluff of the Mississippi—one swing in
the pure ether for every swing over the green grass; or let me oscillate in it
beneath the cool dome of St. Peter's; or drop me in it, as in a balloon, from
the zenith, with the whole firmament to rock and expatiate in; and I would
not exchange my coarse canvas hammock for the grand state-bed, like a
stately coach-and-four, in which they tuck in a king when he passes a night
at Blenheim Castle.

When you have the requisite room, you always have "spreaders" in your
hammock; that is, two horizontal sticks, one at each end, which serve to
keep the sides apart, and create a wide vacancy between, wherein you can
turn over and over—lay on this side or that; on your back, if you please;
stretch out your legs; in short, take your ease in your hammock; for of all
inns, your bed is the best.

But when, with five hundred other hammocks, yours is crowded and
jammed in on all sides, on a frigate berth-deck, the third from above; when

"*spreaders*" are prohibited by an express edict from the Captain's cabin; and every man about you is jealously watchful of the rights and privileges of his own proper hammock, as settled by law and usage; *then* your hammock is your Bastile and canvas jug; into which, or out of which, it is very hard to get; and where sleep is but a mockery and a name.

Eighteen inches a man is all they allow you; eighteen inches in width; in *that* you must swing. Dreadful! they give you more swing than that at the gallows.

During warm nights in the Tropics, your hammock is as a stew-pan; where you stew and stew, till you can almost hear yourself hiss. Vain are all stratagems to widen your accommodations. Let them catch you insinuating your boots or other articles in the head of your hammock, by way of a "spreader." Near and far, the whole rank and file of the row to which you belong feel the encroachment in an instant, and are clamorous till the guilty one is found out, and his pallet brought back to its bearings.

In platoons and squadrons, they all lie on a level; their hammock *clews* crossing and recrossing in all directions, so as to present one vast field-bed, midway between the ceiling and the floor; which are about five feet asunder.

One extremely warm night, during a calm, when it was so hot that only a skeleton could keep cool (from the free current of air through its bones), after being drenched in my own perspiration, I managed to wedge myself out of my hammock; and with what little strength I had left, lowered myself gently to the deck. Let me see now, thought I, whether my ingenuity can not devise some method whereby I can have room to breathe and sleep at the same time. I have it. I will lower my hammock underneath all these others; and then—upon that separate and independent level, at least—I shall have the whole berth-deck to myself. Accordingly, I lowered away my pallet to the desired point—about three inches from the floor—and crawled into it again.

But, alas! this arrangement made such a sweeping semicircle of my hammock, that, while my head and feet were at par, the small of my back was settling down indefinitely; I felt as if some gigantic archer had hold of me for a bow.

But there was another plan left. I triced up my hammock with all my strength, so as to bring it wholly *above* the tiers of pallets around me. This done, by a last effort, I hoisted myself into it; but alas! it was much worse than before. My luckless hammock was stiff and straight as a board; and there I was—laid out in it, with my nose against the ceiling, like a dead man's against the lid of his coffin.

So at last I was fain to return to my old level, and moralize upon the folly, in all arbitrary governments, of striving to get either *below* or *above* those whom legislation has placed upon an equality with yourself.

Speaking of hammocks, recalls a circumstance that happened one night in the Neversink. It was three or four times repeated, with various but not fatal results.

The watch below was fast asleep on the berth-deck, where perfect silence was reigning, when a sudden shock and a groan roused up all hands; and the hem of a pair of white trowsers vanished up one of the ladders at the fore-hatchway.

We ran toward the groan, and found a man lying on the deck; one end of his hammock having given way, pitching his head close to three twenty-four-pound cannon shot, which must have been purposely placed in that position. When it was discovered that this man had long been suspected of being an *informer* among the crew, little surprise and less pleasure were evinced at his narrow escape.

Chapter 21

One Reason why Men-of-war's-men are, generally, Short-lived

I CAN NOT QUIT this matter of the hammocks without making mention of a grievance among the sailors that ought to be redressed. In a man-of-war at sea, the sailors have *watch and watch;* that is, through every twenty-four hours, they are on and off duty every four hours. Now, the hammocks are piped down from the nettings (the open space for stowing them, running round the top of the bulwarks) a little after sunset, and piped up again when the forenoon watch is called, at eight o'clock in the morning; so that during the daytime they are inaccessible as pallets. This would be all well enough, did the sailors have a complete night's rest; but every other night at sea, one watch have only four hours in their hammocks. Indeed, deducting the time allowed for the other watch to turn out; for yourself to arrange your hammock, get into it, and fairly get asleep; it may be said that, every other night, you have but three hours' sleep in your hammock. Having then been on deck for twice four hours, at eight o'clock in the morning your *watch-below* comes round, and you are not liable to duty until noon. Under like circumstances, a merchant seaman goes to his bunk, and has the benefit of a good long sleep. But in a man-of-war you can do no such thing; your hammock is very neatly stowed in the nettings, and there it must remain till nightfall.

But perhaps there is a corner for you somewhere along the batteries on

82

the gun-deck, where you may enjoy a snug nap. But as no one is allowed to recline on the larboard side of the gun-deck (which is reserved as a corridor for the officers when they go forward to their smoking-room at the *bridle-port*), the starboard side only is left to the seamen. But most of this side, also, is occupied by the carpenters, sail-makers, barbers, and coopers. In short, so few are the corners where you can snatch a nap during daytime in a frigate, that not one in ten of the watch, who have been on deck eight hours, can get a wink of sleep till the following night. Repeatedly, after by good fortune securing a corner, I have been roused from it by some functionary commissioned to keep it clear.

Off Cape Horn, what before had been very uncomfortable became a serious hardship. Drenched through and through by the spray of the sea at night, I have sometimes slept standing on the spar-deck—and shuddered as I slept—for the want of sufficient sleep in my hammock.

During three days of the stormiest weather, we were given the privilege of the *berth-deck* (at other times strictly interdicted), where we were permitted to spread our jackets, and take a nap in the morning after the eight hours' night exposure. But this privilege was but a beggarly one, indeed. Not to speak of our jackets—used for blankets—being soaking wet, the spray, coming down the hatchways, kept the planks of the berth-deck itself constantly wet; whereas, had we been permitted our hammocks, we might have swung dry over all this deluge. But we endeavored to make ourselves as warm and comfortable as possible, chiefly by close stowing, so as to generate a little steam, in the absence of any fire-side warmth. You have seen, perhaps, the way in which they box up subjects intended to illustrate the winter lectures of a professor of surgery. Just so we laid; heel and point, face to back, dove-tailed into each other at every ham and knee. The wet of our jackets, thus densely packed, would soon begin to distill. But it was like pouring hot water on you to keep you from freezing. It was like being "packed" between the soaked sheets in a Water-cure Establishment.

Such a posture could not be preserved for any considerable period without shifting side for side. Three or four times during the four hours I would be startled from a wet doze by the hoarse cry of a fellow who did the duty of a corporal at the after-end of my file, "*Sleepers ahoy! stand by to slew round!*" and, with a double shuffle, we all rolled in concert, and found ourselves facing the taffrail instead of the bowsprit. But, however you turned, your nose was sure to stick to one or other of the steaming backs on your two flanks. There was some little relief in the change of odor consequent upon this.

But what is the reason that, after battling out eight stormy hours on deck at night, men-of-war's-men are not allowed the poor boon of a dry four hours' nap during the day following? What is the reason? The Commodore, Captain, and First Lieutenant, Chaplain, Purser, and scores of others, have *all night in*, just as if they were staying at a hotel on shore. And the junior Lieutenants not only have their cots to go to at any time; but as only one of them is required to head the watch, and there are so many of them among whom to divide that duty, they are only on deck four hours to twelve hours below. In some cases the proportion is still greater. Whereas, with *the people* it is four hours in and four hours off continually.

What is the reason, then, that the common seamen should fare so hard in this matter? It would seem but a simple thing to let them get down their hammocks during the day for a nap. But no; such a proceeding would mar the uniformity of daily events in a man-of-war. It seems indispensable to the picturesque effect of the spar-deck, that the hammocks should invariably remain stowed in the nettings between sunrise and sundown. But the chief reason is this—a reason which has sanctioned many an abuse in this world—*precedents are against it;* such a thing as sailors sleeping in their hammocks in the daytime, after being eight hours exposed to a night-storm, was hardly ever heard of in the navy. Though, to the immortal honor of some captains be it said, the fact is upon navy record that, off Cape Horn, they *have* vouchsafed the morning hammocks to their crew. Heaven bless such tender-hearted officers; and may they and their descendants—ashore or afloat—have sweet and pleasant slumbers while they live, and an undreaming siesta when they die.

It is concerning such things as the subject of this chapter that special enactments of Congress are demanded. Health and comfort—so far as duly attainable under the circumstances—should be legally guaranteed to the man-of-war's-man; and not left to the discretion or caprice of their commanders.

Chapter 22

Wash-day, and House-cleaning in a Man-of-war

BESIDES THE OTHER TRIBULATIONS connected with your hammock, you must keep it snow-white and clean; who has not observed the long rows of spotless hammocks exposed in a frigate's nettings, where, through the day, their outsides, at least, are kept airing?

Hence it comes that there are regular mornings appointed for the scrubbing of hammocks; and such mornings are called *scrub-hammock-mornings;* and desperate is the scrubbing that ensues.

Before daylight the operation begins. All hands are called, and at it they go. Every deck is spread with hammocks, fore and aft; and lucky are you if you can get sufficient superficies to spread your own hammock in. Down on their knees are five hundred men, scrubbing away with brushes and brooms; jostling, and crowding, and quarreling about using each other's suds; when all their Purser's soap goes to create one indiscriminate yeast.

Sometimes you discover that, in the dark, you have been all the while scrubbing your next neighbor's hammock instead of your own. But it is too late to begin over again; for now the word is passed for every man to advance with his hammock, that it may be tied to a net-like frame work of clothes-lines, and hoisted aloft to dry

That done, without delay you get together your frocks and trowsers, and on the already flooded deck embark in the laundry business. You have

85

no special bucket or basin to yourself—the ship being one vast wash-tub, where all hands wash and rinse out, and rinse out and wash, till at last the word is passed again, to make fast your clothes, that they, also, may be elevated to dry.

Then on all three decks the operation of holy-stoning begins, so called from the queer name bestowed upon the principal instruments employed. These are ponderous flat stones with long ropes at each end, by which the stones are slidden about, to and fro, over the wet and sanded decks; a most wearisome, dog-like, galley-slave employment. For the by-ways and corners about the masts and guns, smaller stones are used, called *prayer-books*; inasmuch as the devout operator has to down with them on his knees.

Finally, a grand flooding takes place, and the decks are remorselessly thrashed with dry swabs. After which an extraordinary implement—a sort of leathern hoe called a *"squilgee"*—is used to scrape and squeeze the last dribblings of water from the planks. Concerning this "squilgee," I think something of drawing up a memoir, and reading it before the Academy of Arts and Sciences. It is a most curious affair.

By the time all these operations are concluded it is *eight bells*, and all hands are piped to breakfast upon the damp and every-way disagreeable decks.

Now, against this invariable daily flooding of the three decks of a frigate, as a man-of-war's-man, White-Jacket most earnestly protests. In sunless weather it keeps the sailor's quarters perpetually damp; so much so, that you can scarce sit down without running the risk of getting the lumbago. One rheumatic old sheet-anchor-man among us was driven to the extremity of sewing a piece of tarred canvas on the seat of his trowsers.

Let those neat and tidy officers who so love to see a ship kept spick and span clean; who institute vigorous search after the man who chances to drop the crumb of a biscuit on deck, when the ship is rolling in a sea-way; let all such swing their hammocks with the sailors, and they would soon get sick of this daily damping of the decks.

Is a ship a wooden platter, that it is to be scrubbed out every morning before breakfast, even if the thermometer be at zero, and every sailor goes barefooted through the flood with the chilblains? And all the while the ship carries a doctor, well aware of Boerhaave's great maxim *"keep the feet dry."* He has plenty of pills to give you when you are down with a fever, the consequences of these things; but enters no protest at the outset as it is his duty to do—against the cause that induces the fever.

During the pleasant night watches, the promenading officers, mounted on their high-heeled boots, pass dry-shod, like the Israelites, over the decks; but by daybreak the roaring tide sets back, and the poor sailors are almost overwhelmed in it, like the Egyptians in the Red Sea.

Oh! the chills, colds, and agues that are caught. No snug stove, grate, or fire-place to go to; no, your only way to keep warm is to keep in a blazing passion, and anathematize the custom that every morning makes a wash-house of a man-of-war.

Look at it. Say you go on board a line-of-battle-ship: you see every thing scrupulously neat; you see all the decks clear and unobstructed as the side-walks of Wall Street of a Sunday morning; you see no trace of a sailor's dormitory; you marvel by what magic all this is brought about. And well you may. For consider, that in this unobstructed fabric nearly one thousand mortal men have to sleep, eat, wash, dress, cook, and perform all the ordinary functions of humanity. The same number of men ashore would expand themselves into a township. Is it credible, then, that this extraordinary neatness, and especially this *unobstructedness* of a man-of-war, can be brought about, except by the most rigorous edicts, and a very serious sacrifice, with respect to the sailors, of the domestic comforts of life? To be sure, sailors themselves do not often complain of these things; they are used to them; but man can become used even to the hardest usage. And it is because he *is* used to it, that sometimes he does not complain of it.

Of all men-of-war, the American ships are the most excessively neat, and have the greatest reputation for it. And of all men-of-war the general discipline of the American ships is the most arbitrary.

In the English navy, the men liberally mess on tables, which, between meals, are triced up out of the way. The American sailors mess on the deck, and peck up their broken biscuit, or *midshipmen's nuts*, like fowls in a barn-yard.

But if this unobstructedness in an American fighting-ship be, at all hazards, so desirable, why not imitate the Turks? In the Turkish navy they have no mess-chests; the sailors roll their mess things up in a rug, and thrust them under a gun. Nor do they have any hammocks; they sleep any where about the decks in their *gregoes*. Indeed, come to look at it, what more does a man-of-war's-man absolutely require to live in than his own skin? That's room enough; and room enough to turn in, if he but knew how to shift his spine, end for end, like a ramrod, without disturbing his next neighbor.

Among all men-of-war's men, it is a maxim that over-neat vessels are Tartars to the crew; and perhaps it may be safely laid down that, when you see such a ship, some sort of tyranny is not very far off.

In the Neversink, as in other national ships, the business of *holy-stoning* the decks was often prolonged, by way of punishment to the men, particularly of a raw, cold morning. This is one of the punishments which a lieutenant of the watch may easily inflict upon the crew, without infringing the statute which places the power of punishment solely in the hands of the Captain.

The abhorrence which men-of-war's-men have for this protracted *holy-stoning* in cold, comfortless weather—with their bare feet exposed to the splashing inundations—is shown in a strange story, rife among them, curiously tinctured with their proverbial superstitions.

The First Lieutenant of an English sloop of war, a severe disciplinarian, was uncommonly particular concerning the whiteness of the quarter-deck. One bitter winter morning at sea, when the crew had washed that part of the vessel, as usual, and put away their holy-stones, this officer came on deck, and after inspecting it, ordered the *holy-stones* and *prayer-books* up again. Once more slipping off the shoes from their frosted feet, and rolling up their trowsers, the crew kneeled down to their task; and in that suppliant posture, silently invoked a curse upon their tyrant; praying, as he went below, that he might never more come out of the ward-room alive. The prayer seemed answered; for being shortly after visited with a paralytic stroke at his breakfast-table, the First Lieutenant next morning was carried out of the ward-room feet foremost, dead. As they dropped him over the side—so goes the story—the marine sentry at the gangway turned his back upon the corpse.

To the credit of the humane and sensible portion of the roll of American navy-captains, be it added, that *they* are not so particular in keeping the decks spotless at all times, and in all weathers; nor do they torment the men with scraping bright-wood and polishing ring-bolts; but give all such gingerbread-work a hearty coat of black paint, which looks more warlike, is a better preservative, and exempts the sailors from a perpetual annoyance.

Chapter 23

Theatricals in a Man-of-war

T HE NEVERSINK had summered out her last Christmas on the
Equator; she was now destined to winter out the Fourth of July
not very far from the frigid latitudes of Cape Horn.

It is sometimes the custom in the American Navy to celebrate this national holiday by doubling the allowance of spirits to the men; that is, if
the ship happen to be lying in harbor. The effects of this patriotic plan may
be easily imagined: the whole ship is converted into a dram-shop; and the
intoxicated sailors reel about, on all three decks, singing, howling, and
fighting. This is the time that, owing to the relaxed discipline of the ship,
old and almost forgotten quarrels are revived, under the stimulus of drink;
and, fencing themselves up between the guns—so as to be sure of a clear
space with at least three walls—the combatants, two and two, fight out
their hate, cribbed and cabined like soldiers dueling in a sentry-box. In a
word, scenes ensue which would not for a single instant be tolerated by the
officers upon any other occasion. This is the time that the most venerable
of quarter-gunners and quarter-masters, together with the smallest apprentice boys, and men never known to have been previously intoxicated during
the cruise—this is the time that they all roll together in the same muddy
trough of drunkenness.

In emulation of the potentates of the Middle Ages, some Captains augment the din by authorizing a grand jail-delivery of all the prisoners who, on that auspicious Fourth of the month, may happen to be confined in the ship's prison—"*the brig.*"

But from scenes like these the Neversink was happily delivered. Besides that she was now approaching a most perilous part of the ocean—which would have made it madness to intoxicate the sailors—her complete destitution of *grog*, even for ordinary consumption, was an obstacle altogether insuperable, even had the Captain felt disposed to indulge his man-of-war's-men by the most copious libations.

For several days previous to the advent of the holiday, frequent conferences were held on the gun-deck touching the melancholy prospects before the ship.

"Too bad—too bad!" cried a top-man. "Think of it, shipmates—a Fourth of July without grog!"

"I'll hoist the Commodore's pennant at half-mast that day," sighed the signal-quarter-master.

"And I'll turn my best uniform jacket wrong side out, to keep company with the pennant, old Ensign," sympathetically responded an after-guard's-man.

"Ay, do!" cried a forecastle-man. "I could almost pipe my eye to think on't."

"No grog on de day dat tried men's souls!" blubbered Sunshine, the galley-cook.

"Who would be a *Jankee* now?" roared a Hollander of the fore-top, more Dutch than sour-crout.

"Is this the *riglar* fruits of liberty?" touchingly inquired an Irish waister of an old Spanish sheet-anchor-man.

You will generally observe that, of all Americans, your foreign-born citizens are the most patriotic—especially toward the Fourth of July.

But how could Captain Claret, the father of his crew, behold the grief of his ocean children with indifference? He could not. Three days before the anniversary—it still continuing very pleasant weather for these latitudes—it was publicly announced that free permission was given to the sailors to get up any sort of theatricals they desired, wherewith to honor the Fourth.

Now, some weeks prior to the Neversink's sailing from home—nearly three years before the time here spoken of—some of the seamen had clubbed together, and made up a considerable purse, for the purpose of purchasing a theatrical outfit; having in view to diversify the monotony of lying in foreign harbors for weeks together, by an occasional display on the boards

—though if ever there was a continual theatre in the world, playing by night and by day, and without intervals between the acts, a man-of-war is that theatre, and her planks are the *boards* indeed.

The sailors who originated this scheme had served in other American frigates, where the privilege of having theatricals was allowed to the crew. What was their chagrin, then, when, upon making an application to the Captain, in a Peruvian harbor, for permission to present the much-admired drama of "*The Ruffian Boy*," under the Captain's personal patronage, that dignitary assured them that there were already enough *ruffian boys* on board, without conjuring up any more from the green-room.

The theatrical outfit, therefore, was stowed down in the bottom of the sailors' bags, who little anticipated *then* that it would ever be dragged out while Captain Claret had the sway.

But immediately upon the announcement that the embargo was removed, vigorous preparations were at once commenced to celebrate the Fourth with unwonted spirit. The half-deck was set apart for the theatre, and the signal-quarter-master was commanded to loan his flags to decorate it in the most patriotic style.

As the stage-struck portion of the crew had frequently during the cruise rehearsed portions of various plays, to while away the tedium of the night-watches, they needed no long time now to perfect themselves in their parts.

Accordingly, on the very next morning after the indulgence had been granted by the Captain, the following written placard, presenting a broad-side of staring capitals, was found tacked against the main-mast on the gun-deck. It was as if a Drury-Lane bill had been posted upon the London Monument:

CAPE HORN THEATRE.

Grand Celebration of the Fourth of July.

DAY PERFORMANCE.

UNCOMMON ATTRACTION.

THE OLD WAGON PAID OFF!

JACK CHASE........PERCY ROYAL-MAST.

STARS OF THE FIRST MAGNITUDE.

For this time only,

THE TRUE YANKEE SAILOR.

The managers of the Cape Horn Theatre beg leave to inform the inhabitants of the Pacific and Southern Oceans that, on the afternoon of the Fourth of July, 184–, they will have the honor to present the admired drama of

THE OLD WAGON PAID OFF!

Commodore Bougee .... *Tom Brown, of the Fore-top.*
Captain Spy-glass .... *Ned Brace, of the After-Guard.*
Commodore's Cockswain .... *Joe Bunk, of the Launch.*
Old Luff .... *Quarter-master Coffin.*
Mayor .... *Seafull, of the Forecastle.*
PERCY ROYAL-MAST .... JACK CHASE.
Mrs. Lovelorn .... *Long-locks, of the After-Guard.*
Toddy Moll .... *Frank Jones.*
Gin and Sugar Sall................ *Dick Dash.*
Sailors, Marines, Bar-keepers, Crimps, Aldermen, Police-officers, Soldiers, Landsmen generally.

Long live the Commodore! ‖ Admission Free.

To conclude with the much-admired song by Dibdin, altered to suit all American Tars, entitled

THE TRUE YANKEE SAILOR.

True Yankee Sailor (in costume), Patrick Flinegan,
Captain of the Head.

Performance to commence with "Hail Columbia," by the Brass Band. Ensign rises at three bells, P.M. No sailor permitted to enter in his shirt-sleeves. Good order is expected to be maintained. The Master-at-arms and Ship's Corporals to be in attendance to keep the peace.

At the earnest entreaties of the seamen, Lemsford, the gun-deck poet, had been prevailed upon to draw up this bill. And upon this one occasion his literary abilities were far from being underrated, even by the least intellectual person on board. Nor must it be omitted that, before the bill was placarded, Captain Claret, enacting the part of censor and grand chamberlain, ran over a manuscript copy of "*The Old Wagon Paid Off,*" to see whether it contained any thing calculated to breed disaffection against lawful authority among the crew. He objected to some parts, but in the end let them all pass.

The morning of The Fourth—most anxiously awaited—dawned clear and fair. The breeze was steady; the air bracing cold; and one and all the sailors anticipated a gleeful afternoon. And thus was falsified the prophecies of certain old growlers averse to theatricals, who had predicted a gale of wind that would quash all the arrangements of the green-room.

As the men whose regular turns, at the time of the performance, would come round to be stationed in the tops, and at the various halyards and running ropes about the spar-deck, could not be permitted to partake in the celebration, there accordingly ensued, during the morning, many amusing scenes of tars who were anxious to procure substitutes at their posts. Through the day, many anxious glances were cast to windward; but the weather still promised fair.

At last *the people* were piped to dinner; two bells struck; and soon after, all who could be spared from their stations hurried to the half-deck. The capstan bars were placed on shot-boxes, as at prayers on Sundays, furnishing seats for the audience, while a low stage, rigged by the carpenter's gang, was built at one end of the open space. The curtain was composed of a large ensign, and the bulwarks round about were draperied with the flags of all nations. The ten or twelve members of the brass band were ranged in a row at the foot of the stage, their polished instruments in their hands, while the consequential Captain of the Band himself was elevated upon a gun-carriage.

At three bells precisely a group of ward-room officers emerged from the after-hatchway, and seated themselves upon camp-stools, in a central position, with the stars and stripes for a canopy. *That* was the royal box. The sailors looked round for the Commodore; but neither Commodore nor Captain honored *the people* with their presence.

At the call of a bugle the band struck up *Hail Columbia*, the whole audience keeping time, as at Drury Lane, when *God Save the King* is played after a great national victory.

At the discharge of a marine's musket the curtain rose, and four sailors, in the picturesque garb of Maltese mariners, staggered on the stage in a feigned state of intoxication. The truthfulness of the representation was much heightened by the roll of the ship.

"The Commodore," "Old Luff," "The Mayor," and "Gin and Sugar Sall," were played to admiration, and received great applause. But at the first appearance of that universal favorite, Jack Chase, in the chivalric character of "*Percy Royal-Mast*," the whole audience simultaneously rose to their feet, and greeted him with three hearty cheers, that almost took the main-top-sail aback.

Matchless Jack, *in full fig*, bowed again and again, with true quarter-deck grace and self-possession; and when five or six untwisted strands of rope and bunches of oakum were thrown to him, as substitutes for bouquets, he took them one by one, and gallantly hung them from the buttons of his jacket.

"Hurrah! hurrah! hurrah!—go on! go on!—stop hollering—hurrah! —go on!—stop hollering—hurrah!" was now heard on all sides, till at last, seeing no end to the enthusiasm of his ardent admirers, Matchless Jack stepped forward, and, with his lips moving in pantomime, plunged into the thick of the part. Silence soon followed, but was fifty times broken by uncontrollable bursts of applause. At length, when that heart-thrilling scene came on, where Percy Royal-Mast rescues fifteen oppressed sailors from the watch-house, in the teeth of a posse of constables, the audience leaped to their feet, overturned the capstan bars, and to a man hurled their hats on the stage in a delirium of delight. Ah Jack, that was a ten-stroke indeed!

The commotion was now terrific; all discipline seemed gone forever; the Lieutenants ran in among the men, the Captain darted from his cabin, and the Commodore nervously questioned the armed sentry at his door as to what the deuce *the people* were about. In the midst of all this, the trumpet of the officer-of-the-deck, commanding the top-gallant sails to be taken in, was almost completely drowned. A black squall was coming down on the weather-bow, and the boatswain's mates bellowed themselves hoarse at the main-hatchway. There is no knowing what would have ensued, had not the bass drum suddenly been heard, calling all hands to quarters, a summons not to be withstood. The sailors pricked their ears at it, as horses at the sound of a cracking whip, and confusedly stumbled up the ladders to their stations. The next moment all was silent but the wind, howling like a thousand devils in the cordage.

"Stand by to reef all three top-sails!—settle away the halyards!—haul out—so: make fast!—aloft, top-men! and reef away!"

Thus, in storm and tempest terminated that day's theatricals. But the sailors never recovered from the disappointment of not having the "*True Yankee Sailor*" sung by the Irish Captain of the Head.

And here White-Jacket must moralize a bit. The unwonted spectacle of the row of gun-room officers mingling with "the people" in applauding a mere seaman like Jack Chase, filled me at the time with the most pleasurable emotions. It is a sweet thing, thought I, to see these officers confess a human brotherhood with us, after all; a sweet thing to mark their cordial appreciation of the manly merits of my matchless Jack. Ah! they are noble fellows all round, and I do not know but I have wronged them sometimes in my thoughts.

Nor was it without similar pleasurable feelings that I witnessed the temporary rupture of the ship's stern discipline, consequent upon the tumult of the theatricals. I thought to myself, this now is as it should be. It is good to shake off, now and then, this iron yoke round our necks. And after having once permitted us sailors to be a little noisy, in a harmless way—somewhat merrily turbulent—the officers can not, with any good grace, be so excessively stern and unyielding as before. I began to think a man-of-war a man-of-peace-and-good-will, after all. But, alas! disappointment came.

Next morning the same old scene was enacted at the gangway. And beholding the row of uncompromising-looking officers there assembled with the Captain, to witness punishment—the same officers who had been so cheerfully disposed over night—an old sailor touched my shoulder, and said, "See, White-Jacket, all round they have *shipped their quarter-deck faces again*. But this is the way."

I afterward learned that this was an old man-of-war's-man's phrase, expressive of the facility with which a sea-officer falls back upon all the severity of his dignity, after a temporary suspension of it.

Chapter 24

Introductory to Cape Horn

A ND NOW, through drizzling fogs and vapors, and under damp, double-reefed top-sails, our wet-decked frigate drew nearer and nearer to the squally Cape.

Who has not heard of it? Cape Horn, Cape Horn—a *horn* indeed, that has tossed many a good ship. Was the descent of Orpheus, Ulysses, or Dante into Hell, one whit more hardy and sublime than the first navigator's weathering of that terrible Cape?

Turned on her heel by a fierce West Wind, many an outward-bound ship has been driven across the Southern Ocean to the Cape of Good Hope —*that* way to seek a passage to the Pacific. And that stormy Cape, I doubt not, has sent many a fine craft to the bottom, and told no tales. At those ends of the earth are no chronicles. What signify the broken spars and shrouds that, day after day, are driven before the prows of more fortunate vessels? or the tall masts, imbedded in icebergs, that are found floating by? They but hint the old story—of ships that have sailed from their ports, and never more have been heard of.

Impracticable Cape! You may approach it from this direction or that —in any way you please—from the East, or from the West; with the wind astern, or abeam, or on the quarter; and still Cape Horn is Cape Horn. Cape Horn it is that takes the conceit out of fresh-water sailors, and steeps in a still salter brine the saltest. Woe betide the tyro; the foolhardy, Heaven preserve!

Your Mediterranean captain, who with a cargo of oranges has hitherto made merry runs across the Atlantic, without so much as furling a t'-gallant-sail, oftentimes, off Cape Horn, receives a lesson which he carries to the grave; though the grave—as is too often the case—follows so hard on the lesson that no benefit comes from the experience.

Other strangers who draw nigh to this Patagonia termination of our Continent, with their souls full of its shipwrecks and disasters—top-sails cautiously reefed, and every thing guardedly snug—these strangers at first unexpectedly encountering a tolerably smooth sea, rashly conclude that the Cape, after all, is but a bugbear; they have been imposed upon by fables, and founderings and sinkings hereabouts are all cock-and-bull stories.

"Out reefs, my hearties; fore and aft set t'-gallant-sails! stand by to give her the fore-top-mast stun'-sail!"

But, Captain Rash, those sails of yours were much safer in the sail-maker's loft. For now, while the heedless craft is bounding over the billows, a black cloud rises out of the sea; the sun drops down from the sky; a horrible mist far and wide spreads over the water.

"Hands by the halyards! Let go! Clew up!"

Too late.

For ere the ropes' ends can be cast off from the pins, the tornado is blowing down to the bottom of their throats. The masts are willows, the sails ribbons, the cordage wool; the whole ship is brewed into the yeast of the gale.

And now, if, when the first green sea breaks over him, Captain Rash is not swept overboard, he has his hands full, be sure. In all probability his three masts have gone by the board, and, raveled into list, his sails are floating in the air. Or, perhaps, the ship *broaches to*, or is *brought by the lee*. In either case, Heaven help the sailors, their wives, and their little ones; and Heaven help the underwriters.

Familiarity with danger makes a brave man braver, but less daring. Thus with seamen: he who goes the oftenest round Cape Horn goes the most circumspectly. A veteran mariner is never deceived by the treacherous breezes which sometimes waft him pleasantly toward the latitude of the Cape. No sooner does he come within a certain distance of it—previously fixed in his own mind—than all hands are turned to setting the ship in storm-trim; and, never mind how light the breeze, down come his t'-gallant-yards. He "bends" his strongest storm-sails, and lashes every thing on deck securely. The ship is then ready for the worst; and if, in reeling round the headland, she receives a broadside, it generally goes well with her. If ill, all hands go to the bottom with quiet consciences.

Among sea-captains, there are some who seem to regard the genius of the Cape as a willful, capricious jade, that must be courted and coaxed into complaisance. First, they come along under easy sail; do not steer boldly for the headland, but tack this way and that—sidling up to it. Now they woo the Jezebel with a t'-gallant-studding-sail; anon, they deprecate her wrath with double-reefed-top-sails. When, at length, her unappeasable fury is fairly aroused, and all round the dismantled ship the storm howls and howls for days together, they still persevere in their efforts. First, they try unconditional submission; furling every rag and *heaving to;* laying like a log, for the tempest to toss wheresoever it pleases.

This failing, they set a *spencer* or *try-sail*, and shift on the other tack. Equally vain! The gale sings as hoarsely as before. At last, the wind comes round fair; they drop the fore-sail; square the yards, and scud before it: their implacable foe chasing them with tornadoes, as if to show her insensibility to the last.

Other ships, without encountering these terrible gales, spend week after week endeavoring to turn this boisterous world-corner against a continual head-wind. Tacking hither and thither, in the language of sailors, they *polish* the Cape by beating about its edges so long.

Le Mair and Schouten, two Dutchmen, were the first navigators who weathered Cape Horn. Previous to this, passages had been made to the Pacific by the Straits of Magellan; nor, indeed, at that period, was it known to a certainty that there was any other route, or that the land now called Terra Del Fuego was an island. A few leagues southward from Terra Del Fuego is a cluster of small islands, the Diegoes; between which and the former island are the Straits of Le Mair, so called in honor of their discoverer, who first sailed through them into the Pacific. Le Mair and Schouten, in their small, clumsy vessels, encountered a series of tremendous gales, the prelude to the long train of similar hardships which most of their followers have experienced. It is a significant fact, that Schouten's vessel, the *Horne,* which gave its name to the Cape, was almost lost in weathering it.

The next navigator round the Cape was Sir Francis Drake, who, on Raleigh's Expedition, beholding for the first time, from the Isthmus of Darien, the "goodlie South Sea," like a true-born Englishman, vowed, please God, to sail an English ship thereon; which the gallant sailor did, to the sore discomfiture of the Spaniards on the coasts of Chili and Peru.

But perhaps the greatest hardships on record, in making this celebrated passage, were those experienced by Lord Anson's squadron in 1736. Three remarkable and most interesting narratives record their disasters and sufferings. The first, jointly written by the carpenter and gunner of the Wager; the second, by young Byron, a midshipman in the same ship; the third, by the chaplain of the Centurion. White-Jacket has them all; and they are fine reading of a boisterous March night, with the casement rattling in your ear, and the chimney-stacks blowing down upon the pavement, bubbling with rain-drops.

But if you want the best idea of Cape Horn, get my friend Dana's unmatchable "Two Years Before the Mast." But you can read, and so you must have read it. His chapters describing Cape Horn must have been written with an icicle.

At the present day the horrors of the Cape have somewhat abated. This is owing to a growing familiarity with it; but, more than all, to the improved condition of ships in all respects, and the means now generally in use of preserving the health of the crews in times of severe and prolonged exposure.

Chapter 25

The Dog-days off Cape Horn

COLDER AND COLDER; we are drawing nigh to the Cape. Now gregoes, pea jackets, monkey jackets, reefing jackets, storm jackets, oil jackets, paint jackets, round jackets, short jackets, long jackets, and all manner of jackets, are the order of the day, not excepting the immortal white jacket, which begins to be sturdily buttoned up to the throat, and pulled down vigorously at the skirts, to bring them well over the loins.

But, alas! those skirts were lamentably scanty; and though, with its quiltings, the jacket was stuffed out about the breasts like a Christmas turkey, and of a dry cold day kept the wearer warm enough in that vicinity, yet about the loins it was shorter than a ballet-dancer's skirts; so that while my chest was in the temperate zone, close adjoining the torrid, my hapless thighs were in Nova Zembla, hardly an icicle's toss from the Pole.

Then, again, the repeated soakings and dryings it had undergone, had by this time made it shrink woefully all over, especially in the arms, so that the wristbands had gradually crawled up near to the elbows; and it required an energetic thrust to push the arm through, in drawing the jacket on.

I endeavored to amend these misfortunes by sewing a sort of canvass ruffle round the skirts, by way of a continuation or supplement to the original work, and by doing the same with the wristbands.

This is the time for oil-skin suits, dread-naughts, tarred trowsers and overalls, sea-boots, comforters, mittens, woolen socks, Guernsey frocks, Havre shirts, buffalo-robe shirts, and moose-skin drawers. Every man's jacket is his wigwam, and every man's hat his caboose.

Perfect license is now permitted to the men respecting their clothing. Whatever they can rake and scrape together they put on—swaddling themselves in old sails, and drawing old socks over their heads for night-caps. This is the time for smiting your chest with your hand, and talking loud to keep up the circulation.

Colder, and colder, and colder, till at last we spoke a fleet of icebergs bound North. After that, it was one incessant "*cold snap*," that almost snapped off our fingers and toes. Cold! It was cold as *Blue Flujin*, where sailors say fire freezes.

And now coming up with the latitude of the Cape, we stood southward to give it a wide berth, and while so doing were becalmed; ay, becalmed off Cape Horn, which is worse, far worse, than being becalmed on the Line.

Here we lay forty-eight hours, during which the cold was intense. I wondered at the liquid sea, which refused to freeze in such a temperature. The clear, cold sky overhead looked like a steel-blue cymbal, that might ring, could you smite it. Our breath came and went like puffs of smoke from pipe-bowls. At first there was a long, gauky swell, that obliged us to furl most of the sails, and even send down t'-gallant-yards, for fear of pitching them overboard.

Out of sight of land, at this extremity of both the inhabitable and un-inhabitable world, our peopled frigate, echoing with the voices of men, the bleating of lambs, the cackling of fowls, the gruntings of pigs, seemed like Noah's old ark itself, becalmed at the climax of the Deluge.

There was nothing to be done but patiently to await the pleasure of the elements, and "whistle for a wind," the usual practice of seamen in a calm. No fire was allowed, except for the indispensable purpose of cooking, and heating bottles of water to toast Selvagee's feet. He who possessed the largest stock of vitality, stood the best chance to escape freezing. It was horrifying. In such weather any man could have undergone amputation with great ease, and helped take up the arteries himself.

Indeed, this state of affairs had not lasted quite twenty-four hours, when the extreme frigidity of the air, united to our increased tendency to inactivity, would very soon have rendered some of us subjects for the surgeon and his mates, had not a humane proceeding of the Captain suddenly impelled us to vigorous exercise.

And here be it said, that the appearance of the Boatswain, with his silver whistle to his mouth, at the main hatchway of the gun-deck, is always regarded by the crew with the utmost curiosity, for this betokens that some general order is about to be promulgated through the ship. What now? is the question that runs on from man to man. A short preliminary whistle is then given by "Old Yarn," as they call him, which whistle serves to collect round him, from their various stations, his four mates. Then Yarn, or Pipes, as leader of the orchestra, begins a peculiar call, in which his assistants join. This over, the order, whatever it may be, is loudly sung out and prolonged, till the remotest corner echoes again. The Boatswain and his mates are the town-criers of a man-of-war.

The calm had commenced in the afternoon; and the following morning the ship's company were electrified by a general order, thus set forth and declared: "*D'ye hear there, fore and aft! all hands skylark!*"

This mandate, nowadays never used except upon very rare occasions, produced the same effect upon the men that Exhilarating Gas would have done, or an extra allowance of "grog." For a time, the wonted discipline of the ship was broken through, and perfect license allowed. It was a Babel here, a Bedlam there, and a Pandemonium every where. The Theatricals were nothing compared with it. Then the fainthearted and timorous crawled to their hiding-places, and the lusty and bold shouted forth their glee. Gangs of men, in all sorts of outlandish habiliments, wild as those worn at some crazy carnival, rushed to and fro, seizing upon whomsoever they pleased—warrant-officers and dangerous pugilists excepted—pulling and hauling the luckless tars about, till fairly baited into a genial warmth. Some were made fast to, and hoisted aloft with a will; others, mounted upon oars, were ridden fore and aft on a rail, to the boisterous mirth of the spectators, any one of whom might be the next victim. Swings were rigged from the tops, or the masts; and the most reluctant wights being purposely selected, spite of all struggles, were swung from East to West, in vast arcs of circles, till almost breathless. Hornpipes, fandangoes, Donnybrook-jigs, reels, and quadrilles, were danced under the very nose of the most mighty captain, and upon the very quarter-deck and poop. Sparring and wrestling, too, were all the vogue; *Kentucky bites* were given, and the *Indian hug* exchanged. The din frightened the sea-fowl, that flew by with accelerated wing.

It is worth mentioning that several casualties occurred, of which, however, I will relate but one. While the "skylarking" was at its height, one of the fore-top-men—an ugly-tempered devil of a Portuguese, looking on—swore that he would be the death of any man who laid violent hands upon his inviolable person. This threat being overheard, a band of desperadoes, coming up from behind, tripped him up in an instant, and in the twinkling of an eye the Portuguese was straddling an oar, borne aloft by an uproarious multitude, who rushed him along the deck at a rail-road gallop. The living mass of arms all round and beneath him was so dense, that every time he inclined to one side he was instantly pushed upright, but only to fall over again, to receive another push from the contrary direction. Presently, disengaging his hands from those who held them, the enraged seaman drew from his bosom an iron belaying-pin, and recklessly laid about him to right and left. Most of his persecutors fled; but some eight or ten still stood their ground, and, while bearing him aloft, endeavored to wrest the weapon from his hands. In this attempt, one man was struck on the head, and dropped insensible. He was taken up for dead, and carried below to Cuticle, the surgeon, while the Portuguese was put under guard. But the wound did not prove very serious; and in a few days the man was walking about the deck, with his head well bandaged.

This occurrence put an end to the "skylarking," further head-breaking being strictly prohibited. In due time the Portuguese paid the penalty of his rashness at the gangway; while once again the officers *shipped their quarter-deck faces.*

Chapter 26

The Pitch of the Cape

ERE THE CALM had yet left us, a sail had been discerned from the fore-top-mast-head, at a great distance, probably three leagues or more. At first it was a mere speck, altogether out of sight from the deck. By the force of attraction, or something else equally inscrutable, two ships in a calm, and equally affected by the currents, will always approximate, more or less. Though there was not a breath of wind, it was not a great while before the strange sail was descried from our bulwarks; gradually, it drew still nearer.

What was she, and whence? There is no object which so excites interest and conjecture, and, at the same time, baffles both, as a sail, seen as a mere speck on these remote seas off Cape Horn.

A breeze! a breeze! for lo! the stranger is now perceptibly nearing the frigate; the officer's spy-glass pronounces her a full-rigged ship, with all sail set, and coming right down to us, though in our own vicinity the calm still reigns.

She is bringing the wind with her. Hurrah! Ay, there it is! Behold how mincingly it creeps over the sea, just ruffling and crisping it.

Our top-men were at once sent aloft to loose the sails, and presently they faintly began to distend. As yet we hardly had steerage-way. Toward sunset the stranger bore down before the wind, a complete pyramid of canvass.

104

Never before, I venture to say, was Cape Horn so audaciously insulted. Stun'-sails alow and aloft; royals, moon-sails, and every thing else. She glided under our stern, within hailing distance, and the signal-quarter-master ran up our ensign to the gaff.

"Ship ahoy!" cried the Lieutenant of the Watch, through his trumpet.

"Halloa!" bawled an old fellow in a green jacket, clapping one hand to his mouth, while he held on with the other to the mizzen-shrouds.

"What ship's that?"

"The Sultan, Indiaman, from New York, and bound to Callao and Canton, sixty days out, all well. What frigate's that?"

"The United States ship Neversink, homeward bound."

"Hurrah! hurrah! hurrah!" yelled our enthusiastic countryman, transported with patriotism.

By this time the Sultan had swept past, but the Lieutenant of the Watch could not withhold a parting admonition.

"D'ye hear? You'd better take in some of your flying-kites there. Look out for Cape Horn!"

But the friendly advice was lost in the now increasing wind. With a suddenness by no means unusual in these latitudes, the light breeze soon became a succession of sharp squalls, and our sail-proud braggadocio of an Indiaman was observed to let every thing go by the run, his t'-gallant stun'-sails and flying-jib taking quick leave of the spars; the flying-jib was swept into the air, rolled together for a few minutes, and tossed about in the squalls like a foot-ball. But the wind played no such pranks with the more prudently managed canvass of the Neversink, though before many hours it was stirring times with us.

About midnight, when the starboard watch, to which I belonged, was below, the boatswain's whistle was heard, followed by the shrill cry for "*All hands take in sail!* jump, men, and save ship!"

Springing from our hammocks, we found the frigate leaning over to it so steeply, that it was with difficulty we could climb the ladders leading to the upper deck.

Here the scene was awful. The vessel seemed to be sailing on her side. The main-deck guns had several days previous been run in and housed, and the port-holes closed, but the lee carronades on the quarter-deck and forecastle were plunging through the sea, which undulated over them in milk-white billows of foam. With every lurch to leeward the yard-arm-ends seemed to dip in the sea, while forward the spray dashed over the bows in cataracts, and drenched the men who were on the fore-yard. By this time the deck was alive with the whole strength of the ship's company, five hundred men, officers and all, mostly clinging to the weather bulwarks. The occasional phosphorescence of the yeasting sea cast a glare upon their uplifted faces, as a night fire in a populous city lights up the panic-stricken crowd.

In a sudden gale, or when a large quantity of sail is suddenly to be furled, it is the custom for the First Lieutenant to take the trumpet from whoever happens then to be officer of the deck. But Mad Jack had the trumpet that watch; nor did the First Lieutenant now seek to wrest it from his hands. Every eye was upon him, as if we had chosen him from among us all, to decide this battle with the elements, by single combat with the spirit of the Cape; for Mad Jack was the saving genius of the ship, and so proved himself that night. I owe this right hand, that is this moment flying over my sheet, and all my present being to Mad Jack. The ship's bows were now butting, battering, ramming, and thundering over and upon the head seas, and with a horrible wallowing sound our whole hull was rolling in the trough of the foam. The gale came athwart the deck, and every sail seemed bursting with its wild breath.

All the quarter-masters, and several of the forecastle-men, were swarming round the double-wheel on the quarter-deck. Some jumping up and down, with their hands upon the spokes; for the whole helm and galvanized keel were fiercely feverish, with the life imparted to them by the tempest.

"Hard *up* the helm!" shouted Captain Claret, bursting from his cabin like a ghost in his night-dress.

"Damn you!" raged Mad Jack to the quarter-masters; "hard *down*— hard *down*, I say, and be damned to you!"

Contrary orders! but Mad Jack's were obeyed. His object was to throw the ship into the wind, so as the better to admit of close-reefing the top-sails. But though the halyards were let go, it was impossible to clew down the yards, owing to the enormous horizontal strain on the canvass. It now blew a hurricane. The spray flew over the ship in floods. The gigantic masts seemed about to snap under the world-wide strain of the three entire top-sails.

"Clew down! clew down!" shouted Mad Jack, husky with excitement, and in a frenzy, beating his trumpet against one of the shrouds. But, owing to the slant of the ship, the thing could not be done. It was obvious that before many minutes something must go—either sails, rigging, or sticks, perhaps the hull itself, and all hands.

Presently a voice from the top exclaimed that there was a rent in the main-top-sail. And instantly we heard a report like two or three muskets discharged together; the vast sail was rent up and down like the Vail of the Temple. This saved the main-mast; for the yard was now clewed down with comparative ease, and the top-men laid out to stow the shattered canvass. Soon, the two remaining top-sails were also clewed down and close reefed.

Above all the roar of the tempest and the shouts of the crew, was heard the dismal tolling of the ship's bell—almost as large as that of a village church—which the violent rolling of the ship was occasioning. Imagination can not conceive the horror of such a sound in a night-tempest at sea.

"Stop that ghost!" roared Mad Jack; "away, one of you, and wrench off the clapper!"

But no sooner was this ghost gagged, than a still more appalling sound was heard, the rolling to and fro of the heavy shot, which, on the gun-deck, had broken loose from the gun-racks, and converted that part of the ship into an immense bowling-alley. Some hands were sent down to secure them; but it was as much as their lives were worth. Several were maimed; and the midshipmen who were ordered to see the duty performed reported it impossible, until the storm abated.

The most terrific job of all was to furl the main-sail, which, at the commencement of the squalls, had been clewed up, coaxed and quieted as much as possible with the bunt-lines and slab-lines. Mad Jack waited some time for a lull, ere he gave an order so perilous to be executed. For to furl this enormous sail, in such a gale, required at least fifty men on the yard; whose weight, superadded to that of the ponderous stick itself, still further jeopardized their lives. But there was no prospect of a cessation of the gale, and the order was at last given.

At this time a hurricane of slanting sleet and hail was descending upon us; the rigging was coated with a thin glare of ice, formed within the hour.

"Aloft, main-yard-men! and all you main-top-men! and furl the main-sail!" cried Mad Jack.

I dashed down my hat, slipped out of my quilted jacket in an instant, kicked the shoes from my feet, and, with a crowd of others, sprang for the rigging. Above the bulwarks (which in a frigate are so high as to afford much protection to those on deck) the gale was horrible. The sheer force of the wind flattened us to the rigging as we ascended, and every hand seemed congealing to the icy shrouds by which we held.

"Up—up, my brave hearties!" shouted Mad Jack; and up we got, some way or other, all of us, and groped our way out on the yard-arms.

"Hold on, every mother's son!" cried an old quarter-gunner at my side. He was bawling at the top of his compass; but in the gale, he seemed to be whispering; and I only heard him from his being right to windward of me.

But his hint was unnecessary; I dug my nails into the *jack-stays*, and swore that nothing but death should part me and them until I was able to turn round and look to windward. As yet, this was impossible; I could scarcely hear the man to leeward at my elbow; the wind seemed to snatch the words from his mouth and fly away with them to the South Pole.

All this while the sail itself was flying about, sometimes catching over our head, and threatening to tear us from the yard in spite of all our hugging. For about three quarters of an hour we thus hung suspended right over the rampant billows, which curled their very crests under the feet of some four or five of us clinging to the lee-yard-arm, as if to float us from our place.

Presently, the word passed along the yard from windward, that we were ordered to come down and leave the sail to blow, since it could not be furled. A midshipman, it seemed, had been sent up by the officer of the deck to give the order, as no trumpet could be heard where we were.

Those on the weather yard-arm managed to crawl upon the spar and scramble down the rigging; but with us, upon the extreme leeward side, this feat was out of the question; it was, literally, like climbing a precipice to get to windward in order to reach the shrouds; besides, the entire yard was now encased in ice, and our hands and feet were so numb that we dared not trust our lives to them. Nevertheless, by assisting each other, we contrived to throw ourselves prostrate along the yard, and embrace it with our arms and legs. In this position, the stun'-sail-booms greatly assisted in securing our hold. Strange as it may appear, I do not suppose that, at this moment, the slightest sensation of fear was felt by one man on that yard. We clung to it with might and main; but this was instinct. The truth is, that, in circumstances like these, the sense of fear is annihilated in the unutterable sights that fill all the eye, and the sounds that fill all the ear. You become identified with the tempest; your insignificance is lost in the riot of the stormy universe around.

Below us, our noble frigate seemed thrice its real length—a vast black wedge, opposing its widest end to the combined fury of the sea and wind.

At length the first fury of the gale began to abate, and we at once fell to pounding our hands, as a preliminary operation to going to work; for a gang of men had now ascended to help secure what was left of the sail; we somehow packed it away, at last, and came down.

About noon the next day, the gale so moderated that we shook two reefs out of the top-sails, set new courses, and stood due east, with the wind astern.

Thus, all the fine weather we encountered after first weighing anchor on the pleasant Spanish coast, was but the prelude to this one terrific night; more especially, that treacherous calm immediately preceding it. But how could we reach our long-promised homes without encountering Cape Horn? by what possibility avoid it? And though some ships have weathered it without these perils, yet by far the greater part must encounter them. Lucky it is that it comes about midway in the homeward-bound passage, so that the sailors have time to prepare for it, and time to recover from it after it is astern.

But, sailor or landsman, there is some sort of a Cape Horn for all. Boys! beware of it; prepare for it in time. Gray-beards! thank God it is passed. And ye lucky livers, to whom, by some rare fatality, your Cape Horns are placid as Lake Lemans, flatter not yourselves that good luck is judgment and discretion; for all the yolk in your eggs, you might have foundered and gone down, had the Spirit of the Cape said the word.

Chapter 27

Some Thoughts growing out of Mad Jack's Countermanding his Superior's Order

IN TIME OF PERIL, like the needle to the load-stone, obedience, irrespective of rank, generally flies to him who is best fitted to command. The truth of this seemed evinced in the case of Mad Jack, during the gale, and especially at that perilous moment when he countermanded the Captain's order at the helm. But every seaman knew, at the time, that the Captain's order was an unwise one in the extreme; perhaps worse than unwise.

These two orders, given by the Captain and his Lieutenant, exactly contrasted their characters. By putting the helm *hard up*, the Captain was for *scudding*; that is, for flying away from the gale. Whereas, Mad Jack was for running the ship into its teeth. It is needless to say that, in almost all cases of similar hard squalls and gales, the latter step, though attended with more appalling appearances, is, in reality, the safer of the two, and the most generally adopted.

Scudding makes you a slave to the blast, which drives you headlong before it; but *running up into the wind's eye* enables you, in a degree, to hold it at bay. Scudding exposes to the gale your stern, the weakest part of your hull; the contrary course presents to it your bows, your strongest part. As with ships, so with men; he who turns his back to his foe gives him an advantage. Whereas, our ribbed chests, like the ribbed bows of a frigate, are as bulkheads to dam off an onset.

That night, off the pitch of the Cape, Captain Claret was hurried forth from his disguises, and, at a manhood-testing conjuncture, appeared in his true colors. A thing which every man in the ship had long suspected that night was proved true. Hitherto, in going about the ship, and casting his glances among the men, the peculiarly lustreless repose of the Captain's eye—his slow, even, unnecessarily methodical step, and the forced firmness of his whole demeanor—though, to a casual observer, seemingly expressive of the consciousness of command and a desire to strike subjection among the crew—all this, to some minds, had only been deemed indications of the fact that Captain Claret, while carefully shunning positive excesses, continually kept himself in an uncertain equilibrio between soberness and its reverse; which equilibrio might be destroyed by the first sharp vicissitude of events.

And though this is only a surmise, nevertheless, as having some knowledge of brandy and mankind, White-Jacket will venture to state that, had Captain Claret been an out-and-out temperance man, he would never have given that most imprudent order to *hard up* the helm. He would either have held his peace, and stayed in his cabin, like his gracious majesty the Commodore, or else have anticipated Mad Jack's order, and thundered forth "Hard down the helm!"

To show how little real sway at times have the severest restrictive laws, and how spontaneous is the instinct of discretion in some minds, it must here be added, that though Mad Jack, under a hot impulse, had countermanded an order of his superior officer before his very face, yet that severe Article of War, to which he thus rendered himself obnoxious, was never enforced against him. Nor, so far as any of the crew ever knew, did the Captain even venture to reprimand him for his temerity.

It has been said that Mad Jack himself was a lover of strong drink. So he was. But here we only see the virtue of being placed in a station constantly demanding a cool head and steady nerves, and the misfortune of filling a post that does *not* at all times demand these qualities. So exact and methodical in most things was the discipline of the frigate, that, to a certain extent, Captain Claret was exempted from personal interposition in many of its current events, and thereby, perhaps, was he lulled into security, under the enticing lee of his decanter.

But as for Mad Jack, he must stand his regular watches, and pace the quarter-deck at night, and keep a sharp eye to windward. Hence, at sea, Mad Jack tried to make a point of keeping sober, though in very fine weather he was sometimes betrayed into a glass too many; and got himself into difficulties, as has been mentioned elsewhere. But with Cape Horn before him, he took the temperance pledge outright, till that perilous promontory should be far astern.

The leading incident of the gale irresistibly invites the question, Are there incompetent officers in the American navy?—that is, incompetent to the due performance of whatever duties may devolve upon them. But in that gallant marine, which, during the Late War, gained so much of what is called *glory*, can there possibly be to-day incompetent officers?

As in the camp ashore, so on the quarter-deck at sea—the trumpets of one victory drown the muffled drums of a thousand defeats. And, in degree, this holds true of those events of war which are neuter in their character, neither making renown nor disgrace. Besides, as a long array of ciphers, led by but one solitary numeral, swell, by mere force of aggregation, into an immense arithmetical sum, even so, in some brilliant actions, do a crowd of officers, each inefficient in himself, aggregate renown when banded together, and led by a numeral Nelson or a Wellington. And the renown of such heroes, by outliving themselves, descends as a heritage to their subordinate survivors. One large brain and one large heart have virtue sufficient to magnetize a whole fleet or an army. And if all the men who, since the beginning of the world, have mainly contributed to the warlike successes or reverses of nations, were now mustered together, we should be amazed to behold but a handful of heroes. For there is no heroism in merely running in and out a gun at a port-hole, enveloped in smoke or vapor, or in firing off muskets in platoons at the word of command. This kind of merely manual valor is often born of trepidation at the heart. There may be men, individually craven, who, united, may display even temerity. Yet it would be false to deny that, in some instances, the lowest privates have acquitted themselves with even more gallantry than their commodores. True heroism is not in the hand, but in the heart and the head.

But are there incompetent officers in the gallant American navy? For an American, the question is of no grateful cast. White-Jacket must again evade it, by referring to an historical fact in the history of a kindred marine, which, from its long standing and magnitude, furnishes many more examples of all kinds than our own. And this is the only reason why it is ever referred to in this narrative. I thank God I am free from all national invidiousness.

It is indirectly on record in the books of the English Admiralty, that in the year 1808—after the death of Lord Nelson—when Lord Collingwood commanded on the Mediterranean station, and his broken health induced him to solicit a furlough, that out of a list of upward of one hundred admirals, not a single officer was found who was deemed qualified to relieve the applicant with credit to the country. This fact Collingwood sealed with his life; for, hopeless of being recalled, he shortly after died, worn out, at his post. Now, if this was the case in so renowned a marine as England's, what must be inferred with respect to our own? But herein no special disgrace is involved. For the truth is, that to be an accomplished and skillful naval generalissimo needs natural capabilities of an uncommon order. Still more, it may safely be asserted, that, worthily to command even a frigate, requires a degree of natural heroism, talent, judgment, and integrity, that is denied to mediocrity. Yet these qualifications are not only required, but demanded; and no one has a right to be a naval captain unless he possesses them.

Regarding Lieutenants, there are not a few Selvagees and Paper Jacks in the American navy. Many Commodores know that they have seldom taken a line-of-battle ship to sea, without feeling more or less nervousness when some of the Lieutenants have the deck at night.

According to the last Navy Register (1849), there are now 68 Captains in the American navy, collectively drawing about $300,000 annually from the public treasury; also, 97 Commanders, drawing about $200,000; and 327 Lieutenants, drawing about half a million; and 451 Midshipmen (including Passed-midshipmen), also drawing nearly half a million. Considering the known facts, that some of these officers are seldom or never sent to sea, owing to the Navy Department being well aware of their inefficiency; that others are detailed for pen-and-ink work at observatories, and solvers of logarithms in the Coast Survey; while the really meritorious officers, who are accomplished practical seamen, are known to be sent from ship to ship, with but a small interval of a furlough; considering all this, it is not too much to say, that no small portion of the million and a half of money above mentioned is annually paid to national pensioners in disguise, who live on the navy without serving it.

Nothing like this can be even insinuated against the "*forward officers*"— Boatswains, Gunners, &c.; nor against the *petty officers*—Captains of the Tops, &c.; nor against the able seamen in the navy. For if any of *these* are found wanting, they are forthwith disrated or discharged.

True, all experience teaches that, whenever there is a great national establishment, employing large numbers of officials, the public must be reconciled to support many incompetent men; for such is the favoritism and nepotism always prevailing in the purlieus of these establishments, that some incompetent persons are always admitted, to the exclusion of many of the worthy.

Nevertheless, in a country like ours, boasting of the political equality of all social conditions, it is a great reproach that such a thing as a common seaman rising to the rank of a commissioned officer in our navy, is nowadays almost unheard-of. Yet, in former times, when officers have so risen to rank, they have generally proved of signal usefulness in the service, and sometimes have reflected solid honor upon the country. Instances in point might be mentioned.

Is it not well to have our institutions of a piece? Any American landsman may hope to become President of the Union—commodore of our squadron of states. And every American sailor should be placed in such a position, that he might freely aspire to command a squadron of frigates.

But if there is good reason to believe, that there are some incompetent officers in our navy; we have still better, and more abundant reason to know, that there are others, whom both nature and art have united in eminently qualifying for it; and whom the service does not so much honor, as they may be said to honor it.

And the only purpose of this chapter is, to point out as the peculiar desert of individuals, that generalized reputation, which most men, perhaps, are apt to ascribe in the gross, to one and all the members of a popular military establishment.

Chapter 28

Edging Away

RIGHT BEFORE THE WIND! Ay, blow, blow, ye breezes; so long as *ye* stay fair, and *we* are homeward bound, what care the jolly crew?

It is worth mentioning here that, in nineteen cases out of twenty, a passage from the Pacific round the Cape is almost sure to be much shorter, and attended with less hardship, than a passage undertaken from the Atlantic. The reason is, that the gales are mostly from the westward, also the currents.

But, after all, going before the wind in a frigate, in such a tempest, has its annoyances and drawbacks, as well as many other blessings. The disproportionate weight of metal upon the spar and gun decks induces a violent rolling, unknown to merchant ships. We rolled and rolled on our way, like the world in its orbit, shipping green seas on both sides, until the old frigate dipped and went into it like a diving-bell.

The hatchways of some armed vessels are but poorly secured in bad weather. This was peculiarly the case with those of the Neversink. They were merely spread over with an old tarpaulin, cracked and rent in every direction.

In fair weather, the ship's company messed on the gun-deck; but as this was now flooded almost continually, we were obliged to take our meals upon the berth-deck, the next one below. One day, the messes of the starboard-watch were seated here at dinner; forming little groups, twelve or fifteen men in each, reclining about the beef-kids and their pots and pans; when all of a sudden the ship was seized with such a paroxysm of rolling that, in a single instant, every thing on the berth-deck—pots, kids, sailors, pieces of beef, bread-bags, clothes-bags, and barges—were tossed indiscriminately from side to side. It was impossible to stay one's self; there was nothing but the bare deck to cling to, which was slippery with the contents of the kids, and heaving under us as if there were a volcano in the frigate's hold. While we were yet sliding in uproarious crowds—all seated—the windows of the deck opened, and floods of brine descended, simultaneously with a violent lee-roll. The shower was hailed by the reckless tars with a hurricane of yells; although, for an instant, I really imagined we were about being swamped in the sea, such volumes of water came cascading down.

A day or two after, we had made sufficient Easting to stand to the northward, which we did, with the wind astern; thus fairly turning the corner without abating our rate of progress. Though we had seen no land since leaving Callao, Cape Horn was said to be somewhere to the West of us; and though there was no positive evidence of the fact, the weather encountered might be accounted pretty good presumptive proof.

The land near Cape Horn, however, is well worth seeing, especially Staten Land. Upon one occasion, the ship in which I then happened to be sailing drew near this place from the northward, with a fair, free wind, blowing steadily, through a bright translucent day, whose air was almost musical with the clear, glittering cold. On our starboard beam, like a pile of glaciers in Switzerland, lay this Staten Land, gleaming in snow-white barrenness and solitude. Unnumbered white albatross were skimming the sea near by, and clouds of smaller white wings fell through the air like snowflakes. High, towering in their own turbaned snows, the far-inland pinnacles loomed up, like the border of some other world. Flashing walls and crystal battlements, like the diamond watch-towers along heaven's furthest frontier.

After leaving the latitude of the Cape, we had several storms of snow; one night a considerable quantity laid upon the decks, and some of the sailors enjoyed the juvenile diversion of snow-balling. Woe unto the "middy" who that night went forward of the booms. Such a target for snow-balls! The throwers could never be known. By some curious sleight in hurling the missiles, they seemed to be thrown on board by some hoydenish seanymphs outside the frigate.

At daybreak Midshipman Pert went below to the surgeon with an alarming wound, gallantly received in discharging his perilous duty on the forecastle. The officer of the deck had sent him on an errand, to tell the boatswain that he was wanted in the captain's cabin. While in the very act of performing the exploit of delivering the message, Mr. Pert was struck on the nose with a snow-ball of wondrous compactness. Upon being informed of the disaster, the rogues expressed the liveliest sympathy. Pert was no favorite.

After one of these storms, it was a curious sight to see the men relieving the uppermost deck of its load of snow. It became the duty of the captain of each gun to keep his own station clean; accordingly, with an old broom, or "squilgee," he proceeded to business, often quarreling with his next-door neighbors about their scraping their snow on his premises. It was like Broadway in winter, the morning after a storm, when rival shop-boys are at work cleaning the sidewalk.

Now and then, by way of variety, we had a fall of hail-stones, so big that sometimes we found ourselves dodging them.

The Commodore had a Polynesian servant on board, whose services he had engaged at the Society Islands. Unlike his countrymen, Wooloo was of a sedate, earnest, and philosophic temperament. Having never been outside of the tropics before, he found many phenomena off Cape Horn, which absorbed his attention, and set him, like other philosophers, to feign theories corresponding to the marvels he beheld. At the first snow, when he saw the deck covered all over with a white powder, as it were, he expanded his eyes into stew-pans; but upon examining the strange substance, he decided that this must be a species of superfine flour, such as was compounded into his master's "*duffs*," and other dainties. In vain did an experienced natural philosopher belonging to the fore-top maintain before his face, that in this hypothesis Wooloo was mistaken; Wooloo's opinion remained unchanged for some time.

As for the hailstones, they transported him; he went about with a bucket, making collections, and receiving contributions, for the purpose of carrying them home to his sweet-hearts for glass beads; but having put his bucket away, and returning to it again, and finding nothing but a little water, he accused the by-standers of stealing his precious stones.

This suggests another story concerning him. The first time he was given a piece of "duff" to eat, he was observed to pick out very carefully every raisin, and throw it away, with a gesture indicative of the highest disgust. It turned out that he had taken the raisins for bugs.

In our man-of-war, this semi-savage, wandering about the gun-deck in his barbaric robe, seemed a being from some other sphere. His tastes were our abominations: ours his. Our creed he rejected: his we. We thought him a loon: he fancied us fools. Had the case been reversed; had we been Polynesians and he an American, our mutual opinion of each other would still have remained the same. A fact proving that neither was wrong, but both right.

Chapter 29

The Night-watches

THOUGH LEAVING the Cape behind us, the severe cold still continued, and one of its worst consequences was the almost incurable drowsiness induced thereby during the long night-watches. All along the decks, huddled between the guns, stretched out on the carronade slides, and in every accessible nook and corner, you would see the sailors wrapped in their monkey jackets, in a state of half-conscious torpidity, lying still and freezing alive, without the power to rise and shake themselves.

"Up—up, you lazy dogs!" our good-natured Third Lieutenant, a Virginian, would cry, rapping them with his speaking trumpet. "Get up, and stir about."

But in vain. They would rise for an instant, and as soon as his back was turned, down they would drop, as if shot through the heart.

Often I have lain thus, when the fact, that if I laid much longer I would actually freeze to death, would come over me with such overpowering force as to break the icy spell, and starting to my feet, I would endeavor to go through the combined manual and pedal exercise to restore the circulation. The first fling of my benumbed arm generally struck me in the face, instead of smiting my chest, its true destination. But in these cases one's muscles have their own way.

In exercising my other extremities, I was obliged to hold on to something, and leap with both feet; for my limbs seemed as destitute of joints as a pair of canvass pants spread to dry, and frozen stiff.

When an order was given to haul the braces—which required the strength of the entire watch, some two hundred men—a spectator would have supposed that all hands had received a stroke of the palsy. Roused from their state of enchantment, they came halting and limping across the decks, falling against each other, and, for a few moments, almost unable to handle the ropes. The slightest exertion seemed intolerable; and frequently a body of eighty or a hundred men, summoned to brace the main-yard, would hang over the rope for several minutes, waiting for some active fellow to pick it up and put it into their hands. Even then, it was some time before they were able to do any thing. They made all the motions usual in hauling a rope, but it was a long time before the yard budged an inch. It was to no purpose that the officers swore at them, or sent the midshipmen among them to find out who those "*horse-marines*" and "*sogers*" were. The sailors were so enveloped in monkey jackets, that in the dark night there was no telling one from the other.

"Here, *you*, sir!" cries little Mr. Pert, eagerly catching hold of the skirts of an old sea-dog, and trying to turn him round, so as to peer under his tarpaulin. "Who are *you*, sir? What's your name?"

"Find out, Milk-and-Water," was the impertinent rejoinder.

"Blast you! you old rascal; I'll have you licked for that! Tell me his name, some of you!" turning round to the bystanders.

"Gammon!" cries a voice at a distance.

"Hang me, but I know *you*, sir! and here's at you!" and, so saying, Mr. Pert drops the impenetrable unknown, and makes into the crowd after the bodiless voice. But the attempt to find an owner for that voice is quite as idle as the effort to discover the contents of the monkey jacket.

And here sorrowful mention must be made of something which, during this state of affairs, most sorely afflicted me. Most monkey jackets are of a dark hue; mine, as I have fifty times repeated, and say again, was white. And thus, in those long, dark nights, when it was my quarter-watch on deck, and not in the top, and others went skulking and "sogering" about the decks, secure from detection—their identity undiscoverable—my own hapless jacket forever proclaimed the name of its wearer. It gave me many a hard job, which otherwise I should have escaped. When an officer wanted a man for any particular duty—running aloft, say, to communicate some slight order to the captains of the tops—how easy, in that mob of incognitoes, to individualize "*that white jacket*," and dispatch him on the errand. Then, it would never do for me to hang back when the ropes were being pulled.

Indeed, upon all these occasions, such alacrity and cheerfulness was I obliged to display, that I was frequently held up as an illustrious example of activity, which the rest were called upon to emulate. "Pull—pull! you lazy lubbers! Look at White-Jacket, there; pull like him!"

Oh! how I execrated my luckless garment; how often I scoured the deck with it to give it a tawny hue; how often I supplicated the inexorable Brush, captain of the paint-room, for just one brushful of his invaluable pigment. Frequently, I meditated giving it a toss overboard; but I had not the resolution. Jacketless at sea! Jacketless so near Cape Horn! The thought was unendurable. And, at least, my garment was a jacket in name, if not in utility.

At length I essayed a "swap." "Here, Bob," said I, assuming all possible suavity, and accosting a mess-mate with a sort of diplomatic assumption of superiority, "suppose I was ready to part with this 'grego' of mine, and take yours in exchange—what would you give me to boot?"

"Give you to *boot?*" he exclaimed, with horror; "I wouldn't take your infernal jacket for a gift!"

How I hailed every snow-squall; for then—blessings on them!—many of the men became *white jackets* along with myself; and, powdered with the flakes, we all looked like millers.

We had six lieutenants, all of whom, with the exception of the First Lieutenant, by turns headed the watches. Three of these officers, including Mad Jack, were strict disciplinarians, and never permitted us to lay down on deck during the night. And, to tell the truth, though it caused much growling, it was far better for our health to be thus kept on our feet. So promenading was all the vogue. For some of us, however, it was like pacing in a dungeon; for, as we had to keep at our stations—some at the halyards, some at the braces, and elsewhere—and were not allowed to stroll about indefinitely, and fairly take the measure of the ship's entire keel, we were fain to confine ourselves to the space of a very few feet. But the worst of this was soon over. The suddenness of the change in the temperature consequent on leaving Cape Horn, and steering to the northward with a ten-knot breeze, is a noteworthy thing. To-day, you are assailed by a blast that seems to have edged itself on icebergs; but in a little more than a week, your jacket may be superfluous.

One word more about Cape Horn, and we have done with it.

Years hence, when a ship-canal shall have penetrated the Isthmus of Darien, and the traveler be taking his seat in the cars at Cape Cod for Astoria, it will be held a thing almost incredible that, for so long a period, vessels bound to the Nor'-west Coast from New York should, by going round Cape Horn, have lengthened their voyages some thousands of miles. "In those unenlightened days" (I quote, in advance, the language of some future philosopher), "entire years were frequently consumed in making the voyage to and from the Spice Islands, the present fashionable watering-place of the beau-monde of Oregon." Such must be our national progress.

Why, sir, that boy of yours will, one of these days, be sending your grandson to the salubrious city of Jeddo to spend his summer vacations.

Chapter 30

A Peep through a Port-hole at the Subterranean Parts of a Man-of-war

WHILE NOW RUNNING RAPIDLY AWAY from the bitter coast of Patagonia, battling with the night-watches—still cold —as best we may; come under the lee of my white jacket, reader, while I tell of the less painful sights to be seen in a frigate.

A hint has already been conveyed concerning the subterranean depths of the Neversink's hold. But there is no time here to speak of the *spirit-room*, a cellar down in the after-hold, where the sailor "grog" is kept; nor of the *cable-tiers*, where the great hawsers and chains are piled, as you see them at a large ship-chandler's on shore; nor of the grocer's vaults, where tierces of sugar, molasses, vinegar, rice, and flour are snugly stowed; nor of the *sail-room*, full as a sail-maker's loft ashore—piled up with great top-sails and top-gallant-sails, all ready-folded in their places, like so many white vests in a gentleman's wardrobe; nor of the copper and copper-fastened *magazine*, closely packed with kegs of powder, great-gun and small-arm cartridges; nor of the immense *shot-lockers*, or subterranean arsenals, full as a bushel of apples with twenty-four-pound balls; nor of the *bread-room*, a large apartment, tinned all round within to keep out the mice, where the hard biscuit destined for the consumption of five hundred men on a long voyage is stowed away by the cubic yard; nor of the vast iron *tanks* for fresh water in the hold, like the reservoir lakes at Fairmount, in

Philadelphia; nor of the *paint-room*, where the kegs of white-lead, and casks of linseed oil, and all sorts of pots and brushes, are kept; nor of the *armoror's smithy*, where the ship's forges and anvils may be heard ringing at times; I say I have no time to speak of these things, and many more places of note.

But there is one very extensive warehouse among the rest that needs special mention—*the ship's Yeoman's store-room*. In the Neversink it was down in the ship's basement, beneath the berth-deck, and you went to it by way of the *Fore-passage*, a very dim, devious corridor, indeed. Entering —say at noonday—you find yourself in a gloomy apartment, lit by a solitary lamp. On one side are shelves, filled with balls of *marline, ratlin-stuff, seizing-stuff, spun-yarn*, and numerous twines of assorted sizes. In another direction you see large cases containing heaps of articles, reminding one of a shoe-maker's furnishing-store—wooden *serving-mallets, fids, toggles*, and *heavers*; iron *prickers* and *marling-spikes*; in a third quarter you see a sort of hardware shop—shelves piled with all manner of hooks, bolts, nails, screws, and *thimbles*; and, in still another direction, you see a block-maker's store, heaped up with lignum-vitæ sheeves and wheels.

Through low arches in the bulk-head beyond, you peep in upon distant vaults and catacombs, obscurely lighted in the far end, and showing immense coils of new ropes, and other bulky articles, stowed in tiers, all savoring of tar.

But by far the most curious department of these mysterious store-rooms is the armory, where the pikes, cutlasses, pistols, and belts, forming the arms of the boarders in time of action, are hung against the walls, and suspended in thick rows from the beams overhead. Here, too, are to be seen scores of Colt's patent revolvers, which, though furnished with but one tube, multiply the fatal bullets, as the naval cat-o'-nine-tails, with a cannibal cruelty, in one blow nine times multiplies a culprit's lashes; so that, when a sailor is ordered one dozen lashes, the sentence should read one hundred and eight. All these arms are kept in the brightest order, wearing a fine polish, and may truly be said to *reflect* credit on the Yeoman and his mates.

Among the lower grade of officers in a man-of-war, that of Yeoman is not the least important. His responsibilities are denoted by his pay. While the *petty officers*, quarter-gunners, captains of the tops, and others, receive but fifteen and eighteen dollars a month—but little more than a mere able seaman—the Yeoman in an American line-of-battle ship receives forty dollars, and in a frigate thirty-five dollars per month.

He is accountable for all the articles under his charge, and on no account must deliver a yard of twine or a tenpenny nail to the boatswain or carpenter, unless shown a written requisition and order from the Senior Lieutenant. The Yeoman is to be found burrowing in his under-ground storerooms all the day long, in readiness to serve licensed customers. But in the counter, behind which he usually stands, there is no place for a till to drop the shillings in, which takes away not a little from the most agreeable part of a storekeeper's duties. Nor, among the musty, old account-books in his desk, where he registers all expenditures of his stuffs, is there any cash or check book.

The Yeoman of the Neversink was a somewhat odd specimen of a Troglodite. He was a little old man, round-shouldered, bald-headed, with great goggle-eyes, looking through portentous round spectacles, which he called his *barnacles*. He was imbued with a wonderful zeal for the naval service, and seemed to think that, in keeping his pistols and cutlasses free from rust, he preserved the national honor untarnished.

After *general quarters*, it was amusing to watch his anxious air as the various *petty officers* restored to him the arms used at the martial exercises of the crew. As successive bundles would be deposited on his counter, he would count over the pistols and cutlasses, like an old housekeeper telling over her silver forks and spoons in a pantry before retiring for the night. And often, with a sort of dark lantern in his hand, he might be seen poking into his furthest vaults and cellars, and counting over his great coils of ropes, as if they were all jolly puncheons of old Port and Madeira.

By reason of his incessant watchfulness and unaccountable bachelor oddities, it was very difficult for him to retain in his employment the various sailors who, from time to time, were billeted with him to do the duty of subalterns. In particular, he was always desirous of having at least one steady, faultless young man, of a literary taste, to keep an eye to his account-books, and swab out the armory every morning. It was an odious business this, to be immured all day in such a bottomless hole, among tarry old ropes and villainous guns and pistols. It was with peculiar dread that I one day noticed the goggle-eyes of *Old Revolver*, as they called him, fastened upon me with a fatal glance of good-will and approbation. He had somehow heard of my being a very learned person, who could both read and write with extraordinary facility; and, moreover, that I was a rather reserved youth, who kept his modest, unassuming merits in the background. But though, from the keen sense of my situation as a man of war's-man, all this about my keeping myself in the *back* ground was true enough, yet I had no idea of hiding my diffident merits *under* ground. I became alarmed at the old

Yeoman's goggling glances, lest he should drag me down into tarry perdition in his hideous store-rooms. But this fate was providentially averted, owing to mysterious causes which I never could fathom.

Chapter 31

The Gunner under Hatches

AMONG SUCH A CROWD of marked characters as were to be met with on board our frigate, many of whom moved in mysterious circles beneath the lowermost deck, and at long intervals flitted into sight like apparitions, and disappeared again for whole weeks together, there were some who inordinately excited my curiosity, and whose names, callings, and precise abodes I industriously sought out, in order to learn something satisfactory concerning them.

While engaged in these inquiries, often fruitless, or but partially gratified, I could not but regret that there was no public printed Directory for the Neversink, such as they have in large towns, containing an alphabetic list of all the crew, and where they might be found. Also, in losing myself in some remote, dark corner of the bowels of the frigate, in the vicinity of the various store-rooms, shops, and warehouses, I much lamented that no enterprising tar had yet thought of compiling a *Hand-book of the Neversink*, so that the tourist might have a reliable guide.

Indeed, there were several parts of the ship under hatches shrouded in mystery, and completely inaccessible to the sailor. Wondrous old doors, barred and bolted in dingy bulk-heads, must have opened into regions full of interest to a successful explorer.

They looked like the gloomy entrances to family vaults of buried dead;

and when I chanced to see some unknown functionary insert his key, and enter these inexplicable apartments with a battle-lantern, as if on solemn official business, I almost quaked to dive in with him, and satisfy myself whether these vaults indeed contained the moldering relics of by-gone old Commodores and Post-captains. But the habitations of the living commodore and captain—their spacious and curtained cabins—were themselves almost as sealed volumes, and I passed them in hopeless wonderment, like a peasant before a prince's palace. Night and day armed sentries guarded their sacred portals, cutlass in hand; and had I dared to cross their path, I would infallibly have been cut down, as if in battle. Thus, though for a period of more than a year I was an inmate of this floating box of live-oak, yet there were numberless things in it that, to the last, remained wrapped in obscurity, or concerning which I could only lose myself in vague speculations. I was as a Roman Jew of the Middle Ages, confined to the Jews' quarter of the town, and forbidden to stray beyond my limits. Or I was as a modern traveler in the same famous city, forced to quit it at last without gaining ingress to the most mysterious haunts—the innermost shrine of the Pope, and the dungeons and cells of the Inquisition.

But among all the persons and things on board that puzzled me, and filled me most with strange emotions of doubt, misgivings, and mystery, was the Gunner—a short, square, grim man, his hair and beard grizzled and singed, as if with gunpowder. His skin was of a flecky brown, like the stained barrel of a fowling-piece, and his hollow eyes burned in his head like blue-lights. He it was who had access to many of those mysterious vaults I have spoken of. Often he might be seen groping his way into them, followed by his subalterns, the old quarter-gunners, as if intent upon laying a train of powder to blow up the ship. I remembered Guy Fawkes and the Parliament-house, and made earnest inquiry whether this gunner was a Roman Catholic. I felt relieved when informed that he was not.

A little circumstance which one of his *mates* once told me heightened the gloomy interest with which I regarded his chief. He told me that, at periodical intervals, his master the Gunner, accompanied by his phalanx, entered into the great Magazine under the Gun-room, of which he had sole custody and kept the key, nearly as big as the key of the Bastile, and provided with lanterns, something like Sir Humphrey Davy's Safety-lamp for coal mines, proceeded to turn, end for end, all the kegs of powder and packages of cartridges stored in this innermost explosive vault, lined throughout with sheets of copper. In the vestibule of the Magazine, against the paneling, were several pegs for slippers, and, before penetrating further than that vestibule, every man of the gunner's-gang silently removed his shoes, for fear that the nails in their heels might possibly create a spark, by striking against the coppered floor within. Then, with slippered feet and with hushed whispers, they stole into the heart of the place.

This turning of the powder was to preserve its inflammability. And surely it was a business full of direful interest, to be buried so deep below the sun, handling whole barrels of powder, any one of which, touched by the smallest spark, was powerful enough to blow up a whole street of warehouses.

The gunner went by the name of *Old Combustibles*, though I thought this an undignified name for so momentous a personage, who had all our lives in his hand.

While we lay in Callao, we received from shore several barrels of powder. So soon as the *launch* came alongside with them, orders were given to extinguish all lights and all fires in the ship; and the master-at-arms and his corporals inspected every deck to see that this order was obeyed; a very prudent precaution, no doubt, but not observed at all in the Turkish navy. The Turkish sailors will sit on their gun-carriages, tranquilly smoking, while kegs of powder are being rolled under their ignited pipe-bowls. This shows the great comfort there is in the doctrine of these Fatalists, and how such a doctrine, in some things at least, relieves men from nervous anxieties. But we are all Fatalists at bottom. Nor need we so much marvel at the heroism of that army officer, who challenged his personal foe to bestride a barrel of powder with him—the match to be placed between them—and be blown up in good company, for it is pretty certain that the whole earth itself is a vast hogshead, full of inflammable materials, and which we are always bestriding; at the same time, that all good Christians believe that at any minute the last day may come, and the terrible combustion of the entire planet ensue.

As if impressed with a befitting sense of the awfulness of his calling, our gunner always wore a fixed expression of solemnity, which was heightened by his grizzled hair and beard. But what imparted such a sinister look to him, and what wrought so upon my imagination concerning this man, was a frightful scar crossing his left cheek and forehead. He had been almost mortally wounded, they said, with a sabre-cut, during a frigate engagement in the last war with Britain.

He was the most methodical, exact, and punctual of all the forward officers. Among his other duties, it pertained to him, while in harbor, to see that at a certain hour in the evening one of the great guns was discharged from the forecastle, a ceremony only observed in a flag-ship. And always at the precise moment you might behold him blowing his match, then applying it; and with that booming thunder in his ear, and the smell of the powder in his hair, he retired to his hammock for the night. What dreams he must have had!

The same precision was observed when ordered to fire a gun to *bring to* some ship at sea; for, true to their name, and preserving its applicability, even in times of peace, all men-of-war are great bullies on the high seas. They domineer over the poor merchantmen, and with a hissing hot ball sent bowling across the ocean, compel them to stop their headway at pleasure.

It was enough to make you a man of method for life, to see the gunner superintending his subalterns, when preparing the main-deck batteries for a great national salute. While lying in harbor, intelligence reached us of the lamentable casualty that befell certain high officers of state, including the acting Secretary of the Navy himself, some other member of the President's cabinet, a Commodore, and others, all engaged in experimenting upon a new-fangled engine of war. At the same time with the receipt of this sad news, orders arrived to fire minute-guns for the deceased head of the naval department. Upon this occasion the gunner was more than usually cere-monious, in seeing that the long twenty-fours were thoroughly loaded and rammed down, and then accurately marked with chalk, so as to be dis-charged in undeviating rotation, first from the larboard side, and then from the starboard.

But as my ears hummed, and all my bones danced in me with the reverberating din, and my eyes and nostrils were almost suffocated with the smoke, and when I saw this grim old gunner firing away so solemnly, I thought it a strange mode of honoring a man's memory who had himself been slaughtered by a cannon. Only the smoke, that, after rolling in at the port-holes, rapidly drifted away to leeward, and was lost to view, seemed truly emblematical touching the personage thus honored, since that great non-combatant, the Bible, assures us that our life is but a vapor, that quickly passeth away.

Chapter 32

A Dish of Dunderfunk

IN MEN-OF-WAR, the space on the uppermost deck, round about the main-mast, is the Police-office, Court-house, and yard of execution, where all charges are lodged, causes tried, and punishment administered. In frigate phrase, to be *brought up to the mast*, is equivalent to being presented before the grand-jury, to see whether a true bill will be found against you.

From the merciless, inquisitorial *baiting*, which sailors, charged with offences, too often experience *at the mast*, that vicinity is usually known among them as the *bull-ring*.

The main-mast, moreover, is the only place where the sailor can hold formal communication with the captain and officers. If any one has been robbed; if any one has been evilly entreated; if any one's character has been defamed; if any one has a request to present; if any one has aught important for the executive of the ship to know—straight to the main-mast he repairs; and stands there—generally with his hat off—waiting the pleasure of the officer of the deck, to advance and communicate with him. Often, the most ludicrous scenes occur, and the most comical complaints are made.

One clear, cold morning, while we were yet running away from the Cape, a raw-boned, crack-pated Down Easter, belonging to the Waist, made his appearance at the mast, dolefully exhibiting a blackened tin pan, bearing a few crusty traces of some sort of a sea-pie, which had been cooked in it.

"Well, sir, what now?" said the Lieutenant of the Deck, advancing.

"They stole it, sir; all my nice *dunderfunk*, sir; they did, sir," whined the Down Easter, ruefully holding up his pan.

"Stole your *dundlefunk!* what's that?"

"*Dunderfunk*, sir, *dunderfunk*; a cruel nice dish as ever man put into him."

"Speak out, sir; what's the matter?"

"My *dunderfunk*, sir—as elegant a dish of *dunderfunk* as you ever see, sir—they stole it, sir!"

"Go forward, you rascal!" cried the Lieutenant, in a towering rage, "or else stop your whining. Tell me, what's the matter?"

"Why, sir, them 'ere two fellows, Dobs and Hodnose, stole my *dunder-funk*."

"Once more, sir, I ask what that *dundledunk* is? Speak!"

"As cruel a nice—"

"Be off, sir! sheer!" and muttering something about *non compos mentis*, the Lieutenant stalked away; while the Down Easter beat a melancholy retreat, holding up his pan like a tambourine, and making dolorous music on it as he went.

"Where are you going with that tear in your eye, like a traveling rat?" cried a top-man.

"Oh! he's going home to Down East," said another; "so far eastward, you know, *shippy*, that they have to pry up the sun with a handspike."

To make this anecdote plainer, be it said that, at sea, the monotonous round of salt beef and pork at the messes of the sailors—where but very few of the varieties of the season are to be found—induces them to adopt many contrivances in order to diversify their meals. Hence the various sea-rolls, made dishes, and Mediterranean pies, well known by man-of-war's-men—Scouse, Lob-scouse, Soft-Tack, Soft-Tommy, Skillagalee, Burgoo, Dough-boys, Lob-Dominion, Dog's-Body, and lastly, and least known, *Dunderfunk*; all of which come under the general denomination of *Manavalins*.

Dunderfunk is made of hard biscuit, hashed and pounded, mixed with beef fat, molasses, and water, and baked brown in a pan. And to those who are beyond all reach of shore delicacies, this *dunderfunk*, in the feeling language of the Down Easter, is certainly "*a cruel nice dish.*"

Now the only way that a sailor, after preparing his *dunderfunk*, could get it cooked on board the Neversink, was by slily going to *Old Coffee*, the ship's cook, and bribing him to put it into his oven. And as some such dishes or other are well known to be all the time in the oven, a set of unprincipled gourmands are constantly on the look-out for the chance of stealing them. Generally, two or three league together, and while one engages *Old Coffee* in some interesting conversation touching his wife and family at home, another snatches the first thing he can lay hands on in the oven, and rapidly passes it to the third man, who at his earliest leisure disappears with it.

In this manner had the Down Easter lost his precious pie, and afterward found the empty pan knocking about the forecastle.

Chapter 33

A Flogging

IF YOU BEGIN THE DAY with a laugh, you may, nevertheless, end it with a sob and a sigh.

Among the many who were exceedingly diverted with the scene between the Down Easter and the Lieutenant, none laughed more heartily than John, Peter, Mark, and Antone—four sailors of the starboard-watch. The same evening these four found themselves prisoners in the "brig," with a sentry standing over them. They were charged with violating a well-known law of the ship—having been engaged in one of those tangled, general fights sometimes occurring among sailors. They had nothing to anticipate but a flogging, at the captain's pleasure.

Toward evening of the next day, they were startled by the dread summons of the boatswain and his mates at the principal hatchway—a summons that ever sends a shudder through every manly heart in a frigate:

"All hands witness punishment, ahoy!"

The hoarseness of the cry, its unrelenting prolongation, its being caught up at different points, and sent through the lowermost depths of the ship; all this produces a most dismal effect upon every heart not calloused by long habituation to it.

However much you may desire to absent yourself from the scene that ensues, yet behold it you must; or, at least, stand near it you must; for the

134

regulations enjoin the attendance of the entire ship's company, from the corpulent Captain himself to the smallest boy who strikes the bell.

"*All hands witness punishment, ahoy!*"

To the sensitive seaman that summons sounds like a doom. He knows that the same law which impels it—the same law by which the culprits of the day must suffer; that by that very law he also is liable at any time to be judged and condemned. And the inevitableness of his own presence at the scene; the strong arm that drags him in view of the scourge, and holds him there till all is over; forcing upon his loathing eye and soul the sufferings and groans of men who have familiarly consorted with him, eaten with him, battled out watches with him—men of his own type and badge—all this conveys a terrible hint of the omnipotent authority under which he lives. Indeed, to such a man the naval summons to witness punishment carries a thrill, somewhat akin to what we may impute to the quick and the dead, when they shall hear the Last Trump, that is to bid them all arise in their ranks, and behold the final penalties inflicted upon the sinners of our race.

But it must not be imagined that to all men-of-war's-men this summons conveys such poignant emotions; but it is hard to decide whether one should be glad or sad that this is not the case; whether it is grateful to know that so much pain is avoided, or whether it is far sadder to think that, either from constitutional hard-heartedness or the multiplied searings of habit, hundreds of men-of-war's-men have been made proof against the sense of degradation, pity, and shame.

As if in sympathy with the scene to be enacted, the sun, which the day previous had merrily flashed upon the tin pan of the disconsolate Down Easter, was now setting over the dreary waters, veiling itself in vapors. The wind blew hoarsely in the cordage; the seas broke heavily against the bows; and the frigate, staggering under whole top-sails, strained as in agony on her way.

"*All hands witness punishment, ahoy!*"

At the summons the crew crowded round the main-mast; multitudes eager to obtain a good place on the booms, to overlook the scene; many laughing and chatting, others canvassing the case of the culprits; some maintaining sad, anxious countenances, or carrying a suppressed indignation in their eyes; a few purposely keeping behind to avoid looking on; in short, among five hundred men, there was every possible shade of character.

All the officers—midshipmen included—stood together in a group on the starboard side of the main-mast; the First Lieutenant in advance, and the surgeon, whose special duty it is to be present at such times, standing close by his side.

Presently the Captain came forward from his cabin, and stood in the centre of this solemn group, with a small paper in his hand. That paper was the daily report of offences, regularly laid upon his table every morning or evening, like the day's journal placed by a bachelor's napkin at breakfast.

"Master-at-arms, bring up the prisoners," he said.

A few moments elapsed, during which the Captain, now clothed in his most dreadful attributes, fixed his eyes severely upon the crew, when suddenly a lane formed through the crowd of seamen, and the prisoners advanced—the master-at-arms, rattan in hand, on one side, and an armed marine on the other—and took up their stations at the mast.

"You John, you Peter, you Mark, you Antone," said the Captain, "were yesterday found fighting on the gun-deck. Have you any thing to say?"

Mark and Antone, two steady, middle-aged men, whom I had often admired for their sobriety, replied that they did not strike the first blow; that they had submitted to much before they had yielded to their passions; but as they acknowledged that they had at last defended themselves, their excuse was overruled.

John—a brutal bully, who, it seems, was the real author of the disturbance—was about entering into a long extenuation, when he was cut short by being made to confess, irrespective of circumstances, that he had been in the fray.

Peter, a handsome lad about nineteen years old, belonging to the mizzentop, looked pale and tremulous. He was a great favorite in his part of the ship, and especially in his own mess, principally composed of lads of his own age. That morning two of his young mess-mates had gone to his bag, taken out his best clothes, and, obtaining the permission of the marine sentry at the "brig," had handed them to him, to be put on against being summoned to the mast. This was done to propitiate the Captain, as most captains love to see a tidy sailor. But it would not do. To all his supplications the Captain turned a deaf ear. Peter declared that he had been struck twice before he had returned a blow. "No matter," said the Captain, "you struck at last, instead of reporting the case to an officer. I allow no man to fight on board here but myself. *I* do the fighting."

"Now, men," he added, "you all admit the charge; you know the penalty. Strip! Quarter-masters, are the gratings rigged?"

The gratings are square frames of barred wood-work, sometimes placed over the hatch-ways. One of these squares was now laid on the deck, close to the ship's bulwarks, and while the remaining preparations were being made, the master-at-arms assisted the prisoners in removing their jackets and shirts. This done, their shirts were loosely thrown over their shoulders.

At a sign from the Captain, John, with a shameless leer, advanced, and stood passively upon the grating, while the bare-headed old quarter-master, with gray hair streaming in the wind, bound his feet to the cross-bars, and, stretching out his arms over his head, secured them to the hammock-nettings above. He then retreated a little space, standing silent.

Meanwhile, the boatswain stood solemnly on the other side, with a green bag in his hand, from which taking four instruments of punishment, he gave one to each of his mates; for a fresh "cat," applied by a fresh hand, is the ceremonious privilege accorded to every man-of-war culprit.

At another sign from the Captain, the master-at-arms, stepping up, removed the shirt from the prisoner. At this juncture a wave broke against the ship's side, and dashed the spray over his exposed back. But though the air was piercing cold, and the water drenched him, John stood still, without a shudder.

The Captain's finger was now lifted, and the first boatswain's-mate advanced, combing out the nine tails of his *cat* with his hand, and then, sweeping them round his neck, brought them with the whole force of his body upon the mark. Again, and again, and again; and at every blow, higher and higher rose the long, purple bars on the prisoner's back. But he only bowed over his head, and stood still. Meantime, some of the crew whispered among themselves in applause of their ship-mate's nerve; but the greater part were breathlessly silent as the keen scourge hissed through the wintery air, and fell with a cutting, wiry sound upon the mark. One dozen lashes being applied, the man was taken down, and went among the crew with a smile, saying, "D—n me! it's nothing when you're used to it! Who wants to fight?"

The next was Antone, the Portuguese. At every blow he surged from side to side, pouring out a torrent of involuntary blasphemies. Never before had he been heard to curse. When cut down, he went among the men, swearing to have the life of the Captain. Of course, this was unheard by the officers.

Mark, the third prisoner, only cringed and coughed under his punishment. He had some pulmonary complaint. He was off duty for several days after the flogging; but this was partly to be imputed to his extreme mental misery. It was his first scourging, and he felt the insult more than the injury. He became silent and sullen for the rest of the cruise.

The fourth and last was Peter, the mizzen-top lad. He had often boasted that he had never been degraded at the gangway. The day before his cheek had worn its usual red, but now no ghost was whiter. As he was being secured to the gratings, and the shudderings and creepings of his dazzlingly white back were revealed, he turned round his head imploringly; but his weeping entreaties and vows of contrition were of no avail. "I would not forgive God Almighty!" cried the Captain. The fourth boatswain's-mate advanced, and at the first blow, the boy, shouting *"My God! Oh! my God!"* writhed and leaped so as to displace the gratings, and scatter the nine tails of the scourge all over his person. At the next blow he howled, leaped, and raged in unendurable torture.

"What are you stopping for, boatswain's-mate?" cried the Captain. "Lay on!" and the whole dozen was applied.

"I don't care what happens to me now!" wept Peter, going among the crew, with blood-shot eyes, as he put on his shirt. "I have been flogged once, and they may do it again, if they will. Let them look out for me now!"

"Pipe down!" cried the Captain, and the crew slowly dispersed.

Let us have the charity to believe them—as we do—when some Captains in the Navy say, that the thing of all others most repulsive to them, in the routine of what they consider their duty, is the administration of corporal punishment upon the crew; for, surely, not to feel scarified to the quick at these scenes would argue a man but a beast.

You see a human being, stripped like a slave; scourged worse than a hound. And for what? For things not essentially criminal, but only made so by arbitrary laws.

Chapter 34

Some of the Evil Effects of Flogging

THERE ARE INCIDENTAL CONSIDERATIONS touching this matter of flogging, which exaggerate the evil into a great enormity. Many illustrations might be given, but let us be content with a few.

One of the arguments advanced by officers of the Navy in favor of corporal punishment is this: it can be inflicted in a moment; it consumes no valuable time; and when the prisoner's shirt is put on, *that* is the last of it. Whereas, if another punishment were substituted, it would probably occasion a great waste of time and trouble, besides thereby begetting in the sailor an undue idea of his importance.

Absurd, or worse than absurd, as it may appear, all this is true; and if you start from the same premises with these officers, you must admit that they advance an irresistible argument. But in accordance with this principle, captains in the Navy, to a certain extent, inflict the scourge—which is ever at hand—for nearly all degrees of transgression. In offences not cognizable by a court martial, little, if any, discrimination is shown. It is of a piece with the penal laws that prevailed in England some sixty years ago, when one hundred and sixty different offences were declared by the statute-book to be capital, and the servant-maid who but pilfered a watch was hung beside the murderer of a family.

It is one of the most common punishments for very trivial offences in the Navy, to "stop" a seaman's *grog* for a day or a week. And as most seamen so cling to their *grog*, the loss of it is generally deemed by them a very serious penalty. You will sometimes hear them say, "I would rather have my wind *stopped* than my *grog!*"

But there are some sober seamen that would much rather draw the money for it, instead of the grog itself, as provided by law; but they are too often deterred from this by the thought of receiving a scourging for some inconsiderable offence, as a substitute for the stopping of their spirits. This is a most serious obstacle to the cause of temperance in the Navy. But, in many cases, even the reluctant drawing of his grog can not exempt a prudent seaman from ignominy; for besides the formal administering of the "*cat*" at the gangway for petty offences, he is liable to the "colt," or rope's-end, a bit of *ratlin-stuff*, indiscriminately applied—without stripping the victim—at any time, and in any part of the ship, at the merest wink from the Captain. By an express order of that officer, most boatswain's mates carry the "colt" coiled in their hats, in readiness to be administered at a minute's warning upon any offender. This was the custom in the Never-sink. And until so recent a period as the administration of President Polk, when the historian Bancroft, Secretary of the Navy, officially interposed, it was an almost universal thing for the officers of the watch, at their own discretion, to inflict chastisement upon a sailor, and this, too, in the face of the ordinance restricting the power of flogging solely to Captains and Courts Martial. Nor was it a thing unknown for a Lieutenant, in a sudden outburst of passion, perhaps inflamed by brandy, or smarting under the sense of being disliked or hated by the seamen, to order a whole watch of two hundred and fifty men, at dead of night, to undergo the indignity of the "colt."

It is believed that, even at the present day, there are instances of Commanders still violating the law, by delegating the power of the colt to subordinates. At all events, it is certain that, almost to a man, the Lieutenants in the Navy bitterly rail against the officiousness of Bancroft, in so materially abridging their usurped functions by snatching the colt from their hands. At the time, they predicted that this rash and most ill-judged interference of the Secretary would end in the breaking up of all discipline in the Navy. But it has not so proved. These officers *now* predict that, if the "cat" be abolished, the same unfulfilled prediction would be verified.

Concerning the license with which many captains violate the express laws laid down by Congress for the government of the Navy, a glaring instance may be quoted. For upward of forty years there has been on the American Statute-book a law prohibiting a Captain from inflicting, on his own authority, more than twelve lashes at one time, and for one offence. If more are to be given, the sentence must be passed by a Court Martial. Yet, for nearly half a century, this law has been frequently, and with almost perfect impunity, set at naught: though of late, through the exertions of Bancroft and others, it has been much better observed than formerly; indeed, at the present day, it is generally respected. Still, while the Neversink was lying in a South American port, on the cruise now written of, the seamen belonging to another American frigate informed us that their captain sometimes inflicted, upon his own authority, eighteen and twenty lashes. It is worth while to state that this frigate was vastly admired by the shore ladies for her wonderfully neat appearance. One of her forecastle-men told me that he had used up three jack-knives (charged to him on the books of the purser) in scraping the belaying-pins and the combings of the hatchways.

It is singular that while the Lieutenants of the Watch in American men-of-war so long usurped the power of inflicting corporal punishment with the *colt*, few or no similar abuses were known in the English Navy. And though the captain of an English armed ship is authorized to inflict, at his own discretion, *more* than a dozen lashes (I think three dozen), yet it is to be doubted whether, upon the whole, there is as much flogging at present in the English Navy as in the American. The chivalric Virginian, John Randolph of Roanoke, declared, in his place in Congress, that on board of the American man-of-war that carried him out Embassador to Russia he had witnessed more flogging than had taken place on his own plantation of five hundred African slaves in ten years. Certain it is, from what I have personally seen, that the English officers, as a general thing, seem to be less disliked by their crews than the American officers by theirs. The reason probably is, that many of them, from their station in life, have been more accustomed to social command; hence, quarter-deck authority sits more naturally on them. A coarse, vulgar man, who happens to rise to high naval rank by the exhibition of talents not incompatible with vulgarity, invariably proves a tyrant to his crew. It is a thing that American man-of-war's-men have often observed, that the Lieutenants from the Southern States, the descendants of the old Virginians, are much less severe, and much more gentle and gentlemanly in command, than the Northern officers, as a class

According to the present laws and usages of the Navy, a seaman, for the most trivial alleged offences, of which he may be entirely innocent, must, without a trial, undergo a penalty the traces whereof he carries to the grave; for to a man-of-war's-man's experienced eye the marks of a naval scourging with the "*cat*" are through life discernible. And with these marks on his back, this image of his Creator must rise at the Last Day. Yet so untouchable is true dignity, that there are cases wherein to be flogged at the gangway is no dishonor; though, to abase and hurl down the last pride of some sailor who has piqued him, be sometimes the secret motive, with some malicious officer, in procuring him to be condemned to the lash. But this feeling of the innate dignity remaining untouched, though outwardly the body be scarred for the whole term of the natural life, is one of the hushed things, buried among the holiest privacies of the soul; a thing between a man's God and himself; and forever undiscernible by our fellow-men, who account *that* a degradation which seems so to the corporal eye. But what torments must that seaman undergo who, while his back bleeds at the gangway, bleeds agonized drops of shame from his soul! Are we not justified in immeasurably denouncing this thing? Join hands with me, then; and, in the name of that Being in whose image the flogged sailor is made, let us demand of Legislators, by what right they dare profane what God himself accounts sacred.

Is it lawful for you to scourge a man that is a Roman? asks the intrepid Apostle, well knowing, as a Roman citizen, that it was not. And now, eighteen hundred years after, is it lawful for you, my countrymen, to scourge a man that is an American? to scourge him round the world in your frigates?

It is to no purpose that you apologetically appeal to the general depravity of the man-of-war's-man. Depravity in the oppressed is no apology for the oppressor; but rather an additional stigma to him, as being, in a large degree, the effect, and not the cause and justification of oppression.

Chapter 35

Flogging not Lawful

I T IS NEXT TO IDLE, at the present day, merely to denounce an iniquity. Be ours, then, a different task.

If there are any three things opposed to the genius of the American Constitution, they are these: irresponsibility in a judge, unlimited discretionary authority in an executive, and the union of an irresponsible judge and an unlimited executive in one person.

Yet by virtue of an enactment of Congress, all the Commodores in the American Navy are obnoxious to these three charges, so far as concerns the punishment of the sailor for alleged misdemeanors not particularly set forth in the Articles of War.

Here is the enactment in question.

XXXII. *Of the Articles of War.*—"All crimes committed by persons belonging to the Navy, which are not specified in the foregoing articles, shall be punished according to the laws and customs in such cases at sea."

This is the article that, above all others, puts the scourge into the hands of the Captain, calls him to no account for its exercise, and furnishes him with an ample warrant for inflictions of cruelty upon the common sailor, hardly credible to landsmen.

By this article the Captain is made a legislator, as well as a judge and an executive. So far as it goes, it absolutely leaves to his discretion to decide what things shall be considered crimes, and what shall be the penalty; whether an accused person has been guilty of actions by him declared to be crimes; and how, when, and where the penalty shall be inflicted.

In the American Navy there is an everlasting suspension of the Habeas Corpus. Upon the bare allegation of misconduct, there is no law to restrain the Captain from imprisoning a seaman, and keeping him confined at his pleasure. While I was in the Neversink, the Captain of an American sloop of war, from undoubted motives of personal pique, kept a seaman confined in the brig for upward of a month.

Certainly the necessities of navies warrant a code for its government more stringent than the law that governs the land; but that code should conform to the spirit of the political institutions of the country that ordains it. It should not convert into slaves some of the citizens of a nation of free-men. Such objections can not be urged against the laws of the Russian Navy (not essentially different from our own), because the laws of that Navy, creating the absolute one-man power in the Captain, and vesting in him the authority to scourge, conform in spirit to the territorial laws of Russia, which is ruled by an autocrat, and whose courts inflict the *knout* upon the subjects of the land. But with us it is different. Our institutions claim to be based upon broad principles of political liberty and equality. Whereas, it would hardly affect one iota the condition on shipboard of an American man-of-war's-man, were he transferred to the Russian Navy and made a subject of the Czar.

As a sailor, he shares none of our civil immunities; the law of our soil in no respect accompanies the national floating timbers grown thereon, and to which he clings as his home. For him our Revolution was in vain; to him our Declaration of Independence is a lie.

It is not sufficiently borne in mind, perhaps, that though the naval code comes under the head of the martial law, yet, in time of peace, and in the thousand questions arising between man and man on board ship, this code, to a certain extent, may not improperly be deemed municipal. With its crew of 800 or 1000 men, a three-decker is a city on the sea. But in most of these matters between man and man, the Captain, instead of being a magistrate, dispensing what the law promulgates, is an absolute ruler, mak-ing and unmaking law as he pleases.

It will be seen that the XXth of the Articles of War provides, that if any person in the Navy negligently perform the duties assigned him, he shall suffer such punishment as a court martial shall adjudge; but if the offender be a private (common sailor), he may, at the discretion of the Captain, be put in irons or flogged. It is needless to say, that in cases where an officer commits a trivial violation of this law, a court martial is seldom or never called to sit upon his trial; but in the sailor's case, he is at once condemned to the lash. Thus, one set of sea-citizens is exempted from a law that is hung in terror over others. What would landsmen think, were the State of New York to pass a law against some offence, affixing a fine as a penalty, and then add to that law a section restricting its penal operation to mechanics and day laborers, exempting all gentlemen with an income of one thousand dollars? Yet thus, in the spirit of its practical operation, even thus, stands a good part of the naval laws wherein naval flogging is involved.

But a law should be "universal," and include in its possible penal operations the very judge himself who gives decisions upon it; nay, the very judge who expounds it. Had Sir William Blackstone violated the laws of England, he would have been brought before the bar over which he had presided, and would there have been tried, with the counsel for the crown reading to him, perhaps, from a copy of his own *Commentaries*. And should he have been found guilty, he would have suffered like the meanest subject, "according to law."

How is it in an American frigate? Let one example suffice. By the Articles of War, and especially by Article I., an American Captain may, and frequently does, inflict a severe and degrading punishment upon a sailor, while he himself is forever removed from the possibility of undergoing the like disgrace; and, in all probability, from undergoing any punishment whatever, even if guilty of the same thing—contention with his equals, for instance—for which he punishes another. Yet both sailor and captain are American citizens.

Now, in the language of Blackstone, again, there is a law, "coeval with mankind, dictated by God himself, superior in obligation to any other, and no human laws are of any validity if contrary to this." That law is the Law of Nature; among the three great principles of which Justinian includes "that to every man should be rendered his due." But we have seen that the laws involving flogging in the Navy do *not* render to every man his due, since in some cases they indirectly exclude the officers from any punishment whatever, and in all cases protect them from the scourge, which is inflicted upon the sailor. Therefore, according to Blackstone and Justinian, those laws have no binding force; and every American man-of-war's-man would be morally justified in resisting the scourge to the uttermost; and, in so resisting, would be religiously justified in what would be judicially styled "the act of mutiny" itself.

If, then, these scourging laws be for any reason necessary, make them binding upon all who of right come under their sway; and let us see an honest Commodore, duly authorized by Congress, condemning to the lash a transgressing Captain by the side of a transgressing sailor. And if the Commodore himself prove a transgressor, let us see one of his brother Commodores take up the lash against *him*, even as the boatswain's mates, the navy executioners, are often called upon to scourge each other.

Or will you say that a navy officer is a man, but that an American-born citizen, whose grandsire may have ennobled him by pouring out his blood at Bunker Hill—will you say that, by entering the service of his country as a common seaman, and standing ready to fight her foes, he thereby loses his manhood at the very time he most asserts it? Will you say that, by so doing, he degrades himself to the liability of the scourge, but if he tarries ashore in time of danger, he is safe from that indignity? All our linked states, all four continents of mankind, unite in denouncing such a thought.

We plant the question, then, on the topmost argument of all. Irrespective of incidental considerations, we assert that flogging in the navy is opposed to the essential dignity of man, which no legislator has a right to violate; that it is oppressive, and glaringly unequal in its operations; that it is utterly repugnant to the spirit of our democratic institutions; indeed, that it involves a lingering trait of the worst times of a barbarous feudal aristocracy; in a word, we denounce it as religiously, morally, and immutably *wrong*.

No matter, then, what may be the consequences of its abolition; no matter if we have to dismantle our fleets, and our unprotected commerce should fall a prey to the spoiler, the awful admonitions of justice and humanity demand that abolition without procrastination; in a voice that is not to be mistaken, demand that abolition to-day. It is not a dollar-and-cent question of expediency; it is a matter of *right and wrong*. And if any man can lay his hand on his heart, and solemnly say that this scourging is right, let that man but once feel the lash on his own back, and in his agony you will hear the apostate call the seventh heavens to witness that it is *wrong*. And, in the name of immortal manhood, would to God that every man who upholds this thing were scourged at the gangway till he recanted.

Chapter 36

Flogging not Necessary

B UT WHITE-JACKET is ready to come down from the lofty mast-head of an eternal principle, and fight you—Commodores and Captains of the navy—on your own quarter-deck, with your own weapons, at your own paces.

Exempt yourselves from the lash, you take Bible oaths to it that it is indispensable for others; you swear that, without the lash, no armed ship can be kept in suitable discipline. Be it proved to you, officers, and stamped upon your foreheads, that herein you are utterly wrong.

"Send them to Collingwood," said Lord Nelson, "and *he* will bring them to order." This was the language of that renowned Admiral, when his officers reported to him certain seamen of the fleet as wholly ungovernable. "Send them to Collingwood." And who was Collingwood, that, after these navy rebels had been imprisoned and scourged without being brought to order, Collingwood could convert them to docility?

Who Admiral Collingwood was, as an historical hero, history herself will tell you; nor, in whatever triumphal hall they may be hanging, will the captured flags of Trafalgar fail to rustle at the mention of that name. But what Collingwood was as a disciplinarian on board the ships he commanded perhaps needs to be said. He was an officer, then, who held in abhorrence all corporal punishment; who, though seeing more active service than any sea-officer of his time, yet, for years together, governed his men without inflicting the lash.

But these seamen of his must have been most exemplary saints to have proved docile under so lenient a sway. Were they saints? Answer, ye jails and alms-houses throughout the length and breadth of Great Britain, which, in Collingwood's time, were swept clean of the last lingering villain and pauper to man his majesty's fleets.

Still more, *that* was a period when the uttermost resources of England were taxed to the quick; when the masts of her multiplied fleets almost transplanted her forests, all standing to the sea; when British press-gangs not only boarded foreign ships on the high seas, and boarded foreign pier-heads, but boarded their own merchantmen at the mouth of the Thames, and boarded the very fire-sides along its banks; when Englishmen were knocked down and dragged into the navy, like cattle into the slaughter-house, with every mortal provocation to a mad desperation against the service that thus ran their unwilling heads into the muzzles of the enemy's cannon. *This* was the time, and *these* the men that Collingwood governed without the lash.

I know it has been said that Lord Collingwood began by inflicting severe punishments, and afterward ruling his sailors by the mere memory of a by-gone terror, which he could at pleasure revive; and that his sailors knew this, and hence their good behavior under a lenient sway. But, granting the quoted assertion to be true, how comes it that many American Captains, who, after inflicting as severe punishment as ever Collingwood could have authorized—how comes it that *they*, also, have not been able to maintain good order without subsequent floggings, after once showing to the crew with what terrible attributes they were invested? But it is notorious, and a thing that I myself, in several instances, *know* to have been the case, that in the American navy, where corporal punishment has been most severe, it has also been most frequent.

But it is incredible that, with such crews as Lord Collingwood's—composed, in part, of the most desperate characters, the rakings of the jails—it is incredible that such a set of men could have been governed by the mere *memory* of the lash. Some other influence must have been brought to bear; mainly, no doubt, the influence wrought by a powerful brain, and a determined, intrepid spirit over a miscellaneous rabble.

It is well known that Lord Nelson himself, in point of policy, was averse to flogging; and that, too, when he had witnessed the mutinous effects of government abuses in the navy—unknown in our times—and which, to the terror of all England, developed themselves at the great mutiny of the Nore: an outbreak that for several weeks jeopardized the very existence of the British navy.

But we may press this thing nearly two centuries further back, for it is a matter of historical doubt whether, in Robert Blake's time, Cromwell's great admiral, such a thing as flogging was known at the gangways of his victorious fleets. And as in this matter we can not go further back than to Blake, so we can not advance further than to our own time, which shows Commodore Stockton, during the recent war with Mexico, governing the American squadron in the Pacific without employing the scourge.

But if of three famous English Admirals one has abhorred flogging, another almost governed his ships without it, and to the third it may be supposed to have been unknown, while an American Commander has, within the present year almost, been enabled to sustain the good discipline of an entire squadron in time of war without having an instrument of scourging on board, what inevitable inferences must be drawn, and how disastrous to the mental character of all advocates of navy flogging, who may happen to be navy officers themselves.

It can not have escaped the discernment of any observer of mankind, that, in the presence of its conventional inferiors, conscious imbecility in power often seeks to carry off that imbecility by assumptions of lordly severity. The amount of flogging on board an American man-of-war is, in many cases, in exact proportion to the professional and intellectual incapacity of her officers to command. Thus, in these cases, the law that authorizes flogging does but put a scourge into the hand of a fool. In most calamitous instances this has been shown.

It is a matter of record, that some English ships of war have fallen a prey to the enemy through the insubordination of the crew, induced by the witless cruelty of their officers; officers so armed by the law that they could inflict that cruelty without restraint. Nor have there been wanting instances where the seamen have ran away with their ships, as in the case of the Hermione and Danae, and forever rid themselves of the outrageous inflictions of their officers by sacrificing their lives to their fury.

Events like these aroused the attention of the British public at the time. But it was a tender theme, the public agitation of which the government was anxious to suppress. Nevertheless, whenever the thing was privately discussed, these terrific mutinies, together with the then prevailing insubordination of the men in the navy, were almost universally attributed to the exasperating system of flogging. And the necessity for flogging was generally believed to be directly referable to the impressment of such crowds of dissatisfied men. And in high quarters it was held that if, by any mode, the English fleet could be manned without resource to coercive measures, then the necessity of flogging would cease.

"If we abolish either impressment or flogging, the abolition of the other will follow as a matter of course." This was the language of the Edinburgh Review at a still later period, 1824.

If, then, the necessity of flogging in the British armed marine was solely attributed to the impressment of the seamen, what faintest shadow of reason is there for the continuance of this barbarity in the American service, which is wholly freed from the reproach of impressment?

It is true that, during a long period of non-impressment, and even down to the present day, flogging has been, and still is, the law of the English navy. But in things of this kind England should be nothing to us, except an example to be shunned. Nor should wise legislators wholly govern themselves by precedents, and conclude that, since scourging has so long prevailed, some virtue must reside in it. Not so. The world has arrived at a period which renders it the part of Wisdom to pay homage to the prospective precedents of the Future in preference to those of the Past. The Past is dead, and has no resurrection; but the Future is endowed with such a life, that it lives to us even in anticipation. The Past is, in many things, the foe of mankind; the Future is, in all things, our friend. In the Past is no hope; the Future is both hope and fruition. The Past is the text-book of tyrants; the Future the Bible of the Free. Those who are solely governed by the Past stand like Lot's wife, crystallized in the act of looking backward, and forever incapable of looking before.

Let us leave the Past, then, to dictate laws to immovable China; let us abandon it to the Chinese Legitimists of Europe. But for us, we will have another captain to rule over us—that captain who ever marches at the head of his troop and beckons them forward, not lingering in the rear, and impeding their march with lumbering baggage-wagons of old precedents. *This* is the Past.

But in many things we Americans are driven to a rejection of the maxims of the Past, seeing that, ere long, the van of the nations must, of right, belong to ourselves. There are occasions when it is for America to make precedents, and not to obey them. We should, if possible, prove a teacher to posterity, instead of being the pupil of by-gone generations. More shall come after us than have gone before; the world is not yet middle-aged.

Escaped from the house of bondage, Israel of old did not follow after the ways of the Egyptians. To her was given an express dispensation; to her were given new things under the sun. And we Americans are the peculiar, chosen people—the Israel of our time; we bear the ark of the liberties of the world. Seventy years ago we escaped from thrall; and, besides our first birth-right—embracing one continent of earth—God has given to us, for a future inheritance, the broad domains of the political pagans, that shall yet come and lie down under the shade of our ark, without bloody hands being lifted. God has predestinated, mankind expects, great things from our race; and great things we feel in our souls. The rest of the nations must soon be in our rear. We are the pioneers of the world; the advance-guard, sent on through the wilderness of untried things, to break a new path in the New World that is ours. In our youth is our strength; in our inexperience, our wisdom. At a period when other nations have but lisped, our deep voice is heard afar. Long enough have we been skeptics with regard to ourselves, and doubted whether, indeed, the political Messiah had come. But he has come in *us*, if we would but give utterance to his promptings. And let us always remember that with ourselves, almost for the first time in the history of earth, national selfishness is unbounded philanthropy; for we can not do a good to America but we give alms to the world.

Chapter 37

Some superior old "London Dock" from the Wine-coolers of Neptune

W E HAD JUST SLID into pleasant weather, drawing near to the Tropics, when all hands were thrown into a wonderful excitement by an event that eloquently appealed to many palates.

A man at the fore-top-sail-yard sung out that there were eight or ten dark objects floating on the sea, some three points off our lee-bow.

"Keep her off three points!" cried Captain Claret, to the quarter-master at the *cun*.

And thus, with all our batteries, store-rooms, and five hundred men, with their baggage, and beds, and provisions, at one move of a round bit of mahogany, our great-embattled ark edged away for the strangers, as easily as a boy turns to the right or left in pursuit of insects in the field.

Directly the man on the top-sail-yard reported the dark objects to be hogsheads. Instantly all the top-men were straining their eyes, in delirious expectation of having their long *grog-fast* broken at last, and that, too, by what seemed an almost miraculous intervention. It was a curious circumstance that, without knowing the contents of the hogsheads, they yet seemed certain that the staves encompassed the thing they longed for.

Sail was now shortened, our headway was stopped, and a cutter was lowered, with orders to tow the fleet of strangers alongside. The men sprang to their oars with a will, and soon five goodly puncheons lay wallowing in the sea, just under the main-chains. We got overboard the slings, and hoisted them out of the water.

It was a sight that Bacchus and his bacchanals would have gloated over. Each puncheon was of a deep-green color, so covered with minute barnacles and shell-fish, and streaming with sea-weed, that it needed long searching to find out their bung-holes; they looked like venerable old *loggerhead-turtles.* How long they had been tossing about, and making voyages for the benefit of the flavor of their contents, no one could tell. In trying to raft them ashore, or on board of some merchant-ship, they must have drifted off to sea. This we inferred from the ropes that lengthwise united them, and which, from one point of view, made them resemble a section of a sea-serpent. They were *struck* into the gun-deck, where the eager crowd being kept off by sentries, the cooper was called with his tools.

"Bung up, and bilge free!" he cried, in an ecstasy, flourishing his driver and hammer.

Upon clearing away the barnacles and moss, a flat sort of shell-fish was found, closely adhering, like a California-shell, right over one of the bungs. Doubtless this shell-fish had there taken up his quarters, and thrown his own body into the breach, in order the better to preserve the precious contents of the cask. The by-standers were breathless, when at last this puncheon was canted over and a tin-pot held to the orifice. What was to come forth? salt-water or wine? But a rich purple tide soon settled the question, and the lieutenant assigned to taste it, with a loud and satisfactory smack of his lips, pronounced it Port!

"Oporto!" cried Mad Jack, "and no mistake!"

But, to the surprise, grief, and consternation of the sailors, an order now came from the quarter-deck to "strike the strangers down into the main-hold!" This proceeding occasioned all sorts of censorious observations upon the Captain, who, of course, had authorized it.

It must be related here that, on the passage out from home, the Neversink had touched at Madeira; and there, as is often the case with men-of-war, the Commodore and Captain had laid in a goodly stock of wines for their own private tables, and the benefit of their foreign visitors. And although the Commodore was a small, spare man, who evidently emptied but few glasses, yet Captain Claret was a portly gentleman, with a crimson face, whose father had fought at the battle of the Brandywine, and whose brother had commanded the well-known frigate named in honor of that engagement. And his whole appearance evinced that Captain Claret himself had fought many Brandywine battles ashore in honor of his sire's memory, and commanded in many bloodless Brandywine actions at sea.

It was therefore with some savor of provocation that the sailors held forth on the ungenerous conduct of Captain Claret, in stepping in between them and Providence, as it were, which by this lucky windfall, they held, seemed bent upon relieving their necessities; while Captain Claret himself, with an inexhaustible cellar, emptied his Madeira decanters at his leisure.

But next day all hands were electrified by the old familiar sound—so long hushed—of the drum rolling to grog.

After that the port was served out twice a day, till all was expended.

Chapter 38

The Chaplain and Chapel in a Man-of-war

T**HE NEXT DAY** was Sunday; a fact set down in the almanac, spite of merchant seamen's maxim, that *there are no Sundays off soundings. No Sundays off soundings*, indeed! No Sundays on shipboard! You may as well say there should be no Sundays in churches; for is not a ship modeled after a church? has it not three spires—three steeples? yea, and on the gun-deck, a bell and a belfry? And does not that bell merrily peal every Sunday morning, to summon the crew to devotions?

At any rate, there were Sundays on board this particular frigate of ours, and a clergyman also. He was a slender, middle-aged man, of an amiable deportment and irreproachable conversation; but I must say, that his sermons were but ill calculated to benefit the crew. He had drank at the mystic fountain of Plato; his head had been turned by the Germans; and this I will say, that White-Jacket himself saw him with Coleridge's Biographia Literaria in his hand.

Fancy, now, this transcendental divine standing behind a gun-carriage on the main-deck, and addressing five hundred salt-sea sinners upon the psychological phenomena of the soul, and the ontological necessity of every sailor's saving it at all hazards. He enlarged upon the follies of the ancient philosophers; learnedly alluded to the Phædon of Plato; exposed the follies of Simplicius's Commentary on Aristotle's "De Cœlo," by arraying against that clever Pagan author the admired tract of Tertullian—*De Præscriptionibus Hæreticorum*—and concluded by a Sanscrit invocation. He was particularly hard upon the Gnostics and Marcionites of the second century of the Christian era; but he never, in the remotest manner, attacked the every-day vices of the nineteenth century, as eminently illustrated in our man-of-war world. Concerning drunkenness, fighting, flogging, and oppression— things expressly or impliedly prohibited by Christianity—he never said aught. But the most mighty Commodore and Captain sat before him; and in general, if, in a monarchy, the state form the audience of the church, little evangelical piety will be preached. Hence, the harmless, non-committal abstrusities of our Chaplain were not to be wondered at. He was no Massillon, to thunder forth his ecclesiastical rhetoric, even when a Louis le Grand was enthroned among his congregation. Nor did the chaplains who preached on the quarter-deck of Lord Nelson ever allude to the guilty Felix, nor to Delilah, nor practically reason of righteousness, temperance, and judgment to come, when that renowned Admiral sat, sword-belted, before them.

During these Sunday discourses, the officers always sat in a circle round the chaplain, and, with a business-like air, steadily preserved the utmost propriety. In particular, our old Commodore himself made a point of looking intensely edified; and not a sailor on board but believed that the Commodore, being the greatest man present, must alone comprehend the mystic sentences that fell from our parson's lips.

Of all the noble lords in the ward-room, this lord-spiritual, with the exception of the Purser, was in the highest favor with the Commodore, who frequently conversed with him in a close and confidential manner. Nor, upon reflection, was this to be marveled at, seeing how efficacious, in all despotic governments, it is for the throne and altar to go hand-in-hand.

The accommodations of our chapel were very poor. We had nothing to sit on but the great gun-rammers and capstan-bars, placed horizontally upon shot-boxes. These seats were exceedingly uncomfortable, wearing out our trowsers and our tempers, and, no doubt, impeded the conversion of many valuable souls.

To say the truth, man-of-war's-men, in general, make but poor auditors upon these occasions, and adopt every possible means to elude them. Often the boatswain's-mates were obliged to drive the men to service, violently swearing upon these occasions, as upon every other.

"Go to prayers, d—n you! To prayers, you rascals—to prayers!" In this clerical invitation Captain Claret would frequently unite.

At this Jack Chase would sometimes make merry. "Come, boys, don't hang back," he would say; "come, let us go hear the parson talk about his Lord High Admiral Plato, and Commodore Socrates."

But, in one instance, grave exception was taken to this summons. A remarkably serious, but bigoted seaman, a sheet-anchor-man—whose private devotions may hereafter be alluded to—once touched his hat to the Captain, and respectfully said, "Sir, I am a Baptist; the chaplain is an Episcopalian; his form of worship is not mine; I do not believe with him, and it is against my conscience to be under his ministry. May I be allowed, sir, *not* to attend service on the half-deck?"

"You will be allowed, sir!" said the Captain, haughtily, "to obey the laws of the ship. If you absent yourself from prayers on Sunday mornings, you know the penalty."

According to the Articles of War, the Captain was perfectly right; but if any law requiring an American to attend divine service against his will be a law respecting the establishment of religion, then the Articles of War are, in this one particular, opposed to the American Constitution, which expressly says, "Congress shall make no law respecting the establishment of religion, or the free exercise thereof." But this is only one of several things in which the Articles of War are repugnant to that instrument. They will be glanced at in another part of the narrative.

The motive which prompts the introduction of chaplains into the Navy can not but be warmly responded to by every Christian. But it does not follow, that because chaplains are to be found in men-of-war, that, under the present system, they achieve much good, or that, under any other, they ever will.

How can it be expected that the religion of peace should flourish in an oaken castle of war? How can it be expected that the clergyman, whose pulpit is a forty-two-pounder, should convert sinners to a faith that enjoins them to turn the right cheek when the left is smitten? How is it to be expected that when, according to the XLII. of the Articles of War, as they now stand unrepealed on the Statute Book, "a bounty shall be paid" (to the officers and crew) "by the United States government of $20 for each person on board any ship of an enemy which shall be sunk or destroyed by any United States ship;" and when, by a subsequent section (vii.), it is provided, among other apportionings, that the chaplain shall receive "two twentieths" of this price paid for sinking and destroying ships full of human beings? How is it to be expected that a clergyman, thus provided for, should prove efficacious in enlarging upon the criminality of Judas, who, for thirty pieces of silver, betrayed his Master?

Although, by the regulations of the Navy, each seaman's mess on board the Neversink was furnished with a Bible, these Bibles were seldom or never to be seen, except on Sunday mornings, when usage demands that they shall be exhibited by the cooks of the messes, when the master-at-arms goes his rounds on the berth-deck. At such times, they usually surmounted a highly polished tin-pot placed on the lid of the chest.

Yet, for all this, the Christianity of man-of-war's-men, and their disposition to contribute to pious enterprises, are often relied upon. Several times subscription papers were circulated among the crew of the Neversink, while in harbor, under the direct patronage of the Chaplain. One was for the purpose of building a seaman's chapel in China; another to pay the salary of a tract-distributor in Greece; a third to raise a fund for the benefit of an African Colonization Society.

Where the Captain himself is a moral man, he makes a far better chaplain for his crew than any clergyman can be. This is sometimes illustrated in the case of sloops of war and armed brigs, which are not allowed a regular chaplain. I have known one crew, who were warmly attached to a naval commander worthy of their love, who have mustered even with alacrity to the call to prayer; and when their Captain would read the Church of England service to them, would present a congregation not to be surpassed for earnestness and devotion by any Scottish Kirk. It seemed like family devotions, where the head of the house is foremost in confessing himself before his Maker. But our own hearts are our best prayer-rooms, and the chaplains who can most help us are ourselves.

Chapter 39

The Frigate in Harbor · The Boats · Grand State Reception of the Commodore

IN GOOD TIME we were up with the parallel of Rio de Janeiro, and, standing in for the land, the mist soon cleared; and high aloft the famed Sugar Loaf pinnacle was seen, our bowsprit pointing for it straight as a die.

As we glided on toward our anchorage, the bands of the various men-of-war in harbor saluted us with national airs, and gallantly lowered their ensigns. Nothing can exceed the courteous etiquette of these ships, of all nations, in greeting their brethren. Of all men, your accomplished duellist is generally the most polite.

We lay in Rio some weeks, lazily taking in stores and otherwise preparing for the passage home. But though Rio is one of the most magnificent bays in the world; though the city itself contains many striking objects; and though much might be said of the Sugar Loaf and Signal Hill heights; and the little islet of Lucia; and the fortified Ilha das Cobras, or Isle of the Snakes (though the only anacondas and adders now found in the arsenals there are great guns and pistols); and Lord Hood's Nose—a lofty eminence said by seamen to resemble his lordship's conch-shell; and the Prays do Flamingo—a noble tract of beach, so called from its having been the resort, in olden times, of those gorgeous birds; and the charming Bay of Botafogo, which, spite of its name, is fragrant as the neighboring Larangieros, or

159

Valley of the Oranges; and the green Gloria Hill, surmounted by the belfries of the queenly Church of Nossa Senora de Gloria; and the iron-gray Benedictine convent near by; and the fine drive and promenade, Passeo Publico; and the massive arch-over-arch aqueduct, Arcos de Carico; and the Emperor's Palace; and the Empress's Gardens; and the fine Church de Candelaria; and the gilded throne on wheels, drawn by eight silken, silverbelled mules, in which, of pleasant evenings, his Imperial Majesty is driven out of town to his Moorish villa of St. Christova—ay, though much might be said of all this, yet must I forbear, if I may, and adhere to my one proper object, *the world in a man-of-war*.

Behold, now, the Neversink under a new aspect. With all her batteries, she is tranquilly lying in harbor, surrounded by English, French, Dutch, Portuguese, and Brazilian seventy-fours, moored in the deep-green water, close under the lee of that oblong, castellated mass of rock, Ilha das Cobras, which, with its port-holes and lofty flag-staffs, looks like another man-of-war, fast anchored in the bay. But what is an insular fortress, indeed, but an embattled land-slide into the sea from the world's Gibraltars and Quebecs? And what a main-land fortress but a few decks of a line-of-battle ship transplanted ashore? They are all one—all, as King David, men-of-war from their youth.

Ay, behold now the Neversink at her anchors, in many respects presenting a different appearance from what she presented at sea. Nor is the routine of life on board the same.

At sea there is more to employ the sailors, and less temptation to violations of the law. Whereas, in port, unless some particular service engages them, they lead the laziest of lives, beset by all the allurements of the shore, though perhaps that shore they may never touch.

Unless you happen to belong to one of the numerous boats, which, in a man-of-war in harbor, are continually plying to and from the land, you are mostly thrown upon your own resources to while away the time. Whole days frequently pass without your being individually called upon to lift a finger; for though, in the merchant-service, they make a point of keeping the men always busy about something or other, yet, to employ five hundred sailors when there is nothing definite to be done wholly surpasses the ingenuity of any First Lieutenant in the Navy.

As mention has just been made of the numerous boats employed in harbor, something more may as well be put down concerning them. Our frigate carried a very large boat—as big as a small sloop—called a *launch*, which was generally used for getting off wood, water, and other bulky articles. Besides this, she carried four boats of an arithmetical progression in point of size—the largest being known as the first cutter, the next largest the second cutter, then the third and fourth cutters. She also carried a Commodore's Barge, a Captain's Gig, and a "dingy," a small yawl, with a crew of apprentice boys. All these boats, except the "dingy," had their regular crews, who were subordinate to their cockswains, or steersmen—*petty officers*, receiving pay in addition to their seaman's wages.

The *launch* was manned by the old Tritons of the forecastle, who were no ways particular about their dress, while the other boats—commissioned for genteeler duties—were rowed by young fellows, mostly, who had a dandy eye to their personal appearance. Above all, the officers see to it that the Commodore's Barge and the Captain's Gig are manned by gentlemanly youths, who may do credit to their country, and form agreeable objects for the eyes of the Commodore or Captain to repose upon as he tranquilly sits in the stern, when pulled ashore by his barge-men or gig-men, as the case may be. Some sailors are very fond of belonging to the boats, and deem it a great honor to be a *Commodore's bargeman;* but others, perceiving no particular distinction in that office, do not court it so much.

On the second day after arriving at Rio, one of the gig-men fell sick, and, to my no small concern, I found myself temporarily appointed to his place.

"Come, White-Jacket, rig yourself in white—that's the gig's uniform to-day; you are a gig-man, my boy—give ye joy!" This was the first announcement of the fact that I heard; but soon after it was officially ratified.

I was about to seek the First Lieutenant, and plead the scantiness of my wardrobe, which wholly disqualified me to fill so distinguished a station, when I heard the bugler call away the "gig;" and, without more ado, I slipped into a clean frock, which a messmate doffed for my benefit, and soon after found myself pulling off his High Mightiness, the Captain, to an English seventy-four.

As we were bounding along, the cockswain suddenly cried "Oars!" At the word every oar was suspended in the air, while our Commodore's barge floated by, bearing that dignitary himself. At the sight, Captain Claret removed his chapeau, and saluted profoundly, our boat laying motionless on the water. But the barge never stopped; and the Commodore made but a slight return to the obsequious salute he had received.

We then resumed rowing, and presently I heard "Oars!" again; but from another boat, the second cutter, which turned out to be carrying a Lieutenant ashore. It was now Captain Claret's turn to be honored. The cutter lay still, and the Lieutenant off hat; while the Captain only nodded, and we kept on our way.

This naval etiquette is very much like the etiquette at the Grand Porte of Constantinople, where, after washing the Sublime Sultan's feet, the Grand Vizier avenges himself on an Emir, who does the same office for him.

When we arrived aboard the English seventy-four, the Captain was received with the usual honors, and the gig's crew were conducted below, and hospitably regaled with some spirits, served out by order of the officer of the deck.

Soon after, the English crew went to quarters; and as they stood up at their guns, all along the main-deck, a row of beef-fed Britons, stalwart-looking fellows, I was struck with the contrast they afforded to similar sights on board of the Neversink.

For on board of us our "*quarters*" showed an array of rather slender, lean-cheeked chaps. But then I made no doubt, that, in a sea-tussle, these lantern-jawed varlets would have approved themselves as slender Damascus blades, nimble and flexible; whereas these Britons would have been, per-haps, as sturdy broadswords. Yet every one remembers that story of Saladin and Richard trying their respective blades; how gallant Richard clove an anvil in twain, or something quite as ponderous, and Saladin elegantly severed a cushion; so that the two monarchs were even—each excelling in his way—though, unfortunately for my simile, in a patriotic point of view, Richard whipped Saladin's armies in the end.

There happened to be a lord on board of this ship—the younger son of an earl, they told me. He was a fine-looking fellow. I chanced to stand by when he put a question to an Irish captain of a gun; upon the seaman's inadvertently saying *sir* to him, his lordship looked daggers at the slight; and the sailor, touching his hat a thousand times, said, "Pardon, your honor; I meant to say *my lord*, sir!"

I was much pleased with an old white-headed musician, who stood at the main hatchway, with his enormous bass drum full before him, and thumping it sturdily to the tune of "God Save the King!" though small mercy did he have on his drum-heads. Two little boys were clashing cym-bals, and another was blowing a fife, with his cheeks puffed out like the plumpest of his country's plum-puddings.

When we returned from this trip, there again took place that ceremo-nious reception of our captain on board the vessel he commanded, which always had struck me as exceedingly diverting.

In the first place, while in port, one of the quarter-masters is always stationed on the poop with a spy-glass, to look out for all boats approaching, and report the same to the officer of the deck; also, who it is that may be coming in them; so that preparations may be made accordingly. As soon, then, as the gig touched the side, a mightily shrill piping was heard, as if some boys were celebrating the Fourth of July with penny whistles. This proceeded from a boatswain's mate, who, standing at the gangway, was thus honoring the Captain's return after his long and perilous absence.

The Captain then slowly mounted the ladder, and gravely marching through a lane of "side-boys," so called—all in their best bibs and tuckers, and who stood making sly faces behind his back—was received by all the Lieutenants in a body, their hats in their hands, and making a prodigious scraping and bowing, as if they had just graduated at a French dancing-school. Meanwhile, preserving an erect, inflexible, and ram-rod carriage, and slightly touching his chapeau, the Captain made his ceremonious way to the cabin, disappearing behind the scenes, like the pasteboard ghost in Hamlet.

But these ceremonies are nothing to those in homage of the Commodore's arrival, even should he depart and arrive twenty times a day. Upon such occasions, the whole marine guard, except the sentries on duty, are marshaled on the quarter-deck, presenting arms as the Commodore passes them; while their commanding officer gives the military salute with his sword, as if making masonic signs. Meanwhile, the boatswain himself —not a *boatswain's mate*—is keeping up a persevering whistling with his silver pipe; for the Commodore is never greeted with the rude whistle of a boatswain's subaltern; *that* would be positively insulting. All the Lieutenants and Midshipmen, besides the Captain himself, are drawn up in a phalanx, and off hat together; and the *side-boys*, whose number is now increased to ten or twelve, make an imposing display at the gangway; while the whole brass band, elevated upon the poop, strike up "See! the Conquering Hero comes!" At least, this was the tune that our Captain always hinted, by a gesture, to the captain of the band, whenever the Commodore arrived from shore. It conveyed a complimentary appreciation, on the Captain's part, of the Commodore's heroism during the Late War.

To return to the gig. As I did not relish the idea of being a sort of body-servant to Captain Claret—since his gigmen were often called upon to scrub his cabin floor, and perform other duties for him—I made it my particular business to get rid of my appointment in his boat as soon as possible, and the next day after receiving it, succeeded in procuring a substitute, who was glad of the chance to fill the position I so much undervalued.

And thus, with our counterlikes and dislikes, most of us man-of-war's-men harmoniously dove-tail into each other, and, by our very points of opposition, unite in a clever whole, like the parts of a Chinese puzzle. But as, in a Chinese puzzle, many pieces are hard to place, so there are some unfortunate fellows who can never slip into their proper angles, and thus the whole puzzle becomes a puzzle indeed, which is the precise condition of the greatest puzzle in the world—this man-of-war world itself.

Chapter 40

Some of the Ceremonies in a Man-of-war unnecessary and injurious

T HE CEREMONIALS OF A MAN-OF-WAR, some of which have been described in the preceding chapter, may merit a reflection or two.

The general usages of the American Navy are founded upon the usages that prevailed in the Navy of monarchical England more than a century ago; nor have they been materially altered since. And while both England and America have become greatly liberalized in the interval; while shore pomp in high places has come to be regarded by the more intelligent masses of men as belonging to the absurd, ridiculous, and mock-heroic; while that most truly august of all the majesties of earth, the President of the United States, may be seen entering his residence with his umbrella under his arm, and no brass band or military guard at his heels, and unostentatiously taking his seat by the side of the meanest citizen in a public conveyance; while this is the case, there still lingers in American men-of-war all the stilted etiquette and childish parade of the old-fashioned Spanish court of Madrid. Indeed, so far as the things that meet the eye are concerned, an American Commodore is by far a greater man than the President of twenty millions of freemen.

But we plain people ashore might very willingly be content to leave these commodores in the unmolested possession of their gilded penny whistles, rattles, and gewgaws, since they seem to take so much pleasure in them, were it not that all this is attended by consequences to their subordinates in the last degree to be deplored.

While hardly any one will question that a naval officer should be surrounded by circumstances calculated to impart a requisite dignity to his position, it is not the less certain that, by the excessive pomp he at present maintains, there is naturally and unavoidably generated a feeling of servility and debasement in the hearts of most of the seamen who continually behold a fellow-mortal flourishing over their heads like the archangel Michael with a thousand wings. And as, in degree, this same pomp is observed toward their inferiors by all the grades of commissioned officers, even down to a midshipman, the evil is proportionately multiplied.

It would not at all diminish a proper respect for the officers, and subordination to their authority among the seamen, were all this idle parade—only ministering to the arrogance of the officers, without at all benefiting the state—completely done away. But to do so, we voters and lawgivers ourselves must be no respecters of persons.

That saying about *leveling upward, and not downward*, may seem very fine to those who can not see its self-involved absurdity. But the truth is, that, to gain the true level, in some things, we *must* cut downward; for how can you make every sailor a commodore? or how raise the valleys, without filling them up with the superfluous tops of the hills?

Some discreet, but democratic, legislation in this matter is much to be desired. And by bringing down naval officers, in these things at least, without affecting their legitimate dignity and authority, we shall correspondingly elevate the common sailor, without relaxing the subordination, in which he should by all means be retained.

Chapter 41

A Man-of-war Library

NOWHERE DOES TIME PASS more heavily than with most man-of-war's-men on board their craft in harbor.

One of my principal antidotes against *ennui* in Rio, was reading. There was a public library on board, paid for by government, and intrusted to the custody of one of the marine corporals, a little, dried-up man, of a somewhat literary turn. He had once been a clerk in a Post-office ashore; and, having been long accustomed to hand over letters when called for, he was now just the man to hand over books. He kept them in a large cask on the berth-deck, and, when seeking a particular volume, had to capsize it like a barrel of potatoes. This made him very cross and irritable, as most all Librarians are. Who had the selection of these books, I do not know, but some of them must have been selected by our Chaplain, who so pranced on Coleridge's "*High German horse.*"

Mason Good's Book of Nature—a very good book, to be sure, but not precisely adapted to tarry tastes—was one of these volumes; and Machiavel's Art of War—which was very dry fighting; and a folio of Tillotson's Sermons—the best of reading for divines, indeed, but with little relish for a main-top-man; and Locke's Essays—incomparable essays, every body knows, but miserable reading at sea; and Plutarch's Lives—superexcellent biographies, which pit Greek against Roman in beautiful style, but then,

167

in a sailor's estimation, not to be mentioned with the *Lives of the Admirals;* and Blair's Lectures, University Edition—a fine treatise on rhetoric, but having nothing to say about nautical phrases, such as "*splicing the main-brace,*" "*passing a gammoning,*" "*puddinging the dolphin,*" and "*making a Carrick-bend;*" besides numerous invaluable but unreadable tomes, that might have been purchased cheap at the auction of some college-professor's library.

But I found ample entertainment in a few choice old authors, whom I stumbled upon in various parts of the ship, among the inferior officers. One was "*Morgan's History of Algiers,*" a famous old quarto, abounding in picturesque narratives of corsairs, captives, dungeons, and sea-fights; and making mention of a cruel old Dey, who, toward the latter part of his life, was so filled with remorse for his cruelties and crimes that he could not stay in bed after four o'clock in the morning, but had to rise in great trepidation and walk off his bad feelings till breakfast time. And another venerable octavo, containing a certificate from Sir Christopher Wren to its authenticity, entitled "*Knox's Captivity in Ceylon, 1681*"—abounding in stories about the Devil, who was superstitiously supposed to tyrannize over that unfortunate land: to mollify him, the priests offered up buttermilk, red cocks, and sausages; and the Devil ran roaring about in the woods, frightening travelers out of their wits; insomuch that the Islanders bitterly lamented to Knox that their country was full of devils, and, consequently, there was no hope for their eventual well-being. Knox swears that he himself heard the Devil roar, though he did not see his horns; it was a terrible noise, he says, like the baying of a hungry mastiff.

Then there was Walpole's Letters—very witty, pert, and polite—and some odd volumes of plays, each of which was a precious casket of jewels of good things, shaming the trash nowadays passed off for dramas, containing "The Jew of Malta," "Old Fortunatus," "The City Madam," "Volpone," "The Alchymist," and other glorious old dramas of the age of Marlow and Jonson, and that literary Damon and Pythias, the magnificent, mellow old Beaumont and Fletcher, who have sent the long shadow of their reputation, side by side with Shakspeare's, far down the endless vale of posterity. And may that shadow never be less! but as for St. Shakspeare, may his never be more, lest the commentators arise, and settling upon his sacred text, like unto locusts, devour it clean up, leaving never a dot over an I.

I diversified this reading of mine, by borrowing Moore's "*Loves of the Angels*" from Rose-water, who recommended it as "*de charmingest of wolumes;*" and a Negro Song-book, containing *Sittin' on a Rail, Gumbo*

Squash, and *Jim along Josey*, from Broadbit, a sheet-anchor-man. The sad taste of this old tar, in admiring such vulgar stuff, was much denounced by Rose-water, whose own predilections were of a more elegant nature, as evinced by his exalted opinion of the literary merits of the *"Loves of the Angels."*

I was by no means the only reader of books on board the Neversink. Several other sailors were diligent readers, though their studies did not lie in the way of belles-lettres. Their favorite authors were such as you may find at the book-stalls around Fulton Market; they were slightly physiological in their nature. My book experiences on board of the frigate proved an example of a fact which every book-lover must have experienced before me, namely, that though public libraries have an imposing air, and doubtless contain invaluable volumes, yet, somehow, the books that prove most agreeable, grateful, and companionable, are those we pick up by chance here and there; those which seem put into our hands by Providence; those which pretend to little, but abound in much.

Chapter 42

Killing Time in a Man-of-war in Harbor

READING WAS BY NO MEANS the only method adopted by my shipmates in whiling away the long, tedious hours in harbor. In truth, many of them could not have read, had they wanted to ever so much; in early youth their primers had been sadly neglected. Still, they had other pursuits; some were expert at the needle, and employed their time in making elaborate shirts, stitching picturesque eagles, and anchors, and all the stars of the federated states in the collars thereof; so that when they at last completed and put on these shirts, they may be said to have hoisted the American colors.

Others excelled in *tattooing*, or *pricking*, as it is called in a man-of-war. Of these prickers, two had long been celebrated, in their way, as consummate masters of the art. Each had a small box full of tools and coloring matter; and they charged so high for their services, that at the end of the cruise they were supposed to have cleared upward of four hundred dollars. They would *prick* you to order a palm-tree, an anchor, a crucifix, a lady, a lion, an eagle, or any thing else you might want.

The Roman Catholic sailors on board had at least the crucifix pricked on their arms, and for this reason: If they chanced to die in a Catholic land, they would be sure of a decent burial in consecrated ground, as the priest would be sure to observe the symbol of Mother Church on their persons.

They would not fare as Protestant sailors dying in Callao, who are shoved under the sands of St. Lorenzo, a solitary, volcanic island in the harbor, overrun with reptiles, their heretical bodies not being permitted to repose in the more genial loam of Lima.

And many sailors not Catholics were anxious to have the crucifix painted on them, owing to a curious superstition of theirs. They affirm— some of them—that if you have that mark tattooed upon all four limbs, you might fall overboard among seven hundred and seventy-five thousand white sharks, all dinnerless, and not one of them would so much as dare to smell at your little finger.

We had one fore-top-man on board, who, during the entire cruise, was having an endless cable *pricked* round and round his waist, so that, when his frock was off, he looked like a capstan with a hawser coiled round about it. This fore-top-man paid eighteen pence per link for the cable, besides being on the smart the whole cruise, suffering the effects of his repeated puncturings; so he paid very dear for his cable.

One other mode of passing time while in port was cleaning and polishing your *bright-work;* for it must be known that, in men-of-war, every sailor has some brass or steel of one kind or other to keep in high order—like house-maids, whose business it is to keep well-polished the knobs on the front-door railing and the parlor-grates.

Excepting the ring-bolts, eye-bolts, and belaying-pins scattered about the decks, this bright-work, as it is called, is principally about the guns, embracing the "*monkey-tails*" of the carronades, the screws, *prickers*, little irons, and other things.

The portion that fell to my own share I kept in superior order, quite equal in polish to Rogers's best cutlery. I received the most extravagant encomiums from the officers; one of whom offered to match me against any brasier or brass-polisher in her British majesty's Navy. Indeed, I devoted myself to the work body and soul, and thought no pains too painful, and no labor too laborious, to achieve the highest attainable polish possible for us poor lost sons of Adam to reach.

Upon one occasion, even, when woolen rags were scarce, and no burned-brick was to be had from the ship's-yeoman, I sacrificed the corners of my woolen shirt, and used some dentrifice I had, as substitutes for the rags and burned-brick. The dentifrice operated delightfully, and made the threading of my carronade screw shine and grin again, like a set of false teeth in an eager heiress-hunter's mouth.

Still another mode of passing time, was arraying yourself in your best "*togs*" and promenading up and down the gun-deck, admiring the shore scenery from the port-holes, which, in an amphitheatrical bay like Rio— belted about by the most varied and charming scenery of hill, dale, moss, meadow, court, castle, tower, grove, vine, vineyard, aqueduct, palace, square, island, fort—is very much like lounging round a circular cos- morama, and ever and anon lazily peeping through the glasses here and there. Oh! there is something worth living for, even in our man-of-war world; and one glimpse of a bower of grapes, though a cable's length off, is almost satisfaction for dining off a shank-bone salted down.

This promenading was chiefly patronized by the marines, and par- ticularly by Colbrook, a remarkably handsome and very gentlemanly corporal among them. He was a complete lady's man; with fine black eyes, bright red cheeks, glossy jet whiskers, and a refined organization of the whole man. He used to array himself in his regimentals, and saunter about like an officer of the Cold-Stream Guards, strolling down to his club in St. James's. Every time he passed me, he would heave a senti- mental sigh, and hum to himself "*The girl I left behind me.*" This fine corporal afterward became a representative in the Legislature of the State of New Jersey; for I saw his name returned about a year after my return home.

But, after all, there was not much room, while in port, for promenading, at least on the gun-deck, for the whole larboard side is kept clear for the benefit of the officers, who appreciate the advantages of having a clear stroll fore and aft; and they well know that the sailors had much better be crowded together on the other side than that the set of their own coat-tails should be impaired by brushing against their tarry trowsers.

One other way of killing time while in port is playing checkers; that is, when it is permitted; for it is not every navy captain who will allow such a scandalous proceeding. But, as for Captain Claret, though he *did* like his glass of Madeira uncommonly well, and was an undoubted descendant from the hero of the Battle of the Brandywine, and though he sometimes showed a suspiciously flushed face when superintending in person the flogging of a sailor for getting intoxicated against his particular orders, yet I will say for Captain Claret that, upon the whole, he was rather indulgent to his crew, so long as they were perfectly docile. He allowed them to play checkers as much as they pleased. More than once I have known him, when going forward to the fore-castle, pick his way carefully among scores of canvass checker-cloths spread upon the deck, so as not to tread upon the men—the checker-men and man-of-war's-men included; but, in a certain sense, they were both one; for, as the sailors used their checker-men, so, at quarters, their officers used these man-of-war's-men.

But Captain Claret's leniency in permitting checkers on board his ship might have arisen from the following little circumstance, confidentially communicated to me. Soon after the ship had sailed from home, checkers were prohibited; whereupon the sailors were exasperated against the Captain, and one night, when he was walking round the forecastle, bim! came an iron belaying-pin past his ears; and while he was dodging that, bim! came another, from the other side; so that, it being a very dark night, and nobody to be seen, and it being impossible to find out the trespassers, he thought it best to get back into his cabin as soon as possible. Some time after—just as if the belaying-pins had nothing to do with it—it was indirectly rumored that the checker-boards might be brought out again, which—as a philosophical shipmate observed—showed that Captain Claret was a man of a ready understanding, and could understand a hint as well as any other man, even when conveyed by several pounds of iron.

Some of the sailors were very precise about their checker-cloths, and even went so far that they would not let you play with them unless you first washed your hands, especially if so be you had just come from tarring down the rigging.

Another way of beguiling the tedious hours, is to get a cosy seat somewhere, and fall into as snug a little revery as you can. Or if a seat is not to be had—which is frequently the case—then get a tolerably comfortable *stand-up* against the bulwarks, and begin to think about home and bread and butter—always inseparably connected to a wanderer—which will very soon bring delicious tears into your eyes; for every one knows what a luxury is grief, when you can get a private closet to enjoy it in, and no Paul Prys intrude. Several of my shore friends, indeed, when suddenly overwhelmed by some disaster, always make a point of flying to the first oyster-cellar, and shutting themselves up in a box, with nothing but a plate of stewed oysters, some crackers, the castor, and a decanter of old Port.

Still another way of killing time in harbor, is to lean over the bulwarks, and speculate upon where, under the sun, you are going to be that day next year, which is a subject full of interest to every living soul; so much so, that there is a particular day of a particular month of the year, which, from my earliest recollections, I have always kept the run of, so that I can even now tell just where I was on that identical day of every year past since I was twelve years old. And, when I am all alone, to run over this almanac in my mind is almost as entertaining as to read your own diary, and far more interesting than to peruse a table of logarithms on a rainy afternoon. I always keep the anniversary of that day with lamb and peas, and a pint of Sherry, for it comes in Spring. But when it came round in the Neversink, I could get neither lamb, peas, nor Sherry.

But perhaps the best way to drive the hours before you four-in-hand, is to select a soft plank on the gun-deck, and go to sleep. A fine specific, which seldom fails, unless, to be sure, you have been sleeping all the twenty-four hours beforehand.

Whenever employed in killing time in harbor, I have lifted myself up on my elbow and looked around me, and seen so many of my shipmates all employed at the same common business; all under lock and key; all hopeless prisoners like myself; all under martial law; all dieting on salt beef and biscuit; all in one uniform; all yawning, gaping, and stretching in concert, it was then that I used to feel a certain love and affection for them, grounded, doubtless, on a fellow-feeling.

And though, in a previous part of this narrative, I have mentioned that I used to hold myself somewhat aloof from the mass of seamen on board the Neversink; and though this was true, and my real acquaintances were comparatively few, and my intimates still fewer, yet, to tell the truth, it is quite impossible to live so long with five hundred of your fellow-beings, even if not of the best families in the land, and with morals that would not be spoiled by further cultivation; it is quite impossible, I say, to live with five hundred of your fellow-beings, be they who they may, without feeling a common sympathy with them at the time, and ever after cherishing some sort of interest in their welfare.

The truth of this was curiously corroborated by a rather equivocal acquaintance of mine, who, among the men, went by the name of "Shakings." He belonged to the fore-hold, whence, of a dark night, he would sometimes emerge to chat with the sailors on deck. I never liked the man's looks; I protest it was a mere accident that gave me the honor of his acquaintance, and generally I did my best to avoid him, when he would come skulking, like a jail-bird, out of his den into the liberal, open air of the sky. Nevertheless, the anecdote this *holder* told me is well worth preserving, more especially the extraordinary frankness evinced in his narrating such a thing to a comparative stranger.

The substance of his story was as follows: Shakings, it seems, had once been a convict in the New York State's Prison at Sing Sing, where he had been for years confined for a crime, which he gave me his solemn word of honor he was wholly innocent of. He told me that, after his term had expired, and he went out into the world again, he never could stumble upon any of his old Sing Sing associates without dropping into a public house and talking over old times. And when fortune would go hard with him, and he felt out of sorts, and incensed at matters and things in general, he told me that, at such time, he almost wished he was back again in Sing Sing, where he was relieved from all anxieties about what he should eat and drink, and was supported, like the President of the United States and Prince Albert, at the public charge. He used to have such a snug little cell, he said, all to himself, and never felt afraid of house-breakers, for the walls were uncommonly thick, and his door was securely bolted for him, and a watchman was all the time walking up and down in the passage, while he himself was fast asleep and dreaming. To this, in substance, the *holder* added, that he narrated this anecdote because he thought it applicable to a man-of-war, which he scandalously asserted to be a sort of State Prison afloat.

Concerning the curious disposition to fraternize and be sociable, which this Shakings mentioned as characteristic of the convicts liberated from his old homestead at Sing Sing, it may well be asked, whether it may not prove to be some feeling, somehow akin to the reminiscent impulses which influenced them, that shall hereafter fraternally reunite all us mortals, when we shall have exchanged this State's Prison man-of-war world of ours for another and a better.

From the foregoing account of the great difficulty we had in killing time while in port, it must not be inferred that on board of the Neversink in Rio there was literally no work to be done. At long intervals the *launch* would come alongside with water-casks, to be emptied into iron tanks in the hold. In this way nearly fifty thousand gallons, as chronicled in the books of the master's mate, were decanted into the ship's bowels—a ninety days' allowance. With this huge Lake Ontario in us, the mighty Neversink might be said to resemble the united continent of the Eastern Hemisphere—floating in a vast ocean herself, and having a Mediterranean floating in her.

Chapter 43

Smuggling in a Man-of-war

IT IS IN A GOOD DEGREE owing to the idleness just described, that, while lying in harbor, the man-of-war's-man is exposed to the most temptations, and gets into his saddest scrapes. For though his vessel be anchored a mile from the shore, and her sides are patrolled by sentries night and day, yet these things can not entirely prevent the seductions of the land from reaching him. The prime agent in working his calamities in port is his old arch-enemy, the ever-devilish god of grog.

Immured as the man-of-war's-man is, serving out his weary three years in a sort of sea-Newgate, from which he can not escape, either by the roof or burrowing under ground, he too often flies to the bottle to seek relief from the intolerable ennui of nothing to do, and nowhere to go. His ordinary government allowance of spirits, one gill per diem, is not enough to give a sufficient fillip to his listless senses; he pronounces his grog basely *watered*; he scouts at it, as *thinner than muslin*; he craves a more vigorous *nip at the cable*, a more sturdy *swig at the halyards*; and if opium were to be had, many would steep themselves a thousand fathoms down in the densest fumes of that oblivious drug. Tell him that the delirium tremens and the mania-a-potu lie in ambush for drunkards, he will say to you, "Let them bear down upon me, then, before the wind; any thing that smacks of life is better than to feel Davy Jones's chest-lid on your nose." He is reckless as an avalanche; and though his fall destroy himself and others, yet a ruinous commotion is better than being frozen fast in unendurable solitudes. No wonder, then, that he goes all lengths to procure the thing he craves; no wonder that he pays the most exorbitant prices, breaks through all law, and braves the ignominious lash itself, rather than be deprived of his stimulus.

Now, concerning no one thing in a man-of-war, are the regulations more severe than respecting the smuggling of grog, and being found intoxicated. For either offence there is but one penalty, invariably enforced; and that is, the degradation of the gangway.

All conceivable precautions are taken by most frigate-executives to guard against the secret admission of spirits into the vessel. In the first place, no shore-boat whatever is allowed to approach a man-of-war in a foreign harbor without permission from the officer of the deck. Even the *bum-boats*, the small craft licensed by the officers to bring off fruit for the sailors, to be bought out of their own money—these are invariably inspected before permitted to hold intercourse with the ship's company. And not only this, but every one of the numerous ship's boats—kept almost continually plying to and from the shore—are similarly inspected, sometimes each boat twenty times in the day.

This inspection is thus performed: The boat being descried by the quarter-master from the poop, she is reported to the deck-officer, who thereupon summons the master-at-arms, the ship's Chief of Police. This functionary now stations himself at the gangway, and as the boat's crew, one by one, come up the side, he personally overhauls them, making them take off their hats, and then, placing both hands upon their heads, draws his palms slowly down to their feet, carefully feeling all unusual protuberances. If nothing suspicious is felt, the man is let pass; and so on, till the whole boat's crew, averaging about sixteen men, are examined. The Chief of Police then descends into the boat, and walks from stem to stern, eyeing it all over, and poking his long rattan into every nook and cranny. This operation concluded, and nothing found, he mounts the ladder, touches his hat to the deck-officer, and reports the boat *clean;* whereupon she is hauled out to the booms.

Thus it will be seen that not a man of the ship's company ever enters the vessel from shore without it being rendered next to impossible, apparently, that he should have succeeded in smuggling any thing. Those individuals who are permitted to board the ship without undergoing this ordeal, are only persons whom it would be preposterous to search—such as the

Commodore himself, the Captain, Lieutenants, &c., and gentlemen and ladies coming as visitors.

For any thing to be clandestinely thrust through the lower port-holes at night, is rendered very difficult, from the watchfulness of the quarter-master in hailing all boats that approach, long before they draw alongside, and the vigilance of the sentries, posted on platforms overhanging the water, whose orders are to fire into a strange boat which, after being warned to withdraw, should still persist in drawing nigh. Moreover, thirty-two-pound shot are slung to ropes, and suspended over the bows, to drop a hole into and sink any small craft, which, spite of all precautions, by strategy should succeed in getting under the bows with liquor by night. Indeed, the whole power of martial law is enlisted in this matter; and every one of the numerous officers of the ship, besides his general zeal in enforcing the regulations, adds to that a personal feeling, since the sobriety of the men abridges his own cares and anxieties.

How then, it will be asked, in the face of an argus-eyed police, and in defiance even of bayonets and bullets, do man-of-war's-men contrive to smuggle their spirits? Not to enlarge upon minor stratagems—every few days detected, and rendered naught (such as rolling up, in a neckerchief, a long, slender "skin" of grog, like a sausage, and in that manner ascending to the deck out of a boat just from shore; or openly bringing on board cocoa-nuts and melons, procured from a knavish bum-boat, filled with spirits, instead of milk or water)—we will only mention here two or three other modes, coming under my own observation.

While in Rio, a fore-top-man, belonging to the second cutter, paid down the money, and made an arrangement with a person encountered at the Palace-landing ashore, to the following effect. Of a certain moonless night, he was to bring off three gallons of spirits, *in skins*, and moor them to the frigate's anchor-buoy—some distance from the vessel—attaching something heavy, to sink them out of sight. In the middle watch of the night, the fore-top-man slips out of his hammock, and by creeping along in the shadows, eludes the vigilance of the master-at-arms and his mates, gains a port-hole, and softly lowers himself into the water, almost without creating a ripple—the sentries marching to and fro on their overhanging platform above him. He is an expert swimmer, and paddles along under the surface, every now and then rising a little, and lying motionless on his back to breathe—little but his nose exposed. The buoy gained, he cuts the skins adrift, ties them round his body, and in the same adroit manner makes good his return.

This feat is very seldom attempted, for it needs the utmost caution, address, and dexterity; and no one but a super-expert burglar, and faultless Leander of a swimmer, could achieve it.

From the greater privileges which they enjoy, the *"forward officers,"* that is, the Gunner, Boatswain, &c., have much greater opportunities for successful smuggling than the common seamen. Coming alongside one night in a cutter, Yarn, our boatswain, in some inexplicable way, contrived to slip several skins of brandy through the air-port of his own state-room. The feat, however, must have been perceived by one of the boat's crew, who immediately, on gaining the deck, sprung down the ladders, stole into the boatswain's room, and made away with the prize, not three minutes before the rightful owner entered to claim it. Though, from certain circumstances, the thief was known to the aggrieved party, yet the latter could say nothing, since he himself had infringed the law. But the next day, in the capacity of captain of the ship's executioners, Yarn had the satisfaction (it was so to him), of standing over the robber at the gangway; for, being found intoxicated with the very liquor the boatswain himself had smuggled, the man had been condemned to a flogging.

This recalls another instance, still more illustrative of the knotted, trebly intertwisted villainy, accumulating at a sort of compound interest in a man-of-war. The cockswain of the Commodore's barge takes his crew apart, one by one, and cautiously sounds them as to their fidelity—not to the United States of America, but to himself. Three individuals, whom he deems doubtful—that is, faithful to the United States of America—he procures to be discharged from the barge, and men of his own selection are substituted; for he is always an influential character, this cockswain of the Commodore's barge. Previous to this, however, he has seen to it well, that no Temperance men—that is, sailors who do not draw their government ration of grog, but take the money for it—he has seen to it, that none of these *balkers* are numbered among his crew. Having now proved his men, he divulges his plan to the assembled body; a solemn oath of secrecy is obtained, and he waits the first fit opportunity to carry into execution his nefarious designs.

At last it comes. One afternoon the barge carries the Commodore across the Bay to a fine water-side settlement of noblemen's seats, called Praya Grande. The Commodore is visiting a Portuguese marquis, and the pair linger long over their dinner in an arbor in the garden. Meanwhile, the cockswain has liberty to roam about where he pleases. He searches out a place where some choice *red-eye* (brandy) is to be had, purchases six large bottles, and conceals them among the trees. Under the pretence of filling the boat-keg with water, which is always kept in the barge to refresh the crew, he now carries it off into the grove, knocks out the head, puts the bottles inside, reheads the keg, fills it with water, carries it down to the boat, and audaciously restores it to its conspicuous position in the middle, with its bung-hole up. When the Commodore comes down to the beach, and they pull off for the ship, the Cockswain, in a loud voice, commands the nearest man to take that bung out of the keg—that precious water will spoil. Arrived alongside the frigate, the boat's crew are overhauled, as usual, at the gangway; and nothing being found on them, are passed. The master-at-arms now descending into the barge, and finding nothing suspicious, reports it *clean*, having put his finger into the open bung of the keg and tasted that the water was pure. The barge is ordered out to the booms, and deep night is waited for, ere the Cockswain essays to snatch the bottles from the keg.

But, unfortunately for the success of this masterly smuggler, one of his crew is a weak-pated fellow, who, having drank somewhat freely ashore, goes about the gun-deck throwing out profound, tipsy hints concerning some unutterable proceeding on the ship's anvil. A knowing old sheet-anchor-man, an unprincipled fellow, putting this, that, and the other together, ferrets out the mystery; and straightway resolves to reap the goodly harvest which the Cockswain has sowed. He seeks him out, takes him to one side, and addresses him thus:

"Cockswain, you have been smuggling off some *red-eye*, which at this moment is in your barge at the booms. Now, Cockswain, I have stationed two of my mess-mates at the port-holes, on that side of the ship; and if they report to me that you, or any of your bargemen, offer to enter that barge before morning, I will immediately report you as a smuggler to the officer of the deck."

The Cockswain is astounded; for, to be reported to the deck-officer as a smuggler, would inevitably procure him a sound flogging, and be the disgraceful *breaking* of him as a petty officer, receiving four dollars a month beyond his pay as an able seaman. He attempts to bribe the other to secrecy, by promising half the profits of the enterprise; but the sheet-anchor-man's integrity is like a rock; he is no mercenary, to be bought up for a song. The Cockswain, therefore, is forced to swear that neither himself, nor any of his crew, shall enter the barge before morning. This done, the sheet-anchor-man goes to his confidants, and arranges his plans. In a word, he succeeds in introducing the six brandy bottles into the ship; five of which he sells at eight dollars a bottle; and then, with the sixth, between two guns, he secretly regales himself and confederates; while the helpless Cockswain, stifling his rage, bitterly eyes them from afar.

Thus, though they say that there is honor among thieves, there is little among man-of-war smugglers.

Chapter 44

A Knave in Office in a Man-of-war

THE LAST SMUGGLING STORY now about to be related also occurred while we lay in Rio. It is the more particularly presented, since it furnishes the most curious evidence of the almost incredible corruption pervading nearly all ranks in some men-of-war.

For some days, the number of intoxicated sailors collared and brought up to the mast by the master-at-arms, to be reported to the deck-officers—previous to a flogging at the gangway—had, in the last degree, excited the surprise and vexation of the Captain and senior officers. So strict were the Captain's regulations concerning the suppression of grog-smuggling, and so particular had he been in charging the matter upon all the Lieutenants, and every under-strapper official in the frigate, that he was wholly at a loss how so large a quantity of spirits could have been spirited into the ship, in the face of all these checks, guards, and precautions.

Still additional steps were adopted to detect the smugglers; and Bland, the master-at-arms, together with his corporals, were publicly harangued at the mast by the Captain in person, and charged to exert their best powers in suppressing the traffic. Crowds were present at the time, and saw the master-at-arms touch his cap in obsequious homage, as he solemnly assured the Captain that he would still continue to do his best; as, indeed, he said, he had always done. He concluded with a pious ejaculation, expressive of his personal abhorrence of smuggling and drunkenness, and his fixed resolution, so help him Heaven, to spend his last wink in setting up by night, to spy out all deeds of darkness.

"I do not doubt you, master-at-arms," returned the Captain; "now go to your duty." This master-at-arms was a favorite of the Captain's.

The next morning, before breakfast, when the market-boat came off (that is, one of the ship's boats regularly deputed to bring off the daily fresh provisions for the officers)—when this boat came off, the master-at-arms, as usual, after carefully examining both her and her crew, reported them to the deck-officer to be free from suspicion. The provisions were then hoisted out, and among them came a good-sized wooden box, addressed to "Mr. ——, Purser of the United States ship Neversink." Of course, any private matter of this sort, destined for a gentleman of the ward-room, was sacred from examination, and the master-at-arms commanded one of his corporals to carry it down into the Purser's state-room. But recent occurrences had sharpened the vigilance of the deck-officer to an unwonted degree, and seeing the box going down the hatchway, he demanded what that was, and whom it was for.

"All right, sir," said the master-at-arms, touching his cap; "stores for the Purser, sir."

"Let it remain on deck," said the Lieutenant. "Mr. Montgomery!" calling a midshipman, "ask the Purser whether there is any box coming off for him this morning."

"Ay, ay, sir," said the middy, touching his cap.

Presently he returned, saying that the Purser was ashore.

"Very good, then; Mr. Montgomery, have that box put into the 'brig,' with strict orders to the sentry not to suffer any one to touch it."

"Had I not better take it down into my mess, sir, till the Purser comes off?" said the master-at-arms, deferentially.

"I have given my orders, sir!" said the Lieutenant, turning away.

When the Purser came on board, it turned out that he knew nothing at all about the box. He had never so much as heard of it in his life. So it was again brought up before the deck-officer, who immediately summoned the master-at-arms.

"Break open that box!"

"Certainly, sir!" said the master-at-arms; and, wrenching off the cover, twenty-five brown jugs, like a litter of twenty-five brown pigs, were found snugly nestled in a bed of straw.

"The smugglers are at work, sir," said the master-at-arms, looking up.

"Uncork and taste it," said the officer.

The master-at-arms did so; and, smacking his lips after a puzzled fashion, was a little doubtful whether it was American whisky or Holland gin; but he said he was not used to liquor.

"Brandy; I know it by the smell," said the officer; "return the box to the brig."

"Ay, ay, sir," said the master-at-arms, redoubling his activity.

The affair was at once reported to the Captain, who, incensed at the audacity of the thing, adopted every plan to detect the guilty parties. Inquiries were made ashore; but by whom the box had been brought down to the market-boat there was no finding out. Here the matter rested for a time.

Some days after, one of the boys of the mizzen-top was flogged for drunkenness, and, while suspended in agony at the gratings, was made to reveal from whom he had procured his spirits. The man was called, and turned out to be an old superannuated marine, one Scriggs, who did the cooking for the marine-sergeants and master-at-arms' mess. This marine was one of the most villainous-looking fellows in the ship, with a squinting, pick-lock, gray eye, and hang-dog gallows gait. How such a most unmartial vagabond had insinuated himself into the honorable marine corps was a perfect mystery. He had always been noted for his personal uncleanliness, and among all hands, fore and aft, had the reputation of being a notorious old miser, who denied himself the few comforts, and many of the common necessaries of a man-of-war life.

Seeing no escape, Scriggs fell on his knees before the Captain, and confessed the charge of the boy. Observing the fellow to be in an agony of fear at the sight of the boatswain's mates and their lashes, and all the striking parade of public punishment, the Captain must have thought this a good opportunity for completely pumping him of all his secrets. This terrified marine was at length forced to reveal his having been for some time an accomplice in a complicated system of underhand villainy, the head of which was no less a personage than the indefatigable chief of police, the master-at-arms himself. It appeared that this official had his confidential agents ashore, who supplied him with spirits, and in various boxes, packages, and bundles —addressed to the Purser and others—brought them down to the frigate's boats at the landing. Ordinarily, the appearance of these things for the Purser and other ward-room gentlemen occasioned no surprise; for almost every day some bundle or other is coming off for them, especially for the Purser; and, as the master-at-arms was always present on these occasions, it was an easy matter for him to hurry the smuggled liquor out of sight, and, under pretence of carrying the box or bundle down to the Purser's room, hide it away upon his own premises.

The miserly marine, Scriggs, with the pick-lock eye, was the man who clandestinely sold the spirits to the sailors, thus completely keeping the master-at-arms in the background. The liquor sold at the most exorbitant prices; at one time reaching twelve dollars the bottle in cash, and thirty dollars a bottle in orders upon the Purser, to be honored upon the frigate's arrival home. It may seem incredible that such prices should have been given by the sailors; but when some man-of-war's-men crave liquor, and it is hard to procure, they would almost barter ten years of their lifetime for but one solitary "*tot*," if they could.

The sailors who became intoxicated with the liquor thus smuggled on board by the master-at-arms, were, in almost numberless instances, officially seized by that functionary and scourged at the gangway. In a previous place it has been shown how conspicuous a part the master-at-arms enacts at this scene.

The ample profits of this iniquitous business were divided between all the parties concerned in it; Scriggs, the marine, coming in for one third. His cook's mess-chest being brought on deck, four canvass bags of silver were found in it, amounting to a sum something short of as many hundred dollars.

The guilty parties were scourged, double-ironed, and for several weeks were confined in the "brig," under a sentry; all but the master-at-arms, who was merely cashiered and imprisoned for a time, with bracelets at his wrists. Upon being liberated, he was turned adrift among the ship's company; and, by way of disgracing him still more, was thrust into the *waist*, the most inglorious division of the ship.

Upon going to dinner one day, I found him soberly seated at my own mess; and at first I could not but feel some very serious scruples about dining with him. Nevertheless, he was a man to study and digest; so, upon a little reflection, I was not displeased at his presence. It amazed me, however, that he had wormed himself into the mess, since so many of the other messes had declined the honor; until at last, I ascertained that he had induced a mess-mate of ours, a distant relation of his, to prevail upon the cook to admit him.

Now it would not have answered for hardly any other mess in the ship to have received this man among them, for it would have torn a huge rent in their reputation; but our mess, A. No. 1—the Forty-two-pounder Club

—was composed of so fine a set of fellows; so many captains of tops, and quarter-masters—men of undeniable mark on board ship—of long-established standing and consideration on the gun-deck; that, with impunity, we could do so many equivocal things, utterly inadmissible for messes of inferior pretension. Besides, though we all abhorred the monster of Sin itself, yet, from our social superiority, highly rarified education in our lofty top, and large and liberal sweep of the aggregate of things, we were in a good degree free from those useless, personal prejudices, and galling hatreds against conspicuous *sinners*—not *Sin*—which so widely prevail among men of warped understandings and unchristian and uncharitable hearts. No; the superstitions and dogmas concerning Sin had not laid their withering maxims upon our hearts. We perceived how that evil was but good disguised, and a knave a saint in his way; how that in other planets, perhaps, what we deem wrong, may there be deemed right; even as some substances, without undergoing any mutations in themselves, utterly change their color, according to the light thrown upon them. We perceived that the anticipated millennium must have begun upon the morning the first worlds were created; and that, taken all in all, our man-of-war world itself was as eligible a round-sterned craft as any to be found in the Milky Way. And we fancied that though some of us, of the gun-deck, were at times condemned to sufferings and slights, and all manner of tribulation and anguish, yet, no doubt, it was only our misapprehension of these things that made us take them for woeful pains instead of the most agreeable pleasures. I have dreamed of a sphere, says Pinzella, where to break a man on the wheel is held the most exquisite of delights you can confer upon him; where for one gentleman in any way to vanquish another, is accounted an everlasting dishonor; where to tumble one into a pit after death, and then throw cold clods upon his upturned face, is a species of contumely, only inflicted upon the most notorious criminals.

But whatever we mess-mates thought, in whatever circumstances we found ourselves, we never forgot that our frigate, bad as it was, was home-ward-bound. Such, at least, were our reveries at times, though sorely jarred, now and then, by events that took our philosophy aback. For after all, philosophy—that is, the best wisdom that has ever in any way been revealed to our man-of-war world—is but a slough and a mire, with a few tufts of good footing here and there.

But there was one man in the mess who would have naught to do with our philosophy—a churlish, ill-tempered, unphilosophical, superstitious old bear of a quarter-gunner; a believer in Tophet, for which he was accordingly preparing himself. Priming was his name; but methinks I have spoken of him before.

Besides, this Bland, the master-at-arms, was no vulgar, dirty knave. In him—to modify Burke's phrase—vice *seemed*, but only seemed, to lose half its seeming evil by losing all its apparent grossness. He was a neat and gentlemanly villain, and broke his biscuit with a dainty hand. There was a fine polish about his whole person, and a pliant, insinuating style in his conversation, that was, socially, quite irresistible. Save my noble captain, Jack Chase, he proved himself the most entertaining, I had almost said the most companionable man in the mess. Nothing but his mouth, that was somewhat small, Moorish-arched, and wickedly delicate, and his snaky, black eye, that at times shone like a dark-lantern in a jeweler-shop at midnight, betokened the accomplished scoundrel within. But in his conversation there was no trace of evil; nothing equivocal; he studiously shunned an indelicacy, never swore, and chiefly abounded in passing puns and witticisms, varied with humorous contrasts between ship and shore life, and many agreeable and racy anecdotes, very tastefully narrated. In short— in a merely psychological point of view, at least—he was a charming blackleg. Ashore, such a man might have been an irreproachable mercantile swindler, circulating in polite society.

But he was still more than this. Indeed, I claim for this master-at-arms a lofty and honorable niche in the Newgate Calender of history. His intrepidity, coolness, and wonderful self-possession in calmly resigning himself to a fate that thrust him from an office in which he had tyrannized over five hundred mortals, many of whom hated and loathed him, passed all belief; his intrepidity, I say, in now fearlessly gliding among them, like a disarmed sword-fish among ferocious white-sharks; this, surely, bespoke no ordinary man. While in office, even, his life had often been secretly attempted by the seamen whom he had brought to the gangway. Of dark nights they had dropped shot down the hatchways, destined "to damage his pepper-box," as they phrased it; they had made ropes with a hangman's noose at the end, and tried to *lasso* him in dark corners. And now he was adrift among them, under notorious circumstances of superlative villainy, at last dragged to light; and yet he blandly smiled, politely offered his cigar-holder to a perfect stranger, and laughed and chatted to right and left, as if springy, buoyant, and elastic, with an angelic conscience, and sure of kind friends wherever he went, both in this life and the life to come.

While he was lying ironed in the "brig," gangs of the men were sometimes overheard whispering about the terrible reception they would give him when he should be set at large. Nevertheless, when liberated, they seemed confounded by his erect and cordial assurance, his gentlemanly sociability and fearless companionableness. From being an implacable police-man, vigilant, cruel, and remorseless in his office, however polished in his phrases, he was now become a disinterested, sauntering man of leisure, winking at all improprieties, and ready to laugh and make merry with any one. Still, at first, the men gave him a wide berth, and returned scowls for his smiles; but who can forever resist the very Devil himself, when he comes in the guise of a gentleman, free, fine, and frank? Though Goëthe's pious Margaret hates the Devil in his horns and harpooneer's tail, yet she smiles and nods to the engaging fiend in the persuasive, winning, oily, wholly harmless Mephistophiles. But, however it was, I, for one, regarded this master-at-arms with mixed feelings of detestation, pity, admiration, and something opposed to enmity. I could not but abominate him when I thought of his conduct; but I pitied the continual gnawing which, under all his deftly-donned disguises, I saw lying at the bottom of his soul. I admired his heroism in sustaining himself so well under such reverses. And when I thought how arbitrary the *Articles of War* are in defining a man-of-war villain; how much undetected guilt might be sheltered by the aristocratic awning of our quarter-deck; how many florid pursers, ornaments of the ward-room, had been legally protected in defrauding *the people*, I could not but say to myself, Well, after all, though this man is a most wicked one indeed, yet is he even more luckless than depraved.

Besides, a studied observation of Bland convinced me that he was an organic and irreclaimable scoundrel, who did wicked deeds as the cattle browse the herbage, because wicked deeds seemed the legitimate operation of his whole infernal organization. Phrenologically, he was without a soul. Is it to be wondered at, that the devils are irreligious? What, then, thought I, who is to blame in this matter? For one, I will not take the Day of Judgment upon me by authoritatively pronouncing upon the essential criminality of any man-of-war's-man; and Christianity has taught me that, at the last day, man-of-war's-men will not be judged by the *Articles of War*, nor by the *United States Statutes at Large*, but by immutable laws, ineffably beyond the comprehension of the honorable Board of Commodores and Navy Commissioners.

But though I will stand by even a man-of-war thief, and defend him from being seized up at the gangway, if I can—remembering that my Savior once hung between two thieves, promising one life-eternal—yet I would not, after the plain conviction of a villain, again let him entirely loose to prey upon honest seamen, fore and aft all three decks. But this did Captain Claret; and though the thing may not perhaps be credited, nevertheless, here it shall be recorded.

After the master-at-arms had been adrift among the ship's company for several weeks, and we were within a few days' sail of home, he was summoned to the mast, and publicly reinstated in his office as the ship's chief of police. Perhaps Captain Claret had read the Memoirs of Vidocq, and believed in the old saying, *set a rogue to catch a rogue*. Or, perhaps, he was a man of very tender feelings, highly susceptible to the soft emotions of gratitude, and could not bear to leave in disgrace a person who, out of the generosity of his heart, had, about a year previous, presented him with a rare snuff-box, fabricated from a sperm-whale's tooth, with a curious silver hinge, and cunningly wrought in the shape of a whale; also a splendid gold-mounted cane, of a costly Brazilian wood, with a gold plate, bearing the Captain's name and rank in the service, the place and time of his birth, and with a vacancy underneath—no doubt providently left for his heirs to record his decease.

Certain it was that, some months previous to the master-at-arms' disgrace, he had presented these articles to the Captain, with his best love and compliments; and the Captain had received them, and seldom went ashore without the cane, and never took snuff but out of that box. With some Captains, a sense of propriety might have induced them to return these presents, when the generous donor had proved himself unworthy of having them retained; but it was not Captain Claret who would inflict such a cutting wound upon any officer's sensibilities, though long-established naval customs had habituated him to scourging *the people* upon an emergency.

Now had Captain Claret deemed himself constitutionally bound to decline all presents from his subordinates, the sense of gratitude would not have operated to the prejudice of justice. And, as some of the subordinates of a man-of-war captain are apt to invoke his good wishes and mollify his conscience by making him friendly gifts, it would perhaps have been an excellent thing for him to adopt the plan pursued by the President of the United States, when he received a present of lions and Arabian chargers from the Sultan of Muscat. Being forbidden by his sovereign lords and masters, the imperial people, to accept of any gifts from foreign powers, the President sent them to an auctioneer, and the proceeds were deposited in the Treasury. In the same manner, when Captain Claret received his snuff-box and cane, he might have accepted them very kindly, and then sold them off to the highest bidder, perhaps to the donor himself, who in that case would never have tempted him again.

Upon his return home, Bland was paid off for his full term, not deducting the period of his suspension. He again entered the service in his old capacity.

As no further allusion will be made to this affair, it may as well be stated now that, for the very brief period elapsing between his restoration and being paid off in port by the Purser, the master-at-arms conducted himself with infinite discretion, artfully steering between any relaxation of discipline—which would have awakened the displeasure of the officers—and any unwise severity—which would have revived, in ten-fold force, all the old grudges of the seamen under his command.

Never did he show so much talent and tact as when vibrating in this his most delicate predicament; and plenty of cause was there for the exercise of his cunningest abilities; for, upon the discharge of our man-of-war's-men at home, should he *then* be held by them as an enemy, as free and independent citizens they would waylay him in the public streets, and take purple vengeance for all his iniquities, past, present, and possible in the future. More than once a master-at-arms ashore has been seized by night by an exasperated crew, and served as Origen served himself, or as his enemies served Abelard.

But though, under extreme provocation, *the people* of a man-of-war have been guilty of the maddest vengeance, yet, at other times, they are very placable and milky-hearted, even to those who may have outrageously abused them; many things in point might be related, but I forbear.

This account of the master-at-arms can not better be concluded than by denominating him, in the vivid language of the Captain of the Fore-top, as *"the two ends and middle of the thrice-laid strand of a bloody rascal,"* which was intended for a terse, well-knit, and all-comprehensive assertion, without omission or reservation. It was also asserted that, had Tophet itself been raked with a fine-tooth comb, such another ineffable villain could not by any possibility have been caught.

Chapter 45

Publishing Poetry in a Man-of-war

A DAY OR TWO after our arrival in Rio, a rather amusing incident occurred to a particular acquaintance of mine, young Lemsford, the gun-deck bard.

The great guns of an armed ship have blocks of wood, called *tompions*, painted black, inserted in their muzzles, to keep out the spray of the sea. These tompions slip in and out very handily, like covers to butter firkins.

By advice of a friend, Lemsford, alarmed for the fate of his box of poetry, had latterly made use of a particular gun on the main-deck, in the tube of which he thrust his manuscripts, by simply crawling partly out of the port-hole, removing the tompion, inserting his papers, tightly rolled, and making all snug again. Little Quoin, the quarter-gunner, was on the "sick-list" then.

Breakfast over, Lemsford and I were reclining in the main-top—where, by permission of my noble master, Jack Chase, I had invited him—when, of a sudden, we heard a cannonading. It was our own ship.

"Ah!" said a top-man, "returning the shore salute they gave us yesterday."

"O Lord!" cried Lemsford, "my *Songs of the Sirens!*" and he ran down the rigging to the batteries; but just as he touched the gun-deck, gun No. 20—his literary strong box—went off with a terrific report.

"Well, my after-guard Virgil," said Jack Chase to him, as he slowly returned up the rigging, "did you get it? You need not answer; I see you were too late. But never mind, my boy; no printer could do the business for you better. That's the way to publish, White-Jacket," turning to me— "fire it right into 'em; every canto a twenty-four-pound shot; *hull* the blockheads, whether they will or no. And mind you, Lemsford, when your shot does the most execution, you hear the least from the foe. A killed man can not even lisp."

"Glorious Jack!" cried Lemsford, running up and snatching him by the hand, "say that again, Jack! look me in the eyes. By all the Homers, Jack, you have made my soul mount like a balloon! Jack, I'm a poor devil of a poet. Not two months before I shipped aboard here, I published a volume of poems, very aggressive on the world, Jack. Heaven knows what it cost me. I published it, Jack, and the cursed publisher sued me for damages; my friends looked sheepish; one or two who liked it were non-committal; and as for the addle-pated mob and rabble, they thought they had found out a fool. Blast them, Jack, what they call the public is a monster, like the idol we saw in Owhyhee, with the head of a jackass, the body of a baboon, and the tail of a scorpion!"

"I don't like that," said Jack; "when I'm ashore, I myself am part of the public."

"Your pardon, Jack; you are not. You are then a part of the people, just as you are aboard the frigate here. The public is one thing, Jack, and the people another."

"You are right," said Jack; "right as this leg. Virgil, you are a trump; you are a jewel, my boy. The public and the people! Ay, ay, my lads, let us hate the one and cleave to the other."

Chapter 46

The Commodore on the Poop, and one of "the People" under the Hands of the Surgeon

A DAY OR TWO after the publication of Lemsford's "Songs of the Sirens," a sad accident befell a mess-mate of mine, one of the captains of the mizzen-top. He was a fine little Scot, who, from the premature loss of the hair on the top of his head, always went by the name of *Baldy*. This baldness was no doubt, in great part, attributable to the same cause that early thins the locks of most man-of-war's-men—namely, the hard, unyielding, and ponderous man-of-war and navy-regulation tarpaulin hat, which, when new, is stiff enough to sit upon, and indeed, in lieu of his thumb, sometimes serves the common sailor for a bench.

Now, there is nothing upon which the Commodore of a squadron more prides himself than upon the celerity with which his men can handle the sails, and go through with all the evolutions pertaining thereto. This is especially manifested in harbor, when other vessels of his squadron are near, and perhaps the armed ships of rival nations.

Upon these occasions, surrounded by his post-captain satraps—each of whom in his own floating island is king—the Commodore domineers over all—emperor of the whole oaken archipelago; yea, magisterial and magnificent as the Sultan of the Isles of Sooloo.

But, even as so potent an emperor and Cæsar to boot as the great Don of Germany, Charles the Fifth, was used to divert himself in his dotage by watching the gyrations of the springs and cogs of a long row of clocks, even so does an elderly Commodore while away his leisure in harbor, by what is called "*exercising guns*," and also "*exercising yards and sails;*" causing the various spars of all the ships under his command to be "braced," "topped," and "cock billed" in concert, while the Commodore himself sits, something like King Canute, on an arm-chest on the poop of his flag-ship.

But far more regal than any descendant of Charlemagne, more haughty than any Mogul of the East, and almost mysterious and voiceless in his authority as the Great Spirit of the Five Nations, the Commodore deigns not to verbalize his commands; they are imparted by signal.

And as for old Charles the Fifth, again, the gay-pranked, colored suits of cards were invented, to while away his dotage, even so, doubtless, must these pretty little signals of blue and red spotted *bunting* have been devised to cheer the old age of all Commodores.

By the Commodore's side stands the signal-midshipman, with a sea-green bag swung on his shoulder (as a sportsman bears his game-bag), the signal-book in one hand, and the signal-spy-glass in the other. As this signal-book contains the Masonic signs and tokens of the navy, and would therefore be invaluable to an enemy, its binding is always bordered with lead, so as to insure its sinking in case the ship should be captured. Not the only book this, that might appropriately be bound in lead, though there be many where the author, and not the bookbinder, furnishes the metal.

As White-Jacket understands it, these signals consist of variously-colored flags, each standing for a certain number. Say there are ten flags, representing the cardinal numbers—the red flag, No. 1; the blue flag, No. 2; the green flag, No. 3, and so forth; then, by mounting the blue flag over the red, that would stand for No. 21: if the green flag were set underneath, it would then stand for 213. How easy, then, by endless transpositions, to multiply the various numbers that may be exhibited at the mizzen-peak, even by only three or four of these flags.

To each number a particular meaning is applied. No. 100, for instance, may mean, "*Beat to quarters.*" No. 150, "*All hands to grog.*" No. 2000, "*Strike top-gallant-yards.*" No. 2110, "*See any thing to windward?*" No. 2800, "*No.*"

And as every man-of-war is furnished with a signal-book, where all these things are set down in order, therefore, though two American frigates —almost perfect strangers to each other—came from the opposite Poles, yet at a distance of more than a mile they could carry on a very liberal conversation in the air.

When several men-of-war of one nation lie at anchor in one port, forming a wide circle round their lord and master, the flag-ship, it is a very interesting sight to see them all obeying the Commodore's orders, who meanwhile never opens his lips.

Thus was it with us in Rio, and hereby hangs the story of my poor mess-mate Baldy.

One morning, in obedience to a signal from our flag-ship, the various vessels belonging to the American squadron then in harbor simultaneously loosened their sails to dry. In the evening, the signal was set to furl them. Upon such occasions, great rivalry exists between the First Lieutenants of the different ships; they vie with each other who shall first have his sails stowed on the yards. And this rivalry is shared between all the officers of each vessel, who are respectively placed over the different top-men; so that the main-mast is all eagerness to vanquish the fore-mast, and the mizzen-mast to vanquish them both. Stimulated by the shouts of their officers, the sailors throughout the squadron exert themselves to the utmost.

"Aloft, top-men! lay out! furl!" cried the First Lieutenant of the Neversink.

At the word the men sprang into the rigging, and on all three masts were soon climbing about the yards, in reckless haste, to execute their orders.

Now, in furling top-sails or courses, the point of honor, and the hardest work, is in the *bunt*, or middle of the yard; this post belongs to the first captain of the top.

"What are you 'bout there, mizzen-top-men?" roared the First Lieutenant, through his trumpet. "D—n you, you are clumsy as Russian bears! don't you see the main-top-men are nearly off the yard? Bear a hand, bear a hand, or I'll stop your grog all round! You, Baldy! are you going to sleep there in the bunt?"

While this was being said, poor Baldy—his hat off, his face streaming with perspiration—was franticly exerting himself, piling up the ponderous folds of canvass in the middle of the yard; ever and anon glancing at victorious Jack Chase, hard at work at the main-topsail-yard before him.

At last, the sail being well piled up, Baldy jumped with both feet into the *bunt*, holding on with one hand to the chain "*tie*," and in that manner was violently treading down the canvass, to pack it close.

"D—n you, Baldy, why don't you move, you crawling caterpillar?" roared the First Lieutenant.

Baldy brought his whole weight to bear on the rebellious sail, and in his frenzied heedlessness let go his hold on the *tie*.

"You, Baldy! are you afraid of falling?" cried the First Lieutenant.

At that moment, with all his force, Baldy jumped down upon the sail; the *bunt-gasket* parted; and a dark form dropped through the air. Lighting upon the *top-rim*, it rolled off; and the next instant, with a horrid crash of all his bones, Baldy came, like a thunder-bolt, upon the deck.

Aboard of most large men-of-war there is a stout oaken platform, about four feet square, on each side of the quarter-deck. You ascend to it by three or four steps; on top, it is railed in at the sides, with horizontal brass bars. It is called *the Horse Block;* and there the officer of the deck usually stands, in giving his orders at sea.

It was one of these horse blocks, now unoccupied, that broke poor Baldy's fall. He fell lengthwise across the brass bars, bending them into elbows, and crushing the whole oaken platform, steps and all, right down to the deck in a thousand splinters.

He was picked up for dead, and carried below to the surgeon. His bones seemed like those of a man broken on the wheel, and no one thought he would survive the night. But with the surgeon's skillful treatment he at last promised recovery. Surgeon Cuticle devoted all his science to this case.

A curious frame-work of wood was made for the maimed man; and placed in this, with all his limbs stretched out, Baldy lay flat on the floor of the Sick-bay, for many weeks. Upon our arrival home, he was able to hobble ashore on crutches; but from a hale, hearty little man, with bronzed cheeks, he was become a mere dislocated skeleton, white as foam; but ere this, perhaps, his broken bones are healed and whole in the last repose of the man-of-war's-man.

Not many days after Baldy's accident in furling sails—in this same frenzied manner, under the stimulus of a shouting officer—a seaman fell from the main-royal-yard of an English line-of-battle ship near us, and buried his ankle-bones in the deck, leaving two indentations there, as if scooped out by a carpenter's gouge.

The royal-yard forms a cross with the mast, and falling from that lofty cross in a line-of-battle ship is almost like falling from the cross of St. Paul's; almost like falling as Lucifer from the well-spring of morning down to the Phlegethon of night.

In some cases, a man, hurled thus from a yard, has fallen upon his own shipmates in the tops, and dragged them down with him to the same destruction with himself.

Hardly ever will you hear of a man-of-war returning home after a cruise, without the loss of some of her crew from aloft, whereas similar accidents in the merchant service—considering the much greater number of men employed in it—are comparatively few.

Why mince the matter? The death of most of these man-of-war's-men lies at the door of the souls of those officers, who, while safely standing on deck themselves, scruple not to sacrifice an immortal man or two, in order to show off the excelling discipline of the ship. And thus do *the people* of the gun-deck suffer, that the Commodore on the poop may be glorified.

Chapter 47

An Auction in a Man-of-war

SOME ALLUSION HAS BEEN MADE to the weariness experienced by the man-of-war's-man while lying at anchor; but there are scenes now and then that serve to relieve it. Chief among these are the Purser's auctions, taking place while in harbor. Some weeks, or perhaps months, after a sailor dies in an armed vessel, his bag of clothes is in this manner sold, and the proceeds transferred to the account of his heirs or executors.

One of these auctions came off in Rio, shortly after the sad accident of Baldy.

It was a dreamy, quiet afternoon, and the crew were listlessly lying around, when suddenly the Boatswain's whistle was heard, followed by the announcement, "D'ye hear there, fore and aft! Purser's auction on the spar-deck!"

At the sound, the sailors sprang to their feet and mustered round the main-mast. Presently up came the Purser's steward, marshaling before him three or four of his subordinates, carrying several clothes' bags, which were deposited at the base of the mast.

Our Purser's steward was a rather gentlemanly man in his way. Like many young Americans of his class, he had at various times assumed the most opposite functions for a livelihood, turning from one to the other with all the facility of a light-hearted, clever adventurer. He had been a clerk in a steamer on the Mississippi River; an auctioneer in Ohio; a stock actor at the Olympic Theatre in New York; and now he was Purser's steward in the Navy. In the course of this diversified career his natural wit and waggery had been highly spiced, and every way improved; and he had acquired the last and most difficult art of the joker, the art of lengthening his own face while widening those of his hearers, preserving the utmost solemnity while setting them all in a roar. He was quite a favorite with the sailors, which, in a good degree, was owing to his humor; but likewise to his off-hand, irresistible, romantic, theatrical manner of addressing them.

With a dignified air, he now mounted the pedestal of the main-top-sail sheet-bitts, imposing silence by a theatrical wave of his hand; meantime, his subordinates were rummaging the bags, and assorting their contents before him.

"Now, my noble hearties," he began, "we will open this auction by offering to your impartial competition a very superior pair of old boots;" and so saying, he dangled aloft one clumsy cowhide cylinder, almost as large as a fire bucket, as a specimen of the complete pair.

"What shall I have now, my noble tars, for this superior pair of sea-boots?"

"Where's t'other boot?" cried a suspicious-eyed waister. "I remember them 'ere boots. They were old Bob's the quarter-gunner's; there was two on 'em, too. I want to see t'other boot."

"My sweet and pleasant fellow," said the auctioneer, with his blandest accents, "the other boot is not just at hand, but I give you my word of honor that it in all respects corresponds to the one you here see—it does, I assure you. Yes: I solemnly guarantee, my noble sea-fencibles," he added, turning round upon all, "that the other boot is the exact counterpart of this. Now, then, say the word, my fine fellows. What shall I have? Ten dollars, did you say?" politely bowing toward some indefinite person in the background.

"No; ten cents," responded a voice.

"Ten cents! ten cents! gallant sailors, for this noble pair of boots," exclaimed the auctioneer, with affected horror; "I must close the auction, my tars of Columbia; this will never do. But let's have another bid; now, come," he added, coaxingly and soothingly. "What is it? One dollar? One dollar, then—one dollar; going at one dollar; going, going—going. Just see how it vibrates"—swinging the boot to and fro—"this superior pair of sea-boots vibrating at one dollar; wouldn't pay for the nails in their heels; going, going—*gone!*" And down went the boots.

"Ah, what a sacrifice! what a sacrifice!" he sighed, tearfully eyeing the solitary fire-bucket, and then glancing round the company for sympathy.

"A sacrifice, indeed!" exclaimed Jack Chase, who stood by; "Purser's Steward, you are Mark Antony over the body of Julius Cæsar."

"So I am, so I am," said the auctioneer, without moving a muscle. "And look!" he exclaimed, suddenly seizing the boot, and exhibiting it on high, "look, my noble tars, if you have tears, prepare to shed them now. You all do know this boot. I remember the first time ever old Bob put it on. 'Twas on a winter evening, off Cape Horn, between the starboard carron-ades—that day his precious grog was stopped. Look! in this place a mouse has nibbled through; see what a rent some envious rat has made; through this another filed, and, as he plucked his cursed rasp away, mark how the bootleg gaped. This was the unkindest cut of all. But whose are the boots?" suddenly assuming a business-like air; "yours? yours? yours?"

But not a friend of the lamented Bob stood by.

"Tars of Columbia," said the auctioneer, imperatively, "these boots must be sold; and if I can't sell them one way, I must sell them another. How much *a pound*, now, for this superior pair of old boots? going by *the pound* now, remember, my gallant sailors! what shall I have? one cent, do I hear? going now at one cent a pound—going—going—going—*gone!*"

"Whose are they? Yours, Captain of the Waist? Well, my sweet and pleasant friend, I will have them weighed out to you when the auction is over."

In like manner all the contents of the bags were disposed of, embracing old frocks, trowsers, and jackets, the various sums for which they went being charged to the bidders on the books of the Purser.

Having been present at this auction, though not a purchaser, and seeing with what facility the most dismantled old garments went off, through the magical cleverness of the accomplished auctioneer, the thought occurred to me, that if ever I calmly and positively decided to dispose of my famous white jacket, this would be the very way to do it. I turned the matter over in my mind a long time.

The weather in Rio was genial and warm, and that I would ever again need such a thing as a heavy quilted jacket—and such a jacket as the white one, too—seemed almost impossible. Yet I remembered the American coast, and that it would probably be Autumn when we should arrive there. Yes, I thought of all that, to be sure; nevertheless, the ungovernable whim seized me to sacrifice my jacket and recklessly abide the consequences. Besides, was it not a horrible jacket? To how many annoyances had it subjected me? How many scrapes had it dragged me into? Nay, had it not once jeopardized my very existence? And I had a dreadful presentiment that, if I persisted in retaining it, it would do so again. Enough! I will sell it, I muttered; and, so muttering, I thrust my hands further down in my waistband, and walked the main-top in the stern concentration of an inflexible purpose. Next day, hearing that another auction was shortly to take place, I repaired to the office of the Purser's steward, with whom I was upon rather friendly terms. After vaguely and delicately hinting at the object of my visit, I came roundly to the point, and asked him whether he could slip my jacket into one of the bags of clothes next to be sold, and so dispose of it by public auction. He kindly acquiesced, and the thing was done.

In due time all hands were again summoned round the main-mast; the Purser's steward mounted his post, and the ceremony began. Meantime, I lingered out of sight, but still within hearing, on the gun-deck below, gazing up, unperceived, at the scene.

As it is now so long ago, I will here frankly make confession that I had privately retained the services of a friend—Williams, the Yankee pedagogue and peddler—whose business it would be to linger near the scene of the auction, and, if the bids on the jacket loitered, to start it roundly himself; and if the bidding then became brisk, he was continually to strike in with the most pertinacious and infatuated bids, and so exasperate competition into the maddest and most extravagant overtures.

A variety of other articles having been put up, the white jacket was slowly produced, and, held high aloft between the auctioneer's thumb and fore-finger, was submitted to the inspection of the discriminating public.

Here it behooves me once again to describe my jacket; for, as a portrait taken at one period of life will not answer for a later stage; much more this jacket of mine, undergoing so many changes, needs to be painted again and again, in order truly to present its actual appearance at any given period.

A premature old age had now settled upon it; all over it bore melancholy scars of the masoned-up pockets that had once trenched it in various directions. Some parts of it were slightly mildewed from dampness; on one side several of the buttons were gone, and others were broken or cracked; while, alas! my many mad endeavors to rub it black on the decks had now imparted to the whole garment an exceedingly untidy appearance. Such as it was, with all its faults, the auctioneer displayed it.

"You venerable sheet-anchor-men! and you, gallant fore-top-men! and you, my fine waisters! what do you say now for this superior old jacket? Buttons and sleeves, lining and skirts, it must this day be sold without reservation. How much for it, my gallant tars of Columbia? say the word, and how much?"

"My eyes!" exclaimed a fore-top-man, "don't that 'ere bunch of old swabs belong to Jack Chase's pet? Arn't that *the white jacket?*"

"*The white jacket!*" cried fifty voices in response; "*the white jacket!*" The cry ran fore and aft the ship like a slogan, completely overwhelming the solitary voice of my private friend Williams, while all hands gazed at it with straining eyes, wondering how it came among the bags of deceased mariners.

"Ay, noble tars," said the auctioneer, "you may well stare at it; you will not find another jacket like this on either side of Cape Horn, I assure you. Why, just look at it! How much, now? Give me a bid—but don't be rash; be prudent, be prudent, men; remember your Purser's accounts, and don't be betrayed into extravagant bids."

"Purser's Steward!" cried Grummet, one of the quarter-gunners, slowly shifting his quid from one cheek to the other, like a ballast-stone, "I won't bid on that 'ere bunch of old swabs, unless you put up ten pounds of soap with it."

"Don't mind that old fellow," said the auctioneer. "How much for the jacket, my noble tars?"

"Jacket!" cried a dandy *bone-polisher* of the gun-room. "The sail-maker was the tailor, then. How many fathoms of canvass in it, Purser's Steward?"

"How much for this *jacket?*" reiterated the auctioneer, emphatically.

"*Jacket* do you call it!" cried a captain of the hold. "Why not call it a white-washed man-of-war schooner? Look at the port-holes, to let in the air of cold nights."

"A reg'lar herring-net," chimed in Grummet.

"Gives me the *fever-nagur* to look at it," echoed a mizzen-top-man.

"Silence!" cried the auctioneer. "Start it now—start it, boys; any thing you please, my fine fellows! it *must* be sold. Come, what ought I to have on it, now?"

"Why, Purser's Steward," cried a waister, "you ought to have new sleeves, a new lining, and a new body on it, afore you try to shove it off on a green-horn."

"What are you busin' that 'ere garment for?" cried an old sheet-anchor-man. "Don't you see it's a 'uniform mustering jacket'—three buttons on one side, and none on t'other?"

"Silence!" again cried the auctioneer. "How much, my sea-fencibles, for this superior old jacket?"

"Well," said Grummet, "I'll take it for cleaning-rags at one cent."

"Oh, come, give us a bid! say something, Columbians."

"Well, then," said Grummet, all at once bursting into genuine indignation, "if you want us to say something, then heave that bunch of old swabs overboard, *say I*, and show us something worth looking at."

"No one will give me a bid, then? Very good; here, shove it aside. Let's have something else there."

While this scene was going forward, and my white jacket was thus being abused, how my heart swelled within me! Thrice was I on the point of rushing out of my hiding-place, and bearing it off from derision; but I lingered, still flattering myself that all would be well, and the jacket find a purchaser at last. But no, alas! there was no getting rid of it, except by rolling a forty-two-pound shot in it, and committing it to the deep. But though, in my desperation, I had once contemplated something of that sort, yet I had now become unaccountably averse to it, from certain involuntary superstitious considerations. If I sink my jacket, thought I, it will be sure to spread itself into a bed at the bottom of the sea, upon which I shall sooner or later recline, a dead man. So, unable to conjure it into the possession of another, and withheld from burying it out of sight forever, my jacket stuck to me like the fatal shirt on Nessus.

Chapter 48

Purser, Purser's Steward, and Postmaster in a Man-of-war

A S THE PURSER'S STEWARD so conspicuously figured at the unsuccessful auction of my jacket, it reminds me of how important a personage that official is on board of all men-of-war. He is the right-hand man and confidential deputy and clerk of the Purser, who intrusts to him all his accounts with the crew, while, in most cases, he himself, snug and comfortable in his state-room, glances over a file of newspapers instead of overhauling his ledgers.

Of all the non-combatants of a man-of-war, the Purser, perhaps, stands foremost in importance. Though he is but a member of the gun-room mess, yet usage seems to assign him a conventional station somewhat above that of his equals in navy rank—the Chaplain, Surgeon, and Professor. Moreover, he is frequently to be seen in close conversation with the Commodore, who, in the Neversink, was more than once known to be slightly jocular with our Purser. Upon several occasions, also, he was called into the Commodore's cabin, and remained closeted there for several minutes together. Nor do I remember that there ever happened a cabinet meeting of the ward room barons, the Lieutenants, in the Commodore's cabin, but the Purser made one of the party. Doubtless the important fact of the Purser having under his charge all the financial affairs of a man-of-war, imparts to him the great importance he enjoys. Indeed, we find in every government—monarchies and republics alike—that the personage at the head of the finances invariably occupies a commanding position. Thus, in point of station, the Secretary of the Treasury of the United States is deemed superior to the other heads of departments. Also, in England, the real office held by the great Premier himself is—as every one knows—that of First Lord of the Treasury.

Now, under this high functionary of state, the official known as the Purser's Steward was head clerk of the frigate's fiscal affairs. Upon the berth-deck he had a regular counting-room, full of ledgers, journals, and day-books. His desk was as much littered with papers as any Pearl Street merchant's, and much time was devoted to his accounts. For hours together you would see him, through the window of his subterranean office, writing by the light of his perpetual lamp.

Ex-officio, the Purser's Steward of most ships is a sort of Postmaster, and his office the Post-office. When the letter-bags for the squadron—almost as large as those of the United States mail—arrived on board the Neversink, it was the Purser's Steward that sat at his little window on the berth-deck and handed you your letter or paper—if any there were to your address. Some disappointed applicants among the sailors would offer to buy the epistles of their more fortunate shipmates, while yet the seal was unbroken—maintaining that the sole and confidential reading of a fond, long, domestic letter from any man's home, was far better than no letter at all.

In the vicinity of the office of the Purser's Steward are the principal store-rooms of the Purser, where large quantities of goods of every description are to be found. On board of those ships where goods are permitted to be served out to the crew for the purpose of selling them ashore, to raise money, more business is transacted at the office of a Purser's Steward in one *Liberty-day* morning than all the dry goods shops in a considerable village would transact in a week.

Once a month, with undeviating regularity, this official has his hands more than usually full. For, once a month, certain printed bills, called Mess-bills, are circulated among the crew, and whatever you may want from the Purser—be it tobacco, soap, duck, dungeree, needles, thread, knives, belts, calico, ribbon, pipes, paper, pens, hats, ink, shoes, socks, or whatever it may be—down it goes on the mess-bill, which, being the next day returned to the office of the Steward, the "slops," as they are called, are served out to the men and charged to their accounts.

Lucky is it for man-of-war's-men that the outrageous impositions to which, but a very few years ago, they were subjected from the abuses in this department of the service, and the unscrupulous cupidity of many of the Pursers—lucky is it for them that *now* these things are in a great degree done away. The Pursers, instead of being at liberty to make almost what they pleased from the sale of their wares, are now paid by regular stipends laid down by law.

Under the exploded system, the profits of some of these officers were almost incredible. In one cruise up the Mediterranean, the Purser of an American line-of-battle ship was, on good authority, said to have cleared the sum of $50,000. Upon that he quitted the service, and retired into the country. Shortly after, his three daughters—not very lovely—married extremely well.

The ideas that sailors entertain of Pursers is expressed in a rather inelegant but expressive saying of theirs: "The Purser is a conjuror; he can make a dead man chew tobacco"—insinuating that the accounts of a dead man are sometimes subjected to post-mortem charges. Among sailors, also, Pursers commonly go by the name of *nip-cheeses*.

No wonder that on board of the old frigate Java, upon her return from a cruise extending over a period of more than four years, one thousand dollars paid off eighty of her crew, though the aggregate wages of the eighty for the voyage must have amounted to about sixty thousand dollars. Even under the present system, the Purser of a line-of-battle ship, for instance, is far better paid than any other officer, short of Captain or Commodore. While the Lieutenant commonly receives but eighteen hundred dollars, the Surgeon of the fleet but fifteen hundred, the Chaplain twelve hundred, the Purser of a line-of-battle ship receives thirty-five hundred dollars. In considering his salary, however, his responsibilities are not to be overlooked; they are by no means insignificant.

There are Pursers in the Navy whom the sailors exempt from the insinuations above mentioned, nor, as a class, are they so obnoxious to them now as formerly; for one, the florid old Purser of the Neversink—never coming into disciplinary contact with the seamen, and being withal a jovial and apparently good-hearted gentleman—was something of a favorite with many of the crew.

Chapter 49

Rumors of a War, and how they were received by the Population of the Neversink

WHILE LYING in the harbor of Callao, in Peru, certain rumors had come to us touching a war with England, growing out of the long-vexed Northeastern Boundary Question. In Rio these rumors were increased; and the probability of hostilities induced our Commodore to authorize proceedings that closely brought home to every man on board the Neversink his liability at any time to be killed at his gun.

Among other things, a number of men were detailed to pass up the rusty cannon-balls from the shot-lockers in the hold, and scrape them clean for service. The Commodore was a very neat gentleman, and would not fire a dirty shot into his foe.

It was an interesting occasion for a tranquil observer; nor was it altogether neglected. Not to recite the precise remarks made by the seamen while pitching the shot up the hatchway from hand to hand, like schoolboys playing ball ashore, it will be enough to say that, from the general drift of their discourse—jocular as it was—it was manifest that, almost to a man, they abhorred the idea of going into action.

And why should they desire a war? Would their wages be raised? Not a cent. The prize-money, though, ought to have been an inducement. But of all the "rewards of virtue," prize-money is the most uncertain; and this the man-of-war's-man knows. What, then, has he to expect from war?

What but harder work, and harder usage than in peace; a wooden leg or arm; mortal wounds, and death? Enough, however, that by far the majority of the common sailors of the Neversink were plainly concerned at the prospect of war, and were plainly averse to it.

But with the officers of the quarter-deck it was just the reverse. None of them, to be sure, in my hearing at least, verbally expressed their gratification; but it was unavoidably betrayed by the increased cheerfulness of their demeanor toward each other, their frequent fraternal conferences, and their unwonted animation for several days in issuing their orders. The voice of Mad Jack—always a belfry to hear—now resounded like that famous bell of England, Great Tom of Oxford. As for Selvagee, he wore his sword with a jaunty air, and his servant daily polished the blade.

But why this contrast between the forecastle and the quarter-deck, between the man-of-war's-man and his officer? Because, though war would equally jeopardize the lives of both, yet, while it held out to the sailor no promise of promotion, and what is called *glory*, these things fired the breast of his officers.

It is no pleasing task, nor a thankful one, to dive into the souls of some men; but there are occasions when, to bring up the mud from the bottom, reveals to us on what soundings we are, on what coast we adjoin.

How were these officers to gain glory? How but by a distinguished slaughtering of their fellow-men. How were they to be promoted? How but over the buried heads of killed comrades and mess-mates.

This hostile contrast between the feelings with which the common seamen and the officers of the Neversink looked forward to this more than possible war, is one of many instances that might be quoted to show the antagonism of their interests, the incurable antagonism in which they dwell. But can men, whose interests are diverse, ever hope to live together in a harmony uncoerced? Can the brotherhood of the race of mankind ever hope to prevail in a man-of-war, where one man's bane is almost another's blessing? By abolishing the scourge, shall we do away tyranny; *that* tyranny which must ever prevail, where of two essentially antagonist classes in perpetual contact, one is immeasurably the stronger? Surely it seems all but impossible. And as the very object of a man-of-war, as its name implies, is to fight the very battles so naturally averse to the seamen; so long as a man-of-war exists, it must ever remain a picture of much that is tyrannical and repelling in human nature.

Being an establishment much more extensive than the American Navy, the English armed marine furnishes a yet more striking example of this thing, especially as the existence of war produces so vast an augmentation of her naval force compared with what it is in time of peace. It is well known what joy the news of Bonaparte's sudden return from Elba created among crowds of British naval officers, who had previously been expecting to be sent ashore on half-pay. Thus, when all the world wailed, these officers found occasion for thanksgiving. I urge it not against them as *men*—their feelings belonged to their profession. Had they not been naval officers, they had not been rejoicers in the midst of despair.

When shall the time come, how much longer will God postpone it, when the clouds, which at times gather over the horizons of nations, shall not be hailed by any class of humanity, and invoked to burst as a bomb? Standing navies, as well as standing armies, serve to keep alive the spirit of war even in the meek heart of peace. In its very embers and smoulderings, they nourish that fatal fire, and half-pay officers, as the priests of Mars, yet guard the temple, though no god be there.

Chapter 50

The Bay of all Beauties

I HAVE SAID that I must pass over Rio without a description; but just now such a flood of scented reminiscences steals over me, that I must needs yield and recant, as I inhale that musky air.

More than one hundred and fifty miles' circuit of living green hills imbosoms a translucent expanse, so gemmed in by sierras of grass, that among the Indian tribes the place was known as "The Hidden Water." On all sides, in the distance, rise high conical peaks, which at sunrise and sunset burn like vast tapers; and down from the interior, through vineyards and forests, flow radiating streams, all emptying into the harbor.

Talk not of Bahia de Todos os Santos—the Bay of All Saints; for though that be a glorious haven, yet Rio is the Bay of all Rivers—the Bay of all Delights—the Bay of all Beauties. From circumjacent hill-sides, untiring summer hangs perpetually in terraces of vivid verdure; and, embossed with old mosses, convent and castle nestle in valley and glen.

All round, deep inlets run into the green mountain land, and, overhung with wild Highlands, more resemble Loch Katrines than Lake Lemans. And though Loch Katrine has been sung by the bonneted Scott, and Lake Leman by the coroneted Byron; yet here, in Rio, both the loch and the lake are but two wild flowers in a prospect that is almost unlimited. For, behold! far away and away, stretches the broad blue of the water, to yonder soft-swelling hills of light green, backed by the purple pinnacles and pipes of the grand Organ Mountains; fitly so called, for in thunder-time they roll cannonades down the bay, drowning the blended bass of all the cathedrals in Rio. Shout amain, exalt your voices, stamp your feet, jubilate, Organ Mountains! and roll your Te Deums round the world!

What though, for more than five thousand five hundred years, this grand harbor of Rio lay hid in the hills, unknown by the Catholic Portuguese? Centuries ere Haydn performed before emperors and kings, these Organ Mountains played his Oratorio of the Creation, before the Creator himself. But nervous Haydn could not have endured that cannonading choir, since this composer of thunder-bolts himself died at last through the crashing commotion of Napoleon's bombardment of Vienna.

But all mountains are Organ Mountains: the Alps and the Himmelahs; the Appalachian Chain, the Ural, the Andes, the Green Hills and the White. All of them play anthems forever: The Messiah, and Samson, and Israel in Egypt, and Saul, and Judas Maccabeus, and Solomon.

Archipelago Rio! ere Noah on old Ararat anchored his ark, there lay anchored in you all these green, rocky isles I now see. But God did not build on you, isles! those long lines of batteries; nor did our blessed Savior stand godfather at the christening of yon frowning fortress of Santa Cruz, though named in honor of himself, the divine Prince of Peace!

Amphitheatrical Rio! in your broad expanse might be held the Resurrection and Judgment-day of the whole world's men-of-war, represented by the flag-ships of fleets—the flag-ships of the Phœnician armed galleys of Tyre and Sidon; of King Solomon's annual squadrons that sailed to Ophir; whence in after times, perhaps, sailed the Acapulco fleets of the Spaniards, with golden ingots for ballasting; the flag-ships of all the Greek and Persian craft that exchanged the war-hug at Salamis; of all the Roman and Egyptian galleys that, eagle-like, with blood-dripping prows, beaked each other at Actium; of all the Danish keels of the Vikings; of all the musquito craft of Abba Thule, king of the Pelews, when he went to vanquish Artingall; of all the Venetian, Genoese, and Papal fleets that came to the shock at Lepanto; of both horns of the crescent of the Spanish Armada; of the Portuguese squadron that, under the gallant Gama, chastised the Moors, and discovered the Moluccas; of all the Dutch navies led by Van Tromp, and sunk by Admiral Hawke; of the forty-seven French and Spanish sail-of-the-line that, for three months, essayed to batter down Gibraltar; of all Nelson's seventy-fours that thunder-bolted off St. Vincent's, at the Nile, Copenhagen, and Trafalgar; of all the frigate-merchantmen of the East India Company; of Perry's war-brigs, sloops, and schooners that scattered the British armament on Lake Erie; of all the Barbary corsairs captured by Bainbridge; of the war-canoes of the Polynesian kings, Tammahammaha and Pomare—ay! one and all, with Commodore Noah for their Lord High Admiral—in this abounding Bay of Rio these flag-ships might all come to anchor, and swing round in concert to the first of the flood.

Rio is a small Mediterranean; and what was fabled of the entrance to that sea, in Rio in partly made true; for here, at the mouth, stands one of Hercules' Pillars, the Sugar-Loaf Mountain, one thousand feet high, inclining over a little, like the Leaning Tower of Pisa. At its base crouch, like mastiffs, the batteries of Jose and Theodosia; while opposite, you are menaced by a rock-founded fort.

The channel between—the sole inlet to the bay—seems but a biscuit's toss over; you see naught of the land-locked sea within till fairly in the strait. But, then, what a sight is beheld! Diversified as the harbor of Constantinople, but a thousand-fold grander. When the Neversink swept in, word was passed, "Aloft, top-men! and furl the t'-gallant-sails and royals!"

At the sound I sprang into the rigging, and was soon at my perch. How I hung over that main-royal-yard in a rapture! High in air, poised over that magnificent bay, a new world to my ravished eyes, I felt like the foremost of a flight of angels, new-lighted upon earth, from some star in the Milky Way.

Chapter 51

One of "the People" has an Audience with the Commodore and the Captain on the Quarter-deck

W E HAD NOT LAIN in Rio long, when in the innermost recesses of the mighty soul of my noble Captain of the Top—incomparable Jack Chase—the deliberate opinion was formed, and rock-founded, that our ship's company must have at least one day's "*liberty*" to go ashore ere we weighed anchor for home.

Here it must be mentioned that, concerning any thing of this kind, no sailor in a man-of-war ever presumes to be an agitator, unless he is of a rank superior to a mere able-seaman; and no one short of a petty officer—that is, a captain of the top, a quarter-gunner, or boatswain's mate—ever dreams of being a spokesman to the supreme authority of the vessel in soliciting any kind of favor for himself and shipmates.

After canvassing the matter thoroughly with several old quarter-masters and other dignified sea-fencibles, Jack, hat in hand, made his appearance, one fine evening, at the mast, and, waiting till Captain Claret drew nigh, bowed, and addressed him in his own off-hand, polished, and poetical style. In his intercourse with the quarter-deck, he always presumed upon his being such a universal favorite.

"Sir, this Rio is a charming harbor, and we poor mariners—your trusty sea-warriors, valiant Captain! who, with *you* at their head, would board the Rock of Gibraltar itself, and carry it by storm—we poor fellows, valiant

213

Captain! have gazed round upon this ravishing landscape till we can gaze no more. Will Captain Claret vouchsafe one day's liberty, and so assure himself of eternal felicity, since, in our flowing cups, he will be ever after freshly remembered?"

As Jack thus rounded off with a snatch from Shakspeare, he saluted the Captain with a gallant flourish of his tarpaulin, and then, bringing the rim to his mouth, with his head bowed, and his body thrown into a fine negligent attitude, stood a picture of eloquent but passive appeal. He seemed to say, Magnanimous Captain Claret, we fine fellows, and hearts of oak, throw ourselves upon your unparalleled goodness.

"And what do you want to go ashore for?" asked the Captain, evasively, and trying to conceal his admiration of Jack by affecting some haughtiness.

"Ah! sir," sighed Jack, "why do the thirsty camels of the desert desire to lap the waters of the fountain and roll in the green grass of the oasis? Are we not but just from the ocean Sahara? and is not this Rio a verdant spot, noble Captain? Surely you will not keep us always tethered at anchor, when a little more cable would admit of our cropping the herbage! And it is a weary thing, Captain Claret, to be imprisoned month after month on the gun-deck, without so much as smelling a citron. Ah! Captain Claret, what sings sweet Waller:

'But who can always on the billows lie?
The watery wilderness yields no supply.'

Compared with such a prisoner, noble Captain,

'Happy, thrice happy, who, in battle slain,
Press'd in Atrides' cause the Trojan plain!'

Pope's version, sir, not the original Greek."

And so saying, Jack once more brought his hat-rim to his mouth, and slightly bending forward, stood mute.

At this juncture the Most Serene Commodore himself happened to emerge from the after-gangway, his gilded buttons, epaulets, and the gold lace on his chapeau glittering in the flooding sunset. Attracted by the scene between Captain Claret and so well-known and admired a commoner as Jack Chase, he approached, and assuming for the moment an air of pleasant condescension—never shown to his noble barons the officers of the ward-room—he said, with a smile, "Well, Jack, you and your shipmates are after some favor, I suppose—a day's liberty, is it not?"

Whether it was the horizontal setting sun, streaming along the deck, that blinded Jack, or whether it was in sun-worshipping homage of the mighty Commodore, there is no telling; but just at this juncture noble Jack was standing reverentially holding his hat to his brow, like a man with weak eyes.

"Valiant Commodore," said he, at last, "this audience is indeed an honor undeserved. I almost sink beneath it. Yes, valiant Commodore, your sagacious mind has truly divined our object. Liberty, sir; liberty is, indeed, our humble prayer. I trust your honorable wound, received in glorious battle, valiant Commodore, pains you less to-day than common."

"Ah! cunning Jack!" cried the Commodore, by no means blind to the bold sortie of his flattery, but not at all displeased with it. In more respects than one, our Commodore's wound was his weak side.

"I think we must give them liberty," he added, turning to Captain Claret; who thereupon, waving Jack further off, fell into confidential discourse with his superior.

"Well, Jack, we will see about it," at last cried the Commodore, advancing. "I think we must let you go."

"To your duty, captain of the main-top!" said the Captain, rather stiffly. He wished to neutralize somewhat the effect of the Commodore's condescension. Besides, he had much rather the Commodore had been in his cabin. His presence, for the time, affected his own supremacy in his ship. But Jack was noways cast down by the Captain's coldness; he felt safe enough; so he proceeded to offer his acknowledgments.

"'Kind gentlemen,'" he sighed, "'your pains are registered where every day I turn the leaf to read'—Macbeth, valiant Commodore and Captain!—what the Thane says to the noble lords, Rosse and Angus."

And long and lingeringly bowing to the two noble officers, Jack backed away from their presence, still shading his eyes with the broad rim of his hat.

"Jack Chase forever!" cried his shipmates, as he carried the grateful news of liberty to them on the forecastle. "Who can talk to Commodores like our matchless Jack!"

Chapter 52

Something concerning Midshipmen

I

T WAS THE NEXT MORNING after matchless Jack's interview
with the Commodore and Captain, that a little incident occurred, soon
forgotten by the crew at large, but long remembered by the few seamen
who were in the habit of closely scrutinizing every-day proceedings. Upon
the face of it, it was but a common event—at least in a man-of-war—the
flogging of a man at the gangway. But the under-current of circumstances
in the case were of a nature that magnified this particular flogging into a
matter of no small importance. The story itself can not here be related; it
would not well bear recital: enough that the person flogged was a middle-
aged man of the Waist—a forlorn, broken-down, miserable object, truly;
one of those wretched landsmen sometimes driven into the Navy by their
unfitness for all things else, even as others are driven into the work-house.
He was flogged at the complaint of a midshipman; and hereby hangs the
drift of the thing. For though this waister was so ignoble a mortal, yet his
being scourged on this one occasion indirectly proceeded from the mere
wanton spite and unscrupulousness of the midshipman in question—a
youth, who was apt to indulge at times in undignified familiarities with
some of the men, who, sooner or later, almost always suffered from his
capricious preferences.

But the leading principle that was involved in this affair is far too
mischievous to be lightly dismissed.

In most cases, it would seem to be a cardinal principle with a Navy Captain that his subordinates are disintegrated parts of himself, detached from the main body on special service, and that the order of the minutest midshipman must be as deferentially obeyed by the seamen as if proceeding from the Commodore on the poop. This principle was once emphasized in a remarkable manner by the valiant and handsome Sir Peter Parker, upon whose death, on a national arson expedition on the shores of Chesapeake Bay, in 1812 or 1813, Lord Byron wrote his well-known stanzas. "By the god of war!" said Sir Peter to his sailors, "I'll make you touch your hat to a midshipman's coat, if it's only hung on a broomstick to dry!"

That the king, in the eye of the law, can do no wrong, is the well-known fiction of despotic states; but it has remained for the navies of Constitutional Monarchies and Republics to magnify this fiction, by indirectly extending it to all the quarter-deck subordinates of an armed ship's chief magistrate. And though judicially unrecognized, and unacknowledged by the officers themselves, yet this is the principle that pervades the fleet; this is the principle that is every hour acted upon, and to sustain which, thousands of seamen have been flogged at the gangway.

However childish, ignorant, stupid, or idiotic a midshipman, if he but orders a sailor to perform even the most absurd action, that man is not only bound to render instant and unanswering obedience, but he would refuse at his peril. And if, having obeyed, he should then complain to the Captain, and the Captain, in his own mind, should be thoroughly convinced of the impropriety, perhaps of the illegality of the order, yet, in nine cases out of ten, he would not publicly reprimand the midshipman, nor by the slightest token admit before the complainant that, in this particular thing, the midshipman had done otherwise than perfectly right.

Upon a midshipman's complaining of a seaman to Lord Collingwood, when Captain of a line-of-battle ship, he ordered the man for punishment; and, in the interval, calling the midshipman aside, said to him, "In all probability, now, the fault is yours—you know; therefore, when the man is brought to the mast, you had better ask for his pardon."

Accordingly, upon the lad's public intercession, Collingwood, turning to the culprit, said, "This young gentleman has pleaded so humanely for you, that, in the hope you feel a due gratitude to him for his benevolence, I will, for this time, overlook your offence." This story is related by the editor of the Admiral's "Correspondence," to show the Admiral's kind-heartedness.

Now Collingwood was, in reality, one of the most just, humane, and benevolent admirals that ever hoisted a flag. For a sea-officer, Collingwood was a man in a million. But if a man like him, swayed by old usages, could thus violate the commonest principle of justice—with however good motives at bottom—what must be expected from other Captains not so eminently gifted with noble traits as Collingwood?

And if the corps of American midshipmen is mostly replenished from the nursery, the counter, and the lap of unrestrained indulgence at home; and if most of them at least, by their impotency as officers, in all important functions at sea, by their boyish and overweening conceit of their gold lace, by their overbearing manner toward the seamen, and by their peculiar aptitude to construe the merest trivialities of manner into set affronts against their dignity; if by all this they sometimes contract the ill-will of the seamen; and if, in a thousand ways, the seamen can not but betray it— how easy for any of these midshipmen, who may happen to be unrestrained by moral principle, to resort to spiteful practices in procuring vengeance upon the offenders, in many instances to the extremity of the lash; since, as we have seen, the tacit principle in the Navy seems to be that, in his ordinary intercourse with the sailors, a midshipman can do nothing obnoxious to the public censure of his superiors.

"You fellow, I'll get you *licked* before long," is often heard from a midshipman to a sailor who, in some way not open to the judicial action of the Captain, has chanced to offend him.

At times you will see one of these lads, not five feet high, gazing up with inflamed eye at some venerable six-footer of a forecastle-man, cursing and insulting him by every epithet deemed most scandalous and un-endurable among men. Yet that man's indignant tongue is treble-knotted by the law, that suspends death itself over his head should his passion discharge the slightest blow at the boy-worm that spits at his feet.

But since what human nature is, and what it must forever continue to be, is well enough understood for most practical purposes, it needs no special example to prove that, where the merest boys, indiscriminately snatched from the human family, are given such authority over mature men, the results must be proportionable in monstrousness to the custom that authorizes this worse than cruel absurdity.

Nor is it unworthy of remark that, while the noblest-minded and most heroic sea-officers men of the topmost stature, including Lord Nelson himself—have regarded flogging in the Navy with the deepest concern, and not without weighty scruples touching its general necessity, still, one who has seen much of midshipmen can truly say that he has seen but few midshipmen who were not enthusiastic advocates and admirers of scourging. It would almost seem that they themselves, having so recently escaped the posterior discipline of the nursery and the infant school, are impatient to recover from those smarting reminiscences by mincing the backs of full-grown American freemen.

It should not be omitted here, that the midshipmen in the English Navy are not permitted to be quite so imperious as in the American ships. They are divided into three (I think) probationary classes of "volunteers," instead of being at once advanced to a warrant. Nor will you fail to remark, when you see an English cutter officered by one of these volunteers, that the boy does not so strut and slap his dirk-hilt with a Bobadil air, and anticipatingly feel of the place where his warlike whiskers are going to be, and sputter out oaths so at the men, as is too often the case with the little boys wearing best-bower anchors on their lapels in the American Navy.

Yet it must be confessed that at times you see midshipmen who are noble little fellows, and not at all disliked by the crew. Besides three gallant youths, one black-eyed little lad in particular, in the Neversink, was such a one. From his diminutiveness, he went by the name of *Boat Plug* among the seamen. Without being exactly familiar with them, he had yet become a general favorite, by reason of his kindness of manner, and never cursing them. It was amusing to hear some of the older Tritons invoke blessings upon the youngster, when his kind tones fell on their weather-beaten ears. "Ah, good luck to you, sir!" touching their hats to the little man; "you have a soul to be saved, sir!" There was a wonderful deal of meaning involved in the latter sentence. *You have a soul to be saved*, is the phrase which a man-of-war's-man peculiarly applies to a humane and kind-hearted officer. It also implies that the majority of quarter-deck officers are regarded by them in such a light that they deny to them the possession of souls. Ah! but these plebeians sometimes have a sublime vengeance upon patricians. Imagine an outcast old sailor seriously cherishing the purely speculative conceit that some bully in epaulets, who orders him to and fro like a slave, is of an organization immeasurably inferior to himself; must at last perish with the brutes, while he goes to his immortality in heaven.

But from what has been said in this chapter, it must not be inferred that a midshipman leads a lord's life in a man-of-war. Far from it. He lords it over those below him, while lorded over himself by his superiors. It is as if with one hand a school-boy snapped his fingers at a dog, and at the same time received upon the other the discipline of the usher's ferule. And though, by the American Articles of War, a Navy Captain can not, of his own authority, legally punish a midshipman, otherwise than by suspension from duty (the same as with respect to the Ward-room officers), yet this is one of those sea-statutes which the Captain, to a certain extent, observes or disregards at his pleasure. Many instances might be related of the petty mortifications and official insults inflicted by some Captains upon their midshipmen; far more severe, in one sense, than the old-fashioned punishment of sending them to the mast-head, though not so arbitrary as sending them before the mast, to do duty with the common sailors—a custom, in former times, pursued by Captains in the English Navy.

Captain Claret himself had no special fondness for midshipmen. A tall, overgrown young midshipman, about sixteen years old, having fallen under his displeasure, he interrupted the humble apologies he was making, by saying, "Not a word, sir! I'll not hear a word! Mount the netting, sir, and stand there till you are ordered to come down!"

The midshipman obeyed; and, in full sight of the entire ship's company, Captain Claret promenaded to and fro below his lofty perch, reading him a most aggravating lecture upon his alleged misconduct. To a lad of sensibility, such treatment must have been almost as stinging as the lash itself would have been.

In another case a midshipman attempted to carry the day by speaking up to his superior; but in a most unexpected manner he paid the penalty of his indiscretion.

Seeing a reefer's hammock in the quarter-netting, and observing it to be rather equivocally discolored, the Captain demanded to know what particular midshipman was the proprietor of that hammock. When the lad appeared, he said to him, "What do you call that, sir?" pointing at the discoloration.

"Captain Claret," said the unabashed reefer, looking him full in the eye, "you know what that is, sir, as well as I do."

"So I do, sir. Quarter-master! pitch that hammock overboard."

The midshipman started, and, hurrying up to it, turned round, and said, "Captain Claret, I have a purse lashed up here; it's the only safe way I can keep it."

"Did you hear me, quarter-master?" said the Captain; and overboard went the hammock and purse.

The same afternoon, this midshipman reported his *cot-boy* as having neglected to scrub this identical hammock, though repeatedly ordered to do so by his master. Though called a cot-*boy*, the person thus designated happened to be, in fact, a full-grown man. The case being fully laid before the Captain at the mast, and the midshipman's charge having been heard, this cot-boy, spite of his protestations, and altogether through the midshipman's instrumentality, was condemned to a flogging.

Thus it will be seen, that though the Captain permits himself to domineer over a midshipman, and, in cases of personal contact with him, does not scruple to pronounce him an egregious wrong-doer, and treats him accordingly; yet, in *other* cases, involving the immediate relationship between the midshipman and the sailor, he still sustains the principle that a midshipman can neither say nor do any wrong.

It is to be remembered that, wherever these chapters treat of midshipmen, the officers known as passed-midshipmen are not at all referred to. In the American Navy, these officers form a class of young men, who, having seen sufficient service at sea as midshipmen to pass an examination before a Board of Commodores, are promoted to the rank of passed-midshipmen, introductory to that of lieutenant. They are supposed to be qualified to do duty as lieutenants, and in some cases temporarily serve as such. The difference between a passed-midshipman and a midshipman may be also inferred from their respective rates of pay. The former, upon sea-service, receives $750 a year; the latter, $400. There were no passed-midshipmen in the Neversink.

Chapter 53

Sea-faring Persons peculiarly subject to being under the Weather · The Effects of this upon a Man-of-war Captain

IT HAS BEEN SAID that some midshipmen, in certain cases, are guilty of spiteful practices against the man-of-war's-man. But as these midshipmen are presumed to have received the liberal and lofty breeding of gentlemen, it would seem all but incredible that any of their corps could descend to the paltriness of cherishing personal malice against so conventionally degraded a being as a sailor. So, indeed, it would seem. But when all the circumstances are considered, it will not appear extraordinary that some of them should thus cast discredit upon the warrants they wear. Title, and rank, and wealth, and education can not unmake human nature; the same in cabin-boy and commodore, its only differences lie in the different modes of development.

At sea, a frigate houses and homes five hundred mortals in a space so contracted that they can hardly so much as move but they touch. Cut off from all those outward passing things which ashore employ the eyes, tongues, and thoughts of landsmen, the inmates of a frigate are thrown upon themselves and each other, and all their ponderings are introspective. A morbidness of mind is often the consequence, especially upon long voyages, accompanied by foul weather, calms, or head-winds. Nor does this exempt from its evil influence any rank on board. Indeed, high station only ministers to it the more, since the higher the rank in a man-of-war, the less companionship.

It is an odious, unthankful, repugnant thing to dwell upon a subject like this; nevertheless, be it said, that, through these jaundiced influences, even the captain of a frigate is, in some cases, indirectly induced to the infliction of corporal punishment upon a seaman. Never sail under a navy captain whom you suspect of being dyspeptic, or constitutionally prone to hypochondria.

The manifestation of these things is sometimes remarkable. In the earlier part of the cruise, while making a long, tedious run from Mazatlan to Callao on the Main, baffled by light head winds and frequent intermitting calms, when all hands were heartily wearied by the torrid, monotonous sea, a good-natured fore-top-man, by the name of Candy—quite a character in his way—standing in the waist among a crowd of seamen, touched me, and said, "D'ye see the old man there, White-Jacket, walking the poop? Well, don't he look as if he wanted to flog some one? Look at him once."

But to me, at least, no such indications were visible in the deportment of the Captain, though his thrashing the arm-chest with the slack of the spanker-out-haul looked a little suspicious. But any one might have been doing that to pass away a calm.

"Depend on it," said the top-man, "he must somehow have thought I was making sport of *him* a while ago, when I was only taking off old Priming, the gunner's mate. Just look at him once, White-Jacket, while I make believe coil this here rope; if there arn't a dozen in that 'ere Captain's top-lights, my name is *horse-marine*. If I could only touch my tile to him now, and take my Bible oath on it, that I was only taking off Priming, and not *him*, he wouldn't have such hard thoughts of me. But that can't be done; he'd think I meant to insult him. Well, it can't be helped; I suppose I must look out for a baker's dozen afore long."

I had an incredulous laugh at this. But two days afterward, when we were hoisting the main-top-mast stun'-sail, and the Lieutenant of the Watch was reprimanding the crowd of seamen at the halyards for their laziness—for the sail was but just crawling up to its place, owing to the languor of the men, induced by the heat—the Captain, who had been impatiently walking the deck, suddenly stopped short, and darting his eyes among the seamen, suddenly fixed them, crying out, "You, Candy, and be damned to you, you don't pull an ounce, you blackguard! Stand up to that gun, sir; I'll teach you to be grinning over a rope that way, without lending your pound of beef to it. Boatswain's mate, where's your *colt*? Give that man a dozen."

Removing his hat, the boatswain's mate looked into the crown aghast;

the coiled rope, usually worn there, was not to be found; but the next instant it slid from the top of his head to the deck. Picking it up, and straightening it out, he advanced toward the sailor.

"Sir," said Candy, touching and retouching his cap to the Captain, "I was pulling, sir, as much as the rest, sir; I was, indeed, sir."

"Stand up to that gun," cried the Captain. "Boatswain's mate, do your duty."

Three stripes were given, when the Captain raised his finger. "You ——,* do you dare stand up to be flogged with your hat on! Take it off, sir, instantly."

Candy dropped it on deck.

"Now go on, boatswain's mate." And the sailor received his dozen.

With his hand to his back he came up to me, where I stood among the by-standers, saying, "O Lord, O Lord! that boatswain's mate, too, had a spite agin me; he always thought it was *me* that set afloat that yarn about his wife in Norfolk. O Lord! just run your hand under my shirt, will you, White-Jacket? There! didn't he have a spite agin me, to raise such bars as them? And my shirt all cut to pieces, too—arn't it, White-Jacket? Damn me, but these coltings puts the tin in the Purser's pocket. O Lord! my back feels as if there was a red-hot gridiron lashed to it. But I told you so—a widow's curse on him, say I—he thought I meant *him*, and not Priming."

* The phrase here used I have never seen either written or printed, and should not like to be the first person to introduce it to the public.

Chapter 54

"The People" are given "Liberty"

WHENEVER, IN INTERVALS of mild benevolence, or yielding to mere politic dictates, Kings and Commodores relax the yoke of servitude, they should see to it well that the concession seem not too sudden or unqualified; for, in the commoner's estimation, that might argue feebleness or fear.

Hence it was, perhaps, that, though noble Jack had carried the day captive in his audience at the mast, yet more than thirty-six hours elapsed ere any thing official was heard of the "liberty" his shipmates so earnestly coveted. Some of the people began to growl and grumble.

"It's turned out all gammon, Jack," said one.

"Blast the Commodore!" cried another, "he bamboozled you, Jack."

"Lay on your oars a while," answered Jack, "and we shall see; we've struck for liberty, and liberty we'll have! I'm your tribune, boys; I'm your Rienzi. The Commodore must keep his word."

Next day, about breakfast-time, a mighty whistling and piping was heard at the main-hatchway, and presently the boatswain's voice was heard: "D'ye hear there, fore and aft! all you starboard-quarter watch! get ready to go ashore on liberty!"

In a paroxysm of delight, a young mizzen-top-man, standing by at the time, whipped the tarpaulin from his head, and smashed it like a pancake on

225

the deck. "Liberty!" he shouted, leaping down into the berth-deck after his bag.

At the appointed hour, the quarter-watch mustered round the capstan, at which stood our old First Lord of the Treasury and Pay-Master-General, the Purser, with several goodly buck-skin bags of dollars, piled up on the capstan. He helped us all round to half a handful or so, and then the boats were manned, and, like so many Esterhazys, we were pulled ashore by our shipmates. All their lives lords may live in listless state; but give the commoners a holiday, and they out-lord the Commodore himself.

The ship's company were divided into four sections or quarter-watches, only one of which were on shore at a time, the rest remaining to garrison the frigate—the term of liberty for each being twenty-four hours.

With Jack Chase and a few other discreet and gentlemanly top-men, I went ashore on the first day, with the first quarter-watch. Our own little party had a charming time; we saw many fine sights; fell in—as all sailors must—with dashing adventures. But, though not a few good chapters might be written on this head, I must again forbear; for in this book I have nothing to do with the shore further than to glance at it, now and then, from the water; my man-of-war world alone must supply me with the staple of my matter; I have taken an oath to keep afloat to the last letter of my narrative.

Had they all been as punctual as Jack Chase's party, the whole quarter-watch of liberty-men had been safe on board the frigate at the expiration of the twenty-four hours. But this was not the case; and during the entire day succeeding, the midshipmen and others were engaged in ferreting them out of their hiding-places on shore, and bringing them off in scattered detachments to the ship.

They came in all imaginable stages of intoxication; some with blackened eyes and broken heads; some still more severely injured, having been stabbed in frays with the Portuguese soldiers. Others, unharmed, were immediately dropped on the gun-deck, between the guns, where they lay snoring for the rest of the day. As a considerable degree of license is invariably permitted to man-of-war's-men just "off liberty," and as man-of-war's-men well know this to be the case, they occasionally avail themselves of the privilege to talk very frankly to the officers when they first cross the gangway, taking care, meanwhile, to reel about very industriously, so that there shall be no doubt about their being seriously intoxicated, and altogether *non compos* for the time. And though but few of them have cause to feign intoxication, yet some individuals may be suspected of enacting a studied part upon these occasions. Indeed—judging by certain symptoms—even when really inebriated, some of the sailors must have previously determined upon their conduct; just as some persons who, before taking the exhilarating gas, secretly make up their minds to perform certain mad feats while under its influence, which feats consequently come to pass precisely as if the actors were not accountable for them.

For several days, while the other quarter-watches were given liberty, the Neversink presented a sad scene. She was more like a mad-house than a frigate; the gun-deck resounded with frantic fights, shouts, and songs. All visitors from shore were kept at a cable's length.

These scenes, however, are nothing to those which have repeatedly been enacted in American men-of-war upon other stations. But the custom of introducing women on board, in harbor, is now pretty much discontinued, both in the English and American Navy, unless a ship, commanded by some dissolute Captain, happens to lie in some far away, outlandish port, in the Pacific or Indian Ocean.

The British line-of-battle ship, Royal George, which in 1782 sunk at her anchors at Spithead, carried down three hundred English women among the one thousand souls that were drowned on that memorable morning.

When, at last, after all the mad tumult and contention of "Liberty," the reaction came, our frigate presented a very different scene. The men looked jaded and wan, lethargic and lazy; and many an old mariner, with hand upon abdomen, called upon the Flag-staff to witness that there were more *hot coppers* in the Neversink than those in the ship's galley.

Such are the lamentable effects of suddenly and completely releasing *"the people"* of a man-of-war from arbitrary discipline. It shows that, to such, "liberty," at first, must be administered in small and moderate quantities, increasing with the patient's capacity to make a good use of it.

Of course, while we lay in Rio, our officers frequently went ashore for pleasure, and, as a general thing, conducted themselves with propriety. But it is a sad thing to say, that, as for Lieutenant Mad Jack, he enjoyed himself so delightfully for three consecutive days in the town, that, upon returning to the ship, he sent his card to the Surgeon, with his compliments, begging him to drop into his state-room the first time he happened to pass that way in the ward-room.

But one of our Surgeon's mates, a young medico of fine family but slender fortune, must have created by far the strongest impression among the hidalgoes of Rio. He had read Don Quixote, and, instead of curing him of his Quixotism, as it ought to have done, it only made him still more Quixotic. Indeed, there are some natures concerning whose moral maladies the grand maxim of Mr. Similia Similibus Curantur Hahneman does not hold true, since, with them, *like cures* not *like*, but only aggravates *like*. Though, on the other hand, so incurable are the moral maladies of such persons, that the antagonist maxim, *contraria contrariis curantur*, often proves equally false.

Of a warm tropical day, this Surgeon's mate must needs go ashore in his blue cloth boat-cloak, wearing it, with a gallant Spanish toss, over his cavalier shoulder. By noon, he perspired very freely; but then his cloak attracted all eyes, and that was huge satisfaction. Nevertheless, his being knock-kneed, and spavined of one leg, sorely impaired the effect of this hidalgo cloak, which, by-the-way, was somewhat rusty in front, where his chin rubbed against it, and a good deal bedraggled all over, from his having used it as a counterpane off Cape Horn.

As for the midshipmen, there is no knowing what their mammas would have said to their conduct in Rio. Three of them drank a good deal too much; and when they came on board, the Captain ordered them to be sewed up in their hammocks, to cut short their obstreperous capers till sober.

This shows how unwise it is to allow children yet in their teens to wander so far from home. It more especially illustrates the folly of giving them long holidays in a foreign land, full of seductive dissipation. Port for men, claret for boys, cried Dr. Johnson. Even so, men only should drink the strong drink of travel; boys should still be kept on milk and water at home. Middies! you may despise your mother's leading-strings, but they are the *man-ropes*, my lads, by which many youngsters have steadied the giddiness of youth, and saved themselves from lamentable falls. And middies! know this, that as infants, being too early put on their feet, grow up bandy-legged, and curtailed of their fair proportions, even so, my dear middies, does it morally prove with some of you, who prematurely are sent off to sea.

These admonitions are solely addressed to the more diminutive class of midshipmen—those under five feet high, and under seven stone in weight.

Truly, the records of the steerages of men-of-war are full of most melancholy examples of early dissipation, disease, disgrace, and death. Answer, ye shades of fine boys, who in the soils of all climes, the round world over, far away sleep from your homes.

Mothers of men! If your hearts have been cast down when your boys have fallen in the way of temptations ashore, how much more bursting your grief, did you know that those boys were, far from your arms, cabined and cribbed in by all manner of iniquities. But this some of you can not believe. It is, perhaps, well that it is so.

But, hold them fast—all those who have not yet weighed their anchors for the Navy—round and round, hitch over hitch, bind your leading-strings on them, and, clinching a ring-bolt into your chimney-jam, moor your boys fast to that best of harbors, the hearth-stone.

But if youth be giddy, old age is staid; even as young saplings, in the litheness of their limbs, toss to their roots in the fresh morning air; but, stiff and unyielding with age, mossy trunks never bend. With pride and pleasure be it said, that, as for our old Commodore, though he might treat himself to as many "*liberty days*" as he pleased, yet throughout our stay in Rio he conducted himself with the utmost discretion.

But he was an old, old man; physically, a very small man; his spine was as an unloaded musket-barrel—not only attenuated, but destitute of a solitary cartridge, and his ribs were as the ribs of a weasel.

Besides, he was Commodore of the fleet, supreme lord of the Commons in Blue. It beseemed him, therefore, to erect himself into an ensample of virtue, and show the gun-deck what virtue was. But alas! when Virtue sits high aloft on a frigate's poop, when Virtue is crowned in the cabin a Commodore, when Virtue rules by compulsion, and domineers over Vice as a slave, then Virtue, though her mandates be outwardly observed, bears little interior sway. To be efficacious, Virtue must come down from aloft, even as our blessed Redeemer came down to redeem our whole man-of-war world; to that end, mixing with its sailors and sinners as equals.

Chapter 55

Midshipmen entering the Navy early

T HE ALLUSION in the preceding chapter to the early age at which some of the midshipmen enter the Navy, suggests some thoughts relative to more important considerations.

A very general modern impression seems to be, that, in order to learn the profession of a sea-officer, a boy can hardly be sent to sea too early. To a certain extent, this may be a mistake. Other professions, involving a knowledge of technicalities and things restricted to one particular field of action, are frequently mastered by men who begin after the age of twenty-one, or even at a later period of life. It was only about the middle of the seventeenth century that the British military and naval services were kept distinct. Previous to that epoch the king's officers commanded indifferently either by sea or by land.

Robert Blake, perhaps one of the most accomplished, and certainly one of the most successful Admirals that ever hoisted a flag, was more than half a century old (fifty-one years) before he entered the naval service, or had aught to do, professionally, with a ship. He was of a studious turn, and, after leaving Oxford, resided quietly on his estate, a country gentleman, till his forty-second year, soon after which he became connected with the Parliamentary army.

The historian Clarendon says of him, "He was the first man that made it manifest that the science (seamanship) might be attained in less time than was imagined." And doubtless it was to his shore sympathies that the well-known humanity and kindness which Blake evinced in his intercourse with the sailors is in a large degree to be imputed.

Midshipmen sent into the Navy at a very early age are exposed to the passive reception of all the prejudices of the quarter-deck in favor of ancient usages, however useless or pernicious; those prejudices grow up with them, and solidify with their very bones. As they rise in rank, they naturally carry them up, whence the inveterate repugnance of many Commodores and Captains to the slightest innovations in the service, however salutary they may appear to landsmen.

It is hardly to be doubted that, in matters connected with the general welfare of the Navy, government has paid rather too much deference to the opinions of the officers of the Navy, considering them as men almost born to the service, and therefore far better qualified to judge concerning any and all questions touching it than people on shore. But in a nation under a liberal Constitution, it must ever be unwise to make too distinct and peculiar the profession of either branch of its military men. True, in a country like ours, nothing is at present to be apprehended of their gaining political rule; but not a little is to be apprehended concerning their perpetuating or creating abuses among their subordinates, unless civilians have full cognizance of their administrative affairs, and account themselves competent to the complete overlooking and ordering them.

We do wrong when we in any way contribute to the prevailing mystification that has been thrown about the internal affairs of the national sea-service. Hitherto those affairs have been regarded even by some high state functionaries as things beyond their insight—altogether too technical and mysterious to be fully comprehended by landsmen. And this it is that has perpetuated in the Navy many evils that otherwise would have been abolished in the general amelioration of other things. The army is sometimes remodeled, but the Navy goes down from generation to generation almost untouched and unquestioned, as if its code were infallible, and itself a piece of perfection that no statesman could improve. When a Secretary of the Navy ventures to innovate upon its established customs, you hear some of the Navy officers say, "What does this landsman know about our affairs? Did he ever head a watch? He does not know starboard from larboard, girt-line from back-stay."

While we deferentially and cheerfully leave to navy officers the sole conduct of making and shortening sail, tacking ship, and performing other nautical maneuvres, as may seem to them best; let us beware of abandoning to their discretion those general municipal regulations touching the well-being of the great body of men before the mast; let us beware of being too much influenced by their opinions in matters where it is but natural to suppose that their long-established prejudices are enlisted.

Chapter 56

A Shore Emperor on board a Man-of-war

WHILE WE LAY in Rio, we sometimes had company from shore; but an unforeseen honor awaited us. One day, the young Emperor, Don Pedro II., and suite—making a circuit of the harbor, and visiting all the men-of-war in rotation—at last condescendingly visited the Neversink.

He came in a splendid barge, rowed by thirty African slaves, who, after the Brazilian manner, in concert rose upright to their oars at every stroke; then sank backward again to their seats with a simultaneous groan.

He reclined under a canopy of yellow silk, looped with tassels of green, the national colors. At the stern waved the Brazilian flag, bearing a large diamond figure in the centre, emblematical, perhaps, of the mines of precious stones in the interior; or, it may be, a magnified portrait of the famous "Portuguese diamond" itself, which was found in Brazil, in the district of Tejuco, on the banks of the Rio Belmonte.

We gave them a grand salute, which almost made the ship's live-oak *knees* knock together with the tremendous concussions. We manned the yards, and went through a long ceremonial of paying the Emperor homage. Republicans are often more courteous to royalty than royalists themselves. But doubtless this springs from a noble magnanimity.

At the gangway, the Emperor was received by our Commodore in

233

person, arrayed in his most resplendent coat and finest French epaulets. His servant had devoted himself to polishing every button that morning with rotten-stone and rags—your sea air is a sworn foe to metallic glosses; whence it comes that the swords of sea-officers have, of late, so rusted in their scabbards that they are with difficulty drawn.

It was a fine sight to see this Emperor and Commodore complimenting each other. Both wore *chapeaux-de-bras*, and both continually waved them. By instinct, the Emperor knew that the venerable personage before him was as much a monarch afloat as he himself was ashore. Did not our Commodore carry the sword of state by his side? For though not borne before him, it must have been a sword of state, since it looked far too lustrous ever to have been his fighting sword. *That* was naught but a limber steel blade, with a plain, serviceable handle, like the handle of a slaughter-house knife.

Who ever saw a star when the noon sun was in sight? But you seldom see a king without satellites. In the suite of the youthful Emperor came a princely train; so brilliant with gems, that they seemed just emerged from the mines of the Rio Belmonte.

You have seen cones of crystallized salt? Just so flashed these Portuguese Barons, Marquises, Viscounts, and Counts. Were it not for their titles, and being seen in the train of their lord, you would have sworn they were eldest sons of jewelers all, who had run away with their fathers' cases on their backs.

Contrasted with these lamp-lustres of Barons of Brazil, how waned the gold lace of our barons of the frigate, the officers of the gun-room! and compared with the long, jewel-hilted rapiers of the Marquises, the little dirks of our cadets of noble houses—the middies—looked like gilded tenpenny nails in their girdles.

But there they stood! Commodore and Emperor, Lieutenants and Marquises, middies and pages! The brazen band on the poop struck up; the marine guard presented arms; and high aloft, looking down on this scene, all *the people* vigorously hurraed. A top-man next me on the main-royal-yard removed his hat, and diligently manipulated his head in honor of the event; but he was so far out of sight in the clouds, that this ceremony went for nothing.

A great pity it was, that in addition to all these honors, that admirer of Portuguese literature, Viscount Strangford, of Great Britain—who, I believe, once went out Embassador Extraordinary to the Brazils—it was a pity that he was not present on this occasion, to yield his tribute of "A

Stanza to Braganza!" For our royal visitor was an undoubted Braganza, allied to nearly all the great families of Europe. His grandfather, John VI., had been King of Portugal; his own sister, Maria, was now its queen. He was, indeed, a distinguished young gentleman, entitled to high consideration, and that consideration was most cheerfully accorded him.

He wore a green dress-coat, with one regal morning-star at the breast, and white pantaloons. In his chapeau was a single, bright, golden-hued feather of the Imperial Toucan fowl, a magnificent, omnivorous, broad-billed bandit bird of prey, a native of Brazil. Its perch is on the loftiest trees, whence it looks down upon all humbler fowls, and, hawk-like, flies at their throats. The Toucan once formed part of the savage regalia of the Indian caciques of the country, and, upon the establishment of the empire, was symbolically retained by the Portuguese sovereigns.

His Imperial Majesty was yet in his youth; rather corpulent, if any thing, with a care-free, pleasant face, and a polite, indifferent, and easy address. His manners, indeed, were entirely unexceptionable.

Now here, thought I, is a very fine lad, with very fine prospects before him. He is supreme Emperor of all these Brazils; he has no stormy night-watches to stand; he can lay abed of mornings just as long as he pleases. Any gentleman in Rio would be proud of his personal acquaintance, and the prettiest girl in all South America would deem herself honored with the least glance from the acutest angle of his eye.

Yes: this young Emperor will have a fine time of this life, even so long as he condescends to exist. Every one jumps to obey him; and see, as I live, there is an old nobleman in his suit—the Marquis d'Acarty they call him, old enough to be his grandfather—who, in the hot sun, is standing bare-headed before him, while the Emperor carries his hat on his head.

"I suppose that old gentleman, now," said a young New England tar beside me, "would consider it a great honor to put on his Royal Majesty's boots; and yet, White-Jacket, if yonder Emperor and I were to strip and jump overboard for a bath, it would be hard telling which was of the blood royal when we should once be in the water. Look you, Don Pedro II.," he added, "how do you come to be Emperor? Tell me that. You can not pull as many pounds as I on the main-topsail-halyards; you are not as tall as I; your nose is a pug, and mine is a cut-water; and how do you come to be a 'brigand,' with that thin pair of spars? A *brigand*, indeed!"

"*Braganza*, you mean," said I, willing to correct the rhetoric of so fierce a republican, and, by so doing, chastise his censoriousness.

"Braganza! *bragger* it is," he replied; "and a bragger, indeed. See that feather in his cap! See how he struts in that coat! He may well wear a green one, top-mates—he's a green-looking swab at the best."

"Hush, Jonathan," said I; "there's the *First Luff* looking up. Be still! the Emperor will hear you;" and I put my hand on his mouth.

"Take your hand away, White-Jacket," he cried; "there's no law up aloft here. I say, you Emperor—you green-horn in the green coat, there—look you, you can't raise a pair of whiskers yet; and see what a pair of homeward-bounders I have on my jowls! *Don Pedro*, eh? What's that, after all, but plain Peter—reckoned a shabby name in my country. Damn me, White-Jacket, I wouldn't call my dog Peter!"

"Clap a stopper on your jaw-tackle, will you?" cried Ringbolt, the sailor on the other side of him. "You'll be getting us all into darbies for this."

"I won't trice up my red rag for nobody," retorted Jonathan. "So you had better take a round turn with yours, Ringbolt, and let me alone, or I'll fetch you such a swat over your figure-head, you'll think a Long Wharf truck-horse kicked you with all four shoes on one hoof! You Emperor—you counter-jumping son of a gun—cock your weather eye up aloft here, and see your betters! I say, top-mates, he ain't any Emperor at all—*I'm* the rightful Emperor. Yes, by the Commodore's boots! they stole me out of my cradle here in the palace at Rio, and put that green-horn in my place. Ay, you timber-head, you, I'm Don Pedro II., and by good rights you ought to be a main-top-man here, with your fist in a tar-bucket! Look you, I say, that crown of yours ought to be on my head; or, if you don't believe *that*, just heave it into the ring once, and see who's the best man."

"What's this hurra's nest here aloft?" cried Jack Chase, coming up the t'-gallant rigging from the top-sail yard. "Can't you behave yourself, royal-yard-men, when an Emperor's on board?"

"It's this here Jonathan," answered Ringbolt; "he's been blackguarding the young nob in the green coat, there. He says Don Pedro stole his hat."

"How?"

"Crown, he means, noble Jack," said a top-man.

"Jonathan don't call himself an Emperor, does he?" asked Jack.

"Yes," cried Jonathan; "that green-horn, standing there by the Commodore, is sailing under false colors; he's an impostor, I say; he wears my crown."

"Ha! ha!" laughed Jack, now seeing into the joke, and willing to humor it; "though I'm born a Briton, boys, yet, by the mast! these Don Pedros are all Perkin Warbecks. But I say, Jonathan, my lad, don't pipe your eye now about the loss of your crown; for, look you, we all wear crowns, from our cradles to our graves, and though in *double-darbies* in the *brig*, the Commodore himself can't unking us."

"A riddle, noble Jack."

"Not a bit; every man who has a sole to his foot has a crown to his head. Here's mine;" and so saying, Jack, removing his tarpaulin, exhibited a bald spot, just about the bigness of a crown-piece, on the summit of his curly and classical head.

Chapter 57

The Emperor Reviews the People at Quarters

I BEG THEIR ROYAL HIGHNESSES' PARDONS all round, but I had almost forgotten to chronicle the fact, that with the Emperor came several other royal Princes—kings for aught we knew—since it was just after the celebration of the nuptials of a younger sister of the Brazilian monarch to some European royalty. Indeed, the Emperor and his suite formed a sort of bridal party, only the bride herself was absent.

The first reception over, the smoke of the cannonading salute having cleared away, and the martial outburst of the brass band having also rolled off to leeward, the people were called down from the yards, and the drum beat to quarters.

To quarters we went; and there we stood up by our iron bull-dogs, while our royal and noble visitors promenaded along the batteries, breaking out into frequent exclamations at our warlike array, the extreme neatness of our garments, and, above all, the extraordinary polish of the *bright-work* about the great guns, and the marvelous whiteness of the decks.

"Que gosto!" cried a Marquis, with several dry goods samples of ribbon, tallied with bright buttons, hanging from his breast

"Que gloria!" cried a crooked, coffee-colored Viscount, spreading both palms.

"Que alegria!" cried a little Count, mincingly circumnavigating a shot-box.

238

"Que contentamento he o meu!" cried the Emperor himself, complacently folding his royal arms, and serenely gazing along our ranks.

Pleasure, Glory, and *Joy*—this was the burden of the three noble courtiers. *And very pleasing indeed*—was the simple rendering of Don Pedro's imperial remark.

"Ay, ay," growled a grim rammer-and-sponger behind me; "it's all devilish fine for you nobs to look at; but what would you say if you had to holy-stone the deck yourselves, and wear out your elbows in polishing this cursed old iron, besides getting a dozen at the gangway, if you dropped a grease-spot on deck in your mess? Ay, ay, devilish fine for you, but devilish dull for us!"

In due time the drums beat the retreat, and the ship's company scattered over the decks.

Some of the officers now assumed the part of cicerones, to show the distinguished strangers the bowels of the frigate, concerning which several of them showed a good deal of intelligent curiosity. A guard of honor, detached from the marine corps, accompanied them, and they made the circuit of the berth-deck, where, at a judicious distance, the Emperor peeped down into the cable-tier, a very subterranean vault.

The Captain of the Main-Hold, who there presided, made a polite bow in the twilight, and respectfully expressed a desire for His Royal Majesty to step down and honor him with a call; but, with his handkerchief to his Imperial nose, his Majesty declined. The party then commenced the ascent to the spar-deck; which, from so great a depth in a frigate, is something like getting up to the top of Bunker Hill Monument from the basement.

While a crowd of the people was gathered about the forward part of the booms, a sudden cry was heard from below; a lieutenant came running forward to learn the cause, when an old sheet-anchor-man, standing by, after touching his hat, hitched up his waistbands, and replied, "I don't know, sir, but I'm thinking as how one o' them 'ere kings has been tumblin' down the hatchway."

And something like this it turned out. In ascending one of the narrow ladders leading from the berth-deck to the gun-deck, the Most Noble Marquis of Silva, in the act of elevating the Imperial coat-tails, so as to protect them from rubbing against the newly-painted combings of the hatchway, this Noble Marquis's sword, being an uncommonly long one, had caught between his legs, and tripped him head over heels down into the fore-passage.

"Onde ides?" (where are you going?) said his royal master, tranquilly peeping down toward the falling Marquis; "and what did you let go of my coat-tails for?" he suddenly added, in a passion, glancing round at the same time, to see if they had suffered from the unfaithfulness of his train-bearer.

"Oh, Lord!" sighed the Captain of the Fore-top, "who would be a Marquis of Silva?"

Upon being assisted to the spar-deck, the unfortunate Marquis was found to have escaped without serious harm; but, from the marked coolness of his royal master, when the Marquis drew near to apologize for his awkwardness, it was plain that he was condemned to languish for a time under the royal displeasure.

Shortly after, the Imperial party withdrew, under another grand national salute.

Chapter 58

A Quarter-deck Officer before the Mast

A S WE WERE SOMEWHAT SHORT-HANDED while we lay in Rio, we received a small draft of men from a United States sloop of war, whose three years' term of service would expire about the time of our arrival in America.

Under guard of an armed Lieutenant and four midshipmen, they came on board in the afternoon. They were immediately mustered in the starboard gangway, that Mr. Bridewell, our First Lieutenant, might take down their names, and assign them their stations.

They stood in a mute and solemn row; the officer advanced, with his memorandum-book and pencil.

My casual friend, Shakings, the holder, happened to be by at the time. Touching my arm, he said, "White-Jacket, this here reminds me of Sing-Sing, when a draft of fellows, in darbies, came on from the State Prison at Auburn for a change of scene like, you know!"

After taking down four or five names, Mr. Bridewell accosted the next man, a rather good-looking person, but, from his haggard cheek and sunken eye, he seemed to have been in the sad habit, all his life, of sitting up rather late at night, and though all sailors do certainly keep late hours enough—standing watches at midnight—yet there is no small difference between keeping late hours at sea and keeping late hours ashore.

"What's your name?" asked the officer, of this rather rakish-looking recruit.

"Mandeville, sir," said the man, courteously touching his cap. "You must remember me, sir," he added, in a low, confidential tone, strangely dashed with servility; "we sailed together once in the old Macedonian, sir. I wore an epaulet then; we had the same state-room, you know, sir. I'm your old chum, Mandeville, sir," and he again touched his cap.

"I remember an *officer* by that name," said the First Lieutenant, emphatically, "and I know *you*, fellow. But I know you henceforth for a common sailor. I can show no favoritism here. If you ever violate the ship's rules, you shall be flogged like any other seaman. I place you in the fore-top; go forward to your duty."

It seemed this Mandeville had entered the Navy when very young, and had risen to be a lieutenant, as he said. But brandy had been his bane. One night, when he had the deck of a line-of-battle ship, in the Mediterranean, he was seized with a fit of mania-a-potu, or something like that; and, being out of his senses for the time, went below and turned into his berth, leaving the deck without a commanding officer. For this unpardonable offence he was broken.

Having no fortune, and no other profession than the sea, upon his disgrace he entered the merchant-service as a chief mate; but his love of strong drink still pursuing him, he was again cashiered at sea, and degraded before the mast by the Captain. After this, in a state of intoxication, he re-entered the Navy at Pensacola as a common sailor. But all these lessons, so biting-bitter to learn, could not cure him of his sin. He had hardly been a week on board the Neversink, when he was found intoxicated with smuggled spirits. They lashed him to the gratings, and ignominiously scourged him under the eye of his old friend and comrade, the First Lieutenant.

This took place while we lay in port, which reminds me of the circumstance, that when punishment is about to be inflicted in harbor, all strangers are ordered ashore; and the sentries at the side have it in strict charge to waive off all boats drawing near.

Chapter 59

A Man-of-war Button divides two Brothers

THE CONDUCT of Mandeville, in claiming the acquaintance of the First Lieutenant under such disreputable circumstances, was strongly contrasted by the behavior of another person on board, placed for a time in a somewhat similar situation.

Among the genteel youths of the after-guard was a lad of about sixteen, a very handsome young fellow, with starry eyes, curly hair of a golden color, and a bright, sunshiny complexion: he must have been the son of some goldsmith. He was one of the few sailors—not in the main-top— whom I used to single out for occasional conversation. After several friendly interviews he became quite frank, and communicated certain portions of his history. There is some charm in the sea, which induces most persons to be very communicative concerning themselves.

We had lain in Rio but a day, when I observed that this lad—whom I shall here call Frank—wore an unwonted expression of sadness, mixed with apprehension. I questioned him as to the cause, but he chose to conceal it. Not three days after, he abruptly accosted me on the gun-deck, where I happened to be taking a promenade.

"I can't keep it to myself any more," he said; "I must have a confidant, or I shall go mad!"

"What is the matter?" said I, in alarm.

"Matter enough—look at this!" and he handed me a torn half sheet of an old New York Herald, putting his finger upon a particular word in a particular paragraph. It was the announcement of the sailing from the Brooklyn Navy-yard of a United States Store Ship, with provisions for the squadron in Rio. It was upon a particular name, in the list of officers and midshipmen, that Frank's finger was placed.

"That is my own brother," said he; "he must have got a reefer's warrant since I left home. Now, White-Jacket, what's to be done? I have calculated that the Store Ship may be expected here every day; my brother will then see me—he an officer and I a miserable sailor that any moment may be flogged at the gangway, before his very eyes. Heavens! White-Jacket, what shall I do? Would you run? Do you think there is any chance to desert? I won't see him, by Heaven, with this sailor's frock on, and he with the anchor button!"

"Why, Frank," said I, "I do not really see sufficient cause for this fit you are in. Your brother is an officer—very good; and you are nothing but a sailor—but that is no disgrace. If he comes on board here, go up to him, and take him by the hand; believe me, he will be glad enough to see you!"

Frank started from his desponding attitude, and fixing his eyes full upon mine, with clasped hands exclaimed, "White-Jacket, I have been from home nearly three years; in that time I have never heard one word from my family, and, though God knows how I love them, yet I swear to you, that though my brother can tell me whether my sisters are still alive, yet, rather than accost him in this *lined-frock*, I would go ten centuries without hearing one syllable from home!"

Amazed at his earnestness, and hardly able to account for it altogether, I stood silent a moment; then said, "Why, Frank, this midshipman is your own brother, you say; now, do you really think that your own flesh and blood is going to give himself airs over you, simply because he sports large brass buttons on his coat? Never believe it. If he does, he can be no brother, and ought to be hanged—that's all!"

"Don't say that again," said Frank, resentfully; "my brother is a noble-hearted fellow; I love him as I do myself. You don't understand me, White-Jacket; don't you see, that when my brother arrives, he must consort more or less with our chuckle-headed reefers on board here? There's that namby-pamby Miss Nancy of a white-face, Stribbles, who, the other day, when Mad Jack's back was turned, ordered me to hand him the spy-glass, as if he were a Commodore. Do you suppose, now, I want my brother to see me a lackey aboard here? By Heaven, it is enough to drive one distracted! What's to be done?" he cried, fiercely.

Much more passed between us, but all my philosophy was in vain, and at last Frank departed, his head hanging down in despondency.

For several days after, whenever the quarter-master reported a sail entering the harbor, Frank was foremost in the rigging to observe it. At length, one afternoon, a vessel drawing near was reported to be the long-expected store ship. I looked round for Frank on the spar-deck, but he was nowhere to be seen. He must have been below, gazing out of a port-hole. The vessel was hailed from our poop, and came to anchor within a biscuit's toss of our batteries.

That evening I heard that Frank had ineffectually endeavored to get removed from his place as an oarsman in the First-Cutter—a boat which, from its size, is generally employed with the *launch* in carrying ship-stores. When I thought that, the very next day, perhaps, this boat would be plying between the store ship and our frigate, I was at no loss to account for Frank's attempts to get rid of his oar, and felt heartily grieved at their failure.

Next morning the bugler called away the First-Cutter's crew, and Frank entered the boat with his hat slouched over his eyes. Upon his return, I was all eagerness to learn what had happened, and, as the communication of his feelings was a grateful relief, he poured his whole story into my ear.

It seemed that, with his comrades, he mounted the store ship's side, and hurried forward to the forecastle. Then, turning anxiously toward the quarter-deck, he spied two midshipmen leaning against the bulwarks, conversing. One was the officer of his boat—was the other his brother? No; he was too tall—too large. Thank Heaven! it was *not* him. And perhaps his brother had not sailed from home, after all; there might have been some mistake. But suddenly the strange midshipman laughed aloud, and that laugh Frank had heard a thousand times before. It was a free, hearty laugh— a brother's laugh; but it carried a pang to the heart of poor Frank.

He was now ordered down to the main-deck to assist in removing the stores. The boat being loaded, he was ordered into her, when, looking toward the gangway, he perceived the two midshipmen lounging upon each side of it, so that no one could pass them without brushing their persons. But again pulling his hat over his eyes, Frank, darting between them, gained his oar. "How my heart thumped," he said, "when I actually *felt* him so near me; but I wouldn't look at him—no! I'd have died first!"

To Frank's great relief, the store ship at last moved further up the bay, and it fortunately happened that he saw no more of his brother while in Rio; and while there, he never in any way made himself known to him.

Chapter 60

A Man-of-war's-man Shot at

T HERE WAS A SEAMAN belonging to the fore-top—a mess-
mate, though not a top-mate of mine, and no favorite of the
Captain's—who, for certain venial transgressions, had been prohibited from going ashore on liberty when the ship's company went.
Enraged at the deprivation—for he had not touched earth in upward of a
year—he, some nights after, lowered himself overboard, with the view of
gaining a canoe, attached by a rope to a Dutch galiot some cables'-length
distant. In this canoe he proposed paddling himself ashore. Not being a
very expert swimmer, the commotion he made in the water attracted the
ear of the sentry on that side of the ship, who, turning about in his walk,
perceived the faint white spot where the fugitive was swimming in the
frigate's shadow. He hailed it; but no reply.

"Give the word, or I fire!"

Not a word was heard.

The next instant there was a red flash, and, before it had completely
ceased illuminating the night, the white spot was changed into crimson.
Some of the officers, returning from a party at the Beach of the Flamingoes,
happened to be drawing near the ship in one of her cutters. They saw the
flash, and the bounding body it revealed. In a moment the top-man was
dragged into the boat, a handkerchief was used for a tourniquet, and the

246

wounded fugitive was soon on board the frigate, when, the surgeon being called, the necessary attentions were rendered.

Now, it appeared, that at the moment the sentry fired, the top-man—in order to elude discovery, by manifesting the completest quietude—was floating on the water, straight and horizontal, as if reposing on a bed. As he was not far from the ship at the time, and the sentry was considerably elevated above him—pacing his platform, on a level with the upper part of the hammock-nettings—the ball struck with great force, with a downward obliquity, entering the right thigh just above the knee, and, penetrating some inches, glanced upward along the bone, burying itself somewhere, so that it could not be felt by outward manipulation. There was no dusky discoloration to mark its internal track, as in the case when a partly-spent ball—obliquely hitting—after entering the skin, courses on, just beneath the surface, without penetrating further. Nor was there any mark on the opposite part of the thigh to denote its place, as when a ball forces itself straight through a limb, and lodges, perhaps, close to the skin on the other side. Nothing was visible but a small, ragged puncture, bluish about the edges, as if the rough point of a tenpenny nail had been forced into the flesh, and withdrawn. It seemed almost impossible, that through so small an aperture, a musket-bullet could have penetrated.

The extreme misery and general prostration of the man, caused by the great effusion of blood—though, strange to say, at first he said he felt no pain from the wound itself—induced the Surgeon, very reluctantly, to forego an immediate search for the ball, to extract it, as that would have involved the dilating of the wound by the knife; an operation which, at that juncture, would have been almost certainly attended with fatal results. A day or two, therefore, was permitted to pass, while simple dressings were applied.

The Surgeons of the other American ships of war in harbor occasionally visited the Neversink, to examine the patient, and incidentally to listen to the expositions of our own Surgeon, their senior in rank. But Cadwallader Cuticle, who, as yet, has been but incidentally alluded to, now deserves a chapter by himself.

Chapter 61

The Surgeon of the Fleet

CADWALLADER CUTICLE, M.D., and Honorary Member of the most distinguished Colleges of Surgeons both in Europe and America, was our Surgeon of the Fleet. Nor was he at all blind to the dignity of his position; to which, indeed, he was rendered peculiarly competent, if the reputation he enjoyed was deserved. He had the name of being the foremost Surgeon in the Navy, a gentleman of remarkable science, and a veteran practitioner.

He was a small, withered man, nearly, perhaps quite, sixty years of age. His chest was shallow, his shoulders bent, his pantaloons hung round skeleton legs, and his face was singularly attenuated. In truth, the corporeal vitality of this man seemed, in a good degree, to have died out of him. He walked abroad, a curious patch-work of life and death, with a wig, one glass eye, and a set of false teeth, while his voice was husky and thick; but his mind seemed undebilitated as in youth; it shone out of his remaining eye with basilisk brilliancy.

Like most old physicians and surgeons who have seen much service, and have been promoted to high professional place for their scientific attainments, this Cuticle was an enthusiast in his calling. In private, he had once been heard to say, confidentially, that he would rather cut off a man's arm than dismember the wing of the most delicate pheasant. In particular, the

248

department of Morbid Anatomy was his peculiar love; and in his state-room below he had a most unsightly collection of Parisian casts, in plaster and wax, representing all imaginable malformations of the human members, both organic and induced by disease. Chief among these was a cast, often to be met with in the Anatomical Museums of Europe, and no doubt an unexaggerated copy of a genuine original; it was the head of an elderly woman, with an aspect singularly gentle and meek, but at the same time wonderfully expressive of a gnawing sorrow, never to be relieved. You would almost have thought it the face of some abbess, for some unspeakable crime voluntarily sequestered from human society, and leading a life of agonized penitence without hope; so marvelously sad and tearfully pitiable was this head. But when you first beheld it, no such emotions ever crossed your mind. All your eyes and all your horrified soul were fast fascinated and frozen by the sight of a hideous, crumpled horn, like that of a ram, downward growing out from the forehead, and partly shadowing the face; but as you gazed, the freezing fascination of its horribleness gradually waned, and then your whole heart burst with sorrow, as you contemplated those aged features, ashy pale and wan. The horn seemed the mark of a curse for some mysterious sin, conceived and committed before the spirit had entered the flesh. Yet that sin seemed something imposed, and not voluntarily sought; some sin growing out of the heartless necessities of the predestination of things; some sin under which the sinner sank in sinless woe.

But no pang of pain, not the slightest touch of concern, ever crossed the bosom of Cuticle when he looked on this cast. It was immovably fixed to a bracket, against the partition of his state-room, so that it was the first object that greeted his eyes when he opened them from his nightly sleep. Nor was it to hide the face, that upon retiring, he always hung his Navy cap upon the upward curling extremity of the horn, for that obscured it but little.

The Surgeon's cot-boy, the lad who made up his swinging bed and took care of his room, often told us of the horror he sometimes felt when he would find himself alone in his master's retreat. At times he was seized with the idea that Cuticle was a preternatural being; and once entering his room in the middle watch of the night, he started at finding it enveloped in a thick, bluish vapor, and stifling with the odors of brimstone. Upon hearing a low groan from the smoke, with a wild cry he darted from the place, and, rousing the occupants of the neighboring state-rooms, it was found that the vapor proceeded from smoldering bunches of Luciter matches, which had become ignited through the carelessness of the Surgeon. Cuticle, almost dead, was dragged from the suffocating atmosphere, and it was several days ere he completely recovered from its effects. This accident took place immediately over the powder magazine; but as Cuticle, during his sickness, paid dearly enough for transgressing the laws prohibiting combustibles in the gun-room, the Captain contented himself with privately remonstrating with him.

Well knowing the enthusiasm of the Surgeon for all specimens of morbid anatomy, some of the ward-room officers used to play upon his credulity, though, in every case, Cuticle was not long in discovering their deceptions. Once, when they had some sago pudding for dinner, and Cuticle chanced to be ashore, they made up a neat parcel of this bluish-white, firm, jelly-like preparation, and placing it in a tin box, carefully sealed with wax, they deposited it on the gun-room table, with a note, purporting to come from an eminent physician in Rio, connected with the Grand National Museum on the Praca d'Acclamacao, begging leave to present the scientific Senhor Cuticle—with the donor's compliments—an uncommonly fine specimen of a cancer.

Descending to the ward-room, Cuticle spied the note, and no sooner read it, than, clutching the case, he opened it, and exclaimed, "Beautiful! splendid! I have never seen a finer specimen of this most interesting disease."

"What have you there, Surgeon Cuticle?" said a Lieutenant, advancing.

"Why, sir, look at it; did you ever see any thing more exquisite?"

"Very exquisite indeed; let me have a bit of it, will you, Cuticle?"

"Let you have a bit of it!" shrieked the Surgeon, starting back. "Let you have one of my limbs! I wouldn't mar so large a specimen for a hundred dollars; but what can you want of it? You are not making collections!"

"I'm fond of the article," said the Lieutenant; "it's a fine cold relish to bacon or ham. You know, I was in New Zealand last cruise, Cuticle, and got into sad dissipation there among the cannibals; come, let's have a bit, if it's only a mouthful."

"Why, you infernal Feejee!" shouted Cuticle, eyeing the other with a confounded expression; "you don't really mean to eat a piece of this cancer?"

"Hand it to me, and see whether I will not," was the reply.

"In God's name, take it!" cried the Surgeon, putting the case into his hands, and then standing with his own uplifted.

"Steward!" cried the Lieutenant, "the castor—quick! I always use plenty of pepper with this dish, Surgeon; it's oystery. Ah! this is really delicious," he added, smacking his lips over a mouthful. "Try it now, Surgeon, and you'll never keep such a fine dish as this, lying uneaten on your hands, as a mere scientific curiosity."

Cuticle's whole countenance changed; and, slowly walking up to the table, he put his nose close to the tin case, then touched its contents with his finger and tasted it. Enough. Buttoning up his coat, in all the tremblings of an old man's rage he burst from the ward-room, and, calling for a boat, was not seen again for twenty-four hours.

But though, like all other mortals, Cuticle was subject at times to these fits of passion—at least under outrageous provocation—nothing could exceed his coolness when actually employed in his eminent vocation. Surrounded by moans and shrieks, by features distorted with anguish inflicted by himself, he yet maintained a countenance almost supernaturally calm; and unless the intense interest of the operation flushed his wan face with a momentary tinge of professional enthusiasm, he toiled away, untouched by the keenest misery coming under a fleet-surgeon's eye. Indeed, long habituation to the dissecting-room and the amputation-table had made him seemingly impervious to the ordinary emotions of humanity. Yet you could not say that Cuticle was essentially a cruel-hearted man. His apparent heartlessness must have been of a purely scientific origin. It is not to be imagined even that Cuticle would have harmed a fly, unless he could procure a microscope powerful enough to assist him in experimenting on the minute vitals of the creature.

But notwithstanding his marvelous indifference to the sufferings of his patients, and spite even of his enthusiasm in his vocation—not cooled by frosting old age itself—Cuticle, on some occasions, would affect a certain disrelish of his profession, and declaim against the necessity that forced a man of his humanity to perform a surgical operation. Especially was it apt to be thus with him, when the case was one of more than ordinary interest. In discussing it, previous to setting about it, he would vail his eagerness under an aspect of great circumspection, curiously marred, however, by continual sallies of unsuppressible impatience. But the knife once in his hand, the compassionless surgeon himself, undisguised, stood before you. Such was Cadwallader Cuticle, our Surgeon of the Fleet.

Chapter 62

A Consultation of Man-of-war Surgeons

I T SEEMS CUSTOMARY for the Surgeon of the Fleet, when any
important operation in his department is on the anvil, and there is
nothing to absorb professional attention from it, to invite his brother
surgeons, if at hand at the time, to a ceremonious consultation upon it. And
this, in courtesy, his brother surgeons expect.

In pursuance of this custom, then, the surgeons of the neighboring
American ships of war were requested to visit the Neversink in a body, to
advise concerning the case of the top-man, whose situation had now become
critical. They assembled on the half-deck, and were soon joined by their
respected senior, Cuticle. In a body they bowed as he approached, and
accosted him with deferential regard.

"Gentlemen," said Cuticle, unostentatiously seating himself on a camp-
stool, handed him by his cot-boy, "we have here an extremely interesting
case. You have all seen the patient, I believe. At first I had hopes that I
should have been able to cut down to the ball, and remove it; but the state
of the patient forbade. Since then, the inflammation and sloughing of the
part has been attended with a copious suppuration, great loss of substance,
extreme debility and emaciation. From this, I am convinced that the ball
has shattered and deadened the bone, and now lies impacted in the medullary
canal. In fact, there can be no doubt that the wound is incurable, and that

amputation is the only resource. But, gentlemen, I find myself placed in a very delicate predicament. I assure you I feel no professional anxiety to perform the operation. I desire your advice, and if you will now again visit the patient with me, we can then return here, and decide what is best to be done. Once more, let me say, that I feel no personal anxiety whatever to use the knife."

The assembled surgeons listened to this address with the most serious attention, and, in accordance with their superior's desire, now descended to the sick-bay, where the patient was languishing. The examination concluded, they returned to the half-deck, and the consultation was renewed.

"Gentlemen," began Cuticle, again seating himself, "you have now just inspected the limb; you have seen that there is no resource but amputation; and now, gentlemen, what do you say? Surgeon Bandage, of the Mohawk, will you express your opinion?"

"The wound is a very serious one," said Bandage—a corpulent man, with a high German forehead—shaking his head solemnly.

"Can any thing save him but amputation?" demanded Cuticle.

"His constitutional debility is extreme," observed Bandage, "but I have seen more dangerous cases."

"Surgeon Wedge, of the Malay," said Cuticle, in a pet, "be pleased to give *your* opinion; and let it be definitive, I entreat:" this was said with a severe glance toward Bandage.

"If I thought," began Wedge, a very spare, tall man, elevating himself still higher on his toes, "that the ball had shattered and divided the whole *femur*, including the *Greater* and *Lesser Trochanter*, the *Linear aspera*, the *Digital fossa*, and the *Intertrochanteric*, I should certainly be in favor of amputation; but that, sir, permit me to observe, is not my opinion."

"Surgeon Sawyer, of the Buccaneer," said Cuticle, drawing in his thin lower lip with vexation, and turning to a round-faced, florid, frank, sensible-looking man, whose uniform coat very handsomely fitted him, and was adorned with an unusual quantity of gold lace; "Surgeon Sawyer, of the Buccaneer, let us now hear *your* opinion, if you please. Is not amputation the only resource, sir?"

"Excuse me," said Sawyer, "I am decidedly opposed to it; for if hitherto the patient has not been strong enough to undergo the extraction of the ball, I do not see how he can be expected to endure a far more severe operation. As there is no immediate danger of mortification, and you say the ball can not be reached without making large incisions, I should support him, I think, for the present, with tonics, and gentle antiphlogistics, locally applied. On no account would I proceed to amputation until further symptoms are exhibited."

"Surgeon Patella, of the Algerine," said Cuticle, in an ill-suppressed passion, abruptly turning round on the person addressed, "will *you* have the kindness to say whether *you* do not think that amputation is the only resource?"

Now Patella was the youngest of the company, a modest man, filled with a profound reverence for the science of Cuticle, and desirous of gaining his good opinion, yet not wishing to commit himself altogether by a decided reply, though, like Surgeon Sawyer, in his own mind he might have been clearly against the operation.

"What you have remarked, Mr. Surgeon of the Fleet," said Patella, respectfully hemming, "concerning the dangerous condition of the limb, seems obvious enough; amputation would certainly be a cure to the wound; but then, as, notwithstanding his present debility, the patient seems to have a strong constitution, he might rally as it is, and by your scientific treatment, Mr. Surgeon of the Fleet"—bowing—"be entirely made whole, without risking an amputation. Still, it is a very critical case, and amputation may be indispensable; and if it *is* to be performed, there ought to be no delay whatever. That is my view of the case, Mr. Surgeon of the Fleet."

"Surgeon Patella, then, gentlemen," said Cuticle, turning round triumphantly, "is clearly of opinion that amputation should be immediately performed. For my own part—individually, I mean, and without respect to the patient—I am sorry to have it so decided. But this settles the question, gentlemen—in my own mind, however, it was settled before. At ten o'clock to-morrow morning the operation will be performed. I shall be happy to see you all on the occasion, and also your juniors" (alluding to the absent *Assistant Surgeons*). "Good-morning, gentlemen; at ten o'clock, remember."

And Cuticle retreated to the Ward-room.

Chapter 63

The Operation

NEXT MORNING, at the appointed hour, the surgeons arrived in a body. They were accompanied by their juniors, young men ranging in age from nineteen years to thirty. Like the senior surgeons, these young gentlemen were arrayed in their blue navy uniforms, displaying a profusion of bright buttons, and several broad bars of gold lace about the wristbands. As in honor of the occasion, they had put on their best coats; they looked exceedingly brilliant.

The whole party immediately descended to the half-deck, where preparations had been made for the operation. A large garrison-ensign was stretched across the ship by the main-mast, so as completely to screen the space behind. This space included the whole extent aft to the bulk-head of the Commodore's cabin, at the door of which the marine-orderly paced, in plain sight, cutlass in hand.

Upon two gun-carriages, dragged amidships, the Death-board (used for burials at sea) was horizontally placed, covered with an old royal-stun'-sail. Upon this occasion, to do duty as an amputation-table, it was widened by an additional plank Two match-tubs, near by, placed one upon another, at either end supported another plank, distinct from the table, whereon was exhibited an array of saws and knives of various and peculiar shapes and sizes; also, a sort of steel, something like the dinner-table implement, together with long needles, crooked at the end for taking up the arteries, and large darning-needles, thread and bee's-wax, for sewing up a wound.

At the end nearest the larger table was a tin basin of water, surrounded by small sponges, placed at mathematical intervals. From the long horizontal pole of a great-gun rammer—fixed in its usual place overhead—hung a number of towels, with "U. S." marked in the corners.

All these arrangements had been made by the "Surgeon's steward," a person whose important functions in a man-of-war will, in a future chapter, be entered upon at large. Upon the present occasion, he was bustling about, adjusting and readjusting the knives, needles, and carver, like an over-conscientious butler fidgeting over a dinner-table just before the convivialists enter.

But by far the most striking object to be seen behind the ensign was a human skeleton, whose every joint articulated with wires. By a rivet at the apex of the skull, it hung dangling from a hammock-hook fixed in a beam above. Why this object was here, will presently be seen; but why it was placed immediately at the foot of the amputation-table, only Surgeon Cuticle can tell.

While the final preparations were being made, Cuticle stood conversing with the assembled Surgeons and Assistant Surgeons, his invited guests.

"Gentlemen," said he, taking up one of the glittering knives and artistically drawing the steel across it; "Gentlemen, though these scenes are very unpleasant, and in some moods, I may say, repulsive to me—yet how much better for our patient to have the contusions and lacerations of his present wound—with all its dangerous symptoms—converted into a clean incision, free from these objections, and occasioning so much less subsequent anxiety to himself and the Surgeon. Yes," he added, tenderly feeling the edge of his knife, "amputation is our only resource. Is it not so, Surgeon Patella?" turning toward that gentleman, as if relying upon some sort of an assent, however clogged with conditions.

"Certainly," said Patella, "amputation is your only resource, Mr. Surgeon of the Fleet; that is, I mean, if you are fully persuaded of its necessity."

The other surgeons said nothing, maintaining a somewhat reserved air, as if conscious that they had no positive authority in the case, whatever might be their own private opinions; but they seemed willing to behold, and, if called upon, to assist at the operation, since it could not now be averted.

The young men, their Assistants, looked very eager, and cast frequent glances of awe upon so distinguished a practitioner as the venerable Cuticle.

"They say he can drop a leg in one minute and ten seconds from the moment the knife touches it," whispered one of them to another.

"We shall see," was the reply, and the speaker clapped his hand to his fob, to see if his watch would be forthcoming when wanted.

"Are you all ready here?" demanded Cuticle, now advancing to his steward; "have not those fellows got through yet?" pointing to three men of the carpenter's gang, who were placing bits of wood under the gun-carriages supporting the central table.

"They are just through, sir," respectfully answered the Steward, touching his hand to his forehead, as if there were a cap-front there.

"Bring up the patient, then," said Cuticle.

"Young gentlemen," he added, turning to the row of Assistant Surgeons, "seeing you here reminds me of the classes of students once under my instruction at the Philadelphia College of Physicians and Surgeons. Ah, those were happy days!" he sighed, applying the extreme corner of his handkerchief to his glass eye. "Excuse an old man's emotions, young gentlemen; but when I think of the numerous rare cases that then came under my treatment, I can not but give way to my feelings. The town, the city, the metropolis, young gentlemen, is the place for you students; at least in these dull times of peace, when the army and navy furnish no inducements for a youth ambitious of rising in our honorable profession. Take an old man's advice, and if the war now threatening between the States and Mexico should break out, exchange your Navy commissions for commissions in the army. From having no military marine herself, Mexico has always been backward in furnishing subjects for the amputation-tables of foreign navies. The cause of science has languished in her hands. The army, young gentlemen, is your best school; depend upon it. You will hardly believe it, Surgeon Bandage," turning to that gentleman, "but this is my first important case of surgery in a nearly three years' cruise. I have been almost wholly confined in this ship to doctor's practice—prescribing for fevers and fluxes. True, the other day a man fell from the mizzen-top-sail yard; but that was merely an aggravated case of dislocations and bones splintered and broken. No one, sir, could have made an amputation of it, without severely contusing his conscience. And mine—I may say it, gentlemen, without ostentation—is peculiarly susceptible."

And so saying, the knife and carver touchingly dropped to his sides, and he stood for a moment fixed in a tender reverie. But a commotion being heard beyond the curtain, he started, and, briskly crossing and recrossing the knife and carver, exclaimed, "Ah, here comes our patient; surgeons, this side of the table, if you please; young gentlemen, a little further off, I beg. Steward, take off my coat—so; my neckerchief now; I must be perfectly unencumbered, Surgeon Patella, or I can do nothing whatever."

These articles being removed, he snatched off his wig, placing it on the gun-deck capstan; then took out his set of false teeth, and placed it by the side of the wig; and, lastly, putting his forefinger to the inner angle of his blind eye, spirted out the glass optic with professional dexterity, and deposited that, also, next to the wig and false teeth.

Thus divested of nearly all inorganic appurtenances, what was left of the Surgeon slightly shook itself, to see whether any thing more could be spared to advantage.

"Carpenter's mates," he now cried, "will you never get through with that job?"

"Almost through, sir—just through," they replied, staring round in search of the strange, unearthly voice that addressed them; for the absence of his teeth had not at all improved the conversational tones of the Surgeon of the Fleet.

With natural curiosity, these men had purposely been lingering, to see all they could; but now, having no further excuse, they snatched up their hammers and chisels, and—like the stage-builders decamping from a public meeting at the eleventh hour, after just completing the rostrum in time for the first speaker—the Carpenter's gang withdrew.

The broad ensign now lifted, revealing a glimpse of the crowd of man-of-war's-men outside, and the patient, borne in the arms of two of his mess-mates, entered the place. He was much emaciated, weak as an infant, and every limb visibly trembled, or rather jarred, like the head of a man with the palsy. As if an organic and involuntary apprehension of death had seized the wounded leg, its nervous motions were so violent that one of the mess-mates was obliged to keep his hand upon it.

The top-man was immediately stretched upon the table, the attendants steadying his limbs, when, slowly opening his eyes, he glanced about at the glittering knives and saws, the towels and sponges, the armed sentry at the Commodore's cabin-door, the row of eager-eyed students, the meagre death's-head of a Cuticle, now with his shirt sleeves rolled up upon his withered arms and knife in hand, and, finally, his eye settled in horror upon the skeleton, slowly vibrating and jingling before him, with the slow, slight roll of the frigate in the water.

"I would advise perfect repose of your every limb, my man," said Cuticle, addressing him; "the precision of an operation is often impaired by the inconsiderate restlessness of the patient. But if you consider, my good fellow," he added, in a patronizing and almost sympathetic tone, and slightly pressing his hand on the limb, "if you consider how much better it is to live with three limbs than to die with four, and especially if you but knew to what torments both sailors and soldiers were subjected before the time of Celsus, owing to the lamentable ignorance of surgery then prevailing, you would certainly thank God from the bottom of your heart that *your* operation has been postponed to the period of this enlightened age, blessed with a Bell, a Brodie, and a Larrey. My man, before Celsus's time, such was the general ignorance of our noble science, that, in order to prevent the excessive effusion of blood, it was deemed indispensable to operate with a red-hot knife"—making a professional movement toward the thigh—"and pour scalding oil upon the parts"—elevating his elbow, as if with a tea-pot in his hand—"still further to sear them, after amputation had been performed."

"He is fainting!" said one of his mess-mates; "quick! some water!" The steward immediately hurried to the top-man with the basin.

Cuticle took the top-man by the wrist, and feeling it a while, observed, "Don't be alarmed, men," addressing the two mess-mates; "he'll recover presently; this fainting very generally takes place." And he stood for a moment, tranquilly eying the patient.

Now the Surgeon of the Fleet and the top-man presented a spectacle which, to a reflecting mind, was better than a church-yard sermon on the mortality of man.

Here was a sailor, who, four days previous, had stood erect—a pillar of life—with an arm like a royal-mast and a thigh like a windlass. But the slightest conceivable finger-touch of a bit of crooked trigger had eventuated in stretching him out, more helpless than an hour-old babe, with a blasted thigh, utterly drained of its brawn. And who was it that now stood over him like a superior being, and, as if clothed himself with the attributes of immortality, indifferently discoursed of carving up his broken flesh, and thus piecing out his abbreviated days? Who was it, that in capacity of Surgeon, seemed enacting the part of a Regenerator of life? The withered, shrunken, one-eyed, toothless, hairless Cuticle; with a trunk half dead—a *memento mori* to behold!

And while, in those soul-sinking and panic-striking premonitions of speedy death which almost invariably accompany a severe gun-shot wound, even with the most intrepid spirits; while thus drooping and dying, this once robust top-man's eye was now waning in his head like a Lapland moon being eclipsed in clouds—Cuticle, who for years had still lived in his withered tabernacle of a body—Cuticle, no doubt sharing in the common self-delusion of old age—Cuticle must have felt his hold of life as secure as the grim hug of a grizzly bear. Verily, Life is more awful than Death; and let no man, though his live heart beat in him like a cannon—let him not hug his life to himself; for, in the predestinated necessities of things, that bounding life of his is not a whit more secure than the life of a man on his death-bed. To-day we inhale the air with expanding lungs, and life runs through us like a thousand Niles; but to-morrow we may collapse in death, and all our veins be dry as the Brook Kedron in a drought.

"And now, young gentlemen," said Cuticle, turning to the Assistant Surgeons, "while the patient is coming to, permit me to describe to you the highly-interesting operation I am about to perform."

"Mr. Surgeon of the Fleet," said Surgeon Bandage, "if you are about to lecture, permit me to present you with your teeth; they will make your discourse more readily understood." And so saying, Bandage, with a bow, placed the two semicircles of ivory into Cuticle's hands.

"Thank you, Surgeon Bandage," said Cuticle, and slipped the ivory into its place.

"In the first place, now, young gentlemen, let me direct your attention to the excellent preparation before you. I have had it unpacked from its case, and set up here from my state-room, where it occupies the spare berth; and all this for your express benefit, young gentlemen. This skeleton I procured in person from the Hunterian department of the Royal College of Surgeons in London. It is a master-piece of art. But we have no time to examine it now. Delicacy forbids that I should amplify at a juncture like this"—casting an almost benignant glance toward the patient, now beginning to open his eyes; "but let me point out to you upon this thigh-bone"—disengaging it from the skeleton, with a gentle twist—"the precise place where I propose to perform the operation. *Here*, young gentlemen, *here* is the place. You perceive it is very near the point of articulation with the trunk."

"Yes," interposed Surgeon Wedge, rising on his toes, "yes, young gentlemen, the point of articulation with the *acetabulum* of the *os innominatum.*"

"Where's your 'Bell on Bones,' Dick?" whispered one of the assistants to the student next him. "Wedge has been spending the whole morning over it, getting out the hard names."

"Surgeon Wedge," said Cuticle, looking round severely, "we will dispense with your commentaries, if you please, at present. Now, young gentlemen, you can not but perceive, that the point of operation being so near the trunk and the vitals, it becomes an unusually beautiful one, demanding a steady hand and a true eye; and, after all, the patient may die under my hands."

"Quick, Steward! water, water; he's fainting again!" cried the two mess-mates.

"Don't be alarmed for your comrade, men," said Cuticle, turning round. "I tell you it is not an uncommon thing for the patient to betray some emotion upon these occasions—most usually manifested by swooning; it is quite natural it should be so. But we must not delay the operation. Steward, that knife—no, the next one—there, that's it. He is coming to, I think"—feeling the top-man's wrist. "Are you all ready, sir?"

This last observation was addressed to one of the Neversink's assistant surgeons, a tall, lank, cadaverous young man, arrayed in a sort of shroud of white canvass, pinned about his throat, and completely enveloping his person. He was seated on a match-tub—the skeleton swinging near his head —at the foot of the table, in readiness to grasp the limb, as when a plank is being severed by a carpenter and his apprentice.

"The sponges, Steward," said Cuticle, for the last time taking out his teeth, and drawing up his shirt sleeve still further. Then, taking the patient by the wrist, "Stand by, now, you mess-mates; keep hold of his arms; pin him down. Steward, put your hand on the artery; I shall commence as soon as his pulse begins to—*now, now!*" Letting fall the wrist, feeling the thigh carefully, and bowing over it an instant, he drew the fatal knife unerringly across the flesh. As it first touched the part, the row of surgeons simultaneously dropped their eyes to the watches in their hands, while the patient lay, with eyes horribly distended, in a kind of waking trance. Not a breath was heard; but as the quivering flesh parted in a long, lingering gash, a spring of blood welled up between the living walls of the wound, and two thick streams, in opposite directions, coursed down the thigh. The sponges were instantly dipped in the purple pool; every face present was pinched to a point with suspense; the limb writhed; the man shrieked; his mess-mates pinioned him; while round and round the leg went the unpitying cut.

"The saw!" said Cuticle.

Instantly it was in his hand.

Full of the operation, he was about to apply it, when, looking up, and turning to the assistant surgeons, he said, "Would any of you young gentle-men like to apply the saw? A splendid subject!"

Several volunteered; when, selecting one, Cuticle surrendered the instrument to him, saying, "Don't be hurried, now; be steady."

While the rest of the assistants looked upon their comrade with glances of envy, he went rather timidly to work; and Cuticle, who was earnestly regarding him, suddenly snatched the saw from his hand. "Away, butcher! you disgrace the profession. Look at *me!*"

For a few moments the thrilling, rasping sound was heard; and then the top-man seemed parted in twain at the hip, as the leg slowly slid into the arms of the pale, gaunt man in the shroud, who at once made away with it, and tucked it out of sight under one of the guns.

"Surgeon Sawyer," now said Cuticle, courteously turning to the surgeon of the Buccaneer, "would you like to take up the arteries? They are quite at your service, sir."

"Do, Sawyer; be prevailed upon," said Surgeon Bandage.

Sawyer complied; and while, with some modesty, he was conducting the operation, Cuticle, turning to the row of assistants, said, "Young gentlemen, we will now proceed with our illustration. Hand me that bone, Steward." And taking the thigh-bone in his still bloody hands, and holding it conspicuously before his auditors, the Surgeon of the Fleet began:

"Young gentlemen, you will perceive that precisely at this spot—*here*—to which I previously directed your attention—at the corresponding spot precisely—the operation has been performed. About here, young gentle-men, *here*"—lifting his hand some inches from the bone—"about *here* the great artery was. But you noticed that I did not use the tourniquet; I never do. The forefinger of my steward is far better than a tourniquet, being so much more manageable, and leaving the smaller veins uncompressed. But I have been told, young gentlemen, that a certain Seignior Seignioroni, a surgeon of Seville, has recently invented an admirable substitute for the clumsy, old-fashioned tourniquet. As I understand it, it is something like a pair of *calipers*, working with a small Archimedes screw—a very clever invention, according to all accounts. For the padded points at the end of the arches"—arching his forefinger and thumb—"can be so worked as to approximate in such a way, as to—but you don't attend to me, young gentlemen," he added, all at once starting.

Being more interested in the active proceedings of Surgeon Sawyer, who was now threading a needle to sew up the overlapping of the stump, the young gentlemen had not scrupled to turn away their attention altogether from the lecturer.

A few moments more, and the top-man, in a swoon, was removed below into the sick-bay. As the curtain settled again after the patient had disappeared, Cuticle, still holding the thigh-bone of the skeleton in his ensanguined hands, proceeded with his remarks upon it; and having concluded them, added, "Now, young gentlemen, not the least interesting consequence of this operation will be the finding of the ball, which, in case of non-amputation, might have long eluded the most careful search. That ball, young gentlemen, must have taken a most circuitous route. Nor, in cases where the direction is oblique, is this at all unusual. Indeed, the learned Hennen gives us a most remarkable—I had almost said an incredible—case of a soldier's neck, where the bullet, entering at the part called Adam's Apple—"

"Yes," said Surgeon Wedge, elevating himself, "the *pomum Adami.*"

"Entering the point called *Adam's Apple,*" continued Cuticle, severely emphasizing the last two words, "ran completely round the neck, and, emerging at the same hole it had entered, shot the next man in the ranks. It was afterward extracted, says Hennen, from the second man, and pieces of the other's skin were found adhering to it. But examples of foreign substances being received into the body with a ball, young gentlemen, are frequently observed. Being attached to a United States ship at the time, I happened to be near the spot of the battle of Ayacucho, in Peru. The day after the action, I saw in the barracks of the wounded a trooper, who, having been severely injured in the brain, went crazy, and, with his own holster-pistol, committed suicide in the hospital. The ball drove inward a portion of his woolen night-cap—"

"In the form of a *cul-de-sac*, doubtless," said the undaunted Wedge.

"For once, Surgeon Wedge, you use the only term that can be employed; and let me avail myself of this opportunity to say to you, young gentlemen, that a man of true science"—expanding his shallow chest a little—"uses but few hard words, and those only when none other will answer his purpose; whereas the smatterer in science"—slightly glancing toward Wedge—"thinks, that by mouthing hard words, he proves that he understands hard things. Let this sink deep in your minds, young gentlemen; and, Surgeon Wedge"—with a stiff bow—"permit me to submit the reflection to yourself. Well, young gentlemen, the bullet was afterward extracted by pulling upon the external parts of the *cul-de-sac*—a simple, but exceedingly beautiful operation. There is a fine example, somewhat similar, related in Guthrie;

but, of course, you must have met with it, in so well-known a work as his Treatise upon Gun-shot Wounds. When, upward of twenty years ago, I was with Lord Cochrane, then Admiral of the fleets of this very country"— pointing shoreward, out of a port-hole—"a sailor of the vessel to which I was attached, during the blockade of Bahia, had his leg—" But by this time the fidgets had completely taken possession of his auditors, especially of the senior surgeons; and turning upon them abruptly, he added, "But I will not detain you longer, gentlemen"—turning round upon all the surgeons— "your dinners must be waiting you on board your respective ships. But, Surgeon Sawyer, perhaps you may desire to wash your hands before you go. There is the basin, sir; you will find a clean towel on the rammer. For myself, I seldom use them"—taking out his handkerchief. "I must leave you now, gentlemen"—bowing. "To-morrow, at ten, the limb will be upon the table, and I shall be happy to see you all upon the occasion. Who's there?" turning to the curtain, which then rustled.

"Please, sir," said the Steward, entering, "the patient is dead."

"The body also, gentlemen, at ten precisely," said Cuticle, once more turning round upon his guests. "I predicted that the operation might prove fatal; he was very much run down. Good-morning;" and Cuticle departed.

"He does not, surely, mean to touch the body?" exclaimed Surgeon Sawyer, with much excitement.

"Oh, no!" said Patella, "that's only his way; he means, doubtless, that it may be inspected previous to being taken ashore for burial."

The assemblage of gold-laced surgeons now ascended to the quarter-deck; the second cutter was called away by the bugler, and, one by one, they were dropped aboard of their respective ships.

The following evening the mess-mates of the top-man rowed his remains ashore, and buried them in the ever-vernal Protestant cemetery, hard by the Beach of the Flamingoes, in plain sight from the bay.

Chapter 64

Man-of-war Trophies

W HEN THE SECOND CUTTER pulled about among the
ships, dropping the surgeons aboard the American men-of-war
here and there—as a pilot-boat distributes her pilots at the
mouth of the harbor—she passed several foreign frigates, two of which, an
Englishman and a Frenchman, had excited not a little remark on board the
Neversink. These vessels often loosed their sails and exercised yards
simultaneously with ourselves, as if desirous of comparing the respective
efficiency of the crews.

When we were nearly ready for sea, the English frigate, weighing her
anchor, made all sail with the sea-breeze, and began showing off her paces
by gliding about among all the men-of-war in harbor, and particularly by
running down under the Neversink's stern. Every time she drew near, we
complimented her by lowering our ensign a little, and invariably she
courteously returned the salute. She was inviting us to a sailing-match; and
it was rumored that, when we should leave the bay, our Captain would
have no objections to gratify her; for, be it known, the Neversink was
accounted the fleetest keeled craft sailing under the American long-pennant.
Perhaps this was the reason why the stranger challenged us.

It may have been that a portion of our crew were the more anxious to
race with this frigate, from a little circumstance which a few of them deemed

265

rather galling. Not many cables'-length distant from our Commodore's cabin lay the frigate President, with the red cross of St. George flying from her peak. As its name imported, this fine craft was an American born; but having been captured during the last war with Britain, she now sailed the salt seas as a trophy.

Think of it, my gallant countrymen, one and all, down the sea-coast and along the endless banks of the Ohio and Columbia—think of the twinges we sea-patriots must have felt to behold the live-oak of the Floridas and the pines of green Maine built into the oaken walls of Old England! But, to some of the sailors, there was a counterbalancing thought, as grateful as the other was galling, and that was, that somewhere, sailing under the stars and stripes, was the frigate Macedonian, a British-born craft which had once sported the battle-banner of Britain.

It has ever been the custom to spend almost any amount of money in repairing a captured vessel, in order that she may long survive to commemorate the heroism of the conqueror. Thus, in the English Navy, there are many Monsieurs of seventy-fours won from the Gaul. But we Americans can show but few similar trophies, though, no doubt, we would much like to be able so to do.

But I never have beheld any of these floating trophies without being reminded of a scene once witnessed in a pioneer village on the western bank of the Mississippi. Not far from this village, where the stumps of aboriginal trees yet stand in the market-place, some years ago lived a portion of the remnant tribes of the Sioux Indians, who frequently visited the white settlements to purchase trinkets and cloths.

One florid crimson evening in July, when the red-hot sun was going down in a blaze, and I was leaning against a corner in my huntsman's frock, lo! there came stalking out of the crimson West a gigantic red-man, erect as a pine, with his glittering tomahawk, big as a broad-ax, folded in martial repose across his chest. Moodily wrapped in his blanket, and striding like a king on the stage, he promenaded up and down the rustic streets, exhibiting on the back of his blanket a crowd of human hands, rudely delineated in red; one of them seemed recently drawn.

"Who is this warrior?" asked I; "and why marches he here? and for what are these bloody hands?"

"That warrior is the *Red-Hot Coal*," said a pioneer in moccasins, by my side. "He marches here to show off his last trophy; every one of those hands attests a foe scalped by his tomahawk; and he has just emerged from Ben Brown's, the painter, who has sketched the last red hand that you see; for last night this *Red-Hot Coal* outburned the *Yellow Torch*, the chief of a band of the Foxes."

Poor savage! thought I; and is this the cause of your lofty gait? Do you straighten yourself to think that you have committed a murder, when a chance-falling stone has often done the same? Is it a proud thing to topple down six feet perpendicular of immortal manhood, though that lofty living tower needed perhaps thirty good growing summers to bring it to maturity? Poor savage! And you account it so glorious, do you, to mutilate and destroy what God himself was more than a quarter of a century in building?

And yet, fellow-Christians, what is the American frigate Macedonian, or the English frigate President, but as two bloody red hands painted on this poor savage's blanket?

Are there no Moravians in the Moon, that not a missionary has yet visited this poor pagan planet of ours, to civilize civilization and christianize Christendom?

Chapter 65

A Man-of-war Race

W E LAY IN RIO SO LONG—for what reason the Commodore only knows—that a saying went abroad among the impatient sailors that our frigate would at last ground on the beef-bones daily thrown overboard by the cooks.

But at last the good tidings came. "All hands up anchor, ahoy!" And bright and early in the morning up came our old iron, as the sun rose in the East.

The land-breeze at Rio—by which alone vessels may emerge from the bay—is ever languid and faint. It comes from gardens of citrons and cloves, spiced with all the spices of the Tropic of Capricorn. And, like that old exquisite, Mohammed, who so much loved to snuff perfumes and essences, and used to lounge out of the conservatories of Khadija, his wife, to give battle to the robust sons of Koriesh; even so this Rio land-breeze comes jaded with sweet-smelling savors, to wrestle with the wild Tartar breezes of the sea.

Slowly we dropped and dropped down the bay, glided like a stately swan through the outlet, and were gradually rolled by the smooth, sliding billows broad out upon the deep. Straight in our wake came the tall main-mast of the English fighting-frigate, terminating, like a steepled cathedral, in the bannered cross of the religion of peace; and straight after *her* came the rainbow banner of France, sporting God's token that no more would he make war on the earth.

Both Englishman and Frenchman were resolved on a race; and we Yankees swore by our top-sails and royals to sink their blazing banners that night among the Southern constellations we should daily be extinguishing behind us in our run to the North.

"Ay," said Mad Jack, "St. George's banner shall be as the *Southern Cross*, out of sight, leagues down the horizon, while our gallant stars, my brave boys, shall burn all alone in the North, like the Great Bear at the Pole! Come on, Rainbow and Cross!"

But the wind was long languid and faint, not yet recovered from its night's dissipation ashore, and noon advanced, with the Sugar-Loaf pinnacle in sight.

Now it is not with ships as with horses; for though, if a horse walk well and fast, it generally furnishes good token that he is not bad at a gallop, yet the ship that in a light breeze is outstripped, may sweep the stakes, so soon as a t'-gallant breeze enables her to strike into a canter. Thus fared it with us. First, the Englishman glided ahead, and bluffly passed on; then the Frenchman politely bade us adieu, while the old Neversink lingered behind, railing at the effeminate breeze. At one time, all three frigates were irregularly abreast, forming a diagonal line; and so near were all three, that the stately officers on the poops stiffly saluted by touching their caps, though refraining from any further civilities. At this juncture, it was a noble sight to behold those fine frigates, with dripping breast-hooks, all rearing and nodding in concert, and to look through their tall spars and wilderness of rigging, that seemed like inextricably-entangled, gigantic cobwebs against the sky.

Toward sundown the ocean pawed its white hoofs to the spur of its helter-skelter rider, a strong blast from the Eastward, and, giving three cheers from decks, yards, and tops, we crowded all sail on St. George and St. Denis.

But it is harder to overtake than outstrip; night fell upon us, still in the rear—still where the little boat was, which, at the eleventh hour, according to a Rabbinical tradition, pushed after the ark of old Noah.

It was a misty, cloudy night; and though at first our look-outs kept the chase in dim sight, yet at last so thick became the atmosphere, that no sign of a strange spar was to be seen. But the worst of it was, that, when last discerned, the Frenchman was broad on our weather-bow, and the Englishman gallantly leading his van.

The breeze blew fresher and fresher; but, with even our main-royal set, we dashed along through a cream-colored ocean of illuminated foam. White-Jacket was then in the top; and it was glorious to look down and see our black hull butting the white sea with its broad bows like a ram.

"We must beat them with such a breeze, dear Jack," said I to our noble Captain of the Top.

"But the same breeze blows for John Bull, remember," replied Jack, who, being a Briton, perhaps favored the Englishman more than the Neversink.

"But how we boom through the billows!" cried Jack, gazing over the top-rail; then, flinging forth his arm, recited,

> " 'Aslope, and gliding on the leeward side,
> The bounding vessel cuts the roaring tide.'

Camoens! White-Jacket, Camoens! Did you ever read him? The Lusiad, I mean? It's the man-of-war epic of the world, my lad. Give me Gama for a Commodore, say I—Noble Gama! And Mickle, White-Jacket, did you ever read of him? William Julius Mickle? Camoens's Translator? A disappointed man though, White-Jacket. Besides his version of the Lusiad, he wrote many forgotten things. Did you ever see his ballad of Cumnor Hall?— No?—Why, it gave Sir Walter Scott the hint of Kenilworth. My father knew Mickle when he went to sea on board the old Romney man-of-war. How many great men have been sailors, White-Jacket! They say Homer himself was once a tar, even as his hero, Ulysses, was both a sailor and a shipwright. I'll swear Shakspeare was once a captain of the forecastle. Do you mind the first scene in *The Tempest*, White-Jacket? And the world-finder, Christopher Columbus, was a sailor! and so was Camoens, who went to sea with Gama, else we had never had the Lusiad, White-Jacket. Yes, I've sailed over the very track that Camoens sailed—round the East Cape into the Indian Ocean. I've been in Don Jose's garden, too, in Macao, and bathed my feet in the blessed dew of the walks where Camoens wandered before me. Yes, White-Jacket, and I have seen and sat in the cave at the end of the flowery, winding way, where Camoens, according to tradition, composed certain parts of his Lusiad. Ay, Camoens was a sailor once! Then, there's Falconer, whose 'Shipwreck' will never founder, though he himself, poor fellow, was lost at sea in the Aurora frigate. Old Noah was the first sailor. And St. Paul, too, knew how to box the compass, my lad! mind you that chapter in Acts? I couldn't spin the yarn better myself. Were you ever in Malta? They called it Melita in the Apostle's day. I have been in Paul's cave there, White-Jacket. They say a piece of it is good for a charm against shipwreck; but I never tried it. There's Shelley, he was quite a sailor. Shelley—poor lad! a Percy, too—but they ought to have let him sleep in his sailor's grave—he was drowned in the Mediterranean, you know, near Leghorn—and not burn his body, as they did, as if he had been a bloody Turk. But many people thought him so, White-Jacket, because he didn't go to mass, and because he wrote Queen Mab. Trelawny was by at the burning; and he was an ocean-rover, too! Ay, and Byron helped put a piece of a keel on the fire; for it was made of bits of a wreck, they say; one wreck burning another! And was not Byron a sailor? an amateur forecastle-man, White-Jacket! so he was; else how bid the ocean heave and fall in that grand, majestic way? I say, White-Jacket, d'ye mind me? there never was a very great man yet who spent all his life inland. A snuff of the sea, my boy, is inspiration; and having been once out of sight of land, has been the making of many a true poet and the blasting of many pretenders; for, d'ye see, there's no gammon about the ocean; it knocks the false keel right off a pretender's bows; it tells him just what he is, and makes him feel it, too. A sailor's life, I say, is the thing to bring us mortals out. What does the blessed Bible say? Don't it say that we main-top-men alone see the marvelous sights and wonders? Don't deny the blessed Bible, now! don't do it! How it rocks up here, my boy!" holding on to a shroud; "but it only proves what I've been saying—the sea is the place to cradle genius! Heave and fall, old sea!"

"And *you*, also, noble Jack," said I, "what are you but a sailor?"

"You're merry, my boy," said Jack, looking up with a glance like that of a sentimental archangel doomed to drag out his eternity in disgrace. "But mind you, White-Jacket, there are many great men in the world besides Commodores and Captains. I've that here, White-Jacket"—touching his forehead—"which, under happier skies—perhaps in yon solitary star there, peeping down from those clouds—might have made a Homer of me. But Fate is Fate, White-Jacket; and we Homers who happen to be captains of tops must write our odes in our hearts, and publish them in our heads. But look! the Captain's on the poop."

It was now midnight; but all the officers were on deck.

"Jib-boom, there!" cried the Lieutenant of the Watch, going forward and hailing the headmost look-out. "D'ye see any thing of those fellows now?"

"See nothing, sir."

"See nothing, sir," said the Lieutenant, approaching the Captain, and touching his cap.

"Call all hands!" roared the Captain. "This keel sha'n't be beat while I stride it."

All hands were called, and the hammocks stowed in the nettings for the rest of the night, so that no one could lie between blankets.

Now, in order to explain the means adopted by the Captain to insure us the race, it needs to be said of the Neversink, that, for some years after being launched, she was accounted one of the slowest vessels in the American Navy. But it chanced upon a time, that, being on a cruise in the Mediterranean, she happened to sail out of Port Mahon in what was then supposed to be very bad trim for the sea. Her bows were rooting in the water, and her stern kicking up its heels in the air. But, wonderful to tell, it was soon discovered that in this comical posture she sailed like a shooting-star; she outstripped every vessel on the station. Thenceforward all her Captains, on all cruises, *trimmed her by the head;* and the Neversink gained the name of a clipper.

To return. All hands being called, they were now made use of by Captain Claret as make-weights, to trim the ship, scientifically, to her most approved bearings. Some were sent forward on the spar-deck, with twenty-four-pound shot in their hands, and were judiciously scattered about here and there, with strict orders not to budge an inch from their stations, for fear of marring the Captain's plans. Others were distributed along the gun and berth decks, with similar orders; and, to crown all, several carronade guns were unshipped from their carriages, and swung in their breechings from the beams of the main-deck, so as to impart a sort of vibratory briskness and oscillating buoyancy to the frigate.

And thus we five hundred make-weights stood out that whole night, some of us exposed to a drenching rain, in order that the Neversink might not be beaten. But the comfort and consolation of all make-weights is as dust in the balance in the estimation of the rulers of our man-of-war world.

The long, anxious night at last came to an end, and, with the first peep of day, the look-out on the jib-boom was hailed; but nothing was in sight. At last it was broad day; yet still not a bow was to be seen in our rear, nor a stern in our van.

"Where are they?" cried the Captain.

"Out of sight, astern, to be sure, sir," said the officer of the deck.

"Out of sight, *ahead*, to be sure, sir," muttered Jack Chase, in the top.

Precisely thus stood the question: whether we beat them, or whether they beat us, no mortal can tell to this hour, since we never saw them again; but for one, White-Jacket will lay his two hands on the bow-chasers of the Neversink, and take his ship's oath that we Yankees carried the day.

Chapter 66

Fun in a Man-of-war

AFTER THE RACE (our man-of-war Derby) we had many days fine weather, during which we continued running before the Trades toward the north. Exhilarated by the thought of being homeward-bound, many of the seamen became joyous, and the discipline of the ship, if any thing, became a little relaxed. Many pastimes served to while away the *Dog-Watches* in particular. These *Dog-Watches* (embracing two hours in the early part of the evening) form the only authorized play-time for the crews of most ships at sea.

Among other diversions at present licensed by authority in the Neversink, were those of single-stick, sparring, hammer-and-anvil, and head-bumping. All these were under the direct patronage of the Captain, otherwise—seeing the consequences they sometimes led to—they would undoubtedly have been strictly prohibited. It is a curious coincidence, that when a navy captain does not happen to be an admirer of the *Fistiana*, his crew seldom amuse themselves in that way.

Single-stick, as every one knows, is a delightful pastime, which consists in two men standing a few feet apart, and rapping each other over the head with long poles. There is a good deal of fun in it, so long as you are not hit; but a hit—in the judgment of discreet persons—spoils the sport completely. When this pastime is practiced by connoisseurs ashore, they wear heavy, wired helmets, to break the force of the blows. But the only helmets of our tars were those with which nature had furnished them. They played with great gun-rammers.

Sparring consists in playing single-stick with bone poles instead of wooden ones. Two men stand apart, and pommel each other with their fists (a hard bunch of knuckles permanently attached to the arms, and made globular, or extended into a palm, at the pleasure of the proprietor), till one of them, finding himself sufficiently thrashed, cries *enough*.

Hammer-and-anvil is thus practiced by amateurs: Patient No. 1 gets on all-fours, and stays so; while patient No. 2 is taken up by his arms and legs, and his base is swung against the base of patient No. 1, till patient No. 1, with the force of the final blow, is sent flying along the deck.

Head-bumping, as patronized by Captain Claret, consists in two negroes (whites will not answer) butting at each other like rams. This pastime was an especial favorite with the Captain. In the Dog-Watches, Rose-Water and May-Day were repeatedly summoned into the lee waist to tilt at each other, for the benefit of the Captain's health.

May-Day was a full-blooded "*bull-negro*," so the sailors called him, with a skull like an iron tea-kettle, wherefore May-Day much fancied the sport. But Rose-Water, he was a slender and rather handsome mulatto, and abhorred the pastime. Nevertheless, the Captain must be obeyed; so at the word poor Rose-Water was fain to put himself in a posture of defence, else May-Day would incontinently have bumped him out of a port-hole into the sea. I used to pity poor Rose-Water from the bottom of my heart. But my pity was almost aroused into indignation at a sad sequel to one of these gladiatorial scenes.

It seems that, lifted up by the unaffected, though verbally unexpressed applause of the Captain, May-Day had begun to despise Rose-Water as a poltroon—a fellow all brains and no skull; whereas he himself was a great warrior, all skull and no brains.

Accordingly, after they had been bumping one evening to the Captain's content, May-Day confidentially told Rose-Water that he considered him a "*nigger*," which, among some blacks, is held a great term of reproach. Fired at the insult, Rose-Water gave May-Day to understand that he utterly erred; for his mother, a black slave, had been one of the mistresses of a Virginia planter belonging to one of the oldest families in that state. Another insulting remark followed this innocent disclosure; retort followed retort; in a word, at last they came together in mortal combat.

The master-at-arms caught them in the act, and brought them up to the mast. The Captain advanced.

"Please, sir," said poor Rose-Water, "it all come of dat 'ar bumping; May-Day, here, aggravated me 'bout it."

"Master-at-arms," said the Captain, "did you see them fighting?"

"Ay, sir," said the master-at-arms, touching his cap.

"Rig the gratings," said the Captain. "I'll teach you two men that, though I now and then permit you to *play*, I will have no *fighting*. Do your duty, boatswain's mate!" And the negroes were flogged.

Justice commands that the fact of the Captain's not showing any leniency to May-Day—a decided favorite of his, at least while in the ring—should not be passed over. He flogged both culprits in the most impartial manner.

As in the matter of the scene at the gangway, shortly after the Cape Horn theatricals, when my attention had been directed to the fact that the officers had *shipped their quarter-deck faces*—upon that occasion, I say, it was seen with what facility a sea-officer assumes his wonted severity of demeanor after a casual relaxation of it. This was especially the case with Captain Claret upon the present occasion. For any landsman to have beheld him in the lee waist, of a pleasant Dog-Watch, with a genial, good-humored countenance, observing the gladiators in the ring, and now and then indulging in a playful remark—that landsman would have deemed Captain Claret the indulgent father of his crew, perhaps permitting the excess of his kind-heartedness to encroach upon the appropriate dignity of his station. He would have deemed Captain Claret a fine illustration of those two well-known poetical comparisons between a sea-captain and a father, and between a sea-captain and the master of apprentices, instituted by those eminent maritime jurists, the noble Lords Tenterden and Stowell.

But surely, if there is any thing hateful, it is this *shipping of the quarter-deck face* after wearing a merry and good-natured one. How can they have the heart? Methinks, if but once I smiled upon a man—never mind how much beneath me—I could not bring myself to condemn him to the shocking misery of the lash. Oh officers! all round the world, if this quarter-deck face you wear at all, then never unship it for another, to be merely sported for a moment. Of all insults, the temporary condescension of a master to a slave is the most outrageous and galling. That potentate who most condescends, mark him well; for that potentate, if occasion come, will prove your uttermost tyrant.

Chapter 67

White-Jacket arraigned at the Mast

W HEN WITH FIVE HUNDRED OTHERS I made one of the compelled spectators at the scourging of poor Rose-Water, I little thought what Fate had ordained for myself the next day. Poor mulatto! thought I, one of an oppressed race, they degrade you like a hound. Thank God! I am a white. Yet I had seen whites also scourged; for, black or white, all my shipmates were liable to that. Still, there is something in us, somehow, that, in the most degraded condition, we snatch at a chance to deceive ourselves into a fancied superiority to others, whom we suppose lower in the scale than ourselves.

Poor Rose-Water! thought I; poor mulatto! Heaven send you a release from your humiliation!

To make plain the thing about to be related, it needs to repeat what has somewhere been previously mentioned, that in *tacking ship* every seaman in a man-of-war has a particular station assigned him. What that station is, should be made known to him by the First Lieutenant; and when the word is passed to *tack* or *wear*, it is every seaman's duty to be found at his post. But among the various *numbers* and *stations* given to me by the senior Lieutenant, when I first came on board the frigate, he had altogether omitted informing me of my particular place at those times, and, up to the precise period now written of, I had hardly known that I should have had any special place then

277

at all. For the rest of the men, they seemed to me to catch hold of the first rope that offered, as in a merchantman upon similar occasions. Indeed, I subsequently discovered, that such was the state of discipline—in this one particular, at least—that very few of the seamen could tell where their proper stations were, at *tacking* or *wearing*.

"All hands tack ship, ahoy!" such was the announcement made by the boatswain's mates at the hatchways the morning after the hard fate of Rose-Water. It was just eight bells—noon, and springing from my white jacket, which I had spread between the guns for a bed on the main-deck, I ran up the ladders, and, as usual, seized hold of the main-brace, which fifty hands were streaming along forward. When *main-top-sail haul!* was given through the trumpet, I pulled at this brace with such heartiness and good-will, that I almost flattered myself that my instrumentality in getting the frigate round on the other tack, deserved a public vote of thanks, and a silver tankard from Congress.

But something happened to be in the way aloft when the yards swung round; a little confusion ensued; and, with anger on his brow, Captain Claret came forward to see what occasioned it. No one to let go the weather-lift of the main-yard! The rope was cast off, however, by a hand, and the yards, unobstructed, came round.

When the last rope was coiled away, the Captain desired to know of the First Lieutenant who it might be that was stationed at the weather (then the starboard) main-lift. With a vexed expression of countenance the First Lieutenant sent a midshipman for the Station Bill, when, upon glancing it over, my own name was found put down at the post in question.

At the time I was on the gun-deck below, and did not know of these proceedings; but a moment after, I heard the boatswain's mates bawling my name at all the hatchways, and along all three decks. It was the first time I had ever heard it so sent through the furthest recesses of the ship, and well knowing what this generally betokened to other seamen, my heart jumped to my throat, and I hurriedly asked Flute, the boatswain's mate at the fore-hatchway, what was wanted of me.

"Captain wants ye at the mast," he replied. "Going to flog ye, I guess."

"What for?"

"My eyes! you've been chalking your face, hain't ye?"

"What am I wanted for?" I repeated.

But at that instant my name was again thundered forth by the other boatswain's mate, and Flute hurried me away, hinting that I would soon find out what the Captain desired of me.

I swallowed down my heart in me as I touched the spar-deck, for a single instant balanced myself on my best centre, and then, wholly ignorant of what was going to be alleged against me, advanced to the dread tribunal of the frigate.

As I passed through the gangway, I saw the quarter-master rigging the gratings; the boatswain with his green bag of scourges; the master-at-arms ready to help off some one's shirt.

Again I made a desperate swallow of my whole soul in me, and found myself standing before Captain Claret. His flushed face obviously showed him in ill humor. Among the group of officers by his side was the First Lieutenant, who, as I came aft, eyed me in such a manner, that I plainly perceived him to be extremely vexed at me for having been the innocent means of reflecting upon the manner in which he kept up the discipline of the ship.

"Why were you not at your station, sir?" asked the Captain.

"What station do you mean, sir?" said I.

It is generally the custom with man-of-war's-men to stand obsequiously touching their hat at every sentence they address to the Captain. But as this was not obligatory upon me by the Articles of War, I did not do so upon the present occasion, and previously, I had never had the dangerous honor of a personal interview with Captain Claret.

He quickly noticed my omission of the homage usually rendered him, and instinct told me, that to a certain extent, it set his heart against me.

"What station, sir, do you mean?" said I.

"You pretend ignorance," he replied; "it will not help you, sir."

Glancing at the Captain, the First Lieutenant now produced the Station Bill, and read my name in connection with that of the starboard main-lift.

"Captain Claret," said I, "it is the first time I ever heard of my being assigned to that post."

"How is this, Mr. Bridewell?" he said, turning to the First Lieutenant, with a fault-finding expression.

"It is impossible, sir," said that officer, striving to hide his vexation, "but this man must have known his station."

"I have never known it before this moment, Captain Claret," said I.

"Do you contradict my officer?" he returned. "I shall flog you."

I had now been on board the frigate upward of a year, and remained unscourged; the ship was homeward-bound, and in a few weeks, at most, I would be a freeman. And now, after making a hermit of myself in some things, in order to avoid the possibility of the scourge, here it was hanging over me for a thing utterly unforeseen, for a crime of which I was as utterly innocent. But all that was as naught. I saw that my case was hopeless; my solemn disclaimer was thrown in my teeth, and the boatswain's mate stood curling his fingers through the *cat*.

There are times when wild thoughts enter a man's heart, when he seems almost irresponsible for his act and his deed. The Captain stood on the weather-side of the deck. Sideways, on an unobstructed line with him, was the opening of the lee-gangway, where the side-ladders are suspended in port. Nothing but a slight bit of sinnate-stuff served to rail in this opening, which was cut right down to the level of the Captain's feet, showing the far sea beyond. I stood a little to windward of him, and, though he was a large, powerful man, it was certain that a sudden rush against him, along the slanting deck, would infallibly pitch him headforemost into the ocean, though he who so rushed must needs go over with him. My blood seemed clotting in my veins; I felt icy cold at the tips of my fingers, and a dimness was before my eyes. But through that dimness the boatswain's mate, scourge in hand, loomed like a giant, and Captain Claret, and the blue sea seen through the opening at the gangway, showed with an awful vividness. I can not analyze my heart, though it then stood still within me. But the thing that swayed me to my purpose was not altogether the thought that Captain Claret was about to degrade me, and that I had taken an oath with my soul that he should not. No, I felt my man's manhood so bottomless within me, that no word, no blow, no scourge of Captain Claret could cut me deep enough for that. I but swung to an instinct in me—the instinct diffused through all animated nature, the same that prompts even a worm to turn under the heel. Locking souls with him, I meant to drag Captain Claret from this earthly tribunal of his to that of Jehovah, and let Him decide between us. No other way could I escape the scourge.

Nature has not implanted any power in man that was not meant to be exercised at times, though too often our powers have been abused. The privilege, inborn and inalienable, that every man has, of dying himself, and inflicting death upon another, was not given to us without a purpose. These are the last resources of an insulted and unendurable existence.

"To the gratings, sir!" said Captain Claret; "do you hear?"

My eye was measuring the distance between him and the sea.

"Captain Claret," said a voice advancing from the crowd. I turned to see who this might be, that audaciously interposed at a juncture like this. It was the same remarkably handsome and gentlemanly corporal of marines,

Colbrook, who has been previously alluded to, in the chapter describing killing time in a man–of–war.

"I know that man," said Colbrook, touching his cap, and speaking in a mild, firm, but extremely deferential manner; "and I know that he would not be found absent from his station, if he knew where it was."

This speech was almost unprecedented. Seldom or never before had a marine dared to speak to the Captain of a frigate in behalf of a seaman at the mast. But there was something so unostentatiously commanding in the calm manner of the man, that the Captain, though astounded, did not in any way reprimand him. The very unusualness of his interference seemed Colbrook's protection.

Taking heart, perhaps, from Colbrook's example, Jack Chase interposed, and in a manly but carefully respectful manner, in substance repeated the corporal's remark, adding that he had never found me wanting in the top.

Captain Claret looked from Chase to Colbrook, and from Colbrook to Chase—one the foremost man among the seamen, the other the foremost man among the soldiers—then all round upon the packed and silent crew, and, as if a slave to Fate, though supreme Captain of a frigate, he turned to the First Lieutenant, made some indifferent remark, and saying to me *you may go*, sauntered aft into his cabin; while I, who, in the desperation of my soul, had but just escaped being a murderer and a suicide, almost burst into tears of thanksgiving where I stood.

Chapter 68

A Man-of-war Fountain, and other Things

LET US FORGET THE SCOURGE and the gangway a while, and jot down in our memories a few little things pertaining to our man-of-war world. I let nothing slip, however small; and feel myself actuated by the same motive which has prompted many worthy old chroniclers, to set down the merest trifles concerning things that are destined to pass away entirely from the earth, and which, if not preserved in the nick of time, must infallibly perish from the memories of man. Who knows that this humble narrative may not hereafter prove the history of an obsolete barbarism? Who knows that, when men-of-war shall be no more, "White-Jacket" may not be quoted to show to the people in the Millennium what a man-of-war was? God hasten the time! Lo! ye years, escort it hither, and bless our eyes ere we die.

There is no part of a frigate where you will see more going and coming of strangers, and overhear more greetings and gossipings of acquaintances, than in the immediate vicinity of the scuttle-butt, just forward of the main-hatchway, on the gun-deck.

The scuttle-butt is a goodly, round, painted cask, standing on end, and with its upper head removed, showing a narrow, circular shelf within, where rest a number of tin cups for the accommodation of drinkers. Central, within the scuttle-butt itself, stands an iron pump, which, connecting with the immense water-tanks in the hold, furnishes an unfailing supply of the much-admired Pale Ale, first brewed in the brooks of the Garden of Eden, and stamped with the *brand* of our old father Adam, who never knew what wine was. We are indebted to the old vintner Noah for that. The scuttle-butt is the only fountain in the ship; and here alone can you drink, unless at your meals. Night and day an armed sentry paces before it, bayonet in hand, to see that no water is taken away, except according to law. I wonder that they station no sentries at the port-holes, to see that no air is breathed, except according to Navy regulations.

As five hundred men come to drink at this scuttle-butt; as it is often surrounded by officer's servants drawing water for their masters to wash; by the cooks of the range, who hither come to fill their coffee-pots; and by the cooks of the ship's messes to procure water for their *duffs;* the scuttle-butt may be denominated the town-pump of the ship. And would that my fine countryman, Hawthorne of Salem, had but served on board a man-of-war in his time, that he might give us the reading of a *"rill"* from the scuttle-butt.

*   *   *   *   *

As in all extensive establishments—abbeys, arsenals, colleges, treasuries, metropolitan post-offices, and monasteries—there are many snug little niches, wherein are ensconced certain superannuated old pensioner officials; and, more especially, as in most ecclesiastical establishments, a few choice prebendary stalls are to be found, furnished with well-filled mangers and racks; so, in a man-of-war, there are a variety of similar snuggeries for the benefit of decrepit or rheumatic old tars. Chief among these is the office of *mast-man.*

There is a stout rail on deck, at the base of each mast, where a number of *braces, lifts,* and *buntlines* are belayed to the pins. It is the sole duty of the mast-man to see that these ropes are always kept clear, to preserve his premises in a state of the greatest attainable neatness, and every Sunday morning to dispose his ropes in neat *Flemish coils.*

The *main-mast-man* of the Neversink was a very aged seaman, who well deserved his comfortable berth. He had seen more than half a century of the most active service, and, through all, had proved himself a good and faithful man. He furnished one of the very rare examples of a sailor in a green old age; for, with most sailors, old age comes in youth, and Hardship and Vice carry them on an early bier to the grave.

As in the evening of life, and at the close of the day, old Abraham sat at the door of his tent, biding his time to die, so sits our old mast-man on the *coat of the mast*, glancing round him with patriarchal benignity. And that mild expression of his sets off very strangely a face that has been burned almost black by the torrid suns that shone fifty years ago—a face that is seamed with three sabre cuts. You would almost think this old mast-man had been blown out of Vesuvius, to look alone at his scarred, blackened forehead, chin, and cheeks. But gaze down into his eye, and though all the snows of Time have drifted higher and higher upon his brow, yet deep down in that eye you behold an infantile, sinless look, the same that answered the glance of this old man's mother when first she cried for the babe to be laid by her side. That look is the fadeless, ever infantile immortality within.

*   *   *   *   *

The Lord Nelsons of the sea, though but Barons in the state, yet often-times prove more potent than their royal masters; and at such scenes as Trafalgar—dethroning this Emperor and reinstating that—enact on the ocean the proud part of mighty Richard Nevil, the king-making Earl of the land. And as Richard Nevil entrenched himself in his moated old man-of-war castle of Warwick, which, underground, was traversed with vaults, hewn out of the solid rock, and intricate as the wards of the old keys of Calais surrendered to Edward III.; even so do these King-Commodores house themselves in their water-rimmed, cannon-sentried frigates, oaken dug, deck under deck, as cell under cell. And as the old Middle-Age warders of Warwick, every night at curfew, patrolled the battlements, and dove down into the vaults to see that all lights were extinguished, even so do the master-at-arms and ship's corporals of a frigate perambulate all the decks of a man-of-war, blowing out all tapers but those burning in the legalized battle-lanterns. Yea, in these things, so potent is the authority of these sea-wardens, that, though almost the lowest subalterns in the ship, yet should they find the Senior Lieutenant himself sitting up late in his state-room, reading Bowditch's Navigator, or D'Anton "*On Gunpowder and Fire-arms,*" they would infallibly blow the light out under his very nose; nor durst that Grand-Vizier resent the indignity.

But, unwittingly, I have ennobled, by grand historical comparisons, this prying, pettifogging, Irish-informer of a master-at-arms.

You have seen some slim, slip-shod housekeeper, at midnight, ferreting over a rambling old house in the country, starting at fancied witches and ghosts, yet intent on seeing every door bolted, every smouldering ember in the fire-places smothered, every loitering domestic abed, and every light made dark. This is the master-at-arms taking his night-rounds in a frigate.

*   *   *   *   *

It may be thought that but little is seen of the Commodore in these chapters, and that, since he so seldom appears on the stage, he can not be so august a personage, after all. But the mightiest potentates keep the most behind the vail. You might tarry in Constantinople a month, and never catch a glimpse of the Sultan. The Grand Lama of Thibet, according to some accounts, is never beheld by the people. But if any one doubts the majesty of a Commodore, let him know that, according to XLII. of the Articles of War, he is invested with a prerogative which, according to monarchical jurists, is inseparable from the throne—the plenary pardoning power. He may pardon all offences committed in the squadron under his command.

But this prerogative is only his while at sea, or on a foreign station. A circumstance peculiarly significant of the great difference between the stately absolutism of a Commodore enthroned on his poop in a foreign harbor, and an unlaced Commodore negligently reclining in an easy-chair in the bosom of his family at home.

*   *   *   *   *

In the histories of some old states we read of *tasters* being appointed to the court, by way of precaution against poisonings. This taster's business consisted in tasting all dishes previous to his royal master's dining. In modern navies this custom is reversed. Every day, at precisely seven bells of the forenoon watch, (half-past eleven o'clock,) the ship's cook of the Neversink would slowly emerge from the main-hatchway, bearing a capacious tin pan, containing a sample of the salt-beef or pork—as the case might be—that day cooked for the people's messes. Inserted uprightly in the steaming meat would be seen a knife and fork. Advancing to the main-mast, the cook deposits the pan on the belaying rail, and solemnly touching his hat, awaits the pleasure of the officer of the deck. It is a ceremony that attracts all eyes; for of all persons in the world, the sailors in a man-of-war are the most keenly anxious for the dinner-time to come; and Old Coffee's inevitable appearance with his pan, at precisely seven bells, was always hailed by them with delight. To myself, he was better than a clock. Nor was Old Coffee at all blind to the dignity and importance of the ceremony, in which he enacted so conspicuous a part. He preserved the utmost rectitude of carriage; and when it was "Duff Day," he would advance with his tin truncheon borne high aloft, exhibiting a pale, round duff surmounting the blood-red mass of beef;—he looked something like the figure in the old painting of the executioner presenting the head of St. John the Baptist in a charger.

In due time, the officer of the deck draws near, spreads his feet apart at the belaying rails, and squares himself to the inspection. Drawing out the knife and fork from the beef, he cuts himself a choice piece; masticates it rapidly, while looking the cook full in the eye; and if the flavor seems agreeable to him, he sticks the knife and fork into the beef again, and exclaims, "Very good: serve it up." Thus, in a man-of-war, the lords may be said to be tasters to the commons.

The ostensible reason of this ceremony is this, that the officer of the deck may be sure that the ship's cook has faithfully cooked his meat. But as all the meat is not inspected, and the cook may select what piece he pleases for inspection, the test is by no means a thorough one. A picked and pounded bit of the breast is not a fair specimen of a radically tough goose.

Chapter 69

Prayers at the Guns

THE TRAINING-DAYS, or general quarters, now and then taking place in our frigate, have already been described, also the Sunday devotions on the half-deck; but nothing has yet been said concerning the daily morning and evening quarters, when the men silently stand at their guns, and the chaplain simply offers up a prayer.

Let us now enlarge upon this matter. We have plenty of time; the occasion invites; for behold! the homeward-bound Neversink bowls along over a jubilant sea.

Shortly after breakfast the drum beats to quarters; and among five hundred men, scattered over all three decks, and engaged in all manner of ways, that sudden rolling march is magical as the monitory sound to which every good Mussulman at sunset drops to the ground whatsoever his hands might have found to do, and, throughout all Turkey, the people in concert kneel toward their holy Mecca.

The sailors run to and fro—some up the deck-ladders, some down—to gain their respective stations in the shortest possible time. In three minutes all is composed. One by one, the various officers stationed over the separate divisions of the ship then approach the First Lieutenant on the quarter-deck, and report their respective men at their quarters. It is curious to watch their countenances at this time. A profound silence prevails; and, emerging through the hatchway, from one of the lower decks, a slender young officer appears, hugging his sword to his thigh, and advances through the long lanes of sailors at their guns, his serious eye all the time fixed upon the First Lieutenant's—his polar star. Sometimes he essays a stately and graduated step, an erect and martial bearing, and seems full of the vast national importance of what he is about to communicate.

But when at last he gains his destination, you are amazed to perceive that all he has to say is imparted by a Free-mason touch of his cap, and a bow. He then turns and makes off to his division, perhaps passing several brother Lieutenants, all bound on the same errand he himself has just achieved. For about five minutes these officers are coming and going, bringing in thrilling intelligence from all quarters of the frigate; most stoically received, however, by the First Lieutenant. With his legs apart, so as to give a broad foundation for the superstructure of his dignity, this gentleman stands stiff as a pike-staff on the quarter-deck. One hand holds his sabre—an appurtenance altogether unnecessary at the time; and which he accordingly tucks, point backward, under his arm, like an umbrella on a sunshiny day. The other hand is continually bobbing up and down to the leather front of his cap, in response to the reports and salutes of his subordinates, to whom he never deigns to vouchsafe a syllable; merely going through the motions of accepting their news, without bestowing thanks for their pains.

This continual touching of caps between officers on board a man-of-war is the reason why you invariably notice that the glazed fronts of their caps look jaded, lack-lustre, and worn; sometimes slightly oleaginous—though, in other respects, the cap may appear glossy and fresh. But as for the First Lieutenant, he ought to have extra pay allowed to him, on account of his extraordinary outlays in cap fronts; for he it is to whom all day long, reports of various kinds are incessantly being made by the junior Lieutenants; and no report is made by them, however trivial, but caps are touched on the occasion. It is obvious that these individual salutes must be greatly multiplied and aggregated upon the senior Lieutenant, who must return them all. Indeed, when a subordinate officer is first promoted to that rank, he generally complains of the same exhaustion about the shoulder and elbow that La Fayette mourned over, when, in visiting America, he did little else but shake the sturdy hands of patriotic farmers from sunrise to sunset.

The various officers of divisions having presented their respects, and made good their return to their stations, the First Lieutenant turns round, and, marching aft, endeavors to catch the eye of the Captain, in order to touch his own cap to that personage, and thereby, without adding a word of explanation, communicate the fact of all hands being at their guns. He is a sort of retort, or receiver general, to concentrate the whole sum of the information imparted to him, and discharge it upon his superior at one touch of his cap front.

But sometimes the Captain feels out of sorts, or in ill-humor, or is pleased to be somewhat capricious, or has a fancy to show a touch of his omnipotent supremacy; or, peradventure, it has so happened that the First Lieutenant has, in some way, piqued or offended him, and he is not unwilling to show a slight specimen of his dominion over him, even before the eyes of all hands; at all events, only by some one of these suppositions can the singular circumstance be accounted for, that frequently Captain Claret would pertinaciously promenade up and down the poop, purposely averting his eye from the First Lieutenant, who would stand below in the most awkward suspense, waiting the first wink from his superior's eye.

"Now I have him!" he must have said to himself, as the Captain would turn toward him in his walk; "now's my time!" and up would go his hand to his cap; but, alas! the Captain was off again; and the men at the guns would cast sly winks at each other as the embarrassed Lieutenant would bite his lips with suppressed vexation.

Upon some occasions this scene would be repeated several times, till at last Captain Claret, thinking, that in the eyes of all hands, his dignity must by this time be pretty well bolstered, would stalk toward his subordinate, looking him full in the eyes; whereupon up goes his hand to the cap front, and the Captain, nodding his acceptance of the report, descends from his perch to the quarter-deck.

By this time the stately Commodore slowly emerges from his cabin, and soon stands leaning alone against the brass rails of the after-hatchway. In passing him, the Captain makes a profound salutation, which his superior returns, in token that the Captain is at perfect liberty to proceed with the ceremonies of the hour.

Marching on, Captain Claret at last halts near the main-mast, at the head of a group of the ward-room officers, and by the side of the Chaplain. At a sign from his finger, the brass band strikes up the Portuguese hymn. This over, from Commodore to hammock-boy, all hands uncover, and the Chaplain reads a prayer. Upon its conclusion, the drum beats the retreat, and the ship's company disappear from the guns. At sea or in harbor, this ceremony is repeated every morning and evening

By those stationed on the quarter-deck the Chaplain is distinctly heard;

but the quarter-deck gun division embraces but a tenth part of the ship's company, many of whom are below, on the main-deck, where not one syllable of the prayer can be heard. This seemed a great misfortune; for I well knew myself how blessed and soothing it was to mingle twice every day in these peaceful devotions, and, with the Commodore, and Captain, and smallest boy, unite in acknowledging Almighty God. There was also a touch of the temporary equality of the Church about it, exceedingly grateful to a man-of-war's-man like me.

My carronade-gun happened to be directly opposite the brass railing against which the Commodore invariably leaned at prayers. Brought so close together, twice every day, for more than a year, we could not but become intimately acquainted with each other's faces. To this fortunate circumstance it is to be ascribed, that some time after reaching home, we were able to recognize each other when we chanced to meet in Washington, at a ball given by the Russian Minister, the Baron de Bodisco. And though, while on board the frigate, the Commodore never in any manner personally addressed me—nor did I him—yet, at the Minister's social entertainment, we *there* became exceedingly chatty; nor did I fail to observe, among that crowd of foreign dignitaries and magnates from all parts of America, that my worthy friend did not appear so exalted as when leaning, in solitary state, against the brass railing of the Neversink's quarter-deck. Like many other gentlemen, he appeared to the best advantage, and was treated with the most deference in the bosom of his home, the frigate.

Our morning and evening quarters were agreeably diversified for some weeks by a little circumstance, which to some of us at least, always seemed very pleasing.

At Callao, half of the Commodore's cabin had been hospitably yielded to the family of a certain aristocratic-looking magnate, who was going embassador from Peru to the Court of the Brazils, at Rio. This dignified diplomatist sported a long, twirling mustache, that almost enveloped his mouth. The sailors said, he looked like a rat with his teeth through a bunch of oakum, or a St. Jago monkey peeping through a prickly-pear bush.

He was accompanied by a very beautiful wife, and a still more beautiful little daughter, about six years old. Between this dark-eyed little gipsy and our chaplain there soon sprung up a cordial love and good feeling, so much so, that they were seldom apart. And whenever the drum beat to quarters, and the sailors were hurrying to their stations, this little signorita would outrun them all to gain her own quarters at the capstan, where she would stand by the chaplain's side, grasping his hand, and looking up archly in his face.

It was a sweet relief from the domineering sternness of our martial discipline—a sternness not relaxed even at our devotions before the altar of the common God of commodore and cabin-boy—to see that lovely little girl standing among the thirty-two-pounders, and now and then casting a wondering, commiserating glance at the array of grim seamen around her.

Chapter 70

Monthly Muster round the Capstan

BESIDES GENERAL QUARTERS, and the regular morning and evening quarters for prayers on board the Neversink, on the first Sunday of every month we had a grand "*muster round the capstan*," when we passed in solemn review before the Captain and officers, who closely scanned our frocks and trowsers, to see whether they were according to the Navy cut. In some ships, every man is required to bring his bag and hammock along for inspection.

This ceremony acquires its chief solemnity, and, to a novice, is rendered even terrible, by the reading of the Articles of War by the Captain's clerk before the assembled ship's company, who, in testimony of their enforced reverence for the code, stand bareheaded till the last sentence is pronounced.

To a mere amateur reader the quiet perusal of these Articles of War would be attended with some nervous emotions. Imagine, then, what *my* feelings must have been, when, with my hat deferentially in my hand, I stood before my lord and master, Captain Claret, and heard these Articles read as the law and gospel, the infallible, unappealable dispensation and code, whereby I lived, and moved, and had my being on board of the United States ship Neversink.

Of some twenty offences—made penal—that a seaman may commit, and which are specified in this code, thirteen are punishable by death.

"*Shall suffer death!*" This was the burden of nearly every Article read by the Captain's clerk; for he seemed to have been instructed to omit the longer Articles, and only present those which were brief and to the point.

"*Shall suffer death!*" The repeated announcement falls on your ear like the intermitting discharge of artillery. After it has been repeated again and again, you listen to the reader as he deliberately begins a new paragraph; you hear him reciting the involved, but comprehensive and clear arrangement of the sentence, detailing all possible particulars of the offence described, and you breathlessly await, whether *that* clause also is going to be concluded by the discharge of the terrible minute-gun. When, lo! it again booms on your ear—*shall suffer death!* No reservations, no contingencies; not the remotest promise of pardon or reprieve; not a glimpse of commutation of the sentence; all hope and consolation is shut out—*shall suffer death!* that is the simple fact for you to digest; and it is a tougher morsel, believe White-Jacket when he says it, than a forty-two-pound cannon-ball.

But there is a glimmering of an alternative to the sailor who infringes these Articles. Some of them thus terminate: "*Shall suffer death, or such punishment as a court-martial shall adjudge.*" But hints this at a penalty still more serious? Perhaps it means "*death, or worse punishment.*"

Your honors of the Spanish Inquisition, Loyola and Torquemada! produce, reverend gentlemen, your most secret code, and match these Articles of War, if you can. Jack Ketch, *you* also are experienced in these things! Thou most benevolent of mortals, who standest by us, and hangest round our necks, when all the rest of this world are against us—tell us, hangman, what punishment is this, horribly hinted at as being worse than death? Is it, upon an empty stomach, to read the Articles of War every morning, for the term of one's natural life? Or is it to be imprisoned in a cell, with its walls papered from floor to ceiling with printed copies, in italics, of these Articles of War?

But it needs not to dilate upon the pure, bubbling milk of human kindness, and Christian charity, and forgiveness of injuries which pervade this charming document, so thoroughly imbued, as a Christian code, with the benignant spirit of the Sermon on the Mount. But as it is very nearly alike in the foremost states of Christendom, and as it is nationally set forth by those states, it indirectly becomes an index to the true condition of the present civilization of the world.

As, month after month, I would stand bareheaded among my shipmates, and hear this document read, I have thought to myself, Well, well, White-Jacket, you are in a sad box, indeed. But prick your ears, there goes another minute-gun. It admonishes you to take all bad usage in good part, and never to join in any public meeting that may be held on the gun-deck for a redress of grievances. Listen:

Art. XIII. "*If any person in the navy shall make, or attempt to make, any mutinous assembly, he shall, on conviction thereof by a court martial, suffer death.*"

Bless me, White-Jacket, are you a great gun yourself, that you so recoil, to the extremity of your breechings, at that discharge?

But give ear again. Here goes another minute-gun. It indirectly admonishes you to receive the grossest insult, and stand still under it:

Art. XIV. "*No private in the navy shall disobey the lawful orders of his superior officer, or strike him, or draw, or offer to draw, or raise any weapon against him, while in the execution of the duties of his office, on pain of death.*"

Do not hang back there by the bulwarks, White-Jacket; come up to the mark once more; for here goes still another minute-gun, which admonishes you never to be caught napping:

Part of Art. XX. "*If any person in the navy shall sleep upon his watch, he shall suffer death.*"

Murderous! But then, in time of peace, they do not enforce these blood-thirsty laws? Do they not, indeed? What happened to those three men on board an American armed vessel a few years ago, quite within your memory, White-Jacket; yea, while you yourself were yet serving on board this very frigate, the Neversink? What happened to those three Americans, White-Jacket—those three men, even as you, who once were alive, but now are dead? "*Shall suffer death!*" those were the three words that hung those three men.

Have a care, then, have a care, lest you come to a sad end, even the end of a rope; lest, with a black-and-blue throat, you turn a dumb diver after pearl-shells; put to bed forever, and tucked in, in your own hammock, at the bottom of the sea. And there you will lie, White-Jacket, while hostile navies are playing cannon-ball billiards over your grave.

By the main-mast! then, in a time of profound peace, I am subject to the cut-throat martial law! And when my own brother, who happens to be dwelling ashore, and does not serve his country as I am now doing—when he is at liberty to call personally upon the President of the United States, and express his disapprobation of the whole national administration, here am I, liable at any time to be run up at the yard-arm, with a necklace, made by no jeweler, round my neck!

A hard case, truly, White-Jacket; but it can not be helped. Yes; you live under this same martial law. Does not every thing around you din the fact in your ears? Twice every day do you not jump to your quarters at the sound of a drum? Every morning, in port, are you not roused from your hammock by the *reveille*, and sent to it again at nightfall by the *tattoo*? Every Sunday are you not commanded in the mere matter of the very dress you shall wear through that blessed day? Can your shipmates so much as drink their "tot of grog?" nay, can they even drink but a cup of water at the scuttle-butt, without an armed sentry standing over them? Does not every officer wear a sword instead of a cane? You live and move among twenty-four-pounders, White-Jacket; the very cannon-balls are deemed an ornament around you, serving to embellish the hatchways; and should you come to die at sea, White-Jacket, still two cannon-balls would bear you company when you would be committed to the deep. Yea, by all methods, and devices, and inventions, you are momentarily admonished of the fact that you live under the Articles of War. And by virtue of them it is, White-Jacket, that, without a hearing and without a trial, you may, at a wink from the Captain, be condemned to the scourge.

Speak you true? Then let me fly!

Nay, White-Jacket, the landless horizon hoops you in.

Some tempest, then, surge all the sea against us! hidden reefs and rocks, arise and dash the ship to chips! I was not born a serf, and will not live a slave! Quick! cork-screw whirlpools, suck us down! world's end whelm us!

Nay, White-Jacket, though this frigate laid her broken bones upon the Antarctic shores of Palmer's Land; though not two planks adhered; though all her guns were spiked by sword-fish blades, and at her yawning hatch-ways mouth-yawning sharks swam in and out; yet, should you escape the wreck and scramble to the beach, this Martial Law would meet you still, and snatch you by the throat. Hark!

Art. XLII. Part of Sec. 3.—"*In all cases where the crews of the ships or vessels of the United States shall be separated from their vessels by the latter being wrecked, lost, or destroyed, all the command, power, and authority given to the officers of such ships or vessels shall remain, and be in full force, as effectually as if such ship or vessel were not so wrecked, lost, or destroyed.*"

Hear you that, White-Jacket! I tell you there is no escape. Afloat or wrecked the Martial Law relaxes not its gripe. And though, by that self-same warrant, for some offence therein set down, you were indeed to "suffer death," even then the Martial Law might hunt you straight through the other world, and out again at its other end, following you through all eternity, like an endless thread on the inevitable track of its own point, passing unnumbered needles through.

Chapter 71

The Genealogy of the Articles of War

AS THE ARTICLES OF WAR form the ark and constitution of the penal laws of the American Navy, in all sobriety and earnestness it may be well to glance at their origin. Whence came they? And how is it that one arm of the national defences of a Republic comes to be ruled by a Turkish code, whose every section almost, like each of the tubes of a revolving pistol, fires nothing short of death into the heart of an offender? How comes it that, by virtue of a law solemnly ratified by a Congress of freemen, the representatives of freemen, thousands of Americans are subjected to the most despotic usages, and, from the dock-yards of a republic, absolute monarchies are launched, with the "glorious stars and stripes" for an ensign? By what unparalleled anomaly, by what monstrous grafting of tyranny upon freedom did these Articles of War ever come to be so much as heard of in the American Navy?

Whence came they? They can not be the indigenous growth of those political institutions, which are based upon that arch-democrat Thomas Jefferson's Declaration of Independence? No; they are an importation from abroad, even from Britain, whose laws we Americans hurled off as tyrannical, and yet retained the most tyrannical of all.

But we stop not here; for these Articles of War had their congenial origin in a period of the history of Britain when the Puritan Republic had

297

yielded to a monarchy restored; when a hangman Judge Jeffreys sentenced a world's champion like Algernon Sidney to the block; when one of a race —by some deemed accursed of God—even a Stuart, was on the throne; and a Stuart, also, was at the head of the Navy, as Lord High Admiral. One, the son of a King beheaded for encroachments upon the rights of his people, and the other, his own brother, afterward a king, James II., who was hurled from the throne for his tyranny. This is the origin of the Articles of War; and it carries with it an unmistakable clew to their despotism.*

Nor is it a dumb thing that the men who, in democratic Cromwell's time, first proved to the nations the toughness of the British oak and the hardihood of the British sailor—that in Cromwell's time, whose fleets struck terror into the cruisers of France, Spain, Portugal, and Holland, and the corsairs of Algiers and the Levant; in Cromwell's time, when Robert Blake swept the Narrow Seas of all the keels of a Dutch Admiral who insultingly carried a broom at his fore-mast; it is not a dumb thing that, at a period deemed so glorious to the British Navy, these Articles of War were unknown.

Nevertheless, it is granted that some laws or other must have governed Blake's sailors at that period; but they must have been far less severe than those laid down in the written code which superseded them, since, according

---

* The first Naval Articles of War in the English language were passed in the thirteenth year of the reign of Charles the Second, under the title of "*An act for establishing Articles and Orders for the regulating and better Government of his Majesty's Navies, Ships-of-War, and Forces by Sea.*" This act was repealed, and, so far as concerned the officers, a modification of it substituted, in the twenty-second year of the reign of George the Second, shortly after the Peace of Aix la Chapelle, just one century ago. This last act, it is believed, comprises, in substance, the Articles of War at this day in force in the British Navy. It is not a little curious, nor without meaning, that neither of these acts explicitly empowers an officer to inflict the lash. It would almost seem as if, in this case, the British lawgivers were willing to leave such a stigma out of an organic statute, and bestow the power of the lash in some less solemn, and perhaps less public manner. Indeed, the only broad enactments directly sanctioning naval scourging at sea are to be found in the United States Statute Book and in the "Sea Laws" of the absolute monarch, Louis le Grand, of France.[1]

Taking for their basis the above-mentioned British Naval Code, and ingrafting upon it the positive scourging laws, which Britain was loth to recognize as organic statutes, our American lawgivers, in the year 1800, framed the Articles of War now governing the American Navy. They may be found in the second volume of the "United States Statutes at Large," under chapter xxxiii.—"An act for the *better* government of the Navy of the United States."

---

[1] For reference to the latter (L'Ord. de la Marine), *vide* Curtis's "Treatise on the Rights and Duties of Merchant-Seamen, according to the General Maritime Law," Part ii., c. i.

to the father-in-law of James II., the Historian of the Rebellion, the English Navy, prior to the enforcement of the new code, was full of officers and sailors who, of all men, were the most republican. Moreover, the same author informs us that the first work undertaken by his respected son-in-law, then Duke of York, upon entering on the duties of Lord High Admiral, was to have a grand re-christening of the men-of-war, which still carried on their sterns names too democratic to suit his high-tory ears.

But if these Articles of War were unknown in Blake's time, and also during the most brilliant period of Admiral Benbow's career, what inference must follow? That such tyrannical ordinances are not indispensable—even during war—to the highest possible efficiency of a military marine.

Chapter 72

*"Herein are the good Ordinances of the Sea, which wise Men,
who voyaged round the World, gave to our Ancestors, and
which constitute the Books of the Science of good Customs."*
—The Consulate of the Sea

THE PRESENT USAGES of the American Navy are such that,
though there is no government enactment to that effect, yet, in
many respects, its Commanders seem virtually invested with the
power to observe or violate, as seems to them fit, several of the Articles of
War.

According to Article XV., *"No person in the Navy shall quarrel with any
other person in the Navy, nor use provoking or reproachful words, gestures, or
menaces, on pain of such punishment as a court-martial shall adjudge."*

"Provoking or reproachful words!" Officers of the Navy, answer me!
Have you not, many of you, a thousand times violated this law, and addressed to men, whose tongues were tied by this very Article, language
which no landsman would ever hearken to without flying at the throat of
his insulter? I know that worse words than *you* ever used are to be heard
addressed by a merchant-captain to his crew; but the merchant-captain
does not live under this XV.th Article of War.

Not to make an example of him, nor to gratify any personal feeling,
but to furnish one certain illustration of what is here asserted, I honestly
declare that Captain Claret, of the Neversink, repeatedly violated this law
in his own proper person.

According to Article III., no officer, or other person in the Navy, shall be guilty of "oppression, fraud, profane swearing, drunkenness, or any other scandalous conduct."

Again let me ask you, officers of the Navy, whether many of you have not repeatedly, and in more than one particular, violated this law? And here, again, as a certain illustration, I must once more cite Captain Claret as an offender, especially in the matter of profane swearing. I must also cite four of the lieutenants, some eight of the midshipmen, and nearly all the seamen.

Additional Articles might be quoted that are habitually violated by the officers, while nearly all those *exclusively* referring to the sailors are un-scrupulously enforced. Yet those Articles, by which the sailor is scourged at the gangway, are not one whit more laws than those *other* Articles, binding upon the officers, that have become obsolete from immemorial disuse; while still other Articles, to which the sailors alone are obnoxious, are observed or violated at the caprice of the Captain. Now, if it be not so much the severity as the certainty of punishment that deters from trans-gression, how fatal to all proper reverence for the enactments of Congress must be this disregard of its statutes.

Still more. This violation of the law, on the part of the officers, in many cases involves oppression to the sailor. But throughout the whole naval code, which so hems in the mariner by law upon law, and which invests the Captain with so much judicial and administrative authority over him—in most cases entirely discretionary—not one solitary clause is to be found which in any way provides means for a seaman deeming himself aggrieved to obtain redress. Indeed, both the written and unwritten laws of the American Navy are as destitute of individual guarantees to the mass of seamen as the Statute Book of the despotic Empire of Russia.

Who put this great gulf between the American Captain and the American sailor? Or is the Captain a creature of like passions with ourselves? Or is he an infallible archangel, incapable of the shadow of error? Or has a sailor no mark of humanity, no attribute of manhood, that, bound hand and foot, he is cast into an American frigate shorn of all rights and defences, while the notorious lawlessness of the Commander has passed into a proverb, familiar to man-of-war's-men, *the law was not made for the Captain!* Indeed, he may almost be said to put off the citizen when he touches his quarter-deck; and, almost exempt from the law of the land himself, he comes down upon others with a judicial severity unknown on the national soil. With the Articles of War in one hand, and the cat o'-nine-tails in the other, he stands an undignified parody upon Mohammed enforcing Moslemism with the sword and the Koran.

The concluding sections of the Articles of War treat of the naval courts-martial before which officers are tried for serious offences as well as the seamen. The oath administered to members of these courts—which sometimes sit upon matters of life and death—explicitly enjoins that the members shall not "*at any time divulge the vote or opinion of any particular member of the court, unless required so to do before a court of justice in due course of law.*"

Here, then, is a Council of Ten and a Star Chamber indeed! Remember, also, that though the sailor is sometimes tried for his life before a tribunal like this, in no case do his fellow-sailors, his peers, form part of the court. Yet that a man should be tried by his peers is the fundamental principle of all civilized jurisprudence. And not only tried by his peers, but his peers must be unanimous to render a verdict; whereas, in a court-martial, the concurrence of a majority of conventional and social superiors is all that is requisite.

In the English Navy, it is said, they had a law which authorized the sailor to appeal, if he chose, from the decision of the Captain—even in a comparatively trivial case—to the higher tribunal of a court-martial. It was an English seaman who related this to me. When I said that such a law must be a fatal clog to the exercise of the penal power in the Captain, he, in substance, told me the following story.

A top-man guilty of drunkenness being sent to the gratings, and the scourge about to be inflicted, he turned round and demanded a court-martial. The Captain smiled, and ordered him to be taken down and put into the "brig." There he was kept in irons some weeks, when, despairing of being liberated, he offered to compromise at two dozen lashes. "Sick of your bargain, then, are you?" said the Captain. "No, no! a court-martial you demanded, and a court-martial you shall have!" Being at last tried before the bar of quarter-deck officers, he was condemned to two hundred lashes. What for? for his having been drunk? No! for his having had the insolence to appeal from an authority, in maintaining which the men who tried and condemned him had so strong a sympathetic interest.

Whether this story be wholly true or not, or whether the particular law involved prevails, or ever did prevail, in the English Navy, the thing, nevertheless, illustrates the ideas that man-of-war's-men themselves have touching the tribunals in question.

What can be expected from a court whose deeds are done in the darkness of the recluse courts of the Spanish Inquisition? when that darkness is solemnized by an oath on the Bible? when an oligarchy of epaulets sits upon the bench, and a plebeian top-man, without a jury, stands judicially naked at the bar?

In view of these things, and especially in view of the fact that, in several cases, the degree of punishment inflicted upon a man-of-war's-man is absolutely left to the discretion of the court, what shame should American legislators take to themselves, that with perfect truth we may apply to the entire body of American man-of-war's-men that infallible principle of Sir Edward Coke: "*It is one of the genuine marks of servitude to have the law either concealed or precarious.*" But still better may we subscribe to the saying of Sir Matthew Hale in his History of the Common Law, that "*the Martial Law, being based upon no settled principles, is, in truth and reality, no law, but something indulged rather than allowed as a law.*"

I know it may be said that the whole nature of this naval code is purposely adapted to the war exigencies of the Navy. But waiving the grave question that might be raised concerning the moral, not judicial, lawfulness of this arbitrary code, even in time of war; be it asked, why is it in force during a time of peace? The United States has now existed as a nation upward of seventy years, and in all that time the alleged necessity for the operation of the naval code—in cases deemed capital—has only existed during a period of two or three years at most.

Some may urge that the severest operations of the code are tacitly made null in time of peace. But though with respect to several of the Articles this holds true, yet at any time any and all of them may be legally enforced. Nor have there been wanting recent instances, illustrating the spirit of this code, even in cases where the letter of the code was not altogether observed. The well-known case of a United States brig furnishes a memorable example, which at any moment may be repeated. Three men, in a time of peace, were then hung at the yard-arm, merely because, in the Captain's judgment, it became necessary to hang them. To this day the question of their complete guilt is socially discussed.

How shall we characterize such a deed? Says Blackstone, "If any one that hath commission of martial authority doth, in time of peace, hang, or otherwise execute any man by color of martial law, this is murder; for it is against Magna Charta."*

Magna Charta! We moderns, who may be landsmen, may justly boast of civil immunities not possessed by our forefathers; but our remoter forefathers who happened to be mariners may straighten themselves even in their ashes to think that their lawgivers were wiser and more humane in

* Commentaries, b. i., c. xiii.

their generation than our lawgivers in ours. Compare the sea-laws of our Navy with the Roman and Rhodian ocean ordinances; compare them with the "Consulate of the Sea;" compare them with the Laws of the Hanse Towns; compare them with the ancient Wisbury laws. In the last we find that they were ocean democrats in those days. "If he strikes, he ought to receive blow for blow." Thus speak out the Wisbury laws concerning a Gothland sea-captain.

In final reference to all that has been said in previous chapters touching the severity and unusualness of the laws of the American Navy, and the large authority vested in its commanding officers, be it here observed, that White-Jacket is not unaware of the fact, that the responsibility of an officer commanding at sea—whether in the merchant service or the national marine —is unparalleled by that of any other relation in which man may stand to man. Nor is he unmindful that both wisdom and humanity dictate that, from the peculiarity of his position, a sea-officer in command should be clothed with a degree of authority and discretion inadmissible in any master ashore. But, at the same time, these principles—recognized by all writers on maritime law—have undoubtedly furnished warrant for clothing modern sea-commanders and naval courts-martial with powers which exceed the due limits of reason and necessity. Nor is this the only instance where right and salutary principles, in themselves almost self-evident and infallible, have been advanced in justification of things, which in themselves are just as self-evidently wrong and pernicious.

Be it here, once and for all, understood, that no sentimental and theoretic love for the common sailor; no romantic belief in that peculiar noble-heartedness and exaggerated generosity of disposition fictitiously imputed to him in novels; and no prevailing desire to gain the reputation of being his friend, have actuated me in any thing I have said, in any part of this work, touching the gross oppression under which I know that the sailor suffers. Indifferent as to who may be the parties concerned, I but desire to see wrong things righted, and equal justice administered to all.

Nor, as has been elsewhere hinted, is the general ignorance or depravity of any race of men to be alleged as an apology for tyranny over them. On the contrary, it can not admit of a reasonable doubt, in any unbiased mind conversant with the interior life of a man-of-war, that most of the sailor iniquities practiced therein are indirectly to be ascribed to the morally debasing effects of the unjust, despotic, and degrading laws under which the man-of-war's-man lives.

Chapter 73

Night and Day Gambling in a Man-of-war

MENTION HAS ALREADY BEEN MADE that the game of draughts, or checkers, was permitted to be played on board the Neversink. At the present time, while there was little or no ship-work to be done, and all hands, in high spirits, were sailing homeward over the warm, smooth sea of the tropics; so numerous became the players, scattered about the decks, that our First Lieutenant used ironically to say that it was a pity they were not tesselated with squares of white and black marble, for the express benefit and convenience of the players. Had this gentleman had his way, our checker-boards would very soon have been pitched out of the ports. But the Captain—unusually lenient in some things—permitted them, and so Mr. Bridewell was fain to hold his peace.

But, although this one game was allowable in the frigate, all kinds of gambling were strictly interdicted, under the penalty of the gangway; nor were cards or dice tolerated in any way whatever. This regulation was indispensable, for, of all human beings, man-of-war's-men are perhaps the most inclined to gambling. The reason must be obvious to any one who reflects upon their condition on shipboard. And gambling—the most mischievous of vices any where—in a man-of-war operates still more perniciously than on shore. But quite as often as the law against smuggling

305

spirits is transgressed by the unscrupulous sailors, the statutes against cards and dice are evaded.

Sable night, which, since the beginning of the world, has winked and looked on at so many deeds of iniquity—night is the time usually selected for their operations by man-of-war gamblers. The place pitched upon is generally the berth-deck, where the hammocks are swung, and which is lighted so stintedly as not to disturb the sleeping seamen with any obtruding glare. In so spacious an area the two lanterns swinging from the stanchions diffuse a subdued illumination, like a night-taper in the apartment of some invalid. Owing to their position, also, these lanterns are far from shedding an impartial light, however dim, but fling long angular rays here and there, like burglar's dark-lanterns in the fifty-acre vaults of the West India Docks on the Thames.

It may well be imagined, therefore, how well adapted is this mysterious and subterranean Hall of Eblis to the clandestine proceedings of gamblers, especially as the hammocks not only hang thickly, but many of them swing very low, within two feet of the floor, thus forming innumerable little canvass glens, grottoes, nooks, corners, and crannies, where a good deal of wickedness may be practiced by the wary with considerable impunity.

Now the master-at-arms, assisted by his mates, the ship's corporals, reigns supreme in these bowels of the ship. Throughout the night these policemen relieve each other at standing guard over the premises; and, except when the watches are called, they sit in the midst of a profound silence, only invaded by trumpeter's snores, or the ramblings of some old sheet-anchor-man in his sleep.

The two ship's corporals went among the sailors by the names of Leggs and Pounce; Pounce had been a policeman, it was said, in Liverpool; Leggs, a turnkey attached to "The Tombs" in New York. Hence their education eminently fitted them for their stations; and Bland, the master-at-arms, ravished with their dexterity in prying out offenders, used to call them his two right hands.

When man-of-war's-men desire to gamble, they appoint the hour, and select some certain corner, in some certain shadow, behind some certain hammock. They then contribute a small sum toward a joint fund, to be invested in a bribe for some argus-eyed shipmate, who shall play the part of a spy upon the master-at-arms and corporals while the gaming is in progress. In nine cases out of ten these arrangements are so cunning and comprehensive, that the gamblers, eluding all vigilance, conclude their game unmolested. But now and then, seduced into unwariness, or perhaps, from parsimony, being unwilling to employ the services of a spy, they are suddenly lighted upon by the constables, remorselessly collared, and dragged into the *brig*, there to await a dozen lashes in the morning.

Several times at midnight I have been startled out of a sound sleep by a sudden, violent rush under my hammock, caused by the abrupt breaking up of some nest of gamblers, who have scattered in all directions, brushing under the tiers of swinging pallets, and setting them all in a rocking commotion.

It is, however, while laying in port that gambling most thrives in a man-of-war. Then the men frequently practice their dark deeds in the light of the day, and the additional guards which, at such times, they deem indispensable, are not unworthy of note. More especially, their extra precautions in engaging the services of several spies, necessitate a considerable expenditure, so that, in port, the diversion of gambling rises to the dignity of a nabob luxury.

During the day the master-at-arms and his corporals are continually prowling about on all three decks, eager to spy out iniquities. At one time, for example, you see Leggs switching his magisterial rattan, and lurking round the fore-mast on the spar-deck; the next moment, perhaps, he is three decks down, out of sight, prowling among the cable-tiers. Just so with his master, and Pounce his coadjutor; they are here, there, and every where, seemingly gifted with ubiquity.

In order successfully to carry on their proceedings by day, the gamblers must see to it that each of these constables is relentlessly dogged wherever he goes; so that, in case of his approach toward the spot where themselves are engaged, they may be warned of the fact in time to make good their escape. Accordingly, light and active scouts are selected to follow the constable about. From their youthful alertness and activity, the boys of the mizzen-top are generally chosen for this purpose.

But this is not all. On board of most men-of-war there is a set of sly, knavish foxes among the crew, destitute of every principle of honor, and on a par with Irish informers. In man-of-war parlance, they come under the denomination of *fancy-men* and *white-mice*. They are called *fancy-men*, because, from their zeal in craftily reporting offenders, they are presumed to be regarded with high favor by some of the officers. Though it is seldom that these informers can be certainly individualized, so secret and subtle are they in laying their information, yet certain of the crew, and especially certain of the marines, are invariably suspected to be *fancy-men* and *white-mice*, and are accordingly more or less hated by their comrades.

Now, in addition to having an eye on the master-at-arms and his aids, the day-gamblers must see to it, that every person suspected of being a *white-mouse* or *fancy-man*, is likewise dogged wherever he goes. Additional scouts are retained constantly to snuff at their trail. But the mysteries of man-of-war vice are wonderful; and it is now to be recorded, that, from long habit and observation, and familiarity with the *guardo moves* and *maneuvres* of a frigate, the master-at-arms and his aids can almost invariably tell when any gambling is going on by day; though, in the crowded vessel, abounding in decks, tops, dark places, and outlandish corners of all sorts, they may not be able to pounce upon the identical spot where the gamblers are hidden.

During the period that Bland was suspended from his office as master-at-arms, a person who, among the sailors, went by the name of Sneak, having been long suspected to have been a *white-mouse*, was put in Bland's place. He proved a hang-dog, sidelong catch-thief, but gifted with a marvelous perseverance in ferreting out culprits; following in their track like an inevitable Cuba blood-hound, with his noiseless nose. When disconcerted, however, you sometimes heard his bay.

"The muffled dice are somewhere around," Sneak would say to his aids; "there are them three chaps, there, been dogging me about for the last half hour. I say, Pounce, has any one been scouting around *you* this morning?"

"Four on 'em," says Pounce. "I know'd it; I know'd the muffled dice was rattlin'!"

"Leggs!" says the master-at-arms to his other aid, "Leggs, how is it with *you*—any spies?"

"Ten on 'em," says Leggs. "There's one on 'em now—that fellow stitching a hat."

"Halloo, you sir!" cries the master-at-arms, "top your boom and sail large, now. If I see you about me again, I'll have you up to the mast."

"What am I a doin' now?" says the hat-stitcher, with a face as long as a rope-walk. "Can't a feller be workin' here, without being 'spected of Tom Coxe's traverse, up one ladder and down t'other?"

"Oh, I know the moves, sir; I have been on board a *guardo*. Top your boom, I say, and be off, or I'll have you hauled up and riveted in a clinch—both fore-tacks over the main-yard, and no bloody knife to cut the seizing. Sheer! or I'll pitch into you like a shin of beef into a beggar's wallet."

It is often observable, that, in vessels of all kinds, the men who talk the most sailor lingo are the least sailor-like in reality. You may sometimes hear even marines jerk out more salt phrases than the Captain of the Forecastle himself. On the other hand, when not actively engaged in his vocation, you would take the best specimen of a seaman for a landsman. When you see a fellow yawing about the docks like a homeward-bound Indiaman, a long Commodore's pennant of black ribbon flying from his mast-head, and fetching up at a grog-shop with a slew of his hull, as if an Admiral were coming alongside a three-decker in his barge; you may put that man down for what man-of-war's-men call a *damn-my-eyes-tar*, that is, a humbug. And many damn-my-eyes humbugs there are in this man-of-war world of ours.

Chapter 74

The Main-top at Night

THE WHOLE OF OUR RUN from Rio to the Line was one delightful yachting, so far as fine weather and the ship's sailing were concerned. It was especially pleasant when our quarter-watch lounged in the main-top, diverting ourselves in many agreeable ways. Removed from the immediate presence of the officers, we there harmlessly enjoyed ourselves, more than in any other part of the ship. By day, many of us were very industrious, making hats or mending our clothes. But by night we became more romantically inclined.

Often Jack Chase, an enthusiastic admirer of sea-scenery, would direct our attention to the moonlight on the waves, by fine snatches from his catalogue of poets. I shall never forget the lyric air with which, one morning, at dawn of day, when all the East was flushed with red and gold, he stood leaning against the top-mast shrouds, and, stretching his bold hand over the sea, exclaimed, "Here comes Aurora: top-mates, see!" And, in a liquid, long-lingering tone, he recited the lines,

> "With gentle hand, as seeming oft to pause,
> The purple curtains of the morn she draws."

"Commodore Camoens, White-Jacket.—But bear a hand there; we must rig out that stun'-sail boom—the wind is shifting."

From our lofty perch, of a moonlight night, the frigate itself was a glorious sight. She was going large before the wind, her stun'-sails set on both sides, so that the canvass on the main-mast and fore-mast presented the appearance of two majestic, tapering pyramids, more than a hundred feet broad at the base, and terminating in the clouds with the light copestone of the royals. That immense area of snow-white canvass sliding along the sea was indeed a magnificent spectacle. The three shrouded masts looked like the apparitions of three gigantic Turkish Emirs striding over the ocean.

Nor, at times, was the sound of music wanting, to augment the poetry of the scene. The whole band would be assembled on the poop, regaling the officers, and incidentally ourselves, with their fine old airs. To these, some of us would occasionally dance in the *top*, which was almost as large as an ordinary-sized parlor. When the instrumental melody of the band was not to be had, our nightingales mustered their voices, and gave us a song.

Upon these occasions Jack Chase was often called out, and regaled us, in his own free and noble style, with the "*Spanish Ladies*"—a favorite thing with British man-of-war's-men—and many other salt-sea ballads and ditties, including,

> "Sir Patrick Spens was the best sailor
> That ever sailed the sea."

Also,

> "And three times around spun our gallant ship;
> Three times around spun she;
> Three times around spun our gallant ship,
> And she went to the bottom of the sea—
> The sea, the sea, the sea,
> And she went to the bottom of the sea!"

These songs would be varied by sundry *yarns* and *twisters* of the top-men. And it was at these times that I always endeavored to draw out the oldest Tritons into narratives of the war-service they had seen. There were but few of them, it is true, who had been in action; but that only made their narratives the more valuable.

There was an old negro, who went by the name of Tawney, a sheet-anchor-man, whom we often invited into our top of tranquil nights, to hear him discourse. He was a staid and sober seaman, very intelligent, with a fine, frank bearing, one of the best men in the ship, and held in high estimation by every one.

It seems that, during the last war between England and America, he had, with several others, been "impressed" upon the high seas, out of a New England merchantman. The ship that impressed him was an English frigate, the Macedonian, afterward taken by the Neversink, the ship in which we were sailing.

It was the holy Sabbath, according to Tawney, and, as the Briton bore down on the American—her men at their quarters—Tawney and his countrymen, who happened to be stationed at the quarter-deck battery, respectfully accosted the captain—an old man by the name of Cardan—as he passed them, in his rapid promenade, his spy-glass under his arm. Again they assured him that they were not Englishmen, and that it was a most bitter thing to lift their hands against the flag of that country which harbored the mothers that bore them. They conjured him to release them from their guns, and allow them to remain neutral during the conflict. But when a ship of any nation is running into action, it is no time for argument, small time for justice, and not much time for humanity. Snatching a pistol from the belt of a boarder standing by, the Captain leveled it at the heads of the three sailors, and commanded them instantly to their quarters, under penalty of being shot on the spot. So, side by side with his country's foes, Tawney and his companions toiled at the guns, and fought out the fight to the last; with the exception of one of them, who was killed at his post by one of his own country's balls.

At length, having lost her fore and main-top-masts, and her mizzen-mast having been shot away to the deck, and her fore-yard lying in two pieces on her shattered forecastle, and in a hundred places having been *hulled* with round shot, the English frigate was reduced to the last extremity. Captain Cardan ordered his signal quarter-master to strike the flag.

Tawney was one of those who, at last, helped pull him on board the Neversink. As he touched the deck, Cardan saluted Decatur, the hostile commander, and offered his sword; but it was courteously declined. Perhaps the victor remembered the dinner parties that he and the English-man had enjoyed together in Norfolk, just previous to the breaking out of hostilities—and while both were in command of the very frigates now crippled on the sea. The Macedonian, it seems, had gone into Norfolk with dispatches. *Then* they had laughed and joked over their wine, and a wager of a beaver hat was said to have been made between them upon the event of the hostile meeting of their ships.

Gazing upon the heavy batteries before him, Cardan said to Decatur, "This is a seventy-four, not a frigate; no wonder the day is yours!"

This remark was founded upon the Neversink's superiority in guns. The Neversink's main-deck-batteries then consisted, as now, of twenty-four-pounders; the Macedonian's of only eighteens. In all, the Neversink numbered fifty-four guns and four hundred and fifty men; the Macedonian, forty-nine guns and three hundred men; a very great disparity, which, united to the other circumstances of this action, deprives the victory of all claims to glory beyond those that might be set up by a river-horse getting the better of a seal.

But if Tawney spoke truth—and he was a truth-telling man—this fact seemed counterbalanced by a circumstance he related. When the guns of the Englishman were examined, after the engagement, in more than one instance the wad was found rammed against the cartridge, without intercepting the ball. And though, in a frantic sea-fight, such a thing might be imputed to hurry and remissness, yet Tawney, a stickler for his tribe, always ascribed it to quite a different and less honorable cause. But, even granting the cause he assigned to have been the true one, it does not involve any thing inimical to the general valor displayed by the British crew. Yet, from all that may be learned from candid persons who have been in sea-fights, there can be but little doubt that on board of all ships, of whatever nation, in time of action, no very small number of the men are exceedingly nervous, to say the least, at the guns; ramming and sponging at a venture. And what special patriotic interest could an impressed man, for instance, take in a fight, into which he had been dragged from the arms of his wife? Or is it to be wondered at that impressed English seamen have not scrupled, in time of war, to cripple the arm that has enslaved them?

During the same general war which prevailed at and previous to the period of the frigate-action here spoken of, a British flag-officer, in writing to the Admiralty, said, "Every thing appears to be quiet in the fleet; but, in preparing for battle last week, several of the guns in the after part of the ship were found to be spiked;" that is to say, rendered useless. Who had spiked them? The dissatisfied seamen. Is it altogether improbable, then, that the guns to which Tawney referred were manned by men who purposely refrained from making them tell on the foe; that, in this one action, the victory America gained was partly won for her by the sulky insubordination of the enemy himself?

During this same period of general war, it was frequently the case that the guns of English armed ships were found in the mornings with their breechings cut over night. This maiming of the guns, and for the time incapacitating them, was only to be imputed to that secret spirit of hatred to the service which induced the spiking above referred to. But even in cases where no deep-seated dissatisfaction was presumed to prevail among the crew, and where a seaman, in time of action, impelled by pure fear, "shirked from his gun;" it seems but flying in the face of Him who made such a seaman what he constitutionally was, to sew *coward* upon his back, and degrade and agonize the already trembling wretch in numberless other ways. Nor seems it a practice warranted by the Sermon on the Mount, for the officer of a battery, in time of battle, to stand over the men with his drawn sword (as was done in the Macedonian), and run through on the spot the first seaman who showed a semblance of fear. Tawney told me that he distinctly heard this order given by the English Captain to his officers of divisions. Were the secret history of all sea-fights written, the laurels of sea-heroes would turn to ashes on their brows.

And how nationally disgraceful, in every conceivable point of view, is the IV. of our American Articles of War: "If any person in the Navy shall pusillanimously cry for quarter, he shall suffer death." Thus, with death before his face from the foe, and death behind his back from his countrymen, the best valor of a man-of-war's-man can never assume the merit of a noble spontaneousness. In this, as in every other case, the Articles of War hold out no reward for good conduct, but only compel the sailor to fight, like a hired murderer, for his pay, by digging his grave before his eyes if he hesitates.

But this Article IV. is open to still graver objections. Courage is the most common and vulgar of the virtues; the only one shared with us by the beasts of the field; the one most apt, by excess, to run into viciousness. And since Nature generally takes away with one hand to counterbalance her gifts with the other, excessive animal courage, in many cases, only finds room in a character vacated of loftier things. But in a naval officer, animal courage is exalted to the loftiest merit, and often procures him a distinguished command.

Hence, if some brainless bravo be Captain of a frigate in action, he may fight her against invincible odds, and seek to crown himself with the glory of the shambles, by permitting his hopeless crew to be butchered before his eyes, while at the same time that crew must consent to be slaughtered by the foe, under penalty of being murdered by the law. Look at the engagement between the American frigate Essex with the two English cruisers, the Phœbe and Cherub, off the Bay of Valparaiso, during the late war. It is admitted on all hands that the American Captain continued to fight his crippled ship against a greatly superior force; and when, at last, it became physically impossible that he could ever be otherwise than vanquished in the end; and when, from peculiarly unfortunate circumstances, his men merely stood up to their nearly useless batteries to be dismembered and blown to pieces by the incessant fire of the enemy's long guns. Nor, by thus continuing to fight, did this American frigate, one iota, promote the true interests of her country. I seek not to underrate any reputation which the American Captain may have gained by this battle. He was a brave man; *that* no sailor will deny. But the whole world is made up of brave men. Yet I would not be at all understood as impugning his special good name. Nevertheless, it is not to be doubted, that if there were any common-sense sailors at the guns of the Essex, however valiant they may have been, those common-sense sailors must have greatly preferred to strike their flag, when they saw the day was fairly lost, than postpone that inevitable act till there were few American arms left to assist in hauling it down. Yet had these men, under these circumstances, "pusillanimously cried for quarter," by the IV. Article of War they might have been legally hung.

According to the negro, Tawney, when the Captain of the Macedonian —seeing that the Neversink had his vessel completely in her power—gave the word to strike the flag, one of his officers, a man hated by the seamen for his tyranny, howled out the most terrific remonstrances, swearing that, for his part, he would not give up, but was for sinking the Macedonian alongside the enemy. Had he been Captain, doubtless he would have done so; thereby gaining the name of a hero in this world;—but what would they have called him in the next?

But as the whole matter of war is a thing that smites common sense and Christianity in the face; so every thing connected with it is utterly foolish, unchristian, barbarous, brutal, and savoring of the Feejee Islands, cannibalism, saltpetre, and the devil.

It is generally the case in a man-of-war when she strikes her flag that all discipline is at an end, and the men for a time are ungovernable. This was so on board of the English frigate. The spirit-room was broken open, and buckets of grog were passed along the decks, where many of the wounded were lying between the guns. These mariners seized the buckets, and, spite of all remonstrances, gulped down the burning spirits, till, as Tawney said, the blood suddenly spirted out of their wounds, and they fell dead to the deck.

The negro had many more stories to tell of this fight; and frequently he would escort me along our main-deck batteries—still mounting the same guns used in the battle—pointing out their ineffaceable indentations and scars. Coated over with the accumulated paint of more than thirty years, they were almost invisible to a casual eye; but Tawney knew them all by heart; for he had returned home in the Neversink, and had beheld these scars shortly after the engagement.

One afternoon, I was walking with him along the gun-deck, when he paused abreast of the main-mast. "This part of the ship," said he, "we called the *slaughter-house* on board the Macedonian. Here the men fell, five and six at a time. An enemy always directs its shot here, in order to hurl over the mast, if possible. The beams and carlines overhead in the Macedonian *slaughter-house* were spattered with blood and brains. About the hatchways it looked like a butcher's stall; bits of human flesh sticking in the ring-bolts. A pig that ran about the decks escaped unharmed, but his hide was so clotted with blood, from rooting among the pools of gore, that when the ship struck the sailors hove the animal overboard, swearing that it would be rank cannibalism to eat him."

Another quadruped, a goat, lost its fore legs in this fight.

The sailors who were killed—according to the usual custom—were ordered to be thrown overboard as soon as they fell; no doubt, as the negro said, that the sight of so many corpses lying around might not appall the survivors at the guns. Among other instances, he related the following. A shot entering one of the port-holes, dashed dead two thirds of a gun's crew. The captain of the next gun, dropping his lock-string, which he had just pulled, turned over the heap of bodies to see who they were; when, perceiving an old mess-mate, who had sailed with him in many cruises, he burst into tears, and, taking the corpse up in his arms, and going with it to the side, held it over the water a moment, and eying it, cried, "Oh God! Tom!"—"D—n your prayers over that thing! overboard with it, and down to your gun!" roared a wounded Lieutenant. The order was obeyed, and the heart-stricken sailor returned to his post.

Tawney's recitals were enough to snap this man-of-war world's sword in its scabbard. And thinking of all the cruel carnal glory wrought out by naval heroes in scenes like these, I asked myself whether, indeed, that was a glorious coffin in which Lord Nelson was entombed—a coffin presented to him, during life, by Captain Hallowell; it had been dug out of the main-mast of the French line-of-battle ship L'Orient, which, burning up with British fire, destroyed hundreds of Frenchmen at the battle of the Nile.

Peace to Lord Nelson where he sleeps in his moldering mast! but rather would I be urned in the trunk of some green tree, and even in death have the vital sap circulating round me, giving of my dead body to the living foliage that shaded my peaceful tomb.

Chapter 75

"Sink, Burn, and Destroy"
—Printed Admiralty orders in time of war

AMONG INNUMERABLE *"yarns and twisters"* reeled off in our main-top during our pleasant run to the North, none could match those of Jack Chase, our captain.

Never was there better company than ever-glorious Jack. The things which most men only read of, or dream about, he had seen and experienced. He had been a dashing smuggler in his day, and could tell of a long nine-pounder rammed home with wads of French silks; of cartridges stuffed with the finest gunpowder tea; of cannister-shot full of West India sweet-meats; of sailor frocks and trowsers, quilted inside with costly laces; and table legs, hollow as musket barrels, compactly stowed with rare drugs and spices. He could tell of a wicked widow, too—a beautiful receiver of smuggled goods upon the English coast—who smiled so sweetly upon the smugglers when they sold her silks and laces, cheap as tape and ginghams. She called them gallant fellows, hearts of game; and bade them bring her more.

He could tell of desperate fights with his British majesty's cutters, in midnight coves upon a stormy coast; of the capture of a reckless band, and their being drafted on board a man-of-war; of their swearing that their chief was slain; of a writ of habeas corpus sent on board for one of them for a debt—a reserved and handsome man—and his going ashore, strongly suspected of being the slaughtered captain, and this a successful scheme for his escape.

But more than all, Jack could tell of the battle of Navarino, for he had been a captain of one of the main-deck guns on board Admiral Codrington's flag-ship, the Asia. Were mine the style of stout old Chapman's Homer, even then I would scarce venture to give noble Jack's own version of this fight, wherein, on the 20th of October, A.D. 1827, thirty-two sail of Englishmen, Frenchmen, and Russians, attacked and vanquished in the Levant an Ottoman fleet of three ships-of-the-line, twenty-five frigates, and a swarm of fire ships and hornet craft.

"We bayed to be at them," said Jack; "and when we *did* open fire, we were like dolphin among the flying-fish. 'Every man take his bird' was the cry, when we trained our guns. And those guns all smoked like rows of Dutch pipe-bowls, my hearties! My gun's crew carried small flags in their bosoms, to nail to the mast in case the ship's colors were shot away. Stripped to the waistbands, we fought like skinned tigers, and bowled down the Turkish frigates like nine-pins. Among their shrouds—swarming thick with small-arm men, like flights of pigeons lighted on pine-trees—our marines sent their leaden pease and gooseberries, like a shower of hail-stones in Labrador. It was a stormy time, my hearties! The blasted Turks pitched into the old Asia's hull a whole quarry of marble shot, each ball one hundred and fifty pounds. They knocked three port-holes into one. But we gave them better than they sent. 'Up and at them, my bull-dog!' said I, patting my gun on the breech; 'tear open hatchways in their Moslem sides!' White-Jacket, my lad, you ought to have been there. The bay was covered with masts and yards, as I have seen a raft of snags in the Arkansas River. Showers of burned rice and olives from the exploding foe fell upon us like manna in the wilderness. '*Allah! Allah! Mohammed! Mohammed!*' split the air; some cried it out from the Turkish port-holes; others shrieked it forth from the drowning waters, their top-knots floating on their shaven skulls, like black-snakes on half-tide rocks. By those top-knots they believed that their Prophet would drag them up to Paradise, but they sank fifty fathoms, my hearties, to the bottom of the bay. 'Ain't the bloody 'Hometons going to strike yet?' cried my first loader, a Guernsey man, thrusting his neck out of the port-hole, and looking at the Turkish line-of-battle ship near by. That instant his head blew by me like a bursting Paixhan shot, and the flag of Ned Knowles himself was hauled down forever. We dragged his hull to one side, and avenged him with the cooper's anvil, which, endways, we rammed home; a mess-mate shoved in the dead man's bloody Scotch cap for the wad, and sent it flying into the line-of-battle ship. By the god of war! boys, we hardly left enough of that craft to boil a pot of water with. It was a hard day's work—a sad day's work, my hearties. That night, when all was over, I slept sound enough, with a box of cannister shot for my pillow! But you ought to have seen the boat-load of Turkish flags one of our captains carried home; he swore to dress his father's orchard in colors with them, just as our spars are dressed for a gala day."

"Though you tormented the Turks at Navarino, noble Jack, yet you came off yourself with only the loss of a splinter, it seems," said a top-man, glancing at our captain's maimed hand.

"Yes; but I and one of the Lieutenants had a narrower escape than that. A shot struck the side of my port-hole, and sent the splinters right and left. One took off my hat rim clean to my brow; another *razeed* the Lieutenant's left boot, by slicing off the heel; a third shot killed my powder-monkey without touching him."

"How, Jack?"

"It *whizzed* the poor babe dead. He was seated on a *cheese of wads* at the time, and after the dust of the powdered bulwarks had blown away, I noticed he yet sat still, his eyes wide open. '*My little hero!*' cried I, and I clapped him on the back; but he fell on his face at my feet. I touched his heart, and found he was dead. There was not a little finger mark on him."

Silence now fell upon the listeners for a time, broken at last by the Second Captain of the Top.

"Noble Jack, I know you never brag, but tell us what you did yourself that day?"

"Why, my hearties, I did not do quite as much as my gun. But I flatter myself it was that gun that brought down the Turkish Admiral's main-mast; and the stump left wasn't long enough to make a wooden leg for Lord Nelson."

"How? but I thought, by the way you pull a lock-string on board here, and look along the sight, that you can steer a shot about right—hey, Jack?"

"It was the Admiral of the Fleet—God Almighty—who directed the shot that dismasted the Turkish Admiral," said Jack; "I only pointed the gun."

"But how did you feel, Jack, when the musket-ball carried away one of your hooks there?"

"Feel! only a finger the lighter. I have seven more left, besides thumbs; and they did good service, too, in the torn rigging the day after the fight;

for you must know, my hearties, that the hardest work comes after the guns are run in. Three days I helped work, with one hand, in the rigging, in the same trowsers that I wore in the action; the blood had dried and stiffened; they looked like glazed red morocco."

Now, this Jack Chase had a heart in him like a mastodon's. I have seen him weep when a man has been flogged at the gangway; yet, in relating the story of the Battle of Navarino, he plainly showed that he held the God of the blessed Bible to have been the British Commodore in the Levant, on the bloody 20th of October, A.D. 1827. And thus it would seem that war almost makes blasphemers of the best of men, and brings them all down to the Feejee standard of humanity. Some man-of-war's-men have confessed to me, that as a battle has raged more and more, their hearts have hardened in infernal harmony; and, like their own guns, they have fought without a thought.

Soldier or sailor, the fighting man is but a fiend; and the staff and body-guard of the Devil musters many a baton. But war at times is inevitable. Must the national honor be trampled under foot by an insolent foe?

Say on, say on; but know you this, and lay it to heart, war-voting Bench of Bishops, that He on whom we believe *himself* has enjoined us to turn the left cheek if the right be smitten. Never mind what follows. That passage you can not expunge from the Bible; that passage is as binding upon us as any other; that passage embodies the soul and substance of the Christian faith; without it, Christianity were like any other faith. And that passage will yet, by the blessing of God, turn the world. But in some things we must turn Quakers first.

But though unlike most scenes of carnage, which have proved useless murders of men, Admiral Codrington's victory undoubtedly achieved the emancipation of Greece, and terminated the Turkish atrocities in that toma-hawked state, yet who shall lift his hand and swear that a Divine Providence led the van of the combined fleets of England, France, and Russia at the battle of Navarino? For if this be so, then it led the van against the Church's own elect—the persecuted Waldenses in Switzerland—and kindled the Smithfield fires in bloody Mary's time.

But all events are mixed in a fusion indistinguishable. What we call Fate is even, heartless, and impartial; not a fiend to kindle bigot flames, nor a philanthropist to espouse the cause of Greece. We may fret, fume, and fight; but the thing called Fate everlastingly sustains an armed neutrality.

Yet though all this be so, nevertheless, in our own hearts, we mold the whole world's hereafters; and in our own hearts we fashion our own gods.

Each mortal casts his vote for whom he will to rule the worlds; I have a voice that helps to shape eternity; and my volitions stir the orbits of the furthest suns. In two senses, we are precisely what we worship. Ourselves are Fate.

Chapter 76

The Chains

W HEN WEARIED with the tumult and occasional contention of the gun-deck of our frigate, I have often retreated to a port-hole, and calmed myself down by gazing broad off upon a placid sea. After the battle-din of the last two chapters, let us now do the like, and, in the sequestered fore-chains of the Neversink, tranquillize ourselves, if we may.

Notwithstanding the domestic communism to which the seamen in a man-of-war are condemned, and the publicity in which actions the most diffident and retiring in their nature must be performed, there is yet an odd corner or two where you may sometimes steal away, and, for a few moments, almost be private.

Chief among these places is the *chains*, to which I would sometimes hie during our pleasant homeward-bound glide over those pensive tropical latitudes. After hearing my fill of the wild yarns of our top, here would I recline—if not disturbed—serenely concocting information into wisdom.

The chains designates the small platform outside of the hull, at the base of the large shrouds leading down from the three mast-heads to the bulwarks. At present they seem to be getting out of vogue among merchant-vessels, along with the fine, old-fashioned quarter-galleries, little turret-like appurtenances, which, in the days of the old Admirals, set off the angles of an armed ship's stern. Here a naval officer might lounge away an hour after action, smoking a cigar, to drive out of his whiskers the villainous smoke of the gunpowder. The picturesque, delightful stern-gallery, also, a broad balcony overhanging the sea, and entered from the Captain's cabin, much as you might enter a bower from a lady's chamber; this charming balcony, where, sailing over summer seas in the days of the old Peruvian viceroys, the Spanish cavalier Mendanna, of Lima, made love to the Lady Isabella, as they voyaged in quest of the Solomon Islands, the fabulous Ophir, the Grand Cyclades; and the Lady Isabella, at sunset, blushed like the Orient, and gazed down to the gold-fish and silver-hued flying-fish, that wove the woof and warp of their wakes in bright, scaly tartans and plaids underneath where the Lady reclined; this charming balcony—exquisite retreat—has been cut away by Vandalic innovations. Ay, that claw-footed old gallery is no longer in fashion; in Commodore's eyes, is no longer genteel.

Out on all furniture fashions but those that are past! Give me my grand-father's old arm-chair, planted upon four carved frogs, as the Hindoos fabled the world to be supported upon four tortoises; give me his cane, with the gold-loaded top—a cane that, like the musket of General Washington's father and the broad-sword of William Wallace, would break down the back of the switch-carrying dandies of these spindle-shank days; give me his broad-breasted vest, coming bravely down over the hips, and furnished with two strong-boxes of pockets to keep guineas in; toss this toppling cylinder of a beaver overboard, and give me my grandfather's gallant, gable-ended, cocked hat.

But though the quarter-galleries and the stern-gallery of a man-of-war are departed, yet the *chains* still linger; nor can there be imagined a more agreeable retreat. The huge blocks and lanyards forming the pedestals of the shrouds divide the chains into numerous little chapels, alcoves, niches, and altars, where you lazily lounge—outside of the ship, though on board. But there are plenty to divide a good thing with you in this man-of-war world. Often, when snugly seated in one of these little alcoves, gazing off to the horizon, and thinking of Cathay, I have been startled from my repose by some old quarter-gunner, who, having newly painted a parcel of match-tubs, wanted to set them to dry.

At other times, one of the tattooing artists would crawl over the bul-warks, followed by his sitter; and then a bare arm or leg would be extended, and the disagreeable business of "*pricking*" commence, right under my eyes; or an irruption of tars, with ditty-bags or sea-reticules, and piles of old trowsers to mend, would break in upon my seclusion, and, forming a sewing-circle, drive me off with their chatter.

But once—it was a Sunday afternoon—I was pleasantly reclining in a particularly shady and secluded little niche between two lanyards, when I heard a low, supplicating voice. Peeping through the narrow space between the ropes, I perceived an aged seaman on his knees, his face turned seaward, with closed eyes, buried in prayer. Softly rising, I stole through a port-hole, and left the venerable worshiper alone.

He was a sheet-anchor-man, an earnest Baptist, and was well known, in his own part of the ship, to be constant in his solitary devotions in the *chains*. He reminded me of St. Anthony going out into the wilderness to pray.

This man was captain of the starboard bow-chaser, one of the two long twenty-four-pounders on the forecastle. In time of action, the command of that iron Thalaba the Destroyer would devolve upon *him*. It would be his business to "train" it properly; to see it well loaded; the grape and can-nister rammed home; also, to "prick the cartridge," "take the sight," and give the word for the match-man to apply his wand; bidding a sudden hell to flash forth from the muzzle, in wide combustion and death.

Now, this captain of the bow-chaser was an upright old man, a sincere, humble believer, and he but earned his bread in being captain of that gun; but how, with those hands of his begrimed with powder, could he break that *other* and most peaceful and penitent bread of the Supper? though in that hallowed sacrament, it seemed, he had often partaken ashore. The omission of this rite in a man-of-war—though there is a chaplain to preside over it, and at least a few communicants to partake—must be ascribed to a sense of religious propriety, in the last degree to be commended.

Ah! the best righteousness of our man-of-war world seems but an un-realized ideal, after all; and those maxims which, in the hope of bringing about a Millennium, we busily teach to the heathen, we Christians our-selves disregard. In view of the whole present social frame-work of our world, so ill adapted to the practical adoption of the meekness of Chris-tianity, there seems almost some ground for the thought, that although our blessed Savior was full of the wisdom of heaven, yet his gospel seems lacking in the practical wisdom of earth—in a due appreciation of the neces-sities of nations at times demanding bloody massacres and wars; in a proper estimation of the value of rank, title, and money. But all this only the more crowns the divine consistency of Jesus; since Burnet and the best theolo-gians demonstrate, that his nature was not merely human—was not that of a mere man of the world.

Chapter 77

The Hospital in a Man-of-war

AFTER RUNNING with a fine steady breeze up to the Line, it fell calm, and there we lay, three days enchanted on the sea. We were a most puissant man-of-war, no doubt, with our five hundred men, Commodore and Captain, backed by our long batteries of thirty-two and twenty-four pounders; yet, for all that, there we lay rocking, helpless as an infant in the cradle. Had it only been a gale instead of a calm, gladly would we have charged upon it with our gallant bowsprit, as with a stout lance in rest; but, as with mankind, this serene, passive foe—unresisting and irresistible—lived it out, unconquered to the last.

All these three days the heat was excessive; the sun drew the tar from the seams of the ship; the awnings were spread fore and aft; the decks were kept constantly sprinkled with water. It was during this period that a sad event occurred, though not an unusual one on shipboard. But in order to prepare for its narration, some account of a part of the ship called the "*sick-bay*" must needs be presented.

The *sick-bay* is that part of a man-of-war where the invalid seamen are placed; in many respects it answers to a public hospital ashore. As with most frigates, the sick-bay of the Neversink was on the berth-deck—the third deck from above. It was in the extreme forward part of that deck, embracing the triangular area in the bows of the ship. It was, therefore, a subterranean vault, into which scarce a ray of heaven's glad light ever penetrated, even at noon.

In a sea-going frigate that has all her armament and stores on board, the floor of the berth-deck is partly below the surface of the water. But in a smooth harbor, some circulation of air is maintained by opening large auger-holes in the upper portion of the sides, called "air-ports," not much above the water level. Before going to sea, however, these air-ports must be closed, caulked, and the seams hermetically sealed with pitch. These places for ventilation being shut, the sick-bay is entirely barred against the free, natural admission of fresh air. In the Neversink, a few lungsful were forced down by artificial means. But as the ordinary *wind-sail* was the only method adopted, the quantity of fresh air sent down was regulated by the force of the wind. In a calm there was none to be had, while in a severe gale the wind-sail had to be hauled up, on account of the violent draught blowing full upon the cots of the sick. An open-work partition divided our sick-bay from the rest of the deck, where the hammocks of the watch were slung; it, therefore, was exposed to all the uproar that ensued upon the watches being relieved.

An official, called the surgeon's steward, assisted by subordinates, presided over the place. He was the same individual alluded to as officiating at the amputation of the top-man. He was always to be found at his post, by night and by day.

This surgeon's steward deserves a description. He was a small, pale, hollow-eyed young man, with that peculiar Lazarus-like expression so often noticed in hospital attendants. Seldom or never did you see him on deck, and when he *did* emerge into the light of the sun, it was with an abashed look, and an uneasy, winking eye. The sun was not made for *him*. His nervous organization was confounded by the sight of the robust old sea-dogs on the forecastle and the general tumult of the spar-deck, and he mostly buried himself below in an atmosphere which long habit had made congenial.

This young man never indulged in frivolous conversation; he only talked of the surgeon's prescriptions; his every word was a bolus. He never was known to smile; nor did he even look sober in the ordinary way; but his countenance ever wore an aspect of cadaverous resignation to his fate. Strange! that so many of those who would fain minister to our own health should look so much like invalids themselves.

Connected with the sick-bay, over which the surgeon's steward presided—but removed from it in place, being next door to the counting-room of the purser's steward—was a regular apothecary's shop, of which he kept the key. It was fitted up precisely like an apothecary's on shore, displaying tiers of shelves on all four sides filled with green bottles and gallipots; beneath were multitudinous drawers, bearing incomprehensible gilded inscriptions in abbreviated Latin.

He generally opened his shop for an hour or two every morning and evening. There was a Venetian blind in the upper part of the door, which he threw up when inside, so as to admit a little air. And there you would see him, with a green shade over his eyes, seated on a stool, and pounding his pestle in a great iron mortar that looked like a howitzer, mixing some jallapy compound. A smoky lamp shed a flickering, yellow-fever tinge upon his pallid face and the closely-packed regiments of gallipots.

Several times when I felt in need of a little medicine, but was not ill enough to report myself to the surgeon at his levees, I would call of a morning upon his steward at the Sign of the Mortar, and beg him to give me what I wanted; when, without speaking a word, this cadaverous young man would mix me my potion in a tin cup, and hand it out through the little opening in his door, like the boxed-up treasurer giving you your change at the ticket-office of a theatre.

But there was a little shelf against the wall of the door, and upon this I would set the tin cup for a while, and survey it; for I never was a Julius Cæsar at taking medicine; and to take it in this way, without a single attempt at disguising it; with no counteracting little morsel to hurry down after it; in short, to go to the very apothecary's in person, and there, at the counter, swallow down your dose, as if it were a nice mint-julep taken at the bar of a hotel—*this* was a bitter bolus indeed. But, then, this pallid young apothecary charged nothing for it, and *that* was no small satisfaction; for is it not remarkable, to say the least, that a shore apothecary should actually charge you money—round dollars and cents—for giving you a horrible nausea?

My tin cup would wait a long time on that little shelf; yet "Pills," as the sailors called him, never heeded my lingering, but in sober, silent sadness continued pounding his mortar or folding up his powders; until at last some other customer would appear, and then, in a sudden frenzy of resolution, I would gulp down my sherry-cobbler, and carry its unspeakable flavor with me far up into the frigate's main-top. I do not know whether it was the wide roll of the ship, as felt in that giddy perch, that occasioned it, but I always got sea sick after taking medicine and going aloft with it. Seldom or never did it do me any lasting good.

Now the Surgeon's Steward was only a subordinate of Surgeon Cuticle himself, who lived in the ward-room among the Lieutenants, Sailing-master, Chaplain, and Purser.

The Surgeon is, by law, charged with the business of overlooking the general sanitary affairs of the ship. If any thing is going on in any of its departments which he judges to be detrimental to the healthfulness of the crew, he has a right to protest against it formally to the Captain. When a man is being scourged at the gangway, the Surgeon stands by; and if he thinks that the punishment is becoming more than the culprit's constitution can well bear, he has a right to interfere and demand its cessation for the time.

But though the Navy regulations nominally vest him with this high discretionary authority over the very Commodore himself, how seldom does he exercise it in cases where humanity demands it! Three years is a long time to spend in one ship, and to be at swords' points with its Captain and Lieutenants during such a period, must be very unsocial and every way irksome. No otherwise than thus, at least, can the remissness of some surgeons in remonstrating against cruelty be accounted for.

Not to speak again of the continual dampness of the decks consequent upon flooding them with salt water, when we were driving near to Cape Horn, it needs only to be mentioned that, on board of the Neversink, men known to be in consumptions gasped under the scourge of the boatswain's mate, when the Surgeon and his two attendants stood by and never interposed. But where the unscrupulousness of martial discipline is maintained, it is in vain to attempt softening its rigor by the ordaining of humanitarian laws. Sooner might you tame the grizzly bear of Missouri than humanize a thing so essentially cruel and heartless.

But the Surgeon has yet other duties to perform. Not a seaman enters the Navy without undergoing a corporal examination, to test his soundness in wind and limb.

One of the first places into which I was introduced when I first entered on board the Neversink was the sick-bay, where I found one of the Assistant Surgeons seated at a green-baize table. It was his turn for visiting the apartment. Having been commanded by the deck officer to report my business to the functionary before me, I accordingly hemmed, to attract his attention, and then catching his eye, politely intimated that I called upon him for the purpose of being accurately laid out and surveyed.

"Strip!" was the answer, and, rolling up his gold-laced cuff, he proceeded to manipulate me. He punched me in the ribs, smote me across the chest, commanded me to stand on one leg and hold out the other horizontally. He asked me whether any of my family were consumptive; whether I ever felt a tendency to a rush of blood to the head; whether I was gouty; how often I had been bled during my life; how long I had been ashore; how long I had been afloat; with several other questions which have altogether slipped my memory. He concluded his interrogatories with this extraordinary and unwarranted one—"Are you pious?"

It was a leading question which somewhat staggered me, but I said not a word; when, feeling of my calves, he looked up and incomprehensibly said, "I am afraid you are not."

At length he declared me a sound animal, and wrote a certificate to that effect, with which I returned to the deck.

This Assistant Surgeon turned out to be a very singular character, and when I became more acquainted with him, I ceased to marvel at the curious question with which he had concluded his examination of my person.

He was a thin, knock-kneed man, with a sour, saturnine expression, rendered the more peculiar from his shaving his beard so remorselessly, that his chin and cheeks always looked blue, as if pinched with cold. His long familiarity with nautical invalids seemed to have filled him full of theological hypoes concerning the state of their souls. He was at once the physician and priest of the sick, washing down his boluses with ghostly consolation, and among the sailors went by the name of The Pelican, a fowl whose hanging pouch imparts to it a most chop-fallen, lugubrious expression.

The privilege of going off duty and lying by when you are sick, is one of the few points in which a man-of-war is far better for the sailor than a merchantman. But, as with every other matter in the Navy, the whole thing is subject to the general discipline of the vessel, and is conducted with a severe, unyielding method and regularity, making no allowances for exceptions to rules.

During the half hour preceding morning quarters, the Surgeon of a frigate is to be found in the sick-bay, where, after going his rounds among the invalids, he holds a levee for the benefit of all new candidates for the sick-list. If, after looking at your tongue, and feeling of your pulse, he pronounces you a proper candidate, his secretary puts you down on his books, and you are thenceforth relieved from all duty, and have abundant leisure in which to recover your health. Let the boatswain blow; let the deck officer bellow; let the captain of your gun hunt you up; yet, if it can be answered by your mess-mates that you are "*down on the list*," you ride it all out with impunity. The Commodore himself has then no authority over you. But you must not be too much elated, for your immunities are only secure while you are immured in the dark hospital below. Should you venture to get a mouthful of fresh air on the spar-deck, and be there discovered by an officer, you will in vain plead your illness; for it is quite impossible, it seems, that any true man-of-war invalid can be hearty enough to crawl up the ladders. Besides, the raw sea air, as they will tell you, is not good for the sick.

But, notwithstanding all this, notwithstanding the darkness and closeness of the Sick-bay, in which an alleged invalid must be content to shut himself up till the Surgeon pronounces him cured, many instances occur, especially in protracted bad weather, where pretended invalids will submit to this dismal hospital durance, in order to escape hard work and wet jackets.

There is a story told somewhere of the Devil taking down the confessions of a woman on a strip of parchment, and being obliged to stretch it longer and longer with his teeth, in order to find room for all the lady had to say. Much thus was it with our Surgeon's Steward, who had to lengthen out his manuscript Sick-list, in order to accommodate all the names which were presented to him while we were off the pitch of Cape Horn. What sailors call the "*Cape Horn Fever*," alarmingly prevailed; though it disappeared altogether when we got into fine weather, which, as with many other invalids, was solely to be imputed to the wonder-working effects of an entire change of climate.

It seems very strange, but it is really true, that off Cape Horn some "*sogers*" of sailors will stand cupping, and bleeding, and blistering, before they will budge. On the other hand, there are cases where a man actually sick and in need of medicine will refuse to go on the Sick-list, because in that case his allowance of *grog* must be stopped.

On board of every American man-of-war, bound for sea, there is a goodly supply of wines and various delicacies put on board—according to law—for the benefit of the sick, whether officers or sailors. And one of the chicken-coops is always reserved for the Government chickens, destined for a similar purpose. But, on board of the Neversink, the only delicacies given to invalid sailors was a little sago or arrow-root, and they did not get *that* unless severely ill; but, so far as I could learn, no wine, in any quantity, was ever prescribed for them, though the Government bottles often went into the Ward-room, for the benefit of indisposed officers.

And though the Government chicken-coop was replenished at every port, yet not four pair of drum-sticks were ever boiled into broth for sick sailors. Where the chickens went, some one must have known; but, as I can not vouch for it myself, I will not here back the hardy assertion of the men, which was that the pious Pelican—true to his name—was extremely fond of poultry. I am the still less disposed to believe this scandal, from the continued leanness of the Pelican, which could hardly have been the case did he nourish himself by so nutritious a dish as the drum-sticks of fowls, a diet prescribed to pugilists in training. But who can avoid being suspicious of a very suspicious person? Pelican! I rather suspect you still.

Chapter 78

Dismal Times in the Mess

I T WAS ON THE FIRST DAY of the long, hot calm which we had on the Equator, that a mess-mate of mine, by the name of Shenly, who had been for some weeks complaining, at length went on the Sick-list.

An old gunner's mate of the mess—Priming, the man with the hare-lip, who, true to his tribe, was charged to the muzzle with bile, and, moreover, rammed home on top of it a wad of sailor superstition—this gunner's mate indulged in some gloomy and savage remarks—strangely tinged with genuine feeling and grief—at the announcement of the sickness of Shenly, coming as it did not long after the almost fatal accident befalling poor Baldy, captain of the mizzen-top, another mess-mate of ours, and the dreadful fate of the amputated fore-top-man whom we buried in Rio, also our mess-mate.

We were cross-legged seated at dinner, between the guns, when the sad news concerning Shenly was first communicated.

"I know'd it, I know'd it," said Priming, through his nose. "Blast ye, I told ye so; poor fellow! But dam'me, I know'd it. This comes of having *thirteen* in the mess. I hope he arn't dangerous, men? Poor Shenly! But, blast it, it warn't till White-Jacket there comed into the mess that these here things began. I don't believe there'll be more nor three of us left by the time we strike soundings, men. But how is he now? Have you been down to see him, any on ye? Damn you, you Jonah! I don't see how you can sleep in your hammock, knowing as you do that by making an odd number in the mess you have been the death of one poor fellow, and ruined Baldy for life, and here's poor Shenly keeled up. Blast you, and your jacket, say I."

"My dear mess-mate," I cried, "don't blast me any more, for Heaven's sake. Blast my jacket you may, and I'll join you in *that;* but don't blast *me;* for if you do, I shouldn't wonder if I myself was the next man to keel up."

"Gunner's mate!" said Jack Chase, helping himself to a slice of beef, and sandwiching it between two large biscuits—"Gunner's mate! White-Jacket there is my particular friend, and I would take it as a particular favor if you would *knock off* blasting him. It's in bad taste, rude, and unworthy a gentleman."

"Take your back away from that 'ere gun-carriage, will ye now, Jack Chase?" cried Priming, in reply, just then Jack happening to lean up against it. "Must I be all the time cleaning after you fellows? Blast ye! I spent an hour on that 'ere gun-carriage this very mornin'. But it all comes of White-Jacket there. If it warn't for having one too many, there wouldn't be any crowding and jamming in the mess. I'm blessed if we ar'n't about chock a' block here! Move further up there, I'm sitting on my leg!"

"For God's sake, gunner's mate," cried I, "if it will content you, I and my jacket will leave the mess."

"I wish you would, and be —— to you!" he replied.

"And if he does, you will mess alone, gunner's mate," said Jack Chase.

"That you will," cried all.

"And I wish to the Lord you'd let me!" growled Priming, irritably rubbing his head with the handle of his sheath-knife.

"You are an old bear, gunner's mate," said Jack Chase.

"I am an old Turk," he replied, drawing the flat blade of his knife between his teeth, thereby producing a whetting, grating sound.

"Let him alone, let him alone, men," said Jack Chase. "Only keep off the tail of a rattlesnake, and he'll not rattle."

"Look out he don't bite, though," said Priming, snapping his teeth; and with that he rolled off, growling as he went.

Though I did my best to carry off my vexation with an air of indifference, need I say how I cursed my jacket, that it thus seemed the means of fastening on me the murder of one of my shipmates, and the probable murder of two more. For, had it not been for my jacket, doubtless, I had yet been a member of my old mess, and so have escaped making the luckless odd number among my present companions.

All I could say in private to Priming had no effect; though I often took him aside, to convince him of the philosophical impossibility of my having been accessary to the misfortunes of Baldy, the buried sailor in Rio, and Shenly. But Priming knew better; nothing could move him; and he ever afterward eyed me as virtuous citizens do some notorious underhand villain going unhung of justice.

Jacket! jacket! thou hast much to answer for, jacket!

Chapter 79

How Man-of-war's-men Die at Sea

SHENLY, MY SICK MESS-MATE, was a middle-aged, handsome, intelligent seaman, whom some hard calamity, or perhaps some unfortunate excess, must have driven into the Navy. He told me he had a wife and two children in Portsmouth, in the state of New Hampshire. Upon being examined by Cuticle, the surgeon, he was, on purely scientific grounds, reprimanded by that functionary for not having previously appeared before him. He was immediately consigned to one of the invalid cots as a serious case. His complaint was of long standing; a pulmonary one, now attended with general prostration.

The same evening he grew so much worse, that, according to man-of-war usage, we, his mess-mates, were officially notified that we must take turns at sitting up with him through the night. We at once made our arrangements, allotting two hours for a watch. Not till the third night did my own turn come round. During the day preceding, it was stated at the mess that our poor mess-mate was run down completely; the surgeon had given him up.

At four bells (two o'clock in the morning), I went down to relieve one of my mess-mates at the sick man's cot. The profound quietude of the calm pervaded the entire frigate through all her decks. The watch on duty were dozing on the carronade-slides, far above the sick-bay; and the watch below were fast asleep in their hammocks, on the same deck with the invalid.

Groping my way under these two hundred sleepers, I entered the hospital. A dim lamp was burning on the table, which was screwed down to the floor. This light shed dreary shadows over the white-washed walls of the place, making it look like a whited sepulchre under ground. The wind-sail had collapsed, and lay motionless on the deck. The low groans of the sick were the only sounds to be heard; and as I advanced, some of them rolled upon me their sleepless, silent, tormented eyes.

"Fan him, and keep his forehead wet with this sponge," whispered my mess-mate, whom I came to relieve, as I drew near to Shenly's cot, "and wash the foam from his mouth; nothing more can be done for him. If he dies before your watch is out, call the Surgeon's steward; he sleeps in that hammock," pointing it out. "Good-by, good-by, mess-mate," he then whispered, stooping over the sick man; and so saying, he left the place.

Shenly was lying on his back. His eyes were closed, forming two dark-blue pits in his face; his breath was coming and going with a slow, long-drawn, mechanical precision. It was the mere foundering hull of a man that was before me; and though it presented the well-known features of my mess-mate, yet I knew that the living soul of Shenly never more would look out of those eyes.

So warm had it been during the day, that the Surgeon himself, when visiting the sick-bay, had entered it in his shirt sleeves; and so warm was now the night, that even in the lofty top I had worn but a loose linen frock and trowsers. But in this subterranean sick-bay, buried in the very bowels of the ship, and at sea cut off from all ventilation, the heat of the night calm was intense. The sweat dripped from me as if I had just emerged from a bath; and stripping myself naked to the waist, I sat by the side of the cot, and with a bit of crumpled paper—put into my hand by the sailor I had relieved—kept fanning the motionless white face before me.

I could not help thinking, as I gazed, whether this man's fate had not been accelerated by his confinement in this heated furnace below; and whether many a sick man round me might not soon improve, if but permitted to swing his hammock in the airy vacancies of the half-deck above, open to the port-holes, but reserved for the promenade of the officers.

At last the heavy breathing grew more and more irregular, and gradually dying away, left forever the unstirring form of Shenly.

Calling the Surgeon's steward, he at once told me to rouse the master-at-arms, and four or five of my mess-mates. The master-at-arms approached, and immediately demanded the dead man's bag, which was accordingly dragged into the bay. Having been laid on the floor, and washed with a bucket of water which I drew from the ocean, the body was then dressed in a white frock, trowsers, and neckerchief, taken out of the bag. While this was going on, the master-at-arms—standing over the operation with his rattan, and directing myself and mess-mates—indulged in much discursive levity, intended to manifest his fearlessness of death.

Pierre, who had been a "*chummy*" of Shenly's, spent much time in tying the neckkerchief in an elaborate bow, and affectionately adjusting the white frock and trowsers; but the master-at-arms put an end to this by ordering us to carry the body up to the gun-deck. It was placed on the death-board (used for that purpose), and we proceeded with it toward the main hatchway, awkwardly crawling under the tiers of hammocks, where the entire watch-below was sleeping. As, unavoidably, we rocked their pallets, the man-of-war's-men would cry out against us; through the mutterings of curses, the corpse reached the hatchway. Here the board slipped, and some time was spent in readjusting the body. At length we deposited it on the gun-deck, between two guns, and a union-jack being thrown over it for a pall, I was left again to watch by its side.

I had not been seated on my shot-box three minutes, when the messenger-boy passed me on his way forward; presently the slow, regular stroke of the ship's great bell was heard, proclaiming through the calm the expiration of the watch; it was four o'clock in the morning.

Poor Shenly! thought I, that sounds like your knell! and here you lie becalmed, in the last calm of all!

Hardly had the brazen din died away, when the Boatswain and his mates mustered round the hatchway, within a yard or two of the corpse, and the usual thundering call was given for the watch below to turn out.

"All the starboard-watch, ahoy! On deck there, below! Wide awake there, sleepers!"

But the dreamless sleeper by my side, who had so often sprung from his hammock at that summons, moved not a limb; the blue sheet over him lay unwrinkled.

A mess-mate of the other watch now came to relieve me; but I told him I chose to remain where I was till daylight came.

Chapter 80

The Last Stitch

JUST BEFORE DAYBREAK, two of the sail-maker's gang drew near, each with a lantern, carrying some canvass, two large shot, needles, and twine. I knew their errand; for in men-of-war the sail-maker is the undertaker.

They laid the body on deck, and, after fitting the canvass to it, seated themselves, cross-legged like tailors, one on each side, and, with their lanterns before them, went to stitching away, as if mending an old sail. Both were old men, with grizzled hair and beard, and shrunken faces. They belonged to that small class of aged seamen who, for their previous long and faithful services, are retained in the Navy more as pensioners upon its merited bounty than any thing else. They are set to light and easy duties.

"Ar'n't this the fore-top-man, Shenly?" asked the foremost, looking full at the frozen face before him.

"Ay, ay, old Ringrope," said the other, drawing his hand far back with a long thread, "I thinks it's him; and he's further aloft now, I hope, than ever he was at the fore-truck. But I only hopes; I'm afeard this ar'n't the last on him!"

"His hull here will soon be going out of sight below hatches, though, old Thrummings," replied Ringrope, placing two heavy cannon-balls in the foot of the canvass shroud.

"I don't know that, old man; I never yet sewed up a shipmate but he spooked me arterward. I tell ye, Ringrope, these 'ere corpses is cunning. You think they sinks deep, but they comes up agin as soon as you sails over 'em. They lose the number of their mess, and their mess-mates sticks their spoons in the rack; but no good—no good, old Ringrope; they ar'n't dead yet. I tell ye, now, ten best-bower-anchors wouldn't sink this 'ere top-man. He'll be soon coming in the wake of the thirty-nine spooks what spooks me every night in my hammock—jist afore the mid-watch is called. Small thanks I gets for my pains; and every one on 'em looks so 'proachful-like, with a sail-maker's needle through his nose. I've been thinkin', old Ring-rope, it's all wrong that 'ere last stitch we takes. Depend on't, they don't like it—none on 'em."

I was standing leaning over a gun, gazing at the two old men. The last remark reminded me of a superstitious custom generally practiced by most sea-undertakers upon these occasions. I resolved that, if I could help it, it should not take place upon the remains of Shenly.

"Thrummings," said I, advancing to the last speaker, "you are right. That last thing you do to the canvass is the very reason, be sure of it, that brings the ghosts after you, as you say. So don't do it to this poor fellow, I entreat. Try once, now, how it goes not to do it."

"What do you say to the youngster, old man?" said Thrummings, hold-ing up his lantern into his comrade's wrinkled face, as if deciphering some ancient parchment.

"I'm agin all innowations," said Ringrope; "it's a good old fashion, that last stitch; it keeps 'em snug, d'ye see, youngster. I'm blest if they could sleep sound, if it wa'n't for that. No, no, Thrummings! no innowations; I won't hear on't. I goes for the last stitch!"

"S'pose you was going to be sewed up yourself, old Ringrope, would you like the last stitch then? You are an old gun, Ringrope; you can't stand looking out at your port-hole much longer," said Thrummings, as his own palsied hands were quivering over the canvass.

"Better say that to yourself, old man," replied Ringrope, stooping close to the light to thread his coarse needle, which trembled in his withered hands like the needle in a compass of a Greenland ship near the Pole. "You ain't long for the sarvice. I wish I could give you some o' the blood in my veins, old man!"

"Ye ain't got ne'er a tea-spoonful to spare," said Thrummings. "It will go hard, and I wouldn't want to do it; but I'm afear'd I'll have the sewing on ye up afore long!"

"Sew *me* up? Me dead and you alive, old man?" shrieked Ringrope. "Well, I've he'rd the parson of the old Independence say as how old age was deceitful; but I never seed it so true afore this blessed night. I'm sorry for ye, old man—to see you so innocent-like, and Death all the while turning in and out with you in your hammock, for all the world like a hammockmate."

"You lie! old man," cried Thrummings, shaking with rage. "It's *you* that have Death for a hammock-mate; it's *you* that will make a hole in the shot-locker soon."

"Take that back!" cried Ringrope, huskily, leaning far over the corpse, and, needle in hand, menacing his companion with his aguish fist. "Take that back, or I'll throttle your lean bag of wind for ye!"

"Blast ye! old chaps, ain't ye any more manners than to be fighting over a dead man?" cried one of the sail-maker's mates, coming down from the spar-deck. "Bear a hand!—bear a hand! and get through with that job!"

"Only one more stitch to take," muttered Ringrope, creeping near the face.

"Drop your '*palm*,' then, and let Thrummings take it; follow me—the foot of the main-sail wants mending—must do it afore a breeze springs up. D'ye hear, old chap! I say, drop your *palm*, and follow me."

At the reiterated command of his superior, Ringrope rose, and, turning to his comrade, said, "I take it all back, Thrummings, and I'm sorry for it, too. But mind ye, take that 'ere last stitch, now; if ye don't, there's no tellin' the consekenses."

As the mate and his man departed, I stole up to Thrummings, "Don't do it—don't do it, now, Thrummings—depend on it, it's wrong!"

"Well, youngster, I'll try this here one without it for jist this here once; and if, arter that, he don't spook me, I'll be dead agin the last stitch as long as my name is Thrummings."

So, without mutilation, the remains were replaced between the guns, the union jack again thrown over them, and I reseated myself on the shot-box.

Chapter 81

How they Bury a Man-of-war's-man at Sea

QUARTERS OVER IN THE MORNING, the boatswain and his four mates stood round the main hatchway, and after giving the usual whistle, made the customary announcement—"*All hands bury the dead, ahoy!*"

In a man-of-war, every thing, even to a man's funeral and burial, proceeds with the unrelenting promptitude of the martial code. And whether it is *all hands bury the dead!* or *all hands splice the main-brace*, the order is given in the same hoarse tones.

Both officers and men assembled in the lee waist, and through that bareheaded crowd the mess-mates of Shenly brought his body to the same gangway where it had thrice winced under the scourge. But there is something in death that ennobles even a pauper's corpse; and the Captain himself stood bareheaded before the remains of a man whom, with his hat on, he had sentenced to the ignominious gratings when alive.

"*I am the resurrection and the life!*" solemnly began the Chaplain, in full canonicals, the prayer-book in his hand.

"Damn you! off those booms!" roared a boatswain's mate to a crowd of top-men, who had elevated themselves to gain a better view of the scene

"*We commit this body to the deep!*" At the word, Shenly's mess-mates tilted the board, and the dead sailor sank in the sea.

341

"Look aloft," whispered Jack Chase. "See that bird! it is the spirit of Shenly."

Gazing upward, all beheld a snow-white, solitary fowl, which—whence coming no one could tell—had been hovering over the main-mast during the service, and was now sailing far up into the depths of the sky.

Chapter 82

What remains of a Man-of-war's-man after his Burial at Sea

UPON EXAMINING SHENLY'S BAG, a will was found, scratched in pencil, upon a blank leaf in the middle of his Bible; or, to use the phrase of one of the seamen, in the midships, atween the Bible and Testament, where the Pothecary (Apocrypha) uses to be.

The will was comprised in one solitary sentence, exclusive of the dates and signatures: "*In case I die on the voyage, the Purser will please pay over my wages to my wife, who lives in Portsmouth, New Hampshire.*"

Besides the testator's, there were two signatures of witnesses.

This last will and testament being shown to the Purser, who, it seems, had been a notary, or surrogate, or some sort of cosy chamber practitioner in his time, he declared that it must be "proved." So the witnesses were called, and after recognizing their hands to the paper; for the purpose of additionally testing their honesty, they were interrogated concerning the day on which they had signed—whether it was *Banyan Day*, or *Duff Day*, or *Swamp-seed Day;* for among the sailors on board a man-of-war, the land terms, *Monday, Tuesday, Wednesday*, are almost unknown. In place of these they substitute nautical names, some of which are significant of the daily bill of fare at dinner for the week.

The two witnesses were somewhat puzzled by the attorney-like questions of the Purser, till a third party came along, one of the ship's barbers,

343

and declared, of his own knowledge, that Shenly executed the instrument on a *Shaving Day*; for the deceased seaman had informed him of the circumstance, when he came to have his beard reaped on the morning of the event.

In the Purser's opinion, this settled the question; and it is to be hoped that the widow duly received her husband's death-earned wages.

Shenly was dead and gone; and what was Shenly's epitaph?

—"D. D."—

opposite his name in the Purser's books, in *"Black's best Writing Fluid"*— funereal name and funereal hue—meaning "Discharged, Dead."

Chapter 83

A Man-of-war College

I N OUR MAN-OF-WAR WORLD, Life comes in at one gangway
and Death goes overboard at the other. Under the man-of-war scourge,
curses mix with tears; and the sigh and the sob furnish the bass to the
shrill octave of those who laugh to drown buried griefs of their own.
Checkers were played in the waist at the time of Shenly's burial; and as the
body plunged, a player swept the board. The bubbles had hardly burst,
when all hands were *piped down* by the Boatswain, and the old jests were
heard again, as if Shenly himself were there to hear.

This man-of-war life has not left me unhardened. I can not stop to weep
over Shenly now; that would be false to the life I depict; wearing no mourn-
ing weeds, I resume the task of portraying our man-of-war world.

Among the various other vocations, all driven abreast on board of the
Neversink, was that of the schoolmaster. There were two academies in the
frigate. One comprised the apprentice boys, who, upon certain days of the
week, were indoctrinated in the mysteries of the primer by an invalid corporal of marines, a slender, wizzen-cheeked man, who had received a liberal
infant-school education.

The other school was a far more pretentious affair a sort of army and
navy seminary combined, where mystical mathematical problems were
solved by the midshipmen, and great ships-of-the-line were navigated over

imaginary shoals by unimaginable observations of the moon and the stars, and learned lectures were delivered upon great guns, small arms, and the curvilinear lines described by bombs in the air.

"*The Professor*" was the title bestowed upon the erudite gentleman who conducted this seminary, and by that title alone was he known throughout the ship. He was domiciled in the Ward-room, and circulated there on a social par with the Purser, Surgeon, and other *non-combatants* and Quakers. By being advanced to the dignity of a peerage in the Ward-room, Science and Learning were ennobled in the person of this Professor, even as divinity was honored in the Chaplain enjoying the rank of a spiritual peer.

Every other afternoon, while at sea, the Professor assembled his pupils on the half-deck, near the long twenty-four pounders. A bass drum-head was his desk, his pupils forming a semicircle around him, seated on shot-boxes and match-tubs.

They were in the jelly of youth, and this learned Professor poured into their susceptible hearts all the gentle, gunpowder maxims of war. Presidents of Peace Societies and Superintendents of Sabbath Schools, must it not have been a most interesting sight?

But the Professor himself was a noteworthy person. A tall, thin, spectacled man, about forty years old, with a student's stoop in his shoulders, and wearing uncommonly scanty pantaloons, exhibiting an undue proportion of his boots. In early life he had been a cadet in the military academy of West Point; but, becoming very weak-sighted, and thereby in a good manner disqualified for active service in the field, he had declined entering the army, and accepted the office of Professor in the Navy.

His studies at West Point had thoroughly grounded him in a knowledge of gunnery; and, as he was not a little of a pedant, it was sometimes amusing, when the sailors were at quarters, to hear him criticise their evolutions at the batteries. He would quote Dr. Hutton's Tracts on the subject, also, in the original, "*The French Bombardier*," and wind up by Italian passages from the "*Prattica Manuale dell' Artiglieria.*"

Though not required by the Navy regulations to instruct his scholars in aught but the application of mathematics to navigation, yet besides this, and besides instructing them in the theory of gunnery, he also sought to root them in the theory of frigate and fleet tactics. To be sure, he himself did not know how to splice a rope or furl a sail; and, owing to his partiality for strong coffee, he was apt to be nervous when we fired salutes; yet all this did not prevent him from delivering lectures on cannonading and "breaking the enemy's line."

He had arrived at his knowledge of tactics by silent, solitary study, and earnest meditation in the sequestered retreat of his state-room. His case was somewhat parallel to the Scotchman's—John Clerk, Esq., of Eldin—who, though he had never been to sea, composed a quarto treatise on fleet-fighting, which to this day remains a text-book; and he also originated a nautical maneuvre, which has given to England many a victory over her foes.

Now there was a large black-board, something like a great-gun target —only it was square—which during the professor's lectures was placed upright on the gun-deck, supported behind by three boarding-pikes. And here he would chalk out diagrams of great fleet engagements; making marks, like the soles of shoes, for the ships, and drawing a dog-vane in one corner to denote the assumed direction of the wind. This done, with a cutlass he would point out every spot of interest.

"Now, young gentlemen, the board before you exhibits the disposition of the British West Indian squadron under Rodney, when, early on the morning of the 9th of April, in the year of our blessed Lord 1782, he discovered part of the French fleet, commanded by the Count de Grasse, lying under the north end of the Island of Dominica. It was at this juncture that the Admiral gave the signal for the British line to prepare for battle, and stand on. D'ye understand, young gentlemen? Well, the British van having nearly fetched up with the centre of the enemy—who, be it remembered, were then on the starboard tack—and Rodney's centre and rear being yet becalmed under the lee of the land—the question I ask you is, What should Rodney now do?"

"Blaze away, by all means!" responded a rather confident reefer,—Mr. Pert,—who had zealously been observing the diagram.

"But, sir, his centre and rear are still becalmed, and his van has not yet closed with the enemy."

"Wait till he *does* come in range, and *then* blaze away," said the reefer.

"Permit me to remark, Mr. Pert, that '*blaze away*' is not a strictly technical term; and also permit me to hint, Mr. Pert, that you should consider the subject rather more deeply before you hurry forward your opinion."

This rebuke not only abashed Mr. Pert, but for a time intimidated the rest; and the professor was obliged to proceed, and extricate the British fleet by himself. He concluded by awarding Admiral Rodney the victory, which must have been exceedingly gratifying to the family pride of the surviving relatives and connections of that distinguished hero.

"Shall I clean the board, sir?" now asked Mr. Pert, brightening up.

"No, sir; not till you have saved that crippled French ship in the corner.

That ship, young gentlemen, is the Glorieuse; you perceive she is cut off from her consorts, and the whole British fleet is giving chase to her. Her bowsprit is gone; her rudder is torn away; she has one hundred round shot in her hull, and two thirds of her men are dead or dying. What's to be done? the wind being at northeast by north?"

"Well, sir," said Mr. Dash, a chivalric young gentleman from Virginia, "I wouldn't strike yet; I'd nail my colors to the main-royal-mast! I would, by Jove!"

"That would not save your ship, sir; besides, your main-mast has gone by the board."

"I think, sir," said Mr. Slim, a diffident youth, "I think, sir, I would haul back the fore-top-sail."

"And why so? of what service would *that* be, I should like to know, Mr. Slim?"

"I can't tell exactly; but I think it would help her a little," was the timid reply.

"Not a whit, sir—not one particle; besides, you can't haul back your fore-top-sail—your fore-mast is lying across your forecastle."

"Haul back the main-top-sail, then," suggested another.

"Can't be done; your main-mast, also, has gone by the board!"

"Mizzen-top-sail?" meekly suggested little Boat-Plug.

"Your mizzen-top-mast, let me inform you, sir, was shot down in the first of the fight!"

"Well, sir," cried Mr. Dash, "I'd tack ship, any way; bid 'em good-by with a broadside; nail my flag to the keel, if there was no other place; and blow my brains out on the poop!"

"Idle, idle, sir! worse than idle! you are carried away, Mr. Dash, by your ardent Southern temperament! Let me inform you, young gentleman, that this ship," touching it with his cutlass, "can *not* be saved."

Then, throwing down his cutlass, "Mr. Pert, have the goodness to hand me one of those cannon-balls from the rack."

Balancing the iron sphere in one hand, the learned professor began fingering it with the other, like Columbus illustrating the rotundity of the globe before the Royal Commission of Castilian Ecclesiastics.

"Young gentlemen, I resume my remarks on the passage of a shot *in vacuo*, which remarks were interrupted yesterday by general quarters. After quoting that admirable passage in 'Spearman's British Gunner,' I then laid it down, you remember, that the path of a shot *in vacuo* describes a parabolic curve. I now add that, agreeably to the method pursued by the illustrious

Newton in treating the subject of curvilinear motion, I consider the *trajec-tory* or curve described by a moving body in space as consisting of a series of right lines, described in successive intervals of time, and constituting the diagonals of parallelograms formed in a vertical plane between the vertical deflections caused by gravity and the production of the line of motion which has been described in each preceding interval of time. This must be obvious; for, if you say that the passage *in vacuo* of this cannon-ball, now held in my hand, would describe otherwise than a series of right lines, &c., then you are brought to the *Reductio ad Absurdum*, that the diagonals of parallelo-grams are—"

"All hands reef top-sails!" was now thundered forth by the boatswain's mates. The shot fell from the professor's palm; his spectacles dropped on his nose, and the school tumultuously broke up, the pupils scrambling up the ladders with the sailors, who had been overhearing the lecture.

Chapter 84

Man-of-war Barbers

THE ALLUSION to one of the ship's barbers in a previous chapter, together with the recollection of how conspicuous a part they enacted in a tragical drama soon to be related, leads me now to introduce them to the reader.

Among the numerous artists and professors of polite trades in the Navy, none are held in higher estimation or drive a more profitable business than these barbers. And it may well be imagined that the five hundred heads of hair and five hundred beards of a frigate should furnish no small employment for those to whose faithful care they may be intrusted. As every thing connected with the domestic affairs of a man-of-war comes under the supervision of the martial executive, so certain barbers are formally licensed by the First Lieutenant. The better to attend to the profitable duties of their calling, they are exempted from all ship's duty except that of standing nightwatches at sea, mustering at quarters, and coming on deck when all hands are called. They are rated as *able seamen* or *ordinary seamen*, and receive their wages as such; but in addition to this, they are liberally recompensed for their professional services. Herein their rate of pay is fixed for every sailor manipulated—so much per quarter, which is charged to the sailor, and credited to his barber on the books of the Purser.

It has been seen that while a man-of-war barber is shaving his customers at so much per chin, his wages as a seaman are still running on, which makes him a sort of *sleeping partner* of a sailor; nor are the sailor wages he receives altogether to be reckoned as earnings. Considering the circumstances, however, not much objection can be made to the barbers on this score. But there were instances of men in the Neversink receiving government money in part pay for work done for private individuals. Among these were several accomplished tailors, who nearly the whole cruise sat cross-legged on the half-deck, making coats, pantaloons, and vests for the quarter-deck officers. Some of these men, though knowing little or nothing about sailor duties, and seldom or never performing them, stood upon the ship's books as ordinary seamen, entitled to ten dollars a month. Why was this? Previous to shipping they had divulged the fact of their being tailors. True, the officers who employed them upon their wardrobes paid them for their work, but some of them in such a way as to elicit much grumbling from the tailors. At any rate, these makers and menders of clothes did not receive from some of these officers an amount equal to what they could have fairly earned ashore by doing the same work. It was a considerable saving to the officers to have their clothes made on board.

The men belonging to the carpenter's gang furnished another case in point. There were some six or eight allotted to this department. All the cruise they were hard at work. At what? Mostly making chests of drawers, canes, little ships and schooners, swifts, and other elaborated trifles, chiefly for the Captain. What did the Captain pay them for their trouble? Nothing. But the United States government paid them; two of them (the mates) at nineteen dollars a month, and the rest receiving the pay of able seamen, twelve dollars.

To return.

The regular days upon which the barbers shall exercise their vocation are set down on the ship's calendar, and known as *shaving days*. On board of the Neversink these days are Wednesdays and Saturdays; when, immediately after breakfast, the barbers' shops were opened to customers. They were in different parts of the gun-deck, between the long twenty-four pounders. Their furniture, however, was not very elaborate, hardly equal to the sumptuous appointments of metropolitan barbers. Indeed, it merely consisted of a match-tub, elevated upon a shot-box, as a barber's chair for the patient. No Psyche glasses; no hand-mirror; no ewer and basin; no comfortable padded footstool; nothing, in short, that makes a shore "*shave*" such a luxury.

Nor are the implements of these man-of-war barbers out of keeping with the rude appearance of their shops. Their razors are of the simplest patterns, and, from their jaggedness, would seem better fitted for the preparing and harrowing of the soil than for the ultimate reaping of the crop. But this is no matter for wonder, since so many chins are to be shaven, and a razor-case holds but two razors. For only two razors does a man-of-war barber have, and, like the marine sentries at the gangways in port, these razors go off and on duty in rotation. One brush, too, brushes every chin, and one lather lathers them all. No private brushes and boxes; no reservations whatever.

As it would be altogether too much trouble for a man-of-war's-man to keep his own shaving-tools and shave himself at sea, and since, therefore, nearly the whole ship's company patronize the ship's barbers, and as the seamen must be shaven by evening quarters of the days appointed for the business, it may be readily imagined what a scene of bustle and confusion there is when the razors are being applied. First come, first served, is the motto; and often you have to wait for hours together, sticking to your position (like one of an Indian file of merchants' clerks getting letters out of the post-office), ere you have a chance to occupy the pedestal of the match-tub. Often the crowd of quarrelsome candidates wrangle and fight for precedency, while at all times the interval is employed by the garrulous in every variety of ship-gossip.

As the shaving days are unalterable, they often fall upon days of high seas and tempestuous winds, when the vessel pitches and rolls in a frightful manner. In consequence, many valuable lives are jeopardized from the razor being plied under such untoward circumstances. But these sea-barbers pride themselves upon their sea-legs, and often you will see them standing over their patients, with their feet wide apart, and scientifically swaying their bodies to the motion of the ship, as they flourish their edge-tools about the lips, nostrils, and jugular.

As I looked upon the practitioner and patient at such times, I could not help thinking that, if the sailor had any insurance on his life, it would certainly be deemed forfeited should the president of the Company chance to lounge by and behold him in that imminent peril. For myself, I accounted it an excellent preparation for going into a sea-fight, where fortitude in standing up to your gun and running the risk of all splinters, comprise part of the practical qualities that make up an efficient man-of-war's-man.

It remains to be related, that these barbers of ours had their labors considerably abridged by a fashion prevailing among many of the crew, of wearing very large whiskers; so that, in most cases, the only parts needing a shave were the upper lip and suburbs of the chin. This had been more or less the custom during the whole three years' cruise; but for some time previous to our weathering Cape Horn, very many of the seamen had redoubled their assiduity in cultivating their beards, preparatory to their return to America. There they anticipated creating no small impression by their immense and magnificent *homeward-bounders*—so they called the long fly-brushes at their chins. In particular, the more aged sailors, embracing the Old Guard of sea grenadiers on the forecastle, and the begrimed gunner's mates and quarter-gunners, sported most venerable beards of an exceeding length and hoariness, like long, trailing moss hanging from the bough of some aged oak. Above all, the Captain of the Forecastle, old Ushant—a fine specimen of a sea sexagenarian—wore a wide, spreading beard, grizzled and gray, that flowed over his breast, and often became tangled and knotted with tar. This Ushant, in all weathers, was ever alert at his duty; intrepidly mounting the fore-yard in a gale, his long beard streaming like Neptune's. Off Cape Horn it looked like a miller's, being all over powdered with frost: sometimes it glittered with minute icicles in the pale, cold, moonlit Patagonian nights. But though he was so active in time of tempest, yet when his duty did not call for exertion, he was a remarkably staid, reserved, silent, and majestic old man, holding himself aloof from noisy revelry, and never participating in the boisterous sports of the crew. He resolutely set his beard against their boyish frolickings, and often held forth like an oracle concerning the vanity thereof. Indeed, at times he was wont to talk philosophy to his ancient companions—the old sheet-anchor-men around him—as well as to the hare-brained tenants of the foretop, and the giddy lads in the mizzen.

Nor was his philosophy to be despised; it abounded in wisdom. For this Ushant was an old man, of strong natural sense, who had seen nearly the whole terraqueous globe, and could reason of civilized and savage, of Gentile and Jew, of Christian and Moslem. The long night-watches of the sailor are eminently adapted to draw out the reflective faculties of any serious-minded man, however humble or uneducated. Judge, then, what half a century of battling out watches on the ocean must have done for this fine old tar. He was a sort of sea-Socrates, in his old age "pouring out his last philosophy and life," as sweet Spenser has it; and I never could look at him, and survey his right reverend beard, without bestowing upon him that title which, in one of his satires, Persius gives to the immortal quaffer of the hemlock—*Magister Barbatus*—the bearded master.

Not a few of the ship's company had also bestowed great pains upon their hair, which some of them—especially the genteel young sailor bucks of the after-guard—wore over their shoulders like the ringleted Cavaliers. Many sailors, with naturally tendril locks, prided themselves upon what they call *love curls*, worn at the side of the head, just before the ear—a custom peculiar to tars, and which seems to have filled the vacated place of the old-fashioned Lord Rodney cue, which they used to wear some fifty years ago.

But there were others of the crew laboring under the misfortune of long, lank, Winnebago locks, or carroty bunches of hair, or rebellious bristles of a sandy hue. Ambitious of redundant mops, these still suffered their carrots to grow, spite of all ridicule. They looked like Huns and Scandinavians; and one of them, a young Down Easter, the unenvied proprietor of a thick crop of inflexible yellow bamboos, went by the name of *Peter the Wild Boy*; for, like Peter the Wild Boy in France, it was supposed that he must have been caught like a catamount in the pine woods of Maine. But there were many fine, flowing heads of hair to counterbalance such sorry exhibitions as Peter's.

What with long whiskers and venerable beards, then, of every variety of cut—Charles the Fifth's and Aurelian's—and endless *goatees* and *imperials*; and what with abounding locks, our crew seemed a company of Merovingians or Long-haired kings, mixed with savage Lombards or Longobardi, so called from their lengthy beards.

Chapter 85

The great Massacre of the Beards

THE PRECEDING CHAPTER fitly paves the way for the present, wherein it sadly befalls White-Jacket to chronicle a calamitous event, which filled the Neversink with long lamentations, that echoed through all her decks and tops. After dwelling upon our redundant locks and thrice-noble beards, fain would I cease, and let the sequel remain undisclosed, but truth and fidelity forbid.

As I now deviously hover and lingeringly skirmish about the frontiers of this melancholy recital, a feeling of sadness comes over me that I can not withstand. Such a heartless massacre of hair! Such a Bartholomew's Day and Sicilian Vespers of assassinated beards! Ah! who would believe it! With intuitive sympathy I feel of my own brown beard while I write, and thank my kind stars that each precious hair is forever beyond the reach of the ruthless barbers of a man-of-war!

It needs that this sad and most serious matter should be faithfully detailed. Throughout the cruise, many of the officers had expressed their abhorrence of the impunity with which the most extensive plantations of hair were cultivated under their very noses; and they frowned upon every beard with even greater dislike. They said it was unseamanlike; not *ship-shape*; in short, it was disgraceful to the Navy. But as Captain Claret said nothing, and as the officers, of themselves, had no authority to preach a crusade against whiskerandoes, the Old Guard on the forecastle still complacently stroked their beards, and the sweet youths of the After-guard still lovingly threaded their fingers through their curls.

Perhaps the Captain's generosity in thus far permitting our beards sprung from the fact that he himself wore a small speck of a beard upon his own imperial cheek; which, if rumor said true, was to hide something, as Plutarch relates of the Emperor Adrian. But, to do him justice—as I always have done—the Captain's beard did not exceed the limits prescribed by the Navy Department.

According to a then recent ordinance at Washington, the beards of both officers and seamen were to be accurately laid out and surveyed, and on no account must come lower than the mouth, so as to correspond with the Army standard—a regulation directly opposed to the theocratical law laid down in the nineteenth chapter and twenty-seventh verse of Leviticus, where it is expressly ordained, "*Thou shalt not mar the corners of thy beard.*" But legislators do not always square their statutes by those of the Bible.

At last, when we had crossed the Northern Tropic, and were standing up to our guns at evening quarters, and when the setting sun, streaming in at the port-holes, lit up every hair, till, to an observer on the quarter-deck, the two long, even lines of beards seemed one dense grove; in that evil hour it must have been, that a cruel thought entered into the heart of our Captain.

A pretty set of savages, thought he, am I taking home to America; people will think them all catamounts and Turks. Besides, now that I think of it, it's against the law. It will never do. They must be shaven and shorn —that's flat.

There is no knowing, indeed, whether these were the very words in which the Captain meditated that night; for it is yet a mooted point among metaphysicians, whether we think in words or whether we think in thoughts. But something like the above must have been the Captain's cogitations. At any rate, that very evening the ship's company were astounded by an extraordinary announcement made at the main-hatchway of the gun-deck, by the Boatswain's mate there stationed. He was afterward discovered to have been tipsy at the time.

"D'ye hear there, fore and aft? All you that have hair on your heads, shave them off; and all you that have beards, trim 'em small!"

Shave off our Christian heads! And then, placing them between our knees, trim small our worshiped beards! The Captain was mad.

But directly the Boatswain came rushing to the hatchway, and, after soundly rating his tipsy mate, thundered forth a true version of the order that had issued from the quarter-deck. As amended, it ran thus:

"D'ye hear there, fore and aft? All you that have long hair, cut it short; and all you that have large whiskers, trim them down, according to the Navy regulations."

This was an amendment, to be sure; but what barbarity, after all! What! not thirty days' run from home, and lose our magnificent homeward-bounders! The homeward-bounders we had been cultivating so long! Lose them at one fell swoop? Were the vile barbers of the gun-deck to reap our long, nodding harvests, and expose our innocent chins to the chill air of the Yankee coast? And our viny locks! were they also to be shorn? Was a grand sheep-shearing, such as they annually have at Nantucket, to take place; and our ignoble barbers to carry off the fleece?

Captain Claret! in cutting our beards and our hair, you cut us the unkindest cut of all! Were we going into action, Captain Claret—going to fight the foe with our hearts of flame and our arms of steel, then would we gladly offer up our beards to the terrific God of War, and *that* we would account but a wise precaution against having them tweaked by the foe. *Then*, Captain Claret, you would but be imitating the example of Alexander, who had his Macedonians all shaven, that in the hour of battle their beards might not be handles to the Persians. But *now*, Captain Claret! when after our long, long cruise, we are returning to our homes, tenderly stroking the fine tassels on our chins, and thinking of father or mother, or sister or brother, or daughter or son; to cut off our beards *now*—the very beards that were frosted white off the pitch of Patagonia—*this* is too bitterly bad, Captain Claret! and, by Heaven, we will not submit. Train your guns inboard, let the marines fix their bayonets, let the officers draw their swords; we *will not* let our beards be reaped—the last insult inflicted upon a vanquished foe in the East!

Where are you, sheet-anchor-men! Captains of the tops! gunner's mates! mariners, all! Muster round the capstan your venerable beards, and while you braid them together in token of brotherhood, cross hands and swear that we will enact over again the mutiny of the Nore, and sooner perish than yield up a hair!

The excitement was intense throughout that whole evening. Groups of tens and twenties were scattered about all the decks, discussing the mandate, and inveighing against its barbarous author. The long area of the gun-deck was something like a populous street of brokers, when some terrible commercial tidings have newly arrived. One and all, they resolved not to succumb, and every man swore to stand by his beard and his neighbor.

Twenty-four hours after—at the next evening quarters—the Captain's eye was observed to wander along the men at their guns—not a beard was shaven!

When the drum beat the retreat, the Boatswain—now attended by all four of his mates, to give additional solemnity to the announcement—repeated the previous day's order, and concluded by saying, that twenty-four hours would be given for all to acquiesce.

But the second day passed, and at quarters, untouched, every beard bristled on its chin. Forthwith Captain Claret summoned the midshipmen, who, receiving his orders, hurried to the various divisions of the guns, and communicated them to the Lieutenants respectively stationed over divisions.

The officer commanding mine turned upon us, and said, "Men, if to-morrow night I find any of you with long hair, or whiskers of a standard violating the Navy regulations, the names of such offenders shall be put down on the report."

The affair had now assumed a most serious aspect. The Captain was in earnest. The excitement increased ten-fold; and a great many of the older seamen, exasperated to the uttermost, talked about *knocking off duty* till the obnoxious mandate was revoked. I thought it impossible that they would seriously think of such a folly; but there is no knowing what man-of-war's-men will sometimes do, under provocation—witness Parker and the Nore.

That same night, when the first watch was set, the men in a body drove the two boatswain's mates from their stations at the fore and main hatch-ways, and unshipped the ladders; thus cutting off all communication between the gun and spar decks, forward of the main-mast.

Mad Jack had the trumpet; and no sooner was this incipient mutiny reported to him, than he jumped right down among the mob, and fearlessly mingling with them, exclaimed, "What do you mean, men? don't be fools! This is no way to get what you want. Turn to, my lads, turn to! Boatswain's mate, ship that ladder! So! up you tumble, now, my hearties! away you go!"

His gallant, off-handed, confident manner, recognizing no attempt at mutiny, operated upon the sailors like magic. They *tumbled up*, as commanded; and for the rest of that night contented themselves with privately fulminating their displeasure against the Captain, and publicly emblazoning every anchor-button on the coat of admired Mad Jack.

Captain Claret happened to be taking a nap in his cabin at the moment of the disturbance; and it was quelled so soon, that he knew nothing of it till it was officially reported to him. It was afterward rumored through the ship that he reprimanded Mad Jack for acting as he did. He maintained that he should at once have summoned the marines, and charged upon the "mutineers." But if the sayings imputed to the Captain were true, he nevertheless refrained from subsequently noticing the disturbance, or attempting to seek out and punish the ringleaders. This was but wise; for there are times when even the most potent governor must wink at transgression, in order to preserve the laws inviolate for the future. And great care is to be taken, by timely management, to avert an incontestable act of mutiny, and so prevent men from being roused, by their own consciousness of transgression, into all the fury of an unbounded insurrection. *Then*, for the time, both soldiers and sailors are irresistible; as even the valor of Cæsar was made to know, and the prudence of Germanicus, when their legions rebelled. And not all the concessions of Earl Spencer, as First Lord of the Admiralty, nor the threats and entreaties of Lord Bridport, the Admiral of the Fleet—no, nor his gracious majesty's plenary pardon in prospective, could prevail upon the Spithead mutineers (when at last fairly lashed up to the mark) to succumb, until deserted by their own mess-mates, and a handful was left in the breach.

Therefore, Mad Jack! you did right, and no one else could have acquitted himself better. By your crafty simplicity, good-natured daring, and off-handed air (as if nothing was happening) you perhaps quelled a very serious affair in the bud, and prevented the disgrace to the American Navy of a tragical mutiny, growing out of whiskers, soap-suds, and razors. Think of it, if future historians should devote a long chapter to the great *Rebellion of the Beards* on board the United States ship Neversink. Why, through all time thereafter, barbers would cut down their spiralized poles, and substitute miniature main-masts for the emblems of their calling.

And here is ample scope for some pregnant instruction, how that events of vast magnitude in our man-of-war world may originate in the pettiest of trifles. But that is an old theme; we waive it, and proceed.

On the morning following, though it was not a regular shaving day, the gun-deck barbers were observed to have their shops open, their match-tub accommodations in readiness, and their razors displayed. With their brushes, raising a mighty lather in their tin pots, they stood eying the passing throng of seamen, silently inviting them to walk in and be served. In addition to their usual implements, they now flourished at intervals a huge pair of sheep-shears, by way of more forcibly reminding the men of the edict which that day must be obeyed, or woe betide them.

For some hours the seamen paced to and fro in no very good humor, vowing not to sacrifice a hair. Beforehand, they denounced that man who should abase himself by compliance. But habituation to discipline is magical; and ere long an old forecastle-man was discovered elevated upon a match-tub, while, with a malicious grin, his barber—a fellow who, from his merciless rasping, was called Blue-Skin—seized him by his long beard, and at one fell stroke cut it off and tossed it out of the port-hole behind him. This forecastle-man was ever afterward known by a significant title—in the main equivalent to that name of reproach fastened upon that Athenian who, in Alexander's time, previous to which all the Greeks sported beards, first submitted to the deprivation of his own. But, spite of all the contempt hurled on our forecastle-man, so prudent an example was soon followed; presently all the barbers were busy.

Sad sight! at which any one but a barber or a Tartar would have wept! Beards three years old; *goatees* that would have graced a Chamois of the Alps; *imperials* that Count D'Orsay would have envied; and *love-curls* and man-of-war ringlets that would have measured, inch for inch, with the longest tresses of The Fair One with the Golden Locks—all went by the board! Captain Claret! how can you rest in your hammock! By this brown beard which now waves from my chin—the illustrious successor to that first, young, vigorous beard I yielded to your tyranny—by this manly beard, I swear, it was barbarous!

My noble captain, Jack Chase, was indignant. Not even all the special favors he had received from Captain Claret, and the plenary pardon extended to him for his desertion into the Peruvian service, could restrain the expression of his feelings. But in his cooler moments, Jack was a wise man; he at last deemed it but wisdom to succumb.

When he went to the barber he almost drew tears from his eyes. Seating himself mournfully on the match-tub, he looked sideways, and said to the barber, who was *slithering* his sheep-shears in readiness to begin: "My friend, I trust your scissors are consecrated. Let them not touch this beard if they have yet to be dipped in holy water; beards are sacred things, barber. Have you no feeling for beards, my friend? think of it;" and mournfully he laid his deep-dyed, russet cheek upon his hand. "Two summers have gone by since my chin has been reaped. I was in Coquimbo then, on the Spanish Main; and when the husbandman was sowing his Autumnal grain on the Vega, I started this blessed beard; and when the vine-dressers were trimming their vines in the vineyards, I first trimmed it to the sound of a flute. Ah! barber, have you no heart? This beard has been caressed by the snow-white hand of the lovely Tomasita of Tombez—the Castilian belle of all Lower Peru. Think of *that*, barber! I have worn it as an officer on the quarter-deck of a Peruvian man-of-war. I have sported it at brilliant fandangoes in Lima. I have been alow and aloft with it at sea. Yea, barber! it has streamed like an Admiral's pennant at the mast-head of this same gallant frigate, the Neversink! Oh! barber, barber! it stabs me to the heart!—Talk not of hauling down your ensigns and standards when vanquished—what is *that*, barber! to striking the flag that Nature herself has nailed to the mast!"

Here noble Jack's feelings overcame him; he drooped from the animated attitude into which his enthusiasm had momentarily transported him; his proud head sunk upon his chest, and his long, sad beard almost grazed the deck.

"Ay! trail your beards in grief and dishonor, oh crew of the Neversink!" sighed Jack. "Barber, come closer—now, tell me, my friend, have you obtained absolution for this deed you are about to commit? You have not? Then, barber, *I* will absolve you; your hands shall be washed of this sin; it is not you, but another; and though you are about to shear off my manhood, yet, barber, I freely forgive you; kneel, kneel, barber! that I may bless you, in token that I cherish no malice!"

So when this barber, who was the only tender-hearted one of his tribe, had kneeled, been absolved, and then blessed, Jack gave up his beard into his hands, and the barber, clipping it off with a sigh, held it high aloft, and, parodying the style of the boatswain's mates, cried aloud, "D'ye hear, fore and aft? This is the beard of our matchless Jack Chase, the noble captain of this frigate's main-top!"

Chapter 86

The Rebels brought to the Mast

THOUGH MANY HEADS OF HAIR were shorn, and many fine beards reaped that day, yet several still held out, and vowed to defend their sacred hair to the last gasp of their breath. These were chiefly old sailors—some of them petty officers—who, presuming upon their age or rank, doubtless thought that, after so many had complied with the Captain's commands, *they*, being but a handful, would be exempted from compliance, and remain a monument of our master's clemency.

That same evening, when the drum beat to quarters, the sailors went sullenly to their guns, and the old tars who still sported their beards stood up, grim, defying, and motionless, as the rows of sculptured Assyrian kings, who, with their magnificent beards, have recently been exhumed by Layard.

When the proper time arrived, their names were taken down by the officers of divisions, and they were afterward summoned in a body to the mast, where the Captain stood ready to receive them. The whole ship's company crowded to the spot, and, amid the breathless multitude, the venerable rebels advanced and unhatted.

It was an imposing display. They were old and venerable mariners; their cheeks had been burned brown in all latitudes, wherever the sun sends a tropical ray. Reverend old tars, one and all; some of them might have been grandsires, with grandchildren in every port round the world. They ought to have commanded the veneration of the most frivolous or magisterial beholder. Even Captain Claret they ought to have humiliated into deference. But a Scythian is touched with no reverential promptings; and, as the Roman student well knows, the august Senators themselves, seated in the Senate-house, on the majestic hill of the Capitol, had their holy beards tweaked by the insolent chief of the Goths.

Such an array of beards! spade-shaped, hammer-shaped, dagger-shaped, triangular, square, peaked, round, hemispherical, and forked. But chief among them all, was old Ushant's, the ancient Captain of the Forecastle. Of a Gothic venerableness, it fell upon his breast like a continual iron-gray storm.

Ah! old Ushant, Nestor of the crew! it promoted my longevity to behold you.

He was a man-of-war's-man of the old Benbow school. He wore a short cue, which the wags of the mizzen-top called his *"plug of pig-tail."* About his waist was a broad boarder's belt, which he wore, he said, to brace his main-mast, meaning his backbone; for at times he complained of rheumatic twinges in the spine, consequent upon sleeping on deck, now and then, during the night-watches of upward of half a century. His sheath-knife was an antique—a sort of old-fashioned pruning-hook; its handle— a sperm whale's tooth—was carved all over with ships, cannon, and anchors. It was attached to his neck by a *lanyard*, elaborately worked into "rose-knots" and "Turks' heads" by his own venerable fingers.

Of all the crew, this Ushant was most beloved by my glorious Captain, Jack Chase, who one day pointed him out to me as the old man was slowly coming down the rigging from the fore-top.

"There, White-Jacket! isn't that old Chaucer's shipman?

"'A dagger hanging by a las hadde he,
About his nekke, under his arm adown;
The hote sommer hadde made his beard all brown.
Hardy he is, and wise; I undertake
With many a tempest has his beard be shake.'

From the Canterbury Tales, White-Jacket! and must not old Ushant have been living in Chaucer's time, that Chaucer could draw his portrait so well?"

Chapter 87

Old Ushant at the Gangway

THE REBEL BEARDS, headed by old Ushant's, streaming like a Commodore's *bougee*, now stood in silence at the mast.

"You knew the order!" said the Captain, eying them severely; "what does that hair on your chins?"

"Sir," said the Captain of the Forecastle, "did old Ushant ever refuse doing his duty? did he ever yet miss his muster? But, sir, old Ushant's beard is his own!"

"What's that, sir? Master-at-arms, put that man into the brig."

"Sir," said the old man, respectfully, "the three years for which I shipped are expired; and though I am perhaps bound to work the ship home, yet, as matters are, I think my beard might be allowed me. It is but a few days, Captain Claret."

"Put him into the brig!" cried the Captain; "and now, you old rascals!" he added, turning round upon the rest, "I give you fifteen minutes to have those beards taken off; if they then remain on your chins, I'll flog you—every mother's son of you—though you were all my own godfathers!"

The band of beards went forward, summoned their barbers, and their glorious pennants were no more. In obedience to orders, they then paraded themselves at the mast, and, addressing the Captain, said, "Sir, our *muzzle-lashings* are cast off!"

Nor is it unworthy of being chronicled, that not a single sailor who complied with the general order but refused to sport the vile *regulation-whiskers* prescribed by the Navy Department. No! like heroes they cried, "Shave me clean! I will not wear a hair, since I can not wear all!"

On the morrow, after breakfast, Ushant was taken out of irons, and, with the master-at-arms on one side and an armed sentry on the other, was escorted along the gun-deck and up the ladder to the main-mast. There the Captain stood, firm as before. They must have guarded the old man thus to prevent his escape to the shore, something less than a thousand miles distant at the time.

"Well, sir, will you have that beard taken off? you have slept over it a whole night now; what do you say? I don't want to flog an old man like you, Ushant!"

"My beard is my own, sir!" said the old man, lowly.

"Will you take it off?"

"It is mine, sir!" said the old man, tremulously.

"Rig the gratings!" roared the Captain. "Master-at-arms, strip him! quarter-masters, seize him up! boatswain's mates, do your duty!"

While these executioners were employed, the Captain's excitement had a little time to abate; and when, at last, old Ushant was tied up by the arms and legs, and his venerable back was exposed—that back which had bowed at the guns of the frigate Constitution when she captured the Guerriere— the Captain seemed to relent.

"You are a very old man," he said, "and I am sorry to flog you; but my orders must be obeyed. I will give you one more chance; will you have that beard taken off?"

"Captain Claret," said the old man, turning round painfully in his bonds, "you may flog me, if you will; but, sir, in this one thing I can *not* obey you."

"Lay on! I'll see his backbone!" roared the Captain in a sudden fury.

"By Heaven!" thrillingly whispered Jack Chase, who stood by, "it's only a halter; I'll strike him!"

"Better not," said a top-mate; "it's death, or worse punishment, remember."

"There goes the lash!" cried Jack. "Look at the old man! By G—d, I can't stand it! Let me go, men!" and with moist eyes Jack forced his way to one side.

"You, boatswain's mate," cried the Captain, "you are favoring that man! Lay on soundly, sir, or I'll have your own *cat* laid soundly on you."

One, two, three, four, five, six, seven, eight, nine, ten, eleven, twelve lashes were laid on the back of that heroic old man. He only bowed over his head, and stood as the Dying Gladiator lies.

"Cut him down," said the Captain.

"And now go and cut your own throat," hoarsely whispered an old sheet-anchor-man, a mess-mate of Ushant's.

When the master-at-arms advanced with the prisoner's shirt, Ushant waived him off with the dignified air of a Brahim, saying, "Do you think, master-at-arms, that I am hurt? I will put on my own garment. I am never the worse for it, man; and 'tis no dishonor when he who would dishonor you, only dishonors himself."

"What says he?" cried the Captain; "what says that tarry old philosopher with the smoking back? Tell it to me, sir, if you dare! Sentry, take that man back to the brig. Stop! John Ushant, you have been Captain of the Forecastle; I break you. And now you go into the brig, there to remain till you consent to have that beard taken off."

"My beard is my own," said the old man, quietly. "Sentry, I am ready."

And back he went into durance between the guns; but after lying some four or five days in irons, an order came to remove them; but he was still kept confined.

Books were allowed him, and he spent much time in reading. But he also spent many hours in braiding his beard, and interweaving with it strips of red bunting, as if he desired to dress out and adorn the thing which had triumphed over all opposition.

He remained a prisoner till we arrived in America; but the very moment he heard the chain rattle out of the hawse-hole, and the ship swing to her anchor, he started to his feet, dashed the sentry aside, and gaining the deck, exclaimed, "At home, with my beard!"

His term of service having some months previous expired, and the ship being now in harbor, he was beyond the reach of naval law, and the officers durst not molest him. But without unduly availing himself of these circumstances, the old man merely got his bag and hammock together, hired a boat, and throwing himself into the stern, was rowed ashore, amid the unsuppressible cheers of all hands. It was a glorious conquest over the Conqueror himself, as well worthy to be celebrated as the Battle of the Nile.

Though, as I afterward learned, Ushant was earnestly entreated to put the case into some lawyer's hands, he firmly declined, saying, "I have won the battle, my friends, and I do not care for the prize-money." But even had he complied with these entreaties, from precedents in similar cases, it is almost certain that not a sou's worth of satisfaction would have been received.

I know not in what frigate you sail now, old Ushant; but Heaven protect your storied old beard, in whatever Typhoon it may blow. And if ever it must be shorn, old man, may it fare like the royal beard of Henry I., of England, and be clipped by the right reverend hand of some Archbishop of Sees.

As for Captain Claret, let it not be supposed that it is here sought to impale him before the world as a cruel, black-hearted man. Such he was not. Nor was he, upon the whole, regarded by his crew with any thing like the feelings which man-of-war's-men sometimes cherish toward signally tyrannical commanders. In truth, the majority of the Neversink's crew—in previous cruises habituated to flagrant misusage—deemed Captain Claret a lenient officer. In many things he certainly refrained from oppressing them. It has been related what privileges he accorded to the seamen respecting the free playing of checkers—a thing almost unheard of in most American men-of-war. In the matter of overseeing the men's clothing, also, he was remarkably indulgent, compared with the conduct of other Navy Captains, who, by sumptuary regulations, oblige their sailors to run up large bills with the Purser for clothes. In a word, of whatever acts Captain Claret might have been guilty in the Neversink, perhaps none of them proceeded from any personal, organic hard-heartedness. What he was, the usages of the Navy had made him. Had he been a mere landsman—a merchant, say—he would no doubt have been considered a kind-hearted man.

There may be some who shall read of this Bartholomew Massacre of beards who will yet marvel, perhaps, that the loss of a few hairs, more or less, should provoke such hostility from the sailors, lash them into so frothing a rage; indeed, come near breeding a mutiny.

But these circumstances are not without precedent. Not to speak of the riots, attended with the loss of life, which once occurred in Madrid, in resistance to an arbitrary edict of the king's, seeking to suppress the cloaks of the Cavaliers; and, not to make mention of other instances that might be quoted, it needs only to point out the rage of the Saxons in the time of William the Conqueror, when that despot commanded the hair on their upper lips to be shaven off—the hereditary mustaches which whole generations had sported. The multitude of the dispirited vanquished were obliged to acquiesce; but many Saxon Franklins and gentlemen of spirit, choosing rather to lose their castles than their mustaches, voluntarily deserted their fire-sides, and went into exile. All this is indignantly related by the stout

Saxon friar, Matthew Paris, in his *Historia Major*, beginning with the Norman Conquest.

And that our man-of-war's-men were right in desiring to perpetuate their beards, as martial appurtenances, must seem very plain, when it is considered that, as the beard is the token of manhood, so, in some shape or other, has it ever been held the true badge of a warrior. Bonaparte's grenadiers were stout whiskerandoes; and perhaps, in a charge, those fierce whiskers of theirs did as much to appall the foe as the sheen of their bayonets. Most all fighting creatures sport either whiskers or beards; it seems a law of Dame Nature. Witness the boar, the tiger, the cougar, man, the leopard, the ram, the cat—all warriors, and all whiskerandoes. Whereas, the peace-loving tribes have mostly enameled chins.

Chapter 88

Flogging through the Fleet

THE FLOGGING OF AN OLD MAN like Ushant, most landsmen will probably regard with abhorrence. But though, from peculiar circumstances, his case occasioned a good deal of indignation among the people of the Neversink, yet, upon its own proper grounds, they did not denounce it. Man-of-war's-men are so habituated to what landsmen would deem excessive cruelties, that they are almost reconciled to inferior severities.

And here, though the subject of punishment in the Navy has been canvassed in previous chapters, and though the thing is every way a most unpleasant and grievous one to enlarge upon, and though I painfully nerve myself to it while I write, a feeling of duty compels me to enter upon a branch of the subject till now undiscussed. I would not be like the man, who, seeing an outcast perishing by the road-side, turned about to his friend, saying, "Let us cross the way; my soul so sickens at this sight, that I can not endure it."

There are certain enormities in this man-of-war world that often secure impunity by their very excessiveness. Some ignorant people will refrain from permanently removing the cause of a deadly malaria, for fear of the temporary spread of its offensiveness. Let us not be of such. The more repugnant and repelling, the greater the evil. Leaving our women and children behind, let us freely enter this Golgotha.

Years ago there was a punishment inflicted in the English, and I believe in the American Navy, called *keel-hauling*—a phrase still employed by man-of-war's-men when they would express some signal vengeance upon a personal foe. The practice still remains in the French national marine, though it is by no means resorted to so frequently as in times past. It consists of attaching tackles to the two extremities of the main-yard, and passing the rope under the ship's bottom. To one end of this rope the culprit is secured; his own shipmates are then made to run him up and down, first on this side, then on that—now scraping the ship's hull under water—anon, hoisted, stunned and breathless, into the air.

But though this barbarity is now abolished from the English and American navies, there still remains another practice which, if any thing, is even worse than *keel-hauling*. This remnant of the Middle Ages is known in the Navy as "*flogging through the fleet.*" It is never inflicted except by authority of a court-martial upon some trespasser deemed guilty of a flagrant offence. Never, that I know of, has it been inflicted by an American man-of-war on the home station. The reason, probably, is, that the officers well know that such a spectacle would raise a mob in any American sea-port.

By XLI. of the Articles of War, a court-martial shall not, "for any one offence not capital," inflict a punishment beyond one hundred lashes. In cases "not capital" this law may be, and has been, quoted in judicial justification of the infliction of more than one hundred lashes. Indeed, it would cover a thousand. Thus: One act of a sailor may be construed into the commission of ten different transgressions, for each of which he may be legally condemned to a hundred lashes, to be inflicted without intermission. It will be perceived, that in any case deemed "capital," a sailor, under the above Article, may legally be flogged to the death.

But neither by the Articles of War, nor by any other enactment of Congress, is there any direct warrant for the extraordinary cruelty of the mode in which punishment is inflicted, in cases of flogging through the fleet. But as in numerous other instances, the incidental aggravations of this penalty are indirectly covered by other clauses in the Articles of War; one of which authorizes the authorities of a ship—in certain indefinite cases—to correct the guilty "*according to the usages of the sea-service.*"

One of these "usages" is the following:

All hands being called "to witness punishment" in the ship to which the culprit belongs, the sentence of the court-martial condemning him is read, when, with the usual solemnities, a portion of the punishment is inflicted. In order that it shall not lose in severity by the slightest exhaustion in the arm of the executioner, a fresh boatswain's mate is called out at every dozen.

As the leading idea is to strike terror into the beholders, the greatest number of lashes is inflicted on board the culprit's own ship, in order to render him the more shocking spectacle to the crews of the other vessels.

The first infliction being concluded, the culprit's shirt is thrown over him; he is put into a boat—the Rogue's March being played meanwhile— and rowed to the next ship of the squadron. All hands of that ship are then called to man the rigging, and another portion of the punishment is inflicted by the boatswain's mates of that ship. The bloody shirt is again thrown over the seaman; and thus he is carried through the fleet or squadron till the whole sentence is inflicted.

In other cases, the launch—the largest of the boats—is rigged with a platform (like a headsman's scaffold), upon which halberds, something like those used in the English army, are erected. They consist of two stout poles, planted upright. Upon the platform stand a Lieutenant, a Surgeon, a Master-at-arms, and the executioners with their "cats." They are rowed through the fleet, stopping at each ship, till the whole sentence is inflicted, as before.

In some cases, the attending surgeon has professionally interfered before the last lash has been given, alleging that immediate death must ensue if the remainder should be administered without a respite. But instead of humanely remitting the remaining lashes, in a case like this, the man is generally consigned to his cot for ten or twelve days; and when the surgeon officially reports him capable of undergoing the rest of the sentence, it is forthwith inflicted. Shylock must have his pound of flesh.

To say, that after being flogged through the fleet, the prisoner's back is sometimes puffed up like a pillow; or to say that in other cases it looks as if burned black before a roasting fire; or to say that you may track him through the squadron by the blood on the bulwarks of every ship, would only be saying what many seamen have seen.

Several weeks, sometimes whole months, elapse before the sailor is sufficiently recovered to resume his duties. During the greater part of that interval he lies in the sick-bay, groaning out his days and nights; and unless he has the hide and constitution of a rhinoceros, he never is the man he was before, but, broken and shattered to the marrow of his bones, sinks into death before his time. Instances have occurred where he has expired the day after the punishment. No wonder that the Englishman, Dr. Granville —himself once a surgeon in the Navy—declares, in his work on Russia, that the barbarian "knout" itself is not a greater torture to undergo than the Navy cat-o'-nine-tails.

Some years ago a fire broke out near the powder magazine in an American national ship, one of a squadron at anchor in the Bay of Naples. The utmost alarm prevailed. A cry went fore and aft that the ship was about to blow up. One of the seamen sprang overboard in affright. At length the fire was got under, and the man was picked up. He was tried before a court-martial, found guilty of cowardice, and condemned to be flogged through the fleet. In due time the squadron made sail for Algiers, and in that harbor, once haunted by pirates, the punishment was inflicted—the Bay of Naples, though washing the shores of an absolute king, not being deemed a fit place for such an exhibition of American naval law.

While the Neversink was in the Pacific, an American sailor, who had deposited a vote for General Harrison for President of the United States, was flogged through the fleet.

Chapter 89

The Social State in a Man-of-war

B UT THE FLOGGINGS at the gangway and the floggings through the fleet, the stealings, highway robberies, swearings, gamblings, blasphemings, thimble-riggings, smugglings, and tipplings of a man-of-war, which throughout this narrative have been here and there sketched from the life, by no means comprise the whole catalogue of evil. One single feature is full of significance.

All large ships of war carry soldiers, called marines. In the Neversink there were something less than fifty, two thirds of whom were Irishmen. They were officered by a Lieutenant, an Orderly Sergeant, two Sergeants, and two Corporals, with a drummer and fifer. The custom, generally, is to have a marine to each gun; which rule usually furnishes the scale for distributing the soldiers in vessels of different force.

Our marines had no other than martial duty to perform; excepting that, at sea, they stood watches like the sailors, and now and then lazily assisted in pulling the ropes. But they never put foot in rigging or hand in tar-bucket.

On the quarter-bills, these men were stationed at none of the great guns; on the station-bills, they had no posts at the ropes. What, then, were they for? To serve their country in time of battle? Let us see. When a ship is running into action, her marines generally lie flat on their faces behind the bulwarks (the sailors are sometimes ordered to do the same), and when the vessel is fairly engaged, they are usually drawn up in the ship's waist—like a company reviewing in the Park. At close quarters, their muskets may pick off a seaman or two in the rigging, but at long-gun distance they must passively stand in their ranks and be decimated at the enemy's leisure. Only in one case in ten—that is, when their vessel is attempted to be boarded by a large party, are these marines of any essential service as fighting-men; with their bayonets they are then called upon to "repel!"

If comparatively so useless as soldiers, why have marines at all in the Navy? Know, then, that what standing armies are to nations, what turn-keys are to jails, these marines are to the seamen in all large men-of-war. Their muskets are their keys. With those muskets they stand guard over the fresh water; over the grog, when doled; over the provisions, when being served out by the Master's mate; over the "brig" or jail; at the Commodore's and Captain's cabin doors; and, in port, at both gangways and forecastle.

Surely, the crowd of sailors, who besides having so many sea-officers over them, are thus additionally guarded by soldiers, even when they quench their thirst—surely these man-of-war's-men must be desperadoes indeed; or else the naval service must be so tyrannical that the worst is feared from their possible insubordination. Either reason holds good, or both, according to the character of the officers and crew.

It must be evident that the man-of-war's-man casts but an evil eye on a marine. To call a man a "horse-marine," is, among seamen, one of the greatest terms of contempt.

But the mutual contempt, and even hatred, subsisting between these two bodies of men—both clinging to one keel, both lodged in one household—is held by most Navy officers as the height of the perfection of Navy discipline. It is regarded as the button that caps the uttermost point on their main-mast.

Thus they reason: Secure of this antagonism between the marine and the sailor, we can always rely upon it, that if the sailor mutinies, it needs no great incitement for the marine to thrust his bayonet through his heart; if the marine revolts, the pike of the sailor is impatient to charge. Checks and balances, blood against blood, *that* is the cry and the argument.

What applies to the relation in which the marine and sailor stand toward each other—the mutual repulsion implied by a system of checks—will, in degree, apply to nearly the entire interior of a man-of-war's discipline. The whole body of this discipline is emphatically a system of cruel cogs and wheels, systematically grinding up in one common hopper all that might minister to the moral well-being of the crew.

It is the same with both officers and men. If a Captain have a grudge against a Lieutenant, or a Lieutenant against a midshipman, how easy to torture him by official treatment, which shall not lay open the superior officer to legal rebuke. And if a midshipman bears a grudge against a sailor, how easy for him, by cunning practices, born of a boyish spite, to have him degraded at the gangway. Through all the endless ramifications of rank and station, in most men-of-war there runs a sinister vein of bitterness, not exceeded by the fire-side hatreds in a family of step-sons ashore. It were sickening to detail all the paltry irritabilities, jealousies, and cabals, the spiteful detractions and animosities, that lurk far down, and cling to the very kelson of the ship. It is unmanning to think of. The immutable ceremonies and iron etiquette of a man-of-war; the spiked barriers separating the various grades of rank; the delegated absolutism of authority on all hands; the impossibility, on the part of the common seaman, of appeal from incidental abuses, and many more things that might be enumerated, all tend to beget in most armed ships a general social condition which is the precise reverse of what any Christian could desire. And though there are vessels, that in some measure furnish exceptions to this; and though, in other ships, the thing may be glazed over by a guarded, punctilious exterior, almost completely hiding the truth from casual visitors, while the worst facts touching the common sailor are systematically kept in the background, yet it is certain that what has here been said of the domestic interior of a man-of-war will, in a greater or less degree, apply to most vessels in the Navy. It is not that the officers are so malevolent, nor, altogether, that the man-of-war's-man is so vicious. Some of these evils are unavoidably generated through the operation of the Naval code; others are absolutely organic to a Navy establishment, and, like other organic evils, are incurable, except when they dissolve with the body they live in.

These things are undoubtedly heightened by the close cribbing and confinement of so many mortals in one oaken box on the sea. Like pears closely packed, the crowded crew mutually decay through close contact, and every plague-spot is contagious. Still more, from this same close confinement—so far as it affects the common sailors—arise other evils, so direful that they will hardly bear even so much as an allusion. What too many seamen are when ashore is very well known; but what some of them become when completely cut off from shore indulgences can hardly be imagined by landsmen. The sins for which the cities of the plain were overthrown still linger in some of these wooden-walled Gomorrahs of the deep. More than once complaints were made at the mast in the Neversink, from which the deck officer would turn away with loathing, refuse to hear them, and command the complainant out of his sight. There are evils in men-of-war, which, like the suppressed domestic drama of Horace Walpole, will neither bear representing, nor reading, and will hardly bear thinking of. The landsman who has neither read Walpole's *Mysterious Mother*, nor Sophocles's *Œdipus Tyrannus*, nor the Roman story of *Count Cenci*, dramatized by Shelley, let that landsman guardedly remain in his ignorance of even worse horrors than these, and forever abstain from seeking to draw aside this veil.

Chapter 90

The Manning of Navies

T HE GALLOWS and the sea refuse nothing," is a very old sea saying; and, among all the wondrous prints of Hogarth, there is none remaining more true at the present day than that dramatic boat-scene, where after consorting with harlots and gambling on tomb-stones, the Idle Apprentice, with the villainous low forehead, is at last represented as being pushed off to sea, with a ship and a gallows in the distance. But Hogarth should have converted the ship's masts themselves into Tyburn-trees, and thus, with the ocean for a background, closed the career of his hero. It would then have had all the dramatic force of the opera of Don Juan, who, after running his impious courses, is swept from our sight in a tornado of devils.

For the sea is the true Tophet and bottomless pit of many workers of iniquity; and, as the German mystics feign Gehennas within Gehennas, even so are men-of-war familiarly known among sailors as "Floating Hells." And as the sea, according to old Fuller, is the stable of brute monsters, gliding hither and thither in unspeakable swarms, even so is it the home of many moral monsters, who fitly divide its empire with the snake, the shark, and the worm.

Nor are sailors, and man-of-war's-men especially, at all blind to a true sense of these things. "*Purser rigged and parish damned,*" is the sailor saying in the American Navy, when the tyro first mounts the linen frock and blue jacket, aptly manufactured for him in a State Prison ashore.

No wonder, that lured by some *crimp* into a service so galling, and, perhaps, persecuted by a vindictive lieutenant, some repentant sailors have actually jumped into the sea to escape from their fate, or set themselves adrift on the wide ocean on the gratings, without compass or rudder.

In one case, a young man, after being nearly cut into dog's meat at the gangway, loaded his pockets with shot and walked overboard.

Some years ago, I was in a whaling ship lying in a harbor of the Pacific, with three French men-of-war alongside. One dark, moody night, a suppressed cry was heard from the face of the waters, and, thinking it was some one drowning, a boat was lowered, when two French sailors were picked up, half dead from exhaustion, and nearly throttled by a bundle of their clothes tied fast to their shoulders. In this manner they had attempted their escape from their vessel. When the French officers came in pursuit, these sailors, rallying from their exhaustion, fought like tigers to resist being captured. Though this story concerns a French armed ship, it is not the less applicable, in degree, to those of other nations.

Mix with the men in an American armed ship; mark how many foreigners there are, though it is against the law to enlist them. Nearly one third of the petty officers of the Neversink were born east of the Atlantic. Why is this? Because the same principle that operates in hindering Americans from hiring themselves out as menial domestics also restrains them, in a great measure, from voluntarily assuming a far worse servitude in the Navy. "*Sailors wanted for the Navy*" is a common announcement along the wharves of our sea-ports. They are always "*wanted*." It may have been, in part, owing to this scarcity of man-of-war's-men, that not many years ago, black slaves were frequently to be found regularly enlisted with the crew of an American frigate, their masters receiving their pay. This was in the teeth of a law of Congress expressly prohibiting slaves in the Navy. This law, indirectly, means black slaves, nothing being said concerning white ones. But in view of what John Randolph of Roanoke said about the frigate that carried him to Russia, and in view of what most armed vessels actually are at present, the American Navy is not altogether an inappropriate place for hereditary bondmen. Still, the circumstance of their being found in it is of such a nature, that to some it may hardly appear credible. The incredulity of such persons, nevertheless, must yield to the fact, that on board of the United States ship Neversink, during the present cruise, there was a Virginian slave regularly shipped as a seaman, his owner receiving his wages. Guinea—such was his name among the crew—belonged to the Purser, who was a southern gentleman; he was employed as his body servant. Never did I feel my condition as a man-of-war's-man so keenly as when seeing this Guinea freely circulating about the decks in citizen's clothes, and, through the influence of his master, almost entirely exempted from the disciplinary degradation of the Caucasian crew. Faring sumptuously in the ward-room; sleek and round, his ebon face fairly polished with content; ever gay and hilarious; ever ready to laugh and joke, that African slave was actually envied by many of the seamen. There were times when I almost envied him myself. Lemsford once envied him outright. "Ah, Guinea!" he sighed, "you have peaceful times; you never opened the book I read in."

One morning, when all hands were called to witness punishment, the Purser's slave, as usual, was observed to be hurrying down the ladders toward the ward-room, his face wearing that peculiar, pinched blueness, which, in the negro, answers to the paleness caused by nervous agitation in the white. "Where are you going, Guinea?" cried the deck-officer, a humorous gentleman, who sometimes diverted himself with the Purser's slave, and well knew what answer he would now receive from him. "Where are you going, Guinea?" said this officer; "turn about; don't you hear the call, sir?" "'Scuse me, massa!" said the slave, with a low salutation; "I can't 'tand it; I can't, indeed, massa!" and, so saying, he disappeared beyond the hatchway. He was the only person on board, except the hospital-steward and the invalids of the sick-bay, who was exempted from being present at the administering of the scourge. Accustomed to light and easy duties from his birth, and so fortunate as to meet with none but gentle masters, Guinea, though a bondman, liable to be saddled with a mortgage, like a horse—Guinea, in India-rubber manacles, enjoyed the liberties of the world.

Though his body-and-soul proprietor, the Purser, never in any way individualized me while I served on board the frigate, and never did me a good office of any kind (it was hardly in his power), yet, from his pleasant, kind, indulgent manner toward his slave, I always imputed to him a generous heart, and cherished an involuntary friendliness toward him. Upon our arrival home, his treatment of Guinea, under circumstances peculiarly calculated to stir up the resentment of a slave-owner, still more augmented my estimation of the Purser's good heart.

Mention has been made of the number of foreigners in the American Navy; but it is not in the American Navy alone that foreigners bear so large a proportion to the rest of the crew, though in no navy, perhaps, have they ever borne so large a proportion as in our own. According to an English estimate, the foreigners serving in the King's ships at one time amounted to one eighth of the entire body of seamen. How it is in the French Navy, I can not with certainty say; but I have repeatedly sailed with English seamen who have served in it.

One of the effects of the free introduction of foreigners into any Navy can not be sufficiently deplored. During the period I lived in the Neversink, I was repeatedly struck by the lack of patriotism in many of my shipmates. True, they were mostly foreigners who unblushingly avowed, that were it not for the difference of pay, they would as lief man the guns of an English ship as those of an American or Frenchman. Nevertheless, it was evident, that as for any high-toned patriotic feeling, there was comparatively very little—hardly any of it—evinced by our sailors as a body. Upon reflection, this was not to be wondered at. From their roving career, and the sundering of all domestic ties, many sailors, all the world over, are like the "Free Companions," who some centuries ago wandered over Europe, ready to fight the battles of any prince who could purchase their swords. The only patriotism is born and nurtured in a stationary home, and upon an immovable hearth-stone; but the man-of-war's-man, though in his voyagings he weds the two Poles and brings both Indies together, yet, let him wander where he will, he carries his one only home along with him: that home is his hammock. *"Born under a gun, and educated on the bowsprit,"* according to a phrase of his own, the man-of-war's-man rolls round the world like a billow, ready to mix with any sea, or be sucked down to death in the Maelstrom of any war.

Yet more. The dread of the general discipline of a man-of-war; the special obnoxiousness of the gangway; the protracted confinement on board ship, with so few "liberty days;" and the pittance of pay (much less than what can always be had in the Merchant Service), these things contrive to deter from the navies of all countries by far the majority of their best seamen. This will be obvious, when the following statistical facts, taken from Macpherson's Annals of Commerce, are considered. At one period, upon the Peace Establishment, the number of men employed in the English Navy was 25,000; at the same time, the English Merchant Service was employing 118,952. But while the necessities of a merchantman render it indispensable that the greater part of her crew be able seamen, the circumstances of a man-of war admit of her mustering a crowd of landsmen, soldiers, and boys in her service. By a statement of Captain Marryat's, in his pamphlet (A.D. 1822) "On the Abolition of Impressment," it appears that, at the close of the Bonaparte wars, a full third of all the crews of his Majesty's fleets consisted of landsmen and boys.

Far from entering with enthusiasm into the King's ships when their country was menaced, the great body of English seamen, appalled at the discipline of the Navy, adopted unheard-of devices to escape its press-gangs. Some even hid themselves in caves, and lonely places inland, fearing to run the risk of seeking a berth in an outward-bound merchantman, that might have carried them beyond sea. In the true narrative of "John Nichol, Mariner," published in 1822 by Blackwood in Edinburgh, and Cadell in London, and which every where bears the spontaneous impress of truth, the old sailor, in the most artless, touching, and almost uncomplaining manner, tells of his "skulking like a thief" for whole years in the country round about Edinburgh, to avoid the press-gangs, prowling through the land like bandits and Burkers. At this time (Bonaparte's wars), according to "Steel's List," there were forty-five regular press-gang stations in Great Britain.*

In a later instance, a large body of British seamen solemnly assembled upon the eve of an anticipated war, and together determined, that in case of its breaking out, they would at once flee to America, to avoid being pressed into the service of their country—a service which degraded her own guardians at the gangway.

At another time, long previous to this, according to an English Navy officer, Lieutenant Tomlinson, three thousand seamen, impelled by the same motive, fled ashore in a panic from the colliers between Yarmouth

---

* Besides this domestic kidnapping, British frigates, in friendly or neutral harbors, in some instances pressed into their service foreign sailors of all nations from the public wharves. In certain cases, where Americans were concerned, when "*protections*" were found upon their persons, these were destroyed; and to prevent the American consul from claiming his sailor countrymen, the press-gang generally went on shore the night previous to the sailing of the frigate, so that the kidnapped seamen were far out to sea before they could be missed by their friends. It is not intended to revive old feuds. In one sense, let by-gones be by-gones. But these things should be known; for in case the English government again goes to war with its fleets, and should again resort to indiscriminate impressment to man them, it is well that both Englishmen and Americans, that all the world be prepared to put down an iniquity outrageous and insulting to God and man. It is hardly to be anticipated, however, that in case of war the English government would again attempt to revive measures, which some of its own statesmen must have deplored from the beginning; and which, at the present day, must surely seem iniquitous to the great body of Englishmen. Indeed, it is perhaps to be doubted, whether Englishmen could again be brought to submit even to domestic impressment.

Roads and the Nore. Elsewhere, he says, in speaking of some of the men on board the King's ships, that "they were most miserable objects." This remark is perfectly corroborated by other testimony referring to another period. In alluding to the lamented scarcity of good English seamen during the wars of 1808, &c., the author of a pamphlet on "Naval Subjects" says, that all the best seamen, the steadiest and best-behaved men, generally succeeded in avoiding the impress. This writer was, or had been, himself a Captain in the British fleet.

Now it may be easily imagined who are the men, and of what moral character they are, who, even at the present day, are willing to enlist as full-grown adults in a service so galling to all shore-manhood as the Navy. Hence it comes that the skulkers and scoundrels of all sorts in a man-of-war are chiefly composed not of regular seamen, but of these "dock-lopers" of landsmen, men who enter the Navy to draw their grog and murder their time in the notorious idleness of a frigate. But if so idle, why not reduce the number of a man-of-war's crew, and reasonably keep employed the rest? It can not be done. In the first place, the magnitude of most of these ships requires a large number of hands to brace the heavy yards, hoist the enormous top-sails, and weigh the ponderous anchor. And though the occasion for the employment of so many men comes but seldom, it is true, yet when that occasion *does* come—and come it may at any moment—this multitude of men are indispensable.

But besides this, and to crown all, the batteries must be manned. There must be enough men to work all the guns at one time. And thus, in order to have a sufficiency of mortals at hand to "sink, burn, and destroy;" a man-of-war—besides, through her vices, hopelessly depraving the volunteer landsmen and ordinary seamen of good habits, who occasionally enlist—must feed at the public cost a multitude of persons, who, if they did not find a home in the Navy, would probably fall on the parish, or linger out their days in a prison.

Among others, these are the men into whose mouths Dibdin puts his patriotic verses, full of sea-chivalry and romance. With an exception in the last line, they might be sung with equal propriety by both English and American man-of-war's-men.

> "As for me, in all weathers, all times, tides, and ends,
>   Naught's a trouble from duty that springs,
>   For my heart is my Poll's, and my rhino's my friend's,
>   And as for my life, it's the king's.

> To rancour unknown, to no passion a slave,
> Nor unmanly, nor mean, nor a railer," &c.

I do not unite with a high critical authority in considering Dibdin's ditties as "slang songs," for most of them breathe the very poetry of the ocean. But it is remarkable that those songs—which would lead one to think that man-of-war's-men are the most care-free, contented, virtuous, and patriotic of mankind—were composed at a time when the English Navy was principally manned by felons and paupers, as mentioned in a former chapter. Still more, these songs are pervaded by a true Mohammedan sensualism; a reckless acquiescence in fate, and an implicit, unquestioning, dog-like devotion to whoever may be lord and master. Dibdin was a man of genius; but no wonder Dibdin was a government pensioner at £200 per annum.

But notwithstanding the iniquities of a man-of-war, men are to be found in them, at times, so used to a hard life; so drilled and disciplined to servitude, that, with an incomprehensible philosophy, they seem cheerfully to resign themselves to their fate. They have plenty to eat; spirits to drink; clothing to keep them warm; a hammock to sleep in; tobacco to chew; a doctor to medicine them; a parson to pray for them; and, to a penniless castaway, must not all this seem as a luxurious Bill of Fare?

There was on board of the Neversink a fore-top-man by the name of Landless, who, though his back was cross-barred, and plaided with the ineffaceable scars of all the floggings accumulated by a reckless tar during a ten years' service in the Navy, yet he perpetually wore a hilarious face, and at joke and repartee was a very Joe Miller.

That man, though a sea-vagabond, was not created in vain. He enjoyed life with the zest of everlasting adolescence; and, though cribbed in an oaken prison, with the turnkey sentries all round him, yet he paced the gun-deck as if it were broad as a prairie, and diversified in landscape as the hills and valleys of the Tyrol. Nothing ever disconcerted him; nothing could transmute his laugh into any thing like a sigh. Those glandular secretions, which in other captives sometimes go to the formation of tears, in *him* were expectorated from the mouth, tinged with the golden juice of a weed, wherewith he solaced and comforted his ignominious days.

"Rum and tobacco!" said Landlass, "what more does a sailor want?"

His favorite song was "*Dibdin's True English Sailor*," beginning,

> "Jack dances and sings, and is always content,
>   In his vows to his lass he'll ne'er fail her;
>   His anchor's atrip when his money's all spent,
>   And this is the life of a sailor."

But poor Landless danced quite as often at the gangway, under the lash, as in the sailor dance-houses ashore.

Another of his songs, also set to the significant tune of *The King, God bless him!* mustered the following lines among many similar ones:

> "Oh, when safely landed in Boston or 'York,
>   Oh how I will tipple and jig it;
>   And toss off my glass while my rhino holds out,
>   In drinking success to our frigate!"

During the many idle hours when our frigate was lying in harbor, this man was either merrily playing at checkers, or mending his clothes, or snoring like a trumpeter under the lee of the booms. When fast asleep, a national salute from our batteries could hardly move him. Whether ordered to the main-truck in a gale; or rolled by the drum to the grog-tub; or commanded to walk up to the gratings and be lashed, Landless always obeyed with the same invincible indifference.

His advice to a young lad, who shipped with us at Valparaiso, embodies the pith and marrow of that philosophy which enables some man-of-war's-men to wax jolly in the service.

"*Shippy!*" said Landless, taking the pale lad by his neckerchief, as if he had him by the halter; "Shippy, I've seen sarvice with Uncle Sam—I've sailed in many *Andrew Millers*. Now take my advice, and steer clear of all trouble. D'ye see, touch your tile whenever a swob (officer) speaks to you. And never mind how much they rope's-end you, keep your red-rag belayed; for you must know as how they don't fancy sea-lawyers; and when the sarving out of slops comes round, stand up to it stiffly; it's only an oh Lord! or two, and a few oh my Gods!—that's all. And what then? Why, you sleeps it off in a few nights, and turns out at last all ready for your grog."

This Landless was a favorite with the officers, among whom he went by the name of "*Happy Jack.*" And it is just such Happy Jacks as Landless that most sea-officers profess to admire; a fellow without shame, without a soul, so dead to the least dignity of manhood that he could hardly be called a man. Whereas, a seaman who exhibits traits of moral sensitiveness, whose demeanor shows some dignity within; this is the man they, in many cases, instinctively dislike. The reason is, they feel such a man to be a continual reproach to them, as being mentally superior to their power. He has no business in a man-of-war; they do not want such men. To them there is an insolence in his manly freedom, contempt in his very carriage. He is unendurable, as an erect, lofty-minded African would be to some slave-driving planter.

Let it not be supposed, however, that the remarks in this and the preceding chapter apply to *all* men-of-war. There are some vessels blessed with patriarchal, intellectual Captains, gentlemanly and brotherly officers, and docile and Christianized crews. The peculiar usages of such vessels insensibly soften the tyrannical rigor of the Articles of War; in them, scourging is unknown. To sail in such ships is hardly to realize that you live under the martial law, or that the evils above mentioned can any where exist.

And Jack Chase, old Ushant, and several more fine tars that might be added, sufficiently attest, that in the Neversink at least, there was more than one noble man-of-war's-man who almost redeemed all the rest.

Wherever, throughout this narrative, the American Navy, in any of its bearings, has formed the theme of a general discussion, hardly one syllable of admiration for what is accounted illustrious in its achievements has been permitted to escape me. The reason is this: I consider, that so far as what is called military renown is concerned, the American Navy needs no eulogist but History. It were superfluous for White-Jacket to tell the world what it knows already. The office imposed upon me is of another cast; and, though I foresee and feel that it may subject me to the pillory in the hard thoughts of some men, yet, supported by what God has given me, I tranquilly abide the event, whatever it may prove.

Chapter 91

Smoking-club in a Man-of-war, with Scenes on the Gun-deck drawing near Home

THERE IS A FABLE about a painter moved by Jove to the painting of the head of Medusa. Though the picture was true to the life, yet the poor artist sickened at the sight of what his forced pencil had drawn. Thus, borne through my task toward the end, my own soul now sinks at what I myself have portrayed. But let us forget past chapters, if we may, while we paint less repugnant things.

Metropolitan gentlemen have their club; provincial gossipers their news-room; village quidnuncs their barber's shop; the Chinese their opium-houses; American Indians their council-fire; and even cannibals their *Noojona*, or Talk-Stone, where they assemble at times to discuss the affairs of the day. Nor is there any government, however despotic, that ventures to deny to the least of its subjects the privilege of a sociable chat. Not the Thirty Tyrants even—the clubbed post-captains of old Athens—could stop the wagging tongues at the street-corners. For chat man must; and by our immortal Bill of Rights, that guarantees to us liberty of speech, chat we Yankees will, whether on board a frigate, or on board our own terra-firma plantations.

In men-of-war, the Galley, or Cookery, on the gun-deck is the grand centre of gossip and news among the sailors. Here crowds assemble to chat away the half hour elapsing after every meal. The reason why this place and these hours are selected rather than others is this: in the neighborhood of the galley alone, and only after meals, is the man-of-war's-man permitted to regale himself with a smoke.

A sumptuary edict, truly, that deprived White-Jacket, for one, of a luxury to which he had long been attached. For how can the mystical motives, the capricious impulses of a luxurious smoker go and come at the beck of a Commodore's command? No! when I smoke, be it because of my sovereign good pleasure I choose so to do, though at so unseasonable an hour that I send round the town for a brasier of coals. What! smoke by a sun-dial? Smoke on compulsion? Make a trade, a business, a vile recurring calling of smoking? And, perhaps, when those sedative fumes have steeped you in the grandest of reveries, and, circle over circle, solemnly rises some immeasurable dome in your soul—far away, swelling and heaving into the vapor you raise—as if from one of Mozart's grandest marches a temple were rising, like Venus from the sea—at such a time, to have your whole Parthenon tumbled about your ears by the knell of the ship's bell announcing the expiration of the half hour for smoking! Whip me, ye Furies! toast me in saltpetre! smite me, some thunder-bolt! charge upon me, endless squadrons of Mamalukes! devour me, Feejees! but preserve me from a tyranny like this.

No! though I smoked like an Indian summer ere I entered the Neversink, so abhorrent was this sumptuary law that I altogether abandoned the luxury rather than enslave it to a time and a place. Herein did I not right, Ancient and Honorable Old Guard of Smokers all round the world?

But there were others of the crew not so fastidious as myself. After every meal, they hied to the galley and solaced their souls with a whiff.

Now a bunch of cigars, all banded together, is a type and a symbol of the brotherly love between smokers. Likewise, for the time, in a community of pipes is a community of hearts. Nor was it an ill thing for the Indian Sachems to circulate their calumet tobacco-bowl—even as our own forefathers circulated their punch-bowl—in token of peace, charity, and good-will, friendly feelings, and sympathizing souls. And this it was that made the gossipers of the galley so loving a club, so long as the vapory bond united them.

It was a pleasant sight to behold them. Grouped in the recesses between the guns, they chatted and laughed like rows of convivialists in the boxes of some vast dining-saloon. Take a Flemish kitchen full of good fellows from Teniers, add a fire side group from Wilkie; throw in a naval sketch from Cruikshank; and then stick a short pipe into every mother's son's mouth, and you have the smoking scene at the galley of the Neversink.

Not a few were politicians; and, as there were some thoughts of a war with England at the time, their discussions waxed warm.

"I tell you what it is, *shippies!*" cried the old captain of gun No. 1 on the forecastle, "if that 'ere President of ourn don't luff up into the wind, by the Battle of the Nile! he'll be getting us into a grand fleet engagement afore the Yankee nation has rammed home her cartridges—let alone blowing the match!"

"Who talks of luffing?" roared a roystering fore-top-man. "Keep our Yankee nation large before the wind, say I, till you come plump on the enemy's bows, and then board him in the smoke," and with that, there came forth a mighty blast from his pipe.

"Who says the old man at the helm of the Yankee nation can't steer his *trick* as well as George Washington himself?" cried a sheet-anchor-man.

"But they say he's a cold water customer, Bill," cried another; "and sometimes o' nights I somehow has a presentation that he's goin' to stop our grog."

"D'ye hear there, fore and aft!" roared the boatswain's mates at the gangway, "all hands tumble up, and 'bout ship!"

"That's the talk!" cried the captain of gun No. 1, as, in obedience to the summons, all hands dropped their pipes and crowded toward the ladders, "and that's what the President must do—go in stays, my lads, and put the Yankee nation on the other tack."

But these political discussions by no means supplied the staple of conversation for the gossiping smokers of the galley. The interior affairs of the frigate itself formed their principal theme. Rumors about the private life of the Commodore in his cabin; about the Captain, in his; about the various officers in the Ward-room; about the *reefers* in the steerage, and their madcap frolickings, and about a thousand other matters touching the crew themselves; all these—forming the eternally shifting, domestic by-play of a man-of-war—proved inexhaustible topics for our quidnuncs.

The animation of these scenes was very much heightened as we drew nearer and nearer our port; it rose to a climax when the frigate was reported to be only twenty-four hours' sail from the land. What they should do when they landed; how they should invest their wages; what they should eat; what they should drink; and what lass they should marry—these were the topics which absorbed them.

"Sink the sea!" cried a forecastle man. "Once more ashore, and you'll never again catch old Boombolt afloat. I mean to settle down in a sail-loft."

"Cable-tier pinches blister all tarpaulin hats!" cried a young after-guard's-man; "I mean to go back to the counter."

"Shipmates! take me by the arms, and swab up the lee-scuppers with me, but I mean to steer a clam-cart before I go again to a ship's wheel. Let the Navy go by the board—to sea again, I won't!"

"Start my soul-bolts, maties, if any more Blue Peters and sailing signals fly at my fore!" cried the Captain of the Head. "My wages will buy a wheel-barrow, if nothing more."

"I have taken my last dose of salts," said the Captain of the Waist, "and after this mean to stick to fresh water. Ay, maties, ten of us Waisters mean to club together and buy a *serving-mallet boat*, d'ye see; and if ever we drown, it will be in the 'raging canal!' Blast the sea, shipmates! say I."

"Profane not the holy element!" said Lemsford, the poet of the gun-deck, leaning over a cannon. "Know ye not, man-of-war's-men! that by the Parthian magi the ocean was held sacred? Did not Tiridates, the Eastern monarch, take an immense land circuit to avoid desecrating the Mediter-ranean, in order to reach his imperial master, Nero, and do homage for his crown?"

"What lingo is that?" cried the Captain of the Waist.

"Who's Commodore Tiddery-eye?" cried the forecastle-man.

"Hear me out," resumed Lemsford. "Like Tiridates, I venerate the sea, and venerate it so highly, shipmates, that evermore I shall abstain from crossing it. In *that* sense, Captain of the Waist, I echo your cry."

It was, indeed, a remarkable fact, that nine men out of every ten of the Neversink's crew had formed some plan or other to keep themselves ashore for life, or, at least, on fresh water, after the expiration of the present cruise. With all the experiences of that cruise accumulated in one intense recol-lection of a moment; with the smell of tar in their nostrils; out of sight of land; with a stout ship under foot, and snuffing the ocean air; with all the things of the sea surrounding them; in their cool, sober moments of reflection; in the silence and solitude of the deep, during the long night-watches, when all their holy home associations were thronging round their hearts; in the spontaneous piety and devotion of the last hours of so long a voyage; in the fullness and the frankness of their souls; when there was naught to jar the well-poised equilibrium of their judgment—under all these circumstances, at least nine tenths of a crew of five hundred man-of-war's-men resolved forever to turn their backs on the sea. But do men ever hate the thing they love? Do men forswear the hearth and the homestead? What, then, must the Navy be?

But, alas for the man-of-war's-man, who, though he may take a Hannibal oath against the service; yet, cruise after cruise, and after forswearing it again and again, he is driven back to the spirit-tub and the gun-deck by his old hereditary foe, the ever-devilish god of grog.

On this point, let some of the crew of the Neversink be called to the stand.

You, Captain of the Waist! and you, seamen of the fore-top! and you, After-guard's-men and others! how came you here at the guns of the North Carolina, after registering your solemn vows at the galley of the Neversink?

They all hang their heads. I know the cause; poor fellows! perjure yourselves not again; swear not at all hereafter.

Ay, these very tars—the foremost in denouncing the Navy; who had bound themselves by the most tremendous oaths—these very men, not three days after getting ashore, were rolling round the streets in penniless drunkenness; and next day many of them were to be found on board of the *guardo* or receiving-ship. Thus, in part, is the Navy manned.

But what was still more surprising, and tended to impart a new and strange insight into the character of sailors, and overthrow some long-established ideas concerning them as a class, was this: numbers of men who, during the cruise, had passed for exceedingly prudent, nay, parsimonious persons, who would even refuse you a patch, or a needleful of thread, and, from their stinginess, procured the name of *Ravelings*—no sooner were these men fairly adrift in harbor, and under the influence of frequent quaffings, than their three-years'-earned wages flew right and left; they summoned whole boarding-houses of sailors to the bar, and treated them over and over again. Fine fellows! generous-hearted tars! Seeing this sight, I thought to myself, Well, these generous-hearted tars on shore were the greatest curmudgeons afloat! it's the bottle that's generous, not they! Yet the popular conceit concerning a sailor is derived from his behavior ashore; whereas, ashore he is no longer a sailor, but a landsman for the time. A man-of-war's-man is only a man-of-war's-man at sea; and the sea is the place to learn what he is. But we have seen that a man-of-war is but this old-fashioned world of ours afloat, full of all manner of characters—full of strange contradictions; and though boasting some fine fellows here and there, yet, upon the whole, charged to the combings of her hatchways with the spirit of Belial and all unrighteousness.

Chapter 92

The last of the Jacket

A LREADY HAS White-Jacket chronicled the mishaps and inconveniences, troubles and tribulations of all sorts brought upon him by that unfortunate but indispensable garment of his. But now it befalls him to record how this jacket, for the second and last time, came near proving his shroud.

Of a pleasant midnight, our good frigate, now somewhere off the Capes of Virginia, was running on bravely, when the breeze, gradually dying, left us slowly gliding toward our still invisible port.

Headed by Jack Chase, the quarter-watch were reclining in the top, talking about the shore delights into which they intended to plunge, while our captain often broke in with allusions to similar conversations when he was on board the English line-of-battle ship, the Asia, drawing nigh to Portsmouth, in England, after the battle of Navarino.

Suddenly an order was given to set the main-top-gallant-stun'-sail, and the halyards not being rove, Jack Chase assigned to me that duty. Now this reeving of the halyards of a main-top-gallant-stun'-sail is a business that eminently demands sharpsightedness, skill, and celerity.

Consider that the end of a line, some two hundred feet long, is to be carried aloft, in your teeth, if you please, and dragged far out on the giddiest of yards, and after being wormed and twisted about through all sorts of intricacies—turning abrupt corners at the abruptest of angles—is to be dropped, clear of all obstructions, in a straight plumb-line right down to the deck. In the course of this business, there is a multitude of sheeve-holes and blocks, through which you must pass it; often the rope is a very tight fit, so as to make it like threading a fine cambric needle with rather coarse thread. Indeed, it is a thing only deftly to be done, even by day. Judge, then, what it must be to be threading cambric needles by night, and at sea, upward of a hundred feet aloft in the air.

With the end of the line in one hand, I was mounting the top-mast shrouds, when our Captain of the Top told me that I had better off jacket; but though it was not a very cold night, I had been reclining so long in the top, that I had become somewhat chilly, so I thought best not to comply with the hint.

Having reeved the line through all the inferior blocks, I went out with it to the end of the weather-top-gallant-yard-arm, and was in the act of leaning over and passing it through the suspended jewel-block there, when the ship gave a plunge in the sudden swells of the calm sea, and pitching me still further over the yard, threw the heavy skirts of my jacket right over my head, completely muffling me. Somehow I thought it was the sail that had flapped, and, under that impression, threw up my hands to drag it from my head, relying upon the sail itself to support me meanwhile. Just then the ship gave another sudden jerk, and, head foremost, I pitched from the yard. I knew where I was, from the rush of the air by my ears, but all else was a nightmare. A bloody film was before my eyes, through which, ghost-like, passed and repassed my father, mother, and sisters. An unutterable nausea oppressed me; I was conscious of gasping; there seemed no breath in my body. It was over one hundred feet that I fell—down, down, with lungs collapsed as in death. Ten thousand pounds of shot seemed tied to my head, as the irresistible law of gravitation dragged me, head foremost and straight as a die, toward the infallible centre of this terraqueous globe. All I had seen, and read, and heard, and all I had thought and felt in my life, seemed intensified in one fixed idea in my soul. But dense as this idea was, it was made up of atoms. Having fallen from the projecting yard-arm end, I was conscious of a collected satisfaction in feeling, that I should not be dashed on the deck, but would sink into the speechless profound of the sea.

With the bloody, blind film before my eyes, there was a still stranger hum in my head, as if a hornet were there; and I thought to myself, Great God! this is Death! Yet these thoughts were unmixed with alarm. Like frost-work that flashes and shifts its scared hues in the sun, all my braided, blended emotions were in themselves icy cold and calm.

So protracted did my fall seem, that I can even now recall the feeling of wondering how much longer it would be, ere all was over and I struck. Time seemed to stand still, and all the worlds seemed poised on their poles, as I fell, soul-becalmed, through the eddying whirl and swirl of the Maelstrom air.

At first, as I have said, I must have been precipitated head foremost; but I was conscious, at length, of a swift, flinging motion of my limbs, which involuntarily threw themselves out, so that at last I must have fallen in a heap. This is more likely, from the circumstance, that when I struck the sea, I felt as if some one had smote me slantingly across the shoulder and along part of my right side.

As I gushed into the sea, a thunder-boom sounded in my ear; my soul seemed flying from my mouth. The feeling of death flooded over me with the billows. The blow from the sea must have turned me, so that I sank almost feet foremost through a soft, seething, foamy lull. Some current seemed hurrying me away; in a trance I yielded, and sank deeper down with a glide. Purple and pathless was the deep calm now around me, flecked by summer lightnings in an azure afar. The horrible nausea was gone; the bloody, blind film turned a pale green; I wondered whether I was yet dead, or still dying. But of a sudden some fashionless form brushed my side— some inert, coiled fish of the sea; the thrill of being alive again tingled in my nerves, and the strong shunning of death shocked me through.

For one instant an agonizing revulsion came over me as I found myself utterly sinking. Next moment the force of my fall was expended; and there I hung, vibrating in the mid-deep. What wild sounds then rang in my ear! One was a soft moaning, as of low waves on the beach; the other wild and heartlessly jubilant, as of the sea in the height of a tempest. Oh soul! thou then heardest life and death: as he who stands upon the Corinthian shore hears both the Ionian and the Ægean waves. The life-and-death poise soon passed; and then I found myself slowly ascending, and caught a dim glimmering of light.

Quicker and quicker I mounted; till at last I bounded up like a buoy, and my whole head was bathed in the blessed air.

I had fallen in a line with the main-mast; I now found myself nearly abreast of the mizzen-mast, the frigate slowly gliding by like a black world in the water. Her vast hull loomed out of the night, showing hundreds of seamen in the hammock-nettings, some tossing over ropes, others madly flinging overboard the hammocks; but I was too far out from them immediately to reach what they threw. I essayed to swim toward the ship; but instantly I was conscious of a feeling like being pinioned in a feather-bed, and, moving my hands, felt my jacket puffed out above my tight girdle with water. I strove to tear it off; but it was looped together here and there, and the strings were not then to be sundered by hand. I whipped out my knife, that was tucked at my belt, and ripped my jacket straight up and down, as if I were ripping open myself. With a violent struggle I then burst out of it, and was free. Heavily soaked, it slowly sank before my eyes.

Sink! sink! oh shroud! thought I; sink forever! accursed jacket that thou art!

"See that white shark!" cried a horrified voice from the taffrail; "he'll have that man down his hatchway! Quick! the *grains!* the *grains!*"

The next instant that barbed bunch of harpoons pierced through and through the unfortunate jacket, and swiftly sped down with it out of sight.

Being now astern of the frigate, I struck out boldly toward the elevated pole of one of the life-buoys which had been cut away. Soon after, one of the cutters picked me up. As they dragged me out of the water into the air, the sudden transition of elements made my every limb feel like lead, and I helplessly sunk into the bottom of the boat.

Ten minutes after, I was safe on board, and, springing aloft, was ordered to reeve anew the stun'-sail-halyards, which, slipping through the blocks when I had let go the end, had unrove and fallen to the deck.

The sail was soon set; and, as if purposely to salute it, a gentle breeze soon came, and the Neversink once more glided over the water, a soft ripple at her bows, and leaving a tranquil wake behind.

Chapter 93

Cable and Anchor all clear

ND NOW THAT THE WHITE JACKET has sunk to the bottom
of the sea, and the blessed Capes of Virginia are believed to be broad
on our bow—though still out of sight—our five hundred souls are
fondly dreaming of home, and the iron throats of the guns round the galley
re-echo with their songs and hurras—what more remains?

Shall I tell what conflicting and almost crazy surmisings prevailed concerning the precise harbor for which we were bound? For, according to
rumor, our Commodore had received sealed orders touching that matter,
which were not to be broken open till we gained a precise latitude of the
coast. Shall I tell how, at last, all this uncertainty departed, and many a foolish prophecy was proved false, when our noble frigate—her longest pennant
at her main—wound her stately way into the innermost harbor of Norfolk,
like a plumed Spanish Grandee threading the corridors of the Escurial toward the throne-room within? Shall I tell how we kneeled upon the holy
soil? How I begged a blessing of old Ushant, and one precious hair of his
beard for a keepsake? How Lemsford, the gun-deck bard, offered up a
devout ode as a prayer of thanksgiving? How saturnine Nord, the magni-
fico in disguise, refusing all companionship, stalked off into the woods, like
the ghost of an old Calif of Bagdad? How I swayed and swung the hearty
hand of Jack Chase, and nipped it to mine with a Carrick bend; yea, and

kissed that noble hand of my liege lord and captain of my top, my sea-tutor and sire?

Shall I tell how the grand Commodore and Captain drove off from the pier-head? How the Lieutenants, in undress, sat down to their last dinner in the ward-room, and the Champagne, packed in ice, spirted and sparkled like the Hot Springs out of a snow-drift in Iceland? How the Chaplain went off in his cassock, without bidding the people adieu? How shrunken Cuticle, the Surgeon, stalked over the side, the wired skeleton carried in his wake by his cot-boy? How the Lieutenant of Marines sheathed his sword on the poop, and, calling for wax and a taper, sealed the end of the scabbard with his family crest and motto—*Denique Cælum?* How the Purser in due time mustered his money-bags, and paid us all off on the quarter-deck—good and bad, sick and well, all receiving their wages; though, truth to tell, some reckless, improvident seamen, who had lived too fast during the cruise, had little or nothing now standing on the credit side of their Purser's accounts?

Shall I tell of the Retreat of the Five Hundred inland; not, alas! in battle-array, as at quarters, but scattered broadcast over the land?

Shall I tell how the Neversink was at last stripped of spars, shrouds, and sails—had her guns hoisted out—her powder-magazine, shot-lockers, and armories discharged—till not one vestige of a fighting thing was left in her, from furthest stem to uttermost stern?

No! let all this go by; for our anchor still hangs from our bows, though its eager flukes dip their points in the impatient waves. Let us leave the ship on the sea—still with the land out of sight—still with brooding darkness on the face of the deep. I love an indefinite, infinite background—a vast, heaving, rolling, mysterious rear!

It is night. The meagre moon is in her last quarter—that betokens the end of a cruise that is passing. But the stars look forth in their everlasting brightness—and *that* is the everlasting, glorious Future, forever beyond us.

We main-top-men are all aloft in the top; and round our mast we circle, a brother-band, hand in hand, all spliced together. We have reefed the last top-sail; trained the last gun; blown the last match; bowed to the last blast; been tranced in the last calm. We have mustered our last round the capstan; been rolled to grog the last time; for the last time swung in our hammocks; for the last time turned out at the sea-gull call of the watch. We have seen our last man scourged at the gangway; our last man gasp out the ghost in the stifling Sick-bay; our last man tossed to the sharks. Our last death-denouncing Article of War has been read; and far inland, in that blessed clime whitherward our frigate now glides, the last wrong in our frigate will be remembered no more; when down from our main-mast comes our Commodore's pennant, when down sinks its shooting stars from the sky.

"By the mark, nine!" sings the hoary old leadsman, in the chains. And thus, the mid-world Equator passed, our frigate strikes soundings at last.

Hand in hand we top-mates stand, rocked in our Pisgah top. And over the starry waves, and broad out into the blandly blue and boundless night, spiced with strange sweets from the long-sought land—the whole long cruise predestinated ours, though often in tempest-time we almost refused to believe in that far-distant shore—straight out into that fragrant night, ever-noble Jack Chase, matchless and unmatchable Jack Chase stretches forth his bannered hand, and, pointing shoreward, cries: "For the last time, hear Camoens, boys!

> 'How calm the waves, how mild the balmy gale!
> The Halcyons call, ye Lusians spread the sail!
> Appeased, old Ocean now shall rage no more;
> Haste, point our bowsprit for yon shadowy shore.
> Soon shall the transports of your natal soil
> O'erwhelm in bounding joy the thoughts of every toil.'"

The End

A S A MAN-OF-WAR that sails through the sea, so this earth that sails through the air. We mortals are all on board a fast-sailing, never-sinking world-frigate, of which God was the shipwright; and she is but one craft in a Milky-Way fleet, of which God is the Lord High Admiral. The port we sail from is forever astern. And though far out of sight of land, for ages and ages we continue to sail with sealed orders, and our last destination remains a secret to ourselves and our officers; yet our final haven was predestinated ere we slipped from the stocks at Creation.

Thus sailing with sealed orders, we ourselves are the repositories of the secret packet, whose mysterious contents we long to learn. There are no mysteries out of ourselves. But let us not give ear to the superstitious, gun-deck gossip about whither we may be gliding, for, as yet, not a soul on board of us knows—not even the Commodore himself; assuredly not the Chaplain; even our Professor's scientific surmisings are vain. On that point, the smallest cabin-boy is as wise as the Captain. And believe not the hypochondriac dwellers below hatches, who will tell you, with a sneer, that our world-frigate is bound to no final harbor whatever; that our voyage will prove an endless circumnavigation of space. Not so. For how can this world-frigate prove our eventual abiding place, when, upon our first embarkation, as infants in arms, her violent rolling—in after life unperceived—makes every soul of us sea-sick? Does not this show, too, that the very air we here inhale is uncongenial, and only becomes endurable at last through gradual habituation, and that some blessed, placid haven, however remote at present, must be in store for us all?

Glance fore and aft our flush decks. What a swarming crew! All told, they muster hard upon eight hundred millions of souls. Over these we have authoritative Lieutenants, a sword-belted Officer of Marines, a Chaplain, a Professor, a Purser, a Doctor, a Cook, a Master-at-arms.

Oppressed by illiberal laws, and partly oppressed by themselves, many of our people are wicked, unhappy, inefficient. We have skulkers and idlers all round, and brow-beaten waisters, who, for a pittance, do our craft's shabby work. Nevertheless, among our people we have gallant fore, main, and mizen top-men aloft, who, well treated or ill, still trim our craft to the blast.

We have a *brig* for trespassers; a bar by our main-mast, at which they are arraigned; a cat-o'-nine-tails and a gangway, to degrade them in their own eyes and in ours. These are not always employed to convert Sin to Virtue, but to divide them, and protect Virtue and legalized Sin from unlegalized Vice.

We have a Sick-bay for the smitten and helpless, whither we hurry them out of sight, and, however they may groan beneath hatches, we hear little of their tribulations on deck; we still sport our gay streamer aloft. Outwardly regarded, our craft is a lie; for all that is outwardly seen of it is the clean-swept deck, and oft-painted planks comprised above the water-line; whereas, the vast mass of our fabric, with all its store-rooms of secrets, forever slides along far under the surface.

When a shipmate dies, straightway we sew him up, and overboard he goes; our world-frigate rushes by, and never more do we behold him again; though, sooner or later, the everlasting under-tow sweeps him toward our own destination.

We have both a quarter-deck to our craft and a gun-deck; subterranean shot-lockers and gunpowder magazines; and the Articles of War form our domineering code.

Oh, shipmates and world-mates, all round! we the people suffer many abuses. Our gun-deck is full of complaints. In vain from Lieutenants do we appeal to the Captain; in vain—while on board our world-frigate—to the indefinite Navy Commissioners, so far out of sight aloft. Yet the worst of our evils we blindly inflict upon ourselves; our officers can not remove them, even if they would. From the last ills no being can save another;

therein each man must be his own saviour. For the rest, whatever befall us, let us never train our murderous guns inboard; let us not mutiny with bloody pikes in our hands. Our Lord High Admiral will yet interpose; and though long ages should elapse, and leave our wrongs unredressed, yet, shipmates and world-mates! let us never forget, that,

> Whoever afflict us, whatever surround,
> Life is a voyage that's homeward-bound!

THE END

Editorial Appendix

HISTORICAL NOTE
By Willard Thorp
TEXTUAL RECORD
By the Editors
RELATED DOCUMENTS

THE FIRST *of the three parts of this* APPENDIX *is a note on the composition, publication, reception, and later critical history of* White-Jacket, *contributed by Willard Thorp. The second, which records textual information, has been prepared by the editors, Harrison Hayford, Hershel Parker, and G. Thomas Tanselle. It consists of a note on the textual history of* White-Jacket *and on the editorial principles of this edition, followed by discussions of certain problematical readings, a list of emendations made in this edition, a report of line-end hyphenation, and a full list of substantive variants between the first American and English editions. The third part reprints the Preface to the English edition and offers a reproduction and transcript of the surviving manuscript fragment, a two-page draft preface. In verifying the information in the* APPENDIX, *the editors have been aided by the bibliographical associate, Richard Colles Johnson, and the editorial assistants, Watson G. Branch and Amy Puett. To insure uniform policy, the same three editors bear full responsibility for establishing the texts in all volumes of the Edition, except when other editors are specifically named (as in the case of certain writings edited from manuscript). Although most of the historical notes have been written by other contributing scholars, the task of writing textual commentary and of preparing the textual lists has been the joint responsibility of the three editors. Hershel Parker is the editor who coordinated the preparation of this volume.*

At appropriate points in the APPENDIX *acknowledgment is made for generous assistance received from scholars not directly connected with the Edition. The editors also wish to recognize the indispensable services of these members of their staff: Virginia Heiserman, Michael Klee, Myra Linden, Joel Myerson, Eugene Perchak, Eileen Peterson, Karleen Redle, R. E. Steinhauer, and the chief proofreader, Justine Smith.*

Historical Note

ELIZABETH SHAW MELVILLE'S memorandum about her husband covers the summer of 1849 in one sentence: "We remained in New York—he wrote 'Redburn' & 'White Jacket.'"[1] These eleven words summarize the activity of five months when Melville was writing his fourth and fifth books at the top of his bent. Between late April or early May, when he began work on *Redburn*, and mid-September, Melville had completed the manuscript of *Redburn*, a book of 390 pages in its American edition, and the 465-page *White-Jacket*. Arrangements for the publication of the first of the two books also went smoothly. On July 2 Harper & Brothers agreed to publish "My First Voyage &c" (as *Redburn* was described in the contract), offering the immediate payment of $300 on account of half profits. Earlier, on June 5 Melville had written his English publisher, Richard Bentley, offering him *Redburn*. He valued the English copyright at £150, he said in this letter. Bentley's terms were "£100 down on the receipt of the sheets, on account of half profits." On July 20 Melville wrote accepting them.

Since Melville was prepared to reach an agreement with Harpers on July 2, 1849, for the publication of *Redburn*, the novel must have been nearly completed by that date. From Melville's July 20 letter to Bentley we learn

---

1. The passage cited is quoted in Leyda's *The Melville Log*, I, 309. See the section on "Sources" at the end of this NOTE, where the documentation is explained.

that it was then going through the press. Evidently the proofreading was not finished until some time in August. This we infer from a letter written to the Secretary of the American Legation in London whom Melville asked to deliver the parcel of proof to Bentley.

The most likely outside limits for the writing of *Redburn* are mid-April to early July, less than three months, a feat remarkable enough, though it could be matched in the history of fiction. The speed with which Melville wrote *White-Jacket* is even more amazing. We know from a letter of Evert A. Duyckinck to his brother George that the new work was in proof stage by September 5. If Melville began *White-Jacket* as soon as *Redburn* was finished, then he completed it in two months or less. During the first month he was also busy with the proof sheets of *Redburn*.

On September 13 Harper & Brothers agreed "to publish a certain manuscript entitled White Jacket &c" and to advance Melville $500. Negotiations with Bentley for the English edition were postponed until Melville could go to London and transact his business in person. When John Murray, who had issued *Typee* and *Omoo*, refused *Mardi*, Melville, through his agent, John Romeyn Brodhead, turned to Bentley, with surprising results. Bentley's terms for the publication of *Mardi* were handsome, the best in fact that Melville ever received from an English house—200 guineas, which he could draw on in advance. But *Mardi* did not sell well in England or America, and Bentley, like other English publishers at the time, was concerned about the uncertain status of copyright on books by American authors. For these two reasons, probably, he offered only £100 for *Redburn*.

Late in the summer of 1849 Melville decided to make a trip to England, for both business and pleasure. His business would be to receive the £100 promised for *Redburn* and to make the best arrangements he could, with Bentley or some other publisher, for *White-Jacket*, the American proofs of which he took with him as the basis for the English edition. (He seems to have had his mind set on the figure of £200 and an advance.) For pleasure he would travel as widely as he could (at one time he hoped to go on to Vienna, Constantinople, Athens, Jerusalem, and Alexandria), attend the theater, meet English men of letters, and see the sights of London. On October 11 he embarked on the *Southampton*, "a regular London liner." As things turned out, Melville's time away from home was less than four months (October 11, 1849, to February 1, 1850). He was watching his expenses more carefully than he need have done, for the sum which he eventually received for *White-Jacket* was substantial. He could have stayed longer. His journal shows that he was homesick for his wife and ten-month-old son Malcolm. He sailed for America on Christmas day, ten days after he finally made terms with Bentley.

The journal provides us with the details of Melville's efforts to secure the best possible arrangements for the English *White-Jacket*. He was persistent and persuasive, even though the copyright situation made this a poor time for an American author to sell his literary wares in England.[2] Melville began with Bentley on November 12 but saw six other publishers before coming back to him on December 15.

Bentley was at Brighton when Melville reached London but wrote that he would come up to town "at any time convenient." They met on November 12. Melville recorded their session in his journal:

> Very polite. Gave me his note for £100 at 60 days for "Redburn." Couldn't do better, he said. He expressed much anxiety & vexation at the state of the Copyright question. Proposed my new book—"White Jacket"—to him & showed him the Table of Contents. He was much pleased with it. And notwithstanding the vexatious & uncertain state of the Copyright matter, he made me the following offer:—to pay me £200 for the first 1000 copies of the book (the privilege of publishing that number). And as we might afterward arrange, concerning subsequent editions. A liberal offer. But he could make no advance.

Melville was determined to have an advance and he immediately started a series of calls on other publishers. On November 14 he saw John Murray, the publisher of *Typee* and *Omoo*. "He was very civil," Melville wrote in his journal, "much vexed about copyright matter.—I proposed '*White Jacket*' to him—he seemed decidedly pleased—& has since sent for the proof sheets, according to agreement." When Melville saw Murray again on November 16, he got the answer he may have expected: "would not be in his line to publish my book." But Murray kindly passed Melville along to Henry Colbourn. The answer from Colbourn came by post the next day (November 17): "The letter simply declines my proposition . . . & on the ground, principally, of the cursed state of the copyright matter. Bad news

---

2. When Melville began to write, prior or simultaneous publication in the United Kingdom was regarded as sufficient to establish copyright for an American book. On June 5, 1849, Sir Frederick Pollock ruled that no foreigner could gain a copyright simply by priority of publication. English publishers who had American works in their lists behaved handsomely under this ruling, often risking piracy in taking American books. Some cited the ruling, of course, when they wished to refuse an American author. Melville frequently ran into this difficulty in trying to market *White-Jacket*.

enough—I shall not see Rome—I'm floored—appetite unimpaired however." The Longmans were next on Melville's list; he visited them on November 19 and the next day received a note from the firm stating that they "abided by their original terms." What these were is not known. That they were not satisfactory to Melville is proved by his continuing his visits. Equipped with a letter of introduction from Richard Henry Dana, Jr., he saw Edward Moxon on November 20, but apparently did not propose the book to him.

At this point Melville received some friendly advice that strengthened his determination to go on with his visits. On November 23 he called on David Davidson, agent of the American publisher John Wiley, to whom he had a letter of introduction from George Duyckinck.[3] Davidson kindly offered to try to get Bentley's note cashed (the £100 at sixty days for *Redburn*). His advice about *White-Jacket* was to "keep pushing" and he mentioned the "names of some more publishers whom I ought to try." Davidson went with him at once to David Bogue and introduced him. "I stated my business. B. was all ears." Melville was pretty sure Bogue would decline, which he did in a note later the same day, "alleging among other reasons, the state of the copyright question.—So we go." The next day (November 24) Melville tried two firms, Chapman & Hall and H. G. Bohn. As he says in his journal, the result of each interview was "No go."

By this time *White-Jacket* had been turned down by six publishers. Melville abandoned his visits, evidently intending to return to Bentley after a brief excursion to Paris, Brussels, and the Rhine country. The day before he boarded the Boulogne boat he saw Davidson again about Bentley's note. Davidson gave him a check on his bankers. Melville deposited £40 for his brother Allan to draw on in New York and waited at the bankers' while "they shoveled the sovereigns over to me in curious style."

The trip to the Continent lasted from November 27 to December 12. On Saturday, December 15, Melville saw Bentley again. At 6 P.M. he made this entry in his journal:

> Hurrah & three cheers! I have just returned from Mr. Bentley's & have concluded an arrangement with him that gives me tomorrow his note for £200. It is to be at 6 months—and I am almost certain I shall be able to get it cashed at once. This takes a load off my heart. The £200 is in anticipation —for the book is not to be published till the 1st of March next. Hence the

3. Wiley had been a member of the firm of Wiley & Putnam when they published *Typee* in 1846. The firm was dissolved in 1848. In that year the firm of John Wiley, in existence today as John Wiley & Sons, was established.

long time of the note. The above-mentioned sum is for the 1st 1000 copies. Subsequent editions (if any) to be jointly divided between us.

The arrangements did not provide for a cash advance, but Melville now had something almost as good: a note for £200 at six months.

Again the generous Davidson helped him out by giving him a check for the note on December 22. This Melville cashed and then "went with the 'funds' to Baring Brothers, &c. in Bishopgate St. & got a letter of credit on America for £180." Evidently Davidson had discounted the note at 10 per cent.[4]

Melville's negotiations for the English and American editions of *Redburn* and *White-Jacket* had paid off handsomely. Harper & Brothers had advanced him $300 on account for *Redburn* on July 2. On September 13 they advanced $500 for *White-Jacket*. Davidson had taken Bentley's £100 note for *Redburn*, possibly without discounting it. Now, at last, the £180 for the English *White-Jacket* was transformed into a letter of credit. Melville's "take" in the four transactions was $2,148 in cash and credit.

When Melville paid his last visit to Bentley, on December 20, they again discussed the publication date of *White-Jacket*. "And we mutually appointed the 23^{d} day of January next (Wednesday) as the day for publishing *here*." (The date was later changed to February 1.) The English edition, titled *White-Jacket; or The World in a Man-of-War*, was first issued in two volumes, bound in blue cloth, and priced at a guinea. Although 1,000 copies were printed, as of March 4, 1852, 629 copies were still on hand, and Bentley's deficit on *White-Jacket* was £173 9s. 6d. In 1853 the remaining sheets of the first printing were issued (two volumes in one, bound in red cloth) with new title pages.

The American edition had to be held back, of course, to ensure prior publication in England. On January 9, 1850, the title page was deposited with the Clerk of the United States Court, Southern District of New York. On March 26 the book itself was deposited. Melville dated the brief Note which prefaced the American edition "New York, *March*, 1850." On March 6 Allan Melville sent a batch of proofs to Evert A. Duyckinck, remarking that "when you have placed the accompanying sheets with those

---

4. Davidson wrote George Duyckinck on December 24 to thank him for introducing Melville to him. He comments with pleasure on their two dinners together but modestly says nothing about the assistance he had rendered Melville. The letter confirms the impression given by the journal that Melville had managed his affairs well. "He has succeeded most admirably in his business here and leaves tomorrow in the Independence" (Melville's *Journal*, p. 159).

you got at the Harpers yesterday you will have a complete copy of 'White-jacket.'" On March 20 the New York *Commercial Advertiser* carried a Harper & Brothers advertisement announcing the date of publication as March 21 (the date also listed by William Demarest in his contemporary record of Harper publications). The March 23 issue of the *Literary World* carried a full-page Harper advertisement, two-thirds of which was devoted to Melville's new book, announced as "just published." *White-Jacket* was launched in America.

The first two printings of the American edition of *White-Jacket* (technically the second edition of the novel) came out during 1850 and totaled 4,534 copies (of which 2,022 were bound in paper wrappers and 2,042 in muslin, with 470 stored as sheets). Purchasers could have the muslin-bound copies at $1.25 or the paper-bound copies in two parts at 50 cents for each part. By the end of April, 1851, a total of 3,714 copies had been sold, and Melville's share of the profits amounted to $612.36.

The American and English texts of *White-Jacket* were not in all respects identical. Studies made during the preparation of the text of the present edition have revealed 181 substantive changes in the text of the English edition. Those made by Melville must have been entered on the American proof sheets he took to England, on the voyage or while he was waiting to get the terms he wanted from some London publisher. A journal entry on December 18 reads: "Spent an hour or so looking over 'White Jacket' preparatory to sending it finally to Bentley—who, though he has paid his money, has not received his wares. At 6 I dine with him." The authorial changes, which certainly must have taken more than "an hour or so" to write in, are treated in the NOTE ON THE TEXT.

In discussing what Melville thought of *White-Jacket* and the profit it might bring him, in reputation and money, one must consider his view of *Redburn* as well. In letters to friends and publishers he frequently spoke of them together. Though *Mardi*, his third book, was not reckoned a disaster by all the reviewers (it was better liked in America than in England), it was certainly no success in the bookstores. When Melville began writing his next book, *Redburn*, he could not afford to indulge his taste for "poetry and wildness" (Evert A. Duyckinck's words for *Mardi*). Though few of the reviews of *Mardi* were in, he had seen enough to make him turn back to his sea adventures for material. The whaling voyages he had partially used in *Typee, Omoo*, and *Mardi* (*Moby-Dick* was in the future). Still left to be exploited were his voyage to Liverpool at the age of twenty and his service on the frigate *United States*, one of the most famous ships of the old navy, from August 17, 1843, to October 14, 1844. Several times Melville mentioned money as his motive. He was most explicit about this in a letter to his father-in-law, Judge Lemuel Shaw (October 6, 1849). *Redburn* had just been published in England and the proofs of *White-Jacket* were ready to be taken to London for the publishers to inspect.

> For Redburn I anticipate no particular reception of any kind. It may be deemed a book of tolerable entertainment;—& may be accounted dull. —As for the other book, it will be sure to be attacked in some quarters. But no reputation that is gratifying to me, can possibly be achieved by either of these books. They are two *jobs*, which I have done for money—being forced to it, as other men are to sawing wood. And while I have felt obliged to refrain from writing the kind of book I would wish to; yet, in writing these two books, I have not repressed myself much—so far as *they* are concerned; but have spoken pretty much as I feel.—Being books, then, written in this way, my only desire for their "success" (as it is called) springs from my pocket, & not from my heart.

Melville used the wood-sawing image again in a letter to Dana (May 1, 1850): "In fact, My Dear Dana, did I not write these books of mine almost entirely for 'lucre'—by the job, as a woodsawyer saws wood—I almost think, I should hereafter—in the case of a sea book—get my M.S.S. neatly & legibly copied by a scrivener—send you that one copy—& deem such a procedure the best publication."

Writing to Evert A. Duyckinck from London (December 14, 1849), Melville comments on the favorable reception of *Redburn* but adds at once: "I am glad of it—for it puts money into an empty purse. But I hope I shall never write such a book again—Tho' when a poor devil writes with duns all round him, & looking over the back of his chair—& perching on his pen & diving in his inkstand—like the devils about St: Anthony—what can you expect of that poor devil?—What but a beggarly 'Redburn!'" This is not the only place Melville speaks jocularly or disparagingly of *Redburn*. In a letter to Dana (October 6, 1849) he had referred to it as "a little nursery tale of mine." Writing in his London journal as he was about to "press English earth after a lapse of ten years," he boasted privately: "*Then* a sailor, *now* H. M. author of 'Peedee,' 'Hullabaloo' & 'Pog-Dog.'"

Here we come on a difference in Melville's attitude toward the two books he had written to fill an empty purse. He used no such terms as "beggarly" or "nursery tale" in any mention of *White-Jacket*. He cared enough about its reputation to suggest to Dana in the letter of October 6, 1849, that he might, if he felt so inclined, come to its defense if it were handled by reviewers in an unfair or ignorant way. "Your name would do a very great deal; but if you choose to keep that out of sight in the matter, well & good."

II

From this same letter we learn that Dana had suggested to Melville that he turn his experiences on the frigate *United States* into a book: "Your hint concerning a man-of-war has, in anticipation, been acted on. A printed copy of the book is before me. As it will not appear for some two or three months, may I beg of you, that you will consider this communication confidential? The reason is obvious." We pick up a few more facts about the composition of *White-Jacket* in Melville's letters to Dana, but these and some other bits of information in letters to publishers are all we have, aside from the evidence in the book itself.

Yet indirectly and by inference we learn a great deal about how Melville organized and wrote *White-Jacket*. It was, in the end, one of the most carefully put together of his novels.

Three circumstances in happy conjunction made the writing go smoothly. Melville's memories of the routine of shipboard life and of several exciting events which took place during his fourteen months on the *United States* were sharp and he was able to use them at will. He had read or, while writing the novel, got his hands on a number of books and articles that provided him with scenes which he subtly incorporated into the book, transforming them to suit his purposes. From these he also gathered arguments and historical facts to give weight to some chapters, particularly those with propagandistic intent. Finally—and this we infer from studying the structure of the novel—he had a plan for its composition, and this plan worked well. We are aware, chapter by chapter, of his sense of direction. Episodes, descriptions, and propaganda are made to fall into place naturally.

What, then, is the relation between the fictional cruise of the *Neversink* and the actual voyage Melville made on the *United States* in 1843–44? Since this voyage is one of the most completely documented in American naval history, we can check Melville's use of remembered fact in a great many instances. In the National Archives in Washington one may examine the "Log Book of the U.S. Frigate United States" (July 1, 1843–October 13, 1844); the ship's "General Muster Roll . . . from 1st July '43 to 30 June '44 inclusive"; and the manuscript journal kept by Midshipman William Sharp, the most valuable item in it being the three-page list of officers with which Sharp begins his account of the voyage. Also in the National Archives are the Pacific Squadron Letters of this period.

At the Library of Congress is another journal, kept by Midshipman Alonzo C. Jackson. It was begun at Norfolk on November 3, 1841, and terminated at Callao on June 8, 1844, when he was transferred to the *Savannah*. Jackson's claim to fame is his noting the arrival on board of Herman Melville.[5] (Sharp's journal mentions the fact. The log does not.) Charles Roberts Anderson discovered and published, in 1937, the anonymous *Journal of a Cruise to the Pacific Ocean, 1842–1844, in the Frigate UNITED STATES*. It is the liveliest and most informative of the three journals. Another important document, not hitherto examined, is the Medical & Surgical Journal of the frigate *United States*, now in the Princeton University Library. By examining it we can check the fidelity of Melville's accounts of accidents and deaths on board and the day-by-day treatment of the sick.

Two other documents should be mentioned. One of the midshipmen on this cruise was Samuel R. Franklin. In 1898 he published his *Memories of a Rear-Admiral*. Franklin had read *White-Jacket* and speaks admiringly of it. After fifty years his memories of the cruise were shaky, but his comments on some of the officers and men whom Melville introduced into the book are helpful. Another shipmate, Harrison Robertson, Captain's Clerk (No. 76 on the muster roll), owned a copy of *White-Jacket* in which he wrote marginalia within a year of its publication. Robertson was contemptuous of Melville's departure from fact, but his comment on the nature of the book was more acute than he could have realized: "The author probably has made his book, not from personal experience wholly, but has patched together scraps picked up from some other person's journal, or conversation."[6]

Although Melville was using the voyage of the *United States* covertly as a "model" and a storehouse of data, it was necessary for him to disguise the fact. He had caustic things to say about abuses and evils on shipboard, and caricatured some of the officers. Consequently he did not wish readers to identify his *Neversink* with the *United States*. In the brief remarks prefatory to the English and American editions, he says that in 1843 he shipped on an American frigate, then lying in a harbor of the Pacific Ocean. He does not

5. "Friday Aug. 18 [1843] / Moderate breezes and clear. Shipped Herman Melville and Griffith Williams (O.S.). Suspended Wm Hoffman [sic] Boatswain from duty for disrespectful conduct to the officer of the deck." (Hoff figures in *White-Jacket* as Yarn, the boatswain, in Chapter 43, "Smuggling in a Man-of-war.")

6. Leyda, *The Melville Log*, I, 442. The copy is now in the Lilly Library.

name the frigate.[7] To his friend Dana, who was eager to know the real names of the officers to whom Melville had given such satirical names as Captain Claret, Surgeon Cuticle, and Mad Jack, he wrote (May 1, 1850), refusing to put "on pen-&-ink record over my name, the real names of the individuals who officered the frigate. . . . If you think it worth knowing, —I will tell you all, when I next have the pleasure of seeing you face to face."

But aside from his use of actual persons—sufficiently disguised, he hoped, to prevent common identification—Melville had little reason to expect that the actual ship would be known to many readers. The real voyage is transformed in many important particulars. White-Jacket begins his account at Callao (three months before the *United States* dropped anchor at Boston) not at Honolulu, where Melville shipped on a cruise that lasted fourteen months. The fictional voyage ends not at Boston but Norfolk. As the entries in the log make clear, the *United States* rounded Cape Horn without unusual difficulty. The *Neversink* might have foundered in a gale of hurricane strength if Mad Jack had not countermanded Captain Claret's dangerously stupid order. The *United States* was anchored in the harbor of Rio de Janeiro briefly, August 16–24, 1844. The *Neversink* lingers in Rio for so long a time that the sailors said "our frigate would at last ground on the beef-bones daily thrown overboard by the cooks." Melville had twenty-seven chapters, more than one-fourth of the book, to fill with invented ship and shore adventures in Rio.

What, then, did Melville transfer from the actual voyage to the imagined one? Chiefly, descriptions of the routine of life in a man-of-war: standing watches, sleeping and eating, the monthly reading at the capstan of the Articles of War, gambling, smuggling, and floggings.[8] Yet even with such matters, familiar to everyone on the ship, Melville departed from fact when it suited his purpose. A good example is "A Drought in a Man-of-war" (Chapter 14). It is alleged there that not many days out of port a rumor was set afloat that the frigate's supply of grog had not been renewed. The disappointed sailors invented a satisfactory substitute made from Eau de Cologne, brown sugar, and a drop of tar, for flavor. The *United States* was never, of course, short of whisky. Two days after Melville came on board the log carried this entry:

> Wood 10,000 sticks. Water 46,500 galls. Bread 42,000 lbs.
> Whiskey 4,850 galls. Beef 149 Bbls. Pork 179 Bbls.

7. See also the Revised Fair Copy of Preface, pp. 498–99.

8. Melville first witnessed punishment at 9 A.M. the day after he came on board. Four men were lashed. During his fourteen months at sea he saw 163 of his shipmates punished.

The supply of whisky on board was entered almost as regularly as the amount of beef.

Melville also built chapters around several exciting episodes that actually took place. Among these were the loss overboard of David Black, the cooper (Chapter 17, "Away! Second, Third, and Fourth Cutters, away!") and the race between the five warships leaving the harbor at Rio. Melville gives an international character to this contest (matter-of-factly recorded in the log) by reducing the ships to three, the *Neversink*, an English frigate, and another ship sporting "the rainbow banner of France."

There were five deaths while Melville was on board, all described clinically and at length in the Medical & Surgical Journal. One of these Melville turned to account in his lengthy description of the last illness, death, and burial of Shenly (Chapters 78–82). Melville's shipmate, disguised as Shenly, was Edward Williams, captain's cook, who was admitted to sick bay on June 12, 1844, with a pulmonary disease "of long standing." The Medical Journal reveals that though he was given careful treatment, he was past curing and died on the morning of August 27. "Edward Williams at 6 oclock A.M. appears to be sinking gradually; is not able to speak or move himself; pulse scarcely perceptible and expired at $6\frac{1}{2}$ A.M." White-Jacket's account of the last hours of Shenly accords so well with the surgeon's description that we can believe Melville attended his shipmate Williams and saw him die, or heard a firsthand account of his death.[9]

Whenever Melville needed an officer or seaman, whether to make a single point or build a chapter, he reached into his memory, source books, or imagination, and brought the man forward. We seem to meet new characters on almost every page, most of them bearing picturesque or punning names, such as Old Brush (captain of the paint room), Quoin (one of the quarter-gunners), Prime and Cylinder (gunner's mates). As soon as the book was published, readers began to speculate about the originals of the characters who played the most active roles or who were satirized. The

9. This may be the place to say, since we are consulting the Medical Journal, that Melville was never in sick bay for treatment, possibly a cause for regret on our part; nor was Jack Chase. Commodore Jones was treated for inflammation of the eyelids, bowel trouble, and a cough. Captain Armstrong's headache (a hangover?) was cured by a diet of arrowroot. As we might expect, Lt. Latham B. Avery ("Mad Jack") had more interesting diseases. Over a period of six weeks Surgeon William Johnson labored, successfully, to cure "an abscess on the nates and swelling of the Inguinal glands of the left groin." Though Dr. Johnson was greatly experienced in dealing with such complaints, his venereal cures do seem rather quick and final for those pre-penicillin days.

secrets Melville would not disclose to Dana on paper were known to some contemporaries.[10] Scholars have subsequently identified the originals of more than twenty of the characters. Others could possibly be matched up by further searching in the available documents. The risk in this kind of search results from the fact that Melville often invented a personality for a character with a particular rank or rating. For example, because there was a master-at-arms on board in every ship, it does not follow that Melville's Bland is the master-at-arms of the *United States*. Indeed, we know he was not. Melville "borrowed" some of Bland's traits of character from one of his sources, William McNally's *Evils and Abuses in the Naval and Merchant Service, Exposed* (1839).

Melville needed a commodore on board as a symbol of supreme authority. A few known facts in the career of Commodore Thomas ap Catesby Jones are built into the character of Melville's unnamed commodore. Commodore Jones left the *United States* in January, 1844, having been re-called as a gesture to Mexico for his premature seizure of Monterey in October, 1842. There was no commodore on the frigate during the three-month voyage from Callao to Boston, the period covered by the narrative in *White-Jacket*. In at least one trait Captain James Armstrong resembles Captain Claret.[11] It was common knowledge that he was a hard drinker and sometimes had to be carried to his cabin after dinner. Melville's Lt. "Mad Jack" is a composite character, though the portrait resembles in several particulars—his courage and seamanship and his control of the men—Lt. Latham B. Avery of the *United States*. The purser of the *United States* was Edward Fitzgerald. Like Melville's purser, he was a Southern gentleman (from Virginia) and he also had a slave, Robert Lucas, with him. The fleet surgeon on the *United States* was Dr. William Johnson. He is emphatically not the original of Melville's absurd Surgeon Cuticle.[12] There seems to be little resemblance between Melville's transcendentalist chaplain and the Episcopalian chaplain on the *United States*, the Reverend Theodore

10. For example, in a 21-page memorandum dated July, 1850 (which he never published), Rear Admiral Thomas O. Selfridge, Sr., denounced Melville for traducing the commodore, the captain, the lieutenants, and the midshipmen of the *United States*. Charles Roberts Anderson, "A Reply to Herman Melville's *White-Jacket* by Rear-Admiral Thomas O. Selfridge, Sr.," *American Literature*, VII (May, 1935), 123–44.

11. Armstrong was in command during the first part of the voyage. Cornelius K. Stribling was captain during the period covered by *White Jacket*.

12. Johnson had a distinguished career in the navy. After he retired from the active list, he was named Medical Director. The Medical & Surgical Journal shows that he was a skillful physician and a good administrator.

Bartow. The professor, who has such a difficult time teaching gunnery to the obstreperous midshipmen in the "Man-of-war College" on the *Neversink*, was modeled on Henry Hayes Lockwood. Like Melville's professor, Lockwood was a graduate of West Point. Twelve years after he served on the *United States* he was appointed instructor in infantry tactics at the Naval Academy. The commodore's secretary on the *Neversink* "looked much like an Embassador Extraordinary from Versailles." This statement suggests that Melville remembered that the name of Commodore Jones's secretary was Henri La Reintrie. Asa Curtis, the gunner on the *United States*, was as irascible as Melville's "Old Combustibles." William Hoff, boatswain on the *United States*, was a heavy drinker and was frequently in trouble because of this failing. Melville's boatswain, Yarn, is one of the most expert liquor smugglers on the *Neversink*.

The fictional use Melville made of the deaths of David Black (Bungs) and Edward Williams (Shenly) has already been mentioned. He also brought into the book the crippling accident which happened to James Craddock, seaman, when he fell from the mizzen topsail yard. Craddock becomes Baldy in *White-Jacket*. Again the Medical & Surgical Journal supplies us with several corroborative details. The surgeon did indeed place Craddock in "a curious frame-work of wood" in which all his limbs could be stretched out. Surgeon Johnson had a name for this device: "a fracture box." The accident took place on October 28, 1843. Craddock was not able to go about on crutches until the following March, but he made a better recovery than Baldy, who hobbles ashore at the end of the voyage, "a mere dislocated skeleton, white as foam."

In Chapter 13 ("A Man-of-war Hermit in a Mob") the narrator, White-Jacket, speaks of "our mutual friends, Nord and Williams, who, with Lemsford himself, Jack Chase, and my comrades of the main-top, comprised almost the only persons with whom I unreservedly consorted while on board the frigate." All of these friends, except Lemsford, have been certainly identified and in his case there are some shrewd guesses. Jack Chase, hero of the main-top, is "John J. Chase Capt. Top," entered on the muster roll as No. 513. We know a good deal about this Briton, then 53 years old, whom Melville remembered affectionately all his life and to whom he dedicated *Billy Budd, Sailor*: "To / Jack Chase / Englishman / Wherever that great heart may now be / Here on Earth or harbored in Paradise / Captain of the Maintop / in the year 1843 / in the U.S. Frigate / *United States*." Though Melville borrowed some of the adventures of the fictional Jack Chase, the real Jack Chase did indeed desert his ship (it was not the

United States but the *St. Louis*); however, he was received on board the *United States* at Callao, May 29, 1842, with a request from a Peruvian admiral (in whose service he had shipped) that he be pardoned. Melville enlarged on those facts in Chapter 5, "Jack Chase on a Spanish Quarter-deck."

White-Jacket's friend Nord has been identified as Oliver Russ, who shipped on the *United States* under an alias, Edward Norton.[13] In 1859 Russ wrote to Melville, recalling their shore leave together at Lima and inform-ing him that within three years after the cruise (and without knowing that Melville "would be numbered among the literary writers of the day") he had named a son of his Herman Melville Russ, from "a regard for those qualities which an acquaintance of eighteen months with you led me so much to admire." Nord's and White-Jacket's friend Williams, "a thorough-going Yankee from Maine," who is mentioned only briefly in Chapter 13, must be Griffith Williams. Melville and he enlisted on the same day and appear on the muster roll as Nos. 572 and 573.

Two candidates have been proposed for the role of Lemsford, the poet. Charles Roberts Anderson suggested that his original was the G.W.W. who may possibly have been the scribe who wrote up the log for at least part of the voyage and who may have been the author of *Journal of a Cruise to the Pacific Ocean, 1842–1844, in the Frigate* UNITED STATES.[14] A second candidate is Ephraim Curtiss Hine, No. 339 on the muster roll, whose term on board coincided with eleven of Melville's fourteen months in service. In 1848, nearly four years after their voyage ended, Hine published in Auburn, New York, *The Haunted Barque and Other Poems*. Of the thirty-eight poems in this volume, twenty refer to his life at sea and ten of these celebrate places touched by the *United States* while Hine and Melville were on board. It is therefore possible that he wrote some of these under the "difficulties" Lemsford experienced.[15] Hine would seem the likelier candidate for the honor of being Lemsford, especially since the poem which is a major basis for considering G.W.W. a poet—a poem inscribed during the voyage to "J.J.C. [Jack Chase] by his sincere friend G.W.W."—is in fact by Mrs. Hemans, not by G.W.W.[16]

13. Harrison Hayford, "The Sailor Poet of *White-Jacket*," *Boston Public Library Quarterly*, III (July, 1951), 221–22.

14. Anderson, *Journal of a Cruise*, pp. 13–16. There were two men on board whose initials were G. W. W.: George W. Wallace, an ordinary seaman, and George W. Weir, a private of the marine guard.

15. Hayford, "The Sailor Poet of *White-Jacket*," pp. 222–28.

16. Anderson, *Journal of a Cruise*, p. 15. See also Anderson, *Melville in the South Seas*,

What can we say of Herman Melville as White-Jacket, O.S.? From the official records we learn only the dates of Melville's enlistment and discharge and his muster roll number, 572. He was never under the care of Surgeon Johnson and he never suffered the humiliation of the lash. For one resemblance we have Melville's word. Melville evidently did wear the white jacket, but there was, of course, no need for him to endure any hardships the possession of this "albatross" entailed. He could apparently have got "a *grego*, or sailor's surtout" from the purser's steward at any time. But he told Dana in a letter (May 1, 1850) that there was a white jacket which he kept to the day of his discharge from the ship, at Boston. "You ask me about 'the jacket.' I answer it was a veritable garment—which I suppose is now somewhere at the bottom of Charles river [in Boston]. I was a great fool, or I should have brought such a remarkable fabric (as it really was, to behold) home with me." Still other matters doubtless have some basis in Melville's own experience.[17]

III

In all of his early books Melville appropriated passages from other writers, but the number of his extensive pillages for *White-Jacket* is exceeded only by those in *Moby-Dick*. While he was writing the novel, Melville drew on more than a dozen books and articles. These furnished him germinal ideas for scenes or factual information in at least thirty of his ninety-four chapters.

Since it will not be possible to discuss in detail his use of these sources, I shall list them alphabetically here, with comment, when possible, on how he happened to come on them.

1. Nathaniel Ames, *A Mariner's Sketches, Originally Published in the Manufacturers and Farmers Journal*. Providence, 1830.

As Charles Roberts Anderson discovered, Melville rephrased an episode from this book for a large part of White-Jacket's fall from the top-gallant

---

pp. 366–67, where only Wallace is nominated; also p. 486, n. 27, where Anderson points out that the untitled verses in G. W. W.'s hand were by Mrs. Hemans.

17. Wilson L. Heflin conjectures that the episode in Chapter 59, "A Man-of-war Button divides two Brothers," makes fiction of the fact that Melville, for some reason, failed to meet his cousin Stanwix Ganesvoort, a midshipman on the *Erie*, when their respective ships were anchored at Callao Day in February, 1844. "A Man-of-War Button Divides Two Cousins," *Boston Public Library Quarterly*, III (January, 1951), 51–60.

yardarm in Chapter 92. He borrowed from another passage in Ames (pp. 189–90) to furnish the humorous interruptions in Chapter 81, "How they Bury a Man-of-war's-man at Sea."

Ames was on a South Sea cruise of the *United States* from 1824 to 1827. Possibly this fact interested Melville in the *Sketches*.

2. Articles of War.

One of the principal themes of *White-Jacket* is the archaic and inequitable character of the Articles of War. Melville adverts to the Articles in several chapters and gives them a thorough going-over in 70 and 72. He quotes from them with scrupulous accuracy. The Articles in force when Melville was on board the *United States* were passed by the Sixth Congress on April 23, 1800. In a note to Chapter 71 Melville gives us his source: "They may be found in the second volume of the 'United States Statutes at Large,' under chapter xxxiii."

3. Thomas Hodgskin, "Abolition of Impressment," *Edinburgh Review*, XLI (October, 1824), 154–81.[18]

On or after July 20, 1849, Melville borrowed two volumes of the *Edinburgh Review* (41 and 47) from Evert A. Duyckinck's library. Either he already knew that one article in each volume would be of use to him in writing *White-Jacket* or he soon made this discovery. Hodgskin's article is a review of five books about naval matters but he concentrates heavily on the evils of impressment. Melville picked up at least ten bits of factual information which make "The Manning of Navies" (Chapter 90) impressively learned.

4. Francis Jeffrey, review of *A Selection from the Public and Private Correspondence of Vice-Admiral Lord Collingwood . . . By G. L. Newnham Collingwood, Esq.,* in *Edinburgh Review*, XLVII (May, 1828), 385–418.[19]

Melville made use of Jeffrey's long review in Chapters 27, 36, 52, 74, and 90. To Jeffrey, as to Melville, Collingwood was the perfect model of a naval officer, devoted to the best traditions of the service and a firm but compassionate leader of men. Melville quotes Collingwood's dicta without embellishment. He also appropriated some of Jeffrey's own observations

18. Thomas Philbrick, "Melville's 'Best Authorities,'" *Nineteenth-Century Fiction*, XV (September, 1960), 171–79. In Chapter 36 ("Flogging not Necessary"), Melville lets us know that he had seen this article: "This was the language of the Edinburgh Review at a still later period, 1824."

19. Melville's borrowings are discussed by Philbrick, pp. 173–76.

since the article made use of Collingwood's experiences to expose the incompetence of naval officers.

5. Samuel Leech, *Thirty Years from Home, or A Voice from the Main Deck* . . . Boston, 1843.[20]

In Chapter 74, "The Main-top at Night," Tawney, a Negro sheet-anchor-man, comes into the top; he was often invited there "of tranquil nights, to hear him discourse." This night he tells the top-men stories of his experiences on the *Macedonian*, a British frigate on which he served until the *Neversink* captured her in the War of 1812. Tawney's recollections are straight out of Leech (pp. 127–50), who was on board the *United States* when it reduced the *Macedonian* to a dismasted wreck in October, 1812.

Melville borrowed shorter passages from Leech to help him with four other chapters (16, 33, 88, and 90). It is also conceivable that Chapter 63, "The Operation," was suggested by Leech's description (p. 143) of the surgeon at work after the battle: "We held [Logholm] while the surgeon cut off his leg above the knee. The task was most painful to behold, the surgeon using his knife and saw on human flesh and bones, as freely as the butcher at the shambles does on the carcass of the beast!"

R. H. Dana, Jr., may have brought Leech's book to Melville's attention. From the introduction to a reissue in 1857, we learn that Dana had suggested to Leech that he publish the work: it was "chiefly by my advice that he printed his narrative."[21]

6. *Life on Board a Man-of-War; Including a Full Account of the Battle of Navarino. By a British Seaman.* Glasgow: Blackie, Fullarton, & Co., 1829.

In Chapter 75, "Sink, Burn, and Destroy," Jack Chase reels off another of his "*yarns and twisters*," recounting this time, with becoming modesty, his exploits at the Battle of Navarino (October 20, 1827) when a combined British, French, and Russian fleet defeated the Egyptians and the Turks. Jack was, of course, in the thick of the fight, on board Admiral Codrington's flagship, the *Asia*.

But it so happens that a young Scot was on the *Genoa* in this battle and lived to write his memoirs, the anonymous *Life on Board a Man-of-War*.[22]

20. Charles Roberts Anderson first noted Melville's borrowings from this volume, in *Melville in the South Seas*, pp. 390–94.

21. Robert F. Lucid, "The Influence of *Two Years Before the Mast* on Herman Melville," *American Literature*, XXXI (November, 1959), 244.

22. Though the author of *Life on Board* hides his identity under "By a British Seaman" on the title page, internal evidence shows that he was a Scottish lad. Melville's use of this

Strangely enough he witnessed several of the scenes Jack reels off, and describes them in the same language. The "showers of burned rice and olives from the exploding foe" and the drowning "'Hometons" with their topknots by which "they believed their Prophet would drag them up to Paradise" Melville found in *Life on Board* (p. 148). There are other details of the battle, as seen from the decks of the *Genoa*, which he borrowed for Jack Chase's use. Earlier, the young Scot fell from the fore-yardarm sixty feet into the sea. There are similarities between the description of his sensations (pp. 120–21) and White-Jacket's account of his fall in "The Last of the Jacket."

7. *Life in a Man-of-War or Scenes in "Old Ironsides" During her Cruise in the Pacific. By a Fore-Top-Man*. Philadelphia: Lydia R. Bailey, Printer, 1841.[23]

In 1839 "Fore-Top-Man" sailed for a Pacific cruise on the famous *Constitution* ("Old Ironsides"), a sister ship of the *United States*. This cruise ended at Norfolk in October, 1841. There were no great disasters or heroic events for the author of *Life in a Man-of-War* to record and his book is a prosaic though informative work. Melville skimmed off the author's best scenes and also took many short passages of description and dialogue and the names of several characters. Nine chapters are largely indebted to this book: 14, 23, 32, 37, 41, 43, 47, 90, 91. Among these are some of the most amusing episodes in the novel: "A Drought in a Man-of-war" (Chapter 14); "Theatricals in a Man-of-war" (Chapter 23); "A Dish of Dunderfunk" (Chapter 32); "Smuggling in a Man-of-war" (Chapter 43); and "An Auction in a Man-of-war" (Chapter 47).

Because he had made such extensive use of *Life in a Man-of-War*, Melville at one point planned to acknowledge his debt. In the revised draft of a preface, now in the Houghton Library, he made this sly comment: "The writer has to thank the light-hearted author of a book called 'Scenes in old Ironsides', for recalling to his memory several minute man-of-war technicalities & humorous phrases, that otherwise might have escaped his memory; also, for supplying corroborative, or additional hints for two or three scenes in the following chapters" (see pp. 496, 497 below).

exceedingly scarce book was uncovered by Howard P. Vincent, in *The Tailoring of Melville's WHITE-JACKET* (Evanston, 1970).

23. Keith Huntress, "Melville's Use of a Source for *White-Jacket*," *American Literature*, XVII (March, 1945), 66–74. The book was entered for copyright by Henry James Mercier and William Gallop. Some scholars have assumed that "Fore-Top-Man" was James Mercier. Mr. Huntress does not make this identification.

8. John A. Lockwood, "Flogging in the Navy," *United States Magazine, and Democratic Review*, XXV (August, 1849), 97–115.

This was the first of a series of five articles which appeared anonymously in the *Democratic Review*, in the issues of August through December. The author was Dr. John A. Lockwood (1811–1900), a surgeon in the navy and from 1845 to 1849 surgeon and professor of chemistry at the Naval Academy. In 1856 and 1857, when Melville was on his tour of the Near East, he had several pleasant meetings with Dr. Lockwood, who was then surgeon on the *Constellation*.[24] It is possible that they knew each other at the time of the writing of *White-Jacket*. Lockwood was the brother of Henry Hayes Lockwood, the professor of the novel.

Dr. Lockwood gathered the first three of his articles into an anonymous pamphlet (apparently the type was left standing for this purpose), which was issued late in 1849, with the title *An Essay on Flogging in the Navy; Containing Strictures upon Existing Naval Laws, and Suggesting Substitutes for the Discipline of the Lash*. New York: Pudney & Russell Printers.[25]

At the time he was writing *White-Jacket* Melville could have seen only the August, 1849, installment of "Flogging in the Navy." But he found in it historical information which was just what he needed to add force and weight to "The Genealogy of the Articles of War" (Chapter 71) and to "Herein are the good Ordinances of the Sea . . ." (Chapter 72).[26]

9. William McNally, *Evils and Abuses in the Naval and Merchant Service, Exposed; With Proposals for Their Remedy and Redress*. By William McNally, Formerly of the U.S. Navy. Boston: Published by Cassady and March, For the Author, at No. 8 Wilson's Lane, 1839.[27]

McNally had made several voyages in merchant ships before he enlisted in the navy about 1827. He received promotions and was warranted a

24. Howard C. Horsford, ed., *Journal of a Visit to Europe and the Levant* (Princeton, 1955), p. 113 and *passim*.

25. The pamphlet was clearly aimed at the United States Senate, which had resumed debate in December, 1849, on flogging in the Navy. An amendment attached to the Naval Appropriations Bill which would have abolished flogging was defeated by Southern senators in the 30th Congress. The issue was once more before the Congress in the 31st Session. Flogging was at last abolished on September 28, 1850, the Senate having yielded by the narrow vote of 26 to 24.

26 Melville's borrowings are discussed by Philbrick, "Melville's 'Best Authorities,'" pp 176–79.

27. See Thomas L. Philbrick, "Another Source for *White-Jacket*," *American Literature*, XXIX (January, 1958), 431–39; also, *Billy Budd, Sailor*, ed. Harrison Hayford and Merton M. Sealts, Jr. (Chicago, 1962), pp. 31–32 and p. 154, n. 88.

gunner in 1835. In 1837 he was court-martialed for drunkenness and dismissed from the service. In *Evils and Abuses* he had his revenge. It is the savage book he intended it to be.

Melville found in this work many factual details to fortify his accusations of injustice on board. He also used McNally in the creation of two chapters. The portrait of Bland, the master-at-arms, in Chapter 44, draws on McNally's account of Sterritt, the villainous master-at-arms on the *Fairfield*. The near-mutiny at the time of the "massacre of the beards," which Mad Jack puts down with a stern exhortation as he jumps "right down among the mob" (Chapter 85) is derived from McNally's anecdote about a rebellion on board the *Delaware* in 1829.

Melville muffled the tones of personal bitterness sounded in *Evils and Abuses*. "The end result is not," Philbrick says, "that Melville softened the force of McNally's blows; rather, he turned them from individual members of the Navy to what Melville regarded as the true enemy, the institution itself."

10. John Nicol, *The Life and Adventures of John Nicol, Mariner*. Edinburgh: W. Blackwood, 1822.

In Chapter 90 ("The Manning of Navies") Melville alludes to John Nicol's having to skulk like a thief "for whole years in the country round about Edinburgh, to avoid the press-gangs." Thus we know that Melville was familiar with his fascinating plain tale of picaresque adventures, edited (and possibly written down) by John Howell, an Edinburgh bookbinder and printer.

Melville took more from Nicol than this brief reference to the hazard of impressment.[28] Several items in the yarns Jack Chase reels off in Chapter 75, "Sink, Burn, and Destroy," were lifted from Nicol: the "desperate fights with his British majesty's cutters"; the cooper's anvil which was sent flying into a line-of-battle ship; the powder-monkey "whizzed" to death by a shot which did not touch him; the boatload of Turkish flags which "one of our captains carried home," swearing that he would "dress his father's orchard in colors with them." These and several other items which Melville hands over to Jack Chase were picked up from widely separated passages about other battles that Nicol tells about, to add color to Jack's "twister" about the battle of Navarino. In addition, the incident of the

28. John D. Seelye, "'Spontaneous Impress of Truth'ı Melville's Jack Chase: a Source, an Analogue, a Conjecture," *Nineteenth-Century Fiction*, XX (March, 1966), 367–76. In this study of Melville's indebtedness to Nicol, Seelye used a modern reprint of the book, with a Foreword and Afterword by Alexander Laing (New York, 1936).

discovery of the five puncheons of port afloat in the ocean (Chapter 37) is expanded from Nicol's more restrained account of the recovery of *one* cask of "excellent Port wine" off Cape Horn.

11. *The Penny Cyclopædia of the Society for the Diffusion of Useful Knowledge.* 27 vols. London: Charles Knight, 1833–43.[29] This excellent work, issued by a publisher in whose company Melville dined at the Erectheum Club on December 22, 1849, furnished fifteen passages or allusions in the chapters (60–63) recounting Surgeon Cuticle's operation on the foretopman who was shot while trying to get shore liberty. Melville read with care the articles on "Amputation," "Anatomy," "Gun-Shot Wounds," "William Hunter," and "Tourniquet." Much of the dialogue between Cuticle and the other surgeons, and parts of Cuticle's pompous disquisitions on his method of amputating a leg are lifted from these articles.

The most remarkable thing about these borrowings is the way Melville transforms sober scientific reporting into grim humor. Two examples will have to suffice.

The "Amputation" article discusses the reasons why surgeons in classical times were reluctant to amputate. "And no wonder: when they did venture upon it, the consequences were appalling. They cut through the flesh with a red-hot knife, hoping by this means to prevent a fatal loss of blood. After having performed this operation, they dressed the wound with scalding oil, in order to complete what the burning knife may have left imperfect."

Now hear Surgeon Cuticle attempting to allay the fears of the trembling man whose leg he is about to amputate:

"My man, before Celsus's time, such was the general ignorance of our noble science, that, in order to prevent the excessive effusion of blood, it was deemed indispensable to operate with a red-hot knife"—making a professional movement toward the thigh—"and pour scalding oil upon the parts"—elevating his elbow, as if with a tea-pot in his hand—"still further to sear them, after amputation had been performed."

The *Cyclopædia* article on "Gun-Shot Wounds" records several cases of circuitous passages of bullets in the body. "Dr. Hennen mentions one in which a ball entered at the pomum Adami, ran completely round the neck, and was found close by the aperture at which it had penetrated."

29. Melville's use of this source is my own discovery. Howard P. Vincent believes that Melville also used some of the works cited in the *Cyclopædia* articles.

Cuticle is talking to the surgeons:

"That ball, young gentlemen, must have taken a most circuitous route. Nor, in cases where the direction is oblique, is this at all unusual. Indeed the learned Hennen gives us a most remarkable—I had almost said an incredible —case of a soldier's neck, where the bullet, entering at the part called Adam's Apple—"

"Yes," said Surgeon Wedge, elevating himself, "the *pomum Adami*."

"Entering the point called *Adam's Apple*," continued Cuticle, severely emphasizing the last two words, "ran completely round the neck, and, emerging at the same hole it had entered, shot the next man in the ranks."

I am inclined to believe that Melville drew facts from the *Cyclopædia* article on "Janeiro, Rio de" for his description of the city's beautiful harbor (Chapters 39 and 50). A dozen features which Melville mentions are touched on in the article.

12. Others.

Several minor borrowings, some of them conjectural, must be taken into account. Robert F. Lucid believes that Melville used a few descriptions of life on board which he found in Dana's *Two Years Before the Mast* and added touches to the character of Jack Chase which he took from Dana's handsome English sailor, Bill Jackson. The scene in which White-Jacket narrowly escapes a flogging may owe something to William Leggett's "Brought to the Gangway," published in the New York *Mirror*, April 19, 1834, and collected in Leggett's *Naval Stories* (1834 and 1835).[30] Two suggested sources for White-Jacket's murderous thoughts directed at Captain Claret are "Impressment of Seamen," a sketch in John S. Sleeper's *Tales of the Ocean, and Essays for the Forecastle* (1841), and *Proceedings of the Naval Court Martial in the Case of Alexander Slidell Mackenzie . . .* (1844), p. 39. Perry Miller saw some anticipations of *White-Jacket* in Charles Frederick Briggs's *The Adventures of Harry Franco* (1839). Howard P. Vincent has noted that in White-Jacket's account of his fall from the yardarm some of the most striking images in the undersea part were derived from Schiller's ballad "The Diver," in Lord Lytton's translation.

30. "The Influence of *Two Years Before the Mast* on Herman Melville," 250–55; Page S. Procter, Jr., "A Source for the Flogging Incident in *White-Jacket*," *American Literature*, XXII (May, 1950), 176–77.

IV

In studying the structure of *White-Jacket* one is likely to notice first how carefully Melville links his chapters. The first words of a chapter usually tell us where we are in the narrative and what is coming next. A few opening sentences, chosen at random, will substantiate this point.

"Here, I must frankly tell a story about Jack . . ." (Chapter 5).

"The ceremonials of a man-of-war, some of which have been described in the preceding chapter, may merit a reflection or two" (Chapter 40).

"While we lay in Rio, we sometimes had company from shore; but an unforeseen honor awaited us" (Chapter 56).

Thus we are led on through the book, rather in the way a seventeenth-century French dramatist kept the action running smoothly by *la liaison des scènes*. No characters leave the stage until the next group has emerged from the wings and are ready to speak.

Though he insists in his Preface to the English edition that the work is "not presented as a journal of the cruise," Melville took pains to let his readers know exactly where the *Neversink* was at each stage of her voyage from Callao to Norfolk, again using the opening words of many of the chapters to give the clue. These navigational notes do not always relate to the substance of the chapter. Melville put them in, I think, because he wished his book to appeal to readers of voyage literature who wanted the facts about wind and weather, latitude and longitude. By this device he simulated a voyage.

What were the chapters, eventually so explicitly introduced and linked, to be about? Again we observe that Melville followed a plan. There are six kinds of chapters in the novel, not sawed off like logs but nicely fitted together the way a cabinetmaker joins his pieces of wood.

1. Melville's habit was to make the main title of his books enigmatic and then explain immediately in the subtitle what the reader might expect. The second title of *White-Jacket* is *The World in a Man-of-War*. It is significant, I think, that 40 of his 93 chapter titles contain the phrase "man-of-war." More than a third of the novel reports the routine of life on board— "general training" in preparation for battle, killing time, smuggling, gambling, washday, sleeping, eating, death, and burial at sea. These chapters culminate in "The Social State in a Man-of-war" (Chapter 89). In

Chapter 68 ("A Man-of-war Fountain . . .") Melville tells us that these predominant chapters were to tell all, down to the last detail:

> I let nothing slip, however small; and feel myself actuated by the same motive which has prompted many worthy old chroniclers, to set down the merest trifles concerning things that are destined to pass away entirely from the earth, and which, if not preserved in the nick of time, must infallibly perish from the memories of man.

For these factual chapters Melville drew on his memories, but he also used his sources liberally.

2. But Melville was writing a work of fiction, not a treatise or an autobiography. Consequently he devised a number of chapters to provide his narrative with peaks of suspense and excitement. There are eleven of these, and one notices that they are fairly evenly distributed through the book. Five of them are based on events which Melville must have witnessed, such as the drowning of the cooper (Chapter 17) and the crippling fall of James Craddock (Chapter 46). The other six chapters of this kind he either invented or worked up from episodes he found in his reading. Two of these chapters are what dramatists call "obligatory scenes." If you were describing the passage of Cape Horn in the old sailing days, you had to make it dangerous to the point of near fatality. For this required scene Melville conjured up, from his reading and his imagination, a storm he had not seen, certainly on this voyage. Chapter 67, "White-Jacket arraigned at the Mast," had to be written as a climax to the series of chapters about the barbarism of flogging.

3. There is no towering character like Ahab in *White-Jacket*, nor one so fully drawn as Ishmael, but the number and vividness of the character portrayals are remarkable. No other novel of Melville's can match it in this respect. Since there are eighteen chapters built around a single character or group of characters, we can see that Melville used such chapters deliberately as a device in constructing his narrative. He does not introduce these men aimlessly. In every instance he uses their words and actions not only to give delight but to make a point. Two examples will illustrate his intention. Melville begins his attack on the privileges of rank in Chapter 6. He is still pressing this theme in Chapter 52, now using the behavior of the midshipmen to make his point. "However childish, ignorant, stupid or idiotic a midshipman, if he but orders a sailor to perform even the most absurd action, that man is not only bound to render instant and unanswering obedience, but he would refuse at his peril." The contrasting of Lt. Mad

Jack, a great boozer on shore but "in his saddle on the sea," first with the foppish Lt. Selvagee and then with Captain Claret himself, raises the question of the competence of naval officers. Melville concludes Chapter 27, "Some Thoughts growing out of Mad Jack's Countermanding his Superior's Order," with a direct posing of the question, using statistics from the Navy Register for 1849 to prove that "no small portion of the million and a half of money above mentioned is annually paid [for salaries] to national pensioners in disguise, who live on the navy without serving it."

4. That the serious chapters on flogging (33–36) and on the Articles of War (70–72) were carefully planned for maximum effect can be seen from the way they are placed in the novel and the progress of the arguments in them. The chapters on the evils of flogging are introduced only after the book has run one-third of its course, and there is a humorous episode on each side of the group, as if to assure the reader that the author will not linger too long over this disagreeable business. After the initial chapter on the flogging of John, Peter, Mark, and Antone sets the tone, the chapter titles themselves tell us what the arguments will be: "Some of the Evil Effects of Flogging"; "Flogging not Lawful"; "Flogging not Necessary." The final chapter ends with one of the most eloquent passages in all of Melville's writing, calling on America to abolish this evil thing and so live up to what God has predestined and mankind expects "from our race."[31]

The three chapters on the Articles of War were also adroitly placed approximately two-thirds of the way through the book. Melville begins the sequence with a powerful scene in Chapter 70, "Monthly Muster round the Capstan." As the Articles are read by the captain's clerk, White-Jacket interjects, *sotto voce*, after each reading his bitter comments on cutthroat martial law. The words "*shall suffer death*" toll throughout the scene. In the two chapters that follow, Melville levels at the Articles all the weapons in his arsenal: logic, ridicule, citations from earlier and more just sea laws and the English common law. The final chapter ends, as does the last of the

---

31. Rear-Admiral Franklin was responsible for the belief, stated in early studies of the book, that *White-Jacket* influenced the Congress to abolish flogging. In reviewing the matter, Charles Roberts Anderson found no reference to it in any of the speeches delivered on the question of flogging. "So far from Melville's *White-Jacket* bringing about the movement that resulted in the abolition of flogging in the navy," he concludes, "it was the very currency of this agitation that brought forth [Melville's] attack" (*Melville in the South Seas*, p. 431). However, Melville must have followed the debates in Congress with great interest. A week after flogging was abolished (on September 28, 1850), he wrote in a letter (October 6) to Evert A. Duyckinck: "I am offering up devout jubilations for the abolition of the flogging law."

chapters on flogging, with a rhetorical appeal, this time to "right and salutary principles."

5. Though most of the factual chapters are touched with humor, some of it barbed, Melville evidently thought he needed a few chapters that would be all fun and high spirits. These episodes—there are seven of them—offset the serious chapters and add to the narrative content of the novel. One of them Melville invented—the ceremonial visit of the young emperor, Don Pedro II, on board the *Neversink* while it is anchored at Rio (Chapters 56 and 57). The shipboard sports described in "Fun in a Man-of-war" (Chapter 66)—singlestick, sparring, and hammer-and-anvil—we suppose Melville had witnessed, though some details of this chapter are taken from "The Nigger Pugilists" section in Fore-Top-Man's *Life in a Man-of-War*.

The germs of the other five chapters are to be found, interestingly enough, in *Life in a Man-of-War or Scenes in "Old Ironside."* [32] We glimpse Melville at work here. He had noted at some point the possibilities in these episodes in *Scenes* (they are Fore-Top-Man's best passages) and proceeded to transfer them deftly from the decks of the *Constitution* to the *Neversink*.

6. Finally, there are the dozen or so chapters in which the white jacket itself figures prominently. Two of those chapters frame the novel: Chapter 1 ("The Jacket") and Chapter 92 ("The last of the Jacket"). This Quakerish frock, "white as a shroud," serves to identify its owner wherever he moves, and he is always where the action is. The jacket alienates him from his shipmates. In "The Jacket aloft" (Chapter 19) it comes near to being the death of him, as it does again in "The last of the Jacket" (Chapter 92). This time he rids himself of it, at the risk of his life, and emerges after his terrible baptism a new man, reborn.

These white jacket chapters tie the episodes together and they run like a gleaming thread through the book. They also suggest the alienation that the owner of the jacket suffers, then his growing sense of self-identity and self-sufficiency, and finally his rebirth. There is surely a link between the symbolism of the jacket and what Melville wrote Hawthorne in June, 1851: "Until I was twenty-five, I had no development at all. From my twenty-fifth year I date my life." Herman Melville had his twenty-fifth birthday

32. The sections from this book which Melville used for those chapters are as follows (Fore-Top-Man did not number his sections): for 14, "The Grog Expended" and "The Tar's Substitute for Grog"; for 23, "Fourth of July in a Yankee Frigate"; for 32, "The Galley Marauders"; for 37, a short passage from "The Tar's Substitute for Grog"; for 91, "The Galley Politicians."

on August 1, 1844, shortly before the frigate *United States* entered Rio and
the Bay of All Beauties.

V

The English edition of *White-Jacket*, officially published on January 23,
1850, was probably not ready for actual release to the public until nearer
the first of February, since on the second of February four leading journals
reviewed it. The august *Athenæum* was almost rapturous in its praise of
Melville's "poetry of the Ship," and the review included four excerpts from
the novel, three of them long. Oddly enough the reviewer makes no mention of the chapters about naval abuses. His concern was to "place" Melville
as a writer of sea fiction. The last sentence of the review suggests the tone
of the whole piece:

> To conclude, then,—with a thousand faults, which it were needless
> here to point out, Mr. Melville possesses, also, more vivacity, fancy, colour
> and energy than ninety-nine out of the hundred who undertake to poetize
> or to prate about "sea monsters or land monsters;" and we think that, with
> only the commonest care, he might do brilliant service by enlarging the
> library of fictitious adventure.

On the same day, *John Bull*, greatly pleased with the new work,
observed that Melville is "an improving and a vastly improved writer."
The rattling youngster has grown into a thoughtful man, "who, without
any abatement of his rich and ever sparkling wit, has obtained the mastery
of his own fancy." *John Bull*'s reviewer was particularly impressed with the
way in which Melville had contrived to write a caustic critique upon the
American navy which at the same time "possesses all the attraction of a first
rate sea-novel" and embodies the "author's philosophy of life." The *Spectator*'s reviewer, on February 2, did not agree with Melville's opinions on
naval discipline, but acknowledged that there is not always "a ready answer
to his religious, legal, or constitutional logic." He called attention to the
skill with which Melville's "disquisitions" on various topics are made to
proceed from incidents in the story. "Thus, a flogging gives rise to several
essays on naval punishments, the power regularly granted to naval officers,
and the unconstitutional power they usurp." The fourth review on February 2 was in *Britannia*, a journal which had reviewed *Mardi* with reservations and *Redburn* unfavorably, using the occasion each time to point out
faults in style. The lecture continued in the review of *White-Jacket*.

The two reviews that appeared on February 9 were approving. The

Atlas was particularly pleased by Melville's belief that conditions in the British navy were better than in the American. (This note was frequently sounded by the English reviewers.) The *Literary Gazette* was impressed by two features: the completeness of the picture of life on board a man-of-war and the "embellishments" which give "greater piquancy and effect to the narrative." English readers will find "that Mr. Melville's yarn has got such a hold of them that they neither wish to belay or leave it till they have reached the last strand."

Bentley's Miscellany, a journal issued by Melville's publisher, reviewed *White-Jacket* enthusiastically in its March issue. The reviewer may have been deliberately puffing the work, though in this issue two other books published by Bentley were given rough treatment. The review makes a distinction between the "marine story" as written by Melville and by other writers. The charm of the sea stories of Cooper, Marryat, and Hall is "literal truthfulness." But Mr. Melville "bathes the scene in the hues of a fanciful and reflective spirit, which gives it the interest of a creation of genius." Bentley's reviewer concludes decisively: "We do not hesitate to give to this publication the first place amongst Mr. Melville's productions."

There were at least four notices of *White-Jacket* in London newspapers: the *Daily News* (February 11); the *Morning Post* (February 12); the *Globe and Traveller* (March 4); and the *Morning Herald* (also March 4). The review in the *Morning Post* is said by Hetherington to be the longest of the English reviews.[33]

There was considerable anticipatory interest in the forthcoming publication of *White-Jacket* in this country. (The day was to be March 21.) On March 2 the *Albion* reprinted three extracts copied "from a London newspaper." The *Literary World* printed Chapter 56, "A Shore Emperor on board a Man-of-war," in its issue of March 9. The same chapter (picked up from the *Literary World*) was printed by the *Spirit of the Times* on March 16. N. P. Willis' *Home Journal*, in its issue of March 16, gave its readers two-thirds of Chapter 26, "The Pitch of the Cape," under the title "A Gale off Cape Horn."[34]

---

33. *Melville's Reviewers*, p. 161. Unless otherwise indicated, ensuing quotations from the reviews and statements about them are based on the original sources.

34. Other journals and newspapers printed excerpts after the book appeared. These appearances have been noted: the *Literary American* (April 6, 1850); "Supplement" to the New York *Evening Post* (April 6), nearly two columns in length; *Gazette of the Union; Golden Rule; Odd Fellows' Family Companion* (April 20); and the (English) *Eliza Cook's Journal* (August 3).

When the American reviews began to come in, the *Literary World*, edited by Melville's good friends Evert A. and George Duyckinck, led off with a two-part piece (March 16 and 23) that filled nearly ten columns, six of which are extracts from the book. The first part stresses the uniting of fancy and fact in the work, "rare in any walk, almost unknown on the sea."

> It is this union of culture and experience, of thought and observation, the sharp breeze of the forecastle alternating with the mellow stillness of the library, books and work imparting to each other mutual life, which distinguishes the narratives of the author of Typee from all other productions of their class.

The second part of the review concentrates on the treatment of wrongs and abuses in the navy. In his indignation over these wrongs, "White Jacket is not a blubbering sentimentalist, but he is a man of common sense and common feeling. Therefore, we hold him entitled to his 'blow out' on this matter."

Praise of *White-Jacket* continued in the weekly and monthly journals. On March 30, the *Albion*, edited by the English-born William Young, commended these revelations of inner life on board a frigate as having "more truth than poetry to recommend them." There is "no fiction, no allegory" in the book's startling avowals. The reviewer does not agree with Melville's observations about flogging (the abuses of the practice should be denounced rather than flogging per se), but he commends Melville for admitting candidly that "in English ships of war there is less of tyranny than in his own." In sum, the serious portions of the book must draw the attention of serious men. "In its lighter pages, it bears those inherent marks of fancy, freshness, and power, which the public has determined to find in every work that bears the name of Herman Melville."

The review, the same day, in *Saroni's Musical Times* is of special interest because the reviewer (possibly Saroni himself) had done, as he says, "long and grievous penance in a man-of-war" and could speak from experience of the book's truthfulness. Earlier works about this "bustling little world" had been melodramatic. No one before Melville "lifted the veil which covers the . . . real 'life below stairs.'" Melville has not deemed it worth while "to bind his recollections of the sea with any thread of fiction." He remorselessly "tears the veil of romance which has been cast over the 'world in a man-of-war.'" Yet, "dark as the picture appears in some parts, the author must acknowledge that he has left much the darkest colors untouched upon the pallet." The reviewer cannot agree with Melville that flogging must be abolished at once. He would "dread the experiment."

But he does offer the hope that steam may solve this problem. When vessels are steam-propelled, they will be "manned by hands so comparatively few and select, that less severity may be required in their government." There should be a copy of *White-Jacket* in every village library wherever the English language is spoken, "nay, let a polyglot edition be spread all over the world" so that adventurous youth "may awake from their day-dreams of 'spicy islands' and 'moonlit waters.'"

One of the reviews that appeared in early April was the brief but very favorable notice in W. T. Porter's *Spirit of the Times* (April 6), a journal edited for "the sporting fraternity." The reviewer considers Melville remarkable among modern writers because he can give a large number of readers something that contains "solid nutritive substance" cooked with zest. In this particular work, "the ingenious narrative and abundant incident will attract the crowd of general readers, curiosity will excite the navy corps, and the facts so important and so clearly stated will appeal to our legislators." N. P. Willis' *Home Journal* (a weekly) gave the novel a very long review on April 13. The reviewer, probably Willis himself, touched on several matters: Melville's originality, "vividity," and truthfulness; his ability to depict character; his fresh and abundant humor; his courage in attacking naval abuses. The review (including excerpts) fills five and one-third columns. At this point, taking off from Melville's chapters on naval tyranny, the reviewer continues to fill two more columns with his own disparaging views on our whole military system, the army as well as the navy. The reviewer in the April issue of the *Southern Literary Messenger* could not resist a pun: "*Melville knows the ropes.*" But so did Captain Marryat. What distinguishes Melville from Marryat and all other writers of Melville's class is the way his practical experience of the forecastle unites "with a love of elegant learning and with an educated taste." *Redburn* and *White-Jacket* differ from Melville's preceding works in having a definite purpose in view. *Redburn* aimed at a reform in the discipline of the merchant service. *White-Jacket* directs attention to the subject of flogging in the navy.

The reviewer in the May issue of *Holden's Dollar Magazine*, possibly Charles F. Briggs, was familiar with Melville's actual sea voyages. He was also aware of the fact that "the characters and the ship are drawn under a thin veil of fiction." Because Melville gives his readers the previous history of the *Neversink*, identifying the actual ship will be possible. The reviewer was so delighted with *White-Jacket* that he can say unequivocally that its descriptions are "the finest, most accurate and entertaining of any narrative of sea life that has ever been published; neither Cooper's nor Maryat's [*sic*] will compare with them for fidelity and spirit." The reviewer in the May *Knickerbocker* was glad to "find the author of 'Typee' on the right ground at last." He has abandoned his pseudo-philosophical *rifacciamento* of Carlyle and Emerson. (The reference is, of course, to *Mardi*.) *White-Jacket* should reinstate him in the best good graces of the reading public.[35]

Reviews were still appearing in July. The *Methodist Quarterly Review* was naturally most attentive to what Melville reported about brutalities in the American navy. If what he says about them is true, and the reviewer believes he is being truthful, then they are enough "to sink the whole concern, ships, officers, and all, to perdition." The *Biblical Repository and Classical Review* was also much interested in the book as an exposé of the wickedness of many of our Articles of War in their practical workings, but it ventured a little farther than the *Methodist Quarterly* into criticism. *White-Jacket* is "brim-full of the author's characteristic faults" (such as a swaggering air, extravagant speech, profane expressions), yet "as a sketch of the real world on board a naval ship, from the 'king-commodore to the cabin-boy,' it has wonderful power." The July issue of William Gilmore Simms's *Southern Quarterly Review* carried a six-page review, carefully constructed to make its point. The reviewer is chiefly taken with Melville's theme, passed over by many reviewers, of the petty shipboard regulations which make life a constant misery to the seamen. The reviewer follows this theme through the book, using extracts to secure his point. Melville, he believes, "seeks none of the successes of the artist or romancer. His role is that of the reformer."

Several journals gave *White-Jacket* brief reviews, often little more than notices, but a few of these contain indicative remarks. The reviewer for *Sartain's Magazine* (June, 1850) regrets that he has not been able to read "this inviting volume"! The *Literary American* (April 6) states that "Mr. Melville seems to have been born for the sea, or rather born for writing about it." The New York *Christian Intelligencer* for April 11 praised the book's easy style and noted that it was "well calculated by its incidents and narration to keep up the attention of the reader to the end." The *National Era* (April 25) says that because of Melville's insight into naval abuses, "the book should be placed in the hands of every member of Congress." The *American Whig Review* (April) is inclined to think *White-Jacket* "will be one of the most popular books of this world-renowned *sea author*." To the reviewer in the May issue of the *Christian Examiner* it "is by far the most

---

35. *Littell's Living Age*, a scissors and paste magazine, reprinted on May 4 the favorable review that had appeared in the New York *Tribune* on April 5.

instructive and valuable of his writings." The *Commercial Review* for June was content to copy five recommendatory lines from the London *Morning Post*. The writer of the six-line notice in *Godey's Lady's Book* for June says succinctly: "We like it much." The August 1, 1850, issue of *The Friend* (a temperance journal published in Honolulu) merely copied out the notice in the *National Era*, but it added the useful information that Melville had shipped "as a sailor on board the United States frigate 'United States,' at Honolulu, in 1843, and proceeded to the United States."

Of all these American reviews and notices in magazines only one was predominantly hostile in tone, the short notice in the April issue of the *United States Magazine and Democratic Review*. The reviewer sees the book as "evidently manufactured for the English market." The puffs for English officers, with the left-handed compliments to the American service, "doubtless had their value with Bentley." The narrator was "threatened with a rope's-end in the service, and is now apparently approaching the end of his rope." In one sentence of grudging praise the reviewer admits that the book is highly interesting and "we can afford to wink at the author's weakness."[36]

White-Jacket was widely noticed in the daily press, beginning with the review in the Troy *Daily Budget* on March 21. One by one the city newspapers entered their verdicts: Philadelphia, Buffalo, Springfield, Worcester, Baltimore. Five papers were heard from in New York and three in Boston. Three of the newspaper notices merit attention.

The review in the New York *Tribune* for April 5, 1850 (possibly by George Ripley, a founder of the Brook Farm community), though not long, is remarkably well-balanced and just. Melville has found "ample materials for an entertaining book, and has worked them up into a narrative of great power and interest." Yet his moral and metaphysical reflections are set forth in bad Carlylese and are encumbrances to the narrative. His remarks on naval discipline are entitled to great consideration. "A man of Melville's brain and pen is a dangerous character in the presence of a gigantic humbug, and those who are interested in the preservation of rotten abuses, had better stop that 'chiel from taking notes.'"

The reviewer in the New Bedford *Mercury* (April 4, 1850) rejoices that

---

36. The sneering tone of the review may be accounted for by the fact that the editor, Thomas Prentice Kettell, disliked "Young America," a group of writers with whom Melville was associated. According to Perry Miller, in *The Raven and the Whale*, the reviewing of Melville's books was much affected by "wars" among contemporary literary cliques.

Melville "has once more put foot on the ratlins and donned the tarpaulin," though he is still too much bent "upon airing his literature." The chief item of interest in the review is the revelatory statement that the book is a narrative of the author's "service on board the frigate United States, returning as the flag ship of the Pacific squadron, from Callao to Norfolk." Further, the reviewer tells his readers where to find the names of the actual persons disguised in the fictional account. Let them look in the navy's official "Blue book" for the years when the *United States* was on the Pacific station. Melville's secret was out.

The long "Literary Notice" of *White-Jacket* in the Boston *Post* for April 10, 1850, is important because it takes issue with Melville's attacks on naval abuses, a feature of the book which had been almost invariably praised. The reviewer observes that all the notices of the work he has seen "regard it in a literary light only." It does indeed contain many passages of excellent writing, but on the whole *White-Jacket* assumes to be a didactic rather than an "ornamental" book and must be judged accordingly. Melville abuses the navy so very heartily as to make one doubt "the soundness and knowledge of such a wholesale reformer, such a venomous upholder of abstract right, against that singular mixture of right and wrong, which always has prevailed, and ever must prevail, to some extent, in the administration of terrestrial affairs, whether of religion or government, of ships or armies." Because a man can produce a spirited and beautiful romance like *Typee* or an autobiography like *Redburn*, "running over with a Defoe naturalness and verisimilitude, it does not follow that he is competent to discuss the fitness or unfitness of the 'Articles of War,' the propriety or impropriety of 'Flogging in the Navy,' or the whole system of government and ceremonials of our 'National Marine.'" Discussion of these great practical subjects "requires practical men—men of character, wisdom and experience—not men of theories, fancies and enthusiasm." Let the cobbler stick to his last. Stern as this long review is, it is not a mere personal attack. Mr. Melville has a right to his opinions. The trouble is that his opinions are wrong.

The foregoing summaries of the reviews of *White-Jacket* show that it received nearly universal critical approval. The British liked the book because of its praise of British seamen (from Jack Chase to Admiral Collingwood) and its novel and vivid descriptions of shipboard life. Americans were more interested, naturally, in Melville's attack on naval abuses. They also approved the humanitarian tone of the work and its strong defense of democracy. It was a book in tune with the times. Many reviewers on both sides of the Atlantic thought Melville had proved himself to be the best sea-story writer of his day.

During the next half-dozen years English critics continued to refer to *White-Jacket* with approval. The May, 1854, issue of the *National Miscellany* devoted a nine-page article entirely to *White-Jacket*.[37] The writer seems to have decided that the superiority of the book needed to be confirmed for all time. Life before the mast in the English navy has been described only partially. It is otherwise in America. The reviewer's study of "this remarkable book" satisfies him that "so far as graphic and appropriate language is concerned, there is no living author who can treat such subjects in a style at all approachable to Melville." The aim of the article was to offer a digest of the information about the American naval service which can be gathered from *White-Jacket*. This "digest" is imperfect because the writer did not know (and hardly could have known) that many of the incidents Melville relates were invented or borrowed from his sources.

The last English article to consider the novel in the context of Melville's writing as a whole appeared in the *Dublin University Magazine* in January, 1856 ("A trio of American Sailor-Authors"). The author calls *White-Jacket* Melville's "very best work" and "the best of life-before-the-mast in a ship of war ever yet given to the world."[38]

In this country the novel dropped more quickly from critical attention. Fitz-James O'Brien, in an article on "Our Young Authors" in *Putnam's*, February, 1853, declared that Melville's "later books are a decided falling off." Contrasting *White-Jacket* with the earlier sea novels, O'Brien singles it out as having fewer of Melville's faults than almost any of his works and for its "clear, wholesome satire," and "manly style." Four years later O'Brien again admonished Melville to mend his ways, in "Our Authors and Authorship" (*Putnam's*, April, 1857). That he fails to mention *White-Jacket* in this later article may signify that the novel was already headed for its long oblivion.

We have other evidence of the falling off of interest in *White-Jacket* during Melville's lifetime in the accounts which Harper & Brothers rendered him. The first accounting to give figures of copies bound, sheets on

37. This journal existed from 1853 to 1855, when it merged with *Illustrated London Magazine*.

38. This critic notes that he could point out many instances where Melville "has borrowed remarkable verbal expressions, and even incidents, from nautical books almost unknown to the general reading public (and this he does without a syllable of acknowledgement)."

hand, and sales is dated April 29, 1851; the last was made on March 4, 1887—twenty-two accounts for *White-Jacket*.

Evidently Harpers expected great things of the novel, and during the first year their hopes were justified. In the first account sales are noted as follows: paper, 1,872; cloth, 1,842; copies given away, 125. Of the first two printings of 4,534 copies, Harpers had on hand, on April 29, 1851, a total of 695 copies in various states (sheets, copies bound in paper and cloth). Though sales had gone well thus far, a note in the *Home Journal*'s column of "Literary Items," April 6, 1850, exaggerated the situation: "The first edition of Melville's new work, the 'White Jacket,' was sold as soon as published." And so did the Harper advertisement in the *Literary World* of April 13, 1850, announcing the fifth thousand of *White-Jacket*. Technically the Harper advertisement was not far from the truth: the two impressions of the 1850 edition, 4,534 copies, came close to the "fifth thousand," but not all copies had been sold.

After the good first year, *White-Jacket* sold very slowly. When the six buildings on Cliff Street which constituted the Harper establishment were destroyed by fire on December 10, 1853, the *White-Jacket* stock (272 copies), along with other Melville books, went up in flames. Fortunately the Harpers' stereotype plates were preserved in vaults under the sidewalk. In 1855 Harpers decided to reprint *White-Jacket*, but this, the third printing, consisted of only 257 copies. There was a fourth printing, of 254 copies, in 1860. The fifth and last printing (undated), consisting of 295 copies, occurred between July 24, 1866, and February 13, 1868, bringing the total number printed by Harpers to 5,340.

The sales figures make sad reading. In only two accountings after 1851 do sales go above 100. The low point was the August 1, 1876, figure: four copies sold since the previous year's accounting. When Harpers closed out their account with Melville on March 4, 1887, they had no copies of *White-Jacket* on hand. The book made a profit for Harpers and for its author; not much, but something. Over the 37 years Melville's one-half profit amounted to $969.44.

During Melville's lifetime the 1850 stereotype plates of *White-Jacket* furnished such reprintings of the novel as were called for, until the book went out of print in 1887. The situation changed in 1892, one year after Melville's death. In that year, Arthur Stedman supervised the publication of four Melville books, of which *White-Jacket* was one. As the NOTE ON THE TEXT shows (p. 449), the plates of this United States Book Company edition were traded about among various publishers for many years.

Impressions bearing the imprint of eight other publishers have been recorded. (The "Ninth Impression" of the L. C. Page edition is dated 1950.) Aside from these impressions made from the 1892 plates, *White-Jacket* has been set in type at least six times. Thus it has happened, ironically enough in view of the earlier neglect of the novel, that it has been almost continuously in print in this country since 1892 and for much of the time in England.

A word must be said about two editions of *White-Jacket*, that edited by A. R. Humphreys (Oxford University Press, London, 1966) and that by Hennig Cohen (Holt, Rinehart & Winston, 1967). The Humphreys *White-Jacket* is the first edition in English to be annotated, and as such it has special value. (The translation into German by Walter Weber, Zürich, 1948, was annotated.) Though Mr. Humphreys' Introduction shows that he is aware of the fact that most of Melville's sources have been uncovered, he makes no mention of the source studies in the notes nor does he list them in his Short Guide to Further Reading. Mr. Cohen's *White-Jacket* is not annotated. He takes account of Melville's sources in his Introduction and enters the source studies in his Selected Bibliography. (The texts of these two editions are reviewed below in the NOTE ON THE TEXT.)

In comparison with *Typee, Moby-Dick*, "Benito Cereno," and *Billy Budd*, few translations of *White-Jacket* have been made. The three French editions are *White Jacket (Blouson-Blanc) ou la vie à bord d'un navire de guerre*, translated by Charles Cestre and Armel Guerne (Paris, 1951); *Veste blanche*, an adaptation for children by Eliezer Fournier, with illustrations and color plates (Paris, 1957); and *La Vareuse blanche*, translated by Jacqueline Villaret (Paris, 1967). There are two German translations: *Weissjacke*, translated by Walter Weber (Zürich, 1948); and *Weissjacke, oder die Welt auf einem Kriegsschiff*, translated by Barbara Cramer (Leipzig, 1954). Only one Italian translation has appeared: *Giacchetta bianca: o del mondo d'una nave da guerra*, translated by Luigi Berti (Florence, 1943).

Since the beginning of the Melville revival about 1920, *White-Jacket* has fared well with biographers and critics in America and England. Before the appearance of Charles Roberts Anderson's *Melville in the South Seas* (1939), which carefully separated fact from fiction in *Typee, Omoo*, and *White-Jacket*, most of the biographers were content to read autobiography out of the novel. However, John Freeman, in the first English biography (*Herman Melville*, 1926), thought *White-Jacket* had been underrated as a work of art, and Lewis Mumford (*Herman Melville*, 1929) declared that "apart from Moby-Dick, White-Jacket is, I think, Melville's fullest achievement."

Beginning with William Ellery Sedgwick's *Herman Melville: The Tragedy of Mind* (1944), scholars paid increasing attention to the particular aspects of the novel which accord with their total view of Melville's craft and thought. This is true of such studies as Geoffrey Stone's *Melville* (1949); Richard Chase's *Herman Melville* (1949); Newton Arvin's *Herman Melville* (1950); Ronald Mason's *The Spirit Above the Dust* (1951); and Warner Berthoff's *The Example of Melville* (1962). Special book-length studies which pursue Melville's themes or leading ideas through his works naturally make use of *White-Jacket* to support their arguments. Such studies are William Braswell's *Melville's Religious Thought* (1943); Lawrance Thompson's *Melville's Quarrel with God* (1952); and Edward H. Rosenberry's *Melville and the Comic Spirit* (1955).

Following the lead of Charles Roberts Anderson, the writers of articles have continued to hunt down the sources of *White-Jacket*. As a result of their investigations, we can now see Melville at work on *White-Jacket*, turning from McNally to Fore-Top-Man to Nicol in his search for scenes and factual details to add color and verisimilitude to his novel. These articles have been cited above in the discussion of Melville's sources. There are only a few separate essays on Melville's intention and craft in writing *White-Jacket*. The best of these is Howard P. Vincent's "*White-Jacket*: An Essay in Interpretation" (*New England Quarterly*, September, 1949). Professor Vincent's *The Tailoring of Melville's* WHITE-JACKET (1970) is the first book-length critical study of the imaginative work Melville patched together from his own experiences and from other books.

SOURCES

IN PREPARING THIS HISTORICAL NOTE I have made frequent use of the following sources of information about Melville's life and career as a writer, and all quotations, references, and dates not otherwise footnoted can be found in them: *The Letters of Herman Melville*, ed. Merrell R. Davis and William H. Gilman (New Haven: Yale University Press, 1960); *Journal of a Visit to London and the Continent by Herman Melville 1849–1850*, ed. Eleanor Melville Metcalf (Cambridge: Harvard University Press, 1948); *Journal of a Cruise to the Pacific Ocean, 1842–1844, in the Frigate* UNITED STATES, ed. Charles Roberts Anderson (Durham: Duke University Press, 1937); Charles Roberts Anderson, *Melville in the South Seas* (New York: Columbia University Press, 1939); Jay Leyda, *The Melville Log* (New York: Harcourt, Brace, 1951); Hugh W. Hetherington, *Melville's Reviewers:*

British and American, 1846–1891 (Chapel Hill: University of North Carolina Press, 1961); and Leon Howard, *Herman Melville: A Biography* (Berkeley and Los Angeles: University of California Press, 1951). The same documents may show slight differences in detail as transcribed in these various sources. Other printed sources, as well as unpublished documents, are cited in the text and footnotes. Contemporary reviews have been consulted in their original sources, from which my quotations and conclusions are drawn. The editors of the Northwestern–Newberry Edition furnished me with pertinent information about the Harper & Brothers edition of *White-Jacket* taken from the accounts which the firm sent·Melville between 1851 and 1887. While this Historical Note was being prepared, Howard P. Vincent kindly supplied me with a manuscript copy of *The Tailoring of Melville's White-Jacket* (Evanston: Northwestern University Press, 1970).   He, in turn, saw the first draft of this Note.

Note on the Text

THIS EDITION of *White-Jacket* presents an unmodernized critical text, reconstructed according to the theory of copy-text formulated by Sir Walter Greg.[1] Central to that theory is the distinction between substantive variants (those which affect meaning, such as verbal changes) and accidental variants (those which affect form, such as changes in punctuation and spelling).[2] When an author makes substantive revisions in printed forms of his work, he is not always equally concerned with accidentals. The fact that he does not alter certain accidentals which were not his own but were changes made by the copyist, publisher, or compositor does not amount to an endorsement of those accidentals. Since the aim of a critical edition is to establish a text which represents as nearly as possible the author's intentions, it follows that the formal texture of his work will

1. "The Rationale of Copy-Text," *Studies in Bibliography*, III (1950–51), 19–36. For an application of this method to the period of Melville, see Fredson Bowers, "Some Principles for Scholarly Editions of Nineteenth-Century American Authors," *Studies in Bibliography*, XVII (1964), 223–28; and his "A Preface to the Text," in the Centenary Edition of Hawthorne's *The Scarlet Letter* (Columbus: Ohio State University Press, 1962), pp. xxix–xlvii (reprinted in the later volumes of the Centenary Edition).

2. The line between the two is not rigid, for some changes of punctuation and spelling do affect meaning and accordingly could be classed as substantives.

be most accurately reproduced by adopting as copy-text[3] either the fair-copy manuscript or the first printing based on it. The printed form is chosen if the manuscript does not exist or if the author worked in such a way that corrected proof became in effect the final form of the manuscript. This basic text may then be emended with any later authorial alterations (whether substantive or accidental) and with other obvious corrections. Following this procedure maximizes the probability of keeping authorial readings when evidence is inconclusive as to the source of an alteration in a later authorized edition. The resulting text is *critical* in that it does not correspond exactly to any single authorized edition, but it is closer to the author's intentions—insofar as they are recoverable—than any such edition.

As the preceding HISTORICAL NOTE has shown, the first English edition of *White-Jacket*, though it was published earlier than the first American, was (except for a few added passages) set from the American proof sheets. The American edition was the one set directly from the manuscript Melville supplied, and, lacking that manuscript, the first impression of the American edition becomes the copy-text for the present edition.[4] Any impressions or editions published during Melville's lifetime are a potential source for emendations in this copy-text, since theoretically it would have been possible for Melville to make corrections or changes in them.[5] The two authorized editions—those of Harper & Brothers in the United States and Richard Bentley in England—have been fully collated in the following pattern:

1. American against English Edition
    a. One complete sight collation[6] of the first American impression (1850) against the first issue of the English impression (1850)

3. "Copy-text" is the text accepted as the basis for an edition.

4. The particular copy of the first American impression which served (in the form of a marked Xerox reproduction) as printer's copy is M67–722–122 (see footnote 7). For the passages which first appeared in the English edition, the copy of the first issue of the English edition used as printer's copy is M66–3577 (I) and M66–2471–48 (II).

5. The 1855 condensation published in Henry Howe's *Life and Death on the Ocean* can be ruled out, however, since most of the variants in it are a direct result of the process of condensation, and the others are evidently compositorial errors.

6. Collations between two *editions*, which (because they are printed from different settings of type) cannot be performed on the Hinman Collator, are "sight collations." Those between *impressions* of the same edition are "machine collations"—so called because that machine, by superimposing page images, enables the human collator's eye to see differences, including minute changes not otherwise easily detected, such as resettings and type damage. A "complete sight collation" is one in which both substantive and accidental variants are recorded; a "substantive collation" is one in which only substantive variants

b. One substantive sight collation of the first American impression (1850) against the first issue of the English impression (1850)

c. Two complete sight collations of the first American impression (1850) against the second issue of the English impression (1853)

2. Impressions of the American Edition
Two machine collations of the first impression of this edition (1850) against the last (n.d. [c. 1867])

3. Issues of the English Edition
Two machine collations of the first issue of this edition (1850) against the last (1853)[7]

The text was thus collated for record eight times.[8] In addition, routine procedures in the process of compiling, checking, and preparing the information for publication have resulted in a larger total number of collations.[9]

---

are recorded. The terms *edition, impression (printing), issue,* and *state,* as used here, follow the definitions of Fredson Bowers in *Principles of Bibliographical Description* (Princeton: Princeton University Press, 1949), pp. 379–426.

7. The English edition of *White-Jacket* is in two volumes, the American edition in one. Since each volume of any multivolume work is a separate entity, no bibliographical significance attaches to any particular combination of volumes. In these collations, therefore, no attempt was made to treat presently constituted sets as units, although no set was in fact separated for collation. The copies used for these collations are here recorded by identification number (for books in the Melville Collection, now at The Newberry Library) or by library name and call number (for books not in the Melville Collection): (1a) M66–2471–50 *vs.* M66–2471–48; (1b) M67–722–122 *vs.* M66–2471–48; (1c) M67–103–14 *vs.* M66–2471–47; M66–2471–50 *vs.* Newberry Case Y255M5191; (2) M66–2471–46 *vs.* M66–2471–51; M67–722–85 *vs.* M67–722–145; (3) M66–3288 *vs.* Newberry Case Y255M5191; M66–2471–48 *vs.* M66–2471–47.

8. The number of collations which must be performed in order to detect all significant variations in a given text can never be prescribed with certainty, since chance determines, at least to some extent, the particular copies available for collation. Whether or not variant states of a first impression are detected, for example, depends largely upon whether or not at least one copy of an earlier state is present in the collection of copies assembled for collation; regardless of the size of this collection, there is always the chance that an unknown earlier state is missing. To reduce the element of chance somewhat, the present editors have checked many points in every copy of *White-Jacket* in the Melville Collection at The Newberry Library and have examined numerous copies in other collections. For making copies of *White-Jacket* available, the editors are indebted to William M. Gibson, M. Douglas Sackman, and Howard P. Vincent.

9. Proofreading provided the chief opportunity for making these additional collations. Copies of the first American and the first English editions were simultaneously compared with two sets of the Northwestern–Newberry page proofs, besides this group proofreading, six individual proofreadings were made of the page proofs against copies of the first American edition.

Analysis of the variants (in both substantives and accidentals) disclosed by these collations has resulted in the adoption of 56 emendations in the copy-text; and 39 other emendations, not taken from English variants, have been made by the present editors. In order to make clear the evidence and rationale on which these decisions rest, an account of the textual history of the work is given below, followed by a discussion of the treatment in this text of substantives and accidentals, and an explanation of the editorial apparatus through which the evidence is presented.

THE TEXTS

NO MANUSCRIPT of *White-Jacket* survives (except for a revised fair copy of the Preface—see pp. 489–99), and the closest text to the missing manuscript is not the one published first. Although the English edition was published on January 23, 1850, about two months earlier than the American, it was set (except for a few passages) from proofs of the American edition which Melville took to England with him in October of 1849. What is technically the second edition of the book (New York: Harper & Brothers, 1850), therefore, is the one set directly from Melville's manuscript (whether holograph or scribal is not known). Copies of this American edition dated 1850 on the title page exist in at least two impressions, which can be distinguished in several ways: (1) in one, the quotation from Fuller is on the recto of the leaf following the title leaf, with the Note on the verso, while in the other these positions are reversed (gathering A); (2) in one, gathering U has twelve leaves (including seven leaves of advertisements), while in the other it has eight (including three of advertisements); (3) in one, the first leaf of gathering Q is incorrectly signed "Q*" and the first leaf of T is not signed at all, while in the other these errors are corrected; (4) in one, there are an asterisk and a period in the footnote at 224.22–23[10] (sheet L), a hyphen in "cigar-holder" at 187.35 (sheet K), a period after "her" at 291.7 (sheet P), and a hyphen after "man" in "man-of-war" at 308.5 (sheet P), while in the other these marks of punctuation are absent; (5) in one, no plate damage occurs, for example along the right margins at A239.13–23, A267.23–35, and A452.23–24, and the page numbers 268 and 269 are undamaged, while in the other there is damage at these points. In each case, the readings mentioned second are

10. Reference numbers with prefixed letters refer to page and line of the American edition (A) or the English edition (E); when these letters do not appear, reference is to the Northwestern–Newberry Edition.

the later ones because they persist throughout later printings.[11] The fact that most of the readings listed first usually occur together in the same copies (and most of those listed second usually occur together in other copies), combined with the fact that two of these differences (the changes in gatherings A and U) required reimposition, suggests that there were two impressions of *White-Jacket* in 1850.

Copies exist, however, in which the sheets of the two impressions are mixed; thus in a given copy the presence of the earlier impression of one sheet does not necessarily imply that the copy is of the earlier impression throughout. The copy-text for a critical edition therefore should theoretically be defined as the 1850 Harper printing in which the quotation from Fuller precedes the prefatory Note, gathering U has twelve leaves, Q1 is missigned and T1 unsigned, and the plates are undamaged at a number of points (as listed above). But since there are no textual differences between the two impressions except the changed order of two pages in sheet A and the missing punctuation in sheets K, L, and P, for practical purposes a copy with mixed sheets, but containing the first impression of sheets A, K, L, and P, can serve—as in the present edition—to provide the copy-text.[12]

The Harper edition was printed four more times from these plates between 1850 and 1868 with no deliberate changes; since all of the slight variations resulted from plate damage, none has any textual authority.[13]

11. The advertisements were eliminated entirely from the later printings of *White-Jacket*, but the state of the advertisements (such as the reset text of the advertisement for *Redburn*) in the gathering with eight leaves corresponds to the state of the advertisements in *Moby-Dick* (1851).

12. Historical facts about the dates, sizes, and background of the various printings and editions are given in the HISTORICAL NOTE; precise physical descriptions will appear in the full-scale bibliography to be published in conjunction with the Northwestern–Newberry Edition. The present discussion is not concerned with bibliographical details discovered in the process of collation, unless they bear on textual questions. Type or plate damage, for example, which may distinguish the states within an impression or the impressions within a given year, is not reported here if it does not create a textual variant (as defined in the following footnote) and if the states or impressions involved are not otherwise of textual significance.

13. In the second 1850 printing, although there were at least 26 instances of damage to the plates in addition to those already mentioned, only one could conceivably create a textual ambiguity—the loss of the hyphen in "cigar-holder" at 187.35. The 1855 printing contained two further examples (a missing comma after "things" at 142.10 and a missing hyphen in "fellow-beings" at 174.23), and in 1860 another comma and hyphen were missing (after "printed", 224.22; in "night-cap", 263.27) A final printing, according to the Harper records, occurred between late July, 1866, and mid-February, 1868; examination of the increased plate damage in copies with no date on the title page shows that such

The English edition, unlike the American, was printed only once but was issued at two different times, three years apart. The first issue (2 vols.; London: Richard Bentley, 1850) exists in various states, distinguishable by the relative positions or inking of certain pieces of type in at least nine places. Since the book was printed from type rather than from plates, the shifting (or failure to print) of individual pieces of type does not furnish evidence of an irreversible progression. For example, the absence of the "9" in the page number "319" in the first volume and the absence of a comma after "men" at 94.28 are probably instances of later states (especially since states also exist in which the "9" and the comma print but are out of place), as are the absence of the "t" in "the" at xiv.14 and the absence of "P" in "President" at 294.38, though it is possible that the states in which these types print properly are later. The other variations, usually matters of spacing or inking (such as the inking along the left margin of E11 in the first volume or the inked quadrat preceding "garden" at E1.284.21), do not occur at points where they create substantive differences. In 1853 Bentley issued the remaining sheets of his edition in one-volume form with new title pages (dated 1853); some of the variations present in copies with 1850 title pages (such as the variations in the position of "73" in the page number "173" in the first volume, or the differences in inking of the "s" in "insult" at E1.50.28) also occur in the same states in copies with the 1853 title pages. In addition, a few other variations turn up, not so far discovered in 1850 copies —such as the presence of the second "3" in the page number "33" in the second volume. None of these differences between copies of the English edition—except possibly this adjusting of page numbers—gives any evidence of editorial intervention during the course of printing.

The text of the English edition differs substantively from the American edition at 181 points (there are scores of other changes in spelling and

---

copies belong to the last printing. Of the many new instances of damage, seven came at places where they might affect one's reading of the text: one comma was illegible (after "was", 47.19), and one semicolon appeared to be a comma (after "ship", 180.39), while one period (preceding the dash in 59.25), one exclamation point (244.39), and three hyphens (after "at", 136.11; after "top", 312.23; and in "French-/men", 316.35) entirely disappeared. In this NOTE, when changes are listed within either the American or the English edition, the many instances of battered type or plates and missing letters are not included when it is clear what letter is intended, nor is missing end-punctuation mentioned when the absent mark is a period; and missing hyphens at the ends of lines are not reported when the divided word is not a possible compound. Missing commas, however, which might pass unnoticed, are listed. In other words, type or plate wear is noted only when it could pass unnoticed or be mistaken for intentional revision.

punctuation). Some of these English variants are obviously the result of careless typesetting and proofreading,[14] but seven are corrections of obvious substantive errors in the American edition.[15] Most of the variant readings, however, are neither obvious errors nor corrections of obvious errors. Of these, many are routine compositorial substitutions and casual Anglicizations; others are Melville's own revisions and additions, the most important of which are the insertions of seven passages: six sentences of some 100 words (at 28.22; 191.13–14; 381.31–32; 381.35–40) and six paragraphs totaling 615 words (at 27.26–32; 114.14–22; 285.20–286.16).[16]

The only other edition of *White-Jacket* which appeared during Melville's lifetime[17] was the greatly condensed version of the American edition

14. Among such errors in the English edition are "ring" for "wring" (4.27), "amounted" for "mounted" (16.26), "we" for "be" (27.9), "May" for "Way" (186.20), "remorsely" for "remorselessly" (329.16), and "giving" for "given" (358.6).

15. At 34.13 "sailor's" is corrected to "sailors"; at 318.29 "other" to "others"; at 323.10 "woop and warf" to "woof and warp"; at 378.1 "lined" to "linen"; at 381.4 "were" to "was"; at 382.37 "friends" to "friend's"; and at 385.10 "softens" to "soften".

16. Among these variants (including both authorial and compositorial changes) are a dozen and a half differences in the choice of nouns and verbs (the American "piece" at 231.32, for example, is changed to "place", and "used up" at 141.14 to "worn out"); three dozen in the forms of nouns and verbs (many are the repeated change from "men-" to "man-" in "men-of-war's-men" and "men-of-war's men"); over two dozen in other parts of speech (nearly half of which are substitutions of one adjective for another, such as "dignified" for "perilous" at 25.39); and two dozen in phrasing, ranging from the reversal of the order of words ("I have" at 119.16 becomes "have I", and "the still" at 331.2 becomes "still the") to the rewriting of entire sentences (such as the entries in the LIST OF SUBSTANTIVE VARIANTS at 21.31–32 and 24.22). The largest category of these variants, however, consists of omissions and insertions. Of the 22 omissions in the English edition, 15 are of single words, 5 of a few words each (totaling 13 words), one of a complete sentence (11 words) at 151.9–10, and one of two paragraphs 94 words) at 138.20–27. Although 133 words are thus deleted, the insertions of additional material amount to 757 words. Of the 24 such insertions in the English edition, 11 are of single words, and 6 are of a few words each (totaling 26 words); the remaining 7 (totaling 720 words) are cited in the text above as obviously being Melville's. Comment on the authority of certain individual readings will be found below in the DISCUSSIONS OF ADOPTED READINGS.

17. Several extracts from *White-Jacket* appeared in Evert A. Duyckinck's *Literary World* on March 9, 16, and 23, 1850 (VI, 218–19, 271–72, 297–99); although Melville was in a position to have made revisions in the copy he furnished Duyckinck, a complete collation of these passages with the text of the American edition indicates that he made none. The only differences between the two texts are changes in accidentals (which appear to be either editorial or compositorial) and obvious compositorial errors. (Copies used for collation: M67–2133–1 *vs.* M67–722–108.) The same holds true of the extract printed in the New York *Home Journal* on March 16, 1850, p. 4.

included in Henry Howe's *Life and Death on the Ocean: A Collection of Extraordinary Adventures in the Form of Personal Narratives* (Cincinnati: Henry Howe, 1855). The kinds of changes it introduces cannot be attributed to Melville, and it is of no textual importance.[18]

The first edition to appear after Melville's death was published in New York in 1892 by the United States Book Company. Although no editor's name appeared on the volume, it was part of a series of new editions of Melville supervised by Arthur Stedman. In his introduction to *Typee*, Stedman pointed out that he had some written instructions about that book from Melville himself; and a document in Mrs. Melville's hand, presumably recording directives such as those Stedman was referring to, is presently among Stedman's papers in the Columbia University Library.[19] Although there is no hint of any such instructions in the case of *White-Jacket*, the fact that Stedman had direct contact with the Melville family makes his edition worth examining in more detail than a posthumous edition would normally require. However, although collations of the Stedman text against the first American impression[20] reveal many changes, both in substantives and in

18. Entitled "How They Live on Board of an American Man of War: Being the Experiences of a Sailor in the United States Navy," the condensation consists of 24 pages (pp. 261–84), made up of excerpts from 21 chapters (Chapters 2, 3, 6, 9, 10, 14–16, 25, 30, 31, 33, 48, 67, 68, 74, 84–88). Some of these chapters (such as Chapters 3, 6, 16, 33, 67, 74, and 88) are printed in nearly complete form, while others (such as Chapters 31 and 86) are represented by only a few lines. Since this version is so severely abridged, obviously any omissions—whether of long passages or of short phrases within the selected passages—may be assumed to stem from the aim of condensation. This edition would have textual significance only if substantive differences in the passages printed were demonstrably Melville's own and were not necessitated by the condensation. However, of the substantive variants (excluding omissions) revealed by one collation, three-fourths directly result from the effort to avoid references to omitted parts of the book or to characters' names. These comments on the Howe edition are based on a collation of M67–1794 (a copy of the first American printing) with Gift M66–79 (a copy of the 1860 printing of Howe's book).

19. For further discussion of this document, see the NOTE ON THE TEXT in the Northwestern–Newberry Edition of *Typee*, p. 312.

20. Only two of the substantive variants of the English edition are present (those at 283.11 and 323.10), and the deviations in accidentals from the American edition do not follow the English punctuation—both facts suggesting that Stedman was using the American, not the English, edition as copy-text. But the collations reveal just over a hundred additional substantive differences, ranging from omissions of single words and phrases (over a dozen instances) or of large passages (5 instances, amounting to some 600 words: 45.32–39; 220.20 ff.9, 375.31–376.11) to changes of verb tenses and numbers of nouns (three dozen instances) and possible attempts to improve the choice of words (such as "money-bag" for "monkey-bag" at 39.5, or "squash" for "quash" at 93.14). Many of

accidentals, there is nothing about any of these alterations to suggest that Stedman was following instructions from Melville.

The chief significance of Stedman's United States Book Company edition is that its plates have been used by a long succession of publishers, and perhaps more people have read *White-Jacket* in this edition than in any other. Impressions bearing the imprints of Tait, Sons & Co., Dana Estes & Co., Putnam, A. L. Burt, D. D. Nickerson, L. C. Page, the St. Botolph Society, and Jonathan Cape all utilize these plates. Since this edition of 1892, *White-Jacket* has been set in type at least six times,[21] and some of these editions have been reprinted or issued by more than one publisher—for example, the John Lehmann (Chiltern Library) edition (1952) was issued in the United States by the Grove Press. This edition follows the Harper text, as do the World's Classics (1924) and Pickwick (1928) editions. The Constable edition of *White-Jacket* (1922)—in the collected *Works*—is significant because it is part of the only complete set of Melville's work that has been available to scholars in the past and is therefore often cited as standard. Its text generally follows the Harper edition but incorporates many new changes (mainly in spelling and punctuation).[22]

---

the differences (at least a third) are simply typographical errors (like "robe" for "rope" at 246.9, or "sale" for "sake" at 333.6); and even one of the three long omissions (45.32–39) may have been unintentional (the other two remove material which might be regarded as objectionable). Among the numerous changes in accidentals, the principal categories are the elimination of commas and hyphens and the shift to British spellings (or affectations of British spellings). Copies used for collation: Gift M67-16 (W. M. Gibson copy) *vs.* M67-767-8; Northwestern 813.3M531w1850 *vs.* M67-767-9.

21. The number cannot be stated with assurance, since further editions—which have not been discovered in an extensive search of catalogues, libraries, and bookstores—occasionally still turn up. Details of all these editions will be included in the forthcoming descriptive bibliography. The Melville Collection being formed at The Newberry Library in connection with the preparation of the Northwestern–Newberry Edition contains many of these later editions (and ideally will contain all of them in time). Charles Roberts Anderson, in *Melville in the South Seas* (New York: Columbia University Press, 1939), states that 21 "editions" of *White-Jacket* had been published by 1938 (p. 439); but he is not using "edition" in the sense employed here, as a technical bibliographical term which encompasses all the impressions from a given setting of type.

22. This generalization is based on a partial collation of a copy of the 1850 American edition (M67-2133-1) with a copy of the Constable *White-Jacket* in the Russell & Russell reissue (New York, 1963; M67-722-123). For some background relating to the Constable texts, see Philip Durham, "Prelude to the Constable Edition of Melville," *Huntington Library Quarterly*, XXI (1957–58), 285–89. A compositorial error in the Constable edition, perpetuated in the 1952 Lehmann edition and consequently in the 1952 Grove reissue, has

The fact that there were substantial differences between the original American and English editions has not been generally recognized, although a few bibliographical publications—such as Michael Sadleir's bibliography in Volume XII (1923) of the Constable edition, Jacob Schwartz's *1100 Obscure Points* (1931), and Carroll A. Wilson's *Thirteen Author Collections* (1950)—contained casual allusions to the matter. In 1965 the results of initial collations of *White-Jacket* for the present edition, revealing that Melville had added long passages in the English edition, were announced at a meeting of the Melville Society in Chicago; in 1966 and 1967 two new editions of *White-Jacket* appeared which gave some attention to textual matters. The first was edited by A. R. Humphreys for the Oxford University Press's series of Classic American Texts. Humphreys' work (see his Note on the Text, p. xxvii) was based on the erroneous assumption that the English text represents an earlier stage than the American: "This edition is based on the London text of February 1850 as corrected by the New York text of March, which was set up from it but shows a good many alterations. Many of these are clearly authoritative; others have consequently been accepted here even when it is not clear why they were made, provided they are not evident or probable errors in transmission." The result is that the accidentals of his edition generally follow the English text ("the London one has been taken as the primary authority in this respect"), but the substantives often follow the American. He appends a list of Variant Readings (pp. 428–33), recording 121 of the substantive variants between the Harper and Bentley texts (with an additional 13 entries for Constable variants); this list includes the long passages not present in the Harper text, and it shows that Humphreys in 76 instances chose the Harper reading over the Bentley and four times preferred the Constable to either. The other edition was prepared by Hennig Cohen for Holt, Rinehart & Winston's series of Rinehart Editions. In A Note on this Edition (p. vii), Cohen, confirming the 1965 Northwestern–Newberry discoveries, stated that Melville made alterations in the

---

become a classic contemporary example. The phrase "coiled fish" (NN 393.23) appeared as "soiled fish"; unaware of the error, F. O. Matthiessen, in *American Renaissance* (New York: Oxford University Press, 1941), commented that "hardly anyone but Melville could have created the shudder that results from calling this frightening vagueness some '*soiled* fish of the sea.' The *discordia concors*, the unexpected linking of the medium of cleanliness with filth, could only have sprung from an imagination that had apprehended the terrors of the deep, of the immaterial deep as well as the physical" (p. 392). The compositorial error, together with Matthiessen's unlucky comment, was first pointed out by John W. Nichol, "Melville's '"Soiled" Fish of the Sea,'" *American Literature*, XXI (November, 1949), 338–39.

Harper proof sheets while on the ship bound for England and that these revised proof sheets became the printer's copy for the Bentley edition; the Rinehart edition therefore follows the Harper text as its copy-text. It does not, however, incorporate any emendations but instead records about a third of the variant readings from the Bentley edition, inserted into the text in square brackets. Neither of these editions establishes a definitive text, since neither is based on a study of all the relevant evidence, such as a complete list of variants between the Harper and Bentley editions.

TREATMENT OF SUBSTANTIVES

THE TEXTUAL HISTORY of *White-Jacket* varies slightly from the pattern set by Melville's three preceding books. As in the case of *Omoo*, *Mardi*, and *Redburn*, proofs (somewhat corrected) of the American edition became printer's copy for the English edition. But in those three books there are only a few differences in wording between the American and English texts, while in *White-Jacket* there are many. Melville had much more time to make revisions, and his English publisher, Bentley, after his experience with *Mardi* probably saw more reason to impose modifications.

Melville had the time because he did not hurry the American proof sheets of *White-Jacket* off to England as he had those of the earlier three books but instead took them to London himself. Before he sailed on October 11, 1849, he had evidently made routine corrections in the proofs for the American edition of *White-Jacket*, for according to Evert Duyckinck he was "hard at work with proof of the *new* book"[23] (as distinguished from *Redburn*) on September 5. A month later, on October 6, Melville wrote to Lemuel Shaw, "The other book [*White-Jacket*] I have now in plate-proofs, all ready to go into my trunk."[24] Although the journal which Melville kept on the voyage contains no allusions to the proofs of the book, it was probably inevitable that during three and a half weeks on shipboard he would read them over and make some changes. After his arrival in England, another six weeks elapsed before he furnished Bentley with printer's copy. On December 18 he entered in his journal, "Spent an hour or so looking

23. Quoted in Jay Leyda, *The Melville Log* (New York: Harcourt, Brace & Co., 1951), p. 312.

24. *The Letters of Herman Melville*, ed. Merrell R. Davis and William H. Gilman (New Haven: Yale University Press, 1960), p. 91 (letter 65).

over 'White Jacket' preparatory to sending it finally to Bentley."[25] He was free to make any revisions or additions he wanted to, since the whole book was to be reset for the English edition.

Melville returned to New York on February 1, 1850, roughly a month and a half before the American publication of the book and possibly in time to make more revisions—either to incorporate some of the revised English readings into the American edition or to revise and correct the American edition still further.[26] The fact that the American edition has a different prefatory note dated March, 1850, might seem to support this view, as might the fact that the Harper records show a charge, along with the cost of stereotyping, for 50 hours' alterations. But the spacing of words in the American edition (including the points where the English edition differs) does not show that changes were made, either in standing type or in plates; and the nature of the differences between the two editions does not suggest that the American readings in general are later than the English, though a few may be. The date of the 50 hours' alterations in the American edition, however, is not specified in the Harper account and may well have been before Melville left for England. If so, there are two possibilities: either the revisions involved (or some of them) were not inserted into the proofs for England, with the result that the American readings at these points are later (though none of the American variants seems to be later); or else the revisions did get incorporated into the proofs for England, with the result that they cannot now be identified, since they could not appear as variants between the two editions.[27] In other words, the charge for alterations in the American edition does not furnish evidence which would conclusively determine the sequence of revisions; but it does suggest that Melville's

25. *Journal of a Visit to London and the Continent,* ed. Eleanor Melville Metcalf (Cambridge: Harvard University Press, 1948), p. 76.

26. In revising the proofs of *Moby-Dick* which he sent to London as the basis of the Bentley edition, Melville made several striking corrections of misreadings in the Harper edition. The absence of such corrections among the variants between the Harper and Bentley editions of *White-Jacket* may be due to the greater accuracy of the manuscript, the greater fidelity of the compositors of the Harper edition of *White-Jacket*, or the greater thoroughness of Melville's initial proofreading of the American *White-Jacket*, but the absence could conceivably be due to Melville's correcting the proofs he gave to Bentley, then making the same corrections in the Harper edition after he returned to New York.

27. There remains, of course, the theoretical possibility that revisions were incorporated into both editions in slightly different forms (whether inadvertently or not). Such changes would show up as variants, but neither reading would represent the unrevised proof; in such cases the American reading could be either earlier or later.

revision of *White-Jacket* after the book was first set in type may have been more extensive than is now apparent from a study of the variants between the English and American editions.

An editor must choose the American edition as his copy-text, since it was set from the manuscript Melville supplied. After adopting obvious corrections from the English variants, the editor has two problems. The first is to determine which of the remaining English variants are authorial, and whether to adopt those that are authorial as later or to reject them as earlier than the corresponding American readings. The second is to find and correct any readings that are corrupt in both editions—readings, that is, where the English text follows the American in printing words that cannot be the ones Melville intended.

Seven of the English variants are corrections obviously called for by the context (see p. 447, footnote 15). Whether compositors' errors or slips of the author's pen, the American readings can hardly have been intended by Melville, and whether the correction was made by Melville or by someone at Bentley's is immaterial.

After adopting these obvious corrections from the English edition (and rejecting a few equally obvious errors in it), an editor must consider the large category of variants in which both the American and the English readings make sense in the context. Although many of these English variants are the kinds of differences which can be expected whenever a text is reset in type, they require scrutiny since they could theoretically be Melville's revisions; indeed, some seem unquestionably to be the sort of change which only Melville could have made. These variants can be divided into six groups, ranging from those which are almost certainly not Melville's to those which can confidently be attributed to him. The size of each group, of course, bears no relation to its place in this continuum, for the largest number of individual differences fall into the third category and the largest number of added words into the sixth:

(1) A few variant readings in the English edition, though they make sense, are clearly inferior and can most logically be explained as compositors' errors. The English reading "the muzzles" (42.19–20), for example, instead of "their muzzles", destroys the parallelism with "their teeth" (42.21) and "their touch-holes" (42.21–22) and could easily be a compositor's oversight, influenced by "the port-holes" earlier in the same line; similarly, the omission of "their" before "hands" (36.30) makes the sentence awkward and does not correspond with the phrase "their hands" used twice later in the paragraph. Such readings can safely be rejected.

(2) Some two dozen changes apparently intended to correct grammar or usage, while possibly Melville's, seem more likely to be the work of a reader or compositor at Bentley's. They are not accepted since their origin is uncertain and the Harper readings probably derive from Melville's manuscript. For example, the repeated shift from "men-" to "man-" in "men-of-war's-men" and "men-of-war's men" is not adopted, nor is the alteration of "lay" to "lie" at 235.19.

(3) Roughly half the changes are so unimportant that it is difficult to see why Melville or anyone else went to the trouble of making them; any of these could of course be Melville's, but they are more likely to be routine publisher's changes or compositorial substitutions. Examples are the shifts from "with" to "in" (26.18), "this" to "his" (54.8), "proportionately" to "proportionably" (166.12), and "those" to "these" (211.19). Since there is no strong reason to believe that any of these shifts are characteristic of Melville, no emendations are made in this category.

(4) Stylistic improvements, or attempted improvements (amounting only to half a dozen or so), can more reasonably be attributed to Melville than can the merely grammatical changes; but they also could have resulted from a careful reading by someone at Bentley's, particularly since later Bentley seems to have had such changes made in *The Whale*. The elimination of "that" at 47.22 is a clear syntactic improvement; the shift from "or" to "and" after "smoke" at 112.23 avoids a repetition of "or"; and the omission of "their" before "scraping" at 117.13 removes the awkward repetition of "their". Instances of this kind, when they are obvious improvements of the sort an author with ample time—and inclination—for such revision might make, provide possible grounds for emendation; in *White-Jacket*, however, given Bentley's known practice with *The Whale* and Melville's relative indifference to these matters, the grounds are never compelling.

(5) About two dozen brief changes serve to modify the actual sense of a passage. Some of these changes clarify a statement (often rendering it more consistent with the book as a whole) at points not likely to attract the attention of a publisher's reader, and they can safely be adopted as authorial (for example, those at 11.34, 12.11, 24.22, 141.3, and 191.13–14). Other changes, however, weaken or tone down an expression, and they pose an additional problem—not only whether Melville made a given change but whether, even if he did, it should be adopted as representing his intention. On the one hand, Bentley's known use of a publisher's reader to expurgate and otherwise modify *The Whale* suggests that the

English edition of *White-Jacket* may also have received unusually close attention of this kind. On the other hand, anticipating censorship in advance or acting upon the impulses which later led him to increasingly employ guarded expressions, Melville himself could have made such changes (for example, those at 21.31–32, 77.26, 84.19–20, 87.24, 112.21, 123.7, 135.29, 151.9–10, 156.26–27, 185.14, 288.23). As it turns out, these changes, even when there are some grounds for thinking that they may be Melville's, are not adopted, since they, like his expurgations of *Typee*, can hardly have fitted his conception of the book as an artistic whole. They can more accurately be regarded as adaptations made simply for the sake of his English readers than as revisions intended to supplant the more forceful original American readings. (See the LIST OF SUBSTANTIVE VARIANTS at 4.25, 25.39, 135.29, 143.3, and 194.30.)

(6) The additions of complete sentences and paragraphs which extend and clarify a discussion are unquestionably Melville's own. No one else could have added, in the same vein, the seven passages (enumerated above, p. 447), ranging from 9 to 433 words and totaling over 700 words, which appear only in the English edition. Two of these (381.31–32; 381.35–40) seem calculated to mollify the British, but, like the others, they form a natural elaboration of the subject under discussion. All of these additions are therefore adopted, and the copy-text for such passages is necessarily the Bentley edition.

Besides the emendations taken from the English edition, there is a further—and in *White-Jacket* a minor—class of emendations, involving readings in which the American and English texts concur but which are evidently compositorial misreadings of Melville's manuscript (if not errors in the manuscript itself). In these instances, the emendations restore what Melville must originally have written, or at least intended to write.[28]

No substantive emendations have been made under any other circumstances. If, for example, an English reading fits the sense of a passage as well as the copy-text reading (or is in some respects even better) but cannot be

---

28. Such changes are of course made only when the copy-text reading is unsatisfactory. The emendation must be a word that Melville would have used in the context (judging from his literary practice); it must be a word that improves the sense and fits the tone of the context; and it must be a word that in Melville's hand could have been misread as the word in the copy-text (or that Melville himself could mistakenly have written). Under these three criteria, "woolen" is emended to "wooden" (67.37); "Wood's" to "Hood's" (159.19); "providentially" to "providently" (189.16); "cried" to "cries" (308.29); and "Purser's" to "Surgeon's" (330.15).

convincingly defended as Melville's, then the copy-text reading is retained (see, for instance, the discussion of the reading at xii. 24). In other words, substantive emendations have not been made on the basis of the subjective stylistic judgments of the editors. Since the copy-text is likely to retain more manuscript readings than a later text, there is no choice but to follow it in those few cases which are otherwise indeterminable.

TREATMENT OF ACCIDENTALS

IN THE ABSENCE of a final manuscript, the degree to which the author was responsible for the accidentals—the punctuation and spelling—of a printed text is a matter impossible to settle conclusively. Greg's theory of copy-text provides a method for playing the odds to advantage: adhering to the printed text closest to the manuscript will allow a maximum number of characteristic authorial usages to be retained, since each successive impression or edition offers further opportunities for corruption, in the form of publishers' changes, compositors' errors, or plate damage. Even though changes in the spelling and punctuation of *White-Jacket* were undoubtedly made at Harper & Brothers, the American edition was nevertheless set directly from Melville's manuscript and inevitably preserves more of its accidentals than the English edition, another step removed, could possibly do. Even if some of the variants in accidentals in the English edition are changes that Melville made in the proofs he sent to Bentley, it is impossible to determine just which ones; to accept the English variants which appear to be improvements would be to risk adopting many instances of non-authorial spelling and punctuation on the chance of acquiring a few authorial alterations—and to defeat the purpose of selecting a copy-text on Greg's principles.

Accordingly, the accidentals of the first American impression of *White-Jacket* have been retained in the present edition except in a few unusual instances, even when the spelling and punctuation may appear incorrect or inconsistent by mid-twentieth-century standards. Some of the inconsistencies in the spelling and punctuation may have been in the manuscript, and, although Melville presumably did not intend them, they constitute a suggestive part of his total expression, since patterns of accidentals do affect the texture of a literary work. On the other hand, some of the inconsistencies in accidentals may have resulted either from an imperfectly realized attempt to make the manuscript conform to a house style or from compositorial alterations. To regularize the punctuation and spelling would be to risk choosing nonauthorial forms.[29] Therefore no attempt has been made to impose general consistency on either spelling or punctuation,[30] and any changes have been made sparingly, according to the following guidelines:

SPELLING. The general rule adopted here is to correct spellings which were unacceptable by the standards of 1850, but to retain any acceptable variants. One available guide for decisions about spelling is the 1847 revision of Webster's *American Dictionary of the English Language* (Springfield, Mass., 1848). Webster's was the dictionary used by Harper & Brothers at the time, for Melville remarked, in his letter to Murray on January 28, 1849, that "my printers here 'go for' Webster." The Harper accounts show that Melville ordered at least three copies of Webster's (on April 10 and November 15, 1847, and on November 16, 1848), the third of which could have been the 1848 edition. In any case, the 1848 Webster's can be taken as a generally accepted standard in use in 1849, when Melville was writing *White-Jacket*. Recourse to it and to other contemporary dictionaries (and to editions of American novels and works of travel published in the 1840's by Harpers and other American publishers) has resulted in the retention of a good many anomalous-appearing copy-text forms, such as "Bastile," "Brahim," "breaksman," "Chili," "cue" (for "queue"), "gauky," "glozed," "Mephistophiles," "overhaul" (as in "overhaul trowsers"), "pall" (for "pawl"), "suit" (for "suite"), "waive" (for "wave"), and "wizzen." A few other forms, not found in reliable parallels in such contemporary sources, have been corrected: "braggadacio," "buogee," "Cruickshank," "discription," "Hawthorn," "plum-line," "Shelly," and "Trelwarney." One random misspelling of a name invented by Melville has been regularized (at 336.35, "Shenley" should be "Shenly"). Any changes to bring spelling into conformity with an 1850 standard have been made cautiously so as to preserve the wide latitude allowed in contemporary usage, especially for proper names.

PUNCTUATION. In several instances emendations in punctuation have

29. Melville's habits in the extant manuscripts and letters are not definite enough to offer grounds to emend for consistency (and in any case the letters, not intended for publication, do not provide a parallel situation). Neither is the Harper house styling consistent enough to be helpful in determining precisely what elements of the punctuation of *White-Jacket* resulted from it.

30. For example, no emendations are made to secure consistency in the use (or nonuse) of capital letters; of apostrophes in contractions; of italics or of quotation marks (or both at once) for such items as foreign words, the first occurrence of special terms (nautical terminology, slang, and the like), names of ships, and titles of books.

been made to correct obvious typographical errors, such as the absence of the periods after "years" (141.27) and "deplored" (166.3), and various errors involving the misuse or omission of quotation marks.[31] In only one instance does the punctuation of the Harper text create an ambiguity serious enough to interfere with the meaning of a sentence (229.1), and so to require editorial emendation.

EDITORIAL APPARATUS

THE BASIC EVIDENCE for textual decisions in the present edition is given in the preceding sections of this NOTE and in the four sections which follow it and complete the TEXTUAL RECORD:[32]

DISCUSSIONS OF ADOPTED READINGS. These discussions take up any reading (whether a copy-text reading or an emendation) adopted in the Northwestern–Newberry text which seems to require discussion or explanation beyond the general guidelines already stated. Certain instances of decisions not to emend, as well as some actual emendations, are commented upon.

LIST OF EMENDATIONS. This list records every change made in the copy-text for the present edition, accidentals as well as substantives. The left column gives the Northwestern–Newberry readings, the right column the rejected copy-text readings. Each emendation is followed by a symbol to indicate whether the source is the English edition (E) or the present editors (NN).[33] Items marked with an asterisk are commented on in the DISCUSSIONS OF ADOPTED READINGS.

Forty-three emendations have been made in accidentals, 52 in substantives. Of the accidentals, 20 are corrections made in the English edition,

31. Thus the deletion of double quotation marks at 397.12, together with the insertion of single ones at 397.13 and 397.18, makes clearer who is reciting the verse and follows the practice used elsewhere in the book for such situations. In addition, a single quotation mark is supplied to close the couplet at 270.13. In neither instance does the emendation require a decision affecting the meaning, since in neither does the misuse or omission of quotation marks call into question who is speaking or what is said.

32. On file in the Melville Collection at The Newberry Library is a complete list of variants between the American and the English editions, including both substantives (which are reported in the LIST OF SUBSTANTIVE VARIANTS) and accidentals (which are reported in the LIST OF EMENDATIONS only when they are adopted). Also on file is the evidence for the decisions in the first list of the REPORT OF LINE-END HYPHENATION.

33. The presence of an NN symbol signifies only that the reading does not occur in the two authorized texts; it does not imply that no one has ever thought of it before.

and the other 23 have been made by the present editors; of the substantives, 36 come from the English edition and 16 from the present editors. No emendations of any sort have been made silently; using the LIST OF EMENDATIONS and the REPORT OF LINE-END HYPHENATION, one can reconstruct the copy-text in every detail.[34]

REPORT OF LINE-END HYPHENATION. Since some possible compound words are hyphenated at the ends of lines in the copy-text, the intended forms of these words become a matter for editorial decision. When such a word appears elsewhere in the copy-text in only one form, that form is followed; when its treatment is not consistent (and the inconsistency is an acceptable one, to be retained in the present text), the form which occurs more times in analogous situations is followed. If the word does not occur elsewhere in the copy-text, the form is determined by a survey of similar words, by the usage in the 1848 Webster's, and by any relevant evidence in a Melville manuscript. The first list in the REPORT OF LINE-END HYPHENATION records these decisions, by listing the adopted Northwestern–Newberry forms of possible compounds which are hyphenated at the ends of lines in the copy-text. The second list records the copy-text forms of compounds which are hyphenated at the ends of lines in the Northwestern–Newberry Edition. No editorial decisions are involved in this second list,[35] but the information recorded is essential for reconstructing the copy-text and making exact quotations from the present edition.

LIST OF SUBSTANTIVE VARIANTS. This list is a historical record of all variant substantive readings in the two editions authorized by Melville.[36]

34. That is, every textual detail: features of the styling or design of the copy-text print —such as the length of lines; the form and content of the title page and running titles; the typography and punctuation of the epigraph, chapter numbers, and chapter titles; and the display capitalization of chapter openings and half-titles—are of course not recoverable from these lists. However, in this volume, capitalization of words in the chapter titles, both in the Table of Contents and at the heads of the chapters, follows the somewhat inconsistent capitalization in the Table of Contents of the copy-text. Opening quotation marks are omitted before the display capitals at the beginning of Chapter 2 (p. 6) and Chapter 90 (p. 377). The rule around the playbill on page 92 is supplied.

35. Except in the cases of words hyphenated at the ends of lines in the copy-text as well. These words, which appear in both lists and are marked with daggers, are given in the forms which the present editors adopted but which are obscured by hyphenation at the ends of lines in this edition.

36. Such variants as jails/gaols, suit/suite are considered accidentals whenever the 1848 Webster's or other contemporary dictionaries classify them as interchangeable forms of the same word. Treated as a nontextual feature is the fact that the American edition numbered the chapters I–XCIII and listed them in a single table of contents, whereas the English

The left column gives the readings of the first American impression (and also the Northwestern–Newberry readings when they differ from those of the copy-text). The right column lists the English substantive readings which are at variance with the copy-text. Editions are designated by three symbols: A (American), E (English), and NN (Northwestern–Newberry).

With these lists the reader can examine and reconsider for himself the textual decisions for the present edition and in the process see more clearly the relationships between the texts of *White-Jacket* available during Melville's lifetime and the one which is offered here as a more faithful representation of the author's intentions.

---

edition, in two volumes, numbered them I–XLVII in the first and I–XLVI in the second, with a separate table of contents in each volume.

Discussions of Adopted Readings

I N THESE COMMENTS on emendations and on decisions not to emend, the following symbols are employed:

>A American Edition (1850)
>E English Edition (1850)
>NN Northwestern–Newberry Edition

ix.1–9   Note . . . 1850.]   Since the E Preface is dated October, 1849, while the A Note is dated March, 1850, the Note is retained as representing Melville's later intention. The text of the Preface is printed below, pp. 487–88. For a discussion of the relation between it and the Note, see the comments introducing the revised fair copy of the Preface, pp. 489–92.

xii.24   *Flogging not Necessary*]   The A reading is retained here and at 147.2 because the E reading "Is Flogging necessary?" cannot confidently be accounted for as Melville's revision. If the English reading is assumed to be the later one it is hard to see why either Melville or anyone at Bentley's made a change whose only obvious effect would be to destroy the parallelism with the preceding chapter title. A more likely assumption appears to be that the A reading is in fact the later version, to be accounted for as a revision Melville made to secure parallelism in the two chapter titles. Possibly it was associated with the one word revision at the beginning of the preceding chapter (see discussion of 143.3). Melville may

461

have made the change before he went to England, but not on the proofs he took with him as the basis of the English edition, or he may have made it after his return to New York, when he cut the Preface down to the Note. (The A reading "Flogging not Necessary" is printed as *"Flogging not Necessary"* in conformity with the styling of NN.)

4.25   *Me?* Ah me!]   The absence in E of these three words might be taken as Melville's attempt to eliminate an over-emotional exclamation, perhaps because it is somewhat uncharacteristic of White-Jacket; but since it equally well might be an excision by someone at Bentley's who considered it excessive, the copy-text reading is retained. (A further possibility is that the question mark after *"Me"* was an error for an exclamation point, and that what Melville had intended was a milder lament comparable to "My! oh my!")

27.2   masters-at-arms]   The A and E reading "masters-of-arms" is an obvious slip, since the form "master-at-arms", introduced just above as the title of the official, is employed consistently throughout the book.

28.14–15   Elizabethan, Franklin-warranted]   If the omission of these words from E was not merely by compositorial oversight, possibly they were cut out at Bentley's because the expression "Franklin-warranted" was thought too likely to puzzle English readers. Since the excision seems less likely to be Melville's own, the A reading is retained.

37.18   pantries]   The E reading "pantries" (for "pockets" in A) seems most likely Melville's revision to eliminate the awkward repetition of "pocket" in "pocket-edition" and reinforce the analogy of the pockets of the jacket to "lockers and pantries" at 37.31.

53.2   *Drought*]   NN emends the A and E word "Draught" with the reading *"Drought"*, which is the word that occurs in the table of contents of both A and E. The decision to emend assumes that a "drought" is more likely the idea Melville intended than a "draught", though the latter is also possible in the context. The A reading "DRAUGHT" is printed as *"Drought"* (incorporating the emendation) in conformity with the styling of NN.

58.38   buckets-full]   The anomalous A and E reading "buckets' full" is emended on the analogy of "brushes-full" at 78.28–29.

86.23   sailor's]   The copy-text placing of the apostrophe is retained in this and other instances where literal interpretation of the number involved might favor emendation, and where E sometimes does make the change. Melville's own punctuation in a given case and his practice in general cannot be determined; usage is inconsistent within *White-Jacket*; and in any case idiom does not require literal construction of the sense. See, for example, 256.2, "bee's-wax", 283.11, "officer's servants"; 303.12, "burglar's dark-lanterns"; 323.13, "Commodore's eyes".

113.20–21   97 Commanders . . . 327 Lieutenants]   In both A and E the numbers are given as 297 and 377. Those numbers are errors in transcription, possibly on Melville's part but more likely on that of his copyist or the compositor. On that assumption, NN corrects them to 97 and 327 from Melville's cited source. (His estimates of the approximate total amounts drawn by the several grades were based on figures in this source and are accurate enough, except that the amount he states for midshipmen appears to be about double the actual total.)

114.17   honor]   The English edition, the copy-text for this passage (which does not appear in the American edition), reads "honour" here and at 114.18, but NN emends in accordance with spellings elsewhere in this book and with Melville's known practice. See also the emendation at 286.8 and the NN *Typee*, p. 323.

143.3   It]   The copy-text "It" is retained because priority between that reading and the E "But it" is uncertain. Both openings seem to be Melville's own. Probably the A reading is the later. For anyone at Bentley's to supply the word "But" to open the chapter seems unlikely, while it is highly characteristic for Melville to begin sentences, paragraphs, and even chapters with the word (see the following chapter). Yet it is more likely that Melville would open the chapter with "But" when he was composing and remove it later than that he would open without it and later feel the need to add it. Probably the revision was made at the same time as the change in the title of Chapter 35 (see discussion of xii.24).

189.16   providently]   This required correction of the A and E reading "providentially" was made by Titus Munson Coan in a copy of the Stedman edition of *White-Jacket* now in the Melville Collection at The Newberry Library.

194.30   three or four]   The copy-text reading is retained since there is no way to determine whether the E reading "seven or eight" was ever Melville's at all or, if so, whether it was earlier or later than the A reading. (As it happens, retention of the copy-text reading serves fact and logic, since a message in the United States navy would carry no more than four flags, and since logically four at most would be needed for four-place numbers such as Melville cites. But neither of these considerations is to the point textually because the object is to preserve the author's intended meaning even though it might be wrong and illogical.)

196.19   at last]   The A reading "soon" is plausible if "promised recovery" is taken to mean "showed signs of surviving"; but "at last" fits better with the description in the next paragraph of Baldy's slow and limited recovery. Furthermore, the E reading "hale, hearty little man" five lines later (196.24) is presumably Melville's expansion of the A reading "hale, hearty man" and is additional evidence that this whole passage received his attention as he looked over the proofs.

196.24   little man]   See discussion of 196.19.

199.28   Yes:]   The A reading "And" implies that the auctioneer is going to make an additional point when in fact he merely reiterates what he said in the previous sentence. The superior E reading "Yes:" seems authorial and gives evidence that, in revising the proofs for Bentley, Melville gave minute attention to some passages.

229.1   were,]   The comma after "were" is adopted from E, since the A reading confuses the sense by causing the reader at first to take "far" as one of the complements of the verb, parallel with "cabined" and "cribbed", rather than as a nonrestrictive modifier of "boys" (simply reinforcing for rhetorical effect the idea already established in the preceding paragraph by such phrases as "far away").

234.12   ever]   The word "ever" supplied in E appears to be an authorial insertion to complete the idiom needed to make the exact shade of meaning clear: the sword is not now and can never have been the old Commodore's fighting sword.

262.14   Buccaneer]   The A and E reading "Mohawk" seems to be a slip for "Buccaneer", the name given for Surgeon Sawyer's ship at 253.28 and 253.32. This emendation was suggested by Hennig Cohen in the Rinehart Edition (1967).

263.12, 19   Hennen]   The actual name of the authority cited is "Hennen", but whether or not to adopt this form is a difficult question. In the first occurrence, the name falls at the end of a line in A, on a page where plate damage along the right margin has destroyed half the last letter of the word, leaving only a mark resembling an "r", which could be the left side of either an "r" or an "n" (A310.13); in the second occurrence, ten lines later, the last letter is clearly "r". (In E, "r" appears in both instances.) If an editor could be certain that the broken letter is really "r", then he could argue that the erroneous form of the name, appearing twice, was intended by Melville as a device to characterize Cuticle as inaccurate in his pedantry. On the other hand, if the broken letter is really "n", then the later occurrence of the name with "r" must be simply a compositorial error. Since there are so many uncertainties involved, since the name is in fact "Hennen", and since Melville could hardly have expected a reader to be aware of an intentional distortion of a relatively obscure name, it has seemed proper to consider "Henner" another example of a clearly misspelled proper name (parallel to "Trelwarney" at 271.8) and to emend to the correct form. Although the A and E reading "Lally" for "Larrey" (259.11) might at first seem to support the argument that Melville is consciously distorting the names of medical authorities in Cuticle's speech, the form is more convincingly explained as a misreading of "Larrey" in Melville's manuscript, since the letter "r" in his hand often has a looped peak resembling an "l".

276.1   come]   Though possibly a compositorial substitution, the E reading "come" is adopted as Melville's own restoration of the form he originally intended to have Rose-Water use (since his speech is rendered in dialect). Presumably the copyist or American compositor would be more likely to take Melville's manuscript "come" for "came" (since his a and o are frequently indeterminate) and to conform the verb to the standard past tense than the English compositor (or anyone at Bentley's) would be to make the reverse substitution of the nonstandard form or merely to blunder into so appropriate a change.

294.23, 27, 29   men]   Since the E reading "men" occurs at three points in this passage where the A reading is "sailors" a deliberate change was involved. Both readings are almost certainly Melville's own since the revision, whether from A to E or from E to A, is not the sort anyone at Harper's or Bentley's would be likely to make. NN adopts the E reading as Melville's revision of the A reading on two counts. First, a matter of factual accuracy is involved: technically only two of the three men hanged were "sailors" (i.e., common seamen), the third, Philip Spencer, being an acting midshipman. Second, "men" is also clearly a stylistic improvement.

365.3   No!]   NN retains the A and E reading, assuming that White-Jacket makes the exclamation, since it is in keeping with his emphatic scorn for the "vile *regulation-whiskers*". Possibly, however, the word should be put inside quotation marks as the first word of the speech which follows.

393.1   scared]   Coupled with "hues", the word "scared", though possible, is unusual enough to suggest that a copyist or compositor may have misread Melville's hand. Paleographically plausible readings might be either "scaled" (in reference to the spectrum) or "seared" (in sequence with the heat-cold images).

List of Emendations

I N THIS LIST of changes made in the copy-text by the present editors, the following abbreviations are used to designate the sources of readings:

> A American Edition (1850)
> E English Edition (1850)
> NN Northwestern–Newberry Edition

For further comment on this list, see pp. 458–59 above; for discussions of the emendations marked with an asterisk (*), see the DISCUSSIONS OF ADOPTED READINGS, pp. 461–65. The wavy dash (~) stands for the word cited in the left column and signals that only a punctuation mark is emended. The caret (∧) indicates the absence of a punctuation mark.

	NN READING	COPY-TEXT READING
11.34	merchant-sailor E	sailor
12.11	London ∧ E	~ ;
12.11	in King James's time E	[not present]
18.21	lieutenant ∧ commanding E	~-~
20.11	bougee E	buogee
24.22	The . . . it, E	I never had a good interior look at it but once; and then

	NN Reading	Copy-Text Reading
26.21	sky-larking. E	~,
*27.2	masters-at-arms NN	masters-of-arms
27.26–32	For . . . long. E	[not present]
28.8	people* E	~∧
28.22	*In . . . men." E	[not present]
34.13	sailors E	sailor's
37.3	description E	discription
*37.18	pantries E	pockets
47.32	old∧sheet-anchor-men NN	~-~-~-~
*53.2	*Drought* NN	DRAUGHT
56.4	master-at-arms NN	masters-at-arms
*58.38	buckets-full NN	buckets' full
67.37	wooden NN	woolen
78.13–14	White∧Jacket NN	~-~
79.22	berth-deck, NN	~;
79.22	above; E	~,
105.20	braggadocio E	braggadacio
111.39	many; E	~.
111.39–112.1	and . . . elsewhere. E	[not present]
*113.20–21	97 . . . 327 NN	297 . . . 377
114.14–22	But . . . establishment. E [except for two changes listed below]	[not present]
*114.17	honor NN	honour E [part of passage at 114.14–22]
114.18	honor NN	honour E [part of passage at 114.14–22]
122.5	miles. E	~∧
123.6	white∧jacket E	~-~
141.3	time, E	~.
141.3	and . . . offence. E	[not present]
153.12	section of a E	long
159.17	Ilha E	Ihla

	NN Reading	Copy-Text Reading
159.17	das NN	Dos
159.19	Hood's NN	Wood's
159.22	Botafogo NN	Botofogo
160.14	das NN	Dos
160.17	world's NN	world
161.6	cockswains, E	~∧
161.6	or steersmen E	[not present]
166.3	deplored. E	~∧
184.17	master-at-arms' NN	masters-at-arms'
*189.16	providently NN	providentially
191.13–14	Little . . . then. E	[not present]
191.15	Lemsford E	he
*196.19	at last E	soon
*196.24	little E	[not present]
*199.28	Yes: E	And∧
*229.1	were, E	~ ∧
*234.12	ever E	[not present]
242.16	or something like that; E	[not present]
251.10	eminent NN	imminent
259.11	Larrey NN	Lally
*262.14	Buccaneer NN	Mohawk
*263.12	Hennen NN	Henner
*263.19	Hennen NN	Henner
270.13	tide.' NN	~·∧
271.3	Shelley NN	Shelly
271.4	Shelley NN	Shelly
271.8	Trelawny NN	Trelwarney
*276.1	come E	came
278.31	boatswain's∧ mate E	~-~
283.15	Hawthorne NN	Hawthorn
285,18 –286.16	In . . . goose. E [except for one change listed below]	[not present]

	NN Reading	Copy-Text Reading
286.8	flavor NN	flavour E [part of passage at 285.18–286.16]
*294.23	men E	sailors
*294.27	men E	sailors
*294.29	men E	sailors
308.29	cries NN	cried
318.29	others E	other
323.10	woof E	woop
323.10	warp E	warf
326.14	blowing E	flowing
328.13	it! NN	~ ?
330.15	Surgeon's NN	Purser's
336.35	Shenly E	Shenley
347.25–26	—Mr. Pert,— E	[not present]
349.11	top-sails E	top-sail
357.9	coast? NN	~ !
378.1	linen E	lined
381.4	was E	were
381.31–32	It . . . But E	[not present]
381.32	these E	These
381.35–40	It . . . impressment. E [except for one change listed below]	[not present]
381.38	at NN	as E [part of passage at 381.35–40]
382.37	friend's E	friends
385.10	soften E	softens
387.38	Cruikshank E	Cruickshank
392.2	plumb-line NN	plum-line
397.12	boys!ᴧ NN	~ !"
397.13	"'How NN	" ᴧ~
397.18	toil.'" NN	~ . ᴧ"

Report of Line-End Hyphenation

T HE FIRST LIST below records the forms adopted in the present
edition (NN) for possible compound words which were hyphenated
at line-ends in the copy-text (A) and which the editors had to decide
whether to print as single-word compounds without hyphens or as
hyphenated compounds. The second list records the A reading of possible
compounds which happen to be hyphenated at the ends of lines in the
present edition; any possible compound hyphenated at the end of a line in
NN occurs as one unhyphenated word in A unless it appears in this list.
Those words coincidentally hyphenated between the same elements at line-
ends in both A and NN are listed in the forms which would have been
adopted if they had fallen within a line in NN and are marked with daggers
(†). A slash (/) indicates the line-end break in A in a word with two or more
hyphens.

To make the record of editorial decisions complete, a few words
hyphenated at the ends of lines in A are included in the first list even though
(1) they always appear as one unhyphenated word when they occur within
the line in the copy-text (e.g., "forecastle"), or (2) they always appear
either as a hyphenated compound or as two separate words when they
occur within the line in the copy-text (e.g., "deck-officer" or "deck
officer"). Both lists exclude two classes of line-end hyphenation: (1) those

which unquestionably mark only compositorial syllabication of non-compound words (for example, "in-/asmuch" and "not-/withstanding"), and (2) those which separate two or more elements that could not possibly be run together as one word without a hyphen (e.g., "Dogs-Body" and "First-Cutter" or "father-in-law" and "cock-and-bull"). For further comment on these lists, see p. 459 above.

I. NN *forms of possible compounds which were hyphenated at copy-text line-ends*

xi.8	*Berth-deck*	45.2	head-stones
xii.7	*Short-lived*	45.26	good-humored
4.18	rain-storm	45.27	temper-soothing
9.10	main-mast	46.27	hotel-clerks
9.11	main-yard	48.8	dinner-party
9.36	Quarter-deck	48.26	cot-boys
9.38	main-brace	51.4	†After-guard
10.12	hard-hearted	51.17	midnight
10.17	*silk-/sock-gentry*	52.7	castaways
10.19	gun-deck	52.11	broken-hearted
10.23	hay-seed	53.12	midshipman
10.26	gun-deck	54.19	Main-/top-man
11.15	Mizen-top	54.20	After-guard
14.22	drawing-room	55.26	mess-chests
16.19	merchant-	58.5	*Rose-water*
	seaman's	59.19	match-tub
17.21	sheet-/anchor-	61.12	overboard
	man	62.29	†blaze-away
18.6	long-bearded	62.33	†native-born
19.19	overboard	65.30	long-gun
21.22	flag-officer	65.39	quarter-deck
22.23	state-room	66.26	overboard
25.3	anchor-button	67.4	port-hole
26.26	dressing-gown	67.12	Bowery-boy
26.34	schoolmaster	68.32	gun-carriages
27.3	hatchways	69.13	long-gun
30.2	main-/top-man	69.14	top-gallant
34.20	sea-officer	69.39	quarter-bills
35.7	door-steps	71.8	life-lines
36.26	night-watch	72.39	*Sheet-/anchor men*
37.5	thumb-hole	74.13	castaway
39.9	hiding-place	75.15	three-story

337.9	death-board	384.17	grog-tub
339.1	shipmate	386.2	*Gun-deck*
343.21	attorney-like	386.16	post-captains
344.5	death-earned	387.30	forefathers
346.8	Ward-room	389.3	lee-scuppers
347.7	great-gun	390.7	fore-top
348.9	main-mast	392.15	weather-top-
351.8	quarter-deck		gallant-yard-/arm
351.32	†twenty-four	393.27	mid-deep
353.9	quarter-gunners	396.19	powder-
356.30	main-hatchway		magazine
363.1	grandsires	399.16	gangway
363.21	old-fashioned	399.24	clean-swept
366.26	hawse-hole	399.24	†water-line
370.8	shipmates	399.25	store-rooms
380.22	*bowsprit*		

II. *Copy-text forms of possible compounds which are hyphenated at line-ends in* NN

4.18	bone-dry	42.21	touch-holes
9.4	main-royal	45.33	light-houses
10.3	sailor-like	46.27	market-women
10.24	chicken-coops	47.1	quarter-gunners
10.29	pig-pens	47.31	blue-light
11.19	cot-boys	48.17	non-combatants
18.33	sword-knot	50.14	main-deck
19.5	gold-laced	51.4	†After-guard
21.17	body-servant's	51.38	man-hater
22.4	main-top-/man	58.28	merchant-vessels
22.26	shirt-buttons	59.21	to-morrow
22.28	incense-burning	59.36	half-famished
26.8	hand-saws	62.22	gun-deck
26.12	infant-school	62.29	†blaze-away
26.18	double-reefed	62.33	†native-born
26.37	†grease-spots	65.6	war-horse
28.14	Franklin-	65.35	†long-gun
	warranted	66.38	ramming-pole
36.24	main-/royal-yard	67.13	main-deck
38.4	high-raised	67.38	arm-hole
39.8	mess-chest	68.5	grape-shot
41.37	ship-underlings	68.10	twenty-four

68.23	ward-room	136.25	mizzen-top
68.35	silk-hose	137.9	hammock-
69.34	galley-cooks		nettings
72.17	quarter-casks	141.34	man-of-war's-/
76.17	ocean-wanderers		men
78.28	brushes-full	147.3	mast-head
81.12	twenty-/four-	148.11	pier-heads
	pound	148.14	slaughter-house
84.22	tender-hearted	153.7	*loggerhead-turtles*
87.6	wash-house	153.12	sea-serpent
87.27	barn-yard	153.28	main-hold
88.7	*holy-stoning*	160.6	silver-belled
90.8	man-of-war's-/	162.11	stalwart-looking
	men	163.12	dancing-school
90.18	after-guard's-/	163.34	body-servant
	man	164.1	man-of-war's-/
91.20	night-watches		men
91.24	gun-deck	168.4	*Carrick-bend*
93.30	gun-carriage	174.7	twenty-four
97.4	t'-gallant-/sail	180.19	sheet-/anchor-
97.16	sail-maker's		man
97.37	storm-trim	180.37	sheet-anchor-/
97.38	t'-gallant-/yards		man
103.19	*quarter-deck*	186.2	†long-established
105.3	signal-quarter-/	189.13	gold-mounted
	master	194.15	sea-green
105.21	†stun'-sails	199.20	sea-boots
105.37	†yard-arm-/ends	202.24	sail-maker
106.32	top-sails	202.39	sheet-/anchor-
107.30	main-sail		man
116.28	snow-flakes	213.15	quarter-masters
116.38	sea-nymphs	214.34	ward-room
121.35	ten-knot	216.11	†middle-aged
122.8	watering-place	217.26	†mid-shipman
123.9	*spirit-room*	217.37	†kind-heartedness
123.14	top-sails	220.2	sea-statutes
123.16	copper-fastened	221.2	midshipman's
125.3	store-rooms	221.18	sea-service
125.28	†account-books	221.10	midshipmen
128.23	blue lights	226.22	quarter-watch
128.27	Parliament-house	231.2	well-known
134.9	well-known	232.2	well-being

234.13	slaughter-house	311.34	sheet-/anchor-
234.32	†main-royal-/yard		man
235.8	broad-billed	312.23	mizzen-mast
235.18	night-watches	313.2	twenty-four-/
238.22	shot-box		pounders
242.23	re-entered	313.18	sea-fights
245.5	long-expected	316.33	main-mast
246.3	†mess-mate	317.9	nine-pounder
249.1	state-room	317.11	†sweet-meats
252.14	camp-stool	318.30	†black-snakes
255.17	royal-stun'-/sail	320.15	body-guard
256.10	over-	322.4	†port-hole
	conscientious	322.20	merchant-vessels
257.8	gun-carriages	323.32	match-tubs
258.26	mess-mates	325.16	*sick-bay*
260.9	death-bed	326.15	sick-bay
264.24	quarter-deck	326.28	sea-dogs
268.20	main-mast	328.1	Sailing-master
270.25	world-finder	329.32	sick-list
271.11	forecastle-man	330.20	wonder-working
274.5	homeward-bound	332.13	mess-mate
276.18	good-humored	336.14	dark-blue
276.27	*quarter-deck*	336.15	long-drawn
278.12	good-will	338.5	sail-maker
278.18	weather-lift	340.5	hammock-mate
282.17	main-hatchway	340.31	shot-box
283.4	scuttle-butt	346.13	shot-boxes
283.13	scuttle-butt	350.15	night-watches
284.27	sea-wardens	351.32	†twenty-four
285.28	main-mast	353.24	sheet–/anchor-
294.22	blood-thirsty		men
295.12	twenty-/four-	353.25	fore-top
	pounders	353.31	serious-minded
299.27	main-lift	354.5	old-fashioned
301.34	quarter-deck	355.20	*ship-shape*
302.1	courts-martial	357.5	homeward-
302.23	court-martial		bounders
304.21	self-evident	358.12	to-morrow
304.25	noble-	358.20	man-of-war's-/
	heartedness		men
307.38	*white-mice*	359.19	off-handed
311.29	top-men	359.31	match-tub

360.37	snow-white	388.13	sheet-anchor-/
360.39	quarter-deck		man
363.20	sheath-knife	389.1	after-/guard's-
363.23	rose-knots		man
364.21	*muzzle-lashings*	389.13	gun-deck
365.2	*regulation-*	392.33	yard-arm
	whiskers	394.3	feather-bed
368.11	peace-loving	396.16	battle-array
372.7	court-martial	396.37	death-
382.10	full-grown		denouncing
384.21	man-of-war's-/	398.3	never-sinking
	men	398.12	gun-deck
385.4	slave-driving	398.19	world-frigate
386.11	opium-houses	399.24	†water-line
386.19	terra-firma		

List of Substantive Variants

I N THIS LIST, which is a historical record of the substantive variants in the authorized editions during Melville's lifetime, the following abbreviations are used to designate the sources of readings:

A American Edition (1850–1868)
E English Edition (1850–1853)
NN Northwestern–Newberry Edition

Copy-text (A) readings are listed in the left column and readings differing from them on the right. (In the instances of emendations made by the present editors, the NN reading also appears in the left column to provide a reference to the text.) Features of the styling or design of the American edition are not necessarily followed in the present edition, and such deviations are not recorded here (see the NOTE ON THE TEXT, p. 459, footnote 34). Empty brackets ([ ]) indicate space where a letter or letters failed to print.

vii.1–4	[*epigraph*] A	[*epigraph on title page*] E
ix.1–9	[*note*] A	[*E has instead the preface re-printed below, pp. 487–88*]
xii.24	*Flogging not* NN	
	Flogging not A	Is Flogging E

479

3.14	laying A	spreading E
4.25	*Me?* Ah me! Soaked A	Soaked E
4.27	wring A	ring E
8.15	him A	he E
11.34	merchant-sailor NN sailor A	merchant-sailor E
12.11	in King James's time NN [*not present*] A	in King James's time E
13.21	of oracle A	[*not present*] E
15.21	neck handkerchiefs A	neckerchiefs E
16.26	mounted A	amounted E
16.38	men-of-war's-men A	man-of-war's-men E
21.31–32	Perhaps . . . afloat. A	Why was this? Why not be companionable with his officers? E
21.32	real A	[*not present*] E
21.33	he A	our Commodore E
24.22	The . . . it, NN I never had a good interior look at it but once; and then A	The . . . it, E
25.39	perilous A	dignified E
26.18	with A	in E
27.9	be A	we E
27.26–32	For . . . long. NN [*not present*] A	For . . . long. E
28.14–15	Elizabethan, Franklin- warranted A	[*not present*] E
28.22	*In . . . men." NN [*not present*] A	*In . . . men." E
29.5	men-of-war's A	man-of-war's E
29.10	men-of-war's A	man-of-war's E
34.13	sailors NN sailor's A	sailors E
35.18	a A	the E
36.30	their A	[*not present*] E

37.18	pantries NN	
	pockets A	pantries E
41.30	stationery A	stationary E
42.19	their A	the E
44.2	*Men-of-war's* NN	
	MEN-OF-WAR'S A	MAN-OF-WAR'S E
46.22	a A	[*not present*] E
46.23	child A	children E
47.22	that A	[*not present*] E
54.8	this A	his E
62.30	men-of-war's-men A	man-of-war's-men E
68.22	in A	of E
69.6	men-of-war's-men A	man-of-war's-men E
77.26	still A	still almost E
78.13	dyers A	dyer's E
79.22	frigate A	frigate's E
82.2	*Men-of-war's-men* NN	
	MEN-OF-WAR'S-MEN A	MAN-OF-WAR'S MEN E
84.2	men-of-war's-men A	man-of-war's-men E
84.5	a A	an E
84.19–20	was . . . heard of A	is not a regular thing E
84.29	their A	his E
84.29–30	commanders A	commander E
85.12	superficies A	surface E
85.12	in A	on E
87.24	the most A	perhaps the most E
87.24	arbitrary A	severe E
87.37	men-of-war's-men A	man-of-war's-men E
88.7	men-of-war's-men A	man-of-war's-men E
90.24	*Jankee* A	*Jankee* (Yankee) E
103.19	while A	where E
105.34	previous A	previously E
106.3	yeasting A	yeasty E

108.22	dared A	dare E
111.39–112.1	and . . . elsewhere NN	
	[*not present*] A	and . . . elsewhere E
112.13	swell A	swells E
112.21	or reverses A	[*not present*] E
112.23	smoke or A	smoke and E
114.14–22	But . . . establishment. NN	
	[*not present*] A	But . . . establishment. E
117.13	their scraping A	scraping E
119.16	I have A	have I E
120.26	and, so A	so E
121.37	in a A	in E
123.7	the less painful A	some of the E
123.10	sailor A	sailors' E
135.1	of A	of almost E
135.18	men-of-war's-men A	man-of-war's-men E
135.23	men-of-war's-men A	man-of-war's-men E
135.29	in agony A	if scourged E
138.20–27	Let . . . laws. A	[*not present*] E
141.3	time . . . offence NN	
	time A	time . . . offence E
141.14	used up A	worn out E
143.3	I⊤ A	B⊔⊤ it E
145.27	Blackstone A	a great lawyer E
145.27	again A	[*not present*] E
146.14	in A	in the E
147.2	*Flogging not* NN	
	FLOGGING NOT A	IS FLOGGING E
150.3	resource A	recourse E
150.11	freed A	free E
151.9–10	The . . . rear. A	[*not present*] E
152.11	at A	of E
153.11	the A	[*not present*] E

153.12	section of a NN long A	section of a E
156.26–27	in . . . is A	it is, in some governments, E
161.6	or steersmen NN [*not present*] A	or steersmen E
165.18	Spanish A	[*not present*] E
166.12	proportionately A	proportionably E
173.39	your own A	my E
174.21	best A	best of E
176.17	at A	[*not present*] E
182.4	in A	at E
185.14	almost numberless A	repeated E
186.4	so A	[*not present*] E
186.20	Way A	May E
187.12	jeweler-shop A	jeweller's-shop E
188.10	Goëthe's A	Clanqui's E
188.10	Margaret A	Zantua E
188.12	Mephistophiles A	Don E
188.16	lying A	[*not present*] E
191.11	manuscripts A	manuscript E
191.13–14	Little . . . then. NN [*not present*] A	Little . . . then. E
191.15	Lemsford NN he A	Lemsford E
194.30	three A	seven E
194.30	four A	eight E
196.19	at last NN soon A	at last E
196.24	little NN [*not present*] A	little E
199.28	Yes: NN And A	Yes: E
200.7	, auctioneer . . . muscle A	auctioneer E
202.6	'ere A	ere E

211.19	those A	these E
211.23	and A	and the E
212.17	grander A	more grand E
213.23	itself A	[*not present*] E
217.12	despotic A	certain E
226.36	very A	[ ] E
231.32	piece A	place E
234.12	ever NN [*not present*] A	ever E
234.22	fathers' A	father's E
235.19	lay A	lie E
235.21	all A	[*not present*] E
242.16	or something like that; NN [*not present*] A	or something like that; E
253.37	no A	no more E
256.2	bee's-wax A	bees'-wax E
265.6	the A	a E
265.15	invariably A	invariable E
275.24	aroused A	roused E
276.1	come NN came A	come E
276.12	A's . . . of A	During E
276.27	is any A	be any E
279.5	quarter-master A	quarter-masters E
280.2	as A	[*not present*] E
283.11	officer's A	officers' E
285.20–286.16	In . . . goose. NN [*not present*] A	In . . . goose. E
288.23	invariably A	often E
288.37	having A	have E
294.23	men NN sailors A	men E
294.27	men NN sailors A	men E

294.29	men NN	
	sailors A	men E
300.17	would A	could E
300.17	hearken to A	hear E
300.20	this A	the E
306.12	burglar's A	burglars' E
318.29	others NN	
	other A	others E
323.10	woof NN	
	woop A	woof E
323.10	warp NN	
	warf A	warp E
326.14–15	blowing NN	
	flowing A	blowing E
327.26	a hotel A	an hotel E
329.16	remorselessly A	remorsely E
329.21	went A	he went E
331.2	the still A	still the E
336.25	emerged A	immerged E
338.10	hair A	air E
347.25–26	—Mr. Pert,— NN	
	[*not present*] A	—Mr. Pert,— E
349.11	top-sails NN	
	top-sail A	top-sails E
351.22	elaborated A	elaborate E
358.6	given A	giving E
367.35	whole A	old E
375.21	glazed A	glosed E
378.1	linen NN	
	lined A	linen E
381.4	was NN	
	were A	was E
381.31–32	It . . . But NN	
	[*not present*] A	It . . . But E
381.35–40	It . . . impressment. NN	
	[*not present*] A	It . . . impressment. E

382.37	friend's NN	
	friends A	friend's E
383.33	glandular A	[*not present*] E
385.10	soften NN	
	softens A	soften E
398.15	surmisings A	surmises E

Preface to the English Edition

THE OBJECT of this work is to give some idea of the interior life in a man-of-war. In the year 1843, the author shipped as a common sailor on board of a United States frigate, then lying in a harbour of the Pacific Ocean. After serving on board of this frigate for more than a year, he was discharged, with the rest of the crew, upon the vessel's arrival home. His man-of-war experiences and observations have been incorporated into the present volumes. But these volumes are not presented as a journal of the cruise.

As the object of this work is not to portray the particular man-of-war in which the author sailed, and its officers and crew, but, by illustrative scenes, to paint general life in the Navy, the true name of the frigate is not given. Nor is it here asserted that any of the persons introduced in the following chapters are real individuals. Wherever statements are made in any way concerning the established laws and usages of the Navy, facts have been strictly adhered to. Allusion is sometimes made to events or facts in the past history of Navies. In these cases, no statement is presented unless supported by the best authorities. For the hitherto unrecorded by-play of circumstances in one or two well-known naval actions referred to, the writer is indebted to the seamen into whose mouths these things are put.

The work opens at the frigate's last harbour in the Pacific, just previous to weighing her anchor for the homeward-bound passage, by the way of Cape Horn.

New York, *October*, 1849.

¶ NOTE   The relation between this preface to the English edition (which was headed "PREFACE.") and that to the American edition (headed "NOTE.") is discussed below, pp. 489–92.

Revised Fair Copy of Preface

TWO LEAVES of *White-Jacket* manuscript survive, carrying the two consecutive pages of a semifinal fair copy of the preface that appeared in the English edition. They are preserved in the Melville Collection of the Houghton Library of Harvard University, with the designation Ms Am 188 (392) and the endorsement "Gift of Eleanor Melville Metcalf / Feb 1938". They are reproduced and transcribed here by permission. Each leaf is a half-sheet of the same off-white wove paper and measures approximately 19 × 31.5 cm. The writing, on the recto of the leaves, is in brown ink in the hand of a copyist whose identity can only be inferred from handwriting characteristics.[1] Melville revised the fair copy, also in brown ink. Both the copyist and Melville used pencil at a few points, and minor pencil notations were made later.

In his revision Melville added the heading "Preface", altered words and phrases, changed the paragraphing and punctuation, and canceled one passage after he had tentatively elaborated it. At one point he supplied a word for which the baffled copyist had left a blank, and at another he traced

1. Jay Leyda in *The Melville Log*, I, 317, and Hennig Cohen in the Rinehart edition of *White-Jacket*, p. liii, state that the copyist is Melville's wife, Elizabeth Shaw Melville. (Full citation of these sources is given on pp. 439, 438.) Comparison with Mrs. Melville's hand in other documents, however, indicates that the attribution is incorrect.

over in ink three words the copyist had cautiously entered in pencil. The tendency of Melville's revisions, apart from minor stylistic improvements, was to shorten his original statements and make them less specific, particularly as to the degree of literal fact in the book's presentation of persons and events. In the one or more nonextant versions between this and the printer's copy for the English edition the tendency continued, for in the English preface he shortened his statements further and made them even more vague as to the relation of literal fact and representative truth in the book. He removed his acknowledgment of a debt to "Scenes from Old Ironsides." The trend of his revision toward brevity and away from specific definition of the book's ingredients reached its extreme in the American edition, where he truncated the preface so severely that it apparently no longer qualified for the name and was headed simply "Note." In this note he used only the second, third, and fourth sentences from the preface, and even these he pruned slightly. For some reason he shifted its statements from the third to the first person, so that, unlike the earlier versions, it appeared to be saying simply that the work was autobiographical. All direct comment on the proportion of fact to representative truth had disappeared, and only by implication was any ingredient but the author's first-person "man-of-war experiences and observations" present in the work, in which they were said, in an equivocal retained phrase, to be "incorporated."

The history of this revised fair-copy preface is conjectural. It must have been preceded by at least one draft, from which it was copied, and followed by at least one, which served as printer's copy for the English preface. Since it was inscribed by a copyist, evidently it was originally intended to serve as printer's copy. Melville's revisions on it, too, were written clearly and their intended placing was indicated by carets and guidelines, showing that he still meant it to serve as printer's copy. It is fully legible and has none of the hastily scrawled and virtually illegible words, or even the misspelled words, characteristic of his first and working drafts. He overlooked one word ("refered") misspelled by the copyist and one spelled in a way ("pourtrayed") differing from his own spelling just above ("portray"), and left some vestigial punctuation after his revisions, but these oversights would not have troubled a compositor. The page numbers, 3 and 4 (the 3 altered from an original 1), indicate that at one time the leaves stood, or were numbered to stand, in manuscript sequence preceded only by two leaves. Penciled numbers, 22 and 41 in column at the lower right corner of the second page (not visible in the reproduction), are probably memoranda referring to later pages of the manuscript and hence support the inference that these pages 3 and 4 did once stand in a longer sequence. Although the capitalized word ("Prizer"?) penciled later, probably in a third hand, at the left of the heading (also not visible in the reproduction), may be the name of a compositor to whom the pages were assigned, nothing else in the scanty available evidence suggests that they were in fact ever set in type. Their survival when the rest of the printer's copy for *White-Jacket* was not preserved suggests that they never went to a printer. They bear no terminal dateline, as do both printed versions, English and American. For another thing, if any version was set in type in New York for the American edition in 1849 in time for Melville to take proofs of it to England with him as the basis for the English preface, it cannot have been set from these pages. The reason is that the English preface restores and reallocates some of the words and phrasing left finally canceled in this version ("Nor is it here asserted that" . . . "persons" . . . "in the following chapters" . . . "are real individuals"). Therefore it cannot have been set from American proofs, unless they were proofs which had been set from a revised transcript of this version —a transcript inscribed by Melville rather than a copyist, since only he, copying from this manuscript, could have pieced together the canceled phrasing.

It is possible that this fair copy was made to go with the American proofs Melville took to England, no preface having yet been set in type in New York; that at some time before he delivered the proofs to Bentley in London he had made on the fair copy the revisions that appear on it and in the English preface; and that what he turned over to Bentley was not these undated pages but a copy made from them, dated New York, October, 1849, and including the restored phrasing just referred to, as well as a few further revisions that appear in the English preface. (Minor changes were doubtless made by someone at Bentley's or by the compositor, e.g., "harbour" for "harbor" and "volumes" for "volume".) When Melville returned to New York in February, 1850, the Harper edition presumably still lacked a preface, and, for whatever reasons, he supplied neither these pages, which he must still have had on hand, nor a copy of the English preface, but only the brief three-sentence note drawn from one or the other and dated New York, March, 1850. These manuscript leaves are among the few that survive from Melville's works of the 1850's. They descended through his widow, who probably at some later time penciled the notation "White Jacket" (partially visible in the reproduction) at the right of the heading; to his daughter; then to her daughter, Mrs. Metcalf, who presented them to the Houghton Library.

The form in which the revised fair copy is given below in genetic transcription is designed to show the order in which the copyist and, later, Melville put down the words.[2] It distinguishes between the copyist's inscription (outside the brackets) and Melville's revisions (inside the brackets). It also distinguishes among: (1) words first written down by the copyist or by Melville, (2) words either of them canceled at once and replaced by other words on the same line, (3) words Melville canceled at some later time and replaced by other words inserted above the line or added. Words are transcribed as spelled; none are illegible and only the capitalized word ("Prizer" ?) added in pencil at the left of the heading is conjectural. Some punctuation marks added or altered in revision by Melville may not have been distinguished from the copyist's. Vestigial punctuation, whether or not actually canceled, is reported as canceled along with its accompanying words. Only the text is transcribed, not the extra-textual notations, all of which (except a penciled question mark in the lower left margin of p. 3) have been mentioned above.

SYMBOLS USED

→...→	revision enclosed between arrows was made by copyist at time fair copy was first being inscribed
[...]	revision enclosed in brackets was made by Melville after fair copy was inscribed
{...}	revision enclosed in braces was made by Melville after his first revision
>	the word(s) following were inserted above, with caret
<	the word(s) following were canceled (by lining out)
add	the word(s) following were added, on same line
≫	the canceled word(s) following were restored (by underlining)
/	end of line in manuscript
	all words in roman outside of brackets are in the copyist's hand; all words in roman (and all punctuation) inside brackets are in Melville's hand; all words in italics are editorial

---

2. The two previously published transcriptions are incomplete and inaccurate in details; neither tries to represent the process of inscription. See Leyda and Cohen, as cited in footnote 1 above. No photographic reproduction has until now been published.

GENETIC TRANSCRIPTION

[*First page*]

[Preface]
[*device*]

   The object of this book is to give / some idea of the interior life in a
man-of-war. / In the year 1843, the author shipped as a com- / mon sailor on
board of a United States frigate, / then lying in a harbor of the Sandwich
Islands, / in the Pacific. [<Sandwich . . . the *and add guideline from the to* Pacific
and > (*after* Pacific) ocean.] After serving on board of this / ship [<ship *and*
add in margin frigate] for more than a year, he was discharged, / with the rest
of the crew, upon the vessel's / arrival home. His man-of-war experiences / &
observations have been incorporated into / the present volume; which,
however, in its purely narrative parts, [<in . . . parts *and add guideline*] is not,
in every literal / detail [<in . . . detail > (*with guideline to caret*) presented as]
a mere [<a <mere <*guideline and add* (*after* as) a journal or *and add new*
guideline] log-book of that portion of the / cruise which is treated of. [*add*
guideline to run in next paragraph {<*guideline and add* The volume is more /
descriptive than narrative. *and add bracket restoring paragraph opening*}]

   As the object of the book is not / to paint [<paint > (*with guideline to*
caret) portray] the particular man-of-war in which / the author sailed, & its
officers & crew →< crew → crew,— / but to [<but to > (*with guideline to*
caret) so much as to {<so . . . to *and* <*guideline* ≫ but to}] paint general life in
the navy; the / true name of his [<his > the] frigate, →<,→ & the true names
[<the true names] / of all the persons spoken of in the following / chapters [,]
have been suppressed. Nor is it [*add* here] / asserted, that these persons are real
individ- / uals. [<Nor . . . individuals > (*at top of page with guideline to caret*
and with paragraph indentation) Nor is it, here at least, laid down, that any
{<any > (*with guideline to caret*) the slightest} / occurrence mentioned in the
following pages, is, in a / matter of fact point of view, true. All that is left to /
the reader. {<All . . . reader.} Let Truth vindicate itself, & [<, & > ;] falsehood
will stand / confessed out of its own mouth. / {<falsehood . . . mouth *and alter*
semicolon to period} {*cancel whole insertion* Nor . . . itself.}] The general [> (*before*
The *with guideline to caret and with bracket for paragraph opening*) In some instances
and alter The *to* the] delineation of naval life / has been rendered more true by
allowing / some latitude in the mode of treating /

Nor is it, here at least, laid down, that any
occurrence mentioned in the following pages, is, in a
matter of fact, not of view, true. All that is left to
the reader, Let Truth vindicate itself

Preface
———·i·———

The object of this book is to give
some idea of the interior life in a man-of-war.
In the year 1843, the author shipped as a common sailor on board of a United States frigate,
then lying in a harbor of the Sandwich Islands,
in the Pacific ocean. After serving on board of this
frigate ship for more than a year, he was discharged,
with the rest of the crew, upon the vessel's
arrival home. His man-of-war experiences
& observations have been incorporated into
the present volume; which, however, in its
purely narrative parts, is not, in every literal
detail of these presented as a journal or log-book of that portion of the
cruise which is treated of. The volume is more
descriptive than narrative. It is the object of the book is not
to paint portray the particular man-of-war, in which
the author sailed, & its officers & crew,
but to paint general life in the navy; the
true name of the frigate & the true names
of all the persons spoken of in the following
chapters, have been suppressed. Nor is there
asserted, that these persons are not individuals. The general delineation of naval life
has been rendered more true, by allowing
some latitude in the mode of treating

4

the particular events falling under the author's
personal experience. In all things, a scrupulous
adherence to the broadest spirit of the life to
be pourtrayed, has been faithfully maintained.
~~And~~ Wherever ~~their~~ statements are made, in
any way concerning the established laws &
usages of the navy, facts have been religiously adhered to.

In a word, this book is simply presented as an attempt at a ~~t~~ truthful, generalized picture of naval life;—both quarter-deck
& gun-deck—officer & sailor included.

The writer has to thank the light-
hearted author of a book called "Scenes in
old Ironsides", for ~~recalling to his mind~~
~~several minute man-of-war technicalities &~~
~~humorous phrases, that otherwise might have~~
~~escaped his the memory~~; ~~also, for~~ supplying
corroborative, ~~or additional~~ hints for ~~two or~~
some few ~~three~~ scenes. ~~in the following chapters~~.

~~Collateral~~ Allusion is sometimes made,
— by the author in person, to events, or facts in the
past history of navies. In these cases, no statement is presented unless supported by the best
accessible authorities. For the hitherto unrecorded
bye-play of circumstances in one or two well-known
naval actions referred to, the writer is indebted to the
seamen into whose mouths these things are put.

The book opens at the frigate's last
harbor in the Pacific, just previous to weighing
her anchor for ~~home~~, by the way of Cape Horn.

The homeward-bound Passage.

[*Second page*]

the particular events falling under the author's / personal experience. [<In
some instances . . . experience.] In all things, a scrupulous / adherence to the
[*add in word space left by copyist* broadest] spirit of the life to / be pourtrayed, has
been faithfully maintained. / And wherever [<And *and alter* wherever *to*
Wherever] plain [<plain] statements are made, in / any way concerning the
established laws & / usages of the navy, facts have been religious- / ly adhered
to. / [*add guideline to run in next paragraph*]

    In a word, this book is simply pre- / sented as an attempt at a th →<th→
truthful, general- / ized picture of naval life, — both quarter-deck / &
gun-deck — officer & sailor included. / [*add guideline to run in next paragraph*]

    The writer has to thank the light- / hearted author of a book called
"Scenes in / old Ironsides", for recalling to his memory [(*first in pencil then in
ink*) <his memory >mind] / several minute man-of-war technicalities & /
humorous phrases, that otherwise might have / *next three words in pencil*
escaped his memory [*in ink over copyist's pencil words* escaped his {<his >the}
memory. {<that . . . memory. >;}] also, for [<recalling . . . for *add guideline*]
supplying / corroborative, or additional [<or additional] hints for two or / three
[<two or three *and add* (*in margin with guideline to caret*) some few] scenes in the
following chapters. / [[<in . . . chapters. *and add period after* scenes]

    Collateral allusion [<Collateral *alter* allusion *to* Allusion *and add guideline
to run in this paragraph*] is sometimes made [,] / [—] by the author in person
[>—] to events, or facts in the / past history of navies. In these cases, no state- /
ment is presented unless supported by the best / accessible authorities. For the
hitherto unrecorded / bye-play of circumstances in one or two well-known /
naval actions refered to, the writer is indebted to the / seamen [*add then cancel
comma*] into whose mouths these things are put. /

    The book opens at the frigate's last / harbor in the Pacific[,] just previous
to weighing / her anchor for home, [<home, >(*below, circled, with guideline
to caret*) the homeward-bound passage,] by the way of Cape Horn. /

PARALLEL TEXTS

[*Revised fair copy*]
Preface
　　The object of this
book is to give some idea of the
interior life in a man-of-war. In
the year 1843, the author shipped
as a common sailor on board of a
United States frigate, then lying
in a harbor of the Pacific ocean.
After serving on board of this
frigate for more than a year, he
was discharged, with the rest of
the crew, upon the vessel's
arrival home. His man-of-war
experiences & observations have
been incorporated into the present
volume; which, however, is
not presented as a journal or
log-book of that portion of the
cruise which is treated of. The
volume is more descriptive than
narrative.
　　As the object of the
book is not to portray the
particular man-of-war in which
the author sailed, & its officers
& crew,—but to paint general
life in the navy; the true name
of the frigate &
of all the persons
spoken of in the following chapters,
have been suppressed.
In all things, a scrupulous adherence
to the broadest spirit of the life
to be pourtrayed, has been faithfully
maintained. Wherever statements are
made, in any way concerning the established
laws & usages of the navy, facts have
been religiously adhered to. In a word,
this book is simply presented as an

[*English edition*]
PREFACE.
　　The object of this
work is to give some idea of the
interior life in a man-of-war. In
the year 1843, the author shipped
as a common sailor on board of a
United States frigate, then lying
in a harbour of the Pacific Ocean.
After serving on board of this
frigate for more than a year, he
was discharged, with the rest of
the crew, upon the vessel's
arrival home. His man-of-war
experiences and observations have
been incorporated into the present
volumes. But these volumes are
not presented as a journal of the

cruise.

　　As the object of this
work is not to portray the
particular man-of-war in which
the author sailed, and its officers
and crew, but, by illustrative scenes, to paint
general life in the Navy, the true name
of the frigate is not given. Nor is it
here asserted that any of the persons
introduced in the following chapters
are real individuals.

Wherever statements are
made in any way concerning the established
laws and usages of the Navy, facts have
been strictly adhered to.

attempt at a truthful, generalized
picture of naval life,—both quarter-deck
& gun-deck—officer & sailor included.
The writer has to thank the light-hearted
author of a book called "Scenes in old
Ironsides", for supplying corroborative
hints for some few scenes. Allusion is
sometimes made,—by the author in person—
to events, or facts in the past
history of navies. In these cases,
no statement is presented unless
supported by the best accessible
authorities. For the hitherto unrecorded
bye-play of circumstances in one or two
well-known naval actions refered to,
the writer is indebted to the seamen
into whose mouths these things are put.

The book opens at the frigate's last
harbor in the Pacific, just previous
to weighing her anchor
for the homeward-bound passage,
by the way of Cape Horn.

Allusion is
sometimes made
to events or facts in the past
history of Navies. In these cases,
no statement is presented unless
supported by the best
authorities. For the hitherto unrecorded
by-play of circumstances in one or two
well-known naval actions referred to,
the writer is indebted to the seamen
into whose mouths these things are put.

The work opens at the frigate's last
harbour in the Pacific, just previous
to weighing her anchor
for the homeward-bound passage,
by the way of Cape Horn.

NEW YORK, *October*, 1849.

COLOPHON

THE TEXT *of the Northwestern–Newberry Edition of* THE WRITINGS OF HERMAN MELVILLE *is set in eleven-point Monophoto Bembo, two points leaded. The exceptionally handsome type face is a modern rendering of designs made by Francesco Griffo for the office of Aldus Manutius in Venice and first used for printing, in 1495, of the tract* De Aetna *by Cardinal Pietro Bembo. The display face is Bruce Rogers's Centaur, a twentieth-century design based on and reflective of the late-fifteenth-century Venetian models of Nicolas Jenson.*

This volume was composed by William Clowes & Sons, Ltd., of Beccles, Suffolk, England. It was printed and bound by Kingsport Press, Inc., of Kingsport, Tennessee. The typography and binding design of the edition are by Paul Randall Mize.

PS
2380
.F68
Vol. 5

35,939

CAMROSE LUTHERAN COLLEGE
LIBRARY